Praise for John Ajvide

'Profoundly felt . . . *The Kindness* is a tho………………
SFX

'The power of Lindqvist's storytelling and his passion to promote understanding can't be denied'   *Guardian*

'Warm-hearted, unflinching, utterly immersive'   *Daily Mail*

'A magician of genre fiction'   *Independent*

'Lindqvist is Sweden's answer to Stephen King'   *Daily Mirror*

'Lindqvist has reinvented the vampire novel and made it all the more chilling . . . An immensely readable and highly disturbing book in which grim levels of gore and violence are tempered by an unexpected tenderness'   *Daily Express*

'Reminiscent of Stephen King at his best, there are some truly scary bits in the book that will haunt your dreams. Best read by sunlight'   *Independent on Sunday*

'A very scary tale indeed from a writer who is master of his genre'
Financial Times   .

'Combines an atmospheric coming-of-age story set in Stockholm with a shocking (and very gory) thriller. His vampire is an original, both heart-breakingly pathetic and terrifying. This was a bestseller in Sweden and could be equally big here. Don't miss it'   *The Times*

'A surprising and sometimes delightful reading experience . . . Lindqvist manages to maintain a light touch in an otherwise bleak landscape'   *Sunday Times*

'A compelling horror story, but it's also a finely calibrated tale about the pain of growing up'   *Sunday Telegraph*

JOHN AJVIDE LINDQVIST is a Swedish author, born in 1968. He grew up in Blackeberg, a suburb of Stockholm. He wanted to become something awful and fantastic. First he became a conjurer and came second in the Nordic card trick championship. Then he was a stand-up comedian for twelve years, before writing *Let the Right One In*. That novel became a phenomenal international bestseller and was made into a film and a West End play, both called Let Me In. His books are published in twenty-nine countries worldwide.

ALSO BY JOHN AJVIDE LINDQVIST

Let the Right One In

Handling the Undead

Harbour

Little Star

Let the Old Dreams Die

I Am Behind You

I Always Find You

I Am the Tiger

THE
KINDNESS

John Ajvide Lindqvist

Translated from Swedish
by Marlaine Delargy

riverrun

First published in Sweden in 2021 under the title *Vänligheten* by Ordfront Förlag.
This English translation first published in Great Britain in 2023 by riverrun
This paperback edition published in 2024 by

riverrun

An imprint of

Quercus Editions Limited
Carmelite House
50 Victoria Embankment
London EC4Y 0DZ

An Hachette UK company

A CIP catalogue record for this book is available
from the British Library

Paperback ISBN 978 1 52941 908 5
Ebook ISBN 978 1 52941 907 8

10 9 8 7 6 5 4 3 2 1

Typeset by CC Book Production
Printed and bound in Great Britain by Clays Ltd, Elcograf S.p.A.

Papers used by riverrun are from well-managed forests and other responsible sources.

To Jenny and Love.
Life has been even more fun
since we became friends.

One day many years ago, I was out and about in Norrtälje when suddenly I saw it: the Kindness. There were two builders chatting and laughing, and one patted the other on the shoulder, a car stopped to let someone cross the road, a door was held open, a couple of strangers helped lift a child's buggy onto the bus.

Once I'd noticed the Kindness, I couldn't stop seeing it, because it exists everywhere. People do small things for each other in order to make life easier. Hands reach out, help is offered, something is lifted, an obstacle is removed.

The Kindness can be glimpsed behind our actions and heard behind our words. Have a nice weekend, have a good day, best of luck, take care of yourself. These are simple phrases and in no way binding, but they come from a spring of goodwill. I want you to be happy, whoever you are.

We need the Kindness and we carry out its deeds as something that is self-evident, without even thinking. Eyes meet, smiles are exchanged, thanks are expressed. The Kindness is our defence against disintegration, and we would do well to give it some thought now and again. It is so important, yet at the same time so fragile. What happens if the Kindness crumbles away, and what will become of us?

PROLOGUE
20TH SEPTEMBER 2002

I AM A STORM FROM NOWHERE

I

A girl is standing outside the library in Norrtälje. Her name is Siw Waern, and she is thirteen years old. She looks to the right and left, behind and in front of her as if she is searching for something. She takes a few steps and seems to be leaving, but then she stops, turns around and continues to look to the right and left, behind and in front. She moves her feet up and down on the spot, she shakes her head. It seems to be more a question of *waiting* rather than searching. Siw is waiting for something which will come from an unknown direction.

There is something special about Siw, and perhaps we would have lingered with her anyway, even if it hadn't been for her anxious behaviour. She is slightly below average height, slightly above average weight. You wouldn't call her short and fat, but the tendency is there. Medium-length brown hair with a fringe that hangs down over deep-set eyes. Rounded cheeks and a prominent chin combine to give her a kind of Inuit appearance. You could picture her dressed in sealskin with a harpoon in her hand. In fact, she is wearing a black coat that is rather dated, an impression reinforced by the neon-yellow backpack looped over one shoulder.

She is about to give up again. She takes out her phone and checks the time: 15.43. She gazes at the café outside the library. A mother with a buggy is drinking tea at one table, while a young couple deep in conversation are seated at another. A man carrying a tray is just about to negotiate his way out of the door. Siw gives a slight shrug and spreads her hands wide, then slips her phone into her pocket and sets off, humming an old-fashioned folk song. Not what you would expect from a thirteen-year-old.

After two steps she stops. A Samhall minibus is driving along Billborgsgatan at high speed. The driver is preoccupied with something on the instrument panel, and the vehicle swerves as it passes the video store. Siw spins around to face the café again.

The man with the tray has emerged and is passing between the mother and the buggy on his way to a free table. He turns to edge past and catches the buggy with his hip. The mother must have forgotten to put on the brake, because the nudge sets the buggy in motion. The front wheel goes over the edge of the top step – there are three – and when the back wheels follow, the buggy picks up speed on its downward trajectory.

The mother hasn't yet noticed what has happened, because her view is obscured by the man's body. The buggy bumps down another step and accelerates towards the street, where the Samhall minibus is racing along doing at least fifty kilometres per hour. Two moving objects are going to collide, and the result will be a tragedy.

Only when the buggy lands on the pavement and continues on its journey does the mother see what is happening. Her face contorts into a mask of horror and she lets out a scream of despair. She knocks over her table as she leaps to her feet, knowing it's already too late. Her life is about to fall apart.

The front wheel of the buggy has just passed the edge of the pavement when Siw grabs the handle. The minibus sweeps by no more than half a metre away, making Siw's fringe flutter up from her eyes, which are wide with disbelief.

The child in the buggy is crying. Its mother is sobbing hysterically, hugging Siw so tightly that it takes her breath away. Over the woman's shoulder she can see the man who bumped into the buggy standing with his hands pressed to his mouth. The tray is at his feet. Siw blinks. In that moment she realises that at some quintessential level, she is not human.

2

'Come on! What are you looking at?'

Max waves to Johan, who has taken two steps back to get a better view of the rusty ladder running up the side of the silo. Johan points to a spot thirty metres above the ground, about halfway up. 'Isn't it broken there?'

Max stands beside him and shades his eyes against the low sun with his hand. When he's finished looking, he shrugs. 'So?'

'But that's not good, is it? If it's broken?'

'That's why we've brought the kit.'

Max shakes the bag in which they have gathered together something resembling mountaineering equipment from the tool shed at Max's house. Ropes, carbine hooks, cleats. Johan scratches the back of his neck. 'I'm not sure . . .'

'Shit! Duck!'

7

A van marked 'Odalmannen' is approaching along the quayside, and the boys hurl themselves behind an electricity box. It isn't hard to work out that what they are planning is forbidden. You only have to read the angry yellow sign on the fence, beneath which there is a convenient hollow, just deep enough to allow a slender body to slip through.

Both Max and Johan are slender. Skinny, in fact. Even though they have turned thirteen, they are as fine-limbed as small children – very tall small children. Johan measures one metre seventy-three in his stocking feet, Max one metre seventy-eight, and neither of them has finished growing. They have the same long, narrow, sensitive face, the same medium blond hair and couldn't-care-less style. They could pass for brothers if it weren't for their eyes. Max's are large and such a pale shade of blue that they almost seem transparent, especially when they reflect the sky. Johan's are ordinary, brown, and the shadows beneath them suggest poor sleep. They have been best friends ever since they started school.

'We're either doing this or we're not,' Max says when the van has disappeared and they are standing at the foot of the ladder once more. 'I'm definitely doing it anyway.'

'Okay, okay,' Johan says. 'Don't blame me if we die.'

They each secure a rope around their waist. Max is the best at knots, so he takes care of the tying, finally fixing a carbine hook to the end. 'We keep on fastening the hook to a rung a few steps above us, okay? If the rung you're standing on breaks, then . . .'

'And if the rung the hook is attached to breaks – what then?'

Max stares intently at Johan, for such a long time that Johan has to look away. 'What? What are you staring at?'

'Have you never wished you were dead?'

'Yes – but that doesn't mean I want to die.'

'So, what does it mean?'

Johan shrugs. 'That I don't want to live.'

'How are you going to not live and not be dead? Are you planning on becoming a zombie or something?'

'Can we just do this?'

'Absolutely.'

Without further ado, Max marches up to the ladder and climbs ten steps before attaching the hook for the first time. Johan stays on the ground looking up at him.

They started talking about climbing one of the grain silos in Norrtälje harbour when they were ten years old, after hearing about some boys from the high school who'd done it. The topic had come up from time to time over the years, and it was always Max who brought it up.

Max is the more daring of the two. When they used to play their fantasy games on the hill behind Johan's house on Glasmästarbacken, it was always Max who climbed the highest in any tree, Max who almost fell down the steep drop to Tillfällegatan. He passed his diving certificate when he was twelve, and holidayed with his parents in Mauritius. Johan has never been outside Sweden.

The light behind Max turns him into a shapeless silhouette as he makes his way up the ladder, with a loud clunk every time he swaps the hook to a different rung. Johan weighs his hook in his hand and sighs. Then he walks up to the foot of the ladder.

What he fears most is not the rungs breaking, but the whole ladder coming away from the side of the silo and falling outwards, taking them down with it and crushing them like flies beneath a huge swatter made of rusty iron. However, as he begins to climb, he realises he was wrong. A broken rung would be worse.

Max is leading the way, so he is the one who is testing the ladder's stability. If an accident happens, it is almost certain that Max will be the victim. Admittedly he could fall on top of Johan and they will both tumble to their deaths, but that's unlikely. If anyone is going to die, it's Max.

Johan clambers up a few more steps. He is only five metres above the ground, yet his stomach contracts when he glances over his shoulder. He fastens the carbine hook to the rung above his head that looks the least rusty.

'How's it going?' Max calls to him.

Johan would give him the thumbs up if he dared to let go. Instead, he shouts: 'Nearly caught up!'

'Shall I wait for you?'

'No, it's fine!'

Johan doesn't want Max to see that he's started sweating. His palms are sticking to the rough, rusty iron, and a shudder rises through his chest. He keeps going, tries to complete the train of thought he began a moment ago.

If anyone is going to die, it's Max.

It doesn't exactly cheer him up. In fact, it makes him feel like shit. If Max died, Johan wouldn't have anyone apart from his crazy mother. No one to go to the hill or play video games with, no one to talk to, no one who understands. He would be, to put it briefly, completely fucking alone.

So . . .

So it's better if the ladder comes away and they both get squashed like flies together. It's true that he's often thought and actually said out loud that he doesn't want to live because there's so much crap in his life, but that's not entirely true. As long as Max exists, he can live. Without him, he can't.

When he looks down at the ground after fifteen metres, he's no longer quite so sure. He just wants this to be over. He presses his forehead against the rung in front of him. It's so thin – just as thin as the one he's standing on. Fragile rods of iron that are his only fixed point, his only protection against falling, against his guts being splattered all over the concrete.

'Dear God,' he murmurs, 'dear God, you fucking bastard, please let us both survive this. If you do *something* for me just this once, I'll try to hate you a bit less.'

He closes his eyes as he continues to climb, three, four, five, six steps. And then something happens. Ice-cold fingers grasp his lungs and twist them like dishcloths as he feels himself being dragged downwards. His hands clutch the rung they are holding in a vice-like grip, and as a desperate additional safety measure Johan clamps his teeth around the rung closest to his mouth, presses his body against the ladder and shakes like a whipped dog refusing to let go of its bone. Then he understands. He's forgotten to unclip the carbine hook, and it's now several rungs below him, stopping him from making any progress.

Tears spring to his eyes as his hands refuse to let go, and he breathes in rapid, shallow gasps. If he falls now, the rung the hook is attached to would never withstand his weight. His only option is to go back and unfasten it. He forces himself to open his mouth. He spits out several flakes of rust, then looks down.

Down.

What frightens him the most is the powerful urge to allow it to happen, to let go and fall, get rid of all the crap. No more night vigils to stop his mother from running out into the street stark naked, preaching to anyone who will listen. No more nagging fears about everything going wrong, so that he ends up in foster care. To fall, to hover in the air for a second, then let them cry, all of them.

Even the realisation of this little project means he has to unfasten the hook first. If the rung holds, against all expectation, he might only break his back. He hears Max's voice from high above: 'How fantastic is this?'

At that moment, Johan hates his best friend. Max knows him, knows what his life is like. Max shouldn't expose him to temptation. Max is insensitive and fucking stupid, unless . . . *unless that was the plan all along.* Johan lets out a sob and a couple of tears trickle down his cheeks. Maybe Max wants him to die. Maybe Max is sick of Johan hanging around at his house in the hope of being asked to stay for dinner, sick of playing *Pokémon*, sick of the fantasy games they still play on the hill when there's no one else around. Maybe Max wants to get rid of him, and has chosen this method.

His sorrow switches to anger, which gives him the ability to climb down four rungs and undo the hook.

'Are you too frightened?' Max yells.

'No!' Johan clambers back to the spot where he had his scare, and clips the hook safely above his head.

No! That's a no!

'Listen, the ladder's fine,' Max calls down. 'It's just a bit bent here.'

Johan pushes away his foolish thoughts. It's not clever of Max to expose him to this, but he's not trying to kill him. Besides, Max would be in trouble if Johan died. Regardless of the low value Johan puts on himself, he knows that a dead thirteen-year-old is a big thing. Front-page news in the local paper, at least. Police interviews, one hell of a fuss. He looks down and the temptation is there once again, in a different form. The whole town would be talking about him.

No! That's a NO!

Max said something about the state of the ladder, which means he's reached the point Johan noticed from the ground. Halfway up. It's a long way from where he is now, and he has to get there. He, Johan Andersson, can't do it, which means he has to become someone else, he has to become . . . *Uruk-hai*.

A lot of the games he and Max have played over the years have been inspired by *The Lord of the Rings*. They've read the books and seen the film, and they can't wait for the next one to come out. They've pretended to be elves and hobbits, wizards and Gollum, but above all they've pretended to be orcs. Their terse single-mindedness makes them fun to play.

During a school skiing competition last winter, both he and Max had been on their last legs. They are neither fit nor keen skiers, and with three kilometres to go of a five-kilometre circuit, they'd been on the point of giving up – until Johan whispered to Max: 'We are the fighting Uruk-hai.' Max had grinned and begun to move his poles mechanically, skiing like an orc, purposeful and determined. They had set off along the trail saying things like 'Kill' or 'Destroy', and eventually had reached the end in a decent time.

I am a fighting Uruk-hai.

Johan empties his mind and sees only the tasty little hobbits who have set up camp on the top of the silo in the belief that they are safe. Get there. Attack. Kill. He growls and heaves his bulky orc-body upwards. He can still taste rust in his mouth, which is good because it is very similar to the taste of blood, and it is his immense thirst for blood that drives him on. Tasty little hobbits.

He keeps on going like a fighting Uruk-hai. Every time he moves the hook to a rung above him he lets out a grunt of contempt at this human invention that he is having to use. Without thinking anything but orc-thoughts he reaches the point where the ladder bends to the right.

'That didn't take you long!' Max says from above him, and Johan looks up. Max has let go of the ladder with one hand and is leaning back to get a better view. The sight makes Johan's stomach turn over and his fantasy almost slips, but he can't afford to let that happen. He grits his teeth and hisses: 'I am a fighting Uruk-hai.'

Max frowns and gives a slightly patronising and ambiguous smile. Johan hadn't intended to say the words aloud, they just slipped out. He's noticed a gradual shift lately. Max is six months older than him. Maybe it's not so much about the age difference as about attitude or need, but Max is in the process of leaving the world they've built up together over the past seven years.

Johan has an insoluble dilemma. On the one hand, he has a burning desire to grow up and escape from the apartment and the suffocating atmosphere created by his mother's unpredictable insanity. On the other hand, he doesn't want to leave his fantasies and take on the responsibilities that life as an adult involves. The simplest solution is to go crazy himself, and maybe one day he will.

Max sets off again and Johan lets out a snort. Max can become a boring adult if that's what he wants. Johan will continue to be a fighting Uruk-hai until Aragorn comes along and chops off his head.

Aragorn!

Maybe that fucker is up there with the hobbits? If so, the time for revenge has come – revenge for all the orc blood that bastard half-elf has spilled! Onward, onward!

Johan's fantasy lasts almost all the way. He doesn't look down, he doesn't think about where he is, he just sees the rungs passing by his yellow orc eyes, moving his hands and the hook mechanically while thinking elemental thoughts about blood and revenge. He is just over three metres from the top when Max clambers over the edge and disappears, then lets out a huge laugh. It isn't an expression

14

of joy at his achievement, it's something else. What can possibly be so amusing? Speculation drives a wedge into Johan's fantasy, and it shatters.

I am a fighting . . . I am . . . on a narrow ladder that is going to come away from the silo at any second.

It is *here* it's going to happen, when he's close to the top, so that the fly swat will land on him with the greatest possible force. They're going to have to scrape him off the concrete with a spoon. His hands begin to shake and the extent of the fall opens up in his stomach like a searing pain. He clamps his buttocks together. He's got this far – he's not going to end by shitting himself.

Max is saying something, but Johan can't make out what it is. He takes a deep breath and thinks: *Three metres. Ten rungs. You can do this.* And somehow he does, but when he makes it over the edge he collapses face down on the wonderful flat surface. His head is spinning and in his confusion he thinks he can hear another voice, a voice he vaguely recognises.

'You're something else!' Max says. What does he mean? Johan's achievement may have been greater because he was so much more afraid, but that's hardly something Max is capable of appreciating. Johan raises his head.

There is a metal rail running around the edge of the silo roof; it is even rustier than the ladder. Sitting next to this rail, with his legs actually dangling over the edge, is Marko. He's the one Max was talking to. He's the one who is something else.

Marko joined their class after the summer holidays, just over a month ago. He's from Bosnia and has been in Sweden for two years. The family recently moved to Norrtälje. Coincidentally, they are actually living on Glasmästarbacken, a couple of doors down from Johan, but he has never said more than 'Hi' to Marko. He has also

15

nodded a couple of times to Marko's father, who often sits on the balcony smoking. But here is Marko at the top of the silo, looking as if he's waiting for a bus, calm and composed.

'Did you hear that?' Max says to Johan. 'Marko comes up here, like, *every day*! He just climbs the ladder, and we're kitted out like fucking *mountaineers*.'

Max laughs again, and Marko smiles. On a theoretical level Johan understands that it's funny, but laughter is not the expression of emotion that lies closest to the surface right now. Plus, it could easily turn into projectile vomiting, so he merely gives a weary nod. He doesn't think he's going to be able to stand up. Only now does Max notice there's a problem, and crouches down beside him.

'Are you okay?' he asks. 'Was it horrible?'

'Yes. Yes, it was horrible.'

'I thought so too. I was shit scared.'

'I couldn't tell.'

'You know what I'm like.'

Johan does know. Max has a decent relationship with his parents, but still insists that he will never, ever be like his father. And yet he is very much like his father. Through self-discipline and hard work – as his father often says – he has gone from a simple scaffolder to vice chair of a reasonably large construction company, and is one of the twenty richest people in Norrtälje. He features on the list in the local paper every single year.

This self-discipline is also evident in his expressions of emotion, such as they are. It takes a great deal for Max's father to give even the slightest indication of what he is feeling. When he's really angry he sometimes wrinkles his nose, and that's it. Max is similar in many ways, but, unlike his father, he at least has the ability to laugh.

'I do,' Johan says.

16

'Can you get up?'

'I don't actually know.'

'Do you want a hand? It would be a shame if you didn't see the view.'

With Max's support, Johan gets to his feet. They are standing on a circular roof approximately eight metres across. Johan has temporarily forgotten the formula for working out the surface area. He looks at Marko and nods. 'Hi.'

'Hi,' Marko says, his face expressionless.

'Is it true that you come up here every day?'

'Not every day,' Marko says with a slight accent. 'Maybe . . . every other.'

'Did you make the hole? Under the fence?'

Marko nods. Johan nods back. Max goes over and stands next to Marko. He leans on the rail and spreads his arms out wide. 'Shit!' he says. 'Norrtälje! Fucking Norrtälje!'

Marko tugs at his trouser leg and points to the rail. 'Don't lean over. The rail is very rusty. You'll end up like a pancake.'

Max raises his hands and takes a step back. Only now does Johan notice something unusual about Marko. In school he is always neat and tidy – kind of stiff, somehow. Perfectly ironed shirts buttoned right up to the neck and chinos that look as if they've come from the dry cleaner's that morning. If he was anyone else, he'd be a target for gibes and sneers, but he isn't anyone else. There is an aura of great strength in repose surrounding Marko, and no one dares tease him.

But today he is wearing a creased checked shirt with a hole in one elbow, and a pair of jeans with dirty marks on the knees. Johan can't see his feet because they're dangling over the edge, but he's guessing that Marko isn't in the highly polished shoes he wears to

17

school. The sight of those dangling legs makes him feel dizzy all over again. He goes and stands exactly in the middle of the circle, as far from the edge as possible.

A Samhall minibus is driving along Glasmästarbacken at high speed. If Johan moves his eyes a fraction, he can see his balcony. From this distance you can't tell it's full of crap; his mother is in one of her phases when she refuses to throw anything away. He glances at his watch: 15.42. Any minute now his mother will start pacing back and forth in the apartment, wondering where he's gone.

He looks to the left, towards the trees in Society Park. From this angle their crowns are bushy clouds in shades of yellow as the sun begins to go down. Incredible. He is high above the treetops.

The minibus reaches the bridge and continues into town. Max forms a rifle with his hands and aims at a couple wandering along hand in hand on the far side of the harbour.

'Perfect place for sniping,' he says, squeezing an imaginary trigger.

Marko stands up, raises his eyebrows and says: 'Sniping?'

'Yes . . .' Max replies, glancing at Johan, who slowly shakes his head. Max comes to his senses, blinks. 'I mean . . . no.'

'It's okay,' Marko assures him. 'You don't need to worry. No one in my family has been . . . sniped.'

'Good to know,' Max says feebly. He looks as if he's about to place a hand on Marko's shoulder. Johan rolls his eyes; Max can be such an *idiot*. For example, now he's leaning towards the rail even though Marko told him . . .

Something is wrong. Max's eyes have rolled back in his head and only the whites are visible. His head is jerking from side to side. Marko frowns and takes a step back. 'Max, what's wrong? Be careful . . .'

Johan knows. He has been there on several occasions when Max

18

has had an attack, ever since they were little. When he's seen things that everyone would read about in the local paper the following day – accidents, fires, even a murder. Always events that involved serious injuries or death.

Johan also knows that Max has now lost control of his body, because he is no longer present. Johan ought to rush forward and do something. The problem is that his feet are stuck fast in the middle of the roof and refuse to move. He is physically incapable of approaching the edge.

Max lets go of the rail and falls sideways onto it. There is a sharp crack as the rusty metal snaps and bends outwards under the weight of Max's body. Even though the whole thing is happening in slow motion, Johan doesn't stand a chance of reaching him in time, even if he could move. His jaw drops and he inhales as a scream of impotence swells in his chest. He is going to stand here and watch his best friend die.

Max's right hand reaches out to Johan as his pupils return to their normal position; he can see and understand the situation. Their eyes meet for a second, then something comes flying into their field of vision and the contact is broken. Marko's arm. He grabs hold of Max's wrist and tries to stop him from falling, but the movement has begun, and Max is tall, his outward impetus strong.

Marko does his best to resist, but he is dragged to the edge. He turns his head, stretches out his free arm towards Johan and yells: 'Help!'

For the rest of his life, Johan will despise himself for what happens next. Instead of giving Marko the help he deserves and the traction he needs, Johan allows the scream to take command of him. He screams and actually takes a couple of steps back.

Marko is going over the edge with Max. The golden yellow

sunlight on the treetops loses its glow as the sun drops behind Stallmästarberget, and there is a flash as the last rays catch the town hall's clock tower. This moment will be seared into Johan's brain forever.

In a last desperate attempt, Marko grabs hold of Max's arm with both hands. His right foot finds the base of a post and he throws his body backwards just as his left foot slips toward the edge. Max's upper body is jerked back a few centimetres and hangs in the balance. The two boys form a V-shape that can't quite decide which way it's going to fall. Then Marko's left foot hits something uneven that gives him the purchase he needs. He pulls hard and crashes down onto his back. A fraction of a second later Max follows and lands on his stomach beside him.

Johan's scream is cut off as if someone has flicked a switch. His fists open and close as shame floods his body in dark waves.

You coward. You little fucking coward.

He would give anything to be the one lying next to Max, gasping for air and shaking his head. The one who had risked his own life to save him. They would have shared this for the rest of their lives. He would give anything – but he hadn't given what was asked of him.

The dark waves bring dark thoughts along with them. Johan hates Marko, lying there wallowing in his heroic achievement; he would like to throw him over the edge, make him disappear. When Johan realises what he's thinking, he is even more ashamed. Marko has just saved his best friend's life. If they're still best friends, that is.

Max and Marko look at each other. And start laughing. They laugh and laugh until Max slams down his hand on the cement and pushes himself up onto his knees. He gazes at Marko with shining eyes and says: 'You saved me! You fucking saved me!'

'Yes,' Marko says. 'Yes.'

Max pulls a strange face – almost a grimace. 'You don't get it!' He points to the edge. 'I'd be dead now if it hadn't been for you! At this very moment, right now, I'd be down there with every bone in my body broken. That's what would have happened if you hadn't done what you did.'

'I do get it. It's not complicated,' Marko says.

Max opens and closes his mouth as if there's something he'd like to explain, but can't work out how to do it. In the silence that follows Johan finally manages to squeeze a word out of his constricted throat, and that word is: 'Sorry'.

Max and Marko turn to Johan as if they've forgotten his very existence, and Johan wants to sink through the floor, which is a roof, down into the dark innards of the silo and disappear among whatever shit they store in there. He tugs at the hem of his T-shirt like a toddler and his cheeks flush red as he whispers: 'Forgive me, I . . .'

He can't get the words out, there are too many of them. He can't explain how he froze on the spot because at a quintessential level Max is his life, and the shock of seeing his life disappear in a second was so overwhelming that it blocked him from actually stopping this from happening. Instead, he stares at his feet. He hears footsteps, then Max is standing in front of him.

'Listen,' Max says. Johan looks up; the accusation he is expecting to see in Max's eyes isn't there. Instead, they are shining with a light not unlike the one in Johan's mother's eyes when she has one of her revelations.

'Look at me,' Max says, pointing to himself. 'I'm standing here. I'm not dead. And besides . . .' His gaze turns inwards, which Johan doesn't like at all. For a brief moment he thinks Max is going to start yelling and waving his hands the way his mother does, but Max

21

returns to the present moment and goes on: '. . . I don't know how I would have reacted, okay? I might have done exactly the same as you. It's cool, okay? It's cool.'

Johan nods, even though he doesn't think that Max would have reacted as he did. Max does not have fear as his base element, Max is not a coward. However, Johan is grateful for what his friend has said. It helps a little. Max gestures towards Marko. 'Although it's lucky Marko was here, otherwise I'd have ended up smeared all over the concrete.'

For the first time Johan risks looking at Marko, who is sitting cross-legged on the ground looking quite comfortable. His expression is calm, without a hint of reproach. 'You're a hero, Marko,' Johan says tentatively.

Marko shakes his head. 'My dad is a hero.'

Johan can't reconcile the concept 'hero' with the nervous little man who stands on the balcony chain-smoking, but he nods as if he knows exactly what Marko means. Meanwhile, Max's shoulders have slumped and the light in his eyes has dulled.

'What happened?' Johan asks quietly. 'You saw something, didn't you?'

Max nods, and Johan glances at Marko. As far as Johan is aware, he is the only one who is privy to the secret, and he doesn't know if Max wants to share it with Marko. Personally, that's the last thing Johan wants. Unfortunately Marko gets to his feet and asks the same question: 'So what happened? Are you epileptic or something?'

Max shakes his head. 'I sometimes see things. Things that are going to happen.'

So that's that, but Johan realises that because of what Marko had done, he has the right to know. Taken as a whole, the silo project has been a really crap idea. Johan went along with it in order to get closer to Max, and instead he's achieved the opposite.

'You mean . . . you see into the future?' Marko says.

'Only for a moment. A few seconds before it happens. Sometimes a bit longer.'

Johan is determined to justify his existence, so he joins in. 'It's true. I've been with Max a few times when he's seen something, then it's been in the paper the next day.'

Marko nods slowly. 'Okay.'

Max raises his eyebrows. 'You believe me?'

'Why wouldn't I? What did you see?'

'I already asked him that,' Johan says. Marko gives him a long look which makes Johan take a sudden interest in his shoes once again. He's started to notice that Max is older than him, but somehow Marko seems more like an adult.

Max gazes up at the sky, where the clouds are still lit by the sun, reflecting the glow down onto his face so that it has a spiritual shimmer. 'I saw . . . some steps. A buggy rolling down the steps. And a minibus. From the organisation that . . . sorts out jobs for disabled people . . .'

'Samhall?' Johan says. 'I saw that minibus. Just now.'

'In that case, it must have happened nearby, or . . .' Max rubs his temples and blinks. 'That's the thing. I saw the buggy roll into the road. Bang. The baby was thrown out and the buggy went under the wheels of the minibus. The driver slammed on the brakes, but skidded and drove over the baby's head. That's what I saw.'

'How terrible,' Johan says. 'You don't know where it was?'

'It could have been the steps outside the library, but . . .' Max looks from Marko to Johan and back again, as if he is searching for an explanation on their faces. He rubs his temples again. 'Here's the thing: *it didn't happen*. Don't ask me how I know, but I'm every bit as sure as I was that it was *going* to happen. But it didn't.'

'So . . . you didn't see into the future?' Marko says.

'I did!' Max is angry. 'I did! But something . . . got in the way.'

'Well, that's good,' Johan ventures.

'Of course it is!' Max snaps. 'It's fantastic! But it doesn't make sense. It's as if there's something I can't see. Something that is . . . *something else*.'

ENTEI

THE WIND SPEAKS

There was a time when nothing impeded my progress, and I drifted over the waters in these northern regions like the spirit of God. Sometimes I turned myself into a storm and made the waves huge, sometimes I rested and left the surface of the sea as calm and still as a mirror, but it was the same as when a tree falls in the forest. No one could comment on or observe my actions, because there was no land to stand upon. It was a tedious period, and it went on for a long time.

Then the islands slowly emerged from the sea and I rejoiced. At last something new to look at and play with, tangled thickets of sea buckthorn with leaves to shake. Gradually the land rose after the ice melted away, like a person straightening up after shedding a burden. There were more and more islands; they joined together and formed solid land masses. I had some busy years when I wanted to visit them all, make the tops of the trees quiver. Occasionally I would bring down a tree, just for fun.

Then at last the people came. Oh, the people! I speak from vast experience, and truly I say to you, no animal gives me greater pleasure than people. It may be down to vanity, because no animal engages with me and discusses me the way people do, particularly seafarers and those who live on the coast. However, I think it's something else, namely the combination of sense and stupidity that makes them endlessly interesting.

The rest of the animals do things based on instinct and a simpler thought process. Human beings reason with themselves, struggle with decisions and sometimes feel regret afterwards. What other animal has the capacity to feel *regret*? A human being uses his or her good sense to settle on the best choice, whereupon his or her stupidity often leads him or her to do the exact opposite. Then there's drama, an inexhaustible source of entertainment for an ever-present force like me.

But I am drifting away, as is my nature. I am supposed to be talking about Norrtälje. Long ago, Lake Lommaren was a part of the deep cut into the land which is now the bay known as Norrtäljeviken. That's also where the name comes from – *tälja*, to carve. The bay is carved into Sweden's belly, so to speak. Then the land rose higher and part of the bay became a river, leaving Lommaren as an inland lake.

Fishing boats went out and I buffeted their sails, gave the oarsmen a following wind or a headwind depending on my mood. The people praised me or cursed me. I followed their journeys into the bay and made a point of spreading the smell of herring in the market far and wide. There was movement and activity and traffic to and from Finland, and my volatility was a constant topic of conversation.

However, I must admit that I am vain, and that the town charter in 1622 was a miscalculation. An arms factory was built and many German smiths arrived. So far so good – they wore amusing broad-brimmed hats that I could rip from their heads, but the focus began to shift from the sea to the river, because it was a source of power for both the factory and a number of mills.

27

The river! It was referred to as 'Norrtälje's bloodstream and heart' and 'God's blessing to the residents of Norrtälje'. The river! What do I have to do with the river? Nothing! I can cause ripples on its surface and I can toss the leaves from the trees into it, but unlike the sea, the river is *sufficient unto itself* in a very irritating way. The fishing and sea traffic continued, and it wasn't as if I was forgotten, but my significance was reduced, and masses were no longer celebrated to appease me.

Maybe that was why I didn't do anything when the Russians arrived in 1719. I could easily have raced eastwards and pushed their fleet back to where it had come from. Instead, I provided a fine following wind, and when they had set fire to the town I made sure I travelled between the buildings, feeding the flames. Perhaps this was a slightly exaggerated form of revenge, but I have a passionate nature.

Anyway. The town was gradually rebuilt, and the time for my first speech will soon be over. However, before I fade away, I want to mention one more period in the long history of Norrtälje, namely the bathing epoch. It seems incredible now, but during the late 1800s and early 1900s, the town was the most elegant bathing resort on the east coast.

Oh my goodness! The ladies that disembarked from the SS *Rex* and other vessels in the harbour – there was no shortage of broad-brimmed hats for me to grab hold of! Elegantly clad ladies and gentlemen made their way across the newly built Society Bridge into Society Park where the Society Building lay. Society in all directions! They took cold baths, hot baths and mud baths, and in the evenings there were outdoor concerts where I could whisk away the sheet music, find my way beneath the ladies' wide skirts and tickle the gentlemen's well-tended beards. Those were the days!

Gradually the town's miracle-working mud fell into oblivion. The ships stopped coming and the Society Building was torn down. These days when I travel through the park I have to dodge this way and that between people pushing buggies, and young and old with their eyes glued to screens. My only consolation is a large weathervane that has been erected in my honour.

But a new age is dawning! A ship is approaching the harbour, a ship with a cargo that will be difficult to unload, and will turn many things upside down. My nature is erratic and I love change, not to mention chaos. My time is coming.

NOTHING IS HAPPENING HERE

I

Two women are walking across the lawns where Norrtälje's airfield once lay. As they approach the rampart that was built to protect said airfield, one woman takes out her phone. Look, it's Siw, whom we last saw outside the library when she interrupted a preordained tragedy. The same hand that closed around the handle of a child's buggy sixteen years ago is now moving adroitly across the screen as she manipulates some kind of fantasy figure.

Siw is rounder than she used to be – let's be honest, she's overweight. She has dropped the sense of style she displayed at the age of thirteen, and today she is wearing grey joggers and a faded black hoodie; the logo 'Take me to love' is just about legible. She has Crocs on her feet. Her hair is dyed black, her roots showing a centimetre of her original colour.

It is something of a disappointment to see Siw like this. One could easily have got the impression that she was destined for great things, but it seems as if life has taken its toll on her. However, her eyes are bright and alert, there is nothing cowed about her posture, and what do we know about a person's destiny? The future could still hold great achievements for our Siw.

The other woman is called Anna. She is the same age as Siw, and is clearly not happy with her friend's current activity. She rolls her eyes and tugs irritably at the strap of the small backpack she is wearing. 'Can't you stop messing with that crap?' she says. 'I'm friends with a fucking *Pokémon* zombie.'

'Hang on,' Siw says. 'I'm just going to . . .'

Siw scrolls down her list, finds fat Snorlax and puts him in the rampart's gym. We have now realised this is *Pokémon Go*, and that Siw's Pokémon collection is extensive, as she has reached level thirty-five. Anna points to Snorlax and says: 'You do know that's how we're going to end up, if we don't pull ourselves together.'

Like the boys we saw earlier, these two friends are very similar. Anna is also overweight; she is carrying about twenty kilos that do not sit well on her body. Her hair is also dyed black, but she is more meticulous than Siw when it comes to keeping her roots covered. The women are both equally tall, or rather short, but that's where the immediate resemblance ends.

Anna's eyes are green and slightly bulbous, which gives her a challenging, almost bold expression. This is reinforced by the fact that her full lips and broad mouth automatically settle into an ironic smile. Her nose is large and slightly upturned, so that you can see her nostrils. You wouldn't call her pretty, but there is something striking about her appearance. There is a generosity about Anna. Her hips are wide and her breasts bounce as she moves. You can't avoid *seeing* her.

Siw is also carrying her gym wear in a backpack, because the friends are on their way to Friskis & Svettis. She checks the time on her phone, sees that it is just after five and says: 'It'll have to be a short session today. I need to pick up Alva at six.'

'No problem. Let's just see if there are any hunks in tights, that kind of thing.'

'Hopefully not.'

'What?'

'Seriously, do *you* want the place to be packed out with self-obsessed guys – girls too – staring at us as we . . . bounce around?'

'Don't worry, we won't manage more than ten minutes before we collapse, so it'll definitely be a short session.'

Siw nibbles at a thumbnail and her eyes become suspiciously shiny as she says: 'I really want this. I want to have the courage to go for it.'

'So go for it,' Anna says, then stops dead and slaps her forehead. 'Shit!'

'What's wrong?'

Anna points to the car park outside the gym. It is filled with market stalls, their lanterns lighting up the September twilight. 'I promised to help my sister. What time did you say it was? Five o'clock? I'll do it later. I'd better go and say hello, though.'

Siw and Anna pass through the smells of candy floss, hot dogs and sweets, they walk past stalls offering mobile phone cases, selfie sticks, fun T-shirts and sheepskin slippers, and they eventually stop at a stall selling Americana.

Anna's older sister Lotta has packed her space with all kinds of things reminiscent of a USA that disappeared long ago. There are tin models of cars from the 1950s, Bakelite busts of Elvis, jars of Brylcreem, money boxes in the form of jukeboxes. A huge Confederate flag is displayed on the back wall, and the sound of Johnny Cash singing 'I Walk the Line' is coming out of a pair of speakers.

Lotta is the queen of all she surveys. She is one metre ninety tall, and only just fits under the roof. Her naturally black hair is braided into an aggressive plait that hangs down over her shoulder like a mamba ready to strike. She glares at Anna.

'Where the fuck have you been?' Lotta snaps, waving a hand that is surprisingly small in relation to her large body. 'I had to set this lot up by myself. Hi, Siw.'

Siw responds with a nod and a cautious smile. When she was growing up she often spent time at Anna's farm outside Rimbo, and she has always been slightly afraid of her friend's family. Anna has two brothers and two sisters, all as tall and well-built as their father. 'He must have been sick the day he made me,' as Anna, the exception, says. No doubt she takes after her mother, who is of normal height but compensates with coarse language that used to terrify Siw.

'I'll be back later,' Anna says, jerking her head in the direction of the gym. 'Siw and I are going to work out.'

'Work out?' Lotta says. 'What the fuck for? If you want to lift stuff, there's plenty here.'

'Maybe some people actually care what they look like,' Anna retorts, nodding at Lotta's belly, protruding underneath her cowboy shirt, which has metal collar tips. Lotta puts her hands on her hips and sticks her belly out even further. 'Are you calling me ugly?'

'No, I'm saying you look fucking terrible. See you later.'

'Fuck off.'

This was the normal tone in Anna's family – in fact, her mother was considerably worse – and Siw had never been able to get used to it. The conversation around the dinner table frequently made her blush. She had explained away Anna's language to her own mother with the excuse that the tone back home was 'coarse but warm', even though Siw couldn't find much warmth in the things they said to one another. Anna was less offensive than the rest of them, possibly as a consequence of her association with Siw.

They walk side by side towards the entrance. On the concrete wall a couple of metres to the right, someone has sprayed 'Ballet for Fatties'.

2

'Can I open the door, Mummy?'

Siw takes out the key which is attached to a round piece of wood with the word 'Home' etched on it, and hands it to Alva who has to stand on tiptoe in order to insert it in the lock. Siw can't help grimacing as her daughter struggles to turn the key, but lets her carry on. Finally there is a click and Siw can relax. She takes out the key and discreetly checks that it hasn't been bent by Alva's efforts.

The smell that means home envelops Siw as she steps into the hallway. She closes the door behind her and the tension in her chest eases. She hangs the key on its hook and points to the shoes that Alva has kicked off, then at the shoe rack. As Alva places her shoes in the right place, she asks: 'Why do shoes have to go on the shoe rack?'

'It's all in the name, isn't it? Shoe rack.'

Alva frowns, then nods. The explanation fits in with the way she perceives the world, and for once there is no demand for further clarification. Instead, she demands: 'What's for dinner?'

'Meatballs and mashed potato.'

'*Real* mashed potato?'

'Yes. And real meatballs.'

34

'Good. That's all right.'

Alva has very clear ideas on the way things should be. 'Real' mashed potato is, in fact, powdered mash, because the homemade version might contain lumps, and that is not okay. 'Real' meatballs are also difficult to make, because *real* meatballs are small and perfectly round. Mustard is only mustard if it comes in a plastic bottle. And so on.

Alva disappears into her room while Siw unpacks her sports gear. The only dampness comes from her wet towel, because she didn't make enough effort to work up a sweat. Her muscles can do what's required of them in everyday life, but faced with a range of gym equipment, they quickly kicked back and refused to continue. Their daily task consists mainly of passing goods across a scanner at the supermarket checkout, so Siw has strong hands and forearms, but not much else.

When she hangs the towel up to dry in the bathroom, she discovers that she has difficulty raising her arms, in spite of the brevity of the gym session. But surely that's a good sign? Something is happening.

On the way to the kitchen she pauses for a moment in the living room. She loves every bit of her three-room apartment, but she is particularly fond of her living room. Above the sofa hangs a patch-work quilt made up of different-coloured woven pieces, and on the coffee table there are three candle holders. Humming 'Brännö Serenade', she lights the candles with the long-necked lighter, which, like the key hook, is intended precisely for that purpose. If you were looking for one phrase to describe Siw's apartment, it would indeed be *fit for purpose*. Each item in its place, and no extravagances.

So, what about the rocking chair in the corner? It's decorated with kurbits painting, and seems to be a fine example of handicraft.

Yes, but it was given to Siw by her maternal grandmother when she had to move into a care home, because it used to be Siw's favourite spot when she was little. There is a knitting basket on the floor next to the chair, and Siw promises herself that this evening she will finally get on with Alva's sweater.

She pictures herself sitting in the rocking chair with several candles burning, the needles clicking quietly and Håkan Hellström singing softly from the speakers. A warm rush of pleasure floods her body, and she smiles and shakes her head.

You don't ask for much, do you, Siw?

No, that's the way it is. Certain elements may be lacking in Siw's life, but she has managed to adapt, to accept who she is and what she has, and to appreciate it. In that way, she is an expert in the art of living.

Alva examines her mashed potato, searching for lumps. When she doesn't find any, she spears a meatball and looks at it from every angle before announcing: 'This one isn't perfectly round.'

'In that case we'll have to complain.'

'Do what?'

'Put it in an envelope and send it to Findus with a note: *We are returning your sub-standard meatball. Send us a new one.*'

'You can't put a meatball in an envelope. That's silly.'

'Okay. Give it to me then.'

Alva holds out her fork, shaking her head at her mother's stupidity. When Siw has chewed and swallowed, she says: 'You're right. It wasn't perfectly round. That's terrible.'

'Don't be sarcastic, Mummy.'

'Sorry.'

Siw can't claim that she fully understands her daughter. On the one hand, Alva is incredibly imaginative and can stage advanced

36

role play games with her cuddly toys, while on the other, she is as strict as a puritan and refuses to accept any infringements of the bounds of reality. It is a balancing act, and Siw sometimes stumbles.

Alva is short and slender, her shoulders fragile beneath the blue *Frozen* T-shirt she is wearing. Her brown hair is braided in two thin plaits, framing a small face with a firm chin and a pointed nose. Her blue eyes are often screwed up, and the whole combination gives Alva an impression of sharpness, as if you might cut yourself on her if you're not careful. She is seven years old.

'Has anything happened today?' Siw asks tentatively.

Alva glances at her and apparently decides that Mummy can be forgiven for her attempt at sarcasm. 'Milla's daddy isn't at home because he's in hospital because he fell off the roof.'

'Oh dear. What was he doing up on—'

'Was my daddy in hospital?' Alva interrupts.

Siw sighs. *Here we go again.* 'No. I've already told you. He disappeared.'

'But *before* he disappeared?'

'No. He just disappeared.'

'But where did he go?'

'Nobody knows.'

'Not even his mummy and daddy – my granny and granddad?'

'No, I've told you that as well. They're dead.'

This conversation has been played out in countless variations ever since Alva was old enough to understand that there is something strange about the fact that she doesn't have a daddy. Because Siw had been asked the question in the past by adult acquaintances, she had an elaborate story all ready to dole out to Alva in bite-sized portions. In short, it involved a Finn on a sea crossing, a man who has since proved impossible to trace.

It bothers her that Alva occasionally announces with pride that she is half-Finnish, but it can't be helped. At least it's better than the truth. To Siw's relief, Alva seems to have decided that the topic has been exhausted for now, because she nods to her mother and asks: 'Why is your hair wet?'

'I went to the gym.'

'To do what?'

'Strength training.'

'So you'll be strong?'

'Yes. And a bit thinner.'

Alva screws up her eyes as if she is assessing Siw and finding it unlikely that she will ever achieve different proportions from the ones she has at the moment. When she has finished her assessment, she says: 'Isn't that rather . . . unnecessary?'

Siw lets out a snort and almost chokes on the food in her mouth, but manages to swallow it while exhaling through her nose. When she looks up Alva is frowning at her. She doesn't like being laughed at unless she has told a joke.

'Sorry,' Siw says. 'Auntie Anna was there too.'

Alva is very fond of Anna, and Siw hopes the mention of her will improve the situation. However, Alva is in no mood to be appeased. Her frown deepens, she folds her arms and asks: 'Why do you do *everything* with Auntie Anna?'

'Because she's my best friend.'

Alva's expression softens slightly. 'Has she *always* been your best friend?'

'No. We didn't meet until high school.'

'When you were old.'

'Not that old. I was thirteen.'

'So, what happened? When you met?'

38

3

Siw had a favourite place to spend break times. A week after the incident outside the library she was sitting as usual in 'her' armchair in the corner of the common room, where three sets of sofas and chairs were scattered around the windowless space that resembled a cross between a bunker and a waiting room. Fluorescent lighting. Posters on the walls warning of the dangers of drugs and unprotected sex, including a picture of a suntanned girl on a beach, with the words: 'Holiday romance? Don't forget the condoms!' Someone had added a rather good drawing of an enormous erect cock with a beach bum hairstyle, making its way towards the girl in the sunset.

Siw had a hardback copy of *Crime and Punishment* on her lap, but it was mainly for show. She would really like to be the girl who read Russian authors during break, but at the moment the book was just an excuse to enable her to sit in the corner and observe everyone else. Occasionally she read a few lines, but they didn't make much sense. Her mother had given her the novel, and Siw had accepted it because she liked its physical heaviness.

She wasn't a victim of bullying, even though she was sometimes teased about her weight, but neither was she au fait with the social codes necessary to become part of the centre stage, which was made up of the main seating area. Therefore, she stayed in the wings, observing the performances of star players. Like Anna.

In spite of the fact that Anna had joined the class only a month ago, and from *Rimbo*, for goodness' sake, she had already acquired a swarm of admirers who hung on every word that fell from her thick lips as she joked about teachers, other pupils, herself and

Rimbo. She had a big mouth, both figuratively and literally, and Siw found her simultaneously repulsive and fascinating. So far they hadn't exchanged a single word.

For once it wasn't Anna who was holding court but Sofi, a girl with backcombed hair who wouldn't have looked out of place in an eighties video. In Siw's opinion, she had all the intelligence of a marshmallow. With fluttering manicured hands and a high voice, she was expounding on something that had happened at the bus station over the weekend.

'And he just sat there, like, checking me out and I went, like, *what* and he . . .'

Unconsciously Siw rolled her eyes and shook her head before turning her attention to her book. A voice of a completely different calibre from Sofi's suddenly rang out.

'Hey! You!' Siw looked up and found herself caught in the spotlight of Anna's eyes. She raised her eyebrows. 'Yes, you!' Anna yelled. 'What's your name?'

Siw tried to keep her voice steady. 'Siw.'

'*Siw*,' Anna repeated, as if pronouncing the name caused her physical pain. 'Do you think there's something wrong with the way we talk? Don't we talk *posh* enough for you, *Siiiiw*?'

'You can talk however you want.'

'Can we? *Thank you*, Siw, who doesn't have a life.'

The other girls laughed loudly and Siw lowered her head over her book, a faint flush staining her cheeks. She wasn't the first to have been singled out by Anna, who attacked anyone and anything, but so far she'd escaped by staying in the background.

Part of the explanation for Anna's rapidly rising star was that she had arrived at the school with a reputation. In spite of the fact that she was only fourteen, she was being made to repeat a year: rumour had it that she drank and screwed around, and that everyone under eighteen in Rimbo was scared of her. Among other things, she had attacked a guy riding past her on his moped, because he'd made a nasty comment. He'd fallen off and cracked his skull. That kind of thing. There were also rumours that her family was involved in some sort of criminal activity, but Siw didn't know any more details.

She decided that for the rest of break time, she wasn't even going to look up and risk incurring a further outburst from Anna. After a while she actually managed to concentrate on what she was reading. Some guy called Marmeladov was going on about his own wretchedness, then someone else said something to the person who should have been Marmeladov, but now he suddenly had a different name. This kept happening, which was one of the reasons why Siw found it hard to keep up. Everyone seemed to have up to three different names. She turned back to the first page, where there was a list of characters. Then she heard a different voice above her head. A male voice.

'Move.'

Robert was standing in front of her holding an open laptop. He was in the parallel class to hers, had lots of spots, spiky hair, and was wearing a T-shirt with the logo 'Fuck the law', even though his dad was a police officer. Or maybe that was why. Siw just stared at him.

'Didn't you hear me, Fatso?' He waved the laptop. 'I need somewhere to sit. Shift your fat arse.'

Siw continued to look him in the eye without saying a word. Then Anna's voice sliced through the hum of conversation. 'Hey! Pizza Face!'

The room fell silent. Robert slowly turned around, flipped the laptop shut and took a couple of long strides towards Anna. He was fifteen centimetres taller than her, and twenty kilos heavier. 'Are you talking to me?'

41

Anna nodded and pointed to his crotch. 'I just wanted to tell you that your zip's open.'

Robert did his best, but couldn't help glancing down. The second he bent his neck, Anna said: 'Oh wow – it just zipped itself up! That's amazing! Did you sew it yourself?'

Robert hissed through gritted teeth: 'You fucking . . .'

Anna straightened her shoulders and took a step forward. She jutted out her chin and said: 'Go on, say it. Say the word. If you dare.'

There wasn't a sound in the common room. Everyone's eyes were on Robert, wondering if he would dare to say that word to Anna, and therefore to her whole family. *That* family. He jerked his head and moved his lips as if he were spitting, then he left the room to a chorus of laughter from Anna's posse.

Anna looked over at Siw, who said: 'Thanks, but no thanks.'

'What the fuck do you mean?'

'That I'm perfectly capable of taking care of myself.'

'So I see.'

Anna returned to her group and Siw heard various comments, such as 'thinks she's something else' and 'fucking know-all bitch'. Siw went back to Marmeladov. What a stupid name.

The bell rang. Siw spent thirty seconds finishing the section she was reading. When she looked up the room was empty apart from Anna, who was sitting there staring at her. When they made eye contact Anna stood up, came over and perched on the arm of the nearest sofa.

'Let's hear it,' she said.

'The lesson's starting.'

'So? Let's hear it. How would you have dealt with that idiot, since you're perfectly capable of taking care of yourself? Go on.'

Siw sighed and glanced in the direction of the corridor, which was where she ought to be. 'I would have stayed put. Then he would have said, "Is there something wrong with your hearing, Fatso?", or something along those lines. Then I would have said: 'I hear what you're saying, but I don't understand what it means.' Then he would have said something else and I would have carried on telling him I didn't understand, until he got fed up.'

Anna listened, her eyes getting bigger by the second. When Siw had finished, she shook her head. 'That's the worst idea I've ever heard.'

'Why?'

'You have to crush him, otherwise he'll keep doing it, over and over again.'

'Not too many times. They all get fed up in the end.'

Anna leaned forward, resting her elbows on her knees, and gazed at Siw so intently that Siw felt naked. She didn't want to stand up and expose her body. In the end Anna nodded to herself. 'So, are you a tiny bit psycho? You are, aren't you?'

'Probably, yes.'

'Good to know. What are you reading?'

Siw showed her the cover. She watched Anna, and could see that she read the title without any problem. However, when she reached the author's name, her lips moved. *Fyodor Dostoevsky.* Anna shook her head. 'For fuck's sake,' she said, then stood up and left.

However, something had happened. From then on Siw and Anna nodded to each other whenever they met, but it would take another ten days before they spoke again. Siw was in the library revising for a maths test when Anna plonked herself down in a chair on the opposite side of the table. The aroma of Juicy Fruit chewing gum drifted across when Anna opened her mouth. 'So, what are you doing?'

'Maths test. I'm not very good at maths.'

'Who the fuck is?' Anna replied. She chewed her gum and looked at Siw from under her fringe, as if the next comment was down to her. Siw rested her chin on her hand and waited. Anna drummed her fingers on the table. Her short nails were painted red, but the polish was chipped. Her make-up seemed as if it had been slapped on in a hurry – more an application of war paint than an attempt at beautification. After a while she stopped drumming. 'So, what's a *book review*?'

'What do you mean?'

'Exactly what I said. We're supposed to write a book review in Swedish. What is it?'

'A review of a book.'

Anna stared at Siw as her tongue shot out and licked her lips. 'Are you taking the piss?'

Siw raised her hands. She didn't believe Anna was likely to punch her, but she adopted a pedagogical tone: 'A book review is when you write what you think about a book. A book you've read. Göran went over all this. He told us what to do.'

Göran was their Swedish teacher, and he'd given a detailed explanation of what their reviews should contain. Anna shook her head. 'I wasn't listening. It was so fucking boring.'

'Okay. So have you got a book?'

Anna rummaged in the leopard-print imitation Hermès bag she used for school, dug out a paperback and tossed it on the table. *Hummelhonung [Sweetness]* by Torgny Lindgren. Siw flicked through the pages and saw that it was written in old-fashioned, high-flown language.

'Why have you chosen this one?'

'It's short. Have you read it?'

44

'No. Have you?'

'A bit, but it's so fucking stupid. Nothing that would happen in real life. And I have problems concentrating . . .'

Anna picked up the little book and glared at the cover as if Torgny Lindgren himself was to blame for her difficulties. Siw waited. Eventually Anna put down the book and looked sideways at her in an unexpectedly shy way. She made a gesture as if she were putting her cards on the table. 'The thing is, I've decided to try to . . . get my act together. So far I've just messed around in school, not taken anything seriously. But now I'd like to give it a go, at least.'

'And that's why you've come to me.'

'Yes – you're a psychobitch and you read fyoskodosko whatever his name is. Who else would I come to? None of my friends do that kind of stuff.'

'To be perfectly honest,' Siw said, 'I haven't actually read much fyoskodosko; I carry the book round for appearances' sake.'

'Okay, but at least you've read books. You know what a review is.'

'I do.'

Siw had already written her own review of Stephen King's *The Girl Who Loved Tom Gordon*, which she had also chosen because it was short, but had really liked. It would probably have suited Anna a lot better than Torgny Lindgren.

Siw took out a piece of paper and wrote down a list of bullet points, talking Anna through them. 1) Facts about the book. Search online. 2) Short description of the plot. 3) What you thought of the plot and how it's written. 4) Summary and conclusion.

The longer Siw talked, the more Anna slumped in her seat. When Siw had finished, she said: 'I'll give you a hundred kronor if you write it for me.'

'No.'

'Two hundred.'

'No. But I will help you.'

'Fuck. How did I know you were going to say that?'

'Because you've seen right through me – you know what a kind and helpful person I really am.'

Anna grinned. 'Bullshit. You're a psychobitch and that's all there is to it.'

'Okay, I'll take that as a positive.'

'You do that.'

As Siw was taking things out of her locker the following morning, she heard Anna's voice behind her: 'Hey, psychobitch!'

Siw turned and tried to adopt the same suspicious, passive-aggressive smile as De Niro in *Taxi Driver*. 'You talkin' to me?'

Anna clapped her hands in delight. 'Have you seen it? Isn't it sick?'

Siw hadn't yet used the fashionable new word except in its original meaning, but she said: 'Sick. How come you've seen it?'

'My big brother was watching it – it's his favourite. That and *Scarface* – have you seen that one?'

'No, but I have seen *The Godfather*.'

'My mistake – *that's* his favourite.' Anna took a step back and looked Siw up and down, as if she were a puzzle in which new pieces had appeared, making a reappraisal of the full picture necessary. Fortunately Siw was wearing her grandmother's old Sunday-best coat, and thought she looked pretty cool for once. Anna nodded slowly. 'You're the only girl I know who's seen *Taxi Driver*. Except for my big sister.'

'How many brothers and sisters have you got?'

Anna pulled a face and counted on her fingers. 'One big sister, one little sister. One big brother and one little brother. I'm in the middle. How about you?'

'I'm an only child.'

'Lucky you. Listen, that review . . .'

'Yes?'

A hint of the aggression that was Anna's default setting crept back into her posture, and she glared at Siw the way she'd glared at Torgny Lindgren. Siw sensed that Anna was someone who found it very difficult to ask for anything without getting angry, so she decided to make things easier for her. 'If you need help, then I'll help you. As I said.'

Anna nodded grimly and took no responsibility for her question, since she hadn't asked it, so Siw was forced to go on: 'It's due in the day after tomorrow, so . . . If you want to come over to mine after school, we can work on it.'

'Can't today. Tomorrow?'

'Fine.'

'I mean, you don't have a life anyway, do you?' Siw gave Anna a look that actually made her back off a fraction and wave her hands defensively. 'Sorry, I didn't mean that. I can bring *Scarface* – shall I do that?'

'Good idea.'

*

The man's arms are covered in tattoos. Monsters, devils, plus the names of his children. His back is covered in a well-executed copy of Doré's illustration of the Suicide Tree from Dante's Inferno. *On his way out through the door of the gym's changing room, he turns to the three strangers who are getting changed. 'Have a nice weekend,' he says. Then he leaves.*

47

WINNERS AND LOSERS

I

The word 'nerds' springs to mind when you look at the two young men on the minigolf course. They have brought their own clubs, and each has a little bag in which they carry balls of different grades of hardness and bounce. They are clearly into this in a big way, and you can say what you like about minigolf, but its cool factor is zero. Both men are only just under thirty years old, and have doubtless left such considerations behind them, otherwise they wouldn't be on a minigolf course on a Saturday afternoon in September.

The men are muttering to themselves, making comments on each other's strokes, and there wouldn't be much to arouse our interest if we hadn't met them before. Yes, of course, it's Max and Johan, our daring silo climbers. We bump into them sixteen years later; the silo was demolished six months ago to make room for a new residential development in the harbour area.

It has to be said that they are pretty good – two or at the most three strokes per hole, with the odd hole-in-one. They seem to have

48

played a lot. Let's see what we can learn about them by observing their playing style.

Johan's expression is one of grim determination, as if the game is torture to him. He spends a long time preparing for each stroke, and if the outcome is poor, he nods, lips pressed tightly together, as if he hadn't expected anything else. He *sweeps* the ball away, using his entire body. Even when he absolutely nails a difficult hole, he doesn't show any real pleasure.

Max's game is more erratic. He doesn't put his body into the stroke in the way that Johan does. He pulls a face and sighs when it goes badly, clenches his fist in triumph when it goes well. On one occasion when he makes a real mess of his stroke, he seems to be on the point of throwing his club away, even though it looks newer and more expensive than Johan's.

It is surprising to find them here, especially Max. Given what we learned about his character and family that day on the silo, we might have expected that at the age of twenty-nine he would be pretty successful, well on the way in his career. We might also have assumed that he and Johan would have gone their separate ways many years ago, as so often happens with childhood friends from different backgrounds. Yet here they are, the only players on Norrtälje's minigolf course on a beautiful Saturday afternoon, and we ask ourselves what has brought them to this point. Let's take a closer look.

Both men are still tall and slim. Max isn't exactly muscular, but he seems to be in good physical shape. His appearance is enhanced by a deep tan. Johan is just as sinewy as when he was a boy, and so pale that it must be regarded as something of an achievement after a particularly sunny summer. Max has short hair, while Johan has gathered his long, thinning hair into a man-bun.

There is something disillusioned in Johan's eyes, as if he has seen everything and left it all behind. We mustn't jump to conclusions, but it looks more like bitterness than sorrow. When we turn our attention to Max, we are quite taken aback. His big blue eyes are striking in themselves, but his expression! It's as if there is a thin film over his eyes, the way people look when they are drunk. Max is not under the influence of anything, and yet his expression is *veiled*. What's going on? We dare not guess, but there is an element of madness there – or maybe a deep, suppressed pain.

Max's ball bounces off the low back wall and rolls towards the hole. When it gets there it veers around the edge. It is about to drop in, but completes the movement and continues off to the left.

'Shit!' Max shouts, slashing the air with his club.

'I told you,' Johan says. 'You should have used the number two.'

'It wouldn't have reached the hole.'

'Yes, it would.'

'Wouldn't.'

'Would.'

'Fuck! I was close to my best score of the year there.'

'You should have used the number two.'

They carry on bickering until Max nails the next hole and his mood lightens. He rests the club on his shoulder and squints at the sun, which is going down behind the tops of the fir trees. 'Have you heard that Marko's coming home?'

Johan, who was about to hit the ball, stops in mid-movement and looks up. 'To Norrtälje?'

'Mmm. At the weekend.'

'For . . . for good, or what?'

Max lets out a guffaw as if Johan has said something funny. 'No. That would surprise me. He's coming to help his parents move.'

'Where to?'

'He's bought them a house – near my parents.'

'Wow. He must be doing well.'

'Half a million in bonuses – and that's just so far this year.'

Johan digests this information as he studies his ball, which is lying there waiting for him. 'How do you know all this?'

'He called me. Didn't he call you?'

'No. He didn't call me.'

Johan concentrates on his stroke, twists his body to the side, bounces lightly on his knees and brings the club to the ball in a sweeping movement. He misses the ramp and the ball bounces awkwardly into the channel at the side. That hardly ever happens.

'*You should have used the number two*,' Max sneers, and Johan is struck by a powerful urge to smash him over the head with his club. Instead, he goes and picks up his ball, ready to try again.

2

One afternoon a couple of days after the boys had climbed the silo, Johan's doorbell rang when he was sitting playing *The Wind Waker* on his GameCube. His mother was out, so he paused the game and went to open the door. Marko was standing there.

'Hi,' Johan said.

'Hi,' Marko replied, shifting uncomfortably from foot to foot. 'What are you doing?'

'Playing *The Wind Waker*.'

'Can I . . . have a look?'

Marko's tentative approach was completely different from the stone-faced expression he favoured in school. Johan turned and stared at the apartment; there was stuff piled up everywhere, clothes draped over the back of every chair. Dust bunnies lined the skirting boards; add in a couple of big fat rats and the picture of wretched misery would be complete.

'I'm not sure,' he said. 'We were going to . . . tidy up later.'

'Doesn't matter,' Marko replied. 'I've lived in cellars.'

His response was so disarming that Johan had no choice but to let him in. Marko took off his shoes and padded through the hallway without even glancing at the mess, or wrinkling his nose at the smell emanating from the kitchen. He went into the living room and sat down cross-legged in front of the TV next to the open balcony door, the only spot that was free of crap and dirty laundry. Johan sat down beside him, picked up the control and nodded towards the paused screen.

'Have you played this before?'

Marko shook his head. 'They had PlayStation at one of the camps. I played a bit.'

'PlayStation 2?'

'No, just PlayStation.' Possibly with the intention of alleviating the impression of poverty, Marko pointed in the direction of his apartment and went on: 'We've got a TV, but no . . .' He moved his thumb towards his forefinger several times.

'Remote control?'

'That's it, remote control. No remote control.'

Johan waved in the direction of the clothes, towels and sheets spread all over the sofa, coffee table and armchairs. 'We've got a remote,' he said. 'Somewhere underneath all that.'

Marko smiled and Johan started the game. When he and Max played they usually opted for *Smash Bros* or *Mario Kart* and competed against each other. It felt weird sitting next to someone who was just watching, but after a little while Johan had got used to the situation, and after a while longer he actually liked it. From time to time Marko asked a question about how things worked, and Johan explained.

'This is a Bomb Flower. You have to get rid of it really quickly, because otherwise it explodes and you can get hurt.'

'Can you save it?'

'Mmm, in your bomb bag.'

'Bomb bag?'

'Yes. It's a bit silly.'

When they'd been playing for a few minutes more, Marko said: 'I lied. Before. Well, I didn't *lie*, but I didn't tell the truth.'

'About what?'

'I knew what you were doing. I could hear you. Through the balcony window. I came over because I wanted to see.'

'Okay, that's cool.'

'I just wanted to tell you.'

'It's cool. You speak Swedish *really* well.'

'Do I? I don't know. Who am I supposed to compare myself with? I speak better than my mum. Much better than my dad. Just as well as my little sister. No, better, because I know a lot more words than she does, but then her pronunciation is better than mine.'

'Your pronunciation is perfect.'

'*Hörövarhepp.*'

'Sorry?'

'*Hörövarhepp.* I'm kind of exaggerating now, but – *hörövarhepp.*'

'I don't get it.'

Marko grinned and hissed: '*Sjörövarskepp.* Pirate ship. I still have to make a real effort to pronounce it properly, it doesn't come easy. But soon.'

53

Johan glanced sideways at Marko. 'I hadn't noticed in school, but you're actually . . . quite funny.'

'Thanks,' Marko said. He pointed to the blue cube where the spinning disc could be seen through a window in the lid. 'Is that yours?'

'Yes.'

'Present?'

'No. I bought it myself.'

'How could you afford it?'

Johan hesitated. Since his mother had given up work because of ill health five years ago, they had become poor. Not searching-through-the-bins poor, but enough for Johan to carry it with him like a stigma. He didn't get any pocket money, and the way he chose to earn his own money was the sort of thing poor people did, and not something he liked to share with anyone.

Thinking about it now, he realised that mainly applied to Max. Marko was different. It was partly because he was so straight, so direct, and partly because his own situation seemed pretty similar, so Johan said: 'I collect bottles and jars and return them for the deposit.'

'How do you collect them?'

'I ring people's doorbells, say I'm from the Sea Scouts, we're collecting money for a new boat – do they have any jars or bottles they could donate?'

'The Sea Scouts?'

'Yes – they're like ordinary Scouts, but at sea. I tried a football team to begin with, but it seems as if people prefer the Sea Scouts. For some reason.'

'But . . . you're not a member of the Sea Scouts?'

Johan looked at Marko. In school he gave the impression of being intelligent – *extremely* intelligent, in fact. He was very good at maths and had caught up with all his other subjects at top speed. However, now it turned out that he was a little bit stupid at some level.

'No,' Johan said with exaggerated clarity. 'I am not a member of the Sea Scouts. They're mostly rich kids, I think.'

'So you lie?'

'Yes. I lie. And they give me bottles and jars.'

'Okay.'

Marko turned his attention to the TV, where little Link was speeding across the blue ocean, approaching an island. Johan adjusted his course a fraction and glanced at Marko again. What he hadn't mentioned was that people sometimes gave him money instead, which he was very happy to accept. Or that on a few occasions he *had* rummaged around in bins like the pauper he was, which had enabled him to buy both the console and the games.

'You're very honest, aren't you?' he said.

'Like I said before – who do I compare myself with?'

'Well . . . anybody.'

Marko considered for a moment. 'I always tell the truth.'

'Thought so.'

The island Link was approaching was guarded by several ships flying the skull and crossbones flag. Johan produced the cannon, took aim and fired. As the cannonball flew through the air, he pointed to one of the boats and said: '*Hörövarhepp.*'

The cannonball struck, sinking the enemy vessel. Marko nodded and said: 'The Sea Scouts are attacking.'

Johan burst out laughing and missed the next shot. That was how it began.

Johan nails the last hole and wins the round by four strokes. Max congratulates him. It's not losing he minds so much as the process of losing, the descending curve. Once the loss is a fact, he can take it with equanimity these days. Things had been different when he was young, but the combination of age and Lamictal tablets have lessened his rage towards himself and the world. They gather up their balls and clubs and leave the course with a nod to Lasse, who is just closing up.

'Shall we take a stroll around the market?' Johan suggests. 'I've got a couple of ten kilometres close by.'

Max checks his *Pokémon Go*. He has a few five-kilometre eggs that need tending, but he's not expecting anything special because he's already got everything that's available. However, he shrugs and says okay. He has no plans for the evening.

The two men wander along Gustav Adolfsvägen as dusk begins to fall, lights coming on in the houses on both sides of the street. The air is mild, because the waters of the bay are still holding on to the warmth of late summer and allowing it to drift across the town. A lovely evening with only a hint of earthiness on the breeze, a reminder of the approaching autumn.

As so often happens, Max finds himself harking back to his childhood and youth, remembering how he walked along this same street in the same fading light, but back then everything had seemed mystical and full of promise, as if he were constantly on his way towards a revelation. The smells of which he is now aware are not genuine smells, but markers pointing to a time when he really did experience smells.

This is partly down to the medication he's on. When his psychiatrist prescribed Lamictal, the doctor had explained that the pills would even out his highs and lows. Max would no longer get so depressed, nor would he feel so elated. The extremes of the spectrum would be removed and Max would become the MP3 version of himself.

Maybe it's those extremes he misses. The crazy lust for life and the rash, impulsive projects, like climbing the silo. The pitch-black hours and days when the world sat in his chest like a bowling ball in a bird cage, and all he wanted to do was sink. However, after what had happened to him in Cuba, the swings had become so violent that he no longer dared to be without his medication.

He thinks of Lamictal as a figure, a little troll inside his head that he calls Micke. Micke Littletroll. Micke has a chainsaw, and as soon as he catches sight of a high on its way up or a low on its way down, he starts up the saw and takes the tops off the waves.

Sometimes Max can actually sense it happening, like when he was at a Lars Winnerbäck gig and heard the opening chords of his favourite song, 'Söndermarken'. A feeling of pure joy rose up within him, wanting to take possession of his body, but in a second Micke was there with his chainsaw, and the jubilant choir was chopped down to a small ensemble that applauded politely and murmured: 'How lovely'.

The doctor also explained about the influx of sodium to the neurons and the raising of the threshold for potential action, but the bottom line is that Max feels *lame* all the time, in spite of the fact that he works eleven hours a day. It's interesting that 'Söndermarken' became his favourite song only after he'd started taking Lamictal. It expresses the same longing for a past when everything meant more, the same brooding nostalgia that plagues him. *Dirty white clouds, dentist weather.*

'Have you noticed?' Johan says, pointing to a house opposite Kvisthamra Primary School, where they both spent their early years.

'What?' Max asks, looking at the nondescript plot with a red fence and a Subaru parked on the drive. 'What is it?'

'It's more a matter of what it *isn't*,' Johan says. 'Can't you see? New owners, and the first thing they do is chop down the apple tree. Fucking idiots. Do you remember?'

Max remembers. During the apple season he and Johan would sometimes sit in that tree at break time. The owners were out, and the boys helped themselves to as many apples as they wanted. The main attraction was that it was forbidden to leave the school premises during breaks, and to scrump apples, so they were real gangsters, perched on a branch with their legs dangling down.

Max is on a downward trajectory. Not so bad that Micke needs to step in, but he could have done without the information about the apple tree. As a general rule Max hates change. For example, the demolition of the silo and the development in the harbour area is a constant, ongoing affront to his eyes. Johan is the same, but in a less acute, more teeth-grinding way. *Fucking idiots* is his favourite expression.

'I'd prefer it if you didn't pass on that kind of information,' Max says as they approach Hedlund's tobacconist shop. 'It doesn't do me any good.'

'So are you going to have a nervous breakdown?' Johan asks.

'No, I am not going to have a nervous breakdown, and can you stop being so fucking miserable? It's not my fault Marko didn't call you.'

Johan blows air out between his teeth. 'What do you mean? I don't give a fuck about Marko.'

'Anyway, you've changed your number.'

'You could have given him my new number.'

'I thought you didn't give a fuck about Marko?'

'Yes, but you didn't know that at the time, did you?'

They continue up the hill towards the airfield in silence.

When the sports hall comes into view, Johan stops and takes out his phone. A speckled blue egg can be seen on the screen, with the word 'Oh?' He presses the egg and it begins to vibrate and crack, until a fat, pink figure jumps out, cradling an egg of its own.

'Fuck,' Johan says. 'Fucking Chansey.'

Max rubs his eyes. Even though he is on level thirty-seven and has therefore played considerably more than Johan, who is on level thirty-two, he questions the validity of *Pokémon Go* as a pastime for adults. Maybe the truth is that he and Johan aren't adults, in spite of their careers and apartments. On the other hand, there are several pensioners in the Facebook group Pokémon Go Roslagen who sometimes turn up on raids. And pensioners are definitely adults.

Johan appraises Chansey who, apart from being *fucking Chansey* also has a bagful of stats. Another egg and another 'Oh?' appear on the screen, and Johan presses with unnecessary force. Max did, in fact, pass on Johan's new number to Marko without being asked, but he has no intention of telling Johan, because that would make his friend sad rather than angry.

Max looks up and sees the market sparkling in the car park in front of the sports hall. Events like this always look better from a distance. He has absolutely no desire to join the crowds shuffling past plastic tat from Taiwan.

'Yes!' Johan shouts, raising a clenched fist. 'At last!'

Snorlax is parading across the screen, blue and white and even fatter than Chansey.

'I thought you had him already?'

'No, I didn't *have him already*,' Johan mimics Max. 'So, how many have you got? Seven?'

'Four.'

Johan shakes his head. 'Get a life.'

Get a life. It's the kind of thing people say without thinking, but the concept has seriously started to bother Max over the past few months. He is twenty-nine years old, and is feeling more and more as if he is simply vegetating, waiting for his real life to begin. He has no idea what this real life is supposed to look like.

Vegetating isn't entirely fair. He has two jobs, one as a park keeper and one as a newspaper distributor. On weekdays he gets up at four in the morning, and rarely gets home before six in the evening. He has his own apartment and plenty of money, but lately he has begun to suspect that he works as hard as he does in order to avoid thinking about or tackling *the other thing*, whatever it might be.

Max's life consists of a before and an after. When he set off for Cuba at the age of twenty, his life was mapped out. All he had to do was follow the course until he reached his goal. Then the horror had sunk its claws into him and thick fog had descended; he could barely see his hand in front of him. He had begun to move from day to day without striving to reach any kind of goal; he couldn't do anything else.

As they continue to make their way towards the market, Max glances at Johan, who is busy appraising Snorlax. He seems to be pleased, because for once a smile is playing over his lips. If Max had followed the course that was originally set out for him, Johan wouldn't have been part of the journey, and they would have been strangers by now, instead of meeting up practically every day.

Johan slips the phone back into his pocket and Max says: 'Can I ask you something?'

'Mmm?'

'Do you ever feel as if . . . life is somehow running away from you?'

'Yes. All the time. Why?'

'Shouldn't we try to do something about it?'

'How can we? It's just the natural condition. We live our life, yet at the same time we feel as if we're throwing it away. What was it John Lennon said? Life is what happens while you're busy making other plans.'

'But does it have to be that way?'

'How the fuck should I know?' Johan says as they cross the patch of grass between Carl Bondes väg and the car park. 'What's the alternative?'

Max's nostrils pick up the smell of fast food and sweets, he hears the hum of voices and sees dark bodies moving beneath the coloured lanterns. It occurs to him that all this is merely an imitation, some kind of performance that is being acted out in front of him with the aim of masking the reality, as if real life is hidden inside or behind what he can see.

As they get closer and Max is able to distinguish a myriad of colours and goods for sale, he feels as if something is approaching. In a few moments the mask will be ripped away and the naked reality will be exposed. There is a rushing sound in his ears, emotion swells inside his body . . . and collapses like a souffle that's been taken out of the oven. Micke has done his job.

'What's wrong with you?' Johan asks. 'Is something happening?'

Max is unaware that he has stopped and is standing there with his fists clenched and his mouth open. He smiles apologetically at Johan and shakes his head. 'No, it was just . . . I'm fine.'

61

'Are you sure? You used to look like that when something happened.'

Max still has his visions occasionally, a fleeting glimpse of a car coming off the road or a builder falling from scaffolding, a raised hand holding a knife, but since he started taking Lamictal the experience doesn't possess his entire body as it used to, and the images are no longer so clear. This is mainly a relief. The sudden incidents of awareness, which are not unlike epilepsy, have put him in danger more than once, just like that day on the silo. Lamictal is principally used to control epilepsy, and has the same calming effect on Max's incomprehensible symptoms.

They continue along the wall of the gym, and Johan grins when he sees what someone has sprayed there: 'Ballet for Fatties'. At that moment two overweight, black-haired girls emerge through the main door. Their wide backsides sway beneath their joggers, and Johan jerks his head in the direction of the graffiti. 'Spot on, wouldn't you say?'

Max gazes after the girls. Their hair is wet and they are walking along with their heads close together, deep in conversation. They are as far removed as possible from what he regards as attractive, and yet he feels something he can't put his finger on. Envy, perhaps, as if they have something he will never achieve. Or something else.

*

The elderly couple wander slowly through the market, hand in hand. They stop at a stall selling thirty-seven flavours of liquorice strips. The young man on the till picks up his phone and asks if he can take their picture. His girlfriend doesn't believe that lifelong love exists, but he wants to propose to her, and . . . well, you understand. The couple put their arms around each other and let him take their photo.

62

A TEMPORARY VISIT TO DEATH

I

Max was seven years old the first time it happened. It was late August, he'd just come home from school and was lying on his bed reading the latest Donald Duck paperback, which had arrived in the post that very day. He was the best in his class and could read long passages aloud without stumbling, so Donald Duck was no great challenge.

The window in his big room overlooked the Kvisthamra inlet, and was wide open. He could hear his mother clattering about in the kitchen downstairs; she was making spaghetti carbonara, one of his favourites. He had a pillow behind his back and a blanket over his knees to make things cosy.

He'd just finished reading about Donald's adventure in the Wild West. He lowered the book and looked out of the window; the water was as still as a millpond. Then he became aware of a smell, just like the one when he'd short-circuited an electrical socket by inserting a damp plug. He just had time to think *is *there a fire somewhere?* when his consciousness was taken away from him.

He was no longer on his bed, but inside something that resembled a gigantic bathtub. He had no control over his body, but somehow he knew he was in here because he was playing hide-and-seek. He was curled up on the bottom of the bathtub next to a big propeller with sharp edges. Someone was searching for him.

Max didn't have time to pick up any more of this unfamiliar consciousness. There was a sudden rattling noise and at the very top of his field of vision he saw a large, round object falling down towards him. Instinctively he curled up even tighter and the object, which was a bale of compressed hay, landed right in front of him. Max didn't know why, but a bolt of sheer panic shot through his brain and he opened his mouth to scream. At that moment the propeller began to rotate.

The first sharp edge struck him in the side, knocking the air out of his lungs and slicing his skin open. He tried to get to his feet, but the propeller knocked his legs from under him. The speed increased. If he'd had the presence of mind to lie down flat on his back and let the blades whine past above him, things could have turned out differently, but that wasn't what happened. His kneecaps were sliced off by the spinning edge. The pain was so intense that it made him raise his head to see how bad the damage was. He felt a burning sensation at the back of his head, and then it was over.

Max had slid down from the pillow and kicked off the blanket. He was lying flat on his back on the bed, drenched in sweat. His jaws were clamped together so tightly that it hurt when he relaxed and opened his mouth to take a few short, panting breaths. He opened his equally tightly clenched fists, opened and closed, opened and closed.

64

What? Where? Who?

He had never seen, let alone experienced anything so horrific, not even in his nightmares. He didn't understand what kind of bathtub he'd been in, or who he had been. When the cramp in his body began to ease and his breathing slowed, Max closed his eyes and tried to recall the scene in which he had just found himself.

One thing he knew for sure: he'd been a child, around his own age. He came to this conclusion purely based on the size of his body, and particularly the smallness of the hands resting on his thin, mangled kneecaps. But why would anyone have a giant bathtub with a sharp-bladed propeller in the bottom? How come he'd suddenly had a nightmare that contained stuff he'd never even heard of? Max picked up his book, but he couldn't stop thinking about the child he had become for a while. Who? What? Where?

The following day Max got his answer without asking a question. After dinner his mother and father were sitting out on the patio with a glass of wine. Their sun loungers were just below Max's open window, and when he heard the words 'terrible tragedy', he crept over to listen in.

He couldn't pick up everything they said, but enough to give him a somewhat fragmented picture. A six-year-old child had died in an accident on a farm the previous day. The little boy had hidden in a feed mixer, whatever that was. His father had started up the machine without knowing his son was in there, and had been taken to the local hospital suffering from severe shock.

The final piece of information Max managed to glean was perhaps the most astonishing. This had happened in Björnö, across the inlet outside Max's bedroom window. Only a kilometre or so away as the crow flies. So how had he been able to see it, to *be* there?

He went downstairs and out onto the patio, where his parents let it be known with a subtle shift in their body language that this was *their* time. Max was very good at interpreting these signals, but on this occasion he ignored them and said: 'Mum? Dad? The boy who died, the one you were discussing – I saw it happen.'

'What are you talking about?' his father said, putting down his glass. 'You were at home.'

'I know, but I saw it. In my head.'

'Nonsense,' his mother snapped. She was very sensitive to anything that could be seen as social deviance. Seeing things in one's head definitely fell into that category, but Max wasn't giving up. 'Yesterday. When it happened. I became that little boy just before the propellers began to turn . . .'

'Have people been gossiping about this in school?' his father wondered, his tone making it clear that this was highly inappropriate.

'No – nobody's mentioned it, but I *became* him, it's like I was inside his head and—'

His father held up his hand and said firmly: 'Enough, Max! Mum and I are having a quiet drink, and I don't want to hear your silly stories.'

What Max found most surprising when he returned to his room was the fact that he'd actually thought it was worth trying. Both his mother and father were staunch opponents of any kind of alternative behaviour, which included religious leanings. Supernatural abilities simply didn't exist.

If this *was* a supernatural ability. Max lay down on his bed and his parents' voices died away to a murmur. He placed a hand over his heart and felt his pulse racing. He had once read a Donald Duck story about a magician who could see into the future. His eyes turned into spinning spirals and he was able to say what was going to happen.

But according to Max's parents, the accident had happened *yesterday afternoon* – so at the same time as Max had seen it. Although, of course, he couldn't be sure; the word 'afternoon' covered a lot of hours, but still . . . Something didn't quite fit, and he made a huge effort to try to work it out. Yes! He must have seen into the future a little bit, because he became the six-year-old boy just before the accident. He concentrated, thought back.

He had been scared when the bale of hay came thudding down. The child had understood something that Max knew nothing about. And when the propeller sliced into him, had it hurt? Max searched his memory. Yes, it had hurt, but nowhere near as much as having his kneecaps chopped off should have hurt. It was as if the pain had been confined to his head.

Max covered his eyes with his hands and conducted an experiment. He pictured the block where his father sometimes chopped wood for the fire. He placed his left hand on the block, then he imagined the axe in his right hand.

No. No, no, no.

The thought alone made him want to resist, but he forced himself to swing the axe through the air and bring it down, forced himself to chop off his left index and middle fingers, saw them flip away from the block, saw the blood spurting from the stumps.

Did it hurt? Yes, in a way it did. There was imaginary pain in his imaginary hand. He uncovered his eyes and checked that his left hand was intact. This was how he had felt when the boy in the feed mixer was struck by the blade, but it wasn't something that had *actually* happened to Max. He had experienced imaginary pain and his imaginary death.

He rolled over onto his side and drew his knees up towards his chest as he gazed at the poster of carnivorous dinosaurs on his bedroom wall. Being attacked and eaten by a T-rex had been his worst nightmare. Now he had a new one.

2

Over the years, similar things happened at irregular intervals. The burning smell of an electrical short circuit would fill his nostrils, everything would go black before his eyes, and when his vision returned he was somewhere else, inside someone else.

On the third occasion he was nine years old, watching Sweden's Eurovision Song Contest selection programme with his parents. Nanne Grönvall, with her pixie ears, had just launched into the chorus of 'Jealous' when the smell and the blackout came. Max saw himself sitting on the floor of a living room, pressed against the wall in a corner. Nanne Grönvall was singing on the TV in this room too. In his hands he was holding a shotgun, with the stock propped against the back of an armchair. He wasn't wearing any socks, and his hands clutched the barrel as the muzzle was inserted in his mouth.

'Jealous! I'm so jealous!'
No! Stop! Don't do it!

He was inside the other person's mind, inside the dark despair and loneliness that filled it, but he was incapable of influencing those thoughts, just as a passenger is incapable of using pure strength of will to halt a ferry heading across the sea to Finland. The movement is unstoppable, and Max saw his big toe find its way to the trigger, rest there briefly, then press down and back.

He heard the report, and for a fraction of a second his mouth was filled with the taste of gunpowder before the image was snatched away into the darkness, and he found himself lying on the rug in front of the TV, staring at Nanne Grönvall as she tossed her mane of hair.

'Max! Sweetheart! What happened?'

His mother was crouching beside him, gently shaking his shoulder. Max tried to speak, but just as before his jaws were clamped together so tightly that his lips couldn't form any words, and only a groaning sound emerged.

'What was it, Max?'

His father had dropped to his knees, which Max appreciated in spite of his confused state. His father wasn't the kind of man to allow his feelings to gain the upper hand, but there was a definite note of anxiety in his voice. Max revelled in that anxiety for a moment before hauling himself back up onto the sofa and staring blankly at the TV while his parents exchanged glances.

He was tested for epilepsy, but the results were inconclusive in spite of the fact that his symptoms were largely identical with a *grand mal* attack, albeit short-lived. The doctor who examined him said it was best to wait and see; treatment wasn't implemented until it had happened at least twice. Max didn't mention his previous episodes, particularly as he didn't believe it was anything to do with epilepsy.

A few days later he heard about a neighbour five doors down who had taken his own life during the Eurovision programme. Max didn't need to ask how.

As time went by, Max gained a better understanding of what he called his 'visions'. The closer he was to the actual incident, both emotionally and geographically, the more powerful they were. It was rare for a child to feature, and his first vision had been so strong because the victim was a boy of his own age. The man who'd shot

69

himself had had little in common with Max, but he had been close by.

The most common visions involved suicide. One aspect that surprised Max was that he never saw attempted suicides; he was only connected to the other person's mind when he or she succeeded in their efforts – as if who should die and who should survive was predetermined. The alternative explanation was that his vision kicked in only when the deed was a fait accompli, and that he was seeing everything with a delay.

Whatever the case, one question remained: why? *Why* did he have this gift, and what was the point of it? When he eventually shared his secret with Johan, they speculated about superpowers, mutations and time travel, but failed to come up with anything that made sense. They always ended up with a laconic *because*. Some people are diabetic, others have visions.

When Max saw the child's buggy that was crushed and saved simultaneously, it was his seventeenth vision and the first that didn't end in darkness and death. Well, it did, but then again it didn't. This knowledge, coupled with his own experience of having been a hair's breadth from death, meant that he was shaken and confused when he took the lawnmower out of the storage shed one day towards the end of September, a week after the incident on the top of the silo, to give the grass its final cut of the year.

3

Max was paid one hundred kronor every time he mowed the 1,500-square metre patch of grass sloping down to the Kvisthamra inlet; there was a jetty and a boathouse on the water's edge. The job took him about two hours, and he didn't mind it at all – quite the reverse. Plodding along behind the chugging machine and letting his thoughts run free was quite restful actually. Under normal circumstances, that is. On this particular day he couldn't achieve that sense of calm.

It started when he was getting the mower out. It got stuck on a rake, he lost his temper and yanked it so hard that he almost snapped the handle of the rake. Then the mower wouldn't start. He'd pulled the cord at least ten times and was on the verge of tears when he realised that he'd forgotten to pump the fuel up to the carburettor, something he usually did as a matter of routine.

When he began mowing he thought the machine was too slow, that it was vibrating in his hands in an unpleasant way, and was making too much noise. In an effort to push down the dark lump that was growing in his chest, he took deep breaths as the mower nudged its way down towards the water. This was exactly what he had decided was *not* going to happen; he refused to allow the anxiety to take over.

He had made the decision a few weeks before his eleventh birthday. By that stage he had had four more visions since the Eurovision programme, and the experience was taking its toll. He was terrified at the thought of having to participate when people placed the noose around their neck or drove off an icy road at speed, heading for the tree that would be the last thing they saw on this earth. Terrified.

The faintest smell of smoke, even if it was from someone burning leaves a kilometre away, made him hunch his shoulders and close his eyes, as if that would enable him to ward off the vision that wanted to take him over. When it transpired that it wasn't *that* smell of burning, tears of relief would spring to his eyes.

71

He was always on the alert and found it difficult to concentrate on his work in school. His main respite was the fantasy games he and Johan played on the hill behind Johan's house. When Max became Spiderman or Superman with their superpowers, he was able to forget the gift he actually possessed – at least for a little while. When the game was over, the tension came flooding back.

The turning point came on a summer's day, oddly enough when he was about to cut the grass for the first time that year. Max didn't know it, but during the winter fuel had leaked into the spark plug. Pulling the cord caused a minor explosion in the chamber, with accompanying smoke. When the smell hit Max's nostrils he leapt in the air then ducked, banged his head on the mower's handle, fell over and ended up on his back on the grass. He opened his eyes, gazed up at the clouds drifting across the sky, and thought: *I can't do this anymore.*

He was living in limbo, anxiously waiting for the visions to take possession of him. He was incapable of being present in the moment. Lying there on the grass with a lump forming on his forehead, it suddenly became clear to him that he had two options: either he could step over the line and embrace the anxiety that was his daily bread – flip out completely and be sectioned, medicated into some kind of harmony. Or he could rise above the whole thing, regard the visions as attacks to be endured, but otherwise give them the finger, refuse to let them rule him. He saw a cloud take on the shape of a rearing elephant, and decided on option two.

Once he'd made his choice, the implementation was surprisingly straightforward. Only a week later he fell from some scaffolding and crashed down onto the concrete below. He couldn't avert the attack through willpower, but when he came round and found himself lying on the floor in front of his computer, he simply got up and

72

carried on playing *Civilization* from where he'd left off, without giving the matter another thought.

This new attitude also had consequences in his everyday life. Once he had decided to ignore the worst things that can happen to a person, the things he was forced to experience, he became much more daring. He went in hard when it came to tackling in football, he climbed trees higher than anyone else, and refused to take crap from anyone. So what if he had to roll with the odd punch – that was nothing compared to what he'd gone through.

The decision he'd made beneath a rearing elephant was possibly the smartest thing he'd ever done. His school work recovered, and the respect of his fellow pupils grew. The curve continued on its upward trajectory until the day it drove him to climb the silo, and something happened.

Max carried on mechanically plodding back and forth with the mower, staring at his hands clutching the vibrating handle, and a thought came into his mind: *these hands shouldn't be here.*

The realisation that had struck him on top of the silo was gradually becoming something of an obsession. It was as if the world had been split in two. There was one version where he was cutting grass like any other teenager, and another where his body lay broken and dead in a mortuary, waiting to be cremated. It didn't make sense.

He had tried to follow his original decision beneath the elephant cloud and simply ignore it, but this time his brain refused to co-operate. Over and over again he saw Marko's outstretched hand, felt himself sliding towards the edge, relived Marko's refusal to let go, even though a single centimetre was the difference between life and death. Marko's hand. The power behind Max's back, wanting to drag him down into the abyss. Marko's hand. His grip. The

73

resolve, the courage. He had saved Max's life. The memory settled in his chest like a weight and a barb.

When Max turned the mower towards the shoreline for the third time he saw his father come out onto the patio with the Sunday newspaper and a bottle of beer. Max smiled. In spite of the fact that his father had begun to adopt certain upper-class habits as his wealth increased – tasselled loafers, a well-stocked wine cooler, a Maserati Spyder in the garage – he couldn't bring himself to give up the pleasures of his less affluent background, including a cold Pripps Blå.

He settled down on the sun lounger and opened up the newspaper. Max stopped mowing and headed for the patio. His father didn't look up as he approached, but Max sat down opposite him anyway. 'Dad?'

His father still didn't look up. 'Mmm?'

'I need your help.'

'Mmm-hmm?'

'There's a new boy who's started in my class. His name is Marko, and he's from Bosnia. His dad hasn't got a job, and I wondered if you might be able to . . . sort something out for him.'

His father lowered the newspaper and took off his reading glasses. 'A job?'

'Yes. Johan told me he hasn't got anything, and he's kind of depressed. He really wants to work – for his family and so on.'

'Does he have experience in the construction industry?'

'I don't know, but even if he hasn't, surely there must be something he could do?'

His father sucked one arm of his glasses, a habit he'd acquired in recent years, and stared at Max as if his son were a visual puzzle that must be solved.

74

'So, how come you're . . . involved?'

Max shrugged. 'Marko's a nice kid. It's a shame if his dad is sitting at home getting depressed.'

'We don't need anyone at the moment.'

His father put his glasses back on and was about to return to the newspaper when Max said: 'Please, Dad. This is important.'

There was a lot about his father's reserved behaviour that Max didn't like, but he had to admit that his father understood when something was serious. He was able to appreciate the significance of what was said without probing for the reasons behind it. He gazed at Max for a moment, then nodded. 'Okay, tell him to come over. Then I can see what he's like.'

He pushed his glasses into position with a firm gesture and raised the newspaper so that it formed a barrier between him and his son. Max stood up. 'Thanks, Dad.'

'Mmm.'

*

'Excuse me! Hello – stop!'

The assistant comes rushing out of the ICA supermarket in Kryddan, catches up with the elderly lady and hands over the packet of saffron she left behind. The customer thanks her warmly. Her daughter is coming to visit and she's going to make her favourite meal – saffron chicken. As the name suggests, it wouldn't really work without the saffron. She thanks the assistant once more, gently strokes her cheek.

THE TYRANNY OF GOOD INTENTIONS

I

Johan was sitting on the rock by his front door trying to hit a rusty can with pine cones when Max came racing along on his bike. Eighteen gears. A Monark. Slightly different from Johan's lady's bike with no gears and a chain that came off at regular intervals. When Max stopped and flipped down the support, Johan tried to think of a reason why they couldn't play GameCube. A reason other than the fact that his mother was asleep on the sofa, surrounded by dirty laundry.

'Hi,' Max said, coming over.

'Hi,' Johan replied, throwing another cone that amazingly dropped into the can.

'Shit – have you been practising long?'

'All my life,' Johan said, which made Max frown. Johan was working up to his excuse – one of the controls was broken. However, before he could come out with it, Max asked: 'Do you know if Marko's home?'

'Marko?'

'Yes, Marko. You're friends, aren't you?'

After the *Wind Waker* game Marko had been to Johan's on one more occasion. He'd told Johan about his father, and Johan had passed the information on to Max.

'I've seen him a few times, but I don't keep tabs on where he is.'

'Can we go and see?'

'Why?'

'I've got something. Maybe.'

Johan slid down from the rock, pleased that he didn't have to lie. Together they went in through the entrance next to Johan's and up the stairs to the second floor, where they found the door marked 'Kovac'. Max rang the bell. They could hear the sound of voices from inside, then the door was opened by Marko, who looked enquiringly from Johan to Max.

'Hi,' Max began. 'I was wondering if your dad's home.'

'He is,' Marko replied, as if it were the most natural question in the world. All of a sudden Johan realised what this was about.

'Could I have a word with him?' Max went on.

'You can, but I'll have to translate.'

Max's shoulders slumped. 'Doesn't he speak Swedish?'

'Yes, but not very well. It's best if I help. Come in.'

Johan thought he had a key to Marko's behaviour, the fact that he didn't ask what or why. Because Marko himself was painfully honest and always said it exactly as it was, he assumed that other people had simple, straightforward motives for their actions. Max wanted to meet Marko's father. Okay, then that's what was going to happen.

Max walked in and Marko gave Johan a look that was hard to interpret. Maybe it meant *What are you doing here?*, or *I'm glad you're here*, or a combination of the two.

The apartment was sparsely furnished, and smelled of unfamiliar spices. As they passed through the hallway leading to the living room, a door opened and a girl aged about ten stuck her head out. She had long, black hair framing a face that was almost angelic, apart from a pair of eyebrows so thick that they could have belonged to an adult. These eyebrows were drawn together and a surprisingly deep voice asked: 'Who are you?'

'Friends from school,' Marko informed her.

The girl laughed. 'You haven't got any friends!'

Marko waved his hand in the direction of the girl as if he were swatting away a wasp. 'My little sister. Maria.'

Maria turned her big, luminous green eyes on Johan and Max. She studied them openly from head to toe, then asked: 'Are you dorks?'

Johan had seen her on the hill a few times, but they'd never spoken. Her favourite pastime appeared to be hitting trees with branches while muttering to herself, and he guessed that in her opinion, most people were dorks. Before he could come up with a clever response, Max jumped in. 'Absolutely. We're superdorks.' Maria gave a brief nod and disappeared into her room. Johan caught a glimpse of fabrics in different colours before she closed the door. They continued to the living room. Johan stopped in the doorway and looked around.

Where's all their stuff?

The Kovac family's living room was identical in size and shape to his own, but that was where the resemblance ended. Johan's home was dirty, dusty and cluttered, while this room was spotlessly clean and virtually empty. A sofa, two armchairs, a coffee table, a rug and a television. That was it. There was a cross on the wall, plus a drawing of someone who was presumably Jesus, judging by his unnaturally gentle expression and the halo around his head. Beneath the picture was a little hook with an old-fashioned key hanging on it.

A skinny little man was sitting in one of the armchairs rolling cigarettes with nothing but his fingers. When Marko said: 'Tata,' he looked up. Marko gestured towards Max and Johan and went on in Swedish: 'These are two of my friends from school.' He spoke so slowly and articulated so clearly that it sounded as if he were giving a speech.

The man leapt to his feet, held out his hands and said: 'Hello, hello. Welcome. My name is Goran.' His accent was very strong. Johan took Goran's hand, which was as slender as its owner, but with a surprisingly firm grip. 'Johan,' he said, with a hint of a bow.

When Max had also introduced himself, Goran invited them to sit on the sofa beneath the picture of Jesus, while he returned to his cigarettes. It was like watching a magician. With practised fingers he spread tobacco along the paper, rolled it between his fingers, then sealed it by licking the edge. His movements were rapid, but the resulting cigarette was indistinguishable from one that came out of a packet.

Marko perched on the edge of the other armchair and observed his father's prestidigitation in silence for a few seconds, then said something that began with 'Tata' – which presumably meant Dad – and continued with words that were incomprehensible apart from 'Max'.

This too seemed somehow unnatural to Johan, as if there were another person living inside Marko, a person who expressed him-self in a secret language. Before he'd met Marko he'd never had anything to do with an immigrant, nor had he visited any country outside of Sweden. He glanced at Max who looked perfectly at

79

ease, but then he and his parents went abroad once or twice a year, sometimes to countries Johan had never even heard of.

'What was it you wanted to talk to Dad about?' Marko asked eventually.

'Okay, so . . .' Max linked his hands in his lap. 'My dad . . .'

There was the clink of glass, and Marko's mother emerged from the kitchen carrying a tray with a carafe of juice, several glasses and a plate of Ballerina biscuits. She put the tray down on the table, pointed to herself and said: 'Laura. Marko's mum.'

Laura was at least ten centimetres taller than her husband, and maybe twenty kilos heavier. She had dark shadows beneath her eyes, but she exuded an air of calm that neither Marko's father nor Johan's mother possessed. Johan liked her immediately.

Presumably lured by the sound of clinking glasses, Maria appeared in the doorway. She'd put on a pink tulle tutu over her jeans, and curled up on the arm of her father's chair. She gazed at Johan and Max with those feline eyes, while Laura returned to the kitchen.

'My dad,' Max continued, 'owns a construction company and if . . . if you're looking for a job, he might be able to sort something out.'

Maria attempted to translate for her father, but Marko quickly interrupted. 'You're getting it wrong. Shut up.' He ignored her sullen expression and took over the translation. His father nodded quietly as Laura reappeared carrying a kitchen chair, which she placed between her son and her husband. Goran began to answer Marko, but Laura stopped him. She said something about 'svedski' and pointed to Max.

Goran took a deep breath, closed his eyes for a second, then said in Swedish: 'This . . . job. When I can . . . er . . . start?'

Johan looked at Max, noting with satisfaction that his friend was somewhat taken aback by the direct question, in spite of his wider experience of the world. Max scratched his head. 'Well, I don't exactly know what kind of job it is, but . . . my dad would like to meet you.'

'I expect it's a rubbish job,' Maria announced, reaching for a biscuit. Laura slapped the back of her hand and muttered a rebuke that made the girl sulk even more as Marko translated.

Johan glanced at each of the four members of the Kovac family in turn. He couldn't put his finger on the reason why, but he liked them, both as a group and as individuals. Even Maria. Beneath that spiky exterior he sensed a bright girl with a strong will of her own. He found himself hoping that they would like *him*.

'Juice and biscuits – how lovely,' he said, pouring himself a drink. Max looked at him with something approaching horror. Okay, Johan could hear that he sounded like someone in an old-fashioned children's film, but he wanted to make his position clear. Laura smiled at him, while Maria narrowed her eyes suspiciously. She seemed to be on the point of making a crushing comment when Goran got to his feet and said: 'We go! Now? Yes?'

Laura said something and gestured towards the refreshments, which made Goran sink back in his chair with a sigh. 'I am sorry. I am . . .' He fluttered his fingers in front of him as if he were trying to pluck the right word from the air.

'Keen,' Laura supplied. 'He's very keen.'

2

When Max, Johan, Marko and Goran were putting on their shoes, Maria tugged at her father's shirt and said something that made him shrug. He nodded wearily. Marko turned to Max. 'Is it okay if Maria comes with us?' He widened his eyes and he silently mouthed, *Say no*.

Max was confused by the mixed messages, so Johan answered on his behalf. 'Of course. No problem.' Marko gave him a look – *traitor!* – then turned and issued a sharp command to Maria. She rolled her eyes and stepped out of the pink tutu.

When the little party turned onto Drottning Kristinas väg, Johan realised how happy he was. A feeling of calm suffused his body as he walked along with Max, Marko, Goran and Maria, and he also enjoyed Max's obvious nervousness as he attempted to converse with Goran. Johan focused on Maria. 'So, you're in . . . Year Three?'

'Yes. And you're Year Five?'

Johan didn't take the bait. 'No. Year Four.'

'*Four?*'

'Yes. I've had to repeat three years.' He measured half a metre between his hands. 'I'm this much taller than everybody else in my class. The chairs and desks are too small for me.'

Those feline eyes narrowed. 'You're lying.'

'I am.'

'Because you're in Year *Seven*.'

'Correct.'

Maria nodded, pleased with herself, and the chill between them melted away as she contemplated Johan with a new appreciation. 'Marko never lies.'

'No. I've noticed that.'

'He's so boring.'

'And so nice.'

'Boringly nice.'

They continued in a similar vein all the way to Max's house, while the rest of the group walked along in silence once they'd exhausted the main topic of conversation. Max opened the tall gate and invited them in. Maria took a couple of steps along the gravel path, then stopped dead, put her hands on her hips and stared up at the impressive three-hundred-square-metre, two-storey house, and exclaimed: 'Fuck! You must be super rich!'

'Not really.' Max scratched the back of his neck. 'My dad, I mean, it's his job . . .'

'He started out as a scaffolder,' Johan explained to Goran, who was clearly overwhelmed by such excess. Marko looked enquiringly at Johan, who clarified: 'Scaffolding. The metal poles and boards builders stand on.'

Marko translated for his father, who nodded thoughtfully as he contemplated what Johan had always regarded as the epitome of sheer ostentation.

'Yes,' Max agreed. 'He was a scaffolder. That's right.'

Goran smiled indulgently and Johan realised that he understood exactly what they were trying to do by bringing Max's father down to a more acceptable level. Johan also realised this was completely pointless. Max's father might have started out as an ordinary labourer, but this was his house. This was what he had achieved, while Goran was out of work.

Johan felt a sudden spurt of rage against the way of the world. As a child he had been uncomfortable with the enormous disparity in the standard of living between himself and Max, but had suppressed his unease with the aim of enjoying the privileges that came with having a friend from a wealthy family. Now that discomfort came rushing back with full force.

As they walked towards the heavy oak front door, Johan could see Goran's shoulders slumping more and more. Even though Marko's father was an adult, and a *hero* according to his son, Johan had a powerful urge to put his arm around those sagging shoulders. Of course, that was unthinkable, as well as misguided.

Max opened the door and waved them inside. Maria was first, but at least this time she managed to refrain from swearing as she spun around, taking in the opulence that wealth can provide.

It had been a long time since Johan had reflected on Max's home, but looking through the eyes of the Kovac family, he realised how *big* everything was – not only the space, but the objects filling that space. The aesthetic wasn't so different from the Kovacs' home – apart from the size, needless to say.

The shoe rack in the hallway was made for twenty pairs of shoes, and an entire regiment could have hung up their coats on the hooks above. The crystal chandelier suspended from the ceiling at a height of some six metres would not have looked out of place in an opera house. The staircase was wide, with a sturdy banister and thick carpet. Taken as a whole, the house gave Johan the impression that it belonged to a person who was half a metre taller than everyone else, with an army of friends and a need for space. Maybe that was how Max's father saw himself – or how he wanted to appear.

'Come through,' Max said. 'I think Dad's on the terrace.'

He'd already kicked off his shoes and led the way. As Johan and Marko knelt down to untie their laces, Marko whispered: 'The terrace?'

'The . . . patio?'

'Okay – what's the difference?'

'No idea.'

Goran and Maria had also removed their shoes and followed Johan through the living room, which among other things contained the only plasma TV Johan had seen outside a shop. Forty-two inches, according to Max.

Through the glass doors overlooking the Kvisthamra inlet, they could see Max standing next to his father, who was lying on a sun lounger. Max said something and pointed to the group with Johan as its guide. His father turned his head and his eyes widened. As they emerged onto the terrace he got to his feet and looked them up and down, then said: 'Quite a . . . contingent.'

Once again Maria took the lead and did something completely unexpected. She went up to Max's father, bobbed her head and said, 'Maria,' then fired off a dazzling smile that no one in the world could resist, including Max's father.

'Göran,' he said. 'Welcome.'

'Göran?' Maria repeated. 'That's Dad's name too!'

As if that were the cue he'd been waiting for, Goran stepped forward with his hand outstretched. 'Goran.'

The two men shook hands, then Marko introduced himself. Johan simply raised a hand in greeting. Göran invited them to sit down on the wicker chairs while he perched on the edge of the sun lounger, straight-backed and with his hands resting on his thighs.

'So . . . Goran. I believe you're looking for work?'

'Yes. Work. That's right.'

'What kind of work did you do in . . . your former homeland?'

Goran took a deep breath, then his shoulders dropped and he looked at Marko.

85

'Dad's an engineer,' Marko said. 'He was involved in programming . . . lathes. For the furniture industry.'

'Oh . . . That's not really something I need. Have you ever worked in construction?'

'He's built houses. Ours and one of the neighbours'.'

'Yes,' Goran agreed. 'Big house. Neighbour.'

'Okay,' Göran said. 'And forgive me for asking, how's your Swedish?'

'How's . . . my Swedish?'

'Yes . . . Actually, I think that answers my question.'

Göran glanced at Max, who was sitting with his fists clenched on his lap. Marko noticed the look, and in turn glanced at Johan, who felt obscurely guilty and looked at Maria. An intricate pattern of looks and glances went on for a few seconds, until Maria once again fired off her winning smile and said: 'Daddy will be *super good* at Swedish when he gets a job!'

Marko stared at Göran, who was gazing at Goran as if to assess his qualities. The atmosphere on the terrace had deteriorated, and the only one who didn't appear to notice was Göran, clearly in charge and steering the ship with calm authority.

'Oookaaay,' he said slowly, and Goran began to wring his hands. Johan saw Marko clamp his lips together as he made a huge effort to control himself. There was a loud clap as Göran slapped his thighs. 'How about this? We're working on a project for Samhall out in Görla at the moment. I'll give you a month's trial as a general dogsbody.'

Marko began to translate for his father, then stopped and turned to Göran. His voice was coldly polite as he asked: 'I'm sorry. One word – dogsbody?'

'Yes – little jobs here and there. It'll mostly be clearing up after the others, gathering up spare timber, that kind of thing.'

Goran listened carefully as Marko explained. Johan heard the word 'test' a couple of times, then Marko turned to Göran once more. 'What does "trial" mean – what does it involve?'

'It means if he does well, he can stay on, and in the future he could take on other responsibilities if he proves . . . capable.'

'My father is extremely capable.'

'Yes, but I don't know that.'

Marko was about to say something, but even Max, who'd sat like a stone pillar throughout the entire conversation, must have noticed. He leapt to his feet. 'Is that okay, Goran? Does that suit you?'

'That suits me,' Goran said. 'Suits me very well.' He too stood up and held out his hand to Göran, who took it but remained seated. 'Much thanks,' Goran said. 'Many thanks. I will work hard.'

'Great,' Göran replied. 'I'm sure it'll be fine.'

The details were quickly sorted. Goran could start the very next day if he wished. The pay was low but acceptable, because it could easily be raised in the future. Goran bowed, said thank you again, and ushered Maria back through the house.

Marko also held out his hand as Göran leaned back on his lounger. 'Thank you,' Marko said. 'It's very kind of you.'

Göran gestured towards his son. 'Don't thank me – thank him.'

Arms hanging straight down by his sides, Marko bowed to Max. 'I thank you. And bow down to you.' Max squirmed, and finally even Göran noticed that something was going on beneath the surface. With an amused smile he asked Marko: 'I'm just curious – how come Max has got involved in all this?'

Marko looked Max straight in the eyes before turning to Göran. 'Because your son is a very kind person. A good person. Thank you once again.' With those words he left the terrace.

The meeting had lasted no more than ten minutes, but it would determine and change the direction of many people's lives for several years to come.

*

The young man from Afghanistan is about to do a big shop for the first time. He is standing in front of a bank of trollies looking confused. They are all linked together. It wasn't like this in Kabul. He tugs gently at the first one, but without success. A woman is passing by. 'You need one of these,' she says, and inserts a white plastic token in a slot. When the young man asks in stumbling, hesitant Swedish where he can get such a token, the woman says he can keep hers. She has several.

A HERO EMERGES

I

Marko was nine years old and in a refugee centre outside Alvesta when he realised that his father was a hero. The Kovac family had been in Sweden for just over a year at that point. Before then they had lived in both Germany and the Netherlands, since fleeing from Bosnia in April 1994, when Marko was four years old and Maria two.

Their farm had been in a village a few kilometres to the east of Mostar, in an area dominated by Bosniacs – Muslims. The Kovacs belonged to the Croatian minority who were Catholics, but before the outbreak of the war that wasn't a problem. Quite the reverse, in fact. Friends and neighbours from different religions had a reason to celebrate twice as many high days and holidays. The Kovacs celebrated the end of fasting during Ramadan even though they hadn't fasted themselves, and their Muslim neighbours came over for Christmas, even though they passed on the ham.

Then the war came. Right up to the last minute those who lived in and around Mostar believed that this wasn't something that would affect them; they had lived for so long in peace and harmony, and the area boasted the largest number of mixed marriages in the whole of Yugoslavia. Everyone assumed that the nationalist insanity gripping the country wouldn't gain a foothold here – they were first and foremost neighbours and residents of Mostar.

When the Bosnian Serbs, with the support of Serbia, began to fight for an expansion of Republika Srpska's territory within Bosnia, Croats and Bosnians came together to oppose them. The shells that rained down on Mostar from the surrounding hills hit the supporters of both Jesus and Mohammed, and the snipers didn't care whether their targets swore allegiance to the cross or the crescent moon.

The siege went on for a long time. Several of the city's parks, where so many had stolen their first kiss, became makeshift graveyards because no one dared venture to the cemeteries on the outskirts where the snipers had a clear view, and could knock down the mourners like skittles.

Goran was not one of those who had made his way to the square where weapons were being handed out at the beginning of the siege, but within a couple of months it became impossible to remain on the farm as the Serbs approached from the east. The family moved in with Laura's cousin in central Mostar, to the west of the river, hoping that this was a temporary arrangement.

As the siege went on and the situation worsened, hatred towards those imposing the siege grew. The electricity had been cut off, and there was a shortage of food, water and hygiene products – all because those damned Serbs lay watching and waiting, keeping the city isolated. After coercion and threats, Goran finally felt he had no choice but to pick up a Kalashnikov. He took part in raids and attempted escapes, but always shot over the head of the enemy.

Whatever his opinion of the Serbs' actions and aspirations to power, he didn't want another person's death on his conscience.

So far things were just about bearable, although he hated leaving Laura alone with two small children as much as he hated handling a gun. Then came the next phase of the madness, when Croats and Serbs turned on each other. The background to this development lies outside the parameters of this story, but within just a few months the former allies had become sworn mortal enemies.

The Muslims grouped together on the eastern side of the River Neretva, while the Christians did the same on the western side. The only link was the Stari Most – the Old Bridge. Once a symbol of the city's unity, it was now as appealing as a minefield. The snipers' bullets immediately took out anyone who crossed the border.

On the western side terrible stories of Muslim atrocities against Croat civilians flourished, and vice versa on the eastern side. Isolated from one another, former neighbours increasingly grew to resemble demons from hell. Goran was one of the few who refused to be carried along on the wave of hysteria, maintaining that they were all simply people who had finished up in an unfortunate situation, whipped up by power-crazed politicians. Was he really supposed to believe that Rashid the baker or Ahmed the mechanic from their village had been transformed into monsters, simply because hot-headed demagogues said so?

The event that would turn Goran into a hero in his son's eyes began when a pickup truck stopped outside the family home, where Goran was on leave. A sergeant knocked on the door and ordered Marko's father to go with him. Goran had no choice but to fetch his gun and join two other ordinary soldiers in the back of the truck, which then set off northwards before turning east, heading for the area where the Kovacs used to live.

It was a cloudy day with rain in the air. The pickup bounced along the road Goran had travelled hundreds of times, now pitted with holes thanks to the frequent shelling. He clutched the barrel of his gun and lowered his head, silently praying that they wouldn't drive over one of the landmines left in the ground after the war against the Serbs.

As they approached the family farm he couldn't help looking up – and immediately wished he hadn't. The Croats had recently gained victory in the area over the Bosniacs, and it seemed as if heavy fighting had taken place on the spot he had recently called his own.

When they had been forced to flee at short notice, Goran had seen no other solution but to release the livestock. The cows, pigs, horses and chickens probably wouldn't survive without human intervention, but better that than to stand and starve to death shut inside the barn, the sty and the henhouse.

If he had been harbouring a faint hope that the animals might still be alive by some miracle, that hope was dashed now. All that remained of the barn were a few blackened beams, scattered across the sooty ground like the devil's Mikado sticks. The henhouse must have suffered a direct hit, because there wasn't even a trace of the cement block on which it had stood. Feathers danced in the air, so presumably the chickens had chosen familiarity over freedom.

Every single window in the farmhouse was smashed. The facade was peppered with bullet holes, and parts of the roof had been blown off. Broken items of furniture that Goran recognised only too well lay strewn around the yard. The home he had inherited from his father and grandfather was a desecrated ruin of its former self, and maybe it was at that moment that Goran gave up the last hope that life would ever return to normal. Tears sprang to his eyes

92

as he reached into his pocket and squeezed the front door key – the last thing he had taken with him.

The pickup continued out towards the fields, heading for a haystack that had been as tall as a double decker bus two years ago, but had rotted and sunk down to no more than a quarter of its previous height. Through the mist Goran could see six men lined up in front of the haystack. He recognised one of them as Faisal, a vet from a neighbouring village who had treated Goran's horses for hoof abscesses, among other things. He didn't know the other men.

The pickup skidded to a halt on the muddy, neglected meadow, and Goran scrambled down along with the other soldiers. Now he realised why the six men were standing so awkwardly. Their hands were bound behind their backs, and their faces bore clear signs of mistreatment. When Goran and Faisal's eyes met, the two men nodded to each other.

The sergeant conferred with two soldiers whose automatic rifles were trained on the six Bosniacs, then he ordered two of the new arrivals to take over guard duty while the original duo returned to their posts.

He waved his hand at the prisoners and said: 'These men – although I don't really want to call them men – these Muslim dogs have been found guilty of planning a cowardly attack on our liaison centre, and have therefore been condemned to death. You are here to carry out the sentence, so . . . get on with it.'

Goran and his two companions looked at one another. Attempting to disrupt the enemy's communication network was a natural strategy in war. It was surprising that the six men hadn't been shot on the spot, which made it more likely that they were actually six people with the wrong religious affiliation who had happened to be in the wrong place. The systematic ethnic cleansing that had been reported from other parts of the former Yugoslavia had not yet reached Mostar, but perhaps this was it. People were to be killed – not for what they had done, but for who they were.

'Kovac!' the sergeant yelled. 'Pick up your gun and get over here!'

The Kalashnikov weighed twice as much as usual in Goran's hands as he went to join the others. He glanced at the Bosniacs, whose eyes were so wide open that the whites glowed against the dark brown, rotting hay behind them. Faisal's cracked and swollen lips contorted in a parody of a smile as he caught Goran's eye and said: 'Goran. It's me. Faisal.'

Goran nodded. Of course it was Faisal, with whom he had often drunk a glass of Slivovitz after a successful treatment. Like most Muslims in the area, he was far from orthodox. And of course, the five men lined up beside him also had names, and had shared a glass or two with a Catholic brother.

'Ready!' the sergeant shouted. The two soldiers exchanged a glance and raised their weapons. 'Kovac! You too!'

For three seconds Goran stood motionless. He knew that this moment, beneath this cloudy sky on this gloomy day, would determine who he was going to be for the rest of his life. Who he was going to be for Laura, for his children and for himself. If he was going to be anyone at all. He allowed the gun to slip through his hands and fall to the ground with a thud.

'Are you refusing to obey orders?' the sergeant roared, drawing his pistol and pointing it at Goran. The snake eye that was the barrel of the sergeant's pistol followed Goran as he took ten paces and positioned himself in front of Faisal.

'If you're going to shoot,' he said to his colleagues, 'then you'll have to shoot me as well. This cannot be the will of God.'

The sergeant let out a harsh bark of laughter. 'Who do you think you are, Kovac? Josef Schulz?'

It is not impossible that it was, in fact, the actions of Josef Schulz that lay behind Goran's decision. The story of the German soldier who had refused to take part in the execution of Yugoslav partisans and instead joined the line of those condemned to death was very popular throughout the country, and was believed to be historically accurate. It seemed as if the two soldiers were also familiar with the tale, because they glanced nervously at each other and lowered their guns a fraction.

'I am not Josef Schulz,' Goran said. 'I am Goran Kovac, and I am acting in accordance with the conscience God has given me.'

At that point Goran did indeed feel touched by divine inspiration. That was the only explanation for the fact that clear, comprehensible words were coming out of his mouth, even though he was so terrified that his legs were threatening to give way beneath him. In order to gather strength, he turned his face up to the sky. And felt the first drops of rain.

'Ready!' the sergeant bellowed again, and the two soldiers raised their guns.

Forgive me, Laura, Goran thought, his face still turned up to the sky as the rain fell more heavily. *But you wouldn't have had a husband if I'd followed orders. You would have had a ghost.*

'Take aim!'

Goran would never be able to make sense of what happened next. Divine intervention, or just unbelievable luck? From one second to the next the heavens opened and the rain came down with such force that it became difficult to breathe. The sergeant and the soldiers were no more than blurred silhouettes through a veil of water. If the sergeant did give the order to fire, his voice was

95

drowned out by a deafening clap of thunder, accompanied almost simultaneously by a phosphorus-white flash that hurt Goran's eyes and made the ground shake.

Nor did he ever find out what was said or done within the execution platoon eight metres away. Maybe superstition or the fear of God had sunk its claws into the sergeant in the face of this demonstration from the powers above, but after a brief period of negotiation, inaudible over the cacophony of the storm, the troops returned to the pickup and drove away.

Goran turned to the six men who were standing there with water running down their faces, gazing at him with something like veneration in their eyes.

'God bless you, Goran,' Faisal said. 'God bless you.'

Goran took out the hunting knife he always carried in his pocket and cut the ropes that bound the men's wrists. Then the seven of them stood in a circle with their arms around one another's shoulders, the rain pouring down their backs as they sent up thanks to their respective gods, which when all is said and done might well be one and the same.

2

A week later the Old Bridge was blown up by a direct hit from a Croat tank, but by then the Kovac family was already on the move. With Faisal's help they negotiated their way through the Bosniac-controlled territory; at more than one roadblock Goran and Laura expressed their belief that there is only one God, and that Mohammed is his messenger.

Eventually they reached Split, where after a strategic bribe they were issued with Croatian passports, and were able to board a ferry to Ancona in Italy. Their five years of wandering through Europe also lie outside the parameters of this narrative, but at last we find them in a refugee centre outside Alvesta, waiting to hear whether they have been granted permanent residence, or 'permament' as Goran insists on calling it.

The evening after the incident in the field, when Goran returned home soaked to the skin after walking several kilometres, he had told Laura what had happened – not with the aim of boasting about his heroism, but to stress the need to flee, because he ran the risk of being executed as a deserter. She had listened with tears in her eyes, alternately praising him for being such a good man and cursing him for being such a bad husband.

Goran had told her exactly what he'd thought at the critical moment: that she wouldn't have had her husband back if he'd obeyed orders, only a ghost. The reproaches had stopped immediately. Laura had rested her forehead against his for a long time, then started packing.

Goran might have saved his eternal soul in front of that haystack, but five years of rootlessness and temporary accommodation had actually brought with them a kind of ghostliness. The most debilitating aspect was not having anything specific to *do*. Laura carried the main responsibility for the children; she did as many household tasks as possible, and made a real effort to learn Swedish. Goran often went out into the forest, picking berries and mushrooms when they were in season. The rest of the time all he could do was collect empty jars in order to reclaim the deposit. Only a shadow remained of the self-sufficient farmer he had been.

Then came the next blow. The family's application for permanent

97

residence was turned down; they were to leave Sweden within seven days. It was as if the air went out of Goran and Laura. They spent a couple of days trailing around the centre like zombies, incapable of coming up with an alternative. The children also became apathetic, and couldn't summon up the energy to go to school.

Three days before they were due to be deported, a new family arrived. Goran was sitting in the communal kitchen with his fifth coffee of the day, with Marko sitting beside him sucking listlessly on a biscuit. There was a sudden flurry of noise in the hallway as the new arrivals dumped their luggage, and after a couple of minutes a man appeared in the doorway. Goran looked up, and the man's eyes widened. 'Goran? Goran! It's you!'

Goran frowned and wearily shook his head, not with the intention of denying his identity, but because he didn't recognise the man, who eagerly drew up a chair, sat down opposite him and took his hands.

'Mansur. Mansur Babic, don't you remember? You saved my life! That day out in the field.'

'Right,' Goran said without enthusiasm. 'I'm glad you made it.'

The conversation was conducted in Bosnian, and Marko joined in. 'Tata? What does he mean?'

Goran and Laura had never told the children what had happened, because they didn't want to add to their fragmentary knowledge of the horrors of war and the ethnic conflicts. Goran said firmly: 'Mansur. We don't talk to the children about the war.'

Mansur pointed to Marko. 'But surely your son has the right to know who his father is?'

Before Goran could object, Mansur told Marko the whole story. The boy listened, his eyes growing bigger and bigger. When Mansur finished by saying: 'And so we stood there in the rain, thanking both

Goran and God,' Marko glanced at his father, who seemed to be sitting up a little straighter.

'Your father is a hero,' Mansur said. 'As great as a hero can possibly be. Never forget that, my boy.'

'You're exaggerating,' Goran said, smiling for the first time since their residence application had been turned down. 'But thank you anyway.'

The conversation turned to the two families' experience of the asylum process. Until recently Mansur and his wife and child had been in hiding, but in view of their daughter's type 1 diabetes, their solicitor had managed to have their case reassessed, and they were now back in the system. When Goran explained the Kovacs' situation, Mansur was horrified. 'To think that a man like you . . . a man like you . . .'

Goran's shoulders had slumped again, but Marko found himself looking at his father with new eyes. He had known only the increasingly broken man, subserviently hauling their bags from one temporary home to the next, bowing and expressing grateful thanks for every crumb that was given to them. Now Marko realised that inside this stooping figure there was another, a man with the straightest back it was possible to imagine. A hero. His daddy. A hero.

'Listen to me,' Mansur said.

The family who had hidden the Babics were good people, and he had their phone number. If they couldn't help, they knew others who would. Mansur struck his chest with a clenched fist and announced in a tone redolent of a sacred vow: 'Goran, I am going to fix this, if it is God's will.' With an apologetic glance at the ceiling, he added: 'I'm going to fix this even if it isn't God's will. But it must be.'

And that was what happened. The Kovacs were 'lucky' – they

were taken in by a family who had an entire basement available, plus Marko and Maria's teachers were willing to give them private tuition, in spite of the fact that it was illegal, while they waited for the laws on asylum seekers to change, and for the family to be given another chance.

That chance came in the autumn of 1999. With the help of a new solicitor, a complex process and various letters of recommendation, they were finally granted their much longed-for 'permament' in December of that year, and were able to look for a decent place to live. They settled in Norrtälje.

Marko's view of his father had changed forever. He turned the heroic tale over and over in his head, constantly adding fresh details. He told Maria, who was frightened by the fact that Goran had almost been shot. That scared Marko too, but it paled before the thrilling images of the men standing in front of the haystack, Goran stepping forward, the raised guns, the rain. One day, someone had done something *big*. And that someone was his father. He would never forget it.

*

A seal has hauled itself out of the River Norrtälje and somehow found its way to the square, where it lollops around the fountain known as Havsstenen, bellowing in fear. People stop, get involved. The police are called. Two officers arrive, scratch their heads, call a vet. With the help of two fishermen, they manage to catch the seal in a tarpaulin and carry it to the mouth of the harbour, followed by hundreds of onlookers. When the seal finally slips into the water, everyone claps and cheers.

LIKE A TICK-TICKING BOMB

I

Ever since his retirement three years ago, Harry Boström has had trouble sleeping. He goes to sleep too late, wakes too early. By the time the clock strikes five on this September morning, he has already been lying awake for half an hour with itchy legs, so he gets out of bed and goes into the kitchen in his underpants. He looks out of the window.

There is no more than a hint of dawn in the sky so far, but through the darkness he can just make out the silhouettes of the cranes that have been erected down by the water. If everything goes according to plan, in a year or so he will no longer have the fragment of a sea view that he currently enjoys. The new building project in Norrtälje harbour will block the narrow aspect between Vegagatan and the inlet. Other residents in the area have held meetings, signed petitions, but Harry knows this is pointless. Are the authorities really going to stop the construction of two thousand homes in order to allow a few pensioners their glimpse of the sea? Hardly. You just have to go along with it.

Harry is so good at going along with things and taking each day as it comes with equanimity that his friends sometimes tease him when they meet up in the newsagent's in the square to bet on a harness race. While the other old men get worked up following the action on the TV screen in the shop, Harry mostly stands there nodding, with a melancholy look on his face. He rarely wins, and the others claim it's because of his lack of engagement. They regard his approach to betting as somewhat random, and needless to say his nickname is Harry Boy.

'Tosse?'

The creak of a wicker basket in the hallway, then an elderly Labrador comes lumbering into the kitchen. Tosse comes up to Harry and rests his head on his master's leg, reconfirming their friendship on this new day. Harry strokes his head, where the number of silver hairs among his black coat is steadily growing.

'Shall we go for a walk?'

Tosse looks up at Harry, his expression suggesting that it's hardly worth the trouble, but then he turns and wanders back into the hallway, where he sits down and waits next to his lead. He has to pee, after all. Harry puts on the same clothes he wore the previous day – and the day before that. Soft jeans, short-sleeved shirt and a sweatshirt that is so faded from washing that the logo – Norrtälje Electrics – has long since disappeared, along with most of the blue colour. Then he puts Tosse on the lead and sets off to meet the world.

Tosse brightens up when they get outside, and begins to reclaim his territory with a certain amount of enthusiasm. Harry wishes he could feel the same way – that this piece of the world was *his*. If he'd ever felt like that, the demolition and construction in the harbour has taken it away from him, and his view changes from one day to the next.

And yet he can't help starting his morning walks by taking a stroll down to the harbour to see what's happened since he was last there, and possibly to commit some minuscule act of sabotage as a meaningless protest – kick a tool that has been left lying around into the sea, hide a pack of junction boxes. Just because.

Tosse knows the routine, and after carrying out the necessary marking in the courtyard, he heads for what used to be the boat club's storage yard, which is now an empty space waiting to be built on.

The sky over the inlet to the east is dark red with a few drifting pink clouds, and Harry says to himself: *It's a beautiful morning.* He doesn't want to lose sight of this simple pleasure among the misty veils of misery. He isn't exactly unhappy, but it's also a long time since he could call himself happy, if ever. Too much loneliness.

Harry is so lost in thought that he doesn't notice when Tosse stops dead, and he almost falls over the dog, who is whimpering reproachfully. Tosse's body is stiff with tension, his tail is rigid, and his fur is twitching. Harry looks up to see what is making his dog react in a way that is so out of character.

A container.

On the very edge of the quayside there is a yellow container that wasn't there yesterday evening. Harry moves closer; Tosse reluctantly accompanies his master, emitting a low growl the whole time.

The container seems to have been unloaded in haste, because one corner is sticking out over the water; it looks as if it was simply dumped ashore. There is no sign of a cargo ship or heavy goods vehicle, but at some point during the night or the early hours of the morning, someone must have left it here.

Harry runs his hand over the smooth surface. No flaking paint, no rust. It looks virtually new, and there is no waybill, no text on

103

the side to indicate where it has come from or where its destination might be. It is simply an anonymous yellow container. Harry knocks on the thick metal, and the sound that bounces back is dull. The container is not empty.

He doesn't know what makes him place his ear against the side. Tosse whimpers and tugs at the lead, desperate to get away, but Harry shushes him. He thinks he hears something from inside the container. A *movement*. He knocks again, presses his ear even closer. Nothing. He can't swear that he heard the sound the first time, but he walks around to the front to check the doors.

A heavy bar secured with an equally substantial padlock makes further investigation impossible. Harry checks that no one is watching, then he hammers on the door and shouts: 'Hello? Is anyone there?' No reply, no movement. He takes a step back and scratches his head. Should he call someone? The police? Like most people, he doesn't want to make a fool of himself, but he really did think he heard something. Maybe just an object shifting its position, but what if, what if . . .

Harry stands there staring at the container for a few more seconds, then turns on his heel and heads home to make that call. Tosse pulls at the lead, only too keen to get away from the area.

Before long Harry will become something of a celebrity in Norr-tälje, and will be forced to tell the story of what happened that morning over and over again. He was the first who saw, and the only one who heard.

2

'Typical fucking Norrtälje.' Johan tosses the local paper onto the counter and points to the picture of the yellow container adorning the front page. 'Have you heard?'

Ove looks up from sorting the bowling balls into weight order before the evening session. He stares at Johan in bewilderment and shakes his head, his mouth hanging open. A long time ago he played for the national team, but even then he was slow on the uptake, bordering on stupid.

'The container,' Johan explains. 'The container they found yesterday. It turns out they can't open it, because there is "a lack of clarity regarding the ownership" of the land it's on.'

As so often, Ove repeats the phrase he doesn't understand. Without putting down the red number twelve he is holding, he says: 'A lack of . . . clarity?'

'Yes. No one seems to know whether that part of the quayside is owned by the council, the construction company or the boat club. How the fuck can they *not* know? This fucking town . . .'

Ove has worked at the bowling hall since it was built twenty years ago, and alongside Johan for the last seven. They understand each other, so Ove returns to his task, secure in the knowledge that Johan is about to launch into one of his tirades, which won't require his participation. Sure enough, Johan gets to his feet and begins to pace back and forth behind the café counter, waving his hand in the direction of the newspaper.

'As soon as something doesn't go to plan, they start running around like headless chickens. The water and sewerage improvements in the smaller communities went to hell in a handcart, and the expansion of high-speed fibre broadband keeps on being postponed, and why? Because no one is *responsible*. When the Norrteljeporten shopping mall turned out to be a series of fucking *hangars* with the Biltema sign stuck in the middle like some kind of cross instead of *buildings capturing the atmosphere of the archipelago*, which is what they promised, whose fault is it? Nobody's, because nobody had any *idea* it was going to be so ugly. Well, go down there and have a look, for fuck's sake! I tell you, that container will stay there until it rusts, because nobody on the council is capable of getting off their backside and dealing with it. Fucking idiots!'

Ove has heard many variations of this monologue over the years. His colleague's hatred for the council needs only a spark to burst into flames, and the closing comment is usually *fucking idiots*. Ove listens without listening, as if he were working beside a waterfall and has grown accustomed to the sound of the cascade. He continues to sort the bowling balls as he thinks about the 1986 championship, when he scored twenty-two strikes in succession. Those were the days.

3

'There could be anything in it.'

Maja from the charcuterie counter taps the picture of the container with her index finger, as if this might somehow enable her to unlock its secrets. She, Siw and Ingela from Bakery have taken an early lunch because they've been working since the store opened – Ingela a couple of hours before that. They are alone in the staff canteen at the ICA Flygfyren supermarket, sitting at a table next to a barred window with a view of a tangle of pipes and tubes that is more reminiscent of the petrochemical industry than everyday grocery shopping.

In line with her new, healthier lifestyle, which includes visits to the gym, Siw has made do with a salad. She's finished it, and is every bit as hungry as before she started. She glances at the newspaper, and a feeling of unease tickles her throat. The container looks so . . . *alone* standing there on the edge of the quayside, and loneliness is dangerous.

Ever since she was a child Siw has had a tendency to imbue inanimate objects with a soul. To her mother's irritation, she would bring home the most random items because they allegedly looked so lonely. A spade in the forest, a fallen branch in a car park. The container gives her the same feeling. It has lost all its container friends, and is now all by itself in the harbour, brooding on its situation.

'Anything at all,' Maja goes on. 'It could be the Russians, dumping radioactive waste or one of those poisons they use to kill people.' Ingela laughs and Maja pulls a face. 'You can laugh, but you won't be laughing when you wake up one morning to find that all of your hair has fallen out.'

Siw tries to maintain a serious expression; she doesn't want to risk winding Maja up any further. With the authority of her fifty-two years, Maja believes she is in the best position to interpret current affairs, and won't tolerate being made fun of by a mere girl of twenty-two. However, the image of Ingela's blonde mane being left on the pillow means Siw can't suppress a snort. Maja glares at her, but before she can speak Ingela says: 'Or else we'll all turn into superheroes. Every single person in Norrtälje!'

When Siw is back on the checkout, listening to the monotonous beep of the scanner, the idea lingers in her mind. As she glances up at the next customer with a friendly 'Hi,' she tries to imagine exactly what superpower this particular person, man or woman, young or old, might acquire. X-ray vision, mind-reading, super-human strength, the ability to become invisible, or something else?

The game keeps her entertained until she finishes her shift, which means this has been a good working day, a day that has passed almost without her noticing.

4

Max's work vehicle is a Toro Workman, an electric buggy that always makes him feel a little ridiculous, since he has to sit with his long legs drawn up towards his chest in order to fit in the cab. 'Not exactly a babe magnet,' as Johan once said. Not that Max is keen to cruise around Norrtälje looking for potential romance, but a little dignity wouldn't go amiss.

He passes over Society Bridge, turns left and continues into the park. When he reaches the open-air stage he stops, takes out his phone and checks whether anyone in the Pokémon Go Roslagen Facebook group has posted anything about an ongoing or future raid.

He doesn't usually play during working hours, but Entei has just been released as a raid boss, and he'd really like to catch it before Johan. Totally absurd, but it is what it is. The only available raid is a level one, a Magikarp, and no one is interested because you can easily manage it on your own.

Max puts his phone away and drives along the quayside. He arrives at the sculpture known as Wind Thingie in *Pokémon Go* and stops again. He gazes across at the quay on the opposite side of the inlet.

The container glows like a beacon in the afternoon sun. Several people have gathered and are knocking on the huge metal box or moving around it like the apes circling the monolith in *2001: A Space Odyssey*. With its bright yellow colour and its straight lines it is a foreign object dropped into the middle of their existence. As far as Max can make out, no one knows anything about it. Suddenly it was simply there, its contents still a mystery because of the dispute regarding the ownership of the land.

It is undeniably exciting, just like when a magician builds up the anticipation before opening a box. Of course, it will be a disappointment when the dispute is settled and the lock can be forced – a few tons of rotting vegetables, maybe a pile of stolen boat engines. It's only the glowing yellow container itself that is suggestive, as evidenced by the interest of the townspeople.

Max tears his gaze away and continues in the direction of the open-air gym. It has been used so much during this dry summer that several pieces of equipment need to be repaired. He gets out of the vehicle with his toolbox, then glances around and takes out his phone again. Three Nanab Berries, for heaven's sake . . .

5

'Are you comfortable, Eira?'

Anna has stabilised Eira Johansson with a couple of pillows to stop her from falling over sideways while she's being fed. Usually Eira can manage to feed herself, but today is one of her bad days, and her hands are shaking as if a constant stream of electricity is passing through her body.

Anna reaches for the plate of beefburger and potatoes. She has already cut the food up into bite-sized pieces, and scoops a mouthful onto the spoon. Eira's lips are tightly clamped together, and she is staring at something further down the table.

'Come on, Eira. You have to eat, otherwise you'll never make it as a professional footballer.'

'Look!' Eira says, raising her hand. Her index finger waves like a metronome as she points to the object she is staring at. 'Look – there!'

Anna lowers the spoon and looks. The daily newspaper is lying on the table, with the picture of the yellow container on the front page. Anna picks it up and shows it to Eira.

'This? The container?'

'Mmm-hmm! That! It's going to be terrible! Absolutely fucking terrible!'

A couple of the other elderly residents in the dining room glance uncomfortably at Eira, who has raised her voice. Her shaking episodes are often accompanied by a tendency to make inappropriate comments. Anna doesn't care – she's used to far worse at home – but for the sake of those around her she says calmly: 'Keep it down, Eira. You know it upsets the others.'

Anna is universally liked and respected by the clients at the Solgläntan nursing home. Almost everyone appreciates her directness, her slightly coarse style, and for those who don't, she tones down her approach. The only one who actively dislikes her is Folke Gunnarsson, but then again, he dislikes virtually everything and everyone, with particular emphasis on 'immigrants and parasites'.

Eira is definitely a member of Anna's fan club, so the gentle reproach has the desired effect. She leans forward and whispers conspiratorially: 'It's all going to go to hell. Everything. It's going to be wonderful.'

'Absolutely,' Anna agrees. 'Something for us all to look forward to. But now you need to eat something.'

Eira's lips are clamped shut once more when Anna lifts the spoon. Anna sighs. 'Open your gob, Eira, otherwise you know what will happen. Six of the best with the carpet beater, then I lock you in the cupboard under the stairs.'

Eira lets out a bark of laughter and her body jerks in the wheelchair. She opens her mouth wide, showing her yellowing false teeth. She chews, smacks her lips with relish, and opens her mouth for more.

★

It is generally well known that the junction of Tullportsgatan and Stockholmsvägen is a contender for the title of Sweden's worst traffic solution. Temporary arrangements with flashing lamps or signs exhorting drivers to move forward when the red light is showing have merely led to confusion. Eventually the powers that be realised that the best measure was no measure at all. Many drivers allow others to take precedence even though they don't have to. The traffic flows smoothly.

RACKETING AROUND THE TOWN

I

Siw and Anna are enjoying the twilight on Siw's balcony. She has a corner apartment on Flygaregatan, so as they sit curled up on the imitation wicker sofa, they have a view of the former airfield which is now a football pitch, plus the pizzeria with the charming name 'Airfield Pizzeria'. Siw has been a regular customer until now.

On the table in front of them is a box of wine – Rawson's Retreat – two glasses, plus a bowl of water with three lit candles floating in it. It is just before eight o'clock, dusk is falling, and the football team that had been training has packed up and left. This is the time Siw likes best, when the day's activities have stopped and darkness comes creeping along. An in-between time, with no demands.

Siw and Anna have spent many evenings like this. They used to call it the 'pre-party', although they hardly ever went out, because Siw isn't comfortable with lots of people around her outside of her working environment. Too many powerful impressions. Anna has

112

accepted this, and does her partying with other, less close friends than Siw.

They are in the middle of discussing who they'd like to live with from the *Lord of the Rings* films when Siw receives a text.

See you tonight? S

She replies: **Sorry. Busy. Another time.**

'Was that Sören?' Anna asks.

'Yes. He wants to see me, but I don't feel like it.'

'How can you *ever* feel like it?'

Siw takes a gulp of her wine and her cheeks flush red. 'Well, he's . . . nice.'

Anna sits up straight and shakes her head. 'Nice? A guy in his forties who refers to you as *fuckbuddies*, and who only wants to squeeze your tits?'

Siw wishes she'd never told Anna that Sören used that word – which she also finds offensive – and that he is unreasonably obsessed with her breasts. He works at the supermarket storage depot, and their relationship has been going on for just under a year, after a drunken incident at a staff party.

'Besides,' Anna says, pouring herself another glass of wine even though she's already had three, 'he only contacts you when there isn't an important match on, and he thinks *all* matches are important. Maybe he just fancied a quickie during half-time? A squeeze and a squirt, then back home for the second half.'

'Anna, please!'

It's true that Sören is very keen on football. His living room is merely an extension of the sixty-five-inch TV screen that dominates one wall, and he subscribes to every sports channel. Siw has to admit that Anna has a point, but she doesn't like having her life reduced in that way. It hurts.

Even though she's tipsy, Anna realises she's gone too far. She sighs and strokes Siw's cheek. 'Oh, sweetheart. You deserve something *special*.'

Siw draws back from Anna's clumsy caress. 'We very rarely get what we deserve.'

During Siw's twenty-nine-year life, Sören is the second long-term relationship she has had, if you can call it a relationship. First there was Niklas, a boy from the motor vehicle programme in school. She hung out with him for their final year, and for a while afterwards. He had red hair, spots, and was almost two metres tall. Siw spent a lot of time in his workshop and watched when he was tinkering with cars. They never actually broke up; whatever they had simply faded away. They saw each other less and less often, and eventually not at all. From a purely theoretical point of view, they are still together.

In both cases Siw has been involved with men who were preoccupied with something other than her, and she has fulfilled the same role as a somewhat neglected pet. 'Love' would be a vague concept for her if she hadn't seen so much of it in films, apart from her love for Alva, and to a certain extent her mother and grandmother.

During a period in high school she had wondered if she might be in love with Anna, but after a drunken evening when they both crash-landed in the same bed, and Anna, half asleep, began stroking her thighs, Siw had realised that she felt nothing, not even a tingle. Before she could ask Anna to stop, her friend fell asleep. The experience was never repeated.

Siw picks up her phone. When Anna hears the *Pokémon Go* music, she groans and face-plants into the cushions.

'There's a raid in Society Park,' Siw informs her. 'It starts in twenty minutes.'

'No,' Anna says, her voice muffled. 'Please, no. What if Alva wakes up?'

'It's a black egg – probably Entei. And if Alva does wake up, which is unlikely, she's fine with me being out for a while. I'll leave her a note.'

Anna sits up and rubs her face. 'If Chris Hemsworth was inside that egg and I could take him home with me . . .' She blinks and breaks off. 'Okay, let's not mess around – I'd definitely go if that was the case. But *Entei*? What the fuck is Entei?'

'A Pokémon I don't have. Because it's new.'

'But why do you want it?'

'Do we have to go through all this again? I collect them. And I can battle with it in the gym.'

'Why?'

'Why does anybody do anything? I'm going. You can stay here and drink by yourself if you want. I'll be back later.'

2

Max and Johan are on a *Pokémon* walk, the usual route that covers most of the centre of Norrtälje and nineteen Poké Stops. They've just passed the statue marking the first deposit of money at the Roslagen Savings Bank, and are continuing towards the library.

Both are wearing short-sleeved checked shirts. The air is as warm as on a summer's evening, but there are no tourists. The people drinking beer outside the sports bar are locals, and Johan says hi to a couple he recognises from the bowling hall.

They spin the library Poké Stop and turn into Stora Brogatan. It is just before eight o'clock, and the Thai restaurant Ran Mae is closing up for the night. When they reach the former post office which became a lighting shop which became a health club and sweep their fingers across their screens in a synchronised movement to take the Poké Stop, Johan shakes his head and lowers his phone.

'Seriously, what are we doing?'

'Playing *Pokémon*,' Max replies, picking up a Pidgey with an excellent curveball.

'But from the wider perspective,' Johan persists. 'Is this really how we're going to spend our evenings? You said before that life is running away from us.'

Max picks up the Stop outside Nordea and ignores a Magikarp wriggling on the ground outside the cake shop on the corner. He already has four Gyarados, one of which is a shiny. He shrugs. 'That was how I felt at that moment, but basically I've more or less given up. Those major goals aren't for me. I'm sticking to small, well-defined goals, like reaching level forty in this.'

'And when you've reached level forty?'

'Well, they're bound to add higher levels at some point.'

When they turn into Hantverkaregatan their phones ping and they open Facebook. A message from Pokémon Go Roslagen: the group is meeting in half an hour for a level-five raid at Wind Thingie in Society Park.

'Yes!' Johan says, forgetting his earlier reservations. 'Entei motherfucker!' They move to high five each other, then burst out laughing. 'How sad are we, on a scale of one to ten?' Johan wonders.

'We're complete dorks,' Max informs him. 'And we choose happiness. That's another way of looking at it.'

Even though she's drunk almost an entire bottle of wine, Anna is steady on her feet as she heads for Society Park with Siw. The only noticeable effect of the alcohol is that the world seems a little softer to her. All the greenery, all those leaves form an embrace ready to receive her with tenderness, and the rustling of the treetops is a pleasant, integral part of the whole. This is the nice part of being tipsy, but she is rarely capable of stopping at that point. Which she realises is a shame.

This evening is going to be an exception, at least for the next hour or so. When Anna wanted to decant some of the wine into a plastic bottle to take with them, Siw flatly refused. They bickered for a while, but in the end Anna gave in and pretended to accept Siw's assertion that it was important not to make a bad impression on the other players. In fact, she had chosen to see this as a positive opportunity, a chance to wander around feeling enjoyably woozy for once.

Siw has started *Pokémon Go* on her phone, then put the phone in her pocket just to get the distance covered registered so that the egg will hatch. Anna has more or less understood how it works, and thinks it is utterly ridiculous that Siw is enslaved to a bunch of invisible fantasy creatures. She herself has only tried out *Angry Birds*, but gave up on the second level because the grunting pigs got on her nerves.

She and Siw have been to the gym three times, and Anna has a persistent ache in her thighs. Fortunately the effects of the alcohol have eased it considerably. She knows that the diet plan is more or less dead in the water because wine and spirits contain lots of calories, but there's nothing she can do about that. Without her regular tipple she would drown in misery, and surely she'll be able to turn at least some of her fat into muscle?

At the roundabout they turn onto Bolkavägen, which is lined with attractive houses. Anna wishes she had a can of spray paint to tag the spotless walls and neat fences. She hates areas like this, and cheers herself up by fantasising about the perverted behaviour that is doubtless going on in the cellars. She has just conjured up a man in chinos and loafers who is stuffing kittens into a microwave when Siw asks: 'Have you been to see Acke recently?'

Anna deletes the mental image of an oven door covered in blood and guts. 'I was there the day before yesterday. Or the day before that. Or yesterday.'

Acke is three years younger than Anna. Her visits to her brother in the local jail are so similar that they all merge together into a glutinous porridge of mostly monosyllabic exchanges in the appropriately porridge-coloured visitors' room. During the two years Acke has been inside, Anna has been to see him around a hundred times. It annoys her that she can't remember exactly when she was last there, and she snaps at Siw with unnecessary sharpness. 'Why?'

Siw pulls away a fraction as if Anna has struck out at her. 'I was just wondering. How is he?'

Anna feels guilty about her aggressive tone, which irritates her even more. 'He carries out his fucking DIY tasks and does his fucking press-ups and talks about his new fucking life that's going to start when he gets out.' They have left the idyllic residential area and reached the car park in front of Jansson's newsagent's. The destructive impulse in Anna's heart takes a break. She nudges Siw's shoulder with hers and says: 'Sorry. I'm just so sick of that idiot.'

'Because you love him.'

'Yes. Otherwise I guess I wouldn't bother.'

Anders, or Acke, is the brother who is closest to Anna. She used to look after him when he was little, and introduced him to the gangster movies that were her and Siw's first shared reference. Unfortunately these movies also inspired him to team up with the Djup brothers.

After a few successful years selling the product the brothers always referred to as 'hay', Acke was finally stopped by customs in Trelleborg. The police, who were called after his rucksack was searched, didn't think that 'hay' was the correct term for the three kilos of weed that had been found. Personal use didn't cut it either, and he got two years.

Siw checks the time. They are in danger of being late for the raid, so when they get to Glasmästarbacken she says: 'We need to hurry if we're going to get there in time.'

'You hurry – how are your thighs?'

'Well, stagger faster then.'

Siw is also in considerable pain from her visits to the gym, and as they pick up speed they both start limping. Anna thinks they look like two shapeless ducks waddling down the hill, and when she laughs a little bit of sour wine comes up her throat and burns her nose. She stops laughing and waddles on towards Society Park.

4

As they approach Wind Thingie they can see that a large group of people have already gathered. Anna has been on a couple of raids with Siw before, and is once again struck by how incredibly random the group calling itself Pokémon Go Roslagen is.

Virtually all ages and types are represented, from ten-year-old boys who don't seem to be entirely in control of their limbs to retired ladies calmly swiping across their screens. There's a beefy teenager Anna recognises from the gym, and a woman of her own age who looks as if she's just recovering from long-term drug abuse. Only little girls are missing.

Some of the men seem to be total dorks who drag themselves away from their unemployment benefit and their computer screens in order to catch Pokémon, but others could easily be fine upstanding office administrators with the National Insurance Bureau. If the group had been placed in front of Anna without comment, she would never have guessed what they have in common, unless, of course, they're a family. And in a way, they probably are. Quiet conversations are going on, people check one another's screens to point something out, the odd burst of laughter is heard. A middle-aged man is explaining something to two little boys.

Beautiful, Anna thinks in spite of herself. *Absolutely fucking stupid. But beautiful.*

It is one minute past the agreed time, and as Siw approaches the gathering she calls out: 'Have you started?'

'No,' replies a tall, slim guy about the same age as Siw and Anna. 'We're waiting for Christina. Oh – talk of the devil . . .'

A woman of about sixty comes bowling along on a mobility scooter. She has taken part in the three raids Anna has been on, and is known as 'Mama's Frog'. She is the top player in Norrtälje – level thirty-nine.

When Mama's Frog reaches the group, she grabs her phone and asks what seems to be the compulsory question of the moment: 'Have you started?'

'No,' the guy says. 'How would we manage without you, Christina?'

Judging by Christina's expression, the remark is welcome, even though it's a lie. Siw has explained that about six people can carry out a level-five raid, and there must be at least thirty here. This fact leads to an activity Anna hasn't witnessed before.

'Blue here!' shouts the same guy, and two other voices call out: 'Yellow!' 'Red!'

Siw walks towards the Blue guy, and Anna whispers: 'What's going on?'

'You can't have more than twenty people on a raid,' Siw explains. 'So we divide ourselves up depending on which team we belong to.'

'And you belong to a *team*?'

'I do. Team Mystic.'

'Fucking hell.'

The guy who has taken on the role of co-ordinator is pretty good-looking, with his angular face, tanned skin and pale blue eyes. When Siw positions herself beside him they remind Anna of the Danish comedy duo Ole & Axel, also known as Long & Short. He nods to Siw, then turns to his friend who looks like an inferior version of himself.

Anna spreads her hands wide, encompassing the twelve people who have gathered around. 'So, you're all Team *Mystic*?'

'Yes,' the friend says. 'And what are you?'

'Team Sportia.'

'Cool.' He returns to his phone without a smile. He has exactly the kind of appearance Anna dislikes the most. Mean, narrow lips and squinty brown eyes in a mousy face.

Just give me a reason, she thinks. *Give me a reason and I'll punch you.*

She turns to Siw to whisper something derogatory about him, but Siw isn't home right now. She is staring open-mouthed at the yellow container on the other side of the inlet.

'What's wrong? Siw, what's wrong?'

Siw doesn't answer. The leader has noticed Siw's behaviour too and looks searchingly at her before turning to the group. 'Okay, in we go!' When Siw still doesn't react, he places a hand on her shoulder.

'Hey – we're starting now.'

Siw blinks and fumbles with her phone to enter the raid. She smiles shyly at the guy and gives him a thumbs up as the counter begins to click down from ninety-seven. He looks at Siw, at the container, back at Siw.

'Excuse me, but . . . what is it?'

'Nothing. It's just that container, I don't know, it's kind of . . .'

'Sinister?'

'Yes. Exactly.'

The friend glances at Anna as if he is *assessing* her. Taking the measure of her and finding her inadequate. It might be her imagination, but she has to make a real effort not to stick her tongue out at him. Instead, she lets out a little snort and turns away.

'I'm Max,' says the guy who seems to be in charge, holding out his hand to Siw.

'Siw.' Anna rolls her eyes as she feels rather than sees how close Siw is to actually curtsying when she shakes his hand. Thank God she doesn't do it, and shortly after that the raid begins.

Anna steps back, contemplating the group gathered around the statue, dabbing at their screens with their fingers. The idea of a sect rather than a family comes to mind, with Wind Thingie as the object of their worship and their phones as prayer books. *Dab, dab dab, give us this day our daily Pokémon.*

'How's it going?' she asks. Siw is completely focused, constantly tapping with her index finger. She nods and carries on tapping. The screen is half filled by a creature that resembles a large, bad-tempered dog with wings – the creature they have all come to capture.

Beautiful, possibly, Anna thinks, *but above all totally fucking crazy.*

Her eye is drawn to the glowing yellow container. A few people are standing around it as if it is their golden calf. Anna doesn't understand what Siw or the guy called Max are talking about. It's just a container, like any other. No doubt there is something inside it. Nothing to worry about.

The raid has entered its next phase. Entei has been conquered, and now they have to capture it. People are staring grimly at their screens, stabbing with their fingers or making circular movements in order to throw white Poké balls. Anna sees Siw hit Entei with an excellent shot, and she mutters, 'Come on, come on,' as the ball jiggles back and forth.

Yes, come on Entei, Anna thinks. *Then we might be able to go home at some point.*

'Shit!' Siw shouts as Entei breaks out of the ball and skips away across the comic-book-green grass. Siw has only one ball left, and purses her lips as she spins it around and around, ready to fire off one last curveball.

'Yes, yes, YES!' shouts Mouseface, holding up his phone triumphantly. 'Entei motherfucker!'

Max obviously hasn't been as lucky as his friend; he lowers his phone and rubs his eyes. Anna can see Mouseface's eyes burning with Schadenfreude, which he doesn't even try to hide. What's the name of the Pokémon fucker that looks exactly like that? *Rattata.*

Siw sighs and her shoulders slump. 'No good?' Max asks, and Siw shakes her head.

'I got him with my last ball!' Mouseface says excitedly, turning his phone around. Entei is there on the screen, framed like a picture. Anna is about to say something sarcastic when Max points to Mouseface. 'This is Johan. He's okay, although it might not seem that way.'

Before Anna can stop her, Siw is pointing at her. 'And this is Anna. The same applies to her.'

Anna is dumbstruck; she can't even think of a smart remark as Johan grins condescendingly at her. This is *not* what usually happens in social situations. Anna is the one who breaks the ice and chips out a channel of conversation into which Siw eventually dips a toe, after lengthy consideration.

Johan puts away his phone. 'Shall we go over and check out that container?'

The question was directed to Max, but both Max and Siw shake their heads with such synchronicity that it looks quite funny. Max glances at Siw. 'What are you feeling?'

'Just . . . unease,' Siw replies. 'As if . . . as if something is going to happen when they open it.'

'I feel the same. So, what is it? What's going to happen?'

'I've no idea, but things are going to change.'

'Yes.'

Johan claps his hands and laughs. 'Will you listen to yourselves! You sound as if you're in some crap horror movie. *I've got a bad feeling, oh I must—*'

'Siw knows these things,' Anna snaps. 'Ever since she was little she's—'

'Quiet!' Siw says with such force that Anna gives a start. This really is an unusual evening.

'What is it you know?' Max asks gently.

'Nothing.' Siw lowers her eyes. 'I don't know anything.'

The other members of Pokémon Go Roslagen have drifted away, leaving the four of them alone beneath the floodlight on the top of Wind Thingie. The issue of whether they should go somewhere together hangs in the air, and with the aim of precluding that particular development, Anna takes Siw's hand and says: 'Okay, so thank you and goodnight.' She nods to Johan and adds; 'Congratulations on catching the bad-tempered dog.'

Siw allows herself to be led away. After a few seconds Max calls after her: 'What's your name? In *Pokémon Go*?'

Siw's cheeks flush red. 'Chaplin's Girl.'

Max smiles. 'I'm RoslagsBowser. Nice to meet you.'

Siw opens and closes her mouth as she searches for a suitable response, and Anna forcibly turns her around before she comes out with something embarrassing. They cut across the grass, heading towards the tennis courts. When they reach the sculpture surrounded by benches, Siw pulls her hand away. 'You're the only one I've ever told. You can't just . . .'

'Sorry. I couldn't help myself when Mouseface didn't believe you. But your squeeze seemed to be the same – he had feelings too!'

'What do you mean, *my squeeze*? He's not my squeeze!'

'Nooo . . .' Anna says slowly, poking Siw in the side with her index finger. 'But you wouldn't mind if he was . . .'

'Stop it!'

They walk along in silence as far as the open-air stage, then Anna cracks. She laughs, shakes her head. 'RoslagsBowser – you know how to pick 'em!'

'Pack it in, Anna – this is embarrassing. He's out of my league.'

'Is he now? And what league do you think you're in?'

'Way down. Division six, or whatever it is. At the bottom.'

Anna grabs Siw by the shoulder and pushes her onto one of the benches in front of stage, then she sits down beside her. 'I don't know if you're fishing for compliments here, or if you're just stupid. You have an amazing aura, Siw. Those eyes . . . You should use them to nail people instead of just staring at the ground. And your smile. If you fired it off instead of standing there biting your lip . . . You've got something, something incredibly appealing. If you'd just let it out.'

'You're very kind, Anna. But you know as well as I do—'

'I know nothing, as certain people say. And please take note – I'm not encouraging you to get together with Max, because then we'd get Mouseface into the bargain.'

'We?'

'Yes, we. That's right, isn't it? And now *we* are going to stagger home and drink, and you're going to tell me all your fantasies about your wonderful life with *RoslagsBowser*.'

*

Two boats meet at the entrance to Norrtälje harbour. One is a simple plastic motor launch driven by an elderly couple. The other is a substantial aluminium Buster with a cabin. A family of five are sitting on deck in chairs and on the cushioned thwarts. When the boats pass, both drivers raise a hand in greeting, even though they don't know each other. That's what you do at sea.

126

HOME

I

Johan was twenty years old when his mother reached the room she had been heading towards for so long – the secure wing on ward 142, Danderyd Hospital. She had been in and out of psychiatric care a number of times, but after an episode during which she chased people around the town square with a fire extinguisher in order to drive out the demons from their bodies, she had been judged a danger to herself and others. However, in the secure wing things got worse rather than better. Without the ability to build protective ramparts of rubbish between herself and the world, she fell into a catatonic state, refusing to leave her bed for long periods of time.

When Johan returned to the apartment on Bergsgatan to clear up, he never got further than the hallway, where he would stand stock still with clenched fists and a lump in his throat. His home had been a mess when he was a child, but now it was a tip consisting of two rooms and a kitchen. Clothes, newspapers and rubbish were piled so high that the detritus came halfway up the windows, and the place stank of everything that had the capacity to stink.

The council. The fucking council.

How was it possible that a person could be allowed to sink so low without anyone reacting? Johan knew that his mother's insanity went in phases, and that she could appear to be more or less normal for several days in succession. She was able to go shopping, pay bills, even visit the hairdresser. But in the end she had crept back to this *hellhole* every single day, where God knows what creatures could be heard scuttling and scrabbling among the crap.

Johan had intended to clean up and take a couple of mementoes from the years when he was growing up, but as he stood there in the hallway with his jaws clamped together, he realised that he wanted nothing to do with his childhood. It could rot away along with everything else in the apartment. He turned on his heel and walked out, determined never to come back.

He stayed on in Norrtälje for a few days in order to deal with the documentation his mother's committal had generated, and during that time he was plagued by an anxiety that could be eased only by wandering around the area near the apartment. He walked up and down Bergsgatan, he hung out in the trees on the hill where he and Max used to play their fantasy games, he glanced at the door of the apartment block, he obsessively scratched his arms; he was terrified that he was losing his mind. He felt a gnawing, tearing yearning, without knowing what he was yearning *for*.

Eventually he thought he'd worked it out. He used half of his meagre savings to employ a company who cleared and cleaned the apartment, more or less restoring it to its original state. The work took three days, and when Johan slowly walked through the empty rooms that smelled only of cleaning products, he knew he'd done the right thing.

He wanted to start again. He wanted to be in the space where he'd lived through his childhood so that he could erase it by living a new life in the same place. He sat cross-legged on the floor of the empty living room for a long time, gazing out of the freshly cleaned windows as twilight fell over the silos in the harbour.

I'm home now.

Over the next day or two he occasionally felt a pang of regret – why hadn't he kept the kitchen table and a couple of chairs, for example? He had rented his sublet apartment in Stockholm fully furnished, so he had no choice but to use a bedding roll and his sleeping bag on the floor of his old room for a while.

With the help of second-hand shops, online auction sites and a certain amount of skip diving, he managed to make the apartment habitable. The only thing missing was a television, and when he received his first month's salary from the bowling hall he went straight to the biggest electrical store in town on Knutby Torg and ploughed the last of his savings into a forty-seven-inch Samsung. The sound when he mounted the TV on the wall was the 'click' that told him he was done. Now life could start over.

2

'You're out of your mind,' Johan says as he inserts the key in the lock. 'They were just so . . . fat, both of them.'

'I think *fat* is overstating things,' Max replies, following him into the apartment. 'Okay, so they were a bit chubby, but fat . . .'

'They were fat, for fuck's sake.' Johan closes the door and

locks it behind him. 'And did you see the way that other one looked at me?'

'No, I can't say I did.'

'She *hated* me. The first time I met her eyes, I just felt . . . this girl *hates* me. Not that I care, but that's how it was.'

Max takes off his Ecco loafers and places them neatly on Johan's virtually empty shoe rack. 'It's just that she's not familiar with your wonderful, tolerant personality.'

'I know you think I'm a cynic, but that's because I tell it like it is – I say *fat*, I say *hates*.'

'You can say what you like, but there was something about Siw. Something I . . . recognised.'

'I'm sure she's okay, even if Siw is a weird name, but that other one . . . What's that word you use? *Becoming*. It's not *becoming* to look down your nose at someone else when you're so fat.'

Max senses that Johan is about to spiral into a lengthy diatribe on whether fat people have the right to exist, and with the aim of cutting him off before he can get going, he says: '*Mario Kart*?'

Over the years Max and Johan have gone through a hundred or more titles on various PlayStation, X-box and Nintendo consoles, but these days when they play against each other it has to be either *Mario Kart* or *Smash Bros*, and only the fifteen-year-old GameCube versions will do.

Johan's GameCube let out its last sigh and spun its last mini-disc back in 2010, but his reverse compatible Wii is alive and well, and fortunately Nintendo has been kind enough to equip the Wii with ports for GameCube controllers. Because that's the point: the controllers.

Like many other gamers, Max and Johan are in agreement that the development of the hand controllers peaked with the GameCube.

Neither Sony nor Microsoft have got anywhere near, and it's best not to mention the Wii controller when Johan is around. According to him, the slim, sensitive joystick might come in handy as a dildo in desperate situations. At least it's capable of vibrating. Sometimes.

But the GameCube controller – that's something else! It's nice to look at with its many colours, it fits perfectly in the hand, and both buttons and levers are in exactly the right place so that playing becomes instinctive, and the controller an extension of the body. The GameCube controller is simply the best, and anyone who thinks otherwise is a fucking idiot, according to Johan.

Max cleans a fingerprint from the *Mario Kart* disc by breathing on it and rubbing it gently with the hem of his T-shirt, then he inserts the disc in the console, which receives it with a contented hum and a click.

'Beer?' Johan asks, heading for the kitchen.

'No thanks.' Max uses the despised Wii controller to start up the game. He hears Johan open the refrigerator door and take a couple of swigs of something that will dull his reflexes and make him incapable of winning. Max considers accepting a beer to put them on the same level, but decides against it. He's had enough of long-drawn-out evenings with too much drinking, talking crap and moaning. A couple of games, then home to bed – that's the plan.

'*Mario Kart! Yo-hoo!*' Mario shouts from the TV screen as Max hears a click and a hiss from the kitchen. Johan comes back into the living room with a can of Carlsberg Sort Guld in his hand. He sits down on the floor next to Max and picks up his controller. The wires won't reach the sofa. They sit cross-legged side by side, so close that their shoulders are touching. Max chooses Koopa / Paratroopa because he likes the red shells, while Johan goes for Waluigi / Wario simply because he likes Waluigi, in spite of the difficult-to-handle bombs that are his special weapon. They start *Mushroom Cup*.

As soon as the countdown to Luigi Circuit begins, that strange sense of calm comes over Max. In the real world everything is on the move, and it's impossible to return to the landscapes of your childhood. If they haven't changed, you have, and nothing is quite the way you remember it. But in gaming it is possible. Luigi Circuit looks exactly the same as it did when Max was thirteen years old; he knows every single turn and shortcut, and the feeling when he sets off with a well-timed dash is identical. It's as if no time at all has passed, and it soothes his restless soul in a way that few other things can do.

Max and Johan race around the bends, sparks flying from their tyres. Johan has a slight lead because his car is faster, but that will change as soon as he is hit by a shell, because its acceleration is crap.

'What was that feeling you were talking about?' Johan asks as he fends off a red shell by tossing a green one behind him. 'Down by the harbour – about the container?'

'I don't know. That's all it is – a feeling. Like in the reptile house at Skansen. You stand there staring into a glass tank, and you can't see it, but you *know* that there's a snake somewhere in there.'

'I've never been to Skansen.' Johan throws a fake item box behind him, which Max easily avoids. 'But you don't literally mean that there might be a snake in that container?'

'No, but there's something in there. Something that shouldn't be let out.'

'I don't really understand,' Johan says, then swears as he is hit by the chain chomper, allowing Max to overtake him. He uses a mushroom to accelerate fast, and comes up alongside Max before going on: 'I mean, you usually just have a feeling about the timing – that something is happening *now*. Not *where* it's happening, or going to happen.'

Johan uses the heavier car to his advantage and forces Max's little buggy onto the grass verge so that he loses speed. Whatever Johan was knocking back in the kitchen, it hasn't kicked in yet, and Max has to take the bends as tightly as possible in order to keep up.

'No,' Max says. 'It's weird. Maybe it's to do with Siw – after all, she had—'

'A hell of a rack,' Johan chips in, and Max sighs. He doesn't share his friend's fondness for vulgarity and categorical judgements, which Johan refers to as 'telling the truth'. Quite the reverse; it makes him feel as if the world is falling apart, just a little.

Johan glances at Max. 'Sorry. Tourette's. What were you going to say?'

The apology makes the crack in the world shrink. They're on the last lap, and Johan is still well ahead. The item box rewards Max with a green shell, which he throws after Johan. He misses by a hair's breadth.

'Clean up!' Johan shouts. 'Come on – what were you going to say?'

He often blames Tourette's when he realises that an unacceptable frog has leapt out of his mouth, even though he doesn't actually suffer from an uncontrollable compulsion to say horrible things – just good old-fashioned bitterness. Max misses an acceleration plate at the finish line and it's all over. He finishes second.

The next course, Peach Beach, is Max's favourite. It puts him in a better mood, and he decides to ignore Johan's unnecessary remark. When they have passed the first bend and are cruising along among the giant mutant ducks on the shore, he says: 'It's hard to describe. It's as if I *recognise* her.'

133

'Maybe you do. Norrtälje isn't that big. Maybe the two of you have met before. Shit!'

Johan is hit by a red shell and his car flips into the air, leaving Wario and Waluigi waving their arms. It takes him valuable seconds to regain his speed, and he is overtaken by a couple of characters.

'It's not that,' Max explains. 'I know I've never seen her before. And I've never felt like this before.'

'Listen to you – *I've never felt like this before*. Now why does that sound familiar?'

'You're not taking me seriously. It's like . . . like bumping into someone you haven't seen for many years. In spite of the fact that I've never met her before.'

'Chaplin's Girl.'

'Yes.'

Johan glances at Max and grins. 'But she did have a hell of a rack – you have to agree with me there.'

'Yes, Johan. She did.'

'Plenty to get hold of. Apart from the rack, I mean.'

Max has no desire to think or talk about Siw in those terms. When he examines his emotions as he wobbles his way past the ducks' pecking beaks, he finds a different word, one he would never say to Johan. When he was standing next to Siw, that short, overweight – he's prepared to go that far – woman with her messy cloud of hair and her ill-fitting clothes, he had the sense that he was in the presence of something *holy*. He doesn't really understand what he means, but that was how he felt.

He has lost concentration and fallen behind in the race. He pulls himself together and moves forward with the help of some mushrooms. On the last stretch Johan is hit by a blue shell, and Max is able to overtake him just before the finish line. Johan tosses aside the controller and gives full rein to his Tourette's.

3

It is almost midnight by the time Siw manages to get rid of Anna. The fact that the wine box is empty helps. Siw has drunk maybe three glasses, while Anna's consumption is best measured in litres. Towards the end she was slurring badly when she said: 'Listen, that . . . Roslagsloser or whateverhisnamewas . . . haven't you . . . can't you . . . isn't there . . . you know?'

'No, Anna. I don't know.'

'But . . . ah! Ah!' Anna had thumped her forehead with a clenched fist in order to loosen a thought that had got stuck in some corner of her skull. 'You know, what's it called . . . contact! Can't you contact whatshisname through . . . Fashebook?'

'That's not how it works.'

'Not how it works? Fashebook? But that *is* Fashebook! That's what it's for! Contact!'

'Listen, it's late and I've got an early start in the morning.'

'Oh, you're sooo boooring!'

This was a constant refrain on the evenings Siw and Anna spent together. At some point, often quite early, Anna would pull away from Siw in terms of the level of intoxication, and then Siw was *boooring*, letting Anna get drunk all by herself.

Siw brushes flakes of ash off the sofa and sighs when she sees a fresh burn mark. Anna is a 'party' smoker, and whenever alcohol is involved, it's a party. When Siw turns the seat cushion over she finds an old burn that is even bigger, so she turns it back again.

Anna is her oldest and best friend, the only person she can really call a friend, but she wishes Anna would cut back on the booze. Anna herself insists that she doesn't have a problem. Her main argument is that she's never fucked up at work, therefore she has the situation under control. Siw doesn't agree. There are things that can be fucked up apart from work; it's a slippery slope. Regardless of what Anna says, Siw has noticed that her consumption has increased over the years. At some point you reach the edge, and there's nothing to stop you from falling.

Siw places the glasses on the draining board before dismantling the wine box and squashing it. She doesn't want to risk Alva finding it in the morning and asking questions. Alva once found an empty vodka bottle, and cross-examined her mother at length on the possibility of her becoming an alcoholic.

Siw goes into the living room, opens her laptop and clicks on the Facebook icon. When the page comes up she closes it down and rubs her temples. She turns to Spotify instead and starts Håkan Hellström's album *Confessions of a Colic Child* on shuffle, keeping the volume low.

Tears prick her eyes when she hears the strings at the beginning of 'Brännö Serenade', and when Håkan starts to sing she suddenly has a lump in her throat; he asks what a person knows about the moonlight until they've been broken beneath it.

She lowers the volume a little more and gets to her feet. She goes to Alva's room and peeps in. The rocket-shaped night light on the bedside table illuminates the child, curled up on her side with one hand grasping Poffe, a small cuddly fox.

The lump in Siw's throat grows. When Alva was four years old she found the fox tossed in a bush outside the main door of the apartment block, and with a logic that Siw has never managed to

136

counter, Alva had decided that it was a present from her daddy in heaven. He had thrown it down to her, but had missed her window, so it landed in the bush instead. Ever since that day, Poffe – who is also an angel – has been her constant night-time companion, and Alva refuses to go to bed without him.

One day, sweetheart. One day I'll tell you. Siw closes the door and angrily rubs her eyes to stop the tears from coming.

She sits down at her laptop again –

'*You will see your youth rot before you . . .*'

– opens up Facebook, but scrolls through only one page without finding anything before closing it down once more.

What am I doing?

'*And what do you know about love . . .*'

Siw stands up and goes out onto the balcony. She sits down with her hands resting on her thighs and stares at the football pitch, which is now in darkness. This is exactly where she was sitting when she told Anna her secret.

She had been feeling low all afternoon, and had drunk a little too much wine during the evening. According to Anna's viewpoint, it was one of those rare occasions when Siw wasn't being *boooring*. It was quite late when Siw suddenly said: 'I'm going to tell you. About me.'

Anna topped up her glass. 'Go on. I've always wondered.'

Siw took a big gulp, gathered her courage. 'The thing is, I walk around *waiting*, but I don't know what I'm waiting for. No, don't say anything. It's not a man, it's not a quick shag, it's . . . something else. Something completely . . . essential. *Different.*'

'So, what is it?'

'That's what I'm saying – I don't know! When I say "something different", that's exactly what I mean. Something I can't even imagine, precisely because it's something *different* from anything I think I might want. Do you understand what I mean?'

'Not really – is it like, some kind of religious experience?'

'Kind of, but I definitely don't believe it's anything to do with God. It comes to me as . . . I don't know . . . a vision, or a . . . calling from . . . I don't know.'

'Like the owls in Harry Potter, when they bring the letters?'

'Yes! Yes!' Siw had got so excited that she'd spilled wine on her nice cushions without noticing. 'That's it exactly! Harry doesn't even know that Hogwarts exists until he gets the letters! He doesn't know it's right there waiting for him, and that's where he's meant to go.'

'And for the moment you're living in the cupboard under the stairs?'

Tears had sprung to Siw's eyes on that occasion too. She wasn't sure if it was down to self-pity over the difficulty of her situation, or joy at being understood.

'Yes. For the moment I'm living in the cupboard under the stairs.'

'You're crazy. Cheers to that.'

Siw squints at the football pitch. She thinks someone is walking across it towards her, and she catches herself fantasising that it's RoslagsBowser, coming to get her. She blushes, even though no one can see her or her fantasies.

Go on, do it.

Before she can change her mind, she gets up and marches back to her laptop. She opens up Facebook and scrolls down through the Pokémon Go Roslagen group entries until she finds a post from RoslagsBowser. She clicks on his name.

Of course . . .

What had she expected? That she'd have access to all his secrets, photos of him making a V-sign against the perfect sunset? Roslags-Bowser's profile has been created purely for *Pokémon Go*, and contains nothing but his posts on that page. Not even a profile picture. She glares at the uninformative screen as Håkan continues to warble.

'*I dreamed I could sing, but I can't . . .*'

So that's the end of that.

Siw gets up from the sofa and rubs her hands together as if she's trying to get rid of something sticky. Then she sits back down and reads through all of RoslagsBowser's posts on Pokémon Go Roslagen.

*

A woman is standing outside the entrance to Norrtälje Hospital. She is crying. A nurse who has just finished her shift doesn't know why the woman is crying. There are a thousand reasons to cry outside a hospital, and that isn't important here. The important thing is that the nurse goes up to the woman and takes her hand. They stand there for perhaps thirty seconds as the woman's tears abate just a little. She looks at the nurse and nods. The nurse nods back. Then she gently lets go of the woman's hand and goes home to do the housework.

THE SOUND OF A CAR CRASH

I

When she was little, Siw was of average build, tending towards skinny. It wasn't until she was eleven that her figure began to coarsen, through no fault of her own. It just happened. As a girl she had identified with elves and ethereal creatures skipping through life as light as a feather; by the time she was twelve she had to accept that the earth and weight had her in their grip.

She couldn't take to the person who stood naked before her in the mirror. In addition to the mild fear she felt at the sight of the incipient curve of her hips and breasts, which every girl has to deal with, Siw was repulsed by the *coarseness* that had taken over. It was as if an evil spirit had gradually and covertly removed her birdlike skeleton and replaced it with that of an adult human being. She hated, *hated* what she saw, and it took years of struggle with herself before she was able to accept what had happened to her. The elf had turned into a troll. Siw's petite mother Anita said it was her father's genes making their presence felt. As if that was any consolation. Although it was. A tiny bit.

Anita had left Norrtälje to do a teacher training course in Stockholm, and that was where she had met Ulrik, Siw's father-to-be. He was from Norrland in the far north of Sweden, almost two metres tall, broad-chested and with hands that deserved to be referred to as *paws*. Add a black bushy beard and deep-set eyes, and you have a man who ought to make most people run away and hide. Anita didn't do that. Quite the reverse.

'He was so *nice*,' Anita had said so many times that Siw had lost count. 'The nicest person I'd ever met.' As an adult, Siw thought she'd worked it out: it was the contrast that had attracted her mother – the rough giant of a man with a heart of gold. She had seen something similar among hard rockers – the ones with the most piercings and the most terrifying tattoos were often the gentlest souls.

Siw was conceived according to plan when they'd both qualified and taught in high schools for a year. Anita's subject was Swedish, while Ulrik specialised in natural sciences. When Siw was born they managed to rent a three-room apartment in Bagarmossen. Everything was going well. The plan included another baby within three years, then a move to a house in a suburb outside the city.

Then it came. The destroyer of plans, the silent killer. Ulrik received the diagnosis when he was on paternity leave with Siw, who wasn't even one year old. Advanced leukemia. He'd been feeling tired and had been experiencing some pain for a while, but he came from a family where you didn't really complain if you happened to lose a limb. Going to the doctor with vague symptoms wasn't on his radar. When he found blood in his urine he left it a few months before mentioning it to Anita, who immediately drove him to the hospital.

The oncologists gave him no more than two months to live. He hung on for five, because he didn't want to die without hearing his little girl say 'Daddy'. When Siw was fifteen months old, she said the magic word. A week later, Ulrik was dead.

Anita carried Siw from room to room in the apartment, now empty of a future, empty of meaning. She paused in the living room with her sleeping child in her arms. She saw herself, standing there alone. She told Siw later that was when she truly understood the concept of the *single parent*. There and then she decided to move back to Norrtälje, where she at least had some of her childhood friends and, above all, her own mother.

And so Siw spent part of her childhood with Grandma Berit, who stepped in to help out whenever necessary. As Siw grew up and Berit cut down her working hours, Siw often chose to go to her grandmother's rather than staying on for after-school activities.

It was at Berit's house that she learned to love Chaplin. They spent many an afternoon giggling their way through both the great masterpieces and the early short films, which mainly involve people falling over. It wasn't until Siw turned eleven that she was emotionally mature enough to grasp the tragic element, and shed her first tears over *The Kid*. She continued to weep her way through *City Lights* and *Modern Times* along with Berit. They would sit on the sofa with their arms around each other, tears pouring down their faces.

Such excesses were entirely foreign to Anita, and as the years went by and Siw put together her mother's stories, she realised it was all about a self-control that Anita had imposed upon herself in connection with Ulrik's death. Giving her feelings free rein would be like opening the door of the tiger's cage: she would be swallowed up on the spot. She had no tears to shed over fictional characters – no tears at all.

In addition, Anita was a woman of *words* while Berit, like Siw, was a woman of *pictures*. Following the same logic of skipping a generation, ever since Alva was little, and to the delight of her grandmother Anita, she had shown a great interest in books, and had learned to read just after turning five.

Berit, Anita, Siw, Alva. Four generations of women, each one an only child. Coincidence? We will come to that later. It is time to deal with the elephant in the room.

2

It was around the time of the incident outside the library that Siw came up with a word for the gift that had been her companion since the age of seven. She called it *a Hearing*, an indefinite noun. So she could '*get* a Hearing', and during her life she had '*had* several Hearings'.

The first Hearing came a week before her seventh birthday. She had called in at the leisure centre after school to see if anything interesting was happening. Once she had established that it wasn't, she decided to go to see Berit, who was home in the afternoons.

She'd taken no more than ten steps along the pavement outside the leisure centre when she heard the sound of screeching tyres behind her as a car braked. She spun around to see where the vehicle was, and as she completed the movement, she heard a dull thud and a horrible crunch.

She thought she'd been hit and that the pain hadn't yet got through, like when you stub your toe and have time to think 'ouch' before it actually starts hurting. However, the street was deserted. She knew she was being stupid, but felt all over her body anyway just to check that she hadn't been run over – she'd heard it so *clearly*. But there wasn't even a scratch.

When she told her grandmother what had happened, she thought Berit looked oddly at her before saying cheerfully: 'Listen, Siw – why don't we go and have a look at the school leisure centre? I haven't been there for such a long time!'

'It was nothing to do with the leisure centre, it was just—'

'I *really* want to see it! Come on, off we go!'

Siw tried to protest, she didn't want to go back to the chaotic dump she'd left only a few minutes ago, but Berit refused to listen. When they reached the spot where Siw had heard the invisible car, Berit squeezed her hand so tightly that it hurt.

'Ow, Grandma – let go!'

'Sorry, sweetheart, I got a bit carried away.'

When they arrived at the leisure centre things got even weirder. Berit showed little interest in Siw's drawings and explanations; she insisted on talking to the staff about traffic safety. She said she'd been thinking about the proximity of the road – shouldn't they put up a fence, and post a warden in the meantime?

The staff assured her that the children were taught how to behave, that there was a twenty-kilometre per hour limit, plus a speed bump on either side of the entrance. Siw couldn't understand why her grandmother kept insisting; the staff were giving her funny looks, and it was embarrassing. In the end Siw tugged at her hand and managed to persuade her to leave.

Two days later, Wille in Siw's class was hit by a drunk driver who had just landed after a brief flight. He had missed the speed limit sign and just encountered the first speed bump when Wille ran into the road chasing a football. If Wille had been taller, he might have bounced over the bonnet, but as it was, he ended up beneath the wheels of the car and died instantaneously.

That same evening Berit turned up unannounced and shut herself in the kitchen with Anita. Siw spent the next half hour with her ear pressed to the keyhole. The two women spoke quietly, and Siw found it difficult to make anything out. She did, however, hear the word 'responsibility' several times. It seemed as if Berit wanted to tell Siw something, but Anita was against it. Siw assumed it was to do with Wille.

She wasn't stupid. She'd been in the playground when the accident happened, she'd heard the screech of the tyres, the thud, the crunch – all identical to the sounds she had heard two days earlier. Therefore, she had somehow . . . heard into the future.

Berit was cross when she emerged from the kitchen, and Siw sensed that she had lost the argument about what should and shouldn't be revealed. Siw padded after her into the hallway, and as Berit was pulling on her boots, she whispered: 'Grandma, I think I can sort of—'

Berit stroked her hair and interrupted her. 'All in good time, sweetheart. All in good time.'

'What does that mean?'

'It means you're not quite old enough yet.' Berit glanced at the kitchen door, then added: 'According to your mother.'

3

It was over two years before the next Hearing came along, and Siw had almost forgotten about her possible gift. It was the summer holidays, and she and her best friend Saga had been playing spies in Society Park. Saga had a pair of walkie-talkies that they used to keep in contact as they spied on anyone who looked suspicious.

The last dubious character had just left the park, and they were wandering home along the quayside comparing notes.

Suddenly Siw felt a violent blow to her right side, throwing her off balance. Someone was screaming, and she could hear the crackle of fierce flames.

'What's wrong?' Saga asked, frightened by the sudden change in her friend. Siw was staring wide-eyed at the harbour entrance, where there was nothing to see except the perfectly still surface of the water.

'Can't you hear it?' Siw said.

'Hear what?'

'Something's burning – a boat, I think.'

'Where?'

Only then did Siw remember the incident two years earlier. She realised it would be pointless to try to explain. Without even saying goodbye, she left Saga and ran to tell her grandmother. She hadn't gone many steps before she thought she heard voices calling to her.

'Siw! Siw!'

The voice was coming from her hand – she was still clutching one of Saga's walkie-talkies. She turned and sped back to return the precious item.

'Are you playing some kind of game?' Saga wondered.

'I'm afraid not.'

Siw was out of breath by the time she got to Berit's and told her what had happened. Her grandmother, who had been on her knees weeding the front garden, didn't even bother changing her muddy trousers before accompanying Siw to the harbour. She set off at such a pace that Siw had to ask her to slow down. 'Grandma . . . Can I . . . see into . . . or hear into . . . the future?'

Berit glanced at her, pursed her lips and made a decision. 'Yes.'

'Why?'

'That's a long story.'

'I want . . . to hear it.'

'All in good time.'

Siw clenched her fists and clamped her jaws together. She had forgotten the brief conversation she and her grandmother had had in the hallway two years earlier, but she sensed Anita's threatening, admonitory fingers in the background. Suddenly she was struck by a revelation. 'Can *you* hear into the future, Grandma?'

'Yes.'

'And Mum?'

'Yes. But not much.'

'What do you mean, not much?'

They had reached the top of Glasmästarbacken. Berit was on the point of replying when she stopped dead. A pillar of thick, grey smoke was rising into the sky from the harbour.

'But . . .' Siw said. 'But . . .'

Berit took a deep breath, then exhaled with a long sigh. 'Your mother would have been able to hear this, for example. Because it's closer in terms of time. But not what happened to your classmate.'

Siw couldn't take her eyes off the smoke. Agitated cries were coming from the harbour, and the sound of sirens approaching from the town centre rapidly grew louder.

'But . . . but . . .'

'It's different every time,' Berit tried to explain. 'You never know.'

Anita still refused to allow her daughter to be initiated into what Siw began to think of as 'The Secret'. The information that both her mother and grandmother possessed the same gift, albeit to a different extent, put the whole thing in a new light. It didn't seem far-fetched to imagine that her great-grandmother had had it, and *her* mother, all the way back to . . . what? Thinking like that made Siw's brain hurt. During dinner she tried to push her mother.

'*Why* can't I be told?'

'You'll be told when you're older.'

'But I already know that I can see . . . or hear into the future. And so can Grandma. And you.'

'Is that what Grandma said?'

'Yes.'

Anita's lips narrowed to two thin lines. 'Well, in that case you've been told.'

'But there's *more*. I know there's more.'

'Eat your dinner before it goes cold.'

4

The incident that finally made Anita give in took place just over six months later. During the spring term she had enrolled Siw in the community music school so that she could learn to play the flute, and Siw was on the way to her third lesson. She was walking along swinging her flute case in her hand, trying to work out a strategy that would enable her to give up, because she found the lessons extremely difficult and really boring.

She passed the library, glancing longingly at the reading corner where several children were sitting on cushions and in armchairs. She wasn't that keen on reading, but she enjoyed leafing through picture books. One of her dream jobs was to be someone who drew the pictures for children's books, plus *anything* was better than playing 'Little Snail' and getting cramp in her arms and legs.

She dragged her feet through the thick, freshly fallen snow and stopped outside the video store to check out the posters. *Gladiator* looked amazing, but never in a million years would Anita let her watch it. 'Wait until you're older,' Siw whispered, pursing her lips just like her mother. 'Wait until you're a pensioner.'

She tore herself away and continued along the street, kicking out at lumps of ice. After only a few steps she heard a heavy, wet thud right in front of her. She leapt backwards; her reaction was instinctive, but as no snow had splashed up around her and there was nothing to see, she realised that *it* had happened again. But what was it she'd heard? A low groan came from the empty ground, a rattling, dying breath. A cold hand squeezed her heart as she understood.

No cars were coming; she ran across the road and gazed up at the roof of the building that housed the video store. There was no one there, but the roof was covered in thick snow. At some point in the near future, someone would come to clear it, and then . . .

Siw's initial impulse was to run to Berit's house, but she thought back to the last time. She had been too late. The person who was due to clear the roof might be on the way to his fate right now. She stood there at a loss, gazing around as she tried to work out what to do.

Then she spotted them. There were two men with snow shovels on the roof of the building opposite the library, fifty metres away. Without a second thought she raced across the street. Out of the corner of her eye she caught sight of a car skidding towards her. She hurled herself forward and the car missed her by a hair's breadth. She kept on running.

If I . . . she thought as she ran.

If something happened to her, would she know about it before-hand? Would she hear how she died several days in advance, or . . .

would she hear if she was in the *place* where it was going to be? And if so, could she avoid it?

She almost stopped dead when a really mind-blowing thought occurred to her for the first time: if she heard things that were going to happen, how could she prevent them? And if she did, would that mean she'd . . . heard incorrectly? It was too difficult, more difficult than the flute, and her head was pounding as she ran towards the building. The angle meant that she could no longer see the men on the roof, and they were unlikely to hear her if she called out to them.

At that moment a man emerged from a doorway and Siw took the opportunity to slip inside. She stood at the bottom of the stairs and listened; she could hear faint voices and scraping noises. She ran up the stairs, and at the top she was rewarded with the sight of a ladder leading to an open trapdoor, giving access to the roof.

Only when she was halfway up the ladder and needed to grab hold of one of the rungs for support did she realise she was still carrying the stupid flute case. She hesitated, then kept going. If things got tricky, maybe she could use the flute as a whistle, to attract attention. That was more or less what it sounded like when she played anyway.

'*Little snail, be careful . . .*' Siw sang as she heaved herself up from the ladder and onto the roof. A metal gangway with a low rail ran along the ridge off the roof, and Siw shuffled forward so that she could sit on it. She didn't dare stand up.

The two men were down at the bottom of the roof. Both were wearing safety harnesses, roped to the gangway further along. Siw wouldn't have the nerve to work like that, but they looked pretty secure. Why would one of them fall?

'Hello . . . ?' she whispered, and found that her voice didn't work. She was *really* high up, higher than she'd ever been. Ever since she'd spotted the men she'd acted on impulse, *simply rushed off without thinking*, as her mother would have said. She'd given no thought to what would happen when she got onto the roof. What she would say, for example.

'Hello?' she croaked, and one of the men turned towards the sound. When he saw her he shouted, 'Hey! What the hell . . . ?'

The yell was so angry and so loud that Siw gave a start and dropped the flute case. It slithered down the roof and disappeared over the edge. A couple of seconds later she heard a distant thud. Thank God she could now use both hands to cling on.

The man who had shouted at her hauled in his line with a winch attached to his belt, making his way towards her. Siw was so frightened that she was shaking. She didn't like heights, she didn't like being yelled at, she didn't like what her mother was going to say. This had been a terrible idea.

But what else could I do?

Maybe it was the red-faced man who was going to die in an hour, three hours, tomorrow. What should she do? She had to at least try, but as she perched there trembling with fear, her fingers gripping the cold metal so tightly that it hurt, she began to understand her mother's attitude towards *it*.

With a heavy tread that made the gangway shudder, the man came towards Siw. She screwed her eyes tight shut and lowered her head. 'Get down from here, you stupid girl! What the hell do you think you're doing?'

Siw swallowed a lump of saliva and used every scrap of willpower to open her eyes, look up at the man and whisper: 'There's something I have to tell you.'

'What are you saying?' The man crouched down beside her, grabbed her shoulder and shook her. 'Come on, I'll help you down.'

Siw had no idea what happened, but all of a sudden it was as if a red flash of lightning shot through her body. She pulled away, looked the man in the eye and screamed: 'You're going to die! You or him' – she nodded in the direction of the other man, who was standing at the bottom of the roof watching them – 'are going to die!'

The man frowned. 'What are you talking about?'

Siw was on the verge of tears as she stammered: 'Today or tomorrow or another day, one of you, or someone else on this roof, is going to fall.' She let go of the rail for a second and pointed at the video store. 'Over there. Someone is going to fall off the roof and be killed and I don't know if saying this is any use but now I've said it and now you know and now I'd like to get down.'

Siw had expected a barrage of questions about how she could come out with something so stupid; she knew this whole thing was pointless. They would never believe her. But the man remained motionless, sorrow etched on his face. He shook his head slowly. 'Why are you doing this?'

'To warn you. But you don't believe me.'

'Do you think this is funny?'

'No. Not at all.'

'Right. Because what you're describing – as I think you know perfectly well – happened the day before yesterday. To our friend.'

5

'I have no idea what to do with you. You're obviously out of your mind.'

Anita was pacing back and forth in the living room. Siw was

152

sitting on the sofa, wrapped in a blanket. She had started shivering up on the roof, and she couldn't stop.

The man who'd helped her down the ladder had refused to let her go until she gave him the phone number of one of her parents. In a feeble attempt to gain sympathy she'd told him that her daddy was dead. He'd said he was very sorry to hear that, but stood his ground until she came up with the number of the school where Anita worked.

When Siw reached the street, the man followed her and disappeared around the corner. When he came back he was carrying the flute case. It was broken in two, the flute itself was bent, and two of the keys were missing.

'Here,' he said. 'Good job it didn't land on someone's head.'

A tear trickled down Siw's cheek. 'Mmm.'

The man relented. 'Listen, I really don't understand what you were trying to do here, but . . . don't do it again, okay?'

'Okay.'

'Never again?'

'Never again.'

A couple of hours later Berit and Siw were sitting side by side on the sofa like the accused in court. Berit said: 'If you'd let me tell her . . .'

'Oh!' Anita stopped dead and spread her arms wide. 'So this is all *my* fault?'

'I'm not saying that, but if Siw has this gift, which we knew she would have, then she has to know what it is she—'

'The only thing she needs to know is that she mustn't interfere, because there's nothing she can do!'

'Then *that's* what she needs to know,' Berit insisted. 'Even if I don't agree with you.'

'I want to know,' Siw said grimly. 'I'll keep on doing this over and over again until you tell me.'

Berit covered her mouth to hide a smile, while Anita wagged her index finger at Siw as usual. 'I thought you told that nice man you'd never do it again? That's what you said – never again.'

'I lied.'

The air went out of Anita like a pricked balloon. She made a gesture as if she were dumping a burden from her shoulders and said to Berit: 'Tell her whatever you need to tell her – I'm washing my hands of the whole thing.' She stomped out onto the balcony and did something that astonished Siw: she took out a cigarette and lit it.

'Does Mum *smoke*?' she whispered.

'I'm as surprised as you are.'

'Do you think she's a *secret smoker*?' Siw had only a vague idea of what being a secret smoker involved, but she knew it was bad, and according to Mum herself, she *never* did anything bad.

'Okay,' Berit said, taking hold of Siw's hands, which were still cold and stiff. 'Listen to me. Do you know what a sibyl is?'

Thinking her grandmother was referring to the Sibylla hot dogs she loved so much, Siw said, 'A hot dog kiosk.'

Berit rubbed her eyes. 'Let's start again. Thousands of years ago there were some women who could see into the future. They were respected and regarded as holy, but people were also afraid of them – partly because they knew more about the people than the people did themselves – for example, how they were going to die – but also because this business of seeing into the future means you can't escape your fate. Everything is preordained.'

'And is it?'

'I don't believe it is, but those women, who were called sibyls,

154

could predict things that were going to happen many, many years later.'

'Wow!'

'Wow indeed. But with the passing of time this gift has become weaker and weaker, kind of *diluted*, if you understand what I mean. However, it's still basically the same gift, and it is passed on from mother to daughter. If you have it, then you will bear only one child, and that child will be a daughter.'

'So I'm a . . . sibyl?'

'Yes.'

'You said there were *some* women. All those years ago. Are there more sibyls around now?'

'I'm not sure. You and me and your mum are the only ones I know about, and it was the same for my mother, who told me all this. In the past . . . you know what a witch is?'

'Hansel and Gretel and the witch and Blåkulla and—'

Berit shook her head. 'Back in the day, women who were accused of meddling with the dark arts, such as foretelling the future, were called witches, and many of them were killed.'

'How?'

'Do you really need that information?'

'Tell me.'

Siw saw her grandmother glance over at the balcony, where Anita had just stubbed out her cigarette on the railing and flicked the butt down into the car park. This was such a weird day. Berit lowered her voice. 'They were burned at the stake.'

'While they were *alive*?'

'Yes. While they were alive.'

Anita came back in and Siw didn't dare ask any more questions. Later that night when she lay in bed with her eyes wide open,

155

unable to sleep, she realised she could have done without that last snippet.

Her grandmother's account of what Siw was felt like an attack on her identity, but one that she could accept. She read about sibyls and witches in the school library, and found it possible to combine these fairy-tale creatures – which weren't fairy-tale creatures after all – with her own fantasies about elves and fine-limbed woodland beings. It was all part of something *magical*, something that she liked being a part of, even if it was diluted.

When Siw thought back to this period many years later, she wasn't sure if it was comical or tragic that she had so blithely accepted that she was one of the last survivors in a mythological tradition, while at the same time she found it much harder to reconcile herself with the physical transformation from slender to rotund that came at the age of twelve.

The fact that her mind was partly in the hands of forces beyond her control she swallowed with a slurp like a spoonful of boiled egg, while the changes to her body that she couldn't do anything about became a sour boiled sweet that she had to suck on for a long time before it dissolved. It was then that she discovered Håkan Hellström, and when he sang that he was in love with the ugliest girl in the world, she knew he was talking about her.

*

It is the first Monday of the month. Darkness has fallen and the old aeronautical beacon on the roof of the swimming pool is lit. People stop and look up at the beam of light sweeping across Norrtälje. Many experience a vague sense of consolation, a feeling that we can always rely on the fact that something will guide us through the night. That the light will be there when we need it.

THE THORN OF COMMAND

I

There is a thought that has preoccupied Marko ever since he was thirteen years old, a concept that can be summarised in four words: *Return as a winner.* He has imagined countless scenarios over the past sixteen years.

He took the first childish image from *Mario Kart*, which he sometimes played with Johan – the victory parade after the race. Johan always won, and because his characters were Wario and Waluigi and his vehicle was a flashy, shimmering cab, Marko had many opportunities to see Wario leading the cortege and making victory gestures, while the inhabitants of the city danced hula-hula in grass skirts all around him.

Like that, Marko had thought. *Exactly like that.*

As the years went by he had moderated the concept into more realistic terms. It was hardly likely that he would find himself cruising down Stora Brogatan in a gold-plated Merc while the residents of Norrtälje rotated their hips and tossed flowers in his path, even if that was *exactly* what he would have wanted. Preferably with the *Mario Kart* music playing as loudly as possible.

When he was at the School of Economics he had toyed with the idea of a helicopter, but then he wasn't going to be able to obtain permission to land in the main square with people waving and cheering; it would have to be some field on the outskirts, so that scuppered the idea. And why would people be cheering anyway?

Maybe because Marko, from a purely theoretical point of view, ought to be one of the smartest people in Norrtälje. In spite of his financial difficulties, he graduated with top grades in his master's degree from the School of Economics and spent another year studying the analysis of financial markets. Again, he achieved outstanding results. If anyone asked, he would explain with pride that he was a first-generation immigrant. He might have grown up in Sweden, but he wasn't born here. He didn't object if someone called him a Yugo. He was a Yugo, and he *owned* most of those smart-asses.

His career progression was rapid. A couple of short stints with smaller companies where he did well, then he landed with Carnegie investment bank, where he quickly became known as one of the hungriest and most able dealers. With a growing salary and bonuses, the money came rolling in, and he made a point of investing in technology funds.

One evening, after a two-hour workout in the gym at SATS, he sat alone in the sauna, his mind crystal clear, and took a long, hard look at what it was he actually wanted.

Return as a winner, okay. There was nothing wrong with the concept in principle, but what did it really mean, if he disregarded his juvenile fantasies about grass skirts, hula-hula dancing and flying through the air? And *why* was it so important to him? Marko massaged an overstretched tendon in the back of his neck. He thought he knew the answer to the last question.

He had once read a book by Elias Canetti, *Crowds and Power*, because he'd thought it was about manipulating the will of the masses. It turned out to be something else entirely, but it was part of Marko's character to finish what he started, so he ploughed through the eight hundred pages and was rewarded for his trouble to a certain extent, above all with the chapter on 'the thorn of command'.

It was as if the chapter had been written for him, to enable him to better understand himself and his motives. Every command that a human being is forced to obey remains like a thorn in that person's body, and the only way to get rid of that thorn is to pass it on to someone else.

Marko's thorn had been pushed deep into his flesh that afternoon on Max's terrace. His father, Goran, was a hero who had risked death in order to save others and to stand up for his principles. The fact that this man, whom Marko still idolised, should have to kowtow to Max's father, a fat-cat company director sprawling on his sun lounger . . . It stung and burned, the pain never went away, and it drove Marko through all the years that followed.

Marko was intelligent, ambitious and charming and would probably have succeeded in life anyway, but the thorn that made its presence felt made him ruthless. He didn't care whose dead body he trampled over during his one-man crusade to restore his father's dignity.

So that was the *why*. But then came the question of what it involved, how it could be achieved. He lay down on the bench in the sauna, carefully so as not to irritate the tendon. He gazed up at the ceiling, where the steam was drawing billowing patterns. Suddenly he saw it all with such clarity that he sat bolt upright, sending a wave of pain through his shoulder blade. *He would buy Max's house and give it to his parents!*

He showered and dressed quickly, then hurried home to his three-room apartment on Sturegatan to see how viable the project was. The prices of homes in the Kärleksudden area of Norrtälje weren't on the same level as in Djursholm, but they were surprisingly high. After spending a while checking out places that had been sold over the past few years, Marko worked out that the house owned by Max's parents was probably worth between twelve and fourteen million.

He zoomed in on the property on Google Maps. Even the hateful terrace could be seen, and he knew in the depths of his wounded guts that this was it, this was *the thing*. The sight of his own father sitting on that terrace sipping a Slivovitz while gazing out over the Kvisthamra inlet would make the thorn dissolve once and for all.

Twelve to fourteen million was manageable. He could pay half straight away by selling some of his index funds, and the return from his biggest technology fund would take care of interest and further payments. Which left just one tiny problem: persuading them to sell.

The easiest approach would be to make them an offer they couldn't refuse, but what did that mean? Twenty? Twenty-five? That was a lot, even for Marko. Which left the original implication from the film *The Godfather*. He had certain superficial criminal contacts from the world of nightclubs, and in theory he wouldn't have anything against setting them on Göran, but that would be a *fail*. Look at the Yugo, fixing shit with the help of the Yugo mafia. Plus, his father would flatly refuse to accept the gift if he got wind of any such dealings.

Marko sent out feelers via a firm of estate agents, making sure

160

his name wasn't mentioned, and was informed that the owner had no plans to sell. Marko ground his teeth as he pictured Göran lying back on his fucking sun lounger, waving away the agent like an irritating fly.

Definitely not, my good man – out of the question!

This made Marko so angry that he seriously considered the Corleone method, but he came to his senses before he even made a phone call. After mulling over his disappointment for a couple of days he resigned himself to the situation and went for the next best option: he would buy an identical house in the same neighbourhood. It wasn't an ideal scenario, but it would do, and the house he really wanted might become available at some point in the future.

Only at that point did Marko give Max more than a passing thought. They were friends after all, and it wasn't quite the done thing to pinch a friend's childhood home. Once he had calmed down he decided to make the best of what had happened, and to see it as a positive that he wasn't going to hurt Max. But he would certainly have done it, if he'd had the chance. Restoring his father's dignity was more important than anything else.

While checking out property websites for research purposes, he had seen an attractive house only three doors down from Max's parents. Just as big, with the same sea view, and with an even *larger* fucking terrace. Marko revisited the site, took a closer look and joined the bidding. It had started at eleven million, and had now reached twelve point two. Marko decided to cut to the chase and offered thirteen.

He felt almost dizzy when the confirmation came via a phone call: once the formalities were out of the way, Marko would be the owner of a two-storey, 282-square-metre home at Strandvägen 13 in Norrtälje. He rang off, clenched his fist and yelled: 'I *piss* on your terrace, you fucker!'

And the thorn? It wasn't a real thorn, and couldn't be dealt with in that way, but for a moment it felt as if it had returned to the vicious bush from which it had come.

2

In spite of Marko's dream of his glorious return, no one raises an eyebrow at the coal-black Audi A6 as it joins the roundabout from Stockholmsvägen, which is hardly surprising. To the left are the white metal walls of Roslagsporten, and to the right the concrete foundations of the new fire station. The approach to Norrtälje is every bit as inviting as the entrance to a mortuary.

Lana Del Rey is wailing from the car's eleven hidden speakers, and Marko drums along to the beat of 'Summertime Sadness' on the leather-covered steering wheel. He isn't particularly fond of Lana Del Rey, but the deep, caressing sound in the car's well-insulated interior makes it feel *smooth*.

He is wearing beige chinos and a wine-red shirt from Sand. The top two buttons are undone, but it is still tight across his chest; he can bench-press 160 kilos. He is in perfect physical shape, yet he is sitting in an unnatural position because he is clamping his buttocks together in order to avoid shitting himself.

The situation is critical. As Marko passes between Dogger and Circle K he feels such a sharp pain in his belly that he digs his nails into the leather and arches his back in an effort to clamp his buttocks even tighter and avoid a disaster. One more stab of pain and he'll be fucked.

He indicates right, ignores the traffic light that has changed to red, weaves dangerously between other cars in the Flygfyren retail park, and finally slams on the brakes in a disabled parking space right next to the main entrance. Hunched over, he scuttles through the revolving doors, passes the tobacco counter and discovers to his relief that one of the toilets is vacant.

The diarrhoea pours out in a cascade, splashing up onto his backside, and he has to spend quite some time cleaning himself with wet toilet paper. He checks his Patek Philippe watch, then sits down on the toilet lid and rests his head in his hands.

Yeah! Wario wins!

Marko has enough of his Catholic upbringing left within him to consider the idea that this is God's punishment for the sin of pride, thinking he could come riding into town like Jesus on the donkey. However, the truth is that he's nervous. Everyone outside of his family regards Marko as a rock, both physically and mentally, and in many ways he is, but above all he is so adept at hiding any hint of insecurity that it's more a question of ignoring than hiding.

When he has ignored far too many incidents of insecurity, he reaches a critical point where they come together and express themselves as somatic issues. He gets a migraine or a bad stomach. On one occasion he fainted. It was during an especially hectic period at work, when he'd had to make several difficult decisions. He'd worked fourteen hours straight and was about to go to fetch a coffee, when he suddenly found himself lying on the floor. Fortunately it was late in the evening and he was alone in the office. But here's the thing: Marko lay there for a while gazing up at the fluorescent light on the ceiling. When he got to his feet, he was fine. The anxiety was satisfied. He could simply carry on.

He doesn't quite feel the same sitting here on the stinking toilet

163

with his head in his hands. The problem this time is that he doesn't understand *why* he's nervous. He really is returning home as a winner in his Audi, on his way to meet Max and Johan and to view the house he's bought for his parents. So why doesn't he *feel* like a winner?

It must be this town. In Stockholm he has reinvented himself; he can drift around with complete self-assurance in either the trendiest gyms or the clubs around Stureplan; the whole city is open to him. That is not the case in Norrtälje. The town is closed, glaring at him with disapproving eyes, remembering the boy who climbed up the silo one afternoon to make something stupendous out of his pathetic loneliness. *You're not fooling anyone.*

Marko stands up and looks in the mirror, runs his fingers through his hair and adjusts his shirt collar. He smiles at himself and fails to produce the smile that has brought him success in so many different contexts. He tries again; this time it's better. *Let's do this.*

3

Like two naughty kids searching for the best apple tree to scrump from, Max and Johan are standing with their noses pressed to the gate of the house Marko has bought. The gate isn't locked, but they don't want to jump the gun; this is Marko's show.

'How much do you think it went for?' Johan asks.

'I don't know – twelve, maybe?'

Johan lets out a low whistle. 'Jesus, he's done well for himself. Don't you ever . . . you know?'

'No – what?'

'You were supposed to be like him. That was the plan, wasn't it? Before it all went wrong.'

164

'I don't think I would ever have been like Marko.'

'Why not?'

'I didn't have the same . . . I wasn't as unhappy as him.'

Johan draws back his head, revealing the hint of a double chin. 'Marko was *unhappy*?'

'Yes – you know he was. Here he comes.'

The Audi glides almost silently along Gustaf Adolfs väg. Marko is at the wheel, wearing a pair of sunglasses as black as the vehicle he is driving. As he approaches he lowers the window and points to the gate. 'Can you open it?'

'Yeah, yeah. Hello to you too,' Johan mutters, pushing down the handle. He and Max each open their half of the gate, and when the Audi passes through they make exaggerated gestures, welcoming the king to his royal residence. The car stops and Marko clambers out. His physical bulk is better suited to wrestling with mountain gorillas than to disentangling himself from a seat belt.

Max goes to meet him, arms outspread. When Marko hugs him, Max gasps: 'Don't kill me.' Marko grins, lets go, cups his hands over Max's shoulders and gives them a squeeze.

'You're in pretty good shape yourself. Keeping busy?'

Marko turns his attention to Johan, who is standing a couple of metres away with his hands behind his back. 'What are you doing over there? Come here.'

'You come here.'

Marko glances at Max, shrugs and goes up to Johan. He hesitates for a second, as if Johan is a weight he has to lift, then he spreads his arms wide. 'What's wrong?'

'Nothing.'

'So why are you standing like that? Hello, it's Marko. Do you remember me?'

165

'Vaguely.' Johan unclasps his hands. 'Is that better?'

'It'll do. Come here.' Marko hugs Johan, who almost disappears in his embrace, awkwardly patting Marko's back.

'Okay,' Marko says, letting go and rubbing his hands together. 'Shall we see what kind of jerry-built house I've bought?'

The jerry-built house turns out to be a well-constructed sixties property. Certain details remind Max of his family home, and it seems likely that the same architect is responsible for the design.

Marko wanders through the empty rooms, listing all the things he intends to change. The kitchen will be ripped out and modernised, the ordinary windows overlooking the inlet will be replaced by a glass wall, there will be oak parquet flooring throughout, and so on. There is something manic about this litany of home styling, and Max is concerned.

Marko changed during their time at the School of Economics. At secondary school his competitive nature had been focused mainly on doing better than Max, and since Max was the brightest brain in the class, Marko had to push himself to the limit. Even though Marko took the competition seriously, there was an element of fun that led to their becoming friends. They only had each other up at the top, after all.

Marko had sailed through grammar school with top grades, in spite of the fact that Max was no longer there to compete with, but when they met up again at the School of Economics Marko was determined to compete with *everyone*. You can say what you like about that place, but the people who go there are anything but stupid. Once again Marko pushed himself to breaking point. He constantly had dark circles beneath his eyes, and he developed tics at the corners of his eyes and a tendency to fiddle with his right earlobe. If you spoke to him, his expression often became glassy; it was obvious that he was somewhere else.

The three childhood friends have met only a few times since Marko started work, but it has seemed to Max that he's become more stable on each occasion, almost like a normal person, no longer uptight, and with a certain capacity for rest and relaxation. But today something is making him revert to his former self.

'Jesus!'

Johan has opened the door leading to the terrace and gone outside. Max and Marko follow him. The terrace is literally as big as a tennis court, and it's hard to imagine how the previous owners made use of it. In the absence of furniture and other paraphernalia, it looks ridiculously huge.

'I mean, seriously . . .' Max says, gazing at the well-oiled decking. 'What did they use this for?'

'They were going to install a pool, but they couldn't afford it,' Marko informs him. 'So I'm going to do it instead.'

'You're going to install a pool?'

'Mmm. Then Mum and Dad can float around on their lilos and take it easy.'

'Is that what they want?'

'Sorry?'

'Have you checked with them? Asked them what they want?'

Marko tugs at his right earlobe and fixes his eyes on the inlet as he answers. 'They don't know anything about it yet.'

'You mean . . . you've bought this house for them . . . without *telling* them?'

'Exactly.'

Max glances at Johan, who looks away. Max doesn't know what his problem is, why he's being so evasive. Is it just because Marko hadn't called him? Marko moves closer to Max. 'I wanted it finished. Perfect. Then I'll give it to them.'

There is something threatening about Marko's bulk looming over Max, as if he will brook no contradictions, and Max feels uncomfortable. He steps to one side, staring at the enormous expanse of decking, and feels even worse. He raises his head, and the sun's reflection hurts his eyes, before the whole surface of the water in the inlet begins to tilt.

No . . . no . . .

He hears the screech of rough metal, sees a black river pouring out, hears gasping breaths and a fight for life, screams, contorted faces glimpsed among the shadows, pure horror concentrated into a yellow cube.

The container has been opened.

COME, ARMAGEDDON

I

It is less than a week since the container appeared, and during that time the council, the boat club and the construction company SBAB have reached new heights when it comes to inefficiency and the shirking of responsibility.

The council's attitude towards the container was not unlike the one they adopted when the traffic lights on Vätövägen broke, and they failed to repair them in spite of three attempts. The official responsible had claimed in the local newspaper that it was, in fact, a *good* thing that the lights weren't working, because it made people drive more carefully. In the end one of those careful drivers actually crashed into the traffic light itself.

In the same way, the official in charge of matters relating to the harbour had stated that it was a good thing that the container was where it was, because this gave its owner time to come and collect it – as if a container was something you dropped, like a glove on

169

the street, rather than something that had been deliberately dumped there, for some unknown reason.

While the issue was batted from one department to another, where the person concerned was usually out for lunch, away on holiday or simply unavailable, the public's interest grew. The object itself wasn't particularly mysterious, it was simply a yellow container, but it had appeared in the harbour as if at the whim of the gods.

There was plenty of speculation about what might be inside – in workplaces, over coffee, and in the local paper. Probably contraband or industrial waste – that was the general view. Someone came up with a theory about refugees, but this was dismissed, as one of the things they had actually managed to do was to listen to the interior of the container with an electronic stethoscope; not a sound. Since there was no need for an emergency rescue, the wheels of bureaucracy could turn slowly and undisturbed.

During the daytime there were always a number of curious onlookers nearby, and some wit had sprayed 'PLEASE LEAVE!' on one end overnight. A young man attacked the padlock with a hacksaw but was stopped by members of the public, because: 'you never know what kind of crap might be in there'.

As the days went by, a suspicion grew that the council was trying to hide something. Surely it was possible to work out who owned a piece of flat ground? Something else must be going on, and theories about radioactive waste became increasingly prevalent.

The rumours went so far that eventually the council felt it had no choice but to produce a Geiger counter and a man used to handling such equipment. Accompanied by a journalist from the local paper, he took readings from the container and concluded that only normal traces of radioactivity could be detected. The speculation had to find a different direction, but something clearly wasn't right.

Finally, the various parties reached an agreement that was bordering on the magnificent in its complexity. All the indications were that the boat club owned the piece of land in question, at which point the construction company rented it from the club for ten years, then the council leased the relevant ten square metres for one year at a cost of thirty thousand kronor, and accepted all responsibility for the contents of the container.

If the rightful owner didn't make himself known, or couldn't be traced with the help of whatever might be inside, then the container and its contents were now the property of the council. The agreement was celebrated with coffee and cake in the town hall, although there was some discussion about what kind of pig in a poke they might have bought. It *could* be something valuable, for example a few hundred laptops or thousands of mobile phones – and if so, what should be done with them?

Those with a more realistic view pointed out that it was more likely to be boat engines. Lots of people had had their outboard motors stolen during the summer, and if the council was able to return them to their owners, that would be a bonus for the red-green coalition. Everyone toasted the idea with coffee. Boat engines – excellent. The container would be opened the following day.

2

There is quite the party atmosphere down in the harbour, particularly as the opening just happens to be set for a Saturday. No one knows how the public found out about the timing; it's not as if the council made an announcement. No doubt someone said something to someone else, who mentioned it to a couple of others, and so on. Norrtälje is a small town, and word spreads quickly.

It is a chilly autumn day, and a drizzle so fine that it resembles mist dampens everyone's hair and clothes as they stand shivering in the easterly wind coming off the sea. Several have brought Thermos flasks of coffee, and some have even stretched as far as folding chairs. The big topic of conversation, apart from the container itself, is how strange the harbour has become since the silos disappeared. For most people this is the first time they've seen the area from this angle, without the characteristic colossi dominating the landscape.

They talk of the silos with a heavy dose of nostalgia. In spite of the fact that no one can claim that they were anything but as ugly as sin, they kind of *belonged*. For as long as anyone can remember they towered behind the restaurant ship SS *Norrtelje*'s empty, unusable and decaying bulk, which confirmed that yes, now you were in Norr-tälje. Many had watched with sorrow in their hearts as they were demolished to make way for the new harbourside development. Something had been lost, an epoch had come to an end.

Conversation returns to the container, which even on this over-cast day glows so brightly that it's as if it has its very own sun shining down on it. There are jokes about the council's slowness, how the burned-out restaurant on Fejan hasn't been rebuilt because of difficulties with planning permission, how fibre broadband still isn't up to speed in certain parts of the town in spite of the fact that they've been working on it for many years, and as for the water and sewerage system expansion plans – let's not even go there. No one would have been surprised if the container had still been standing in exactly the same spot when the harbourside development was finished.

But today it is going to be opened, and many of those who

have gathered are as excited as children on Christmas Eve. The anticipation has built up over the past week, and if the scheduled opening doesn't happen today, there is a risk of civil unrest. Well, eggs thrown at the council office's windows, that kind of thing.

Nothing to worry about. Five minutes before the designated time a van arrives from Jansson Metals, with the slogan 'We bow to you'. A man in a high-vis jacket climbs out, glances at the assembled throng, shakes his head, opens the back door and lifts out the largest angle grinder most people have ever seen, with a blade the size of an LP record. The man carries his tool towards the crowd, which respectfully parts. He puts the angle grinder down in front of the container, then runs an extension lead to one of the construction company's electricity supply points.

Only now does he appear to realise that he is the focus of everyone's attention, and that maybe he ought to say something before the performance begins. However, all he can come out with is a brusque: 'Stand back! There'll be sparks and stuff!'

When those who are too close have shuffled to a safe distance away, the man mutters something uncomplimentary about the residents of Norrtälje, puts on his goggles and ear defenders, and sets to work.

The padlock hasp is as thick as a thumb, and sparks spray across the ground as a deafening, whining shriek slices through the air. Some of the onlookers cover their ears and close their eyes, while others stand paralysed, staring at the demonstration of the human capacity for destruction. In less than a minute the angle grinder has cut through the padlock, which drops with a clunk. The man switches off the machine and kicks the red-hot padlock over the edge of the quay. It hits the water with a hissing sound.

'Can't wait, can you!' he yells. He seems to be finding the

situation amusing, and he waves his hands like a magician before grabbing hold of the bar. The trick doesn't exactly come off. The bar is heavy and solid; he only manages to pull it away a centimetre or so before it springs back with a loud bang. He kicks the container and shouts: 'Bastard fucking thing!'

'Do you need some help there, Tompa?'

Another man in a high-vis jacket steps out of the crowd and strolls towards Tompa, who mutters and steps aside for the new arrival. The magician has his assistant. Working together, faces red with exertion, they eventually manage to prise away the bar, and the doors open with a sucking noise.

Both Tompa's and the other man's hands fly up to cover their mouths and noses, and it is only a second before the easterly wind blows across the crowd, and everyone does the same.

The stench is indescribable. The entire quayside is enveloped in a cloud of decay, excrement and death. Some manage to run to the edge to throw up into the water, a few vomit where they stand, while others clamp their hands over their mouths and can just about hold it in.

After the stench comes the liquid. A brownish-black sludge flows out of the container and splashes down onto the quayside, filling cracks and hollows in the paving and continuing on its way into the water.

Tompa and the other man are closest to the source, but somehow they have managed not to throw up. They are still standing with their hands pressed to their lips, staring at the inside of the container with eyes wide with fear. Tompa makes a gesture with his right hand; he wants to signal something, but his hand goes limp and drops to his side. He looks at the other man. Their terrified eyes meet, and a silent decision is made.

They walk away from the container; Tompa doesn't even pick up his angle grinder.

When they reach the crowd, someone asks in a muffled voice: 'What was it? What's inside?'

Tompa looks up. There are tears in his eyes. He opens his mouth to answer, then his lips contort in a grimace. He retches, runs to the edge of the quay and vomits into the water. Retches again when he sees his yellow vomit mixing with the filthy liquid from the container, which continues to flow and flow.

OVER BLACK WATERS

I

We sit in the darkness and wait. The only conversations are conducted in a whisper, mouths close to ears. A few hours ago I made the mistake of using the screen of the phone on which I am recording this to light the area around me. Terrible faces emerged from the darkness – hollow-eyed, emaciated, despairing. As if I were sitting here with an army of ghosts. We should have landed in Trelleborg long ago, but the movements of the container tell me that we are still at sea. The air in here is stale, and the holes in the top do not let in enough oxygen. Sometimes someone climbs on another person's shoulders and puts their mouth to a hole, just to breathe fresh air for a little while. Then they change places. Apart from the sporadic glow of screens, we are in pitch darkness. We haven't been given anything to eat or drink since the doors were closed two days ago. We have shared the resources we had, but they are running out. Some claim that others are hiding food and water – the atmosphere has been pretty bad at times. It goes in waves. A wave of irritation when someone is accused of squirrelling away something that should have been shared among us all. A wave of hope when a sound or a movement suggests that we have reached our destination. Or like now: a wave of apathy, with everyone sitting motionless, staring into the darkness. It can drive you mad. I hope no one goes mad. There isn't room for that. There are twenty-eight of us in here. Fourteen men, eight women and six children. God help us all.

THOSE WHERE I COME FROM

I

Marko just manages to catch Max as he crashes down onto the decking. Max's body is twitching and jerking, and Marko looks at Johan in horror. 'What do I do?'

'Lay him down. Carefully.'

Marko gently tips Max backwards until he is lying flat. His eyes are unseeing, but the seizure begins to abate until only his hands are moving, twitching like flounder tossed onto the shore. Marko and Johan crouch down on either side of him.

'This is the second time I've seen him like this,' Marko says. 'The first time was up on the silo – do you remember?'

'How could I *not* remember? You saved his life and I acted like a coward.'

Marko shakes his head. 'You're too hard on yourself.'

'It's a fact.'

'In that case, you're choosing to remember a fact that is too hard.'

Max rubs his face with his hands and looks around in confusion. 'What happened?'

'You got hit on the head by a golf ball,' Johan says. 'What do you think happened? What did you see?'

Max sits up. Glances towards the inlet, a tortured expression on his face. 'That container. It's full of dead bodies. Lots of dead bodies. Men, women, children, all . . . rotten.'

Marko and Johan look at each other. Maybe it's their imagination, the power of suggestion triggered by what Max has said, but they think they can smell putrefaction in the air. Neither of them doubts Max, and they are no more than half a kilometre from the horror he has described.

'Refugees?' Marko asks.

'I don't know. It was dark in there, so I only saw . . . I felt . . .' Max covers his face with his hands and his shoulders shake. Between his fingers he whispers: 'It was terrible.'

Marko and Johan each place a hand on Max's shoulders, and after a while the shaking stops. He draws a deep, shuddering breath, lowers his hands and says: 'There was something *flowing*. Out of the container. Something dark.'

'Bodily fluids, I expect,' Marko says. 'Jesus. Imagine sitting there, locked in until . . . maybe with your family, and to see them . . .' His gaze is fixed on a point in the distance; maybe a memory of his own family's flight has come over him.

'Yes,' Max says. 'But there was something else too. Flowing. I don't know how to explain. Like something . . . metaphysical.'

'Metaphysical?' Johan repeats tentatively. 'How can something metaphysical flow? I mean, it's just a . . . concept.'

'Like I said, I don't know. I don't understand it myself, but that's what I saw. Something flowed out of the container and there was

179

a dreadful stench and I'm sure you're right about the bodily fluids. But at the same time, there was something else.'

They sit in silence, and it is definitely not down to the power of suggestion now: there is a hint of rotting flesh in the air. It's hard to imagine what it must be like down in the harbour, and even more impossible to grasp the situation of those who are the source of the stench.

Men, women, children, all . . . rotten.

We can read in the papers more or less every day about people who drown in the Mediterranean Sea and are washed ashore on Europe's beaches, identifiable or distended beyond recognition. It's in the press. From a purely theoretical point of view it could be fake news, something that doesn't happen. It's different when a whole container-full lands on our doorstep. The state of the world has reached Norrtälje.

Johan breaks the silence and says to Max: 'One thing I don't understand – or another thing – why did you see this? If they're already dead, and they've been dead for so long that their bodies are rotting? You usually see things that are about to happen, don't you? But this has already happened.'

'I don't know. I don't get it. Maybe something else is going to happen as a consequence of this, but I have no idea.'

'Shit,' Marko says, getting to his feet. 'I need a glass of water. Anyone else?'

The others shake their heads. Johan watches Marko's broad back disappear through the glass door and the memory of an almost identical image comes into his mind, when a thirteen-year-old Johan . . .

2

. . . followed Marko through the glass door while Max remained on the terrace with his father. Goran and Maria had already put their shoes on.

'Nice, Marko,' Johan whispered.

'Nice?'

'When you bowed to Max's dad out there. Nice.'

'Nice is not the right word.'

Without elaborating on what the right word might be, Marko carefully laced up his white trainers. Johan secretly watched as his fingers skilfully tied a double knot. He was seriously impressed by the way Marko had handled the situation, how by exaggerating his submissiveness he had bounced the sense of shame and embarrassment away from himself and towards Max's father. Johan had never reflected on the concept of dignity before, because he'd never known anyone who possessed that quality. Now he did.

He was aware that his loyalty should lie with Max, his oldest and best friend who had been completely crushed by Marko, but he just didn't feel that way, which confused him. It was only when he'd left the house with the Kovac family that he understood: they were all heading home to the slums, while Max was still sitting on his flashy terrace with the sea view behind him. Yet another concept that Johan had never reflected on: class. He and Max were best friends, but when it came to the crunch, maybe Johan's loyalty lay elsewhere. With his people.

'What are you thinking about?'

Johan had been walking along deep in thought, and hadn't

noticed that they were now a hundred metres or so from Max's house. Marko's question came like a bolt from the blue.

'About how we kind of . . . somehow . . . belong together.'

'You mean . . . in relation to Max? Is that what you say – "in relation to"?'

'Yes. And yes.'

Johan would have liked to investigate the topic a little further, but thought it was best to leave it. He really wanted to belong to the Kovac family, and above all Marko, but that wasn't something he could actually *say*. Maria slowed down so that she was walking beside him, and said: 'Do you play chess?'

'Well, I know the rules.'

'Do you want to play with me?'

Johan glanced enquiringly at Marko, who shrugged. 'I just have to warn you – she's a lot smarter than she looks. Especially in chess.'

'It's *at* chess,' Maria informed him. 'And you're a lot more stupid than you look, even though you already look pretty stupid.'

'Which is it?' Marko wanted to know. 'At or in?'

'I think either's fine, but *at* is probably best.'

Maria clapped her hands and spun around before turning to Johan once more. 'Shall we have a game when we get home?' Marko made a sharp comment to his sister in Bosnian, but she shook her head and pointed to Johan. 'He *wants* to. You do, don't you?'

'Yes, but does that fit in with your family's plans?'

'Come this evening,' Marko said. 'After six. You're going to lose so badly.'

Maria nodded eagerly to confirm that this was indeed the case. They continued to walk home to their slum. Johan stole the odd glance at the family surrounding him, taking in their presence and his own. He had to make a real effort not to start crying.

After Johan had established that his mother was still sleeping in the middle of the dirty laundry, he drank a glass of O'boy made with milk that was only one day past its use-by date, then went to the hill.

With his hands in his pockets he strolled among the pine trees, benches and bushes where he and Max had spent so much of their childhood. He recalled the games they had played, things that had happened in the limited area that had been their world for a while. He didn't realise it then, but he was essentially walking around and saying goodbye.

Imagine this: after wandering for a while he didn't end up on top of a rock or up a tree, but sitting like a grown-up on the bench overlooking Posthusgatan; it was one of Norrtälje's best viewing points. He rested his elbows on his knees, took a deep breath, then let it out in short gasps. He felt as if there was a lump in his chest.

Over and over again the image of Marko bowing on the terrace came into his mind. Something had flared up inside Johan at that moment, something that had at first resembled pure joy, but had now taken the form of a lump that made it difficult to breathe.

Marko.

When he had made the 'Juice and biscuits – how lovely' comment, it had been a possibly misguided attempt to make the Kovac family like him, but upon examining his motives more closely, he saw that it was above all Marko he wanted to impress. The others were nice and he really did want to *belong*, but Marko was the most important.

It would take a few years of frustration and confusion before

183

Johan both realised and admitted the truth of the matter: he was in love.

3

Just as Marko had promised, Goran was very capable, and after a month's trial he was given a permanent job. Within a year he was on an equal footing with the other builders, and was given increasingly complex tasks as his Swedish improved – although he never did become as 'supergood' as Maria had claimed he would. Laura got a nursing post at the hospital, and after twelve months her Swedish was pretty much on a level with her children's. Life was working out for the Kovac family.

The only cause for concern was Maria. She was always getting into trouble at school, both in class and in the playground. The basic problem was that she thought everyone was much more stupid than she was, and this was not an opinion she kept to herself – quite the reverse. She set tests for the other children on a daily basis, only to pulverise them with her superiority in maths, history, reading – everything.

Of course, she was called racist names that were meant to be demeaning, but Maria simply countered this by saying: 'Look, the foreign kid knows what this word means, but you don't, and you're Swedish – how stupid are you? Look, the foreign kid who learned to count using bananas can do this sum, but you can't – did you fall off the dung heap when you were little?'

She got into fights and fought right back. She constantly had bruises and scratches on her hands and face. If several of her class-mates attacked her at once and Marko happened to be nearby, he would try to intervene, but he would be met by a stream of abuse in both Bosnian and Swedish, telling him to stay out of it.

Things were different with Johan. On the few occasions when he'd had break at the same time as Maria, and been in the vicinity when some other kids had a go at her, she had accepted his help with open arms.

'This is my friend Johan! He's going to smash your faces in! Come on, Johan!'

'I'm not going to smash anyone's face in, but why do you keep picking on Maria?'

'Because she's *horrible*,' said a very Swedish girl, letting go of the chunk of Maria's hair she'd been intending to pull. 'She says nasty things all the time.'

'Is this true, Maria?'

'I tell it like it is – they're all idiots!'

Johan glanced at the three girls who were glaring at Maria. Judging by their upturned little noses, curly blonde hair and dull, angry expressions beneath heavy eyelids, it seemed likely that Maria was right, but he had no intention of giving her that satisfaction. Instead, he said to the girls: 'I don't care what Maria says. What I see is three against one, and that's not okay. If you're so angry, then go for her one at a time – I have no problem with that.'

None of the girls had any desire to confront Maria alone, with her lethal green eyes, and they shuffled away after one of them had muttered 'fucking gay boy' at Johan.

Ah, yes, that. Johan was thirteen years old, still unable to identify the mildly ecstatic unease he felt when he was alone with Marko for what it really was – the agony of love. He only knew that he wanted to be with Marko, be close to him, talk to him, look at him. Because he didn't feel that way about any other boy, and had never had such thoughts about Max, he took the dark, fizzing sensation for fascination.

He was careful not to be too intrusive, but the fact that Maria sometimes invited him round to be comprehensively beaten at chess meant that he saw quite a lot of Marko.

The incident on Max's terrace had changed their roles. In school Marko and Max hung out because they had chosen each other as arch rivals. They never met up in their free time, which Johan and Marko did, mainly to play video games. Max and Johan had drifted apart to a certain extent when they stopped playing fantasy games. A new order had been established, and it would remain more or less unchanged for the two remaining years of middle school.

4

A key event took place during the Christmas holiday in Year 9. Johan's mother, who had been unusually clear-headed during the autumn and early winter, suddenly experienced a revelation one night between Christmas and New Year. It made her run outside and lie down in a snowdrift, from which the angels of the Lord would lift her up to the glories of heaven. When Johan tried to persuade her to come back indoors and get warm, she thought he was a fiend sent by the Devil to tempt her and stop her beatification, and she threw chunks of ice at him.

By that stage Johan had managed to acquire a cheap mobile phone, so he called the hospital while standing guard over his mother, who was rolling around in the snow cackling to herself. When two paramedics arrived and attempted to lift her, she screamed and tried to scratch their faces. They had to strap her onto a stretcher in order to take her to Danderyd.

As Johan stood there watching the ambulance reverse, Laura emerged from the Kovac family's block. Without saying a word, she went over to Johan and placed a hand on his shoulder. He fell into her arms and sobbed as Laura stroked his hair and said quietly: 'Hush . . . it's okay . . . you're coming with me. You can stay with us. For as long as you need to.'

And so it came about that Johan went to live with the Kovacs for two weeks. Not a day went by without him sending up a brief prayer to the God he didn't believe in: *Don't let Mum come home today.*

He slept on a camp bed in Marko's room, and during lengthy whispered conversations in the darkness, the two boys grew close. Marko had started to become popular with the girls, which gave him a lot to think about. Johan, with his non-existent experience, could only contribute on a theoretical level, but they talked. And talked.

Even though Johan loved living with the Kovacs, this proximity to Marko was a double-edged sword. Great satisfaction was mixed with equally great frustration, yet he still couldn't work out what was going on. It was on the tip of his tongue, but the words refused to be said.

One afternoon the family were all out for various reasons, and Johan was alone in the apartment. He wandered around the living room, then stopped and stared at the key hanging below the picture of Jesus, the key to the Kovacs' farm near Mostar. They too had been forced to leave their home because of the insanity around them.

Something drove him into Maria's room. Two important things had happened to Maria over the past six months. She had calmed down, and had even made a couple of friends in the class above

187

her, plus the great beauty that would be both her blessing and her curse had begun to make itself known. Older boys were already looking at her, and Johan disliked that as much as he'd disliked her being bullied in the playground. On some level he felt like her second big brother.

As Maria became more aware of the effect she had on those around her, she grew more coquettish. She began to wear make-up, and dressed in a feminine way. Johan opened her wardrobe door and ran his fingers over her short dresses, tights and sweaters. Before he knew what he was doing, he had picked out the dress that looked the largest, stripped down to his underpants and pulled the dress over his head. It was tight, but he was still skinny, so it was just about okay.

With his heart pounding and a tingle running through his entire body, he went over to the full-length mirror where Maria would spend hours trying out different styles. If anyone came home, he would die on the spot. His face flushed bright red when he looked at his reflection. He pouted, placed his hands on his hips.

Wearing beautiful Maria's clothes wasn't in the least bit exciting – in fact, that part almost made him feel sick; she was a child. Nor was he a cross-dresser, but at long last he fully accepted what it was that he wanted. He wanted Marko to see him *like this*, like one of those girls he fantasised about at night. He wanted Marko to find him desirable.

The penny had finally dropped, and the tight dress rode up Johan's back as he dropped to his knees and rested his forehead on his clasped hands.

Please, he prayed. *It's never going to happen, so please make it go away.*

*

A woman is standing in the main square. She has been feeling sad for three days, although she doesn't know why. She looks at the balcony above the bank, at the railing where the poet Nils Ferlin allegedly once balanced. She thinks about falling from a height, blood flowing, thin nylon ropes. Then a five-year-old girl appears in front of her. 'Hello,' says the girl. 'My name is Matilda. What's your name?' The woman just has time to say her name before the child's mother intervenes and apologises. The girl waves as they walk away, and the woman waves back. She thinks about her name, the name her mother gave her. Such a thing cannot be wasted.

NO WAY BACK

Harry Boström has told the police, the local newspaper, and anyone who was prepared to listen: *he heard a noise from inside the container.* A thud, as if something had fallen on the floor. The authorities had given sufficient credence to his account to listen with an electronic stethoscope, but nothing more. The container had remained closed while a collection of idiots all had their say. And now look.

Along with fifty or so other residents of Norrtälje, Harry is standing behind the police cordon with Tosse on the lead, watching as one stretcher after another carrying bodies wrapped in plastic is conveyed from the container to waiting ambulances. Constant camera flashes light up the grey, overcast day, making the yellow surface of the container flash too, like some kind of warning signal. Every newspaper and news broadcaster is there, and right now Norrtälje is the centre of attention for the whole of Sweden – if not the world.

Harry shakes his head as yet another stretcher is carried past. The body in white plastic is so small that it must be a child. The cameras click, the flashes go crazy, and the scene is illuminated as if by strobe lights. Tosse whimpers anxiously at Harry's feet. He is frightened of thunder and lightning, and is waiting for the crash that is bound to follow. Harry scratches the top of his head and murmurs words of reassurance.

The fact that there aren't even more people gathered to watch this sensationally horrific performance is down to one thing: the stench. The entire city centre is enveloped in a cloud of death and putrefaction, but it is at its worst in the harbour. Many of those present have handkerchiefs or scarves over their mouths and noses, and are screwing up their eyes as if to prevent the miasma from getting in that way.

'Are you Harry Boström?'

A suspiciously well-groomed man in a sky-blue shirt under a navy-blue blazer pushes his way through to Harry. He is holding a microphone with the TV4 logo. A couple of steps behind him is a less coiffured individual with a camera on his shoulder. He is grimacing at the stench, which doesn't seem to bother Mr Sky-blue.

'I am, yes,' Harry says.

'I believe it was you who found the container?' Harry can't deny this, and the reporter goes on: 'You said you heard a noise from inside, but as I understand it, no one took any notice of you. It's not impossible that lives could have been saved if they had – do you have anything to say about that?'

Harry looks from the man to the container, then over towards the town centre. This isn't about loyalty to the local council or the police; it's more a matter of loyalty to the town where Harry has spent his whole life when he answers: 'Well, I'm not so sure about that.'

The reporter raises an eyebrow in exaggerated surprise. 'But I checked out the local paper online on my way over here, and you were quoted directly. You said you heard a noise.'

'Oh, *online*,' Harry says. 'Reporters. A lot of things get twisted, taken out of context these days.'

'But surely you can't deny . . .'

Harry has been so preoccupied with fending off the journalist that he has forgotten about Tosse, who suddenly yanks the lead out of Harry's hand. With uncharacteristic eagerness the dog races towards the container, his lead dancing behind him.

'Tosse!' Harry shouts. 'Tosse! Come back here!'

Mr Sky-blue gesticulates to the cameraman, instructing him to film this unexpected turn of events instead of the unhelpful old man. Harry hurries over to the cordon, but is stopped by a police officer.

'No unauthorised personnel.'

'But my dog . . .'

'My colleague will deal with it.'

Tosse has reached the doors of the container, where he is causing quite a stir. A well-built police officer wearing a mask over his mouth is heading for the dog, and for a second Harry thinks Tosse is going to be shot. Before anyone can stop Tosse, he lies down in front of the container and starts rolling in the sludge that has come pouring out. Harry groans, his face red with embarrassment. Tosse loves rubbing himself in anything that smells disgusting, particularly rotting animal corpses. Harry should have known this would happen.

The police officer grabs the end of the lead. Tosse refuses to get up, so he is dragged away whimpering, his fur painting a smear of sludge on the pale concrete. A few people laugh and Harry is even more embarrassed, as if he has accidentally performed a sketch in a graveyard.

The lead is slapped into his hand and a pair of angry eyes glare at him above the mask. 'Keep your dog under control, for fuck's sake!'

'I'm terribly sorry, Constable. I do apologise.'

The man snorts '*constable*' and strides away. Harry glances around and sees the bastard from TV4 grinning condescendingly, while his colleague still looks disgusted. Tosse is on his feet now, and Harry sets off for home, his head down.

After about a hundred steps Harry realises that the stench is just as strong, because it is walking along behind him. Tosse looks up at him, as if expecting praise for his achievement, or at the very least a pat on the head.

'I'm not touching you until you've had a bath,' Harry informs him.

Tosse's ears droop. He is old enough to understand a number of words, and 'bath' is one of them. He gives himself a good shake and a few drops of the sludge fly off his fur. One of them lands on Harry's hand, and he slowly brings it up to his nose.

Jesus Christ.

If it really was the sound of a human being that Harry heard, then that person must have been surrounded by rotting dead bodies, standing ankle-deep in this sludge. A fraction of a millilitre is enough to make Harry's stomach start churning. He doesn't want to have heard anything anymore. But he did. He *knows* he did. Unfortunately.

OVER BLACK WATERS

2

It is the third day. In this darkness the passage of the hours and the days is abstract. When there is no light and nothing is happening, time has no meaning. We have stopped talking in whispers. We no longer wish to remain hidden, we want to be found, by anyone. Be let out, to face anything. We have banged on the walls of the container, we have screamed. There is not a sound apart from the howling of the wind, and nothing happens apart from the billowing movement, up and down, up and down. If it weren't for the vibration of the engines, the container could simply be floating on the surface of the sea. We are alone in a pitch-dark universe. The latrine drum in the corner is full. It stinks. My wife is complaining about a terrible headache. I have lifted her up so that she can breathe through the airholes, but the headache hasn't eased at all. Our daughter is lying curled up on the floor with her hands over ears, her eyes and lips clamped tight shut. I can't do anything for either of them. I deeply regret the fact that we embarked on this journey.

There was nothing left for us in our homeland, but at least we had our bodies, our lives. Now we no longer have control of them. Our fate is in unknown hands, the hands of people whose names we don't even know. They could just as easily be gods. Indifferent, turning their backs on us. Something unpleasant happened a few hours ago. A little boy started repeating, 'I'm scared, I'm scared, I'm scared, I'm scared . . .' over and over again. I don't know the others, we have simply been thrown together here, but I assume it was the mother who tried to quieten the child. He refused to shut up, and kept on repeating, 'I'm scared, I'm scared . . .' This went on for several minutes, and the boy's lament became a part of the foul air we breathe, a prerequisite for our lives. Then I heard a roar – I can't describe it in any other way. It didn't even sound human, but it must have been a man, bellowing his disgust at the child's fear from the depths of his chest. It was an ancient, animalistic roar, a threat older than humanity itself, which shut the boy up. He must be even more frightened now, but this time into silence. Whichever gods are ruling us, they must let us out. Soon. Otherwise I fear for how things will go.

FROM NORRTÄLJE PRISON
TO LILLA TORGET

I

Sometimes Anna wishes that the visiting arrangements at Norrtälje Prison were the same as in American movies, with people sitting on either side of a pane of glass speaking via a telephone. Fingers touching the glass, only the most important words being said, or no words at all. *You've got five minutes!*

Anna is by nature a pretty positive person, but those half hours with Acke in the Porridge Room, which is what she calls it because of the colour of the walls, take their toll on her mood. She loves her kid brother, but just under two years in this place have done something to him. A new face has been painted over the old one, his eyes have hardened or rather dried out, so they are no longer capable of lighting the spark that she used to see there. Add about ten kilos of muscle, and her kid brother looks like exactly what he is: a career criminal.

'I heard they'd opened that fucking container,' Acke says, his finger tracing a vein in his pumped-up biceps. 'A pile of Afghans or some other crap came tumbling out.'

'They didn't come tumbling out,' Anna says. 'And nobody knows where they're from.'

'Whatever.'

Anna doesn't know how deep Acke's indifference actually goes. Is it a game in order to maintain his image, or a genuine numbness? The clichéd racism is also something he has acquired in jail. In an attempt to change the subject, she says: 'You'll be out in ten days. Any idea what you're going to do?'

Acke shrugs. 'Sort shit out.'

'What shit, exactly?'

'There's stuff to sort out. Shit.'

'Is this . . . illegal shit?'

Acke looks Anna in the eye for so long and with such intensity that she drops her gaze to his sinewy hands. One of her earliest childhood memories is helping one-year-old Acke to learn to walk; she was six at the time. She shuffled along behind him with her back bent as his tiny hands clutched her index fingers. He tottered around the living room, and she felt so big. He was so little.

She swallows a lump of nostalgia that threatens to choke her. 'I have to go. I'm meeting Siw.'

'To do what?'

It is unusual for Acke to show any interest in what Anna is doing, so she gives a more detailed answer than is strictly necessary. 'We've started exercising. At the gym. Two or three times a week.'

'Right. Is she still as fat?'

The brief flash of goodwill is gone. Anna smiles stiffly and says: 'She's about as fat as you're stupid, but at least Siw can drop a few kilos, while your IQ is going nowhere.'

One corner of Acke's mouth twitches. He says: 'Wham, bam,' and Anna finishes off with, 'Thank you, ma'am.' Their meeting ends in relative harmony.

As always when Anna leaves the prison, it is several hundred metres before she stops feeling its walled presence behind her back. She thinks of all the people in there, all the people who once had tiny fingers, trustingly clinging onto other fingers. Those tiny fingers grew bigger and began to carry out the deeds of darkness. Her thoughts are banal, but she can never help thinking them as she leaves all the unquiet souls behind her and walks towards freedom.

2

'How's it going?' Siw asks as they amble alongside the football pitch carrying their sports bags.

'Same old, same old,' Anna replies. 'My brother has the ability to bring me right down. He says he's got stuff to sort out – no doubt the kind of stuff that will get him sent straight back inside. Fuck him. So have you heard anything from RoslagsBowser?'

Siw opens her mouth to say something, and red roses bloom on her cheeks. 'Wow!' Anna yells. 'What's going on with you?'

'Nothing. It's nothing.'

'So why are you blushing like a fourteen-year-old who's been dipping into her parents' supply of booze?'

Siw carries on opening and closing her mouth as if something is stuck to her palate. For once Anna takes pity on her and allows her to keep her little secrets. They always slip out anyway, sooner or later.

When Anna and Siw enter the changing rooms, two women who are a few years older than them but in considerably better shape are busy wriggling into their tights. Before Siw can move away, Anna drops her bag on the bench beside them.

'Hi,' she says. 'How's things?'

'Fine,' one of them says, her lip curling slightly as her gaze sweeps over Anna's bulk. 'How about you?'

'Brilliant, thanks.' Anna slaps her belly. 'A few too many chips, that's all.'

'Right,' says the woman, getting dressed as quickly as she can. Siw has her back to them and is studying the lockers as if she is finding it difficult to choose between forty identical doors. When the two women have gone, she says: 'Do you *have* to?'

'What? I was just making small talk. Socialising.'

'You know what I mean.'

'No. You can't make yourself invisible, however hard you try. So you might as well chat.'

They get changed in silence. Anna is the only person Siw is even remotely comfortable with seeing her naked, but not enough to be able to make small talk. Whenever she and Sören *do it* she makes sure the light is off, and she is pleased it's him, because he is mainly interested in kneading her breasts until she feels like an unnecessary appendage to a lump of dough.

When Siw and Anna have changed into their sweat pants and sweatshirts and locked away their bags, they head up to the gym. The twenty-three steps are enough to make Siw start gasping for air. There is a lift, but there *are* limits.

The weights room is half-full. *Slimfit* women like those in the changing room, pensioners in rehab lifting the lightest weights with a disillusioned expression, middle-aged men tattooed like old sea dogs, and teenage boys with bulging muscles beneath vests that are little more than bits of string.

Anna and Siw take the bull by the horns and start with the most difficult: the stomach. After hooking on twenty kilos Siw leans back in the seat which bears an unpleasant similarity to the gynaecologist's chair. She brings down the bar which squeezes her breasts, pushing them out to the sides, then lifts up, back, up, back, puffing and panting with the exertion.

'Well done, Siw!' Anna says. 'You can manage three more!'

Siw does indeed manage three more, then she falls backwards with a groan and they swap places. She spurs her friend on with cries of encouragement, and even if her words of praise are out of proportion to Anna's achievements, they do help.

After Siw's second stint in the gynae chair she is so exhausted that she simply lies there gasping like a seal. A young lad in a skimpy vest with a baseball cap pulled well down over his eyes comes over.

'Have you finished?'

Anna checks out his V-shaped physique. 'One question. Why are you even *wearing* that vest?'

He chews on a real or imaginary piece of gum. Judging by his blank expression, the question would have been much too difficult if there hadn't been a set answer. 'You have to. You're not allowed in without.'

'But that's what you'd prefer?'

That question clearly doesn't have a set answer. He shakes his head, says, 'Er,' and walks away.

'Please, Anna,' Siw pants. 'Please!'

'What? It was a perfectly simple question. And I got an answer.' Anna lowers her voice, imitating the young man's drawl. '*You have to. I'd rather be naked, but you* have to. *Got it?*'

*

When they have showered and are alone in the changing room packing their bags, Siw says: 'Okay, I'll tell you. And if you laugh at me, I'll walk out of here and you'll never see me again.'

'Fine.'

'I mean it.'

'You don't, but fair enough. Tell me.'

Siw looks around, as if she's afraid that someone has crept in without her noticing. Lowering her voice, she confides; 'I checked out his posts. On Facebook.'

'Perfectly normal – so you found his page?'

'Only his Pokémon page, where he writes to the rest of the group.'

'Slightly less normal, but okay. And?'

'He has a certain tone . . . he's *funny*. He's very funny. And if a little boy or girl with a child's spelling has a question about the game, he's often the first to reply, and he's always really kind and encouraging and tries to sort it out for them. And . . .'

'Yes?' Anna suspects she knows what's coming when Siw blushes again.

'It seems as if . . . I mean, he doesn't actually say so, but it seems as if underneath it all, behind it all . . . I don't think he has a girlfriend.' As if she's been far too bold, Siw flaps her hands and adds: 'I mean, not that I imagine . . . there's no chance that I . . .'

'Stop that,' Anna says. 'So you're in love?'

'I wouldn't say that. But he seems . . . nice.'

Anna sighs. '*He seems nice.* For God's sake, Siw, when are you going to let go of the boards surrounding the rink, get out there on the ice?'

Siw lowers her head and stares at her bag as she answers almost inaudibly: 'When someone comes along and pulls me away.'

Siw fiddles with her phone as they head home. Halfway across the car park she stops. 'There's a raid in the square – Lilla Torget – in twenty minutes.'

'Lilla Torget? That's, like, twenty minutes' walk from here, at least in our condition. I'm not even sure I can make it home.'

'Please yourself, but I'm going.'

Siw's lips are twitching and Anna narrows her eyes suspiciously until the penny drops. 'Aha! Let me guess – RoslagsBowser is going to be there!'

'Possibly.'

'You know he is – he's posted a message, hasn't he?'

'Possibly.'

'Okay, I'm in.'

'You don't have to come.'

'Don't you want me to?'

Siw can't look her in the eye, which is enough of an answer. Anna laughs and slaps her on the bottom. 'Sorry, but there's no way I'm missing this. I promise to be a good girl.'

'You promise?'

'Yes – unless of course Mouseface is there.'

They turn onto Tullportsgatan, because there are more Poké Stops along that route and Siw is short of balls. Anna's thighs are killing her, as if someone has wrapped barbed wire around them, but today she was able to add a further five kilos to the machine. Some progress is being made, in spite of everything. *At what cost?* she thinks as she staggers along after Siw, who keeps swiping her screen and seems oblivious to the pain she must also be feeling. Not only Red Bull gives you wings.

It is a minute or so to three, and a couple of customers are running towards the liquor store, terrified of being robbed of their Saturday evening stupor. A male beggar aged about forty who looks as if he was injured during a war is sitting on the ground saying, 'Hi,' to the people who emerge from the shop with clinking bags; they all ignore him. Anna fishes out her wallet, puts a twenty-kronor note in his cup and receives a brief blessing in return.

'Nice,' Siw says.

Anna shrugs. 'I only really give to people like him – the ones nobody notices.' After another fifty metres they reach the main square, and Anna says: 'Can we stop for a minute? My legs are on fire.'

Siw consults her phone and discovers that they have made speedy progress in spite of everything. They sit down on a bench by the town hall. Anna massages her legs and asks: 'Aren't *you* in pain?'

'Yes, of course, but it's kind of . . . not relevant.'

Not relevant. Very nice. They've known each other a long time, but there are elements of Siw's use of language that really irritate Anna. When she uses words to keep reality at bay. Perhaps with the aim of introducing a little raw reality, Anna says: 'So what do you think about the container?'

'Yuck. I don't know. It's so awful.'

'But you had a feeling. In the park. And so did your guy.'

'He's not my . . .' Siw begins, then realises that it's useless to protest. 'I don't know what it was. It was just a sense that . . . bad things are going to happen. That's all.'

'I mean, twenty-eight rotting bodies is pretty bad.'

'Yes, but it wasn't that. It was about . . . the consequences it will have. Opening the container.'

'What consequences?'

203

'I don't know. I don't think anything has happened yet. Come on, we have to go.'

The brief respite has given Anna's muscles time to stiffen up, and she just about manages to get to her feet and drag herself in the direction of Lilla Torget on legs that feel like tree trunks. May all Pokémon burn in hell, along with her thigh muscles.

The number of Pokémon hunters gathered around the Havstenen sculpture in the square is significantly lower than on the raid in Society Park. Anna immediately spots Max, and . . . yes, Mouse-face is there too. She feels her tongue begin to take the form of a verbal knife.

Max looks up and sees them. 'Hi,' he says with a smile. 'Here we are again.'

'Yes, right, yes,' Siw says, her eloquence skittering away over the cobbles.

'Siw and . . . Anna, wasn't it?' Max points to Mouseface, who is grinning unpleasantly. 'You've already met Johan. This is Marko.'

A tall guy with black hair who has been studying the facade of the bookshop turns around, and Anna almost has to use her hand to prevent her jaw from dropping. Those dark brown eyes. The careless, boyish lock of hair over his forehead. The cheekbones you could sharpen an axe on. The full lips that part to reveal white, even teeth when he smiles and holds out his hand to her. 'Hi. Marko.'

'Anna.' Somehow she keeps her voice steady as her hand disappears into his grip. It is just firm enough, yet she senses a restrained strength behind it. On top of everything else, the guy is ripped. Siw also greets Marko, with a teasing sideways glance at Anna, who feels a bead of sweat escape from her armpit and trickle down her side.

'Okay,' Max says. 'In we go!'

The group isn't very big, so there is no need for teams on this occasion. Anna and Marko stand side by side and watch as the others tap their screens and make adjustments ready for the battle.

'Not your thing?' Marko says.

'No.' Anna has regained something of her equilibrium. 'I just don't get the obsession.'

'Nor me. I tried it for a while, but I just found it boring. I don't have a relationship with those Pokémon, if you know what I mean.'

'Siw has,' Anna says. 'although it's mainly . . .' – she hesitates for half a second, then takes the leap – '. . . a sexual relationship.'

Marko throws back his head and laughs out loud, sending a wave of warmth through Anna's belly. The laughter stops as quickly as it began, and he says: 'Max and Johan are the same. I bet they've got nude pictures of Pikachu at home.'

'Isn't he or she always naked?'

'I guess so. Now you come to mention it.'

We have so much in common, Anna thinks, risking a glance at Marko's profile. The strong eyebrows, the sharply delineated nose, the shadow of stubble. She has rarely seen a man who looks so overtly *male*, but without making a thing of it.

The battle is over, and Anna notices that Siw and Max have consciously or unconsciously positioned themselves next to each other as their fingers fly across their screens in yet another attempt to capture the bad-tempered dog.

'How do you know them?' Anna can't work out what someone like Marko has to do with the others.

'Max and Johan? We've been friends since childhood – well, school friends really.'

'Me and Siw too.'

205

'Which school?'

'Grind.'

'Oh, we went to Kvisthamra. That explains why we've never met.'

Or maybe it's because we come from different planets, Anna thinks. *Would you have noticed me in school? I don't think so.*

Siw and Max succeed almost simultaneously. They both raise their clenched fists in triumph, which makes them look at each other and laugh, followed by a high five. A paradoxical pang of sorrow pierces Anna's heart.

Little Siw, she thinks. *Darling little Siw. I'm keeping all my fingers crossed for you, but it can never work. Can it?* There is something about the way Max and Siw look at each other. *Can it?*

The group is breaking up. Only Siw, Anna, Max, Marko and Johan are left in the square. Marko checks his watch, which looks like something you might be killed for in certain countries. 'I have to go.' He turns to Anna. 'Good to meet you.'

He strides away, and Anna doesn't spend *too* long watching the way his arse moves under his chinos. Instead, she forces herself to focus on Mouseface, who is looking at her in a very odd way.

'What?' she snaps.

Before Johan has time to answer, Max says: 'Listen, the three of us are meeting up to play minigolf tomorrow. Do you two want to come along?'

'Minigolf . . .' Siw begins.

'Absolutely,' Anna jumps in. 'What time?'

Once they've sorted out the time and place, the boys leave and Anna slumps down on one of the benches next to the sculpture. 'Jesus Christ,' she says. 'Sweet Jesus Christ.'

'What are you talking about?'

'I mean, seriously.' Anna waves limply in the direction of the

206

street where Marko disappeared a couple of minutes ago. 'What.
A. Guy.'

*

*This is the second year they have shown up on 12th August, the elderly
couple who spread out a picnic blanket next to the DC3 on the tarmac
at the Norrteljeporten shopping mall. This year it is a young woman
who wonders what they are doing there. Nothing to tell, really. It's just
that they first saw each other inside the DC3 exactly forty-seven years
ago. How come? Well, in those days the plane was in Society Park and
housed a café, which was where the young couple's eyes met for the first
time. Something like that has to be celebrated. It was more comfortable
when the plane was on the lawn in front of the Roslagen Hotel, but what
won't we do for love? The sun hits the silvery fuselage and is reflected in
the young woman's eyes, making her tears sparkle.*

LOOK AT THAT CLOWN!

I

'Mummy, why is it there?'

'What?'

'The con . . . contr . . . cront . . .'

'Container?'

'Mmm.'

Siw and Alva are on their way to Siw's mother Anita, who sounded less than enthusiastic when Siw called and asked her to babysit for a couple of hours. Alva and Anita get along well, but Anita had already looked after her granddaughter the previous afternoon, while Siw was 'out enjoying herself on a Saturday'.

Minigolf isn't Siw's favourite activity, mainly because she's crap at it, but that's what's on offer if she wants to see Max again.

I'm making a fool of myself, on every level.

'Mummy! Concentrate!'

'Sorry, I . . . No one really knows.'

'But the dead people who were inside – why were they there?'

'How do you know all of this?'

'Grandma told me.'

Anita isn't one for digging up the past or opening up about her feelings, but she's happy to go into detail when it comes to current affairs, even with Alva. Siw once caught her reading aloud to five-year-old Alva from the evening paper, telling her all about some gruesome murder. When Siw questioned the suitability of this material, Anita had replied: 'The child needs to know what the world is like.' Alva had found it super-exciting, then had nightmares.

'Grandma says they're refugees. That they fled from war and misery.'

Siw smiles. *War and misery* is one of Anita's favourite expressions, along with *People behave like lunatics* and *It's all down to those mobile phones*. In her opinion, mobile phones firstly make people unaware of their surroundings, secondly ruin their ability to concentrate, and thirdly destroy their brains with radioactive rays.

'She's probably right,' Siw says. 'There must be a good reason why they'd let themselves be shut in like that.'

'Mmm-hmm – unless, of course, they were prisoners,' Alva replies, holding up her index finger in that precocious way of hers. 'Maybe they were going to be sold as *slaves*. Or . . .' – Alva edges closer to Siw and lowers her voice, as if she is about to reveal a great secret – 'they might have been *sliced open*. They've sold their organs. Well, somebody else sold them. And sliced them open.'

'Is this from Grandma as well?'

'Mmm.' Alva takes her obligatory diversion to the swings by Monsterplanket; she has to swing three times before she can continue, like some kind of ritual to keep the world turning on its axis.

Siw spent some time earlier in the morning reading about the container online. No one knows where it came from, or why the victims were inside it. Autopsies will be carried out on the bodies to determine the cause of death, and the container itself has been removed for forensic analysis. She didn't see anything about the deceased being *sliced open*.

On TV4's homepage she found clips of people continuing to speculate, complaining about the stench, and coming out with variations on the theme of 'Who could imagine that something like this could happen *here*?' as if Norrtälje ought to be safe from the miseries of the world, apart from the odd beggar. The final clip, an amusing coda after all the misery, was of a dog rolling in the stinking sludge that had flowed out of the container. Predictably, those who didn't like dogs or were frightened of them had posted countless derogatory comments about dog owners and dogs in general.

Alva comes racing back from the swings, her thin plaits bouncing around her face. The air is chilly, so she is wearing a black bobble hat with the words 'Jansson Metals – We bow to you' on it. Siw has no idea where it came from; Anita hates it because it's so 'unsophisticated', which is probably why Alva has chosen to put it on. She can be mischievous like that.

'Ready?'

'Mmm. Mummy – are you meeting a man?'

'What makes you think that?'

Alva gives an exaggeratedly casual shrug. 'I just do.'

'And what would you say if I was meeting a man?'

'Depends what he's like. What is he like?'

'There is no man.'

'So why did you say there was?'

'I didn't.'

'You did!'

They carry on like this for a minute or two before turning into

Fältvägen and heading for Anita's apartment block. Since Siw's grandmother Berit moved to the Solgläntan nursing home, the four generations of women live in a right-angled triangle within an area of one kilometre. They can't get away from one another.

2

The first thing Anita focuses on when she opens the door is Alva's bobble hat. 'My dear child, why on earth must you walk around with that caparison on your head?'

'What does caparison mean?' Alva demands as she steps inside and kicks off her shoes.

'Well, it's actually a kind of ornamental horse blanket, but in everyday language it's used to describe something that's incredibly ugly.'

'Oh,' says Alva, removing her jacket but keeping the hat on.

Siw is greeted with: 'Here you are again, then.'

'Sorry, Mum,' Siw says quietly. 'Something came up yesterday, and at first I wasn't going to go, but . . . well, I changed my mind.'

'What came up? Where is it you're going?'

Siw curses herself – why didn't she think of a convincing lie on the way over? If she tries to come up with one now, her sharp-eyed mother would see through her immediately, so she says: 'I'm playing minigolf.'

Anita's eyebrows shoot up as far as is humanly possible. 'Playing *minigolf*? You?'

'With a man!' Alva helpfully informs her grandmother.

'Is that true?' Anita nails Siw with her gaze. 'That would explain it.'

'No, it's not like that.'

'Right. So who are you playing with?'

Siw doesn't know why she lets her mother treat her this way, and why it gets under her skin. As soon as Alva mentions a man, Siw's cheeks flush red and she experiences the usual unjustified sense of shame. When Siw doesn't answer right away, Anita spreads her hands in a gesture of resignation, purses her lips and says: 'Olofsson! I should have guessed.'

According to Anna, Anita has a broomstick up her arse, which is what makes her so stiff and judgemental. Berit, on the other hand, is one of Anna's absolute favourites in the nursing home where she works, and she doesn't understand how such a wonderful old lady could have produced such a horrible daughter.

Siw knows that Anna's negative view of Anita is linked to Anita's even more negative view of Anna. As soon as she found out about Siw and Anna's growing friendship she tried to put a stop to it with nasty comments, criticism, and ineffective bans on hanging out together.

When Siw was fifteen she gathered her courage and faced her mother down. So what exactly was her problem with Anna? Okay, so she was foul-mouthed and a bit . . . slovenly, but that wasn't enough to explain Anita's clear antipathy from day one. It then transpired that the cause was Anna's notorious family. Ever since Grandpa Tore Olofsson's career as a conman and later fraudster during the Second World War, the Olofssons from Rimbo had been known as a group of people with fingers in every possible illegal pie.

It was *common knowledge*, at least according to Anita, that they acted as fences for most of the stolen goods circulating in the Norr-tälje area. They resprayed stolen cars, filed off the serial numbers from bicycles and boat engines. When they didn't have their hands full distributing smuggled booze and cigarettes, they busied themselves making their own moonshine and growing cannabis. And that was just what was *common knowledge*. They were probably also dealing hard drugs, especially after they'd teamed up with the Djup brothers, so maybe Siw could understand why Anita wasn't exactly jumping for joy when her daughter began to spend more and more time with Anna Olofsson.

Anita's argument cut no ice with Siw, who said she'd met Anna's family several times and there were really nice – not true – plus, Anna had nothing to do with their criminal activities – largely true, apart from the fact that she sometimes supplied Lithuanian vodka to fourteen-year-olds who were desperate because of some upcoming party. Whatever – she had no intention of letting her mother dictate who she could and couldn't see. That was Siw's first real rebellion against Anita.

'So you're still hanging out with that Olofsson?' Anita says, shaking her head at her daughter's inability to reform.

'Who's *that Olofsson*?' Alva wants to know.

'No one in particular,' Siw tells her.

'*Anna Olofsson*,' Anita says with an expression that suggests she's about to bring up a hairball. 'And for God's sake, take off that *revolting* hat!'

'Aunty Anna?' Alva's face lights up. 'She's *always* at our place. She's so much fun! Although sometimes she gets too drunk.'

Siw can actually feel a dynamo start humming inside her mother, and before it's fully loaded and ready to launch a tirade that will make her late, she says: 'See you at five. Love you,' and slips out of the door. Just before it closes behind her, she hears Alva say: 'By the way, I *love* this hat.'

By the way.

It's good that Alva is so smart. If Siw guesses correctly, over the next few hours her daughter will be subjected to a thorough interrogation on Siw's social life.

3

They meet at their usual place, the bench next to the rampart. From a considerable distance Siw can see that Anna is armed to the teeth, just like she used to be for a Friday night battle at Moberg's when they were teenagers. A loose-fitting white blouse with a push-up bra underneath; the combination hides her belly and draws attention to her breasts. At the same time the blouse is long enough to conceal her thighs, but shows off her shapely calves. Her hair is combed out and fluffed up, and she is wearing so much make-up that it's hard to see what she actually looks like. The first thing Siw says is: 'Bloody hell, Anna.'

'Bloody hell to you too, Siw. All your decent clothes in the wash, are they? Couldn't find your make-up bag?'

Anna is being unnecessarily harsh. Siw has chosen a pair of simple but reasonably elegant black linen trousers with a white T-shirt and her best denim jacket. She would never dream of signalling her intentions as clearly as Anna.

'Looks as if you've forgotten that this is a lost cause,' Siw says.

'Speak for yourself.'

'Seriously? Talk about out of our league . . .'

'Okay, so I admit he's elite series.' Anna gestures in the direction of the football pitch as if she's actually talking about sport. 'But that doesn't preclude a mercy fuck.'

'He didn't strike me as the type who'd go for a mercy fuck.'

214

'What the hell do you know about the mercy fuck type?'

'Nothing, but—'

'Exactly. So shut the fuck up. Let's go.'

They head towards Jansson's newsagent's through the residential area. Today Anna has nothing to say about the perversions of the petite bourgeoisie; she is unusually quiet, concentrating as if she really is preparing for battle.

Siw has seen Anna pull boys from higher leagues on a few occasions, using her body, gestures and eyes to subtly promise pleasures that have eventually persuaded them to make a guest appearance in the local league, but then these were Norrtälje boys. No disrespect to them – well, maybe a bit – but Marko had carried an aura of the city, worldliness and money, quite apart from the fact that he looked like the craggier type of photographic model.

Marko might be a lovely person, but as far as Siw is concerned, he is basically an object. A very attractive object, but nothing to do with Siw, simply something to look at from a distance, like a statue in an exhibition. Before Siw can say something with the aim of derailing Anna's hopeless project, her friend says: 'You and Bowser seemed to be having a lovely time yesterday.'

'We both caught Entei – almost simultaneously,' Siw replies, smiling at the memory.

'Exactly. That was the most important thing. Catching the bad-tempered dog.'

'That's why we were there.'

'Remember, Siw – time to let go.'

'But that's all it was. We were both pleased and yes, it was very nice. But I'm not reading any more into the situation.'

'You've got dressed up, though.'

'You've changed your tune.'

'You look good.'

'Thanks.'

They pass the newsagent's and turn onto Drottning Kristinas väg. When they reach Kvisthamra school, where the three guys they are meeting became friends, Anna says: 'Joking aside. Can you really not admit to yourself that you fancy this Max? That he's someone you could imagine being with?'

'I can,' Siw says, glancing at the playground and imagining Max, fourteen or fifteen years younger, running around or standing in a corner smoking – she doesn't know which. Eventually she adds: 'But I can't actually say it out loud, because then it feels as if I'm . . . jinxing the universe by having big ideas, imagining that I deserve something like that.'

Anna sighs, tucks her arm through Siw's and rests her head on Siw's shoulder. 'What idiots we are,' she says. 'Each in our own way.'

'Mmm. And now we're going to play minigolf.'

Siw feels Anna's grip on her arm tighten, as if she'd forgotten where they're going.

'Jesus. Are you any good?'

'You must be joking,' Siw says. 'I suck.'

'Me too.'

They are approaching the entrance to the minigolf course where the three guys are standing waiting for them. Anna lets go of Siw, raises a hand in greeting and calls out: 'Hi! This is going to be so much fun!'

*

A man who has just finished his weekly visit to his mother in the nursing home is suddenly struck by an idea. He asks a female member of staff if there are any elderly residents who rarely have a visitor. The woman is from Somalia, and finds nothing strange about the question. She introduces him to a man who is forty-three years his senior, and has no family at all. Something begins.

THE BOY WHO HATED
THE COUNCIL

I

The appearance of the bowling hall isn't exactly inviting. If it weren't for the sign saying 'Roslags Bowling' next to the door, you could easily think you were approaching a military storage depot. Grey, flaking corrugated iron, metal steps with a wheelchair ramp. Johan has suggested that they employ a graffiti artist to paint an archipelago landscape like the one above the lanes, but Peter the boss thinks it would be a waste of money, because the building will soon have to be renovated – or pulled down. The insulation is crap and the roof leaks.

Johan goes up the steps, unlocks the main door and deactivates the alarm. The place is in darkness, and only the glow from the ice cream counter enables him to find his way to the control panel so that he can switch on all the lights.

There you go.

In contrast to the off-putting exterior and the poor condition of the building, the inside is . . . yes, Johan would go so far as to call it *cosy*. False ceilings jut out from the walls in the style of an old boathouse, chairs and tables are arranged in groups beneath lamps, and the counter behind which Johan stands is attractively laden with sweets, fizzy drinks, a coffee machine and a golden, glowing warming cabinet. *Time for a Snack!* The lanes shine faintly beneath the fluorescent lights, waiting to be oiled.

Johan has worked here for seven years, and feels considerably more at home in the bowling hall than in the apartment where he grew up. It doesn't seem to matter what he does, he can never shake off a sense of desolation at home, a desolation he never experiences in the bowling hall, even though it's so much bigger and often, like now, completely empty. He feels safe here.

After putting on the coffee he takes a walk around to make sure that nothing got broken during Saturday night, when things can get a bit wild, especially if the place has been hired out for a corporate event. Fortunately everything appears to be in order.

He punches the boxing machine and nothing rattles that shouldn't rattle. It can take a real beating on Fridays and Saturdays when boozed-up men thump their way down to the primal stage and roar like woolly mammoth hunters when they score a direct hit. However, it brings in a decent amount of money, and also contributes to the fact that actual fist fights are rare, because people can take out whatever needs to be taken out on the punch ball rather than each other.

Johan checks the diary and sees that there is a children's party at twelve. Okay, decision made. He wasn't sure about the minigolf since those two fatsos came into the picture, but anything is preferable to a children's party. He has nothing against one child at a time, quite the reverse, but a party is something else altogether.

Ove can take it, especially as he's stupid enough to think children's parties are *fun*. Johan will make it up to him during the afternoon and evening. Let Ove trail around between the lanes consoling weeping kids who've dropped the ball on their foot.

Johan pulls on a pair of clean shoes and walks up and down each lane to make sure that the light barriers are working. Only two weeks ago a four-year-old at a party decided to run after his ball when it rolled off the board. He was halfway along the lane before someone noticed; he could have made it all the way to the pin deck and been mashed up by the machinery if the light barrier hadn't worked and shut everything down before it was too late.

Johan might not be overfond of kids who scream and get mustard and ketchup all over the balls, but he doesn't want to see them crushed to death, at least not on *his* lanes, which he thinks he can call them now that his boss is away on holiday.

Everything is working as it should be, and Johan can settle down in the staffroom and inhale the first coffee of the day – the first of many.

Ove arrives at eight fifteen, and Johan has nothing to say about that: he seems to have done a good job the previous evening. Everything is clean and tidy. Ove nods a greeting, pours himself a coffee and sits down.

'Any problems last night?' Johan asks.

'Nope.' Ove blows on his coffee. 'The usual stuff, people complaining about their scores when they've had one beer too many. Lane two got stuck for a while, but we sorted it, and Carlos is due tomorrow anyway.'

Carlos Martinez is a mechanic who comes in two days a week to service and oversee the machinery, carrying out repairs when necessary. The area behind the pin decks looks like a derelict elves' workshop and contains, among other things, six dismantled machines of the same thirty-year-old model as their own, bought for next to nothing from a hall in Gothenburg that was closing down, to use for spare parts.

'There was a lot of talk about the container, of course,' Ove goes on. 'Poor bastards.'

'They only have themselves to blame,' Johan counters.

'Don't say that.' Ove puts down his cup without taking a sip. 'Don't say that.'

'Okay, but what kind of people take their partners and kids and voluntarily shut themselves up inside a container so they can come to Sweden and live on benefits?'

'Maybe they didn't do it voluntarily.'

'No, but they probably did. And of course, it's terrible, but it doesn't alter the fact that we've been inundated over the past few years, because people will do *anything* to get here.'

'So you think it's a *good* thing that they died?'

'Of course not, but at some point we have to draw a line. We can't help the whole world.'

'You wouldn't say that if Peter was here.'

'Maybe not, but he isn't here, is he?'

Johan is well aware that his views are politically incorrect, and he doesn't often air them in public, but this business of the container has struck a nerve. In all the non-alternative media, the dead are described either as *victims* or *heroes* who have dared to take the leap and fallen at the final hurdle. The word *tragedy* recurs constantly.

It's twenty-eight dead people, that's all. Twice as many die in the Mediterranean every month, and few mourn them these days. Significant measures have been implemented to prevent people from reaching Europe, and simply because these twenty-eight happen to have been washed up in Norrtälje harbour, they are suddenly the most coveted and heart-rending of all. It is pure hypocrisy.

Johan has nothing in particular against foreigners; he's no racist. People like Carlos or the Kovac family are better than many Swedes he knows, but they came to Sweden during a period when there were *conditions*. This is no longer the case, and politicians and the media refuse to acknowledge the fact. The situation has improved slightly in recent months, and whatever the main parties say, Johan believes it's largely down to the Sweden Democrats. That's why he voted for them in the last election, and intends to vote for them in the next.

He hasn't even told Max, because the very words *Sweden Democrats* bring a lot of shit that Johan can't be bothered with. He has no time for the lunatics on certain forums he follows who have now started writing about 'the container solution', saying that this is how *all* refugees should be treated. Bundle them up together, lock them in and let them rot. Such views are entirely alien to Johan.

'You have to understand what I'm saying,' he tells Ove, who has finally dared to sip at his tepid coffee. 'I'd welcome all refugees with open arms if the *system* worked, so maybe I shouldn't have said that they only have themselves to blame . . .'

'Good to know.'

'Yes. But the system doesn't work. There's nowhere for them to live, there are no jobs, there's no proper integration plan, and yet those fucking politicians and civil servants sit on their arses and pretend it's raining. And here in Norrtälje, I can hardly bring myself to say it, do you know what those idiots have done?'

Ove sips his coffee and closes his eyes and Johan launches into yet another tirade about the incompetent fuckers running the local

222

council. He's heard it so many times before, and he will hear it many more times in the future. He really does try to pretend it's raining, that Johan's words are the calming patter of raindrops on a metal roof, but he isn't very successful. The venom in Johan's voice is hard to ignore.

So much hatred, Ove thinks. *Why so much hatred?*

2

Johan was nine years old when he received the final push that would send him rolling towards a black hole of revulsion when it came to the powers that be.

His mother had been beneath the ice for quite some time. She rarely cooked, and as often as he could, Johan made sure he hung around at Max's house until they felt obliged to ask him to stay for tea. He never told anyone about the situation with his mother, because he was so ashamed.

It was an afternoon in early November. Darkness was falling and there was snow in the air as he reluctantly made his way home from school. His mother had been a mess that morning, almost speaking in tongues. He was going to have to see how she was, even though the thought both frightened and disgusted him.

As soon as he opened the door he realised that something was badly wrong. The apartment was as hot as a sauna, and the air felt damp. Sweat immediately broke out on his forehead, and he took off his jacket before creeping through the hallway. He could hear the sound of rushing water, and through the open bathroom door he saw that the hot tap was full on. Clouds of steam drifted into the passageway.

In the kitchen the oven door was open, belting out heat, and all the hotplates were glowing red. Johan closed the door and switched off the hotplates, then went into the bathroom and turned off the tap. In the silence that followed he became aware of a despairing whimper.

I can't do it. I can't.

He really wanted to open the front door, run to the end of the world and fall over the edge, disappear forever. Instead, he tiptoed towards the living room, where the whimpering was coming from. He stopped in the doorway and rested his forehead on the frame.

His mother was standing in the middle of the room without a stitch on, raking her skin with jagged, bitten nails. She was bleeding from countless scratches on her chest, stomach and arms.

Naked. Why does she always have to be naked?

Of all the unpleasant aspects about his mother's episodes, the fact that he almost always had to see her naked was the one that disturbed him most. The revulsion he felt often mutated into a sticky sense of shame, as if he were the one who had done something taboo when the sight was forced upon him.

'Mum . . .' he said, without looking at her.

'I'm freezing,' his mother whimpered. 'Why is it so *cold*?'

'Maybe because you're not wearing any clothes?' Johan suggested as the sweat poured down his back.

'No!' his mother yelled, lashing out at him. 'It's the coldness of death! From inside! It comes from inside! I have to get it OUT!'

Johan recoiled as she threw herself onto the floor, clawing at her vagina while emitting guttural cries of pain or pleasure as her blood spattered the rug. That was the breaking point for Johan. He couldn't stand it any longer. He couldn't stand here watching this for one more second. He pushed himself away from the door

224

frame and with tears in his eyes he ran to the front door, opened it and slammed it behind him, then raced down the stairs and out into the yard.

During the brief time he'd been inside it had started to snow. Tiny crystals whirled through the air, and his sweaty skin became cold in seconds. He was wearing only a thin shirt, because he'd left his jacket in the apartment – with his keys in the pocket. Fortunately he hadn't got around to taking off his shoes.

Fortunately.

What a fortunate boy he was. Icy tears poured down his cheeks and he sobbed helplessly as he rubbed his arms with his hands and rocked on his heels. What was he going to do? Where could he go? His usual solution was to head for Max's house or hide somewhere until it was over, but this time he suddenly *saw himself*. A nine-year-old boy freezing in the snow with nowhere to go.

Help. I need help.

Social services had called round a few times after his mother had been sectioned two years previously. Fat-bottomed women who stank of perfume, and whose main aim seemed to be to get the whole thing dealt with as quickly as possible. Social services was an abstract concept to Johan, but a month or so earlier his class had been on a study visit to the council offices. They had been shown the different departments, and were allowed to ask questions. The council. At least he knew where the offices were.

It took him fifteen minutes to cover the kilometre to Rubingatan, and by the time he arrived he was chilled to the bone. There was a woman sitting at the long reception desk made of pale wood. She was reading something, her face resting on one hand while the other hand twirled a strand of hair around a pencil. Johan walked up to the desk, his chin barely reaching the top. 'I need help.'

225

'I'm sorry?' The woman had only just noticed him.

'I need help, it's my mother, she . . .' It went against the grain to *tell* on his mother like this, but eventually he managed to go on: 'She's hurting herself.'

'She's hurting herself?'

'Yes. She's scratching her skin until she bleeds.'

The woman disentangled the pencil from her hair so that she could use it to scratch the corner of her eye. 'You do know this is the council offices? We can't . . . I mean, it sounds as if she needs to go to the hospital.'

'But she . . . she . . . she's *mad*.'

'Well, that still means she needs to go to the hospital. You'll have to—'

'But I need help!' Johan yelled. The woman frowned. 'Now! Can someone help me, please!'

The woman gave him a funny look, then got to her feet and disappeared through a door. Johan stood there with his fists clenched, his cheeks bright red. He had done the most unforgivable thing. He had *reported* his mother, he'd said she was mad, and it still hadn't been enough.

A minute or so later the woman came back with a red-haired man who had the bushiest eyebrows Johan had ever seen. A substantial belly protruded from beneath a shabby jacket with leather elbow patches; he stank of cigarette smoke.

'So what's this all about?' the man asked.

'My mother.' Johan found it a little easier this time. 'She's mad.'

'Do you mean she's angry with you, or . . .'

'No. She's mad.' When he said it for the third time he thought of the disciple who denied Jesus. He went cold inside and his legs felt weak. 'She's scratching herself.'

226

'Right. The thing is, this is the council offices and . . .'

Johan's legs gave way. He dropped to his knees, rested his forehead on the floor, clasped his hands in prayer and began to yammer: 'Can't you help me, can't you help me, please . . .'

A muted conversation took place. He heard words like *social services* and *family counselling* and *child psychiatry*. The two adults stood there for a long time, conferring above his head while Johan crouched on the floor with ice in his stomach and his clasped hands stretched out in front of him. At long last the man said, with an unmistakable tone of distrust: 'Listen, sonny, can you get up?'

Johan dragged himself to his knees, then to his feet. He had no strength left in his body; his limbs felt numb. He had reached rock bottom, and he was still there.

The man pointed to a hard green sofa next to a plastic palm. 'If you wait over there, we'll contact social services.'

Johan was beyond protest. He shuffled over to the sofa and sat down. It was every bit as uncomfortable as it looked. He placed his hands on his knees and waited. From time to time he glanced out at the snow, which was falling more heavily now. Then he carried on waiting.

It was an hour before one of the perfumed ladies showed up. During that period no one had said a word to Johan or glanced in his direction; no one had asked if he was hungry or thirsty, which he was. Both. He had sat alone with his hands on his knees and dedicated those sixty minutes to hating the council with increasing intensity.

During the years that had passed since the incident with his mother, Johan had come to realise that the man and woman he'd met that day weren't necessarily representative of the council as a whole. He'd had the misfortune of encountering two idiots who were incapable of taking the appropriate action, but it didn't matter. As soon as the subject of the council and its incompetence arose, the feeling came rushing back: he was crouching on the floor in front of two heartless adults, or sitting on the uncomfortable sofa with humiliation coursing through his veins. He had hated, and continued to hate out of sheer instinct.

That was another point in the Sweden Democrats' favour. They hadn't existed back then, and therefore couldn't even be blamed by association for what he had been put through. *No, because they were, like, Nazis in those days*, someone might say, but surely everyone deserves the opportunity to change. Unless they are from the council.

Johan leaves the bowling hall at eleven thirty after applying a rudimentary coat of protective oil to the lanes. It wasn't as if the kids were going to moan when they didn't even know how to bowl properly. He would switch the machine to the professional level before the afternoon's league matches, then wait for the predictable complaints.

With his hands in his pockets he strolls through an autumnal Norrtälje. The leaves on the trees are beginning to change colour, it's not too cold, and he feels more or less okay. He picks up the odd stray Pokémon here and there, spins a few stops. When he passes the Black Egg sculpture which currently belongs to Team Mystic, he notices that there is an empty space and quickly places his Snorlax there, to keep watch and hopefully earn a few coins.

One of the reasons why Max is at a higher level is that he buys items within the game, for real money – mainly incubators so that he can have several on the go at the same time and hatch more eggs. He can afford it. Johan only uses the PokéCoins he earns by keeping watch over gyms, which means he progresses more slowly through the levels. Capitalism exists even in the world of Pokémon.

To be honest, Johan's job is a lot less mobile than Max's, and less suited to egg-hatching. But even if Johan was out and about like Max, he would still be able to have only one or possibly two incubators on the go, and he would lose again. He likes to think in terms of winning and losing, and almost always finds himself on the losing team.

Don't go there.

He passes the community music school and remembers the time in Year Four when he wanted to learn to play the guitar. He dropped the guitar he'd borrowed and cracked it, which meant he wasn't allowed to borrow another one, and buying his own was out of the question because . . .

Don't go there.

When he reaches Society Bridge, which was built so that fine ladies and gentlemen could make their way safely from the steamboats to the bathing facilities, he gazes over towards the harbour. The spot where the container stood is empty, and everything has returned to normal. On Monday construction will recommence so that fine ladies and gentlemen from the upper classes will be able to live in Soltornet and Havstornet and look down on . . .

Don't.

Yes, *do*. Johan clutches the railing and feels a sudden and irrational fear of all those empty-eyed people who will move in and occupy Norrtälje's new prestige harbour development, maybe people from *Stockholm*. Fear turns to rage. People with *money* who contribute to the *tax base* will wander around smiling warmly at one another in the *natural meeting places* that are planned, and Johan finds himself wanting the container back, a blot on the landscape for all those fucking . . .

Calm down.

He is so angry that he stands there tugging at the railing, which doesn't move a millimetre. He lets go and runs a hand over his eyes. He gets agitated very easily, but this is something else. He carries on across the bridge, massaging his temples. When he reaches Society Park he starts to feel calmer; he glances once more at the empty space where the container stood until yesterday.

Of course, this won't be mentioned in the media, but isn't the container yet another shining example of how much better it is to provide help *in situ*? If the poor bastards – as Ove put it – had been helped to achieve at least a minimum standard of living in their own countries, they wouldn't have taken their women and children and shut themselves up in a container. They would have stayed where they belonged and waited for better times. But no one with the power to make decisions seems to understand that.

Fucking idiots.

Max is waiting for him on a bench in front of the open-air stage, and Johan tries to shake off the gloomy thoughts that have taken over his mind.

'Hi,' Max says, waving in the direction of the stage. 'There's a level three going on here. Alolan Raichu. Shall we take it?'

'I haven't got a raid pass,' Johan replies, holding up his phone to prove it. 'I took a couple of ones and twos on the way to work this morning.'

'Can't you . . .'

'No, I can't.'

A raid pass costs five kronor in real money, but it's a matter of principle. Johan has less of a problem with Nintendo than with most big companies, but he has no intention of throwing his hard-earned wages into its greedy Japanese gob in order to acquire an imaginary object.

'You're in a filthy mood,' Max says, putting away his phone.

'I am not in a filthy mood. I'm sticking to my principles.'

'That's often the same thing.'

They set off through the park with *Pokémon Go* running in their pockets to collect any eggs within walking distance, but they don't make any stops because they both have enough balls. Johan jerks his thumb in the direction of the far side of the harbour. 'Could you imagine living there?'

'In the new development? I don't know. Why?'

'I was just overwhelmed by such a feeling of aggression towards the whole project that it almost scared me.'

'You're often angry.'

Johan jumps when a tennis ball slams into the wire fence next to his ear. Two teenage girls are on the court smashing balls at each other with astonishing force. Their bodies move across the sand with ease, and Johan suddenly feels *old*. Old and angry, so he takes the opportunity to bring up something else that is annoying him.

'Why did you invite those girls?'

'Siw and Anna? I just thought it was a good idea.'

'That's no answer. Have you got something going on with that Siw?'

231

'I don't think so.'

'But yesterday at the raid, the two of you were, like . . . I don't know.'

'Like I said before – there's something I . . . recognise in her.'

Johan groans and holds his hands in front of his belly. 'But she's so *fat*.'

They have reached the map of Norrtälje, and are just about to turn onto the track between the café and the rock face. Max strides ahead, then turns and faces Johan. 'Seriously – I want you to stop talking like that.'

'I'm merely stating a fact.'

'Yes, but maybe you could choose some other facts to state? I've got eyes, okay? I know what she looks like.'

'I mean, she's not exactly ugly, but—'

'Seriously, Johan. Stop now.'

Max turns and keeps on going. Johan stays where he is and considers heading back the way he came, but that seems far too childish, so instead he takes out his phone and follows Max while collecting Pokémon. Which isn't childish at all.

When Johan emerges from the passage, Max is waiting for him, and they continue side by side. Johan concentrates on his screen and throws several balls at a Psyduck, which proves worthless.

'So, what do you think about the container?' Max asks. Before Johan has the chance to answer, he adds: 'If you disregard the way the council dealt with it.'

'Well, you're the expert – you saw it happen. And the – what was it you said? – the metaphysical part. I still don't understand what you meant.'

'I'm asking you what you think.'

'I guess I agree with everybody else – it was a gang of people who were trying to enter the country illegally, and it went wrong somehow.'

'Mmm. But why? Surely it should have been just as easy to let them out. Why were they kept locked in?'

'Maybe they hadn't paid.'

'You think someone dumped the container there as an example, a warning? This is what happens if you don't pay?'

'Yes – why not?'

'What kind of people would do that?'

'Now you're just being naive.'

They turn off at the Knut Lindberg memorial and continue up the hill. If Max's assertion that Johan has an unnecessarily negative view of the world is true, then Max's view is unnecessarily positive. He never ceases to be horrified by the terrible atrocities human beings can visit upon one another, while Johan regards this as the natural order of things. Civilisation and brotherly love are merely the render on the exterior of an unstable society; chuck in an earth tremor and the facade cracks.

They reach the minigolf course shortly before twelve, and a minute or so later Marko comes loping down from the more well-to-do area where Max's house is. Max's *and* Marko's houses, Johan corrects himself.

Marko has his hands behind his back, a worried frown creasing his brow, and Johan can't help himself. As so many times in the past, he would like to take Marko in his arms, kiss him and caress him, make all his troubles disappear. Time has changed nothing.

When Marko sees them his face lights up and he gives that broad

233

Zlatan-smile that makes the pain of impossibility flicker in Johan's chest. What individual born of woman could resist that smile? Maybe future laboratory-produced children can be programmed with inbuilt resistance, but for the moment: no one.

'Hi,' Max says. 'How are things?'

'Oh, you know. Mustn't grumble. Best foot forward. Keep on keeping on.'

'Life's a bitch,' Johan adds.

'Exactly.'

This was a game he and Marko used to play when they were teenagers: speaking only in platitudes. It amused them to mock Swedes, while at the same time it formed part of Marko's language learning project. He made a point of checking which expressions were okay and which sounded stupid, and Johan answered to the best of his ability.

'It's been a while,' Max ventures.

'Well, no, it hasn't,' Marko says. 'We met up yesterday, so . . . no.'

The awkwardness Johan felt when they went to Marko's newly purchased home has more or less gone, even if the hopeless longing in his chest is still there. Years have passed, a great deal has been said and has happened, especially in Stockholm, but on some level Marko remains the great love of Johan's life. There is nothing to be done about it. Nothing.

Two rotund figures are approaching from Gjuterivägen. At first Johan can't believe his eyes, but as they come closer he is able to confirm that he wasn't mistaken. Siw looks perfectly all right if you disregard the blubber, but Anna . . . Fucking hell, Johan can't remember when he last saw someone so plastered in make-up, apart from Peppe the Clown whom they sometimes hire for children's parties at the bowling hall.

'I mean, seriously . . .' he says quietly to the others. 'What *does* she look like?'

'Oh well,' Marko replies. 'What will be will be. Hello, girls!'

*

A seven-year-old girl is standing on Society Bridge. Her chin is resting on the railing as she stares down into the fast-flowing waters of the river. There is a flash of silver as the sun's rays catch the back of a salmon. The girl thinks there is treasure hidden all over the world, and that all people are pirates and adventurers searching for that treasure. Then she remembers how terrible pirates are with their cutlasses and hooks, and how dangerous crocodiles are. Tears fill her eyes and she walks away.

POVERTY AND EXCESS

I

Marko spends Saturday night on a camp bed in the middle of the empty living room in his newly purchased house. Johan, Max and his parents have offered him a place to sleep, but he wanted time to think in peace.

Up until the moment when Max said that maybe Marko should check with his parents, ask them what they wanted, the thought had never even struck Marko. Unbelievable. He had simply seen himself fixing everything up, making it top notch, then the big reveal: ta-da! His mum and dad would stand there open-mouthed, possibly with tears in their eyes as they realised how much their son loved them.

But Max's reaction when he mentioned the pool was telling. Marko has absolutely no idea whether his parents would want a pool, and lying in the silence of the empty house, he is forced to admit to himself that he doesn't even know if they want a place like this.

He twists and turns on the camp bed, and the squeaking of the springs bounces off the bare walls. He has often been accused of recklessness, rushing in head first and acting on instinct. That is only half true. He has a thorough knowledge of the stock market, acquired through dedicated study during thousands of hours of unpaid work, but when it comes to buying or selling . . . what can you say? Trading in options and securities requires speedy action, and Marko can throw in millions based on a *feeling* about how things are going to move, while others sit and consider the pros and cons until the opportunity has slipped through their fingers.

So yes, he acts on instinct and can therefore seem rash or even stupid, but his instinct usually leads him in the right direction because it is based on deep knowledge and mature consideration, undertaken in advance. Plus, of course, a general *feeling*. He bought this house in the same way, in a rush and based on a feeling. Thirteen million, thank you very much, off we go.

He turns over again; he can't get comfortable. The squeaking is getting on his nerves; in fact, it seems as if the springs *are* his nerves. Squeaking and whimpering.

It's disturbing to realise that while he has such a clear understanding of the stock market, which to most people is an impenetrable jungle of numbers, his parents, whom he has known for almost thirty years, are a complete mystery to him. He is incapable of predicting their movements or reactions.

Mum and Dad: 1, stock market: 0. Useless fucking bed.

Marko gets up and wanders through the dark interior, visualising how it will look when he's finished the renovations. He drinks directly from the kitchen tap and splashes his face with cold water.

Liberated from Stockholm's whirling currents where decisions must be made instantly, standing over a sink with water dripping from his face, Marko's mind begins to calm down. He realises that

Max is right. He has to discuss this with his parents. He knows roughly what they like, but what if he spends thousands on a cool sofa for the living room, and it turns out that they want to keep their old one? And so on. He has to talk to them. Tomorrow.

The thought sends a fresh flurry of anxiety swirling through his body, and he drinks some more water. It doesn't help, so he drops to the floor and does a hundred press-ups. Then a hundred sit-ups. He is barely out of breath, but the anxiety has eased slightly. He goes back into the living room and flops down on the bed, which lets out a loud squeak of protest.

Remind me not to shop at Jysk again.

He considers texting Max and dropping out of the minigolf, but it might be nice to have a reason to limit the time he spends with his parents. However much he loves them, they can easily make him feel suffocated. He texts his father to say he'll be over at nine in the morning, and that he has something to show them.

He lies flat on his back and glares at a lamp hook on the ceiling, considers hanging himself to get out of the whole thing, but it is only a spontaneous fantasy. Suicide is completely alien to him. Instead, he mentally reviews the contents of his share portfolio. Columns of figures, graphs showing upturn and downturn, the steady progression of the index funds he holds as security, and at some point during this calming activity he falls asleep.

2

In spite of the fact that it's not allowed, Marko parks in the court-yard. He wants to be able to lead his parents from the main door of the apartment block directly to the car and invite them to take their seats as if they are dignitaries. He gets out of the car and runs a hand over its roof before locking it by simply touching the handle. He hasn't been home for six months, but when he enters the foyer the smell is exactly the same as during his childhood, and as he walks up the stairs it's as if he is regressing. Every step up is a step back in time, and by the time he rings the bell he is almost a little boy again.

His mother opens the door. The years have been kind to her. There are strands of grey in her long black hair and a couple of new wrinkles around her eyes, which always have those dark circles beneath them, but her expression is bright, her body moving with ease. She lets Marko in before throwing her arms around him and saying in Bosnian: 'Welcome home, darling.'

'Thanks, Mum,' he replies in Swedish, gently returning her embrace. Laura gasps and says in Swedish, pretending to be horrified: 'But Marko – you're as big as a house!'

'A garden shed, maybe.'

'Mmm. Or one of those new . . . what are they called?'

'Garden studios.'

'That's it. One of those.'

When Marko was growing up it wasn't impossible to talk to his mother about important matters, but in general there was a light-hearted tone between them, while his relationship with his father was more serious. Maria was completely the opposite – jokey with her father, serious and frequently argumentative with her mother. When they sat down for dinner together there was an incredible mixture of emotional levels around the table, and conversations could easily spiral into fierce arguments and raucous laughter.

His father is sitting in the living room, leafing through a manual. On the floor there is a big cardboard box and a couple of chunks of polystyrene, and on the TV stand a brand new forty-seven-inch Samsung. Marko has one exactly the same, except it's the fifty-five-inch model.

'Hi, Dad.'

Goran looks up. His hair is thinner and much greyer since Marko last saw him, and his body seems bent.

'My son,' he says in Bosnian, then switches to Swedish. 'Can you help me with this? The instructions are in Finnish, German, French, and . . . what's this? Dutch. I can't . . . Oh, for goodness' sake!'

Marko rummages in the box and finds the manual in the missing languages. It is slightly suspicious that his father is messing with the new TV at nine o'clock in the morning, and Marko suspects it's a set-up. Marko is meant to dig out the manual then help to install the television, giving them a period of unforced togetherness focused on a concrete project.

And that's what happens. Marko doesn't need the manual in order to connect various cables between the TV, Blu-Ray player and receiver, which impresses Goran no end. When he has finished Goran spreads his arms wide and exclaims: 'My son! How would I manage without you?'

'You seem to have got along perfectly well so far,' Marko says, hugging his father who is small, strong and sinewy, and definitely less straight-backed than he used to be. Laura has come in to admire the miracle that her son has achieved, and Marko turns to them both. 'We're going for a ride. I've got something to show you.'

'Not until we've had coffee,' Laura says firmly, heading back to the kitchen. Marko exchanges a glance with his father, who raises his shoulders and spreads his hands wide. *What can you do?*

*

240

'Have you heard from Maria lately?' Marko asks, helping himself to yet another piece of homemade *loukoumi*. Coffee and a snack turned out not to be such a bad idea after all. Marko hasn't eaten since lunchtime yesterday – a hot dog at Circle K – and he appreciates the taste-memory from his childhood. He licks the sugar from his fingers and dunks the rectangular sweetmeat in his coffee.

'She calls,' Laura replies. 'Regularly. At least once a week.' Marko can't decide if there's a hidden reproach in her words. A month can easily pass between his calls, but he intends to improve in that respect.

'How is she?'

'Don't you talk to each other?'

'It's been a while.'

His father shakes his head gloomily, as if it goes against the natural order of things for siblings not to keep in touch.

Marko did try to stay in contact with Maria when she followed him to Stockholm at the age of eighteen, but certain events created distance between them. At the same time Maria's modelling career took off and hurled her out into the world. If Marko did call, she was usually very distant and very busy. In the end he gave up.

'Is she home?' he asks.

'You mean . . . in Sweden?' Goran still finds it difficult to equate Sweden with home, even though he's lived here for twenty years. 'Yes, she's home. Looking for somewhere to live. And a job.'

'As what?'

His mother and father exchange a glance that is hard to interpret. Laura's brief sigh before she says: 'As an actress,' is considerably easier to interpret.

'What?' Marko can't suppress a groan. 'Not that again!'

'What's the girl supposed to do?' Laura gazes at the ceiling as if she is seeking support from God on high. 'She has nothing but her appearance.'

'I think you're being a bit hard on her,' Goran says.

'I mean, as far as her education goes. She has no qualifications. Nothing.'

Maria had always been smart, but when it came to anything other than chess she had zero patience, and by the time she reached her teenage years she spent most of her time feeling bored and restless. She dutifully started a course in hospitality, focusing on hotels and restaurants, but dropped out as soon as a modelling agency showed an interest in her. She never went back.

'Being attractive doesn't make you a good actor,' Marko points out.

Laura rolls her eyes. 'Tell *her* that.'

'Okay.' Marko brushes the crumbs from his hands. 'Ready?'

'One more top-up.'

Marko's foot begins to jiggle up and down as his mother drinks yet another cup of coffee, with exaggerated relish. His hands are cold, and he realises that he is no longer nervous. He is afraid.

'Good heavens, what a flashy car!' Laura exclaims, bringing her hands together. 'And you've parked in the courtyard! Whatever will the neighbours say?'

'Since when did you care about what the neighbours say?'

'I care a great deal about what the neighbours say.'

Goran looks up at the facade of the apartment block. 'This wasn't a good idea, Marko.'

Fuck the neighbours, Marko feels like saying. *You won't be living here much longer.* Instead, he unlocks the car and opens the front passenger door for his mother, while his father shuffles into the back seat. All the time he is turning the car around and driving out of the courtyard his mother peers out of the side window, as if she is expecting a gob of saliva or something worse to come flying through the air. She doesn't relax until they are out on Glasmästarbacken.

'Where are we going?' Goran wants to know.

'It's a surprise. A really big surprise.'

'I don't like surprises,' Laura informs her son. 'And the bigger they are, the less I like them.'

'You'll like this one,' Marko assures her, suppressing the urge to make the sign of the cross.

As he turns into Drottning Kristinas väg it strikes him that this will be the route he takes in future when he visits his parents. The realisation evokes a pang of nostalgia. Straight on instead of left by Jansson's newsagent's. Two different worlds.

They pass the minigolf course where he is due to meet the others in just over an hour. As far as he can recall he has never played minigolf, but how hard can it be? You have to get a ball into a hole. He is usually a quick learner, and anyway, that's the least of his worries as they approach the house. He pulls up with the front bumper a few centimetres from the gate, and catches his father's eye in the rear-view mirror.

'Dad, can you get out and open the gate?'

'Here? Why? Who lives here?'

'Can you just open it, please?'

While Marko waits for his father to do as he's asked, Laura narrows her eyes and stares at him. 'What are we doing here, Marko?'

'Soon, Mum. Soon.'

With frequent worried glances up at the house, his father has managed to open the gate. Marko glides in and parks on the drive.

243

He takes a deep breath and gets out of the car. Laura is out too before he has the chance to open the door for her.

'What do you think?' Marko says.

His parents are standing with their backs to the house, their posture indicating that they are ready to leave immediately if anyone appears and challenges them. Reluctantly they turn around.

'It's a house,' Goran says. 'A big house. Someone with a lot of money lives here.'

'Wrong.'

'Stop playing games, Marko,' Laura reprimands him sharply. 'Who lives here?'

'You do. You live here.'

Once again Laura's eyes narrow, and she tilts her head on one side. Something in her expression tells Marko that she understands. Unlike his father, who gives himself a little shake and says: 'Can we go home now? This doesn't feel right.'

He is on his way back to the car when Marko stops him and places a bunch of four keys in his hand, then goes through them one at a time: 'Front door. Cellar. Garage. Annexe, which is a fully equipped guest cottage.'

His father still doesn't get it. 'Why have *you* got these keys?'

'Because I've bought this house. For you.'

Goran looks at Laura with something approaching horror. With a silent nod she confirms that *yes, Marko is perfectly capable of doing something like this*. Goran gazes up at the house, his mouth hanging open. He shakes his head, then hands the keys back to Marko.

'No,' he says. 'It's out of the question.'

'What's out of the question?'

'This. We can't live *here*, surely you realise that?'

'Why not?'

'Because it's out of the *question*.'

His father moves towards the car. Laura says in Bosnian: 'Goran, calm down. Let the boy speak.'

'But it's madness,' Goran insists. *'Ludilo.'*

With a certain amount of persuasion Marko eventually manages to get his parents into the house. They creep from room to room as if they are afraid of waking any resident ghosts, and seem to want nothing more than to leave as soon as possible. Laura doesn't even comment on Marko's rickety camp bed in the living room. The only thing that sparks her interest is the kitchen. She stops dead, taking in the generous worktops, the enormous fridge and the induction hob; life would be so much easier in a kitchen like this.

'Marko, Marko . . .' she says.

'Wait. You haven't seen the best yet.' Marko leads them past the camp bed, over to the patio doors. He flings them open and steps outside, his parents following obediently. He spreads his arms wide, showing off the extensive wooden decking, the view of the Kvisthamra inlet. 'Not bad, eh?'

Goran shakes his head and makes a faint whimpering sound, as if to indicate that, in fact, it's *very* bad indeed.

'Tata,' Marko says. 'Imagine a couple of sun loungers out here, where the two of you can sit and drink a glass of wine. A barbecue here – you love to barbecue, and here . . . here . . .' – he waves in the direction of the far corner – 'you can have a pool, if you want.'

Goran places a hand on his forehead; this is clearly the final straw. 'My son. You have lost your mind. A pool? A house like this . . . you don't understand . . . the furniture alone—'

'Dad, it's you who doesn't understand.'

'What don't I understand?'

'I don't mean to boast, but you don't realise how much money

245

I actually have. You only have to say what furniture you'd like, and I'll buy it for you. If it costs half a million, no problem. And if you do want a pool, I'll have one built for you. Please – I want to give this to you.'

Goran is still in denial, but Laura, whether she likes it or not, seems to have accepted the reality. 'How much did it cost?' she asks.

'Thirteen million.'

Goran whimpers again and makes the sign of the cross, as if to beg the Lord's forgiveness for his son's arrogance, but Laura merely gasps and says: 'You've bought us a house. For thirteen million kronor?'

'No – euros.' Before his parents explode, he holds up his hands. 'I'm joking. Kronor.'

'And tell me again – why have you done this?'

'Because you deserve it. Because I love you. Because I want you to have a good life. And if I'm honest . . . this is one of the goals I've worked for all my life. To be able to give you this.'

Laura nods in a way that Marko regards as unnecessarily gloomy. 'Ah.'

'What do you mean, ah?'

'Just ah. I understand.'

'What do you understand?'

'I understand, Marko. It's fine.'

'So . . . ?'

Laura glances at Goran, who is staring at the spot where Marko suggested installing a pool. 'Your father and I need to discuss this.'

'What is there to discuss?'

'There's a great deal to discuss. I don't want to appear ungrateful, my darling, but you must realise this is a lot to . . . how do you say it? Take in. It's a lot to take in all at once.'

246

'You need to return it,' Goran says.

'Dad, buying a house isn't like buying a TV – you know that perfectly well. And by the way, it's good that you bought a new TV. It will fit in perfectly. Serie A.'

For the first time since they arrived at the house, there is a faint glint in Goran's eyes. He nods. 'Serie A.'

For as long as Marko can remember his father has nurtured a passion for the Italian football league, and for reasons unknown to Marko, his team is Lazio. He never misses a match if he can help it.

'Just imagine,' Marko says, pointing to the living room. 'I'll order a great big comfy sofa where you can sit and enjoy a beer while you watch Lazio win the league.'

'Oh my goodness,' Goran says, crossing himself once again as protection against the continued hubris of his son.

His parents decide to walk home, leaving Marko standing on the porch. He is leaning against one of the pillars supporting the balcony outside the master bedroom, one of the many details he had hoped would delight them. Hoped in vain.

The visit certainly hadn't gone according to plan. It had been worse than he could possibly have imagined. And yet he is still optimistic that things will work out in time, when Laura has talked to Goran and made him see that this is real. Marko thinks that is the problem: his father can't picture himself living in a house like this, so therefore he digs his heels in and says it's impossible. On an essential level, it is. For him.

Laura is different. The appreciative look she gave the kitchen, the faint nod of approval on the patio gave Marko the impression that she was at least beginning to visualise what life in this house could be like. He is confident that she will talk Goran around.

However, the visit was a miscalculation on Marko's part. The 'Ta-da!' moment he has dreamed of was never even close. In spite of the fact that the house was a gift, his parents made him feel like a persistent salesman, trying to force them into something they really didn't want.

Fucking Bosnian peasants.

Marko's hand twitches and he almost crosses himself. He believes strongly in the commandment that tells us to honour our father and our mother, but there is a truth in his forbidden thought. Back home in Bosnia, Goran and Laura were farmers before Laura trained to be a nurse, and those peasant farmers are still firmly embedded in their brains. Don't show off, don't crave too much, live simply in peace and harmony. Then the war came and destroyed everything, drove them off their land, but it didn't manage to drive away those inner farmers.

But it will work out, Marko thinks. *It will work out. One day they'll thank me.*

He glances at his watch: five to twelve. He locks the patio doors and the front door, then sets off for the minigolf course.

Getting a ball into a hole. How hard can it be?

Max and Johan are waiting for him by the fence surrounding the course. They say hi, and when Johan does the platitude thing they made up one evening when Johan was staying with him, Marko feels much better.

Then the girls arrive. Even from a distance he can see that the one he talked to the previous evening is wearing more slap than an American Indian on the warpath, and he can't help smiling because this brings back memories. That's what the girls in Norr-tälje looked like when he was king of the pulling jungle. The girls in the nightclubs on Stureplan where he hangs out these days are cool, their make-up is subtle and they pretend to be indifferent, but here comes – and he uses the words with appreciation – a real *Norrtälje slapper*.

Not that she's a girl he would go with in a thousand years, but he's pleased to have the opportunity to renew his acquaintance with *the type*, so when Johan makes a disparaging comment about Anna's appearance, Marko walks towards them with a warm and sincere: 'Hello, girls!'

HOW HARD CAN IT BE?

I

Johan and Max haven't brought their own clubs and balls because that would give them an unfair advantage, so they have to pay full price. As it's nearly the end of the month Johan's finances are in a precarious position, so the cost of fifty kronor is painful. No problem. Marko offers to pay, as long as someone treats him to an ice cream afterwards.

Anna's ridiculously kohl-rimmed eyes sparkle when she looks at Marko as he takes out his oversized wallet and chooses among the cards. To be fair, she is more interested in his physique than in the rich man's trappings in his hands, but what *is* she thinking? Has she looked in the mirror lately?

They choose from the selection of clubs, and Johan swaps the slightly bent one Marko has picked out for a straight one. They head for lane one, where they tee off in alphabetical order. To Johan's amazement, Anna's first stroke is dead straight and rolls onto the green. She seems to share his astonishment. She gives Siw a look that says *did you see that?* before glancing at Marko and setting off for the green.

'Don't walk on the course!' Johan says sharply. It pains him to see Anna's heels digging into the felt.

'What?' she says, twisting around so that the indentation beneath her right foot deepens.

'You're not allowed to walk on the course. It ruins the surface. Have you never played minigolf?'

'Well, yes. My dad had a few courses at home when I was a kid.'

'What the hell are you talking about?'

'Oh, never mind,' Anna says, stepping off the lane. Her ball is only a few centimetres from the hole, and when she reaches the green she spreads her arms wide and says to Johan: 'Okay, Obersturmbannführer – what do I do now?'

'*Now* you can walk on the course, if you go carefully.'

'*Jawohl!*' Anna steps up to the ball and manages to miss the simplest of putts, which is every bit as amazing as her initial success. The ball glides past the hole and settles next to the board. Anna brandishes her club and yells: 'Cock! *Cock!*'

Johan turns to Max and Marko, expecting to exchange a glance confirming that this girl is the pits, but all he sees is Siw looking shyly at Max, who is clearly amused, and Marko grinning like Zlatan Ibrahimovic after he's scored a hat trick.

Johan shakes his head and explains to Anna that she is allowed to move the ball one club length away from the board, which earns him a Nazi salute.

2

Sometimes Siw is embarrassed by Anna in social situations, because her language can be rather colourful. There are a couple more shouts of 'Cock!' before she finally manages to nudge the ball into the hole. Fortunately the boys don't seem to mind – apart from Johan. Siw has to admit that Anna is right: he really does look at her with utter contempt, which arouses Siw's protective instincts.

As Anna moves on, Johan says: 'Take the ball out of the hole! Don't you know *anything*?'

Before Anna can come up with a retort, Siw steps in. 'We've never done this before, okay? You need to be a little more patient.'

'Yes,' Max says. 'Calm down, Johan.'

A spark of warmth begins to glow in Siw's chest, just below her heart. Max took her side against his friend. She can't work out why Johan is his friend – they're so different. Although so are she and Anna, to be fair. Siw would rather lose a little finger than stand there yelling sexual words in a public place.

Johan refrains from further comment and positions himself at the starting point. His stroke is as straight as Anna's, but unlike her, he sinks the ball with his first putt. Siw would have been both delighted and surprised if she'd achieved such a feat, but Johan doesn't even smile as he retrieves his ball.

Marko's turn. Even though he's from a different planet, Siw can't help being charmed by that smile. The guy is a real heartbreaker, but that would mean giving away her heart to be broken, and she has no intention of doing that, it's Max she . . .

Stop right now, you're being ridiculous.

Even though Max isn't from a different planet, appearance-wise

252

he's from a different . . . tribe than her. But she likes the way he looks at her, the way he takes her side. She is grateful for the crumbs from his table.

Marko measures the shot and whacks the ball. It flies through the air several centimetres off the ground, passes over the board and disappears in the long grass. He turns to the others with an expression that clearly says *what the fuck?*

'This isn't normal golf,' Max informs him. 'Your club is not a driver.'

'No,' Johan agrees. 'But he's ended up in the rough.'

Max laughs and Siw also laughs tentatively, although she didn't understand the joke. She catches Anna's teasing look out of the corner of her eye and determinedly ignores her.

'Cock!' Marko yells, which makes Anna burst into exaggerated laughter, enabling Siw to return that look.

3

'Cock!'

Anna could have clapped her hands with delight, partly because Marko has picked up her expression, and partly because she gets to hear him say that word. Sweet Jesus, what she wouldn't give to undo his belt and push her hand down the waistband of his trousers and . . . But she doesn't clap her hands, she merely cackles, which makes Marko raise his eyebrows and fire off that smile. *Sweet Jesus.*

Regardless of what Siw thinks, Anna isn't completely stupid when it comes to Marko. She knows perfectly well that she doesn't have a chance with a guy like him, but that doesn't mean she can't enjoy playing the game, and she's pleased that he's on the same page.

He realises that she's keen on him and he's toying with her, giving her the eye from time to time, playing along. It's fine, and however unlikely it might be, the possibility of a mercy fuck can't be ruled out completely. Sweet Jesus.

Marko spends some time searching in the grass with his arse in the air. Anna catches herself staring at him like an idiot; her tongue isn't quite hanging out, but almost. She forces herself to look away and catches sight of Herr Obersturmbannführer, whose gaze is also fixed on Marko. When Johan becomes aware of Anna's attention he grimaces and focuses on the score sheet, which, of course, he has taken responsibility for in his capacity as organiser.

Marko finds his ball, returns to the start and tees off again – with less force this time, but still hard enough for the ball to slam into the first obstacle and roll back. He does it again, just as hard and nowhere near straight. Hopeless.

'Stupid fucking game!'

Marko's lips are compressed into a thin line as he tries again and again, sometimes sending the ball to the left, sometimes to the right.

'I think that's eight,' Johan says eventually, and Marko responds by hurling his club into the trees.

'We have to return the—' Johan ventures.

'Shut the fuck up,' Marko says, stomping off in the direction of the copse. 'I'll buy them some new clubs. *Proper* clubs.'

Anna can't help smiling. Nice to know he isn't quite perfect. There are cracks, and what is it Siw often says? The cracks let the light in.

4

Marko is fuming as he stumbles around among the fir trees searching for his club. He *hates* losing, and if Max is only half as good as Johan, then he's going to get his butt whipped. Why won't the fucking ball go in a straight line when he hits it straight on? Somewhere in the recesses of his seething brain he knows perfectly well that he is not hitting the ball straight, otherwise it wouldn't behave that way, but that's not how it seems. As far as he can see he is delivering the perfect stroke, but the little red bastard ball has a will of its own that sends in cannoning into the obstacle.

He finds the club, which doesn't seem to have suffered from its flight through the air. He leans against a tree, tries to calm down. If it hadn't been for the visit to the house with Goran and Laura, he might be able to cope with this more easily. He's far from stable.

The only fun aspect of the game is Anna. She is behaving exactly the same as those girls in his youth – that teasing, open flirtation that he enjoys responding to, without any obligations. She is far below the acceptable level, and it would take a desert island and an entire bottle of strong alcohol for him to even think about going there.

He has two friends with benefits in town, girls he arranges to meet at some club. He pays for a few drinks, then it's back to his place for a round of athletic sex with constant changes of position in his Hästens bed. The two of them are more or less identical – both twenty-five, with long medium-blonde hair. Both eight out of ten, while Anna is a maximum four, so . . . no.

Marko places the club on his shoulder like a rifle and blinks. He can't actually remember either of the girls' names right now. He heads back to the course to see Max retrieving his ball from the hole.

'How many strokes?' Marko asks.

'One.'

'Sorry?'

'Hole in one.'

Marko rubs a hand over his eyes. Seventeen holes to go.

5

Max is well aware of Marko's competitive instinct, particularly where the two of them are concerned, and at school it was stimulating to have someone on his own level against whom he could measure himself. Looking at Marko's tortured expression right now, he wishes he could do something. He hadn't known that Marko was *so* bad; it wouldn't even help if Max gave away a couple of shots just to be kind, and besides . . .

The deep satisfaction he feels after the hole in one makes Max realise how much he wants to impress Siw, show how good he is at minigolf. What an idiot. When did a girl last fall for a guy because of his skills with a minigolf club?

Hang on a minute . . .

Does he want Siw to *fall* for him? He might have had a word with Johan because of the way he spoke about Siw, but she is very fat, and he finds it difficult to imagine himself embracing that wobbling mound of flesh. But there's something about her aura that makes him want to get closer to her. Maybe they can become friends, nothing more?

'You're very good,' Siw says.

'Just luck,' Max replies.

'I don't believe that,' she says with a cautious smile. Max returns it and thinks, *Marko's a multi-millionaire, for fuck's sake – he deserves to get beaten at something.* Max is determined to play to the best of his ability.

'Your turn.' Siw sighs, says, 'Oh dear,' and places her ball down. She doesn't strike it as hard as Marko, but her aim is equally crooked. The club moves sideways the second before it meets the ball, sending it repeatedly into the obstacle.

After the fourth stroke Max goes up to her and says: 'Try this. Stand here instead – some people find it helps.' He shows her how to position herself on the other side of the ball and hit it with a backhand. He gently takes her by the shoulders and moves her a fraction closer to the ball. 'Try now. And allow the movement of the club to follow through.'

Siw pushes her hair out of her eyes and goes for it. The ball hits the edge of the opening in the obstacle, and she nods to Max. The next time the ball goes through, misses the hole by a hair's breadth, rebounds off the board and rolls in. Siw flings her arms out, opens her eyes wide, then shouts: 'Yay!' with a smile Max has never seen before.

'So you like *Friends* too?' he asks.

'I love *Friends*.'

'How many?' Johan wants to know, his pen hovering over the score sheet.

'Six,' Max says, and Johan makes a note.

6

The final result: Max: 35 (second best of the year), Johan: 37, Siw: 63, Anna: 72, Marko: 88. After messing up on the next two holes, Marko decided to play the fool, holding the club with one hand, behind his back, closing his eyes and generally refusing to take part in the competition. Now they're sitting at a table outside the clubhouse with ice creams.

'That was fun,' Siw says to Max as she nibbles on her choc ice. 'After you showed me the trick with the backhand . . . Now I know how to do it.'

'Stupid fucking game,' Marko says. 'Completely meaningless.'

'And what games would you designate as meaningful?' asks Johan. He has already finished his Piggelin pear-flavoured lolly.

'Designate,' Marko mocks him, waving his Daim cone in the air. 'I would *designate* Mikado as meaningful. Pass the Pigs, Go Fish – any fucking thing but this.'

'No doubt you're an absolute star at Go Fish?' Anna says.

'I could beat the lot of you, but I have to go.' Marko swallows the last of his Daim. 'I'm around for a few days – I'll be in touch. And girls – how about Tuesday?'

At some point Anna had mentioned that she and Siw go to the gym, which prompted Marko to ask what kind of training they do. Anna couldn't tell him. Okay, so which muscle groups did they focus on? No idea. Marko had offered to join them for a session, act as their personal trainer and demonstrate a few exercises that would make a good combination – an offer that Anna enthusiastically accepted before Siw could object.

Max checks his phone. 'There's a raid at the Frans Lundman memorial in ten minutes. Anyone coming?'

'I have to get back to work,' Johan replies. 'There's a league game. Plus, I haven't got a raid pass, if you remember.'

'I can come,' Siw offers. 'If that's okay.'

'Of course. Perfect. But we need to make a move right now.'

Siw gives Anna a warning glance, but there is nothing to worry about there. Anna stays where she is, licking her ice lolly, and says: 'Have a lovely time.'

Max and Siw hurry off towards Society Park, leaving Anna and Johan alone together. Anna leans casually against one of the beams supporting the corrugated plastic roof and says: 'So, you fancy Marko too'.

Johan stares at her as she slides the lolly in and out of her mouth. He frowns. 'What the hell are you talking about?'

'Oh, come on – it's obvious.'

'Look who's talking.' Johan holds up his thumb and forefinger, less than a centimetre apart. 'You were this close to humping his leg.'

'If only!' Anna says, placing her hand over her heart and fluttering her eyelashes. 'But at least I wasn't trying to hide it – unlike you. You've definitely got the hots for him. What? Didn't you realise?'

Johan is scowling at Anna now as she continues to suck on the dwindling lolly, a trickle of saliva running from one corner of her mouth. He shakes his head. 'You're crazy. I'm going now.'

'Mmm.' Anna winks at him. 'Going for a wank, maybe.'

Johan gets up so quickly that his foot gets stuck and he almost falls over. Anna's mocking laughter follows him out into the street and continues to echo inside his head all the way to the bowling hall. *What a fucking bitch.*

✶

During the past few days a dense darkness has settled over Harry Boström. He has bathed Tosse, but the disgusting smell still lingers on the dog's fur. It seems to Harry that the stench is the smell of his own lonely and futile life. When he attempted to bath the dog yet again, Tosse growled and snapped at him, which has never happened before. Since then Tosse has

259

kept himself to himself, and growls whenever Harry comes anywhere near him. Harry has reached the limit of what is bearable, and he is surprised at how little hesitation he feels as he takes out a plastic carrier bag and a roll of duct tape. He sits down in the armchair, places the bag over his head and wraps the tape tightly around his neck. Only when he begins to sink into unconsciousness does he remember that he has forgotten to put out any food for Tosse. But by then it is too late.

DON'T GO TO STOCKHOLM

I

When Max and Marko moved to Stockholm to study at the School of Economics, Johan was left alone in Norrtälje. He worked at a leisure centre for a few months, until he grew tired of all those shrieking, demanding kids. Then he got a job as a cleaner at the local hospital until he grew tired of all those lonely old people constantly asking for help. He spent a lot of time online, and that was when his eyes were opened to alternative media.

He was nineteen years old, and had no idea what he wanted to do with his life. On top of this, his mother was heading for one of her difficult periods, and was getting very little help. Johan's deep-seated hatred towards the council was reignited, and he walked around with a constantly burning rage inside him.

Since the divorce his father had made a career in property, and lived in a four-room apartment on Skånegatan with his partner Kristina and their seven-year-old son. Johan had visited a few times and knew they had a room dedicated to his father's collection of ice hockey games.

He called and explained the situation. His dad wasn't exactly thrilled, but said they could give it a go, so in the spring of 2009 Johan left Norrtälje for the Södermalm district of Stockholm. His mother was devastated when he told her, but Johan steeled himself and turned a deaf ear. He had to get away from Norrtälje, otherwise he would drown in a sea of bitterness.

He got a job at the Tomteboda mail sorting office, where all that anyone expected of him was to put the right letter in the right compartment. It was a solitary occupation that required no thought whatsoever, and it suited him perfectly.

As soon as he had installed himself in the apartment on Skånegatan, he got in touch with Max and Marko to tell them what had happened. Marko had to study, but Johan and Max met up for a few cheap beers.

'So what are you planning to do with your life?' Max asked as he sipped his fourth beer.

'Something will turn up.'

'But surely you must have *some* kind of ambition?'

The way Max talked had changed during the six months he'd spent at the School of Economics. The Roslagen accent was still there, but he pronounced words as if he were reading a written text, ditching contractions and slang.

The fact that their level of ambition was so different had created a divide between the two of them, a divide that was hard to bridge now that their frames of reference were no longer the same. There was one thing that Johan wanted to do, but it was kind of embarrassing because it was so unrealistic. However, he felt compelled to reveal it so that Max wouldn't think he was satisfied with his current existence.

'I'd like to write.'

'Write what?'

'Oh, you know. Stories.'

'Novels?'

Johan couldn't quite bring himself to utter that impossible word, but now Max had done it for him. 'Mmm.'

Max's face lit up. 'You never mentioned this before!'

'It's a recent idea.'

While writing on the alternative forums Johan had discovered a talent for expressing himself. Killer comparisons and neat sentences came easily to him, and he often received applauding emojis and lots of shares when he wrote about integration policy and the way the country accepted refugees.

He had also written a few short stories, and found that it was harder when he didn't have a set theme to kick against. However, he was very pleased with one of them, about a man with learning difficulties who kills his council social worker then drowns himself in the river.

That was why Johan liked his job at Tomteboda. No one – not children, old people or anyone else – made any claim on his mental capacity. As long as he did what he was supposed to do he was left to himself and the world of his imagination, a considerably more exciting place than the blue-grey sorting office. At the end of the working day he would jot down the ideas that had come to him, and sometimes he would turn them into stories. He had never shown them to anyone else.

'So, how are you planning to move this forward?' Max asked.

'I'm not. I just write.'

'But you have to . . . I mean, I have no idea how you go about it, but surely you have to . . .'

Johan looked out over Fatbur Park and shook his head. Max would never understand. Max was programmed to see life as a ladder, there to be climbed. It was important to set goals, tick them off one at a time until you reached the point where you wanted to be. As far as Johan was concerned, life was more like a lift: you never knew on which floor it would spew out its passengers. You could press the button for the top floor and still be ejected in the basement. All you could do was step inside and hope for the best.

'I don't have to do anything,' he said. 'I'm just going to carry on.'

Max nodded, but behind his slightly tipsy look Johan glimpsed a sense of disappointment or a diminished respect that Max would never express out loud. It was at that moment and in that look that Johan realised they were doomed to drift apart.

2

A week or so later Johan managed to arrange to see the constantly busy Marko. They'd decided to meet at Espresso House on Sveavägen after Johan finished work, a stone's throw from the School of Economics so that Marko could rush back as soon as he'd finished his coffee. Johan arrived first and bagged a good spot with a couple of armchairs.

To Johan's chagrin, when Marko arrived he was accompanied by the most beautiful girl Johan had ever seen. It took him a couple of seconds to recognise Maria, whom he hadn't seen for six months. She'd looked good then, but now she'd changed her hairstyle and make-up and was pretty much perfect. He noticed how people's eyes were drawn to her.

By this time he had accepted his inclination and had even acted upon it a few times, so he felt no sexual attraction towards Maria. However, beauty is always beauty, with its devastating, uplifting effect, and his stomach flipped over as he stood up to greet her.

'You know Maria,' Marko said in the apologetic tone of voice he always used when talking about his sister.

'Absolutely.' Johan didn't know how to behave. It felt presumptuous to think he had the right to touch the sublime, to give Mona Lisa a pat on the shoulder and say: 'How *you* doin'?' Fortunately Maria came to his rescue by giving him a bear hug and saying: 'Hi, bro.'

Johan returned the hug and the awkwardness disappeared. For some years he had been little Maria's only companion. They'd played chess and made up stories about dragons, cannibalistic princesses and sadistic princes, where everyone died in the end. When Marko wasn't home, Johan even forced himself to play with dolls. Those games also frequently spiralled into violence – no thanks to Johan. It was this shared past that mattered, nothing else.

When Johan sat down he discovered that he felt much more comfortable with Maria than with Marko, who always triggered that bubbling anxiety inside him.

'What are you doing here?' he asked Maria as she sat down in an armchair and crossed her legs with deliberate elegance.

'She's moved to Stockholm,' Marko informed him before Maria could answer. 'Thinks she's going to be an actress.'

Maria turned those lethal green eyes on her brother and drawled: 'Marko. Cappuccino.'

Marko raised an eyebrow at Johan, who said he'd have the same.

Marko headed for the counter, with Maria's pulverising gaze firmly fixed on him.

'An actress,' Johan said.

Maria smiled. 'Yes,' she said, with no trace of a drawl. 'I've got a really good chance of getting a big role in a movie.'

'But . . . do you have any training?'

'No.' Maria fired off a smile, which told Johan everything he needed to know about the reasons behind her success. 'I'm a natural. Or so they say.'

'Wow. Congratulations. I hope it works out.'

Maria nodded and lowered her voice. 'Marko thinks I'm completely stupid and naive, but I do realise there's a lot involved, and that nothing is guaranteed. But you have to take your chances when they come along, don't you?'

'Absolutely. Go for it!'

'What are you up to?'

Johan told her about his job, and Maria was considerably more interested than Max had been. She asked about postcodes, the different stages of the sorting process, and transportation by rail. She listened, laughed, told him a few stories of her own, and by the time Marko returned with their coffees it was as if Johan and Maria had been on the verge of revisiting the tale of the princess who ate newborn babies morning, noon and night. As soon as they caught sight of Marko's supercilious expression, they both burst out laughing.

Marko sighed and asked wearily: 'What?'

'Nothing,' Maria replied. 'Nothing you'd learn at the School of Economics, anyway.'

The conversation became less easy with Marko there, and when Maria asked Johan if he'd like to meet up with her one evening, he accepted with alacrity. Marko frowned.

'You won't be drinking, will you?' he said to Maria.

'I will. I'll be drinking fizzy pop. And raspberry juice.'

They met up a week later at Cliff Barnes on Norrtullsgatan. The bar didn't admit anyone under twenty, and the doorman seemed to want to see Maria's ID. She dazzled him with her smile and a warm 'Hi!' as if he were very dear to her, and in the ensuing confusion they slipped inside.

Johan ordered a beer and Maria a mojito, pronouncing it in the Spanish way where the *j* became an *h*, which suggested she'd done it before. There were no tables free, so they stood at the generous bar and picked up the conversation where they'd left off.

Maria told him about the modelling she'd done, and the film she was hoping to appear in. It was a crime thriller based on books Johan had never heard of. Maria would be playing the daughter of the detective inspector who was the main character, a single father since the death of her mother. The best part was that there were *five* books in the series, and if this film went well, they would make more. In the last of the five the daughter's story was more important than the father's.

'Have you read them?' Johan asked.

'The last one,' Maria said with a laugh. 'The one where I'm the main character. But I will read the others when I have time. I'm a bit dyslexic.'

'No you're not – you're just impatient. Try the audiobooks.'

'Good idea.'

A male voice came from the side: 'Excuse me, but I just have to ask – you're a photographic model, aren't you?'

Maria didn't turn her head. 'No, but my boyfriend is, and we have things to discuss, so . . .'

Johan didn't turn his head either, but he could feel the guy's suspicious and envious eyes on him before he walked away.

In fact, it was by no means easy to sustain a conversation with Maria, because they were constantly interrupted by guys wanting to catch her attention. Whenever Johan glanced around the bar he saw men looking away or shamelessly continuing to stare at her, like the spokes attached to the hub of a wheel of hopeless desire.

After the seventh pick-up attempt Maria leaned over to Johan. 'Kiss me.'

Johan licked his lips and moved his face closer to her, then he drew back. 'Sorry. No can do.'

Maria smiled and wiggled her eyebrows. 'That's not the answer I'm used to, but okay. Can you at least stroke my cheek, then?'

'No problem.' Johan gently caressed her with the back of his hand, traced the line of her jaw with his fingers. Finally he cupped her cheek with his palm. She pressed her face against him, closed her eyes.

'I love you,' Johan said.

Maria nodded. Without opening her eyes, she said: 'And I love you. Bro.'

3

The months went by. Johan carried on sorting his letters and packages while his thoughts wandered. A number of ideas had begun to come together, forming something that could become a novel. A story about the destruction of Norrtälje. He made intermittent attempts to write it, but produced nothing more than a series of disparate scenes that were perfectly okay, but a long way from a whole book.

Life with his father and Kristina was going pretty well, even if he felt more like a lodger than a member of the family. He paid three thousand a month for food and accommodation, and consoled himself with the thought that if he really had been a lodger, then he'd found the best deal in the world.

He and his half-brother Henry got along okay. The boy wasn't the type to appreciate Johan's flair for making up stories, but he was a big Lego fan. Johan's own Lego had been a poor collection bought second-hand, while Henry had castles and pirate ships with *instructions*. Johan couldn't help feeling a certain amount of bitterness as he sat with Henry building creations that had been denied him as a child, while they listened to Allan Edwall reading Winnie-the-Pooh.

Just before the summer Johan had turned twenty, and his birthday had been celebrated with a picnic at Djurgården with Max, Marko and Maria. Barbecued chicken, potato salad and a box of white wine. Marko pretended not to notice when Maria poured herself a glass. They toasted Johan, the summer and the future. Maria's film role still hung in the balance, but she would hear for definite by September. It was a lovely day, when even Marko relaxed a little as they reminisced about the past and dreamed of what was to come. It was the last good day they would have together for a long time.

Max and Marko moved back to Norrtälje over the long holiday, and Johan was left alone again. Maria had found a job as a waitress, and spent all her spare time preparing her application to go to drama school in the autumn. Johan rambled around Stockholm, went swimming on the island of Långholmen, and had a brief relationship with an older man he met there.

The summer passed slowly, with sticky, uncomfortable days in the sorting office where the air conditioning had lost the plot and sometimes decided to spew out warm air instead of cold. Johan wore a vest top and stood there sorting the post with sweat pouring from his armpits. He counted the days until Max and Marko's return. He could have taken a day trip to Norrtälje, but he was afraid of bumping into his mother and having to listen to an account of the hell her life had become since he'd left her in the lurch.

In the middle of August he received a postcard from Cuba, where Max was diving with a girl called Linda. Johan had never heard of her. The date was six weeks earlier, so either Cuba's postal system was incredibly slow, or the card had swum across the Atlantic on its own.

The autumn term at the School of Economics began. Johan texted Max, but got no reply. When he eventually got hold of Marko it transpired that Max had turned up for registration, but had completely closed in on himself. All that Marko had been able to get out of him was that he'd been involved in some kind of diving accident in Cuba. The day after registration Max had failed to attend classes, and Marko hadn't seen him since.

Johan called, texted, and even wrote an actual letter, but there was no response. Eventually he tracked down Max's father's number and made a call. He answered immediately.

'Göran Bergwall!' said the authoritative voice on the other end of the line.

'Oh, hi. It's Johan, Johan Andersson, I don't know if you remember me, Max's friend from—'

'I know who you are.'

The tone of voice suggested that he had omitted an *exactly* between *know* and *who*, but Johan ignored this because he needed information. 'I was just wondering if you know anything about Max, only I haven't been able to—'

'He's at home in Norrtälje. Here.'

'Oh, right . . . How is he?'

Something of the authority slipped as Max's father let out a sigh, then said: 'He's in bed. In his room. He doesn't want to talk to anyone.'

'What's happened?'

'He won't say.'

'There was an accident, wasn't there?'

'It seems you know more than me. An accident?'

'Something to do with diving.'

'I've no idea. As I said, he's in bed. Apathetic. That's all I can tell you.'

'And what about his studies?'

This time Göran made no attempt to hide his disappointment. 'He says he's not going back. If there's nothing else . . .'

Johan paced back and forth in his room. He didn't know what to do. Max was one of the few people he had in the world. Should he go to Norrtälje? Something told him he wouldn't get past the front door.

The next few days passed in a state of anxiety; he felt completely at a loss. He did his job, but his thoughts, which normally wandered happily in all directions, were focused on Max. Cuba? A diving accident? The only kind of diving accident Johan knew about was when someone surfaced too quickly; the diver inhales compressed air containing nitrogen, which can damage the organs. But surely that wouldn't cause apathy? Or would it?

Max's postcard, sent from Maria la Gorda, had been written with delicious irony, using a plethora of the trite adjectives Max knew that Johan loved. 'Fantastic sandy beaches.' 'Marvellous little restaurants.' 'Amazing people.' The picture on the front showed

271

the hotel and a number of linked bungalows, with a cross replacing the dot over the i above one of the bungalows. 'This is where we're staying!' Nothing to indicate unhappiness or apathy, so whatever it was must have happened later.

Johan continued to text Max once a day just to show that he was thinking about him, but he never got a reply. This continued for over a week, until Johan was given something else to occupy his mind.

One night when he had gone to bed at ten because he had an early shift and had to be up at five, the doorbell rang. He heard his father's footsteps in the hallway, the sound of the door opening, a quiet conversation.

There was a knock on his door. He said: 'Come in?' pulling the covers up to his chin like a child frightened by Santa Claus. A bulky figure walked in and closed the door behind him as Johan switched on his bedside lamp.

'Marko?'

Marko was standing in the middle of the room, arms by his side, fists clenched as he chewed on his lips. His eyes were black as he stared at Johan, who was seriously scared now. What had he done to incur Marko's rage?

'What's the matter?' He couldn't quite keep his voice steady. To his relief Marko sat down on the bed instead of attacking him.

'Maria,' Marko said through clenched jaws. 'The fucking bastard who was playing her father has raped her.'

'What? When did this happen?'

Some of Marko's rage was turned on Johan. 'What the fuck does that matter? Didn't you hear what I said? She's *seventeen*. And he raped her.'

'Oh my God.'

'Exactly. Oh my God.' A terrifying calmness came over Marko's face as he leaned closer to Johan. 'Are you going to help me?'

'To . . . to do what?'

'To kill him.'

4

Earlier that same evening Marko had gone round to Maria's bedsit in Vårby Gård – a third-hand sublet – and found her drunk. When he realised she'd got into this state on her own, he refused to give up until she told him what was going on. Through slurred words and snotty sobs, the truth gradually emerged.

Two weeks ago she had been invited home by Hans Roos, the actor who was to play her father in the film, in order to go over their lines and 'get a feeling for' certain scenes. Because Maria was doing everything she could to prepare for drama school, she gratefully accepted. The coach she was working with was an ex-teacher from the Calle Flygare drama school; he was always slightly tipsy and took every opportunity to 'accidentally' stumble and grab hold of her for support in inappropriate places.

However, the forty-seven-year-old actor had a glowing career behind him. He had played major roles at the Dramaten theatre in Stockholm and in a number of films, won a Guldbagge award, presented by the Swedish Film Institute, and had even spent time in the USA, where he appeared in both TV series and movies. He was a person Maria definitely felt she could learn from.

She knew that he had a reputation as a ladies' man, not to mention a womaniser, not to mention an absolute pig, but after all, he would be playing her *father*, and if he started touching her up, she would just have to remind him of that.

He was living in a three-room apartment close to Östermalmstorg, rented through an arrangement with Dramaten. Maria's visit got off to a good start; they went over their lines and worked their way through the scenes they had together. Then it began to get terribly *warm* – Maria realised later that Roos had turned up the heating – and no, unfortunately the windows didn't open. Roos stripped down to his vest, while Maria was in a thin T-shirt.

At some point he tried strengthening a scene by gripping her shoulders; only then did she begin to grasp how vulnerable she was. The man was a good thirty centimetres taller than her, he weighed at least twice as much, and a considerable proportion of this weight was made up of muscle, which he presumably wanted to show off – hence the vest. The hands that seized her shoulders were as big as her face.

As if Roos had become aware of the same thing, his skin began to flush red in the heat. He licked the sweat from his upper lip and began to drop hints – about how well Maria could do in the film industry if she made sure she was nice to the right people, and did them certain . . . favours. Roos knew this from his own experience, he had helped lots of girls in the past; did she know for example that . . . He mentioned a name, and Maria said she thought it was time she left. Roos wouldn't hear of it; they'd only just started. Wouldn't she like a glass of wine? Maria had no intention of getting drunk or allowing her drink to be spiked, so she said thanks but no thanks and began to put on her sweater. Roos made a playful movement to stop her. Maria tugged harder to pull it down to her waist, the playful movement became something else, and then everything happened very fast.

In three seconds he changed from a seedy creep into a wild animal with only one goal in mind. He tore off her clothes, and when she tried to scream he clamped his hand so hard over her mouth that her top lip split. He threw her down on the sofa on her stomach, pushed her face into a cushion and thrust into her. Maria's mouth was filled with the taste of blood, she couldn't breathe, and she felt as if she was going to break in two as he pounded into her body with his full weight.

For over a minute Maria thought she was going to die from the pain, lack of oxygen or humiliation. Then he grunted, disgusting slime trickled between her legs and the grip on the back of her head loosened, enabling her to turn her head and take a few gasping breaths. She closed her eyes and stayed where she was, breathing as her vagina burned with revulsion.

Then she smelled smoke. Roos was sitting naked in an armchair smoking a cigarette to celebrate his achievement, gazing at Maria from beneath half-closed eyelids.

'You do understand, don't you?' he said. 'You understand that you don't tell anyone about this, because if you do, your film career will be over before it's even started. You're a smart girl – I'm sure you get it. On the other hand, if you keep your mouth shut and maybe consider doing this again under more . . . mutually agreeable circumstances, then . . .'

The hand holding the cigarette shot up in the air, demonstrating how Maria's career would take off like a rocket, heading for the stars. He sat there while she got dressed, and he was still sitting there when she crept out of the front door, shaking and with hunched shoulders.

It had taken Marko two hours to tease the story out of his weeping sister, while he persuaded her to drink four big glasses of water.

Then he'd helped her to bed, by which stage she'd sobered up enough to take his hand and say: 'Marko, you're not to do anything.'

'Like what?'

'You're not to do anything – promise me.'

Marko had promised, then left her. When he got out into the courtyard he'd punched a tree so hard that he'd broken his little finger.

5

Marko held up his right hand. The little finger had swollen to the same size as his thumb, and was bent at an unnatural angle.

'Okay,' Johan said. 'I'm in.'

Marko nodded. 'There's no one else I can ask, because the thing with Maria is . . . she . . .' Marko lowered his head. His shoulders shook, and Johan realised he was crying. He sat up, put his arm around Marko and rested his forehead on his friend's cheek.

'Shit,' Marko whispered, still weeping silently.

'Yes. Shit.'

Marko's tears ran down Johan's forehead and cheek, then found their way into his mouth. The taste made Johan start crying too. Images filled his mind, images of Maria. His Kid Sister. He straightened up, wiped his eyes and said: 'On one condition. We're not actually going to kill anybody. I can't be a murderer.'

'Not even for Maria's sake?'

'Maybe if I didn't have a choice. But I do.'

'I don't feel as if I have a choice.'

'Okay, but in that case, I can't help you.'

Marko stared at the floor, his jaws working. After a while he said: 'You're right. Plus, he won't suffer. If he dies.'

'We'll just fuck him over.'

'Mmm.'

'How?'

'What do you mean, how?'

'I've seen the bastard in films. He's a big guy, so we need to make sure we have some kind of . . . advantage.'

Marko was well-built back then, but he was a long way from the fit, strong man he would become, and Johan was as skinny as ever. If they simply attacked the man, there was every chance that he would make mincemeat of them.

'You mean a weapon,' Marko said.

'I mean a weapon. Not a gun, but definitely . . . a weapon.'

Johan slipped out of bed and hurried over to the hook where his dressing gown hung. He felt shy in his nakedness, and quickly tied the belt before returning and sitting down next to Marko, who suddenly did something that took Johan by surprise. He looked Johan in the eye and asked: 'Have you got the hots for her?'

'What? No, of course not.'

'Everyone else seems to feel that way.'

'Not me. But I do love her.'

Marko nodded, apparently satisfied with the answer. Johan had one more condition for his participation in the destruction of the bastard who had attacked Maria: they had to be masked. He was willing to take a risk, but he wanted to know there was at least a reasonable chance of getting away with it. Marko reluctantly agreed, and after a while admitted that Johan was right. They couldn't let the pig have the satisfaction of ruining their lives by sending them to jail.

They started planning. Time, location, weapon. Marko's original impulse had been to rush straight round to the apartment and do the deed, but something had made him go to Johan first. Now his burning rage had settled to a steady flame of hatred, he could see that this was a good thing. The chances of fucking the guy over properly were greater if the execution itself wasn't completely chaotic.

As they sat side by side, weighing up the pros and cons of different methods, Johan felt a stab of shame as he realised he was enjoying himself. In spite of the horrific trauma Maria had suffered, it was lovely to sit here with Marko weaving a fantasy, just like he and Max had done when they were kids. The enjoyment factor plummeted when Johan forced himself to recognise that this was for real, something they were actually going to do. Plus, Maria. Her face pushed down into the cushion. The panic. His Kid Sister. The last scrap of enjoyment disappeared.

After half an hour they had come up with a rudimentary plan, to be put into effect three days later. They got to their feet. Before Marko left, he spread his arms wide and gave Johan a long, warm hug. Johan relaxed and allowed himself to revel in Marko's embrace for a moment.

'For our sister,' Marko murmured.

'Yes. For our sister.'

6

The following days gave Johan a greater understanding of Raskolnikov in *Crime and Punishment*. He wandered around in a constant state of slight dizziness, mentally rehearsing what they were going to do, running through the process from different angles and with different outcomes. As he mechanically sorted the post, his normal fantasies disappeared and were replaced by images of the man's face and body, the inevitable sounds, the feeling in his hands. When he went to bed the reel continued to run and he found it difficult to sleep, which made the next day even more dreamlike. And so on.

On the designated day he was in full Raskolnikov mode, brooding over not only his ability to carry out the deed, but whether it was really *justified*. On the latter point he was more successful than Rodion Romanovich Raskolnikov, because Hans Roos definitely deserved what was coming to him, unlike the hapless moneylender. It was, however, harder to work out whether he himself was up to the challenge. He had never struck another person with the aim of causing serious harm. He wasn't at all sure that he would be able to do what was required of him when it came to the crunch.

He longed to see Maria and he was scared of seeing Maria. Scared of what the rape had done to her, scared that he would reveal his and Marko's plans as soon as he looked her in the eye. Having got so far in his self-analysis, he began to examine his motives. Was he really doing this for Maria's sake, when he knew it wasn't what she wanted? Was he doing it for himself? For Marko? Like Marko, he carried a burning hatred towards the bastard who had behaved so appallingly, but wouldn't it be better to persuade Maria to report him to the police?

As evening approached Johan had accepted the dreadful truth: the main reason why he was prepared to risk several years behind bars was because he wanted to do something major with Marko, something they would always share. It would have been better if they could have built a house with their own hands and lived there happily ever after, but in the absence of such a project, grievous bodily harm was the only option on the table.

Marko and Johan met beneath the Mushroom on Stureplan at nine o'clock. They'd checked that Roos was appearing in *A Midsummer Night's Dream* at Dramaten, and that the play finished at about ten. They walked up the hill towards Sibyllegatan side by side. Marko kept his arms stiffly by his sides, as if he were marching. The little finger on his right hand was bandaged. 'What did you get?' Johan asked.

It was almost dark on that late August evening, and there wasn't a soul in sight. Marko shook one arm and a long object slid out of his sleeve. Johan took it and stared at it. He was less than impressed.

'A *rounders* bat? I thought we said a baseball bat?'

'Too big. Hard to conceal. And we're in Sweden, after all. We don't play baseball.'

Johan swung the metre-long club and found it was heavier than the ones they'd used in school, but it was no baseball bat.

'So, are you using the girl's bat?'

'I've never heard of it.'

'The flat version.'

'Oh no, I threw those away. I bought two sets.'

'And the balls?' Johan asked, pushing the bat up his own sleeve as they walked along.

'I kept those. For the tumble dryer.'

Johan's laughter had more than a touch of hysteria.

They had checked out the area around the actor's apartment block in advance and found a good place to lie in wait, behind some bushes in a small park. They could see the main door, but no one could see them from the street. The only drawback was that their chosen location stank of piss and dog shit. They crouched down next to a wall and Marko produced a tin of shoe polish, which they smeared around their eyes before pulling on balaclavas.

Marko looked absolutely terrifying, with the whites of his eyes surrounded by shimmering black polish in the glow of a street lamp. Johan assumed he was equally alarming, but asked anyway: 'How do I look?'

'Like a fucking monster!' It was strange to hear Marko's normal voice emanating from that dark, threatening bulk. 'Fuck, Johan. How did we end up here?'

'You know what I think?' Johan said. 'If we're going to do this, it's best if we don't say anything. If we talk, there's a significant risk that we'll realise how ridiculous this is, then we'll start to have doubts, and then . . .'

'Got it. But I won't have any doubts. That bastard raped Maria. Remember that. Keep it at the forefront of your mind. *Raped*.'

'I know. But still.'

'I'm not saying another word.'

They put on the thin gloves they'd bought specially and waited. At about ten o'clock an elderly lady appeared. She produced a tiny dog from her handbag and placed it on the ground next to the bushes. The dog trotted towards Johan and Marko and cocked its leg, but stiffened when it spotted them and beat a hasty retreat, whimpering. The owner picked it up and consoled it, put it back in her bag and went on her way.

Cars drove past, people came and went with growing infrequency. Johan and Marko changed position to avoid stiffening up, yawned, checked the time on their phones. Johan sat cross-legged on the ground, visualising the sequence of events yet again. First Marko would hit the bastard across the back of the head, then when he wobbled Johan would slam the bat into his knees. Hopefully this would bring him down, enabling them to work on him more systematically.

It was almost one o'clock by the time Roos appeared. He was rather unsteady on his feet; no doubt he had been to the Theatre Bar or some other shithole, drinking with his fucking colleagues. Johan's heart beat faster as he clutched the rounders bat and thought, *The line. Now I'm going to cross the line.* It didn't strike him until he was faced with the real thing. He was about to do something that would make him a different person. A person who had committed an act of violence. If he was capable of it.

Their target had almost reached the door. There was no one else around. Marko and Johan exchanged glances and nodded. It seemed to Johan that his heart was beating so loudly it must be audible on the other side of the street. Crouching down, they ran towards Roos, who was mumbling to himself as he fiddled with the keypad. He really was a big guy.

As they drew closer Johan saw something that Marko had presumably missed. Roos had entered the code and turned to face the door, where Marko's silhouette was reflected in the glass. That must have been what made him duck when Marko swung the bat, which passed over his head and smashed into the entry phone, where a light started flashing.

Roos seemed to have sobered up in a second. He yelled, 'What the fuck!', ripped the bat out of Marko's hands with surprising ease, raised it high in the air and shouted: 'Got a death wish, have you, sonny?'

There was no time for consideration. The man was a few centimetres taller than Johan; there was no way Johan could hit him over the head. As Roos took a step towards Marko, Johan hurled himself forward, brought the bat over his shoulder with considerable force, and slammed it into the man's hateful cock.

He'd never been particularly good at rounders, but occasionally he played the perfect stroke which led to a home run. This was one of those strokes. If the man's testicles had been a ball, they would have gone flying across the pitch, on their way into the forest. *Double* home run.

All the fight went out of Roos. He groaned, dropped the bat and sank to his knees, doubled over in pain. Marko retrieved his bat and raised it above Roos, who was now wriggling around like a snake on a griddle pan.

'Hello?'

Marko paused, looked around. Who had spoken, and why had they said something as banal as *Hello* in the current situation?

'Hello? Is anyone there?'

The voice was coming from the entry phone, and could well have belonged to the lady who'd taken her dog out. Johan and Marko looked at each other. They'd decided not to say a word, partly to ensure that they couldn't be identified by their voices at a later stage, so in silence Marko shattered one of Roos's kneecaps, which of course made him howl with pain.

'Hello? What's going on?'

Johan was still caught up in the endorphin rush from saving Marko, and he swung the bat over and over again at Roos's shoulder until he heard a satisfying crack. Roos shielded his head with his hands and shouted: 'Help! They're trying to kill me!'

A silhouette appeared briefly at a window on the second floor. Someone was bound to call the police, which meant their time was limited. Marko bashed the back of the man's hands repeatedly until one hand came away from the head, enabling Marko to stamp on his fingers until they were jutting out in all directions. Roos screamed and screamed, sometimes with words, sometimes without. *Please don't kill me! Don't you know who I am?*

283

Yes, Johan thought. *We certainly do.*

Marko gestured to Johan, then pointed to his face. Johan spread his hands wide. *What do you mean?* Marko pointed to his face again, then to the man. *Ah.* Johan felt as if he had gone crazy; he was definitely well over the line, along with the Mad Hatter and Hells Angels. *An actor's principal tool and so on.*

With the paradoxical calm of the insane he forced the man's other hand away from his head, and with their combined strength he and Marko forced him onto his back.

A hundred kilos. At least.

Marko stared at the man, his eyes full of hatred, and prepared to deliver the first blow. Roos whimpered: 'No, no . . .', raising a hand to protect himself. Marko knocked it aside and brought the bat down on his mouth. There was a crunching and clattering as teeth were torn out or broken, and blood began to pour from his lips. Marko hit him on the nose, which also broke. More blood. As Marko raised the bat again, flashing blue lights appeared at the end of the street.

Johan thought Marko was about to finish off with a potentially fatal blow to the forehead, but amazingly enough he pulled himself together when Johan held up a warning finger. They both threw down the bats and ran.

They raced along Sibyllegatan and turned into Kommendörsgatan, pulling off their balaclavas and using them to wipe around their eyes. They didn't slow their pace until they reached Humlegården, where they sank down in the shadow of the Linnaeus monument.

They looked at each other. Marko still had black polish around his eyes and his sweaty hair was standing on end; he reminded Johan of a badly turned out emo. Johan gave him a loony smile, and Marko smiled back. Johan was buzzing, he was on the other side of the line where anything was possible, so he took Marko's face between his hands and kissed him. Marko kissed him back.

A desire stronger than he could have imagined took hold of Johan. He was rock hard in a second and began to fumble around with Marko's clothes while moving his tongue inside Marko's mouth. Marko's lips stiffened and he pushed Johan away.

'Stop it! What are you doing?'

'But . . . I thought . . . You kissed . . .'

'The heat of the moment, man. Get a grip – what the fuck is wrong with you?'

'I just . . . I thought . . .'

'Well, you thought wrong. Cool down, for fuck's sake!'

All that buzzing, burning beauty inside Johan was extinguished and sank like a meteorite hitting the ocean. He lowered his head and leaned back against the plinth. After a minute or so Marko turned to him and said: 'Thanks. You saved my arse, but that doesn't mean you get it, okay? Thanks. You're my brother. But from now on, we never speak about anything that's happened tonight. None of it happened. *None of it*. Is that clear?'

7

They got away with it. The attack on Hans Roos made all the front pages, and there was a lot of speculation about the *unknown assailants*. A witness had described one of them as tall and power-fully built, the other smaller and skinnier, but it was hardly enough to identify Marko and Johan. And even if Roos linked what had happened to him with what he'd done to Maria, he wasn't going to go to the police and say: 'The thing is, officer, I raped a girl a couple of weeks ago and . . .'

However, one person who did make the link was Maria. The following day, as soon as the news broke, she called Johan. He'd barely said hello before she asked: 'Was it you two?'

'Was what us two?'

'Don't bother. Was it you?'

'I've no idea what you're talking about.'

'It was you. I know it was you.'

'If you say so. But I still don't know what you mean.'

There was a brief silence. He could hear Maria breathing hard through her nose, then she said: 'Fuck you. There's no film now.'

'Because . . . ?'

'I ought to fucking report you.'

'Are you going to?'

'No, of course not. Fucking idiots.'

She ended the call. Johan remained sitting on his bed, passing his phone from one hand to the other. The feverish enthusiasm that had gripped him after he'd crossed the line and done the unthinkable had disappeared when Marko rejected him. The emptiness had come creeping over him as he slumped by the Linnaeus monument with burning cheeks, and now it had him in its power.

The preparatory fantasy images to which he had devoted himself in the days before the deed had been replaced by memories, which strangely seemed less real than the fantasies. Maybe it was partly because Roos was an actor, and therefore the whole thing was more like a film, but he didn't think so. What Johan had done was so alien to him that it wasn't *realistic* for him to take part in that scene, so in his internal film he merely floated around like a ghostly witness.

It was almost funny. He had participated in a violent assault on another human being, but he felt not a trace of shame or regret. On the other hand, the fact that he had kissed and then tried . . . with Marko . . . he was so ashamed that he could barely bring himself to think about it. How funny was that?

Little more had been said the previous night. After they'd carefully wiped around their eyes and buried the balaclavas and gloves under a bush, they had walked to the subway station at Hötorget, where they had parted with a hug that felt very awkward to Johan.

However much they told themselves that the events of the evening hadn't happened, Johan suspected and feared that they would leave their mark on his and Marko's relationship for a long time to come. Maybe forever.

*

A man has just left his shoes to be soled at the cobbler's next to the Little Bridge. When he comes out of the shop he remains standing for a while with his hands resting on the railing that runs alongside the river. He thinks about the mess in the cobbler's workshop, and becomes convinced that all the man is going to do is to sabotage his favourite shoes. He goes back and says he's changed his mind.

WHEN I WALK BESIDE YOU

It's nice to be alone with Max, of course, to walk beside him on the way to a Pokémon raid as if it were the most natural thing in the world. The only problem is that it makes Siw intensely aware of her physique. During her normal everyday life she has come to terms with her shape, and doesn't think about it any more than is necessary. But now . . . She can feel the rolls of fat spilling over the waistline of her trousers, she can hear the swishing sound as her thighs rub together, and she can see her breasts billowing at the lower edge of her field of vision. At the moment she is anything but comfortable with the way she looks.

Powder, she thinks. *It's going to have to be powder from now on.*

Not that she imagines she has a chance with Max, but let this be her inspiration to finally get her weight down. It is six months since she ordered a substantial quantity of low-calorie meal replacement powder online, and the boxes are still sitting in the cleaning cupboard waiting for inspiration to strike. And now it has.

Powder. Morning, noon and night – powder. And exercise. Yuck.

'What are you thinking about?'

Siw hasn't said anything for a while, and Max's question is so unexpected that she blurts out: 'Powder'.

'Powder?'

'Yes. Powder.'

'What kind of powder?'

'Just powder. It's a peculiar word.'

'Powder . . . Yes, now you come to mention it. Powder.'

'Then again, most words sound weird if you repeat them enough times. Powder, powder.'

Siw is relieved at having dug herself out of a hole, but at the same time the conversation has hit an embarrassingly low point. Hoping to break out of the powder loop, she asks: 'Where do you work?'

'I'm a park keeper – I look after the lawns, trees and shrubs, that kind of thing. And I deliver newspapers – *Norrtelje Tidning* – in the mornings.'

'Wow. So is the keeper's job part time?'

'No. Full time.'

'You work hard.'

'Yes. I work hard.'

From Granliden they cut through a grove of trees to reach Badstugatan, which leads down to the park. Siw pays close attention to a shrub, and thinks it's wonderful, if unexpected, that Max spends his time looking after such things.

'Can I say something?' she says, and wishes she could take back the words. Of course she can say something – they're talking, aren't they? Admittedly it's a rhetorical turn of phrase, but it's still annoying that she's so deferential and so painfully aware of how deferential she is and . . . *Enough, Siw. Get on with it.*

Max makes a vague noise indicating agreement.

'When I saw you for the first time . . . I thought you'd have a more, how shall I put it, *intellectual* profession. Don't take offence, I'm not suggesting there's anything wrong with being a park keeper. I mean, I work on the checkout at Flygfyren, for God's sake, but . . .'

Shut up, Siw.

'Mmm.' Max doesn't seem to be offended. 'That was the plan. I did a year at the Stockholm School of Economics, but . . . stuff happened, and I couldn't carry on.'

It's obvious that he doesn't want to go into detail, and Siw has no intention of pushing him. Besides, they are halfway down the hill to the Frans Lundman memorial, where a number of people from the Pokémon group are waiting.

'Can *I* say something?' Max goes on, and Siw gets a warm feeling in her tummy. She nods. 'When I saw you for the first time, I thought you were involved in something artistic. Maybe not as a job, but as an important part of your life.'

'Oh.' Siw has to turn her head away; she can feel her cheeks beginning to flush red. Max has thought about her, thought she was an artist. The only problem is that she isn't. 'Not really. I knit. Does that count?'

'Of course. As long as you suffer for your art.'

'Oh, I do!'

They have reached the group, and two boys aged about ten shout, 'Max! Max!' and rush over to him to show him a number of Pokémon with perfect IVs that they've captured. Siw watches him secretly as he crouches down next to the boys, their eyes shining when he praises them and explains which attacks they might want to change. Her lips curl in a sad little smile. *He's lovely*, she thinks. *A lovely guy. But I've got no chance.*

The raid begins. Entei is standing on his patch of grass, bellowing as he is attacked from all directions. Siw notices that someone is using Pidgey, incomprehensibly. Maybe someone who's just starting out, if such people exist. Entei falls, and the capture attempts take over. Clenched fists raised in triumph, or sighs when Entei breaks out of the last ball. Siw fires off a pile of Golden Razz Berries and manages to catch Entei on the sixth ball, after three Excellent Curveballs in a row. Max fails. The group disperses with the odd 'Thanks for today' and 'See you' and 'Take care'. Max and Siw are left on their own.

'It's a really nice group,' Siw says. 'Nice atmosphere.'

'Mmm. If the whole world was like Pokémon Go Roslagen, we wouldn't have any problems.'

They wander towards the western side of the park and the quay-side, while Max tells her about a couple of real misfits who came on the raids in the beginning and just stood on the edge of the group without speaking to anyone.

After several raids there was a word here, a sentence there, and eventually whole conversations where it transpired that one was a former heroin addict who'd lost contact with everyone he knew during the process of getting clean – on top of those who'd already died. The other had been badly bullied in school, and didn't have a single friend. Day after day, raid after raid, week after week, the two of them blossomed through being part of a social context where they were accepted and respected as *Pokémon Go* players; anything else was irrelevant. Now it was impossible to distinguish them from the rest of the group; plus, they'd become friends.

'So there you go,' Max says, standing on the edge of the quay with his hands in his pockets. 'Three cheers for Pikachu.'

Siw follows his gaze; he is staring at the empty space where the container used to be. 'What are *you* thinking about?' she asks.

'The container. What was in it.'

'People. Dead people.'

'Yes, but there was something else as well.' Max turns his head and looks searchingly into Siw's eyes. 'Wasn't there?'

OVER BLACK WATERS

3

The latrine drum has overflowed and a sludge of urine and excrement slides across the floor with the movement of the ship. How fortunate that we have run out of water, which limits the amount of urine we produce, how very fortunate. The bad news is that some people are vomiting up the small amount of fluid they have in their bodies, overwhelmed by the stench. There is a constant battle to get up to the holes and breathe in a tiny bit of air that is not suffocating. Someone is always perched on another person's shoulders gasping through the narrow opening, while others fight to get up there themselves. It is hell – I was going to say 'on earth', but it no longer feels as if we are on the earth. Everything that is a part of our existence in a real world – land, air, light, water – has been taken away from us. We are nothing more than faceless bodies waiting for a place that does not exist. Everyone in here would give an arm or a leg to be in the Limbo Dante describes. *Both* arms. And legs. Oh God, just to be able to *breathe* while being burned at the stake. We have to retain a spark of hope. This is what I whisper to my wife and daughter: we must not give up hope, because then there will be nothing left of us if we ever get out of here. I don't know if they can hear me. They don't respond, but I can hear them breathing. They are alive. As long as we are alive, there is hope.

I am becoming increasingly convinced that we are not alone. There is something here *apart from* the twenty-eight people who were shut in this container four days ago. I don't know what it is, but I do know what effect it is having. It happened a few hours ago. I was sitting as usual with my back against the wall of the container, my knees drawn up. Arms by my sides, backs of my hands on the floor. There is no difference in here between sleeping and being awake, but I think I nodded off and was woken by a movement. The ship must have been on its way up or down a wave. The container had tilted in my direction, which meant that the sludge was now covering my palms. I was about to raise them when I felt it. The movement. A wet, jelly-like caress on my left palm, like a jellyfish passing by. It's hard to describe, and of course, I couldn't see anything in the darkness, but I can state with absolute certainty that it was something *living*.

At the same moment as that living thing passed over the palm of my hand, night descended upon me. The dark night of the soul. The struggling, flickering flame of hope I have just been talking about was extinguished, and in its place came a *horror*, the like of which I have never experienced. Everything I have described about life in this container ought to sound like a state of the ultimate horror to most people, and in many ways it is. Physically, mentally, it can't get much worse. And yet. When that thing touched me, I felt a horror that my training at the theological seminary had given me no words to describe. It was deeper and heavier than anything that could be accommodated within my body or my mind, it was the realisation of the utter emptiness of everything, it was the sight of a warm-hearted God roaring in agony in the throes of death, it was the entire cosmos transformed into a scornful smile, it was the *horror* beyond and within everything.

I banged the back of my head against the thick metal wall, I raked my nails down my cheeks until the blood flowed, I wanted to yell, to run, to destroy something or someone, but instead my weakened body sank down into a well of apathy. It took me several hours to climb back up, step by step, in order to continue this recording. An essential part of me remains at the bottom of that well. We are not alone here. We are lost.

THE TRUTH ABOUT ME

I

Max can see that Siw is struggling with herself, that she is finding it difficult to come out with something. Eventually she looks at him shyly, spreads her hands as if she is giving in, accepting whatever might come.

'Ever since I was little,' she begins, 'I've had . . . I call them Hearings. I get a premonition that something is going to happen in a certain place, or a sense of something that has already happened – I never know which. I can hear it in advance. Or afterwards. I know it sounds crazy.'

'No, it doesn't.'

'Anyway. That container . . . It's hard to explain, but I heard it being opened, and it wasn't the opening itself, but what was going to happen as a consequence. That's what I heard. And if it had been in my power, I would have tried to prevent them from opening it. To avert whatever it might be.'

'Have you ever managed to . . . avert an incident?'

'Only once. When I was thirteen.'

'What happened?'

Siw narrows her eyes as she looks suspiciously at Max. 'Do you *believe* me?'

'Yes, I do. Tell me what happened.'

Siw glances at her phone. 'I have to go soon.' Max can see that she is bracing herself, then she adds: 'To relieve the babysitter.'

'You've got children?'

'A daughter. Alva. She's seven.'

'What a lovely name.' Max's eyes flick down to Siw's left hand. 'And . . . a partner?'

'No partner.'

'But what about Alva's father?'

Siw clears her throat and slips her phone into her pocket. 'So anyway, I was thirteen. And I heard some kind of collision outside the library. A big object hitting a smaller one. A woman screaming. That was all. So I went there and waited. I was about to give up, but then a child's buggy . . . What? Whatever's wrong?'

Max's eyes have widened during Siw's account, to the point where he looks insane. His jaw has dropped, reinforcing the impression, but he can't help it. For seventeen years he has sought an explanation for that event, and here it is, standing right in front of him. He almost whispers: 'And the buggy rolled out into the road and a Samhall minibus came along and hit it.'

'Yes, except that I managed to grab the handle of the buggy. So it didn't happen. How can you possibly know this?'

'Because . . . I saw it.'

'Were you *there*?'

'No, I was up on top of the silo. With Johan and Marko.'

'Could you see it from there?'

'No. Or . . .' Max's legs feel wobbly. He gestures to the bench beneath Wind Thingie. 'Shall we sit down for a minute?'

Siw hesitates. 'I'd really like to, but my mum will spend fifteen minutes making me feel like shit for neglecting Alva if I don't leave now.'

'Oh, one of those.'

'Definitely one of those.'

'Well, couldn't we . . . what if we . . . another day, maybe? Meet up for a coffee or something?'

'That would be lovely. I'll be in touch.'

Siw nods quickly a couple of times, feeling her double chin wobble before she turns and walks away. Max is still so paralysed by this new realisation that Siw has gone at least ten steps before he shouts: 'Maybe we should swap numbers then?'

Siw immediately does a U-turn, leaning back before she spins around – a movement Max somehow recognises. She has almost reached him when he works it out: *Chaplin*. Like when he spots a policeman. She's undeniably funny.

'I mean, we don't have to wait for a raid,' Max says. He gives Siw his number; she enters it and calls him. Her number appears on his screen. He saves it in Contacts and holds up his phone to take a photo of her.

Siw covers her face with her hand like the Facehugger in *Alien* and says: 'Noo! Noo!' before she spins around again and hurries away.

Definitely funny.

Max remains sitting on the bench beneath Wind Thingie for a long time, staring at the place where the container stood. He has never imagined that he would find out what happened that day up on the silo, when *something else* stepped in and changed a predetermined course of events. It seems even more unlikely that this *something else* should appear in human form.

He can't decide what he thinks of Siw. She's not beautiful, but there is a beauty about her. She has no immediate aura, but she does have a glow like a dimmed lamp. She isn't excessively talkative, but she seems to have the words, if only they will come out.

Yes. That's it. Siw is a bundle of potential, a whole lot of things she could be that lie dormant within her. If they woke and rose to the surface, she could become a very different person. And on top of all that she has what she calls Hearings in the same way that Max has his Visions. Hearing and sight.

Max has read online about people who claim to have supernatural powers of different kinds, but he has never met anyone. Was that why he felt he *recognised* Siw the first time he saw her? A shared sensitivity to signals in the world that others cannot perceive?

'Me and her,' he murmurs to himself. Just thinking those words is weird. He hasn't been with anyone since Linda, in Cuba. He is too scared. With the help of Lamictal he functions, more or less, but he doesn't trust himself. Associating with other people tends to make him feel cornered, anxious and often exhausted.

It's the aspect of Siw he recognised that has made him operate far beyond his comfort zone over the past few days. When he invited the girls to play minigolf he regretted it almost immediately, but it went well. When Siw said she wanted to come with him on the raid, he almost said he wasn't going. But it went well. So far so good.

In spite of the fact that he is interested in her, mainly because of her gift, he's not sure if he'll call her. She has a daughter, and no doubt a complicated story behind that; she has a difficult mother and presumably had an equally difficult upbringing. He can't cope with getting close to another person. The superficial contact with the members of Pokémon Go Roslagen is the perfect level for him.

He wanders along the quayside, and it is as if a magnetic force turns his head so that he is looking at the empty space where the container stood. He remembers his terrible experience on Marko's terrace when the container was opened. The screams, the screech of metal, the voices. *Horror concentrated into a yellow cube.* One reason why it hit him so hard was that it had something in common with what drew him to Siw – he *recognised* it. He has been there himself.

DEEPER, DEEPER

I

Max achieved his diving certification in Mauritius when he was twelve years old. His mother had been dubious, but the German female instructor had assured her that she had previously trained a couple of other twelve-year-olds, which was the lower age limit for taking the certificate. His father had had no objections.

Max spent four days attending the Sea Urchin Dive Centre in Flic-en-Flac. He studied the theory, familiarised himself with the equipment, then began to dive – offshore at first to learn the basic skills, then in deeper and deeper water until the last day, when he achieved two dives to the maximum depth of twenty-five metres.

He loved it. The reef and the underwater environment were one thing, but above all he adored the physical experience. When the oxygen in his wetsuit was perfectly calibrated so that he neither rose nor sank, but simply hovered in the vast blue ocean, slowly paddling forward with the help of his swim fins, moving up or down above the reef simply by controlling his breathing. Filling his lungs to lift the upper body, exhaling to sink. During the thirty minutes a dive lasted, it was as if he'd discovered a way of existing on this earth that he had never imagined.

He was praised for his calm approach in spite of his young age. The instructor said he had 'the right mindset' to be a good diver, and the certificate issued to him on the final day was the most precious item he had ever brought home from a holiday.

Whenever his parents discussed travel plans in the future, Max did his best to persuade them to spend at least a few days in a place where it was possible to dive. They usually gave in, and he had dived in Thailand, Malaysia, Indonesia and Egypt, among other countries.

The original fascination abated, but never disappeared. As soon as he tumbled backwards off a boat, took a giant step from a diving board or waded out from a shore with the cylinder rubbing against his spine, he began to fizz with anticipation. He was going to revisit the underwater world that lay waiting for him, silent and invisible; he was going to enter the state of weightlessness that made everything that seemed important or difficult up on the surface go away. Thirty, forty minutes of directionless concentration and *peace*.

2

When Max decided to go to Cuba during the summer holiday after his first year at the School of Economics, he hadn't dived for two years. He'd stopped travelling with his parents, so it simply hadn't happened.

He'd been with Linda for three months. She was at the same institution, and they'd met at a student party. It was no great love story, but they got along well and didn't make any major demands of each other. If something developed between them, then so be it. Linda was also a diver and, like Max, she had had her eye on Cuba, principally Maria la Gorda, the most westerly point of the island. The diving there was supposed to be the best in Cuba, mainly because of the rare coral reef formation known as La Pared – The Wall.

The journey from Havana via Viñales turned into a little adventure that brought Max and Linda closer together. They kept up their courage and simply laughed when they found themselves crammed in the lumpy back seat of a *taxi colectivo* with another couple, their luggage banging around alarmingly on an overloaded roof rack. When they were released onto a truly beautiful beach three hours later, it felt like a reward for the ordeal they had endured.

Apart from swimming, hanging out on the beach and being stunned by Photoshop-perfect sunsets, diving was the only activity available. And so they dived, often twice a day; they were each other's buddy and worked their way through all the dive sites. They did three dives at The Wall, which really was something special, a sheer drop of several hundred metres down to the seabed.

Linda came from Lidingö and had grown up in more or less the same financial circumstances as Max, but in a family with 'old money'. While Max's father had acquired certain upper-class mannerisms and attitudes without passing them on to Max, they were an inherent part of Linda's DNA. She didn't complain about the basic nature of the trip, but there was a coolness about her, an unwillingness to let go because it was vulgar.

However, after a few days she began to loosen up – it might have been down to the general *cubana* atmosphere, the diving or the cuba libres they knocked back in the evenings, but she laughed louder and more often, made stupid jokes and was considerably more interested in sex than she was back in Sweden. On the penultimate evening they did it on a sun lounger on the shore, under cover of darkness. Afterwards she ran screaming into the water, waving her arms around. Max was becoming increasingly convinced that their relationship might have a long-term future.

The following day Linda didn't feel great. They'd taken a bottle of rum to the shore the previous night, sat talking and passing the bottle back and forth until it was empty. They'd intended to do one last dive at The Wall, but Linda didn't want to risk vomiting into the regulator, so Max went alone.

3

Max was allocated a solo diver as his buddy, a fat, pallid Englishman aged about fifty who introduced himself as Suggs. 'Like, you know, the guy from Madness.'

As soon as they started to put on the equipment, Max realised that Suggs was an inexperienced diver. He had problems getting into the wetsuit, and almost fell over when the boat veered sideways. He stumbled around bumping into other divers, with a constant refrain of 'Sorry, mate' and 'Sorry, love'.

When it came to assembling the tank, the vest and the regulator, Suggs was totally lost. If he'd ever dived before, then presumably everything had been put together and attached to his body without his input. Max felt sorry for him and checked his regulator and the tank pressure.

'Cheers, mate.'

'But you've done this before, I assume?' Max said.

304

Suggs glanced around and lowered his voice. 'Yeah, sure, but just, like, you know . . . in a pool.'

Great, Max thought. If anything happened, his buddy would be no help at all, while Max would have to take on the responsibility of keeping an eye on his companion instead of enjoying his last dive. Oh well, he'd already seen The Wall three times. He'd just have to suck it up.

The boat slowed and Suggs became increasingly nervous. Max spoke to him calmly in an attempt to avoid the inevitable.

Sure enough . . . As soon as everyone had taken a giant step off the platform and lay floating in the water with their vests inflated, Suggs started hyperventilating. The dive master swam over to him and uttered several sentences in Spanish, which made Suggs turn to Max with a horrified expression on his face. 'What's he sayin', mate?'

Max thought Suggs ought to understand the word *inexperienca*, but he swam closer and continued the therapeutic talk he'd begun on the boat. The other divers drifted around giving Max funny looks; he felt like yelling: 'He's my dive buddy, not my fucking friend!', but he didn't. Oh well, at least it would be a story to tell Linda when he got back.

After a few minutes Suggs's breathing slowed and the dive master gave the signal to descend. Of course, they had to take long breaks because Suggs found it difficult to even out the pressure. He pinched his nose hard until his eyes were bloodshot before giving the thumbs up, which was confusing as it was the accepted signal for ascent. Max gave the 'okay?' sign with his thumb and index finger, to which Suggs responded with a double thumbs up. They continued their descent.

First came thirty metres or so over a smooth surface. Max folded his arms over his chest and relaxed, let himself hover while watching Suggs, who went up a short distance, sank back down again, and waved his arms and legs in order to steer himself. They continued towards the section of the dive that worried Max most in relation to his buddy: the narrow passage of about twenty metres where you had to swim with the reef above your head and no possibility of ascending to the surface. Max placed himself right behind Suggs so that he could intervene if something happened.

Suggs blundered into the walls of the passage, thrashing wildly with his fins. Sand swirled up from the seabed, reducing Max's visibility to only a metre or so ahead. He edged closer to Suggs and was rewarded with a kick in the face that knocked off his mask; fortunately he managed to catch it as it fell. He put it back on and blew out the water, thinking something about *mad dogs and Englishmen*.

They finally emerged. Even though it was his fourth time, Max's stomach flipped when he came out of the opening in The Wall and looked down into the depths, that great expanse of blue, and he felt as if he was going to fall. His diving vest kept him afloat, and if it was damaged, he still had his fins and the buoyancy of the wetsuit, but tell that to the reptilian brain when it finds itself above the abyss.

Max checked on Suggs, who appeared to have been driven crazy by the dizzying experience. He was floundering more than ever. He stuck up his thumbs, and Max responded with the 'perfect' sign. This was going to be a short dive. They'd be lucky if Suggs's oxygen lasted for twenty minutes, the way he was carrying on. Max looked for the others, who were moving further away and higher up The Wall. Visibility was almost thirty metres, but if he wasn't careful, they would soon be out of sight. Suggs was some distance below Max, and he checked the depth gauge. Shit. He'd been so preoccupied that he hadn't noticed that he'd sunk to twenty-eight metres. Not that twenty-five was an absolute limit, but he preferred to stay around there.

When Max let go of the depth gauge he saw that Suggs had dropped even further down, to maybe thirty-five metres. Max had no choice but to swim down and bring him up. He evened out the pressure, turned his body. Suggs was still sinking. Had something happened? Max gave him the question sign and received a thumbs up in reply.

If Max had been able to rub his eyes through the mask, he would have done. If he made the correct sign for ascent – thumbs up – Suggs would merely think he was saying hi. The only possibility was to swim down to a depth Max had never experienced, and haul the Englishman up with him.

Max exhaled and allowed his upper body to drop until he was lying with his fins pointing to the surface, then he took a few strokes. Thirty-three metres. Thirty-four. It looked as if Suggs had finally stopped sinking, and was stable at about forty metres. Thirty-five. Thirty-six. Max caught sight of something *underneath* Suggs and stopped paddling.

A patch of white grew in size and acquired the clear outline of a shark. Max inhaled sharply. His hands flew up to his temples and he *yelled* through the mouthpiece, a shrill tone that made Suggs look up. Max had lost control of his body, and what was meant to be a gesture indicating *underneath you, underneath you* became a limp flapping while the great white, like a single tensed muscle, shot up from the depths.

Max had seen great whites in documentaries and tried to imagine how he would react if he ever had the misfortune of coming across one. The risk was one in a million, allegedly, and *if* it happened, the risk of attack was one in a hundred. Such figures were meaningless

307

now Max found himself just metres from the killing machine; he could see the cold black eyes, the mouth opening to reveal rows of sharp teeth.

Never in his life had he been so afraid, not even when he was about to fall from the silo. His body, his mind turned into a hard knot of pure fear when the shark sank its teeth into Suggs's shoulder and chest. The bite made the Englishman spasm as if he'd been given an electric shock. The regulator flew out of his mouth and fell towards the seabed, a stream of oxygen bubbles rising from the bitten-off tube. The shark jerked its head and Suggs was shaken to and fro like a rag doll, while strands of blood mingled with the bubbles. Suggs scraped at The Wall with his free hand as if he were searching for something to hold on to, something that would allow him to free himself from Death. His fingertips began to bleed as the coral tore the skin, and all the time he was screaming, a trembling sound that spread through the water and seemed to come from every direction.

Everything Max had learned vanished from his mind; there was no room for anything except one key command: *Get away! Now! Up!* He took a deep breath to bring his body into the upright position, then paddled frenetically. *Up! Up!* The last thing he saw was the shark carrying Suggs away, its victim's arms and legs dangling helplessly as it disappeared through a billowing red curtain.

The world had been reduced to two variables: the Shark and the Surface. The pale blue, shimmering surface high above was the place Max had to reach in order to survive, but even though he was pushing so hard that his thigh muscles ached, it didn't seem to be getting any closer.

Max had done his research, he'd trained for an emergency ascent if the regulator became blocked. The most important thing to remember was that all the oxygen expands when a diver is coming up, and the pressure lessens. The oxygen bubbles in the vest expand, giving greater buoyancy, which means the diver rises faster and faster. At the same time the oxygen in the lungs expands, which can lead to serious injuries. Therefore, it is essential to blow air out slowly from the lungs as you ascend.

Max knew all that, but every scrap of knowledge had been erased, leaving only *surface, surface,* which was now getting closer at some speed, as the overfilled vest sent him shooting upwards like a cork.

He had perhaps ten metres left when he felt an intense pain in his chest. The shark had got him too! He jerked and twisted, determined to get away, but there was nothing holding on to him; the pain was coming from inside. Only then did a light begin to flash inside his head, a warning light with the word *AIR* beneath it.

He exhaled in a cascade of bubbles, but when he broke the surface a couple of seconds later, he realised it was too late. His mouth was filled with the taste of iron as blood seeped up from the burst vessels in his lungs. He pulled out the regulator and clamped his lips together as a modicum of sense returned. *Blood. Water. Shark.*

With this thought came the further insight that the recently so desirable Surface was not his salvation. The shark was still down there, and might well be on its way up to rip off his legs. Fear clutched his heart in an iron grip, flooded his body and turned his blood to ice. He didn't dare lower his head to look down. If he saw the shark coming towards him . . .

He tore off the mask so that he could see better; it sank, but he didn't care. The boat was about thirty metres away. He tried to swim, but he had no energy. His chest felt as if it was about to explode with the pain, and the rest of his body was rigid, paralysed.

The oxygen bubbles in the blood . . .

They too expand during a rapid ascent, locking the joints. The skipper was leaning over the gunwale, but Max didn't dare yell to him. His mouth was full of blood; if he tried to shout, the blood would pour out and the shark would pick up his scent. He waved his arms, gave the signal for *help!*, and the skipper straightened up, started the engine and turned the boat.

The period when Max lay floating with knives stabbing his chest as he breathed through his nose, his mouth so full of blood that it made him want to vomit, was the longest in his life. During the incident on the silo time had slowed down, stretched out, but it had been a matter of only a few seconds. This was at least a minute, where every one of those sixty seconds could be the one in which the white shadow came hurtling up and took his life back down to the depths.

But the shadow spared him. One minute later the skipper was able to heave his weak, aching body up onto the platform. The first thing Max did was to spew out the blood, which fanned out across the deck. He lay with his ear pressed to the floor and saw the blood mingle with the water pouring from his suit and vest. Then he lost consciousness.

4

He emerged from the darkness heading for a sound he couldn't identify; it sounded like a gigantic whisk. The darkness thinned out, became a dark red veil. Through the veil he could see a plump body falling, surrounded by bubbles, and a white death-shadow speeding towards him. He gave an involuntary start and opened the red veil that was his eyelid.

He was lying on a sun lounger, beneath a parasol. His wetsuit had been removed, and he was covered by a thin blanket. Linda was kneeling on the sand beside him, her eyes red and puffy from crying. When Max looked at her she seized his hand and said: 'Oh! Oh! How are you feeling?'

Max took in his surroundings. A couple of Cubans were standing close by, their expressions serious, and there was a small group of tourists a little further away, watching what was going on.

'I . . .' It was no good. The pain in his chest made it hard to talk, and even though he was lying on the beach under a blanket, his body still felt cold and stiff.

Am I paralysed?

He stared at his hand, tried to wiggle his fingers. They moved. He focused on his foot, found he could bend his toes. Not paralysed. The whisking sound was getting louder. One of the Cubans crouched down beside him and asked: '*Disculpe, pero tu buddy, qué pasó con el?*'

His buddy. Suggs. They wanted to know what had happened to Suggs. Max raised his head a fraction, squinted into the sunlight. He pointed feebly in the direction of the sea. '*Ti . . . Tiburón. Blanco. Tiburón blanco.*' Great white shark.

The Cubans – Max now recognised one of them as the dive master – glanced at each other then asked if he was sure. *Seguro?* Max nodded, and the small movement was enough to send a shaft of pain through his chest. His high school Spanish wasn't good enough to describe what had happened, and his thoughts were moving as sluggishly through his brain as the blood around his body. All he could manage was: '*Matar. Suggs. El tiburón matar.*' He knew it was grammatically incorrect, but hopefully comprehensible. *Kill. Suggs. Shark kill.*

His mind, impregnated by fear and ready for flight, thought that the object which had just appeared in his peripheral vision was a gigantic bird of prey, coming to snatch him. He had survived the danger from the deep, now it was swooping from the sky. It took him a second or two to work out that it was a helicopter, and his only addled thought was: *Helicopter? Do they have those in Cuba?* before he sank down into the darkness once more.

This time he wasn't out for so long. When he came round he was lying on a stretcher being lifted into the helicopter, and he heard voices talking about *La Habana* and *Decompresión*. His mind was a little clearer, and he understood that he was being taken to Havana and a decompression chamber. *Do they have those in Cuba?*

Linda was having a discussion with someone whose English was as shaky as Max's Spanish. It transpired that she could accompany him in the helicopter, but there was no room for their luggage. After some debate Linda came over to Max and said: 'I understand if you can't talk, but it might be better if I get a cab with our luggage and meet you at the hospital later.'

Max swallowed a gob of saliva that tasted of rusty iron and said: 'You . . . don't need . . .' Linda clearly couldn't hear a word above the noise of the rotor blades. She leaned down so that her ear was almost touching his lips, and Max whispered: 'I'll be. Out of it. You don't. Need.'

'What do you mean?' A shadow of anxiety passed across Linda's face. 'Out of it how?'

'In the chamber. I have to be. Shut inside. The chamber.'

'Yes, for two days, they said. But I want to be there, at the hospital, when you come out. Oh God, Max. Oh God, it's so terrible.'

Max could only nod. *Oh God, it's so terrible* wasn't the half of it. Not even the tiniest fraction of the half of it.

5

Max was unable to enjoy his first trip in a helicopter. The pains in his chest and joints became so severe that they had to give him morphine to ease them, followed by a shot of adrenaline to counteract the effects of the morphine so that his damaged lungs wouldn't stop breathing. It was only his body that needed the helicopter; his mind was soaring high in the air on the wings of the injections.

What happened after they landed on the helipad at Hospital CIMEQ would also remain a vague, confused memory. His lungs were X-rayed and a doctor showed the plates to Max, pointed and explained in decent English that more or less went over Max's head. The blood vessels in the walls of the lungs had burst and he would probably need surgery, but that could wait until after he'd been flown home to Sweden. Max made a weak gesture of protest, sitting in his wheelchair.

'No fly,' he said. '*Peligroso.* Dangerous. Bubbles. Blood.'

The doctor reassured him that the flight wouldn't happen until *after* the decompression process, so there was no risk that the lower air pressure at thirty-five thousand feet would cause further problems with the expanded oxygen in his blood. 'We know these things. *No es peligroso.*'

After being offered a meal of chicken, rice and *frijoles negros*, of which he could manage only a mouthful, they took him to the tank. Max had only ever seen a decompression tank in a picture, and that had been a modern version, equipped like a very small hotel room, verging on pleasant.

This was something completely different. A cylinder made of thick, dark iron, with a single round window roughly the size of a handball in the door, which also sported a large wheel-shaped lock. The door was open. Inside there was nothing but a bunk with a mattress on it, and a bare light bulb hanging from the ceiling. It looked like a torture cell. Max could see a couple of pressure metres on the side, plus a rusty plaque with Cyrillic lettering. So the tank dated back to the 1960s, when the Soviet Union and Cuba were the best of friends.

The doctor apologised, but this was all they had. Slurring his words, Max assured him that he was grateful for the help. He was led in, he lay down on the bunk and the door closed with a deep metallic clang and a sucking noise. He was alone.

A machine started up outside, and he assumed that the inside pressure was now being raised in order to compromise the oxygen bubbles that were causing him so much pain. They would then gradually, one slow bar at a time, lower the pressure until it reached the normal level, and the oxygen was assimilated. *We know these things.*

Forty-eight hours. Max looked up at the curved metal ceiling that was such a dull black that it barely reflected any of the glow from the bulb. Forty-eight hours. If only he'd had the presence of mind to ask for something to read, a Gameboy, anything.

Do they have Gameboy in Cuba? Nintendo?

Meaningless thoughts of this nature occupied Max for the first hour, until the morphine rush subsided and his mind became clearer. Which was unfortunate, because the film entitled *Suggs's Death* began to play in his head. It would run hundreds if not thousands of times during his period in the tank.

Every dreadful, terrifying detail was shown; the camera zoomed in, switched to slow motion, sometimes accompanied by only the silence of the sea, something with the throbbing pulse of the soundtrack to *Jaws*, sometimes with Suggs's screams amplified to the extent that Max felt as if he had surround-sound speakers installed in his brain. It was horrific.

After an hour or so he couldn't stand it any longer. He got up and paced back and forth like a psychologically damaged tiger in a cage that was far too small in some depressing zoo. He pressed his wrists against his eyelids in an attempt to force the images down into the deep sea grave where they belonged, but still they came.

Now it was no longer Suggs, but the great white shark itself, swimming around him and weighing him up with its black eyes, toying with him and showing off its muscular bulk, against which he had about as much chance as a shrew facing a lynx. Or a human being facing a great white. At any moment he would feel those teeth sinking into his flesh, those jaws crushing his bones. The pain would be indescribable and he would be tortured to death, alone in an alien element, and no one would see him as he fell down into the bottomless depths, left to rot in the mud on the seabed.

And again. The shark was approaching. He could see its outline in the distance. Visibility was good. He saw it. He knew there was no chance of escape . . .

Around and around in his Soviet prison, around and around in his thoughts; Max was aware that insanity wasn't far away. He raked his nails across his scalp, he rubbed his face, he waved his hands. His right hand shot up in the air and struck the light bulb, which swung into the wall and shattered. Max dropped his hands and stood perfectly still.

What have I done?

Now the only light came from the tiny window, and that was minimal. The tank was virtually in darkness. Max began to hyper-ventilate, which made the pain in his lungs explode, and he sank

315

to the floor. He crawled over to the door, dragged himself to his feet and pressed the alarm.

After a minute or so the doctor came into the room. Max signalled that he had to be let out. The doctor explained through a pantomime of gestures that this was out of the question unless he was dying. Coming out into normal pressure would cause the equivalent of yet another panic attack like the one he'd suffered earlier. The doctor pointed to his watch, spread his hands and shrugged, pointed to his watch again.

Max went and sat on the bunk and stared out into the darkness. The shark was approaching again, and even though it was underwater Max was aware of the stench of decay from the remains of the carrion between its teeth. It was coming straight for him. His heart contracted with fear, his body was as cold as ice and he was screaming inside with mortal terror. Forty-six hours to go.

6

Those two days in the tank would send Max's life in a new direction. Forty-eight sleepless hours in the company of The Horror turned him into a different person, one who was incapable of completing his studies or thinking about anything but fear for several months after the event. When he finally got up in his boyhood bedroom, he was a person with no worldly ambitions, purely focused on surviving without losing his mind.

He had barely said a word to Linda during the flight home, because everything he had been was struck dumb, and he found it difficult to move or eat because everything, absolutely everything apart from sitting or lying perfectly still, was too painful.

When he hadn't responded to Linda's calls or text messages for a month, she finished with him. It was irrelevant, because she belonged to the outside world, which he couldn't deal with.

As Max stands on the quayside staring at the spot where the container used to be, he knows better than most what the people locked inside must have gone through. Of course, their situation was much, much worse than his own in the tank, because they didn't have a time limit on their living hell, but there were similarities. The horror, the darkness, the threat of insanity.

Max pushes his hands deep in his pockets and gazes at Siw's diminishing figure as she passes the open-air stage. He thinks about her Chaplinesque spin, the way she covered her face with her hand like the Facehugger. He smiles. A possibility, a light in the darkness? Yes, maybe.

*

A drunken man is sitting on one of the benches next to the statue of Nils Ferlin. He studied philosophy a long time ago, and when he contemplates the waters of the river rushing by, he thinks Panta rei. Heraclitus. Everything flows. The simple thought terrifies him. He sees himself and his life trickling away in the darkness, and he takes a deep swig of Koskenkorva vodka in an attempt to douse the burning flame of fear in his chest.

THE POWDER REALLY HELPED ME

I

'Mummy, what *is* that?'

'Food.'

'No it isn't. It looks like O'boy drinking chocolate, although it isn't O'boy. What *is* it?'

'Food.'

'Can I taste?'

Siw passes over the diet shake. Alva sniffs at it suspiciously and pronounces her verdict: 'It smells like chocolate, but weird chocolate.'

Siw is on the third day of her meal replacement diet, which according to what she has read is the worst day. Too true. By the fourth or fifth day the ketone phase kicks in and the body begins to burn its own fat, in the absence of sufficient nutrition. She isn't there yet, and she is plagued by an echoing, corrosive *hunger*.

When Alva raises the glass to her lips, Siw hopes fervently that she won't like the taste. She can't afford to lose one centilitre, or a single one of the six hundred calories she allows herself per day.

Hallelujah. Alva takes a tentative sip, pulls a face and turns her head to the side to get away from the taste. She runs over to the sink and spits it out, shouting: 'Yuck! Eeuw!' She clarifies her opinion by pointing accusingly at the shake. 'That's *disgusting*!'

Siw takes a swig of the grainy liquid, which goes a little way to filling the gaping hole in her stomach. Alva shakes her head. 'How can you drink that?'

'I've told you. It's the only thing I'm eating at the moment.'

With a theatrical gesture of despair, Alva asks: 'But why, Mummy? *Why?*'

'Because I'd like to be a bit thinner.'

'But *why*?'

Alva's inner drama queen takes another step forward. She opens her eyes wide, claps her hands to her mouth, then gasps: 'It's the *guy*! Of course it is! It's the guy, isn't it, Mummy? Is he fit?'

'Alva, eat your cereal. We have to go.'

'Oh! It's the guy!'

Alva remains standing as she shovels down the last of her cornflakes. While she's getting ready for school she continues to bombard Siw with questions. What's his name? Where does he live? What does he do? Does he have a car? Does he like rabbits?

'Why did you ask about the rabbits?' Siw says as they leave the apartment block.

'Because when I get a rabbit, it will be good if he likes it.'

'Alva, I never said—'

'Let's not talk about that now. Does he have any brothers or sisters?'

As they approach the school Siw places a gentle hand on her

daughter's shoulder and crouches down beside her. 'Alva. This guy you've decided I'm seeing – I'd be grateful if you didn't mention him to your friends.'

Alva gives her an accusatory look. 'I'm not stupid, Mummy.'

No, you're not, Siw thinks as she waves goodbye to Alva, who is standing at the window of her classroom. The child pushes her hand under her T-shirt and flips it back and forth, as if her heart is jumping out of her chest, while at the same time she rolls her eyes like someone who is about to swoon with love.

Siw can't help laughing, and the good mood lasts for at least a minute until the hunger begins to gnaw at her again. This is going to be a hard day. On top of everything else she is training with Anna this afternoon and

Fuckfuckfuck

this is the day they arranged for Marko to come along and act as their personal trainer. She's going to make an idiot of herself just so that Anna can check him out. She could go back home, of course, call in sick, pull down the blinds and stay in bed all day, watching *Friends* and eating ice cream. She knows she isn't going to do that.

Siw passes the row of shops that make up the Flygfältet shopping centre. Frank's Paints, Happy Homes, Svanefors. Outside Cervera a sign informs her that they have 'Serviettes for every occasion, 25kr each'. She thinks these are very expensive serviettes, but then they are for *every* occasion. From the pet shop the smell that means *cuddly animals* seeps out, a mixture of wood shavings, hay, food and excrement. That's where Alva has seen the rabbit she will never own, and which she has named Bulgur.

Sportringen, Gant, KappAhl. Siw used to think this was the

ugliest place in the whole of Norrtälje. That was before the Norr-teljeporten shopping mall opened. She turns the corner heading for the staff entrance and glances at the huge photograph displayed on the facade. All of the permanent staff, herself included, standing inside a heart with the words: 'With our hearts in the right place – for a living Roslagen'.

She likes her place of work, but she has a problem with marketing when words like *love*, *warmth* and *heart* are used, as if Flygfyren were a pining lover instead of a place to buy stuff. She finds the other sign more amusing: 'We supply local goods', suggesting that they sell drugs.

The staff entrance is next to the returns desk. Siw swipes her card, keys in the code and walks into the bright red corridor, where she is greeted by the word 'Welcome!'

Thanks. But it's my job, okay?

She passes the bakery, where the aroma of freshly baked bread makes her stomach rumble so loudly that it sounds as if she's swallowed a cat. *The very thought of sinking my teeth into a warm roll. With butter. And cheese. The butter melts and the cheese goes soft and . . .* Siw's mouth is watering. She swallows and continues past the sign proclaiming 'Our Core Values', which as a new employee she read carefully, conscientious as always.

She carries on up the stairs to the changing rooms, along the corridor where a timeline shows Flygfyren's glorious history. She checks her pigeonhole and is disappointed to find it empty. Disappointed? Because there's no information bulletin or shift change in there? No, to her embarrassment she realises she was hoping for a message from Max. Totally absurd, since the pigeonholes are used only for internal mail.

It is three days since she saw him. He said he would call, and he hasn't. Same old story. Siw hasn't called him either, due to the following logic: she was the one who went to the raid in the square, because she saw on Facebook that Roslagsbowser was going. Even if he doesn't know it, she took the first step. Now it's up to him to take the next step.

What about the invitation to play minigolf, then? And the invitation to the raid by the Frans Lundman memorial? And whose idea was it to swap phone numbers?

That's . . . different. Not on the same level as the fact that Siw hurried to the square with aching thighs just to see him. She has gone over and over all this in her mind over the past few days, but now it's time to let it go. She knew from the start that it was hopeless, and now she has to embrace that knowledge once more. She was fine before Max came along, and she's fine now.

Her locker is in the smaller changing room. She puts on her uniform – checked shirt and black trousers – while gazing out of the window that faces the roof. A lone gull is perched on a ventilation drum in the middle of the black expanse of emptiness. The gull is looking around as if it isn't sure what to do next, and Siw gets the idea that it is her soul sitting there.

She goes down the stairs to the store, passing photographs of fellow workers smiling with a touch of hysteria as they demonstrate the correct way to deal with customers. She uses her card to sign in and carries on down.

She nods to her colleagues on charcuterie and cheese before reaching the checkouts. Today she is starting with a left-hand checkout, then right, then finally a stint on Customer Services. She says, 'Hi,' to her colleagues on the other open checkouts before taking her place at number five. Once again, she signs in with her card, and removes the 'Closed' sign. Another working day has begun.

Lunch, which is often the high point of the day, is definitely a low point today. Siw whisks the powder into water that she has heated in the kettle. According to the packet it's supposed to be chicken soup with curry, but the only thing it tastes of is . . . powder. She looks longingly at the baskets of free fruit – *a banana, just one banana* – but controls herself and sits down next to Tanja, who is the same age as her and started at Flygfyren at the same time.

Tanja wrinkles her nose. 'What the hell is *that*?'

'Meal replacement powder.' Siw slurps down a spoonful, which at least gives a feeling of warmth in her empty stomach.

'Are you dieting?'

'Mmm.'

Tanja waves a hand in front of her nose. 'Can't you try the 5:2 or Low Carb, High Fat or something – anything but *that*?'

'I haven't got the self-discipline. I have to go all in, otherwise it doesn't work.'

That's just the way it is. For someone like Tanja, with her freckled nose and a face that was probably very pretty in high school, but is now kind of puffy and would benefit from losing five kilos, a different diet where you take things slowly would no doubt work. But Siw has to jump straight in and go for broke if she's going to have any chance of success. Make a project of it.

Tanja leans forward and scrutinises the pale yellow, runny soup in Siw's bowl. 'I think you've got *enormous* self-discipline if you can eat that shit. How do you do it?'

'Eating this shit doesn't hurt.'

'What?'

'Nothing.'

When Siw has washed up her bowl and sat for a little while on the roof terrace, warming her face in the setting sun, she gets ready to go back to work. It will be nice to change to a right-hand checkout. Her left forearm is aching from passing items across the barcode reader, and she does *not* want to end up with carpal tunnel syndrome at twenty-nine. She wants many more happy years on the checkout!

She has left the staffroom and is heading for the corridor where photos of every member of staff are displayed when she hears a voice.

'Hey, you. Hi.'

Sören is over by the staff fridges in the alcove to the right of the staffroom. He has taken out a plastic box, which he now puts down. Siw gives him a nod and Sören beckons her over as he backs into the alcove. Siw joins him. 'Hi. What do you want?'

Sören checks over her shoulder to make sure no one is in the corridor, then he grips her bum firmly with one hand and starts kneading her right breast with the other. Siw twists away. 'Don't do that.'

'Oh, come on.' He grabs the waistband of her trousers and pulls her close. 'Can't you just . . . you know . . .' He pushes his tongue into his cheek, creating a bulge, and nods meaningfully in the direction of the toilet. He wants a blow job.

An absurd thought passes through Siw's mind as Sören once again reaches for her breast: maybe she should do it, simply because she is so bloody *hungry*. The idea of having something solid in her mouth for a little while . . . And how many calories are there in an ejaculation? Worth the trouble? She can't help giggling.

'What?' Sören says.

Siw pushes the questing hand away. 'Sören, you're such a clown.'

The comment sounds harsher than she'd intended, and has more impact than she'd expected. Sören lets go of her and steps back against the wall, where he goes into a major sulk. Now he really does look like a sad clown. Jesus, he is *so* unattractive – the bushy eyebrows, the swollen lips, the little beer belly. Before she's even decided to say it, the words come out of her mouth: 'Don't call me again.'

The clown now adds a layer of misery on top of the sulkiness. Sören appears to be on the verge of tears. 'Don't be like that, sweetheart, I only wanted—'

'I know what you want, Sören, but that's not what *I* want anymore. You've kneaded these baps for the last time.'

Before he can come up with any further objections, or, God help us, actually starts crying, Siw leaves the alcove and walks down the corridor, where something like a hundred faces on the walls watch her go by. Is that applause she can hear?

2

'High fiiive!'

Anna speaks in the manner of Borat, with a fake Kazakhstan accent as she holds her hand up in the air. Siw smacks her own palm against Anna's with enthusiasm. They're on their way to the gym, and Siw has just told her about the incident with Sören.

'Bloody hell,' Anna goes on. '*You've kneaded these baps for the last time*! Isn't it fantastic when you actually manage to say the right thing in the moment rather than thinking of it half an hour later?

Siw nods. She had been very pleased with herself when she walked away – not so much for the comment, but for what she'd done. Only then did she realise how nice it was to be shot of Sören. For a long time she's been irritated when he contacts her, like being called in to the most boring job in the world.

'So what now? The field is lying fallow, waiting for RoslagsBowser to come along and plough his furrow . . .'

'Anna, be nice. *Please*.'

'I am being nice, I'm just telling it like it is.'

'Those are two irreconcilable elements.'

'What does that mean?'

'You are *not* being nice. Okay, I admit I'm attracted to him, but there's no way he's attracted to me. He said he'd call, and he hasn't. End of story. And it upsets me when you carry on like that.'

Anna pulls Siw close and lays her head on her friend's shoulder. 'Sorry. You know what I'm like. But he might still ring, mightn't he?'

'I'm not letting myself hope.'

'Sorry, darling, but that's your problem right there. Not *letting yourself* do things.'

They pass the entrance to the Contiga Hall where a group of teenagers are tossing a handball around, and continue down the hill to the car park. Marko is sitting on a bench outside the gym, texting. He hasn't seen them yet.

Siw grabs hold of Anna's arm. 'I don't think I can do this.'

'What is it you can't do?'

'I feel so lumpy and clumsy, plus . . . I'm so hungry I already feel as if I'm about to faint.'

'Sorry, Siw, but you have to help me to *let myself* do this. It won't be right for me to show up alone. And surely it's a good thing if he

326

can teach us? Come on, let's do it. I promise to drag you into the shower if you pass out.'

Marko looks up and spots them. Even from a distance of twenty metres the Zlatan-smile shines like a mini-sun across the twilit car park.

'And besides,' Anna whispers, 'he might know something about Max.'

'Don't you dare ask,' a horrified Siw whispers back. 'Don't even *think* about it!'

'Chill out – I can be subtle.'

There are words Siw could use to describe Anna, but subtle is not one of them. She walks towards Marko with something approaching fear in her heart. He greets them with a hug and a kiss on the cheek, which moves Anna to exclaim: 'Wow! Continental!'

3

As Marko goes around demonstrating the various machines to Siw and Anna, the regular gym hunks glance at him first, then nod when their paths cross, as if the general hunkiness makes them brothers. Marko doesn't flash his pecs in a skimpy top as the sexy boys do; he is wearing a plain black T-shirt with the word SATS in white letters on the back.

'The important thing is to keep your spine straight, not to put pressure on any other muscle group apart from the ones the machine is meant to be working.'

Marko is sitting at the pec deck with Siw and Anna standing on either side of him like two admiring hens flanking an impressive rooster. Marko leans forward as he brings the pads together.

'*Not* like this, for example. It puts strain on the back, and can tear the muscles. Like this, slow and steady.'

Marko rests his back against the support and slowly brings the pads towards each other. He's gone for a hundred kilos, but from his gentle movement it's easy to believe that there are no weights at all on the ends of the steel bar. He allows the pads to return to their original position and stands up.

'Your turn.'

Anna happily sits down. It's obvious that Marko's presence and interest are making her feel prettier than usual, but the opposite is true for Siw. She sees herself as an anomaly, something that doesn't belong in the picture and ought to be airbrushed out.

Anna presses on the pads. Needless to say, they don't move a millimetre, which makes her laugh. She has already demonstrated the same cheery attitude on two previous machines, and Siw is slightly embarrassed on her friend's behalf.

'What do you usually go for?' Marko asks, preparing to adjust the weight.

'Fifteen,' says Anna, who actually goes for ten. Siw turns away to avoid seeing the result of Anna's hubris. What is wrong with her? Does she imagine that Marko will think she's Wonder Woman because she goes for fifteen kilos on the pec deck? Which she clearly doesn't, judging by the groaning noises she's making. In her peripheral vision Siw can see Anna's feet waving around and kicking. 'Slow and steady,' Marko reminds her.

'Cock,' Anna says.

When it is Siw's turn, she can't help making a point. She settles for five kilos and easily manages ten reps with smooth, flowing movements and a straight spine, which earns her praise from Marko. Anna pulls a face at Siw, who pulls a face right back.

It takes an hour to complete a more ambitious session than usual. Marko explains that it's normal practice to concentrate on one part of the body during a session – back or legs or chest – but he thinks they'd be better with a more comprehensive programme, since their main focus isn't increasing muscle mass.

'How would you know?' Anna says. 'I might be going for the She-Hulk look.'

'Well, if that's what you want, we can—'

'She's joking,' Siw says. Even though she took it easy with the weights, she thinks she'll probably either throw up or pass out if she has to use one more machine. Her stomach is screaming with hunger, and she feels dizzy.

'What about you?' Anna says to Marko. 'You've hardly been able to do any training yourself.'

'I mainly stick to free weights, so . . .'

'So let's see what you can do.'

'Anna . . .' Siw thinks this performance has gone on long enough. Okay, it was good to be shown what to do by someone who really knows what they're talking about, and Marko has been the embodiment of encouragement and kindness, but Siw feels as if there's something artificial about the whole thing. It's as if she's being forced to participate in a play that makes no sense to her. Unfortunately Marko shrugs and wanders over to the bench.

The last act. Then we'll be let out.

Marko places four twenty-kilo weights on either end of a bar, securing them with a clip before lying down. One hundred and sixty kilos. Siw can't help being fascinated in spite of herself. Surely he can't lift that much?

Anna is standing with her hands clasped to her chest, looking at Marko's outstretched body with an expression that suggests she's

329

having to make a real effort not to leap on top of him and ride a cock horse. So to speak.

Marko unhooks the bar and Siw's eyes widen as she sees it *bend* because of the weights, while Marko keeps his arms straight. She isn't usually impressed by muscles and feats of strength, but this is almost unnatural. She can't take her eyes off Marko as he lowers the bar to his chest, pauses for a second, then raises it again. Anna applauds and Siw shakes her head.

'He just hit him like this, right on the top of his head. He needed, like, an ambulance and everything.'

'Man – what had he done?'

Siw glances to the side and sees two men talking next to a rack of dumbbells. One is wearing a T-shirt with 'Skanska' on it, while the other is wearing high-vis shorts, for some inexplicable reason, like somebody carrying out roadworks in the summer.

'That's the weird part. So, first of all the guy puts two hundred in the cup—'

'*Two hundred?*'

'Yes, and the beggar is, like, thrilled and wants to kiss his hand or something, but the guy just walks off with his bag of booze and half an hour later he's back, right?'

Presumably they're talking about the same beggar Anna gave a twenty-kronor note to a few days ago, the one who usually sits outside the liquor store.

'He must have been, like, thinking about stuff, he's got an empty Explorer bottle in his hand and he, like, hits the beggar on the head with it, the beggar goes down, blood everywhere. And me and Conny were there – you know Conny, right? We like grabbed him and held on to him, because it looked as if he was going to . . . carry on.'

'But why did he do it?'

'We asked him the same question. What the fuck are you doing? And guess what he said? He said the beggar made him feel, like, really *depressed*, for fuck's sake!'

'Sounds weird.'

'Yes, and Conny cut his hand on the broken bottle. You know Conny, right?'

'Conny Andersson?'

'No, Gerhardsson – didn't you do your training together?'

Siw turns her attention back to Marko, who is just replacing the bar on its rests to the accompaniment of Anna's coquettish little claps, hands close to her chest. Marko gets up and gives a little bow before starting to remove the weights.

No encores, please.

'Okay, girls. I hope this has been useful.'

Showered and limp with exhaustion, Siw and Anna are standing next to Marko's car. Siw doesn't know much about such matters, but her first boyfriend claimed that of all the mass-produced cars, the Audi was the one to go for if you could afford it. Marko can obviously afford it. The car looks as if it rolled off the production line this morning.

'Absolutely,' Anna assures him, giving him a pat on the biceps. 'Especially . . . how would you put it, Siw? Visually?'

Siw has no intention of playing that game. 'Thank you so much. It was really valuable. Very kind of you.'

'*De nada*,' Marko says, then clicks his fingers. 'By the way – Saturday. I've bought a house for my parents, and I'm thinking of having a little party. Max and Johan will be there, along with a few friends from Stockholm. You're welcome to join us. If you feel like it.'

'We'll be there,' Anna says.

331

Anna and Marko swap phone numbers so that he can text her the address, then Marko gets into the car, which starts with a purr and glides out of the car park. Marko blows Anna one last kiss, to which she responds with an extravagant kiss of her own. Siw settles for a brief wave.

'Wow,' Anna says, pressing her clenched fists to her heart and rolling her eyes, just like Alva when she and Siw parted company this morning.

'You didn't ask him about Max,' Siw says.

'I didn't get the chance. And you'll be seeing him on Saturday.'

'I'm not sure . . .'

Anna tucks her arm under Siw's and they set off home. Anna gives her a squeeze. 'You *are* sure. And you know why?'

'No.'

'Because you are giving yourself permission, Siw. This time you're letting yourself do it.'

*

An old woman with a wheeled walker is making her way across Elverks Bridge. The seating area outside the café on the island in the middle of the river is full of people, and there isn't much room between the chairs. She reaches a spot where she can't get through, between two well-built men who have their backs to her. People usually move out of the way immediately, but not today.

'Excuse me,' she says.

The two men don't hear her, or they pretend not to hear her. When her second attempt to attract their attention is equally unsuccessful, she takes a deep breath and pushes the walker in between the chairs, which makes the two men leap to their feet.

For a moment it looks as if she's going to get a smack. Then the men register her age, and come to their senses.

FORWARD FACING

I

When Marko glides onto Carl Bondes väg he thinks this wasn't a bad way to spend an hour and a half, even if Anna's constant flirting and innuendo can get a bit much. Oh well, he only has himself to blame. His catastrophic defeat in the minigolf created a need for reparation, and if you're that vain, you have to take the consequences.

Anna and Siw are the kind of people he would never hang out with in Stockholm, but it feels like the right thing to do in Norrtälje. Was it a mistake to invite them to the party? He isn't ashamed of them – in fact, he's proud of the return to his roots that they represent – but he's not sure how they'll cope with his Stockholm friends.

Oh well, what will be will be – he has other things to think about. If he's understood his parents correctly, they are about to tell him whether they are going to accept his gift or not. If not, then he'll have to put the house on the market after Saturday, and regard what is bound to be an enormous loss as the world's most expensive way to hire a party venue. He might as well go full-on oil sheikh and fly in Taylor Swift for a couple of million while he's at it.

He parks obediently in the designated parking area and wanders up the hill to the spot with the best view in town. He and Johan sat here one evening sharing a few beers before they went their separate ways as far as their studies were concerned.

Johan.

Marko is very good at disciplining his thoughts. When he told Johan that the incident with Hans Roos and so on hadn't happened, that was more or less the truth in his own mind. He never thinks about it, doesn't brood. However, he doesn't know if it's his behaviour or Johan's since that night that has created distance between them. Probably a combination of the two, a mirrored gallery where words and expressions, or the lack of them, bounce around and are intensified until the coldness is a fact. He wishes it was different.

Marko sits straight-backed on the bench and gazes out over Norrtälje's roofs, the church spire, the lights of Tullportsgatan and the floodlight shining on the town hall clock. He thinks about Johan and those beers they shared, the cigarette they passed between them while fantasising about a possible future that they would never share. Marko looks up at the stars, and something tickles his right earlobe. A lone tear has found its way down his cheek. He dashes it away and gets to his feet. Time to go down and hear the verdict.

2

For once it is his father who opens the door. He is wearing a freshly ironed shirt buttoned up to the neck; Marko isn't sure how to interpret this.

334

'Tata? Are you going to the Nobel banquet?'

'This is a special evening, my son.'

'In what way?'

'Come into the kitchen.'

Marko takes off his shoes and looks around. Laura always keeps the apartment clean and tidy, but this evening there are two vases of fresh flowers on display. Surely this can't be a sign that they're about to say no – it must be a celebration of their new house. He hopes.

He pads into the kitchen in his stocking feet and stops in the doorway. His father is leaning on the worktop; he waves an arm like a circus ringmaster introducing a new attraction. Laura is sitting at the table in her best dress. Maria is there too.

'The family is gathered together!' Goran says. 'When was the last time? Four years ago?'

'Maria?' Marko says. 'What are you doing here?'

Maria stands up and goes over to him. 'Is that any way to greet your sister after so long?'

'Well, no, I just . . .'

'Come here.'

She presses herself to his chest and he puts his arms around her, pats her clumsily on the shoulder.

'Shit, bro!' Maria says. 'You're built like a house!'

'That's exactly what I said!' Laura exclaims. 'Exactly! And do you know what he said to me?'

Maria ignores her mother and drums her fingers on Marko's chest muscles, still taut from the gym. 'How much do you lift?'

'One sixty, with reps.'

'Mum, you've raised a *monster*!' Maria says.

After more banter in the same vein they all sit down, and Goran is right. There is something special, something ceremonial about

335

the whole thing, and the sense of occasion is underlined by the candelabra with six candles burning in the middle of the table. Marko doesn't know how he feels about the situation. The last time he and Maria spoke it was essentially one long argument about her profligate lifestyle. The fires of conflict are smouldering away, waiting to burst into flame, but right now he needs the answer to a more pressing question.

'Have you made up your minds?' he asks, glancing from Laura to Goran.

'We have,' Laura says.

Goran sits up a little straighter. 'My son. We thank you with all of our proud hearts, and we would be very happy to accept your gift.'

'You want the house?'

Goran nods and relaxes his stiff posture. 'We want the house.'

'What made you decide?'

His parents and sister exchange glances that Marko can't interpret, then Laura speaks. 'It wasn't the only factor, but . . . Maria wants to come and live with us.'

'*What?*' Marko stares at his sister. '*You're* going to live in *Norrtälje?*'

'I grew up here, as you might recall.'

'But . . . But . . .'

Even if the years have left their mark on Maria to a certain extent, and there are a few deep wrinkles at the corners of her eyes, she is still very, very beautiful. Her face, her posture, her whole innate style seems to belong in Norrtälje like a swan in a chicken run.

'But . . . what are you going to *do*?'

'I've got a job. In a café.'

'You're going to work in a *café*?'

'Mmm-hmm.'

336

Marko can't stop himself. One of his father's favourite phrases flashes through his mind, and a second later it has crossed his lips. 'God help us all.'

Maria narrows her eyes, ready for the fight. Goran unintentionally manages to avert it by trotting out his usual old hobby horse: 'And when are the two of you going to find someone to marry?'

Both Goran and Laura think it's a crime against the laws of nature that neither of their children is in a steady relationship. Regardless of anything else they might achieve, this is a constant source of disappointment. Maria glances at Marko and rolls her eyes. He responds by raising his eyebrows, and peace is restored.

Marko is convinced that the real issue for Goran is a desperate longing for grandchildren. His usual gloomy disposition flies out of the window as soon as he is in the company of small children. When he plays with relatives' children it is as if the war never happened, just for a little while, and his dream is a grandchild of his own that he can spoil.

'Tata,' Maria says. 'Not now. Please.'

From earlier conversations with his sister, and things she tells him during the evening, Marko is roughly able to reconstruct her story and interpret her intentions.

She isn't planning on moving to Norrtälje permanently, but she needs – as she puts it – *a decent fucking break*, in order to gather herself. Just gather herself. From a purely practical point of view, many of her possessions are scattered all over the world, but mentally, spiritually, she also feels splintered, geographically dispersed. She hasn't had a proper base since she left home at the age of seventeen. Her memories and experiences are linked to so many different cities on different continents that they are impossible to separate. A life that to outsiders might seem like a series of brightly coloured explosions is to Maria a grey porridge of temporary apartments, hotel rooms, catwalks, photo studios and faces, faces, faces, all equally beautiful and equally meaningless.

Admittedly parts of it have been fun, occasionally euphoric, but these are isolated incidents that tend to flow into one or become diluted in her memory. There is nothing firm to hold on to, no guide rail through the darkness that she can point to and say, *this is the course I followed*. A human being is the sum of his or experiences, and because Maria's experiences are incoherent and abstract, that is also how she feels mentally, and that is why she needs to *gather herself*.

Since coming home she has gone for film and TV roles, and partly due to her fame as an international photographic model, she has been called to a number of auditions. Lots of half-promises, lots of discreet or less discreet invitations on a never-ending carousel that finally threw her off onto a friend's sofa, which is where she is currently living. That was when the curtain fell. Her friend was away, and Maria spent three days lying there with the blinds closed, lost in an internal and external darkness. She ate nothing, drank a little water, didn't answer the phone.

When she got up from the sofa she was empty, but the key difference was that now she knew it. Until that point she had exorcised the emptiness with frantic activity, rushing from one task to the next, from one possibility to another. Always connected, always on the lookout, always spinning around. Eight years inside the tumble dryer. Enough.

'What about the money?' Marko asks, watching a curl of smoke rising from Maria's cigarette to the roof of the balcony. Laura is clearing the table after dinner, and Goran absolutely has to watch the evening news, despite the fact that his children are in the house.

'What money?'

'Don't play dumb, Maria. You must have made money over all these years. A lot of money.'

Maria shrugs. 'Oh, you know . . .'

'Seriously. You were on the cover of *Vogue*, for fuck's sake, that must have—'

Maria taps off the column of ash over the balcony railing and raises her perfectly plucked eyebrows. 'So you knew that?'

'You told me. Several times.'

'Did you buy the magazine?'

'Yes. And I've told you that, don't you remem—'

'What did you think?'

'Fishing for compliments, Maria?'

'Just curious.'

Over the years Maria's face has graced the covers and double-page spreads of several fashion and women's magazines, with *Vogue* as the peak of her achievements. On more than one occasion Marko has walked past a newsagent's and suddenly caught sight of his sister, beautifully made-up and showing off her white, even teeth and her sparkling green eyes.

Maybe he should have felt proud, but the sight usually gave rise to mixed feelings of absurdity and unease. Absurdity because Maria might well be in a different part of the world, they probably hadn't spoken for months, yet here she was, at arm's length. Unease because he couldn't get away from her, as if the covers were a peephole through which she could follow his movements, keep any eye on him like a ubiquitous, ever-present deity.

'What can I say?' he replies. 'I presume you looked good.'

'*Presume?* Do you know who did my make-up? Do you know who the photographer was? I've never—'

'Maria? Hello? This is your brother here. I don't drool over pictures of you. And how's the getting-back-down-to-earth project going?'

Maria concentrates on smoking. Marko almost thinks he hears her breathe *sorry*, so maybe something is changing after all.

'Once again. The money. You must have some tucked away somewhere, otherwise I don't know what—'

'The money, the money. That's your world, Marko. The money.' She flicks the cigarette stub over the balcony and watches as it descends towards the car park in a glowing arc, then rubs her nose and says: 'It's gone.'

Her unconscious gesture makes Marko narrow his eyes. 'Drugs.'

'Drugs?'

'You burned the lot on drugs, didn't you?'

Maria lets out a little laugh that is more like a cough. 'Who are you, the friendly local police officer? Who the hell says *drugs*? Snow, powder, crack, coke, crystal meth, even narcotics would be better, but *drugs*?'

'So it's true.'

'I didn't say that.'

'But it is.'

Maria takes another cigarette out of the yellow Camel packet. Her fingers are shaking and the flame is unsteady as she lights it. A tear shimmers in the corner of her eye and she swallows hard before taking an aggressive drag. She glances towards the living room where Goran is bathed in blue light from the TV, then lowers her voice and says: 'If you must know, I've been clean for two months. And it's hell.'

'But before that?'

'Before that . . .' She peers at her brother through the smoke. 'There are countries I've been in. For a week or more. And I don't have the slightest recollection of them. The past six years . . . If I try really hard, then maybe I can piece together half of them. Max.'

'Oh my God.'

'You have to do it. To cope. To keep up. And to stay thin.'

'But there are plenty of models who are rich, who've moved into another career.'

'Mmm. Unfortunately I'm not one of them.'

'Shit, Maria. This is fucking terrible.'

'Mmm-hmm.' Her eyes sparkle as she adds: 'This is kind of gay.'

The disapproving expression vanishes from Marko's face as he throws back his head and laughs. When the two of them were about ten and twelve, they were obsessed with mondegreens, or what are now called 'Turkhits': mainly songs in Arabic with Swedish words representing what it *sounds* as if they're singing.

The Kovac family had just acquired their first computer, and the two siblings' favourite song was *Hatten är din* (The Hat is Yours), and they would sit there yelling 'Hatten är din, hatt-baby' until Goran and Laura covered their ears with their hands. The song included the line: 'Det här är för jävligt, det tycker vi blir bögigt' – 'This is fucking terrible, this is kind of gay.'

In spite of the fact that Marko hasn't given the songs a thought for many years, he still knows them off by heart after listening to

341

them hundreds of times with Maria. When he's finished laughing, it is Maria who becomes serious. 'I'm clean now, and I'm taking one day at a time, as they say.' She gives her cigarette the careful scrutiny of someone who is smoking a joint. 'That's one of the reasons why I want to live here for a while. To get away from those circles, from all that crap. Do you understand?'

Marko nods, and they stand in silence side by side. The only sounds are the faint hiss of Maria's cigarette, and the murmur of the television newsreader. Eventually Maria flicks away the stub, leans on the balcony rail and gazes at Marko for a few seconds. 'It was you two, wasn't it? Hans Roos?'

'No.'

'It's eight years ago. You can tell me now.'

'It wasn't us.'

Maria sighs and looks over towards the harbour. 'I've sometimes wondered. How things would have been if the film had gone ahead. I've come to the conclusion that they would probably have turned out exactly the same, more or less. You can't get away from yourself, if you know what I mean. You find ways to do what you're going to do, good or bad. So it doesn't matter anymore.'

She lowers her chin, rests it on the hands clutching the railing. The evening air is cool; Marko is wearing a T-shirt, and he rubs the gooseflesh on his arms. The voice from the living room is louder now.

'. . . *the forensic investigation has concluded that a number of people died as a result of violence, in some cases probably self-inflicted. Dehydration and lack of oxygen are also among the causes of death. The police have refused to comment on where the container came from, and refer to* . . .'

'Of course!' Maria exclaims. 'That container – what's happened?'

'I don't know,' Marko says. 'We'd better go in and listen.'

THE CONTAINER

No passports or ID documents have been found on the bodies inside the container, but following the examination of other papers and items among their minimal possessions, it has been possible to conclude that the majority of the dead have come from Syria, and a small number from Afghanistan.

Times of death vary from those who died approximately forty-eight hours before the container was dumped to a small number who were probably alive at that point, and who therefore died shortly before or after it was found. It is hard to be precise, because after a week in the enclosed space the bodies were in an advanced state of decomposition. However, information provided by the life cycle of certain micro-organisms makes it possible to work out a provisional chronology. The deaths definitely did not occur *before* the victims were locked inside the container.

The ID number etched on the container suggests that it might have been loaded in Rotterdam, but as it has been missing from the system for over three years, this cannot be proved. Its last known destination was Rotterdam, but since then it could have been transported several times around the world. Under the radar, so to speak.

The identity of the ship that carried the container has yet to be established. A witness statement from a person who was in the vicinity of Kärleksudden has provided nothing more than a description of the sound of the vessel's engine, because it was a dark night and the ship was travelling without lights. It entered the channel leading to the harbour at just after three o'clock in the morning.

As far as motive goes, one can only speculate. The most likely explanation is that something went wrong. The container was meant to be unloaded elsewhere, perhaps in Kapellskär because it is the nearest large port, but the plan ran into difficulties and they had to abort the mission before completion, eventually dumping their cargo under cover of darkness.

A mobile phone retrieved from the container has been a great help in reconstructing the course of events. It was lying in the sludge covering the bottom of the container, but forensic technicians managed to extract its contents and found an audio file, an eye witness description of what happened during the long journey.

A great deal is still unclear, and the investigation continues with a generous allocation of resources. However, one thing is certain: what the people in the container went through during their voyage is beyond the limit of what it is humanly possible to endure in terms of *horror*.

OVER BLACK WATERS

4

My wife is dead. My daughter is dead. I killed them with my own hands. When they were sleeping or in a state of semi-consciousness, I pinched their noses and covered their mouths, one at a time. First my daughter. Then my wife. They struggled only briefly before sinking down into the sludge. They didn't have the strength to fight back. Or maybe it was what they wanted. I did it to spare them a worse fate. Then I tried to kill myself by banging my head as hard as I could against the wall of the container. I was out for a long time. Then I came back. I think. For the past two days I have considered the possibility that I am already dead. That this is what Death is like.

The container has become the inside of an insane person's brain. This began at about the same time as something in the sludge touched my hand. Immediately after I came to my senses, I heard a ripping, tearing sound. I sacrificed a little of my precious battery to illuminate the source of the noise. A man had slit his wrists open using his teeth, and he was sitting there drinking his own blood with madness in his eyes. I switched off the light.

A little while later I heard thudding and rattling. It almost sounded like the peal of a church bell. I switched on the light. A man was banging another man's face against the wall of the container, over and over again. As the face turned to mush, the pealing of the bell became less and less clearly defined. I switched off the light.

Time passed. I heard a squeaking sound, a bit like a terrified kitten, followed by grunting and thumping. I switched on the light. A man was busy raping one of the young girls. Her head was pressed against the wall of the container, her neck was bent in an unnatural angle. Maybe she was already dead. I also saw that a woman had managed to hang herself from the metal grille covering the airholes. Her body was swinging to and fro in time with the movement of the ship. I switched off the light.

That was when I decided that nothing like that was going to happen to my family, even if that meant quite literally taking matters into my own hands. I shone the light on them one last time, studied their faces, etched with pain, their closed eyes. Then I switched off the light and reached out in the darkness until I found their airways, and sealed them off.

There are only a few of us left alive – me and two other men. One is huddled in a corner. When I shone the light on him for a second his eyes were dead, but I could see his chest heaving. The other man is lying on his back in the sludge, endlessly whispering: 'Satan is Eternity and Eternity is Satan, Satan is Eternity and Eternity . . .' Listen. This is what he sounds like.

The engines are slowing, the sound deepens. The container shudders. It doesn't matter. If we have arrived . . . if we are going to be let out now . . . I am already dead.

BEING AN OLOFSSON

I

'I knew him!'

Berit points to an item in the local paper about a man who has been found dead in an apartment near the harbour. The man's dog was also in the apartment, and had to be destroyed immediately. Berit taps the piece with her finger. 'He did the electricity in our summer cottage. Nice man.'

'How do you know who it was?' Anna asks as she removes the sheets from Berit's bed. Unlike many other clients, she doesn't wet herself during the night, and doesn't even need incontinence pants.

'My dear girl,' Berit says, 'have you never heard of the internet?'

Anna peels off a pillowcase. 'Is it already out there?'

'Everything is always out there,' Berit replies, waving a hand at the slightly antiquated laptop on her bedside table. 'You just have to know where to look.'

'Or maybe you've hacked into the police system.'

'If only. Do you want to know? He's a *celebrity*, for goodness' sake. He's the one who found the container, if you remember.'

'Okay, go on,' Anna says, spreading out a freshly laundered sheet.

'His name was Harry Boström. He had a certain style, back in the day. Always had a flutter on the harness races. When he doesn't turn up at the newsagent's for a few days to place his bet, one of his friends starts to wonder. Goes round there and rings the doorbell. No one answers. Opens the letter box and is hit by the smell. Calls the police. They come along and open the door. It's the friend who wrote about it online, by the way – on *Roslagsporten*. Do you read it?'

'No – I thought that was the name of the new shopping centre?'

'That's Norrteljeporten – keep up, child.'

'If I wasn't so busy changing nappies, I'm sure I'd be as up to date as you,' Anna retorted, tucking in the last corner of the sheet.

'No nappy changing here,' Berit says. 'You can shoot me if I get to that stage.'

'Will do. I'll happily serve twelve to fifteen years behind bars just so you don't have to show anybody your fanny.'

'Do you want to hear the rest, or are you going to stand there making smart remarks?'

Anna turns her attention to the pillowcase. 'Carry on.'

'Okay, so they get into the apartment and the guy is sitting on the sofa with a plastic bag over his head and duct tape wound around his neck. From Flygfyren, where Siw works.'

'The tape?'

'No, the bag, idiot. "Eat, drink and be happy!" it said on it. Nice detail, don't you think?'

'Absolutely. Which convinces me that you've made it up, you old bag.'

Berit chortles delightedly. She loves teasing people, and so does

348

Anna; they are at their happiest when they can banter with each other, because they know exactly how far they can go, and it's a long, long way. Anna often thinks that the time she spends with Siw's grandmother is more like entertainment than work.

Berit is eighty-one years old and has a degenerative muscular condition that means she can't manage any more than short distances with her wheeled walker, or lift anything heavier than a plate. She can just about open the lid of her laptop, and she spends a lot of time online. However, her mind is crystal clear, and her fingers are nimble. She hates the illness that makes her incapable of looking after herself, and she once paraphrased Bodil Malmsten: 'The day my anal sphincter gives up, I'm out of here.' She might be the person Anna likes most in the whole world, apart from Siw, and every morning when she walks into Berit's room she sends up a silent prayer that nothing will have happened during the night, that her friend won't be *out of here*.

'In conclusion,' Berit says, folding her hands on her lap, 'Harry Boström had eaten, drunk and been merry for the last time. The dog, however . . .'

'No,' Anna says, plumping up the pillows in their clean pillow-cases.

'Yes. The fingers and a chunk of one thigh. The *flesh* on the fingers, that is. So the dog must have *peeled*—'

'I get it, Berit. Honestly, I get it.'

'I didn't realise you were so squeamish, child. Anyway. Apparently the dog was completely wild, rabid. It was frothing at the mouth and it flew at the police officers. So when the newspaper says *had to be destroyed immediately* – they shot it.'

Anna brushes her hands together. 'We had a dog like that. Back home. It went crazy and bit my brother Acke. My dad didn't have a gun in the house at the time, so he put the dog in a bin bag and gassed it with the exhaust from some scrap car. It took a hell of a long time and the dog kept thrashing around and howling until . . . well, until it stopped.'

Anna moves towards the door. Berit rests her cheek on one hand and looks at her with twinkling eyes.

'Didn't have a gun in the house at the time,' she repeats. 'One day, my child, maybe on one of your days off, I'd like you to come and sit down and tell me what it was like to grow up as an Olofsson. I can pay you.'

'You don't need to pay me, Berit. But trust me, you don't want to know.'

'Oh yes I do!'

2

Anna's father, the notorious Stig Olofsson, often said that the secret behind a successful fencing operation was perfectly simple. It was just a matter of storage space, nothing else. Then, of course, you needed your contacts, both for the acquisition and distribution of the goods in question, but often you had to hang on to items until they were no longer hot, and then storage was the be all and end all.

Anna doesn't think she's even seen half of the storage facilities in her father's arsenal. There were everything from deserted shacks out in the forest to warehouses in Görla, from a cupboard in a Korean restaurant in Rimbo to a closed-down electrical store in Finsta.

There was also plenty of room on the farm, two kilometres north of Rimbo. It was an old agricultural property with stables, a hay barn, piggery and woodsheds, all equally in need of care and attention. No stolen goods were stored on the farm, apart from in a hidden barn behind the piggery. However, the place was crammed with the legal goods that Stig Olofsson and his family bought and sold. Mainly cars and tractors, tyres and trailers, along with a certain amount of furniture. If you were after a bike or a moped, that was also possible, and you could choose whether you wanted one with an intact serial number, or one with the number filed off for half the price. If you went for the latter option, you had to wait an hour or so while the item was collected. There were often people hanging around in the yard waiting for their purchases while Stig or Anna's older brother Gustav visited the relevant store.

Sometimes the police paid them a visit. They were offered coffee, and after a nice chat the officers would dutifully check the outbuildings and make a note of the registration numbers of the vehicles strewn about. Then they would leave, without having found anything to object to apart from the tread on the tyres of Stig's own car. Anna never understood why they bothered.

Then there was the contraband – smuggled booze and cigarettes kept in one of the aforementioned shacks in the forest, ten minutes' walk away. Stig didn't bother fetching and carrying, he simply escorted the customer to the shack and unlocked the door, then they would stagger away with whatever they could manage. He always referred to this aspect of his business as a 'leisure activity'. His main income came from cars, motorbikes and boat engines, which he exported to the east via Kapellskär.

In spite of rumours to the contrary, the Olofsson family had never been involved in either the production or sale of narcotics. This wasn't so much a matter of moral rectitude as the fact that drugs were the territory of the Djup brothers. You didn't mess with them, unless you fancied 'a little trip' chained to the towbar of their Volvo 740, which they kept specifically for that purpose.

In addition, the Olofsson family and the Djup brothers had a history of good business relations which must not be jeopardised. When it came to the import and export of certain goods, they had shared the risks and even passed on contacts to one another. The Djup brothers were also involved in the smuggling of booze and cigarettes, but on a completely different scale. They turned a blind eye to Stig's little hobby, which mainly involved supplying locals. However, if he ever turned his attention to Norrtälje, there would be trouble.

When Anna was little, she couldn't understand why her parents had had her and her siblings. They showed no interest in the children, who were left to their own devices. As she grew older, she began to suspect that it was because the only time her mother and father weren't at each other's throats was when they were having sex, and the children were an unfortunate by-product of their efforts to achieve a modicum of peace.

Only when she left home at eighteen, to her parents' genuine sorrow, did she realise that they were, in fact, a clan, a tribe who were meant to populate the farm. She and her brothers and sisters had been brought into this world to be the embodiment of the concept 'Olofssons'.

Anna has hardly any memories of her mother and father from her early years. If someone had told her they'd been away until she was seven, she would have found it unlikely but not impossible. Her earliest recollections mainly involve her two older siblings, Gustav and Lotta.

Gustav was five years older than Anna, and it was his job to make sure she didn't get lost in the forest or fall from the hayloft, plus give her something to eat now and again. Lotta, three years older than Anna, helped out reluctantly, with frequent covert pinches and nasty comments. Anna still can't stand her.

When her younger siblings arrived, it became Anna's turn to act as a substitute mother, mainly for Anders, or Acke, the baby of the family. Even when he was tiny, he was hyperactive. Anna sometimes got so tired of chasing after him that she would tie a rope around his waist and attach it to the pole that was used for tethering horses. She made it seem like a game by telling Acke that if he ran in circles until the whole rope was wound around the pole, then in the other direction, he was the Earth that had finished spinning around the sun, and could be released. The Earth would set off, shrieking with delight, giving Anna seven or eight minutes of respite.

Then again . . . Occasionally they would have a nice time together, when Acke finally went to bed after half an hour's struggle, and asked her to tell him a story about Donald Duck. Anna didn't have the gift of being able to make up stories, so she would regurgitate the content of some Donald Duck comic strip she'd laboriously spelled her way through. He would sometimes fall asleep before she'd finished, and when she saw his little head on the pillow and heard his snuffling breaths, she would feel a pain in her heart. *Little brother, what's going to become of you?*

Eventually he was diagnosed with ADHD and embarked on an early criminal career, when he started delivering boxes of cigarettes for the Djup brothers without his father's blessing. Gradually Acke rose through the ranks until he was entrusted with large sums of money in order to be able to finance the import of more serious goods. The business was lucrative until Acke's journey came to an end at the customs post in Trelleborg.

3

Anna's mother Sylvia deserves a chapter of her own. The word 'mum' never crossed her lips unless she was referring to her own mother, *the old bitch*, or Stig's mother, *that fucking cow*, and the children grew up calling her Sylvia, or Sylv – a nickname she'd acquired at school. If one of the kids, possibly inspired by a classmate, tentatively called her 'Mum', they would find themselves on the receiving end of a sharp slap. 'I'm no one's fucking mum, look after yourself, you little bastard!'

This led to a certain amount of confusion. This person called Sylv lived in their house, yelling and shouting, occasionally condescending to do some cooking or even a little cleaning before grabbing her first beer at about seven o'clock. It had to be Starkbock, nothing else would do. She could drink a dozen cans during the course of an evening, but she never appeared to be drunk, or became nastier than she already was – if such a thing had been possible. So who was this woman? When Anna was five years old, she screwed up her courage and asked: 'Who's my mum?'

'How the fuck should I know? Some troll, presumably, given how ugly you are.'

'But who are *you*?'

'Don't you know, idiot? I'm Sylv.'

The piece that finally made sense of the puzzle was the realisation that Anna's mother was very beautiful. When Stig fell in love with her at the age of eighteen she already had the filthiest mouth in Rimbo, but what a mouth! And what a face! She was the hottest girl in town, but the boys behaved as if she was *red hot*, and didn't dare go near her for fear of getting burned.

Stig, who came from a family of macho petty criminals, had no intention of being scared off. Little by little he got closer to those lips until he was finally able to plant his first kiss on them – and what a kiss! Judging by veiled comments from her father and the noises that could be heard from her parents' bedroom, Anna concluded that her mother was something special when it came to sex.

She was also a valuable partner in dealing with money matters. Even the Djup brothers were afraid of her. Whenever they called round to discuss a future project and Stig invited them in for a drink, they always asked: 'Is Sylv home?' If she was, they were happy to have the discussion in the yard. Not that it helped. After a minute or so Sylv would come storming out of the house. 'What are you whispering about, you fucking shits?'

Ewert and Albert Djup would stare at the ground, shuffling their feet, and mumble: 'We didn't want to put you to any trouble . . .'

'Trouble? I have more trouble wiping my backside than dealing with two useless maggots like you. Come in and have a drink, you fucking peasants.'

During the subsequent conversation Sylv would fire off enough insults to flatten fifty people, but the brothers would merely sit there, an embarrassed grin on their faces. When it was time to talk business, they were nicely softened up.

Once when they were about to leave, Anna heard Ewert say to Stig: 'I don't know how you stand it.'

'Oh,' Stig had replied. 'She has her good points. Both front and back.'

'I'm sure she does, but there are limits.'

Sylvia had one redeeming quality. When the children were ill, she became a completely different person. Well, maybe that's a slight exaggeration, but she took care of them, and the curses she uttered in a gentler tone were aimed not at the sick child but at the illness itself, or 'the fucking gyppo' that had passed on the infection. Anna was seven years old before she fell really ill and benefited from the transformation. After that she made a point of being ill as often as she could. She would go out in clothes that were far too thin for the weather, and *definitely* wanted to share chewing gum with the girl in school who was coughing.

Ah, yes, school. Anna didn't find it easy, and in later life she would adopt the mantra: 'I'm not stupid, I just have the misfortune of thinking', which was more or less true. When she managed to concentrate on what she was supposed to be doing, the results could be very good, but it didn't often happen. Her thoughts darted all over the place, settling only sporadically on the task in hand.

She lacked patience, and therefore had problems with recognising patterns, which meant she found it difficult to learn to read. She could cope with short pieces like the speech bubbles in a Donald Duck comic strip, but when it came to anything longer, she couldn't focus, and would have to read the same section over and over again before she could grasp the meaning of the combination of words.

To stop her from falling too far behind, she was provided with a special support tutor, Cecilia, who was twenty-four years old and newly qualified. She and Anna clicked right away. Cecilia came from a similar background – let's call it white trash – and apart from giving Anna support, she also represented the possibility of a different life from the one Anna's parents led.

She became Anna's idol, and during the four hours a week they spent together, Anna learned more than during the whole of the rest of the week. The key point was that Anna really liked Cecilia, which gave her a reason to concentrate and to achieve in order to please her new teacher. Plus, Cecilia was very good at her job, in spite of her youth.

Besides improving Anna's reading skills, Cecilia's presence also led to Anna learning something important about her mother.

4

When Anna had been working with Cecilia for six months, and the effect on Anna's progress was clear both in school and at home – insofar as her parents showed any interest in school – it was time for parents' evening. It was usually Stig who dealt with that kind of thing, because he didn't want to let Sylvia loose on the children's teachers, but on this occasion Sylvia decided to go with him, because she wanted to 'take a look at the miracle worker' who was Anna's support tutor.

Anna dreaded the encounter and feared that Cecilia would never be nice to her again after being chewed up and spat out by her mother. However, Sylvia remained calm while Cecilia talked about Anna's progress and explained the methods she had used. At one point – can you believe it! – Sylvia actually grunted something positive. Then Cecilia moved on to the next parent, and Anna's ordinary teacher, Ann-Katrin, took over. Things then went much as Anna had feared – not that these were real fears, because what did she care about Ann-Katrin, or the fact that Sylvia had expressed the view that she was 'as thick as pig shit'?

The problem that later arose was something Anna couldn't have foreseen. In the car on the way home Sylvia made some comment about Cecilia's appearance, and Stig made the mistake of replying: 'She was certainly easy on the eye'. Anna was used to her parents quarrelling, but the row in the car reached such heights that she stuck her fingers in her ears when Sylvia called her beloved teacher a 'fucking cocksucker' – and worse. About a kilometre from home Stig stopped the car, got out and marched into the forest. Anna watched him disappear among the fir trees. 'Where's Dad going?'

Sylvia slid over into the driving seat, engaged first gear with an alarming screech of metal, and the car leapt forward. 'First he's going to fuck the wood nymph, then he's going to drown himself.'

A few hours later Stig came staggering home, presumably after a visit to the shack. Sylvia received him with the usual barrage of curses, although there was a faint hint of relief there too.

From that day on, Sylvia had a new favourite cudgel with which to beat Stig over the head. According to her, Cecilia, or 'that little whore', was the only woman he had eyes for. If he went to the toilet, it was so that he could 'have a wank and think about the fucking tart'; if he put a log on the fire, he was dreaming of 'shoving his wood into Miss Cocksucker's stove'. The next time Sylvia met Cecilia, she had every intention of kicking her teeth so far down her throat that they'd come out the other end.

One day Anna came home feeling very upset. She shut herself in her room and sobbed with such despairing intensity that Sylvia reacted, for once. She yanked the door open and asked: 'What the fuck is wrong with you?'

'Get out!' Anna yelled, turning her face to the wall.

'I'll go where I want in my own house, thank you.' Sylvia perched on the side of the bed, placed a hand on Anna's hip and gave her a little shake. 'Come on, spit it out.'

Anna wrapped her arms around her stomach, trying to contain a pain that threatened to destroy her. In one breath she gasped:

'Cecilia's leaving because the school can't afford her and I suppose you think that's good because you hate her and I hate you because you hate her!'

In spite of her grief Anna was horrified by what she'd said, and waited for the inevitable blow, physical or verbal. But Sylvia merely got to her feet and left the room.

The following day after school, Anna was crossing the playground on her way home when she met Sylvia marching in the opposite direction. She was in full war paint, with her hair up, and she was wearing the dress she always referred to as her 'fanny flasher'. Anna didn't know what that meant, but it certainly showed off the full length of Sylvia's well-shaped legs.

Anna had started copying her mother's way of talking, so she asked: 'What the fuck are you doing here?' while trying to maintain a sullen expression, even though Sylvia's presence in this environment was always terrifying.

'I'm seeing the headmaster,' Sylvia informed her. 'Why don't you come with me? You might learn something.'

As far as Anna was concerned, *the headmaster* was a remote and almost mythological figure by the name of Per Hallberg. It had never happened to her, but a couple of the boys in her class had been *called to the headmaster's office*, which meant you were in real trouble.

'The headmaster?' Anna spun around and followed her mother at a distance of one metre. 'How come?'

'I've known him for years. He's an acquaintance from the bad old days.'

A door with a pane of frosted glass led into the headmaster's office, and Sylvia marched in without knocking. As if he'd been caught out at something he shouldn't have been doing, Hallberg leapt to his feet and came forward with his hand outstretched. The meeting must have been arranged in advance, because he said: 'Welcome, fru Olofsson.'

Sylvia ignored his hand, plonked herself down on the visitor's armchair and got comfortable. Hallberg leaned towards Anna. 'And this is . . . Anna, I believe?'

Anna nodded and followed the headteacher's gaze as it flicked towards Sylvia's relaxed body. She thought he must be about the same age as her mother, but he seemed older. His hair was thinning, he had dark circles and wrinkles under his eyes, and his jacket looked dusty. He sat down behind his desk, while Anna chose a stool by the door – ready to make a run for it, as always when her mother was involved.

'So, fru Olofsson. As I understand it . . .'

'You can call me Sylvia. Or Sylv, and I'll call you Pelle. Pelle with the Pecker. Do you still like to go around dipping your wick whenever you get the chance?'

The headmaster's eyes widened and his cheeks flushed red as he scrabbled aimlessly through some papers on his desk. 'Perhaps we could stick to the matter in—'

'Do you remember that party when you were so drunk you started groping my bottom? What happened with your nose, by the way?' Sylvia studied his bright red face. 'Still a bit bent, I see. Jesus, you're ugly.'

Hallberg straightened his shoulders and attempted to regain the dignity his position demanded. A younger man looked out of his eyes for a second as he said: 'Sylvia, you can't come here and—'

'I can come here and do what the fuck I like, and now you're going to listen to me.' Sylvia stood up and leaned across the desk, giving Pelle with the Pecker the full benefit of her aggressive decolletage.

360

'My daughter learned fuck all in this shitty school before Cecilia came into the picture.'

Anna was astonished. In one sentence Sylvia had referred to her as her daughter, and called Cecilia by her real name, which hadn't happened once since the parents' evening.

'Our resources . . .' Hallberg gestured helplessly to the documents in front of him.

'You can wipe your arse with your resources. My daughter needs her, and as far as I can make out, she's the only fucking teacher in this place who has anything other than shit for brains. She actually seems competent.'

Hallberg glanced at Anna, who was sitting there open-mouthed, staring at Sylvia. He frowned. 'We just don't have the funds, it's that simple. When we employed Cecilia—'

'Provide even *more* disgusting school dinners, take a pay cut, be a little creative, for fuck's sake, you fucking philanderer.'

Anna had no idea what *philanderer* meant, but it must be something bad, because Hallberg stood up so that his face was level with Sylvia's. 'Listen to me, Sylvia or Sylv or whatever I'm supposed to call you. When we employed Cecilia, the school's financial situation was completely different. I'm very sorry that children with learning difficulties won't be able to access additional support, but we don't have the money. I'm sorry, but that's just the way it is.'

In order to underline his point, the headmaster slammed his fist on the desk before sitting down again. Sylvia also slid back into her armchair, and slowly crossed her legs.

'Okay, Pelle,' she said with alarming calmness. 'Let's not mess around. You know who I am, and you know who this girl's father is. You know what resources we have access to. If you let Cecilia go, that will inevitably lead to a *serious* deterioration in your quality of life.'

Hallberg looked even more stressed now; once again his eyes flicked towards Anna, and once again she realised she was sitting there with her mouth hanging open. Her mother had uttered several consecutive sentences without swearing. The headmaster's lips quivered. 'I know exactly who you are, and threatening me will get you nowhere. If there's no money, then there's no money. I can't personally—'

'There is *always* money, you just have to find it. Okay, so you know who I am, but do you know who this girl's godfather is? Ewert Djup. He's very fond of her, and guess what he said when I told him that her special teacher was being taken away from her? "Maybe I'll have to take that headmaster guy on a little trip." I have no idea what he means, but it sounds nice, don't you think?'

There wasn't a single person who'd grown up in Norrtälje or Rimbo who was unaware of the Djup brothers' methods when it came to those who'd displeased them. There were many backs and backsides flayed to the bone, and if anyone dared to contact the police, the brothers always had a watertight alibi.

The effect on Hallberg was instantaneous. His red face paled. Sweat broke out on his forehead, and his hands were shaking as he began to leaf through the papers on his desk.

'Maybe there's something you'd missed earlier?' Sylvia said.

Hallberg cleared his throat and placed his index finger on a random column of figures. 'There is, actually. This post—'

Sylvia stood up. 'That's what I thought.' She held out her hand. 'Good to see you again, Pelle. Try to keep your pecker in your pants.' The headmaster shook her hand, looking as if he was about to burst into tears.

When Anna and her mother emerged onto the playground, Anna asked: 'Is Uncle Ewert really my godfather?'

'You must be joking. That bastard hates kids.'

Anna got into the car. The scene in the headmaster's office had turned much of what she thought she knew on its head. But Cecilia was staying, that was the most important thing. After a couple of minutes, she took a deep breath. 'Why did you do that? I thought you hated Cecilia.'

'I do. But you don't. You need her. And I'm loyal to you. You're my daughter. You're my family. So I'm loyal to you.'

'Thanks, Mum.'

Sylvia turned her head and looked Anna straight in the eye. 'Do you want a slap?'

5

As Sylvia had predicted, Anna definitely learned something that day. She learned about the power of *fear*. Because she was small, her classmates had tried to bully her, but without success – Anna wasn't afraid to fight. Even older pupils steered clear of her within a few months.

However, punching someone in the face and drawing blood was one thing; it was an act that was enough in itself, but also pointed to the future. *There's more where that came from if you don't leave me alone.* Fear was different. Fear was about an unspoken promise that may or may not be fulfilled. It wasn't about how hard your fists were, but what you could make the other person believe. It was less about facts and more about attitude.

So Anna changed her attitude. From being the snippy girl there was no point in arguing with, she adopted the stance of someone who owned the entire school. By the age of eleven she was so successful that the supposition behind the attitude became a fact. When she strolled around the playground with her entourage, hardly anyone dared look her in the eye without permission, and no one would dream of sitting in her seat in the dining room. The very best seat, by the window.

She operated through a combination of threats and rewards. The currency of violence from home wasn't worth much in the schoolyard, so she made sure she built up her own capital. A mouthy girl was grabbed by the plait and had her face smashed into a tree; a boy who'd thrown a stone at Anna had sand stuffed in his mouth until he threw up. That was it, really. Fear took care of the rest, plus the stories about her which she made sure to spread via her admirers.

On both occasions she was called to the headmaster's office, where she passed on best wishes from her godfather, and was dismissed after a mild reproach. Fear is a fine thing when you're the one controlling it.

The other lesson Anna learned that day was more abstract, and it would be a few years before she fully grasped its significance. It was to do with loyalty, with putting your own wishes aside in favour of a higher purpose, which often involved family. A common origin and a common fate.

Her older sister Lotta could be horrible to her, pinching her and pulling her hair, but God help anyone outside the family who attacked Anna when Lotta was around. Messing with Anna meant messing with the entire Olofsson family, and that could not be tolerated. In later years Anna would have no problem understanding the Sopranos or the Lannisters. It wasn't about power, but about vulnerability. When you are in a vulnerable position, you can't get by without someone you can totally rely on.

Whether Anna wanted it or not, she grew up with this loyalty towards her family etched into her bones. That was what made her keep visiting Acke in prison, jumping in when Lotta needed help, sitting with her younger sister Lena when she fell into one of her depressions, which were as miserable as Lena herself. It wasn't a matter of choice; Anna was compelled to do these things by a loyalty that was greater than herself. *That* was what it was like to grow up as an Olofsson, and that was what she would tell Berit, if they ever had that conversation.

Anna pushes the trolley with clean sheets and pillowcases to number twelve, Folke Gunnarsson's room, and suppresses a sigh. If she's lucky, he won't have filled his nappy so full of shit that it's seeped out, and if she's even luckier, she won't have to listen to his views on immigrants and parasites. The best result of all would be if he'd died during the night, choked by his own bitterness.

Johan, she thinks.

Johan is going to be exactly like this when he's an old man. A bundle of anger stuck in the care system, with no memories other than injustices, a life story consisting only of everything that *didn't* happen.

Anna pushes open the door. 'Good morning, Folke.'

The room stinks of excrement, so no luck there. Nor on the second point. Folke is lying on his side, fists clenched and venom in his eyes. 'That fucking container,' he begins. 'A primary source of infection, you mark my words. Who knows what filth they've brought with them from their shitty countries . . .'

Come, pale death.

365

A woman met a man while she was on holiday in the Gambia. He is now visiting Norrtälje for the first time. He is good-looking and a nice person, and the woman is happy and proud. She wants to show him the best her town has to offer, so they go for a long walk by the river. When they reach the runestone known as Brodds sten, a Swedish man is coming towards them. He pulls a face when he sees the Gambian man, and says: 'How many kilos of bananas did you pay for him?' The woman gets a lump in her throat and her eyes fill with tears. If she'd had a gun, she'd have killed the Swedish man.

LOVE AND HATE

I

Friday evenings are the most lucrative at the bowling hall. This is partly due to people relaxing at the end of the working week, and partly smaller or larger groups celebrating before they hit the town. The venue is fully licensed for the sale of alcohol, but there is rarely any trouble, because people have something to *do*, and can measure themselves against one another with both bowling and, of course, the boxing machine. When Johan is behind the bar he can hear blows, groans, cries of triumph or disappointment, the clack of the balls, the crash of the pins going down, the clinking of glasses. To him, it is a wall of sound representing security and harmony, a warm surface against which to rest his forehead.

Ah, but there is a third category. *Los locos*. The ones who come in during the afternoon, and either alone or as part of a couple plod their way through five, six, seven matches. Blokes, because they are always blokes, who bring three or four urethane balls, both symmetrical and asymmetrical depending on the condition of the lane oil, and thumb holes of different sizes to allow for the swelling of the thumb during a long game.

It is almost seven o'clock and one of the aforementioned blokes, Åke, comes up to the counter after finishing a game. He flexes his fingers with a crack.

'The usual?' Johan says.

'Indeed.'

The usual consists of an IPA, a Famous Grouse chaser, and a plate of hash. Johan sends the order through to Lollo, who is running the kitchen today.

'How did you get on?' he asks.

'Third arrow,' Åke replies, shaking his head. 'But you know what, it was supposed to be Bourbon, but I thought it was more like the Manager's Revenge.'

Complaining about the oil pattern is virtually obligatory, unless they've played a couple of three hundreds, and even then there's usually a certain amount of moaning. Johan knows that Ove has used an oil with a high ratio, almost a tube and therefore easily played, but he doesn't mention this.

'More like Ove's Revenge,' he says instead. 'He was the one who ran the machine today.'

'I should have known.'

Johan almost wishes he'd never come up with the concept of the Manager's Revenge, a random allocation of the oil patterns, and something for the more experienced to get their teeth into on the odd occasion. A cool idea that has given the complaints a recurring refrain. When the game went badly, people used to say that a troll had got hold of the ball, but now the problem is the Manager's Revenge. Unless, of course, it's the shoes, the pinsetter, Murphy's Law, or the fact that life is a bitch.

368

'Okay otherwise?' Johan asks as he measures out the whisky.

'Fine – but did you hear about that shit this afternoon?'

'What shit?' Johan places the glass on the bar. Åke takes a sip before going on.

'Mmm, that's good. So there were these two guys, probably alkies, chatting on that platform down below the bridge – Faktoribron. The benches down there. A bottle of schnapps in a paper bag, having a lovely time. Then something goes wrong and one of them pushes the other into the river.'

'Wow.'

'Yes, but it doesn't end there. So the other one jumps in after him. The water's only about a metre deep there, and he sets about drowning the first guy. Grabs him by the back of the neck and holds his head underwater. The first guy kicks and struggles and tries to free himself, but the second guy is stronger, and eventually he stops struggling. The first guy.'

'Jesus.' Johan takes a bottle of IPA out of the fridge, opens it and puts it on a tray with a glass. 'So he died?'

'Not sure. The cop shop is just across the street, so maybe someone saw something through the window, but anyway a cop shows up and pulls them apart and gets them out of the water, and I don't know how it ended, but I heard he was still alive when the ambulance arrived.'

'But why did he do it – the second guy, I mean?'

'No idea.'

Lollo appears with a plate of hash and beetroot and puts it down in front of Åke, who rubs his hands, then carries his tray over to a table, where he tucks into the hash with great enthusiasm.

There is something rotten in Norrtälje, Johan thinks. It's not a new idea; in fact, it's the idea of all ideas, the dominant idea. He doesn't

369

have time to immerse himself in the usual tangle, because a young man whose eyes can't quite focus arrives to complain that the pinsetter isn't working properly.

'What's the problem?' Johan asks, and receives the crystal-clear analysis: 'Something wrong.'

He checks and discovers that Ove has used a little too much oil, which sticks to the balls, which in turn splash oil onto the pins, so the machine finds it difficult to grip them. Johan cleans the pins and the gripping mechanism, then switches the machine back on.

When he returns to the young man and his two friends, all equally unfocused, the young man says: 'Fucked up the scores.'

'You can have a free game.'

'Yeah,' says the boy, dropping his ball, slick with oil, on the floor. *No more beers for you tonight*, Johan thinks.

Things begin to calm down by nine o'clock. Those who were celebrating in advance have gone on to their parties, the recreational players have finished their recreations, and only the odd enthusiast remains, including Micke Stridh, a former member of the national team, who played so much that his right arm is a couple of centimetres longer than his left, and his body is bent in a pose of constant readiness. Johan can see from his scoreboard that he is only two strikes from a three hundred. Good for him.

'Hi there.'

Johan turns and sees Marko standing there. Without knowing why, he wipes his hands on his jeans, then says, 'Hi,' and holds out his right hand. Marko takes it and pulls Johan towards him in clumsy embrace across the bar.

'What are you doing here?' Johan asks.

Marko lets his gaze roam across the lanes, where Micke Stridh

370

has just achieved another strike. 'I just wanted to see where you work. Nice place.'

'You think?'

'Yes. It's kind of . . . well-used. Homely. I don't know.'

'Cozywozy,' Johan says, using one of their silly childhood expressions, which makes Marko grin. 'Do you play?'

Marko raises his hands in a gesture of resignation. 'I've played a few times, but no thanks. I've been thrashed enough for one week.'

Micke slams home the decisive strike. He clenches his fist and pulls it downwards as if he were ringing a church bell. 'Way to go!' Johan shouts, and Micke gives a small bow.

'Regular customer?' Marko asks.

'You could say that. Bowling built that beautiful body.' Johan nods towards Micke, who wobbles over to the control panel to start a new game.

'You are coming tomorrow, aren't you?'

'Of course. Do I need to bring anything?'

'A cheerful disposition and an empty belly.'

'I can manage the second, but I'm not too sure about the first . . .'

They continue their meaningless banter, and Johan gets the feeling there is something Marko wants to say. When a pause arises, he asks: 'Was there anything in particular you wanted?'

'No, well . . . no. I just wanted to see where you work. Where you spend your time.'

'Why?'

'We're still friends, aren't we? And if I think, *Johan's at work*, now I know where you are. What the place looks like.'

It's not the world's most loving response, but its significance is caring enough to make Johan feel as if he might cry. In order to

371

avoid such an embarrassment, he goes around the bar and leads Marko to the boxing machine.

'This might be more your style,' he says, inserting ten kronor so that the punching ball drops down.

'What do I have to do?'

'Just hit it as hard as you can.'

Marko shrugs, then delivers a blow so forceful that the ball flies up with a deep thud, and the scoreboard shows a figure that is almost the highest it is possible to get.

'Good?' Marko asks.

'The best.'

'Cool. See you tomorrow.'

Marko places the hand that has just mistreated the punching ball on Johan's shoulder, squeezes briefly before he leaves. Johan watches him until he has disappeared through the doors. Then looks at the ball, still quivering slightly from Marko's assault. *Oh, my heart.*

2

When Johan gets home at ten thirty, he goes on Flashback and the discussion thread about the container, which some people are calling the 'Turk Tin'.

He doesn't have much time for that kind of thing. What has happened is a tragedy, and Johan has nothing against the individual refugees. It is the *mass* he doesn't like. For example, he found the pictures of the huge crowd of Afghan men demonstrating in Medborgarplatsen distinctly unpleasant. Sitting there. The horde, the mass, the threat of diluting Swedishness. All with beards.

Even if Johan absolutely loathes politicians, he doesn't loathe Sweden as a concept. Quite the reverse. He loves the idea of Sweden, he is proud of being Swedish, and that is exactly why he doesn't want that Swedishness to disappear into some kind of multicultural soup. In the long term, attacks on Sweden's identity are an attack on his own. It only needs one drop of ink in a glass of water to destroy it.

People on the forum are speculating as to whether the container is part of some biological warfare tactic; there are also comments on the fact that so many of the victims died as a result of violence, and the proclivity for violence demonstrated by other races, and their general inferiority.

Johan isn't getting involved in that either. No doubt Afghans and Syrians can be good people, but they *shouldn't be here*. And if they are going to be here, then the bar must be set very high in terms of integration. Sweden should not give an inch in order to adapt to other cultures. If you visit someone's home as a guest, you don't start making demands about the food, and insisting that everyone say Allahu Akbar before you eat. No, you gratefully accept whatever is offered.

Johan begins to write a piece putting forward the idea that the container ought to act as a brake on a system that is deeply flawed, and revels in his description of the container as a 'yellow boil on the arse of our politicians'. Then he loses interest and deletes the entry without posting it. The bitterness he usually manages to whip up while writing just isn't there.

Now I know where you are. What the place looks like.

Marko wanted to come and see him at work so that he could picture Johan more easily. Which means that Marko sometimes thinks about him. Johan visualises Marko at *his* place of work – not that he knows what it looks like – sitting on a chair, thinking about Johan.

We're still friends, aren't we?

It's just that it's so bloody hard to be friends with someone when all you want to do is shower them with kisses. When Johan was living with the Kovac family, he would sit at the dining table secretly looking at Marko. He would feel those phantom kisses on his lips. If only . . .

The Kovac family definitely weren't fully integrated. They had their Yugloslav food and their Catholic religion, among other things. They celebrated high days and holidays in a different way. Would Johan have wanted to throw them out? No, he wouldn't, and he has accepted this inconsistency in his thinking. *That particular* family can stay and behave as they wish, *purely because it's them.*

He knows it's twisted, and that other people know other immigrant families and would say the same thing, but it is what it is. Johan's private asylum is available only to the Kovac family, however contradictory that might be.

He closes down the internet and opens the folder marked *Stories.* For the past two years he has been working on a novel, although he dare not even think of it in those terms. It's a longish story. It won't become a novel until it's published, and that's never going to happen, because he has no intention of sending it to anyone.

It's about a boy growing up with a mentally ill mother in Norrtälje. That's the framework, but the real theme is parallel worlds. Both the boy and his mother seek refuge from their poverty-stricken existence through fantasies and delusions respectively, and live their real lives in worlds constructed inside their heads. The story ends when the boy returns to Norrtälje as an adult, after his mother's death. He stands in an empty apartment and realises that now only the cold, barren reality remains. Is this preferable?

The last sentence goes like this: 'He stood by the window staring at the tall, nondescript trunks of the pine trees with their pale green crowns. Then he glimpsed a movement among the branches. An angel or a devil poked its nose out and beckoned him. *Come.*' The implication is that the boy is going to be affected by the same illness as his mother, and will continue to live in a parallel world.

The story is sufficiently autobiographical and close to home to make that a good reason for not showing it to anyone else. And yet that's not the main reason. Johan has checked online and discovered that a maximum of two per cent of unsolicited manuscripts sent to publishers are accepted; the rest are rejected.

The very word. *Rejected.* With everything that has gone wrong in Johan's life, being *rejected* would . . . there are many metaphors. The drop, the straw. The glass, the camel's back. As long as he doesn't send his story to anyone, as long as it doesn't get rejected, he can keep believing that he's written something fantastic.

He reads through the first few chapters for the umpteenth time. Changes the odd word, removes a comma. To be honest, there's nothing else he can do. The story is finished.

If I think, Johan's at work, now I know where you are.

Was there a little hint there, the faint hope of a possibility? No, Johan can't let himself think like that. What happened by the Linnaeus monument that day was the most painful rejection he has ever had in his life, and he has no intention of allowing it to happen again.

LIKE A BOUNCING BALL

It is Saturday, and Siw and Alva are playing football on the pitch not too far from their apartment block. Actually, *playing* is overstating the case. Siw passes the ball to Alva, who attempts to kick it. She is in training. After weighing up the pros and cons for several weeks, Alva announced on Friday that she wanted to join the football team made up of girls her own age that she's seen playing on the pitch.

Siw had no objections. For one thing, it's good for Alva to engage in some form of physical activity, and for another, it suits Siw perfectly. Training takes place every Monday and Thursday from six until seven, and the pitch is halfway between home and the gym, so she can do her training while Alva is similarly occupied.

The powder diet has reached the ketogenic phase, and Siw is no longer hungry, although she occasionally feels as if she might faint. The bathroom scales show that she has lost three kilos. Not exactly *The Biggest Loser*, but it's a start. The worst thing is that the diet is so incredibly boring. Siw has never been what you'd call a foodie, but now it's off limits she can imagine nothing more enjoyable than eating real food.

Anything that stops her from thinking about food is welcome, and when Alva said that she wanted to do some training so that she'd be able to manage the actual training, Siw agreed without hesitation. Alva is better at victory gestures and poses than actually striking the ball with her foot. Then again, from what Siw has seen, the other seven-year-olds' training involves running around and playing games as much as football.

Siw kicks the ball gently in Alva's direction. Her daughter adopts the stance of someone who is about to kick down a door, runs a few steps then swings her leg back and then forward. She misses the ball, but the impetus of the movement continues, and she lands flat on her back. It looks very funny, and once she is sure that Alva hasn't hurt herself, Siw turns her head and wipes away the involuntary smile on her lips.

'Oh, for goodness' sake!' Alva says. 'I don't know what to *do*!'

Siw has managed to quell the impulse to laugh. 'I'm no expert, but I think you're supposed to try to keep your eyes on the ball.'

'Keep your eyes on the ball?' Alva says, scrambling to her feet and pretending to hold on to her eyes. 'What does *that* mean?'

'Look at it.'

'I am looking at it! What do you think I'm looking at?'

'Sometimes I think you're looking at your feet.'

'I *never* look at my feet!'

The sound of an engine is approaching from the direction of the Contiga Hall behind Siw. She rolls the ball towards Alva, who stares at it as she measures her shot, draws back her foot and delivers the perfect kick, sending the ball flying past her mother.

'Brilliant! Well done!' Siw exclaims. Alva breaks out into a victory celebration worthy of Ronaldo, and seems to be on the point of pulling off her top as Siw turns to fetch the ball.

A sit-on mower is chugging across the grass, and when Siw

recognises the driver that treacherous flush stains her cheeks red. Oh well, she's playing football, so there's nothing unusual about having red cheeks, is there?

Max raises a hand in greeting and drives up to her. He is wearing a high-vis jacket and a green baseball cap with the word 'Green' on it, which makes sense. His long legs are drawn up, his bony knees sticking out on either side of the wheel. He switches off the engine and Siw says: 'So you work Saturdays too?'

'There's a match this afternoon and the pitch needed mowing, so . . .' Max places his hands on the wheel and rests his chin on them, looking at Siw. 'Listen, I . . .' He is interrupted by Alva, who marches over and asks: 'Who are you?'

'My name is Max. And you must be . . . Alva?'

Alva opens her eyes wide and glances at Siw. 'He knows my name!' She turns her attention back to Max. 'How do you know my name?'

'Your mum told me. And I see you play football – how's it going?'

'Quite badly. But sometimes it goes well.' Alva claps her hands and points at Max, with more than a hint of accusation. 'Are you *the guy*?'

'I don't know. How can I tell if I'm the guy?'

'If you're seeing my mummy, then you're the guy.'

'Alva, please.' Siw's cheeks are about to burst into flames. 'This is something you've made up. There is no guy.'

In order to hide her burning face, she bends down to retrieve the ball. She straightens up a little too quickly, and her head spins. She takes a few wobbly steps, and has to grab hold of the mower to stop herself from falling.

'You see!' Alva says to Max. 'She almost *faints* when you're around.'

'What's wrong?' Max asks.

'I always start the day with a bottle of vodka. No, I just stood up too quickly.'

'Almost faints!' Alva repeats, staggering across the grass like a drunk before collapsing, arms and legs sticking out.

Max tries again. 'Listen, I'm sorry I didn't call you, it's been, it is . . . difficult. For me. Because I . . . oh, it's a long story. But it's not that I don't like you. Because I do.'

'Oh my God!' Alva presses her hands to her heart. 'Oh my God!' Max laughs, and even Siw can't help smiling, even though it's uncomfortable to say the least to have her love life exposed by a seven-year-old.

'Anyway . . .' Max goes on. 'You're coming to Marko's tonight, aren't you? We can talk more then.'

'Okay,' Siw says, once again pretending to run a hand over her face, when in fact she is forcing down the corners of her mouth.

'Bye, Alva. Nice to meet you. Maybe we'll see each other again,' Max says.

'Oh yes! Yes, yes!' Alva shouts with exaggerated ecstasy as Max starts the mower and sets off. Siw does *not* stand there watching him go; instead, she rolls the ball to Alva, who stops it with her foot but doesn't kick it.

'There's no law that says you have to play the fool all the time, you know,' Siw points out.

'Oh yes there is – otherwise you get sent to jail. Mummy?'

'What?'

Alva jerks her head towards Max, who is moving across the pitch in a straight line. 'He's really fit,' she says with the assurance of the connoisseur. 'And he seems nice too. Are you going to a party tonight?'

'We are.'

Alva nods, then makes the kind of comment that always puzzles Siw. Where does she get them from – Anna? Donald Duck? God knows. With her eyes still fixed on Max, Alva whispers theatrically: 'Get in there!'

*

A ten-year-old girl is walking towards the old Society Bridge from the south. She is carrying her phone, and takes a quick selfie which she posts on Snapchat to keep her Snapstreak going. An elderly man is approaching from the opposite direction, pulling a trolley filled with groceries from ICA Kryddan.

They both step onto the bridge at the same time, but because the girl is moving considerably faster, she reaches the crown long before the man. She trips on a piece of wood that is sticking up and drops her phone. It skids across the slippery, sloping surface, on its way to the gap beneath the railing.

The man sees it happen. The phone is coming straight towards him, and all he has to do to stop it falling into the water is to stick out his foot. However, the sight of the girl has reminded him that his grandchildren never come to visit, plus how frightening all this new technology is. He stops dead and watches the phone as it slides over the edge only a couple of centimetres from his foot.

'No, no, nooo!' the girl yells, banging her temples with her fists in sheer frustration. 'Why didn't you do something?'

The man looks at her. And smiles.

MARKO'S PARTY

I

'I could get used to this.'

Lukas gestures with his beer bottle, taking in the Kvisthamra inlet, sparkling in the afternoon sun. He, Markus and Amanda have driven up from Stockholm an hour before the agreed time to 'inspect the property', as they put it. They've toured the house and garden and finally ended up on the terrace, where Marko has laid out enough spirits, wine and beer for twice as many people as have been invited.

'How much did you say?' Markus asks. 'Twelve million?'

'Thirteen,' Marko replies, mixing a Screwdriver for Amanda.

'Shit. And you're just going to *give* it to your parents?'

'I am.'

Amanda takes the drink. 'Thanks. I mean, I can't give my parents anything, because they've already got everything. It's such a shame.'

'Mmm,' Lukas says. 'Then again, I wouldn't even give my parents a dog kennel – they've always been so tight with their money.'

As far as Marko recalls from his time at the School of Economics, Lukas wasn't exactly short of cash. He didn't have to do anything in order to acquire the designer labels he always wore, while Marko worked on a hot dog stand at the weekends to keep up a decent standard.

Markus shakes his head. 'I remember once I took home a bottle of wine for some dinner or something, and it was a decent bottle. My dad just said 'so thoughtful', and stuck it in the door of the fridge. He didn't even put it in the wine cooler – as if it was only good enough to cook with.'

Marko has nothing to add; his own experiences are so radically different from those of his friends from the capital city. They were never particularly close at college, and it is only in later years that they've started to hang out. They frequent the same clubs around Stureplan, they work in roughly the same field, and they're all single by choice.

'I don't think I've ever seen such a big terrace,' Lukas says, waving the bottle around again. 'I went to Johan Persson's place once, and it was . . . No, it definitely wasn't this big.'

'*The* Johan Persson?' Amanda asks.

'Yes – how many Johan Perssons do you know?'

'I was thinking of putting in a pool,' Marko says. 'If Mum and Dad want one.'

'Perfect!' Markus replies. 'In that case, you'll need someone to look after it.'

'I haven't thought that far ahead.'

'I'll give you a number. They're really good. Expensive, but good.'

'Okay.'

'Cheers!' Markus holds out his bottle so that Marko can clink his against it. He puts on a silly voice and says: 'Let's get wasted!'

2

Maria arrives half an hour later. Marko isn't sure if it's an attempt at irony, but she's carrying two giant bags of barbecue flavour crisps. Marko introduces her to his friends, and the atmosphere changes in an entirely predictable way. Lukas and Markus metaphorically stick out their chests, while Amanda behaves as sweetly as possible in order to hide her jealousy. Everything becomes a little stiff and awkward, until Maria shakes the bags and says: 'Can you find me a bowl? Seven years on a starvation diet – tonight I'm eating crisps!'

'Bowls are not among the things I've acquired so far.'

'A bucket, then?'

'You want to put crisps in a bucket?'

'Oh, never mind.' Maria rips open one of the bags and stuffs a handful of crisps in her mouth. She points to the drinks table. 'Fix me a G & T. A strong one.'

Marko is confused by Maria's behaviour. He knows she is capable of cool elegance, but she appears to have opted for a different role, something along the lines of Markus's 'Let's get wasted!', but a lot more convincing. She doesn't seem to be entirely sober, and in direct contravention of her order he pours only a small amount of gin into the glass. Behind him he hears Lukas ask the standard question: 'Are you by any chance a model?'

'Nope,' Maria says through a mouthful of half-chewed crisps. 'I work in a café.'

'But . . . I thought Marko said . . .'

'Marko is a liar. He once said our father was Goran Bregovic.'

'Who?'

'Exactly. What Swede cares about Goran Bregovic? He's an idiot, my brother.'

As Marko adds tonic to the splash of gin, he remembers that there's a good reason why he hasn't spent much time with his sister over the last few years. She doesn't just get on his nerves, she tramples all over them. In spiked shoes.

3

'I saw Siw today. Purely by chance, on the football pitch.'

Max notices that his right shoelace is undone, so he stops and hands the bottle of Valpolicella to Johan, who studies the label before saying: 'I thought you were going to call her?'

'I was, but I . . . didn't get round to it.' Max ties a double knot. The laces of his best shoes are slippery and have a tendency to come undone.

'Why not?' Johan is uncharacteristically interested; Max knows this is because he's nervous about the party, as he is about any social event outside the bowling hall, and would prefer to delay their arrival.

Max straightens up and is about to take back the bottle, but instead he says: 'You might as well hand it over.'

Johan hasn't brought a gift, presumably because he can't afford it, and Max is happy to give up the three-hundred kronor bottle if it helps to calm his nerves. Johan looks at the label again, as if he is seeing the wine in a new light now that it's his to pass on to Marko. 'Thanks. Why?'

'The bottle?'

'No. That Siw.'

384

Johan has a tendency to refer to Siw and Anna as 'That Siw' and 'That Anna', underlining the fact that he doesn't really know them. They have stopped twenty metres from Marko's gate, and Max thinks for a moment before replying: 'It's hard to explain. Deep down I think I'm scared.'

Max is expecting some comment, along the lines of *scared she'll crush you when she lies on top of you?*, but Johan simply asks: 'What do you mean, scared?'

Max would almost have preferred the usual sarcasm. It's difficult to think about these things, but he makes an attempt. 'She gets inside my head. In a way I don't understand. And I don't know if I've got the courage. To let her in.'

Johan nods. Something in his expression changes, and he says: 'Plus, of course, it's hard being in love with a fat blob.'

And with that, everything is back to normal. They continue in silence, and only when Max has pushed open the gate does Johan add: 'Sorry. Tourette's, you know. Just go with the flow. If it's going to happen, it will. Don't think so much. As Marko and I would have said in our platitude game: *Listen to your heart.*'

They can hear voices from the terrace, and instead of going to the front door they head around the back of the house. Max glances at Johan, whose lips are clamped together. He is clutching the neck of the bottle so tightly that his knuckles are white.

As they turn the corner they see Marko and Maria chatting to three people that Johan would probably refer to as typical big city tossers. Medium-length, slicked-back hair using plenty of styling wax for the boys, an ash-blonde pageboy for the girl. Shirts in pale pastel colours tending towards pink; loose-fitting cream designer blouse.

Max recognises only Lukas, who was in the same class in his first

385

year at the School of Economics. Lukas is the first to spot them. 'Max! My man! How's it hanging?' Max makes a vague gesture. *Comme ci, comme ça.*

Maria turns around. She is wearing blue jeans and a black T-shirt, and she is clutching a giant bag of crisps. It only takes a second to see how the land lies, how the two men are following the slightest movement of her body.

As Max and Johan step forward she flings her arms wide, gives Johan a big hug and says: 'Sweetie darling!', before planting a barbecue-flavoured kiss on his lips.

Lukas and Markus exchange glances. An almost imperceptible frown, an equally subtle shrug: *What the fuck?*

4

'Yuck,' says Siw. 'Yuck, yuck, *yuck*.'

'What's yuck?' Anna asks, taking another swig from her hip flask.

'All this,' Siw says, waving a hand at the showy house towering above them as they stand on the drive next to Marko's Audi. There is another Audi parked beside it, also black and almost as new. It's as if the place is hosting a diplomatic summit.

'What's wrong with all this?' Fortunately Anna is not slurring her words, even though she's drunk three glasses of wine on Siw's balcony, topped up with frequent slugs of vodka from the hip flask.

'You know. People. Strangers you have to talk to. Judging us. I can't . . . Shall we go home?'

Anna hands over the hip flask. 'Okay, let's start with a sip of this.'

Siw does as she's told. She feels the heat spreading through her body. Neat booze isn't really her thing, but right now . . . No

386

doubt it's auto-suggestion, but it's as if the liquid is lubricating and loosening the knot in her stomach.

'We're at war, remember that.' Anna replaces the cap on the flask and slips it into her back pocket. 'This is *war*. What Max said to you . . . now it's war. Which has to be won.'

'He just said he liked me.'

'Exactly – and that's *war*. To conquer new territory. Advance. Forward, men! And so on. What was it Alva said?'

'Get in there.'

Anna snorts with laughter, and a drop of saliva lands on Siw's cheek. 'That kid! God, I love her! What more is there to say? Get in there, Siw!'

Fewer people than Siw had feared are gathered on the terrace, but on the other hand the guys from Stockholm look *exactly* like the kind she's been dreading. The second Siw and Anna round the corner of the house, the two men glance at them then raise a quizzical eyebrow at Marko: *Surely they're not supposed to be here?*

Siw seeks refuge in Max's eyes. He is looking at her with warmth, and her heart can't decide whether to beat even faster, or slow right down. For a moment she thinks she's had a sudden attack of arrhythmia.

'Anna!' Marko says. 'Siw! Welcome!'

A girl who was standing with her back to them turns around. Raven hair and startling green eyes, regarding them with interest. She holds out her hand to Anna and says: 'Hi. Maria – Marko's sister.'

Anna takes the hand and shakes it. She shakes her own head at the same time. 'Seriously? Is this some kind of joke?'

'What?' Maria asks.

'I mean, surely no one's allowed to be that fucking beautiful? It's just not fair.'

387

The frank comment seems to knock Maria off balance. In the absence of something to say, she offers Anna the bag she is clutching. 'Crisps?'

'Fantastic,' Anna says, helping herself to a generous handful.

5

Marko is turning over the T-bone steaks on the barbecue. An hour or so has passed since everyone arrived, and so far things are going okay. Admittedly his Stockholm friends are mainly keeping themselves to themselves, with an odd remark thrown in Maria's direction. This is a waste of time, because his sister – much to Marko's surprise – is only interested in talking to Anna.

Maybe her fascination is due to the fact that Anna actually *is* the person that Maria is *appearing* as this evening. They also share a keenness to consume alcohol which doesn't bode well, and make regular visits to the drinks table, where they loudly discuss what 'cocktail' to mix next.

Siw, Max and Johan have formed a little group of their own. Johan looks as if he feels like the third wheel; he keeps shuffling his feet and glancing towards the water, as if death by drowning might be an option. Marko can't help him right now; he has his hands full with the meat. It has been marinading according to Goran's recipe, and the aroma emanating from the Weber barbecue, bought especially for the occasion, is making his mouth water.

Lukas strolls over, one hand in his front pocket, a can of Modus Hoperandi in the other. He lowers his voice. 'Okay, so I get Max and that guy Johan, but those girls? What's that all about? Are they childhood friends too?'

'Nope,' Max says, using the tongs to inspect the underside of a steak. 'I've only known them for a week or so.'

'Right . . . so what's the deal?'

'Deal?'

'Come on, you know what I mean.'

'No, I don't. Explain.'

Lukas holds up his hands in a gesture of resignation as he takes a step back. 'O-kay. Have it your way.'

Marko watches him as he turns and engages Markus's attention for a fresh attempt on Maria. Of course, he knows what Lukas means. Max is capable of behaving and speaking *properly*, while Siw, Anna and Johan are a different breed. *Norrtälje folk.*

But they are in Norrtälje right now, on their turf, which is essentially Marko's too, and he has no intention of letting Lukas question their right to be here. He understands the question, but he does not acknowledge its right to be asked.

6

Anna is having so much fun – firstly because Maria is a party girl, and secondly because it's amazing to chat to someone you normally only see in pictures. *Literally.* Anna occasionally treats herself to a fashion or women's magazine to while away a pleasant hour or two, and she has realised that Maria really is the person she has seen on a number of front covers. It's like being allowed to hang out with a benevolent alien from outer space.

And for once she is with someone who is as keen on drinking as she is. Siw is so fucking boring in that way, while Maria happily knocks back one cocktail after another without getting unpleasantly drunk. It's unbelievable, but Anna has reached the point where she knows she's going to have to slow down if she's going to stay the course all evening. Maria! What a girl!

Anna has realised that she's not the only one who feels that way. Those stuck-up Stockholmers are approaching, with their sticky hair and tight-lipped smiles that seem to want to say: *seeeriously?* They position themselves next to Maria, and before they can come out with some trite phrase, Anna says: 'Lukas and Markus? So what have you done with Matteus and Johannes, the other two gospel writers?' Maria snorts into her rum and Coke.

Markus's smile becomes even tighter. 'You're not the first person to come up with that.'

'Okay. So, do you always come in a pair? Like Laurel and Hardy?'

Maria raises her hand and Anna gives her a high five before taking such a deep slug of her drink that she almost chokes. *Easy now. Let's not lose the plot completely.* Markus and Lukas retire, and to her satisfaction Anna notes that she has *almost* managed to obliterate that supercilious smirk.

Norrtälje: 1, Stockholm: 0

'Lukas and Markus,' Maria says, shaking her head. 'Why did I never think of that?'

'*You're not the fiiirst person to come up with thaaat,*' Anna says, imitating their Stockholm drawl. 'Are you from a . . . religious background?'

'Catholic. Saints, the whole shooting match. How about you?'

'Nihilists. On my mother's side. No joy in life, the whole shooting match.'

'Nili . . . ? What do they believe?'

'Forget it. Fancy another?'

Maria glances over at Max and Siw, who are chatting away while

Johan stands beside them, listening passively. 'I think I need to spend some time with Johan.'

'*Johan?* The guy who . . . ? Are you close?'

'He's been one of the most important people in my life.'

Anna turns her entire body in order to study Johan properly, with this new information in mind. She thinks he looks every bit as spiky and miserable as usual, but she has to admit that his superciliousness is more bearable than Lukas and Markus's attitude. And he has been very important to the sublime Maria.

'No shit,' she says. 'Tell me more.'

7

The Mud Man . . .

Johan gazes out across the inlet while Max and Siw continue to chat. He read somewhere that during the time when Norrtälje was the finest bathing resort on the east coast, the allegedly health-giving mud from the Kvisthamra inlet was the main attraction. People arrived en masse on steamboats to wallow in it, and it was the Mud Man who gathered it every morning, using a long-handled scoop.

The Mud Man. It sounds like the title of a story. Johan can see the man in his mind's eye, bobbing up and down in his skiff. There is a dog with him. A . . . Labrador? No, a mongrel, an indefinable dog, and it is blind in one eye. Its nose is sticking out over the side.

It usually happens spontaneously, but now Johan consciously allows himself to drift away, to give himself up to the images that could form a narrative. Max and Siw are comparing memories of their childhood in Norrtälje, and there is a tone in their conversation that Johan can't bring himself to join in with. A positive, nostalgic tone that he would like to tear apart with filth and sarcasm, but he is sensible and sober enough to realise that it's best to keep quiet. And so he thinks about the Mud Man instead.

What is the problem, the conflict? Didn't people claim that the mud was radioactive, which was seen as an excellent and miraculous quality back then? Assuming this was true, then the man and his dog would have been exposed to huge amounts of radioactivity, and . . . Johan smiles to himself. *Toxic Avenger* in Norrtälje. Maybe . . .

'What are you grinning at?'

Maria rests her forehead on his cheek. Her breath is imbued with a considerable amount of alcohol. Johan puts his arm around her shoulders and kisses the top of her head. 'How's it going?'

'Mmm. Good. Anna is so funny.' Maria ignores the fact that Siw and Max are in the middle of a discussion about how they *must* have seen each other in Society Park at some point. Still maintaining contact with Johan, she prods Siw's shoulder. 'Hey. Your friend. She's really funny.'

'I'm glad you think so,' Siw replies.

'Don't *you* think so? In that case, you must be seriously boring.'

'Leave them alone,' Johan says, using his grip on her shoulders to turn her away. 'They've got a lot to talk about.'

Maria leans back and whispers in his ear on a warm breath: 'Of course they have. Because Max is seriously boring too.'

Johan manoeuvres her a metre or so away from the others. 'Listen, don't you think you ought to slow down a bit? With the drinking?'

'Me?' Maria frees herself from his embrace. She makes a quarter turn, then marches along the gap between two planks of wood without the slightest hesitation. 'Look. *I walk the line*. No problem.'

'Not entirely convincing. You usually have to—'

'Hush,' says Maria. 'Come with me. I want to talk to you.'

Johan is about to give in when Marko announces that the food is ready.

'Later,' he says.

8

Dinner is a spartan affair. T-bone steak and potato salad, eaten off paper plates with plastic cutlery, sitting cross-legged on the terrace. Served with wine from a tetra-pak in plastic glasses. The conversation has become more animated as tongues are loosened by alcohol, and Max sees Johan talking to both Lukas and Amanda. Good, that means he doesn't have to feel responsible for his social wellbeing.

It's funny how Markus, Lukas and Amanda, who from week one at the School of Economics always wanted to lunch at the Sturehof, have no problem with eating as if they were at the Sweden Rock festival. During his years in Stockholm, Max learned a fair amount about the behavioural code relating to status. It can be a more heinous crime to wear the wrong kind of shoes than to throw up on said shoes during Gotland Week. Also, more or less anything is okay, as long as *everyone* does it. Living *la vida cabrón*, *no problemos*.

After they've eaten Marko picks out a Spotify dance mix played through a Bluetooth speaker, and switches on a couple of strings of lights fresh from their packaging. Not exactly Ibiza, but he creates a party atmosphere approximately as spartan as the dinner.

Max goes down the steps to the garden and sits on the bottom one. He gazes out across the lawn, and can't help thinking that it will be a big job for Goran to keep it tidy. He contemplates the overgrown berry bushes and the trees badly in need of pruning, while his thoughts turn to Siw.

He really enjoys talking to her, and the more she relaxes and smiles, the more attractive he finds her. He subconsciously places a picture mount over her, paring away all the excess flesh so that he can see only her pretty face inside the frame. Yes, definitely attractive. Lovely.

And yet it's as if their conversation is conducted on the level of polite interest, like two well-brought-up cousins who don't know each other, but have been pushed together because they're the same age, and suddenly have to find something to say. Maybe it's because they're not talking about *that*, the thing that unites them; maybe *that* is the inflatable elephant in the room that must be punctured before they can begin to get close. But does he even want that? She might be really attractive and nice, but . . .

Two huge hands land on his shoulders and give a couple of squeezes.

'Hi, Marko,' Max says without turning around. Only one person present has hands like that.

'Hi.' Marko sits down beside him. 'What are you thinking about?'

'The lawn.' Max waves his glass in the direction of the broad expanse. 'It's going to be a lot of work for Goran, taking care of this.'

Marko laughs and shakes his head. 'Your job has damaged you for life, you know that?'

'And the shrubs need pruning and those apple trees—'

'*Skål.*' Marko clinks his glass against Johan's. 'And shut the fuck up – it'll be fine. I can employ you, if the worst comes to the worst.' Marko leans back and looks at Max as if he's made a new discovery. 'Seriously – would you be interested?'

'I've got quite a lot on as it is.'

'But in the winter? You're not as busy then, surely?'

'You can't prune in the winter. We'll see. Maybe.'

Marko nods and seems pleased with the realisation that he has a skilled gardener in his circle of friends. He places his hand on the back of Max's neck and squeezes, as if he's claiming ownership. 'You and Siw seem to be getting on well.'

'Yes. She's nice. She's lovely.'

'A bit picky, though? She hardly ate anything.'

'She's on powder.'

'She's on what?'

'Powder – one of those diet things.'

'Ah.' Marko tenses and shows off his right biceps. 'I've done that from time to time. I've never gone along the anabolic steroids route, but—'

He is interrupted by Maria's voice behind them. 'Showing off as usual?' Max looks around and sees Maria making her way down the steps. She is supported by Johan, who smiles apologetically as if Maria's tipsiness is his fault.

Max has always had the feeling that Maria nurtures a barely concealed antipathy towards him, something that has been there from day one. No, that's wrong. Since the day when Max fixed Goran up with a job. Since then Maria has always given him funny looks and been reluctant to talk to him. Things didn't improve when they were in Stockholm. It is what it is.

Max and Marko shuffle to the sides to make room. Johan leads the way, followed by Maria with a hand on his shoulder. She uses the other to ruffle Max's hair in a condescending way as she says: 'Tiddleypom!'

'Maria, you've had enough to drink,' Marko says.

Maria gives Marko the finger behind her back. She swallows the first part of a sentence that ends with: '. . . *not* my father.'

'It's okay,' Johan says. 'I've got her.'

Marko frowns as he watches his sister totter away, still leaning on Johan, before eventually flopping down with her back against a gnarled apple tree about twenty metres away. He gives himself a shake as if to rid himself of unwanted thoughts, then turns to Max. 'So, how much would you charge? Theoretically, of course.'

9

Johan and Maria are surrounded by windfalls. The ground beneath the tree is strewn with apples that have fallen without bringing pleasure to anyone, and in the semi-darkness they simply look like round blobs.

'Apple,' Maria says, picking one up and biting into it, only to spit out the flesh a second later. 'Fuck! Rotten!' She throws the piece of fruit away, and it rolls across the grass like a rejected draft for the Apple logo. 'Bleurrgh!'

She slumps back against the tree, continuing to spit and make disgusted noises, which eventually turn into a whimper.

'So, how are you really?' Johan asks.

'Fitasafiddle.'

'Sorry?'

'Fit . . . as a . . . Oh, forget it. Now, I'm going to ask you a question, and I want you to give me an honest answer.'

She straightens up and her eyes sparkle as they catch the reflection of the lights on the terrace, where the bass beat of an Avicii track has taken over. She leans towards Johan. 'Was it you and Marko?'

'Was what me and Marko?'

'Honest answer, Johan. Was it?'

Johan hasn't had a great deal to drink; he is just on the borderline where instead of being blurred, everything seems much clearer than in normal, everyday life. Maria's question enters his head as if it is passing through a vacuum, insulated from anything else. A straight question that demands a straight answer. 'Yes.'

Maria slams her hand on the ground, squashing a half-rotten apple. While she wipes her palm on the tree trunk, Johan tries to think through the consequences of what he has just admitted. He can't come up with any.

'I knew it,' Maria says. 'I *knew* it. What did you use?'

'Rounders bats.'

It's amazing how easy it is to tell her, now he's started. And liberating. Marko might have said that it hadn't happened, but that isn't how it has seemed to Johan, deep in his soul. It has sat there like a rusty nail, however justified their action might have been. Telling Maria makes the intensity of the sharp pain diminish slightly.

'I mean, Marko I can understand, but you? How could you do something like that?'

'I love you. You know that.'

'Fine . . . that's great, but . . . Aha!' Maria says, slapping herself on the forehead as if, like Newton under a different apple tree, she has suddenly understood. 'Love! Of course! It's always love! Aha!'

'What are you talking about?'

Maria thumps Johan on the shoulder with the spontaneous violence of someone who is drunk. 'Honesty, we said. And of course, you're in love with Marko – or you were back then. Then again, I've known that since . . . since forever, I just didn't think . . . So which is it?'

'Which is what?'

'Is it *were* or *are*?'

397

In the same spirit of simplicity and liberation, Johan replies: 'Are. Am.'

'Ohhhh!' Maria exclaims, not so much embracing Johan as falling on him and covering his cheek with wet kisses. 'That bastard,' she says, pointing to her brother, who is on his way up the steps, 'is as straight as a fucking *ruler*.'

'Yes, so I've learned.'

'The hard way?'

'Definitely the hard way.'

'Ohhh . . .'

'Enough with the kisses, thank you,' Johan says, wiping his wet cheek.

'And it was you,' Maria says, clumsily patting him on the back, 'who was messing with my clothes. What did you do? Try them on?'

'Yes.'

'Hmm.' Maria slumps back against the tree, exhausted by all the confessions and confidences. Johan wonders if he's going to regret this in the morning, but at the moment he thinks it's good to have shared his secrets with someone, and he's glad that someone is Maria. He feels *clean* in a way he hasn't done for a long time.

'Hey Brother' starts up on the terrace, while Maria's breathing slows. The track blends in with the sound of cheering and laughter and applause. Johan checks that Maria is safe, then goes to see what's happening.

10

Anna is dancing, or rather digging the music as hard as it is humanly possible to do in her condition. She has taken off her

398

shoes, tights and blouse, and is dancing in a thin camisole. Her upper body billows and surges, her spare tyres bouncing as her feet perform out-of-time steps across the decking as she informs everyone at the top of her voice that there is nothing in this world she wouldn't do.

Markus, Lukas and Amanda are sitting in a triangle around her, shouting encouragement while filming her on their phones.

'Move that body, shake that booty, baby!'

The drop comes, and Anna wiggles her broad backside, wobbling and tottering so that she nearly falls over. The cheering reaches new heights. Marko has just arrived on the terrace, and if he has felt a growing distaste towards his Stockholm friends during the course of the evening, that feeling is now a lot closer to hatred.

He goes up to Anna in order to put a stop to the degrading spectacle, but when she sees him she spreads her arms wide and takes a few steps backwards, still moving as she calls out: 'Marko! Dance with me, baby!'

Marko gives his so-called friends a withering look; they are still filming like bored tourists who have finally got to see the natives doing something *real*. There is only one way to reduce the level of Anna's humiliation. He steps forward. And begins to dance. Out of the corner of his eye he sees Lukas and Markus lower their phones and grimace at each other.

'Yeah!' Anna is completely unaware of the city-versus-small town drama in which she has the central role. Marko isn't keen on dancing, but he runs through his repertoire of standard moves, which Anna delightedly copies, arms and legs flying in all directions. Her gaze is unfocused and sweat is pouring down her face.

Marko moves closer and manages to catch her when she stumbles and falls forwards. Her body is heavy and slippery in his arms.

She presses her cheek to his stomach and murmurs: 'Oh, Marko. Mmm . . . Marko.'

'I think you need to lie down for a while,' he says.

'Whatever you say, Marko. Whatever you say.'

With one arm draped over his shoulders, she allows herself to be led into the house. She stinks of sweat and booze, and Marko can't stop his lip from curling in disgust. He steers her over to his camp bed, which complains loudly as she flops down. When he tries to lay her on her side, she grabs hold of his shirt and tries to pull him close.

'Stop it, Anna.'

She pouts, runs her tongue over her lips. 'I love you so much, Marko.'

'Mmm. Now lie down.'

He makes a fresh attempt to push her over, but with surprising speed she clamps her hand round the back of his neck and presses her lips to his. This time Marko has to use more force to free himself. 'For fuck's sake, Anna – stop it!'

'But I *love* you,' Anna whimpers.

'Yes, but I don't love you and I never will, so stop it!'

'Never ever? Not even a tiny bit?'

'No. I like you when you're being sensible, but I'll never like you when you're in this state, and that's the end of it.'

Finally Anna goes along with his plea to lie down, but she does so by hurling herself sideways, drawing her knees up to her chest and bursting into tears. Marko spreads his arms wide in a gesture of resignation directed to some divine figure who may be watching him. *I did what I could, okay?*

He suspects things might get even more difficult and embarrassing if he tries to console her, so he leaves the room and goes in search of Siw. On the terrace he flicks a double V-sign at Markus and Amanda, who are gawping at their screens. He looks around for Lukas, but can't see him. He wants all three of them together so he can tell them what complete dickheads they are.

11

'Psst. Hey!'

Maria raises her head, expecting to see Johan, but instead Lukas or Markus or Matteus or Johannes is crouching in front of her. *So many people.* She is about to close her eyes again when someone, whoever it is, grabs her by the shoulders and shakes her.

'It's me. Lukas. I've got some stuff, if you want it.'

Lukas has some stuff. What is the natural follow-up question? Oh yes, that's it.

'What stuff?'

'You know. You seem a little tired . . . I've got something . . . refreshing.'

Maria is aware that she understands what he means, but her brain refuses to engage. She sees a wide expanse of snow before her. Snow is refreshing. Are they going skiing?

'You juss haveto goforit,' she informs him.

'What?'

'But he . . . whassis name . . . your, our national hero, whassis name? Bergmark? Bergsten?'

'Urban Bergsten?'

'Nooo!' Maria snaps. She wants to be left in peace, but Lukas grabs her hand and pulls her to her feet. Keeping one eye on the house, he leads her towards the drive. 'Are we . . . going to the mountains?' she asks him.

Lukas laughs. 'You could say that. Off piste. Powder snow. Pure Chamonix. Have you been there?'

'Of course. Stenmark, that's his name. Ingemar Stenmark. Married to . . . Björn Borg.'

'You talk too much. Here. Get in.'

Lukas opens the car door and Maria knows that this isn't good, there is something not right about this situation, but she is so tired of *walking and walking and walking* that the temptation of the black leather seat is too much for her. She tumbles into the car and sinks into the soft blackness.

The click as the door closes brings her to her senses for a moment. She finds herself sitting in the passenger seat of an expensive car. She's done this before, many times. Through the windscreen she can see the house that her idiot brother has bought. What's going on? Someone must have . . .

The driver's door opens and Lukas slides in. Oh yes. Him. It's always the same. She sniggers to herself. Men with expensive cars. Penis substitutes.

'What is it?' Lukas asks, reaching into his inside pocket.

'Has anybody ever told you your car is a penis substitute?'

Lukas looks genuinely hurt, so maybe someone has. 'I guess so,' he says, taking out a little Ziploc bag of white powder. 'Why?'

'Just a thought.' Maria knows exactly what is going on now. She has been in this situation before. Twice; no, three times. Paris, Milan and . . . Dubai? Nightclub, car park, car, coke. Not Dubai. Rome?

That's not what's important.

Lukas tips out a pile of powder onto a rectangular Biltema plastic ice scraper and begins to divide the pile into lines with the help of a credit card. American Express. Quite right. Biltema, though? Has someone like Lukas ever been to Biltema?

That's not what's important.

Not doing this. That's what's important. She's not going to do this. She's done it before, many times, but she's not going to do it again. There was a decision, a promise. Yes. This is *bad* for her. She's . . . What is she? *Clean.* She is clean. Maria points to the ice scraper and says: 'No. Not doing it. I'm clean. Two months.'

'You've no idea how good this stuff is,' Lukas assures her. 'And it's so fucking pure. Clean, you could say. You've got to try it.'

Maria's mouth is dry and she feels dizzy, as if she's standing on the edge of a precipice and someone is calling to her from way down below. Someone she wants to get to, someone she has missed. A dear friend, the dearest friend of all.

'Just one line,' Lukas cajoles, showing her the ice scraper with the coke divided into four lines. In the other hand he is holding a cut-off straw.

It was to do with money, that's what it was. She's spent so much money on the white powder. That's not the issue here. This is a freebie. The voice from below is pleading now, and Maria feels a sexual tingle. The voice doesn't belong to her friend, but to her lover, the best she's ever had. She bends over the scraper, inserts the straw in one nostril, closes the other with her finger, and inhales two lines.

Off piste, motherfucker!

It is just as Lukas said, top quality and a high degree of purity. As her thoughts were already moving in that direction, her brain links the sudden clarity to snow, and she is speeding down a mountain, her body so light that she is *flying* across the swirling powdery snow.

As if the lines she has inhaled were piano wires, she is sliced in half, into two people. One is confused and muddled, floating around in a tangle of half-thoughts, while the other is crystal clear, capable of thinking faster and better than usual. At the moment, the latter is in charge. She looks at Lukas, who stares back at her as he frantically rubs his nose and says: 'Mmmmm! Good shit!'

Maria says: 'You juss haveto goforit.'

'Your Norrland accent *sucks*,' says Lukas, and a cunning light sparks in his wide-open eyes as he adds: 'Do *you*?'

'Always.' Maria opens the car door. 'But today I'm on holiday. In Chamonix.'

'I'm serious.' Lukas shakes his head, and a stiff strand of his waxed hair falls over one eye. 'Something in return? Just a little touchy-feely maybe?'

Maria stops dead and turns to face Lukas. 'Once upon a time an oil sheikh offered me a million dollars for one night, and I said no.' She nods at the scraper, where the remains of the coke can still be seen. 'So no, I don't think so. But thanks anyway.'

She gets out of the car a lot more elegantly than she got in, and slams the door behind her. *Touchy-feely?* Who the hell uses that expression? She giggles, her body buzzing with energy. She is not going to be groped in some fancy fucking car. She is going to dance!

12

When Anna wakes, she doesn't know where she is at first. The room is unfamiliar, and her throat contracts with fear, the sense of being lost, of maybe never being able to find her way home. When she turns over the bed squeaks, and she remembers. Regret replaces the fear.

The door leading to the terrace opens, and Axwell & Ingrosso cheerfully inform her that the sun is shining and so is she. The sound fades as the door closes. *This sun is so* not *fucking shining.*

Siw's broad silhouette approaches, and she whispers: 'Are you awake?'

'Unfortunately, yes.'

'How are you feeling?'

'Like shit.'

'Marko said . . .'

'What did he say?'

'That you weren't feeling very well.'

Anna sits up and puts her head in her hands. She is still very drunk, and the darkness behind her eyelids is spinning. She doesn't know exactly what happened a little while ago, but she can see fragments, which is more than enough to make her want to bang her head on the floor.

'I've made an idiot of myself,' she says.

'In what way?'

'In every possible way.'

'I thought you'd be used to that.'

Anna makes a hacking sound that could be a laugh. Siw is quite right. This kind of thing has happened before, but this was something else, wasn't it? Unlike Siw, Anna doesn't have much capacity for shame; what's done is done, but that doesn't mean she can't feel embarrassed, at least when she's still in the place where she made a fool of herself.

'Yes, but . . .'

'But what?'

There is something agitated in Siw's tone, and when Anna looks up she sees that Siw is tapping her index fingers together, as she does when she is impatient. *Max.* Everything seems to have gone

405

Siw's way this evening, and of course she is keen to get back to Max instead of standing here arguing with her pathetic friend.

'But what?' Siw says again. It is perfectly clear that she absolutely doesn't want a lengthy answer.

'But nothing. Go. Disappear. Shoo. I'm fine. I just want to lick my wounds in peace. I'm fine.'

'Sure?'

The truth is that Anna would very much like to belch out a tirade on what a mess she is, what Marko said to her and how much it hurt, but Siw is probably in love, and not the person to share all this with. Plus, she's impatient. Anna waves in the direction of the door.

'Go. Say hi to Max.'

When Siw has gone, Anna feels better for a moment, then the darkness comes crowding in again. The room closes in, she is being suffocated. She stands up on unsteady legs. She has to get out, she needs air.

She hurries across the terrace where the Stockholm tossers are busy dancing with one another. She carries on down the steps, and it is only when she feels the grass beneath her feet that she realises she isn't wearing any shoes, and that her blouse seems to be missing. Fuck it. She doesn't mind the cold, and it's not that chilly anyway.

Where can she go in order to suffer in peace? A moonbeam forms a path across the Kvisthamra inlet like a *via dolorosa*, and Anna is drawn towards it. She crosses the sloping lawn and reaches the water's edge, where a jetty leads almost perfectly to the moonpath. She walks along it, her wet feet leaving dark impressions. At the end of the jetty she sinks down. She leans over the edge, splashes her face with water, which helps to clear her mind. She turns onto her side, bathed in moonlight.

I don't love you and I never will.

406

Regret gives way to grief. She knew she didn't have a chance with Marko, but having it spelled out like that really hurts.

I don't love you and I never will.

It hurts, hurts, hurts to be so attracted to another person and to have all her hopes so firmly crushed, forever. Hurts, hurts. Anna looks at the romantic moonpath, and that hurts too. She covers her eyes with her hands like a little girl and bursts into tears.

13

Marko leaves Max on the bench when Siw comes back, because there seems to be something going on up on the terrace. Again. He feels less like a party host than a childminder, keeping an eye on a gang of naughty kids. He takes the steps in two strides.

Avicii's 'Wake Me Up' is booming from the speakers. He doesn't like the track, he doesn't even like Avicii, and the reason for the guy's overrepresentation on his playlist is his tragic death, which gets people going.

And it has certainly got this lot going. Maria is dancing with Markus and Amanda. Unlike Anna, Maria *can* dance, but there is a craziness about her as she makes guttural noises in time with the music, kicking out and air-boxing as if dancing is not enough to express her ecstasy.

Amanda's dancing is apathetic and hesitant, while Markus is in seventh heaven when Maria moves close to him and allows him to put his hands on her hips. No doubt the fuckers will soon start filming too. When Marko goes up to Maria she seizes his hands and shouts: 'Dance with me, bro! Yiiee!'

'Thanks, I've done enough dancing for tonight.' He studies her

407

eyes; the pupils are huge, dilated. He squeezes her hands. 'Have you taken something?'

'What if I have?' Maria tries to pull away, but Marko holds on tight.

'You told me you were clean.'

'Ow, let me go! One little farewell sniff, that's all. Your friend Lukas had such good stuff.'

Marko releases her hands. '*Lukas?*'

'Mmm.' Maria bounces up and down. 'LukasLukasLukas!'

14

Johan has gone for a long walk along the shoreline, sat on a rock for a while, skimmed some stones along the moonpath. Parties aren't his thing. The only positive aspect is the occasional conversation, like the one he had with Maria under the apple tree. Its warmth still lingers in his chest. They no longer have any secrets from each other, and it makes him happy to know that she will be staying in Norrtälje for the immediate future.

When he returns to Marko's garden he can hear a hell of a racket from the terrace. 'Wake Me Up' is playing, and Maria is shrieking with delight over the music. It's nice that she's enjoying herself, but he has no wish to join in. He heads for the jetty. Halfway there he sees something lying at the very end. The silhouette in the moonlight looks like a pile of earth or a bundle of clothes. A fishing net? After a few more steps he realises that the bundle is both moving and crying.

He knows who it is, and is about to turn away when the warmth in his chest makes him stay. Maria had only good things to say about

Anna. Okay, so she was probably just pleased to have a drinking companion, but even so.

Anna's sobbing is so despairing that Johan can't help being moved, in spite of the fact that he doesn't like her. These are the tears of someone who is at rock bottom, tears from the depths of the person she is or wants to be. Johan sits down quietly a metre away, his back against a bollard.

'Hi,' he says. 'What's wrong?'

Anna snivels and turns towards him. He can't see her face, only the moonlight reflected in the tears covering her face. 'Oh. It's you.'

'Yes. Do you want me to go?'

'No, it's fine.' Anna wipes her eyes. 'I'm done.' The tone of her voice indicates that she is far from done.

'What's wrong?' Johan says again. 'Why are you upset?'

'Like you care.'

'Well, let's pretend I do.'

Anna takes a deep breath, looks at the moonpath and exhales in a long, shuddering sigh. 'I know I'm an idiot,' she says. 'But I'm so in love with Marko, and a little while ago he told me . . . I've got no chance. He made it very clear.'

'I know how that feels,' Johan says.

Anna's head jerks back and the moon flashes in the corner of her left eye. 'You mean . . . with Marko?'

'Yes.'

'I was just guessing. When we played minigolf. So you've also been . . . rejected?'

'Oh yes. Big time.'

They sit in silence, listening to the gentle waves lapping against the jetty's wooden poles. A fish splashes in the water, a dog barks on the other side of the inlet.

'I just feel so stupid,' Anna says. 'I threw myself at him, tried to force him to want me, I . . . put myself on the line, and he . . . no thanks, no chance, never ever. What a fucking idiot.'

'You should hear what I did. But with hindsight . . . what the hell, you have to at least *try*, don't you? Even if it feels really hard at the time, maybe you would have regretted it more and for longer if you'd never tried, never . . . put yourself on the line. Maybe.'

Anna wipes her face more thoroughly with a corner of her camisole, and her voice sounds steadier now. 'That's a point. A good point. Thank you for making that point.'

They sit in silence once more and the noise from the terrace grows louder. Johan shuffles half a metre closer to Anna. 'Shall we start again?' He holds out his hand. 'Hi. Johan. Nerd from Norrtälje.'

Anna scrubs at her eyes one last time, then shakes his hand. 'Hi. Anna. Bimbo from Rimbo.'

Before they have time to say any more, the racket becomes impossible to ignore. Shouting and screaming coming closer, and Johan notes with satisfaction that one of the guys from Stockholm is responsible. Heavy feet march along the jetty, and in the milky light he sees Marko carrying one of the tossers, the one called Lukas.

'Fuck's sake, Marko,' Lukas yells. 'My phone, Marko, my phone, I've got *everything* on there!'

With as little effort as if he had a cat in his arms, Marko strides as far as Johan and Anna, then lifts Lukas high above his head and hurls him three metres into the water. While flying through the air Lukas manages one last: 'My phoooone!' before he crashes into the moonpath, which shatters into thousands of sparkling droplets. After a couple of seconds his head breaks the surface of the water. The guy must be a monomaniac – he's still going on about his phone.

'If you come ashore, I'll kill you!' Marko roars.

'Nice throw,' Johan says.

'Ten out of ten,' Anna adds.

Marko looks from one to the other. 'I thought you two fought like cats and dogs?'

'The thing is,' Johan says, 'we've discovered that we have . . . mutual interests.'

15

Max and Siw are standing side by side, leaning on the fence surrounding the veranda. There's a lot going on down by the water. Markus and Amanda have run after Marko and are trying to persuade him to let Lukas come ashore, while Lukas is flailing around as if he's attempting to clamber onto the moonpath so that he can run to the other side of the inlet.

Maria is beside them, dancing to 'Despacito'. She has come out of her frenetic phase and is swaying with her arms wrapped around her body, dreaming and . . . yes, *despacito*. She hasn't even noticed the uproar; she has a contented little smile on her face, as if she is making love to herself, because this is how they do it down in Puerto Rico.

'So,' Max says. 'How about a walk?'

'Fine. Where shall we go?' Siw replies.

'How about . . . everywhere?'

'Let's do it.'

★

It is Saturday night and the tables outside the riverside restaurant are full. There is something odd about the atmosphere. People are talking more

411

loudly than usual, gesticulating more wildly. A glass of beer is knocked over and someone is pushed, which leads to a harder push. Insults rain down. More people get involved. A fist flies through the air, a body falls, taking a table with it. One or two individuals try to defuse the situation, but their eyes too are wild.

TAKE ME AWAY FROM
ALL THE TOMORROWS

I

When Max and Siw have left the house, they both take out their phones and start up *Pokémon Go* with a synchronicity that makes them smile.

'How many incubators have you got on the go?' Max asks.

'Three. How about you?'

'Seven.'

'*Seven?* How much money do you spend on this?'

'Don't ask.'

They walk along Gustaf Adolfs väg and chat about *Pokémon Go* until they reach the crossroads by Jansson's newsagent's. It is after midnight, and Siw ought to go home. If they carry straight on, they will be able to say goodbye outside her house in fifteen minutes; if they turn right down Glasmästarbacken, who knows how long it will be before she gets home. *Tomorrow is another day* and she needs to pick up Alva from her mum's. Before Max has time to make the decision for both of them, Siw turns right.

'That's where Johan lives.' Max points to the long box-like building that looks as if it was imported direct from Rinkeby. 'And Marko. When we were kids. We used to play on the hill behind the block. Although that was before Marko.'

During the evening Max and Siw have told each other about their upbringing in Norrtälje. They have compared experiences of sledging down Kvisthamra hill, and swimming lessons in the freezing cold water in the old pool. They have laughed at memories from schooldays, and the excitement when the postcode lottery came to the main square. They have shared their amazement at the fact that they both remember the *very* local feud with another school. They have a similar sense of humour and a good memory, and the evening has flowed by like a babbling brook.

Each of them has *one* dark or rather radioactive point. As soon as the conversation veers in that direction, they make sure they move away, talk about something else. In Siw's case, it is Alva's father, while Max has no desire to explain why he dropped out of the School of Economics and allowed his life to take a different route.

They pass Society Park and cross the bridge that forms the boundary between the harbour channel and the river. Lanterns shimmer over the tables in front of the riverside restaurant, and they can hear the sound of raised, angry voices and breaking glass.

'I thought that was a quiet place,' Siw says.

'So did I.'

'Weren't Marko's friends supposed to be staying there tonight?'

'Should suit them perfectly. They might feel like another fight.'

'Weren't you friends with that Lukas?'

'Another time, another life.'

Siw has a vague feeling that this is a quotation, and wishes she'd read more. The only thing she ever quotes spontaneously are Håkan

414

Hellström lyrics. She has the urge to say something about being *beaten by a stranger*, but refrains.

The crane in the harbour reaches up into the sky, its single red eye glowing right at the top, as if the construction of the residential area was being carried out by Sauron. Max and Siw continue up the hill. Siw points to the building on the right. 'Did you go to music school?'

'No. You?'

'Yes. Flute. Once, on my way to a lesson . . .' She stops, looks at Max. 'Shall we talk about this now?'

'Yes. Let's do it.'

As they continue towards Vätövägen, Siw tells him how she had a Hearing which ended up with her making her way onto a roof, from which her flute crashed to the ground and broke. All in vain, because the incident she was trying to warn the men about had already happened.

'So you hear things that have already happened too?'

'Yes. Isn't that the case with your, what did you call them, visions?'

'No. it's almost always stuff that's about to happen very soon. Occasionally slightly longer in advance. But how can it . . . I mean . . .'

'This is what I think,' Siw says as they pass the pizzeria, in darkness now. 'In relation to certain events, it's as if time ceases to have any meaning. It's as if I see everything from such an immense *distance* in time that . . . do you understand? If you take, say, a billion years into account, then a day or a week is completely insignificant.'

'You mean, you see things from that perspective?'

'In a way, yes. I don't understand it myself. Then again, I'm also . . .'

'You're what?'

Siw stops again, stares at the ground, moves her feet up and down. All it needs for her to look like an embarrassed little girl is for her to start tugging at the hem of her sweater. Siw tugs at the hem of her sweater and glances shyly at Max. 'I've never told anyone this. Not even Anna. You're not to laugh, or think I'm crazy.'

'I don't think you're crazy.'

'So I'm . . . I'm a sibyl.'

'A *what*?'

'Don't you know what a sibyl is?'

'Well, yes, of course I do, but . . .' *And that's the end of that*, Siw thinks. *He's going to say that sounds insane, or he'll assume I'm some kind of megalomaniac.*

Max completes the sentence. '. . . but that explains it all.'

'You *believe* me?'

'Why not? Don't forget you're talking to someone who can see into the future.'

Siw explains what her grandmother told her – how the gift may have been diluted over the course of thousands of years, how it is passed on from mother to daughter, and how each daughter gives birth to only one daughter. Then she stops. If Max believes what she is saying, then he ought to realise what that means. He must have understood why she's stopped, because he immediately says: 'I like kids, but I've never seen myself as a father.'

'That could change.'

'Not for me. I have a . . . fear. A fear I don't want to pass on to anyone else.'

Siw senses that they are close to the radioactive point, and doesn't press him. Pain passes across his face, so intense that Siw thinks his eyes change colour. In a strained voice he adds: 'I'll tell you one day. But not now.'

They keep walking. During the evening Max has mentioned 'sometime in the future' and 'next time we see each other', and every time Siw's heart has given a little leap of joy at these unconscious hints that there might actually be a future.

'Can I ask a question?' Siw asks, biting her lip as usual. *Don't ask if you can ask.*

'Of course.'

'That business with the buggy. Outside the library. You *saw* it? Just before it happened?'

'Yes, but I didn't see you. That's what's so weird.'

As they approach Vätövägen they turn left and continue past the school while Max talks about the incident on the silo sixteen years earlier. He waves a dismissive hand when Siw wants to hear more about how he almost fell and Marko saved him. He leaves out Johan's behaviour. 'That's the *only* time that something I've seen didn't happen – because you came into the picture. Or rather you weren't in the picture as far as I was concerned, but you know what I mean.'

Siw doesn't say anything for a while. She looks so gloomy that Max asks if she's okay.

'You're definitely going to think I'm crazy now,' she says. 'But I . . . I don't think I'm a human being.'

'You look a lot like a human being to me. In a good way.'

Siw is so absorbed in her thoughts that she doesn't even notice the flirtatious comment. 'I have a human shell and I do everything that human beings do, but on an essential level . . . my presence in this world is not a human presence.'

'You've lost me now. You're walking beside me, you're talking, I can stroke your hair like this. You are present.'

At least Siw notices Max's caress, but she can't enjoy it because what she is trying to describe is her greatest – and vaguest – source of anxiety.

'I've thought about that,' she says. 'That . . . lopsidedness. How can I have a Hearing, hear the sound of something happening, then step in and prevent it? It doesn't make sense, and the only explanation is that my intervention is not a human intervention, but more . . . divine. Don't misunderstand me, but I'm kind of . . . outside the picture, like you said. Like an invisible force, or . . . a storm from nowhere.'

Siw hopes that Max will recognise the Håkan Hellström quotation so that they can start talking about something else, but he's not prepared to drop the subject to which he has given so much thought.

'Forgive me,' Max says, 'but it seems as if this bothers you a great deal. Why?'

They are on Baldersgatan now.

'Because it makes my life feel unreal. As if I'm not really here, as if I might dissolve at any moment. Simply cease to exist, like a soap bubble.'

'I feel the same. Ever since . . . I don't want to go into it now, but I was involved in something in Cuba. And ever since then I've felt an all-pervasive, existential fear of . . . of living itself. Because it's unreal, ephemeral, and I carry the feeling that I'm not really here.'

'I still don't think it's the same thing.'

'Or else it's exactly the same thing.' Max takes a deep breath, hesitates, then decides to come out with it. 'I'm on medication, by the way.'

'What do you take?'

'Lamictal.'

'I was on that for a while, when I was fifteen.'

'This is more . . . long-term.'

418

Siw shrugs. 'Forgive me, I can see this is hard for you, but practically everybody is on some kind of medication these days. It's no big deal.'

She means well, but Max can't help being hurt when the fear that can sometimes paralyse him is treated so casually. As if *the horror* the Lamictal suppresses were comparable to a sore throat that can be cured with a nasal spray. He pushes his hands deep in his pockets, keeps his eyes fixed on the ground. They reach the top of the hill and continue down towards the bus station. Siw is also lost in thought, and doesn't speak until they reach the cycle racks. She clears her throat. 'Do you like Håkan Hellström?'

'No. No, I don't.'

Siw lets out a little gasp. 'Why not?'

'Does there have to be a reason? Okay – he can't sing, he seems completely soft in the head, his lyrics are either pathetic or incomprehensible, and in recent years he appears to have been struck by some kind of megalomania.'

This time there's a sob before Siw says, with tears in her voice: 'Right.'

'I mean, seriously, you can't . . . Lars Winnerbäck, on the other hand. Now there's someone who really can write lyrics. All right, so he's not the world's most entertaining singer, but those lyrics! He might be the best lyricist Sweden has ever produced, and he's also a brilliant guitarist. Can Håkan even play the guitar?'

Siw isn't listening. She is walking one step ahead of him, slowly shaking her head. They pass the runestone and head for the river. Siw lengthens her stride, and Max calls out: 'Don't be stupid, Siw.'

'I'm going home now,' Siw says, breaking into a jog.

'Seriously?' Max stops ten metres before the bridge. 'Just because—'

'Yes.' Another little sob. 'Just because.'

Max spreads his arms wide. Okay, maybe he went a bit too far because he was annoyed about her comment on his medication, but to screw up the entire evening just because Max doesn't like that idiot from Gothenburg . . . In that case, she *is* crazy, if not in the way she fears. It's a shame, but there's nothing Max can do about it.

2

Siw is halfway across the bridge when she stops and looks around. She turns to Max and shouts: 'Here! Somewhere here! There's someone . . .'

Max is about to sit down, and suddenly he keels over on his side onto the grass. The bridge and the river disappear, and he sees himself sitting in a tree, his hands clutching the branches on either side of him. Something is chafing at his neck, there is a noose around it. He looks at the river, flowing past on his right, the bridge ten metres away. Then he lets go and allows himself to fall forwards. There is some slack in the rope, it takes half a second before the line tightens, his head is jerked forward and . . . Max opens his eyes and sees Siw leaning over him with terror in her eyes.

'A tree!' Max gasps. 'On this side of the river, maybe ten metres from the bridge.' He raises himself on one elbow and points. 'In that direction.'

Siw runs while Max staggers to his feet. He rubs his throat, trying to get rid of the sensation that the rope is still there, strangling him. Then he too breaks into a run. Siw is standing underneath a tree, shouting: 'Hello? Don't do it!'

A man is perched in the tree, five metres above the ground.

He's in his fifties, and his eyes are wells of despair, the impression heightened by the purple shadows beneath them. He looks as if he hasn't slept for a week, and he is wearing dirty jeans and a faded T-shirt with the logo *Spola kröken*, the slogan aimed at persuading people to drink less in the seventies and eighties. There is a noose around his neck, and the rope is slack because it is tied around the same branch on which he is sitting. He is aiming to break his neck rather than be strangled.

'Why not?' he says. 'Everything is a silent, empty, black hell. Go away and let me die in peace.'

'We can't do that,' Max informs him. 'We're here now.'

'But it's all meaningless, all of it. What's the point in dragging yourself out of bed for one more day, when there's no fucking meaning and no fucker cares about you?'

'We care about you,' Siw says. 'That's why we came.'

'What do you mean, that's why you came? How did you know I was going to . . . I've been sitting here for half an hour, and I'd finally made up my mind.'

'We knew,' Max says. 'And that's why we came. Surely you don't want us to stand here and watch when you . . . *I* don't want that – do you, Siw?'

'Definitely not. Come down now – you're not going to do this.'

It takes a minute or so, but eventually the man removes the noose from around his neck. They also manage to persuade him to untie the rope from the branch so that he won't decide to come back later. When he's on the ground, Max takes the rope from him and hurls it into the river. The man watches gloomily as it floats away.

'That was a good rope,' he says. 'I used it on the boat.'

The three of them make their way towards Tullportsgatan, and with every step the man's spine is a little straighter.

'So you've got a boat?' Max says. 'Do you go out in the archi-pelago?'

'Yes. Söderarm, that sort of area.'

Max nods. 'That's the best part. And Röder. Those gently curving, striped rocks.'

'And Norruddarna. Have you been out there?'

'Absolutely. Smooth and flat . . .'

'And the pools of rainwater. Wild strawberries everywhere . . .'

The man's voice has a completely different tone now, and there is a dreamy look in his eyes. As they reach the elm tree outside the state-owned liquor store, he says: 'I don't know what I was thinking. If there's nothing else, at least there's always the archipelago. It's just a shame it's such a short season.'

'Surely it's not too late for one last trip this year.'

The man bangs his fist into his palm. 'You're right! I've been so low this last week, but tomorrow I'm going to go for a little Sunday outing. Smell the sea air. Would you two like to come along? There's room.'

'I can't tomorrow,' Siw says. 'Maybe some other time.' She realises this sounds like a standard brush-off, and adds: 'I mean it. I've hardly spent any time in the archipelago.'

'In that case, you have something to look forward to.' The man holds out his hand. 'Charles Karlsson, but everyone calls me Charlie. Those who call me anything, that is.'

Max and Siw introduce themselves and swap phone numbers with Charlie, which cheers him up even more. He doesn't look like the same person who was sitting in a tree ten minutes ago; only the clothes are the same, and even the dark shadows seem a little paler. He seizes Max and Siw's hands in turn in both of his own. 'God bless you both. I'm not a religious person, but still, God bless

422

you. If you hadn't been . . . All the best to you, and may you live happily together for the rest of your lives.'

Charlie heads off down Tullportsgatan, turning to wave at them a couple of times. Max and Siw sink down on the benches by the low wall beneath the elm. They sit in silence, watching the man who would be dead if it hadn't been for the two of them and their combined abilities. When Charlie has disappeared from view, Max says: 'That was quite a blessing.'

'Yes. But possibly a little . . . misguided.'

'Why?'

Siw clamps her lips together and stares at the window of H & M, where a skinny girl in an autumn coat is grinning like a shark at the camera. She seems to have at least eight more teeth than a normal person.

'That was unbelievable,' Max goes on. 'We saved a person's life. Charlie's life. I'm really shaken up. How about you?'

'Yes. Me too. It was . . . big.' Siw picks at her cuticles, then taps her index fingers together before looking Max in the eye. 'I don't care if you think I'm stupid, but this is non-negotiable: you're not to talk about Håkan like that.'

'Is that really what's on your mind when we've just—'

Siw holds up her hand, demanding silence.

'Yes, that is what's on my mind in relation to you. And you're not to talk about Håkan like that. He means so much to me; it's as if you're pissing on something sacred. If you like, you can think of me as a Christian fanatic and Håkan as the Bible, which you're using to wipe your arse. That's the level. Okay?'

'Okay. I get it. I won't—'

'*And!*' The hand comes up again. 'Håkan most certainly *can* play

423

the guitar. Maybe not as well as . . .' – Siw purses her lips – '*Lasse*, but he can play, and he's pretty good.'

'Okay, I—'

'*And!* Seriously – Lars Winnerbäck?' She lowers her voice an octave and sings in a rasping monotone about the leaves lying on the ground, someone sitting in the park contemplating his navel . . . 'What?'

'Careful!' Max admonishes her. 'It's not on the same level as you and Håkan, but . . . just don't go too far, okay?'

'At least I know him well enough to make fun of him – what do you know about Håkan? By the way, I think "Söndermarken" is a brilliant song.'

'My favourite! And there is actually one song by Håkan that I really like.'

'Which one?' Siw sounds as if she doesn't believe him.

'Guess.'

Siw looks him up and down as if assessing his Håkan-calibre, then says: '"Too Late for Edelweiss".'

'Yes – how did you know?'

'Because it's *my* favourite. But you're lying, aren't you? You don't know anything, except maybe "Lena" or "Gothenburg".'

Max clears his throat and sings the first two lines of 'Too Late for Edelweiss', about the sadness of never having known love. He glances at Siw; a smile is growing on her lips. She joins in, harmonising on the third line. Max is about to continue, but pauses when he sees tears shimmering in her eyes. He hesitates as a single tear escapes and trickles down her cheek, then he leans forward and kisses her.

The first kiss. That's a concept: *the first kiss*. A physical line that is crossed, a promise for the future, a memory to keep, a point fixed in time forever: the first kiss.

In Siw's case, the first kiss has often been the last. A snog at a party, some drunk who couldn't find anything better to press his lips against, a bit of slobbering with the tongue, the inevitable squeezing of the tits before he lost interest or passed out. Siw remembers it happening, but can't recall any individuals or faces, just a general perception of saliva, sweat, discomfort and a human need that had nothing to do with love.

The kiss with Max is different. As soon as his lips meet hers, the thought flutters through her mind: *the first kiss*. She may have longed for this moment, but still she is taken by surprise when it actually happens. Yes, something changed between them when they were singing, but she didn't know if he felt the same way, so when his lips touch hers it takes a second or so before she parts them, enough time for Max to freeze and wonder if he's done the wrong thing. Then she opens herself, receives him as if she wants to swallow him. It's a miracle, she isn't thinking *how* and *maybe* and *should*, about the way she's sitting and what she looks like and what is reasonable behaviour with the tongue, she just kisses and kisses.

There is another important point about the first kiss. If those who are kissing are going to become a couple, then the future will hold a great deal of kissing, so you want the first kiss to be *good*. Of course, it is possible to be with someone whose kisses are stiff and boring, but that means some of the pleasure life has to offer will be lost.

Siw had thought of Max as an intellectual and reserved person – not a passionate kisser. It turns out she was wrong. Intellectual maybe, but goodness me, he matches her hunger. His lips are soft and he nibbles gently, covers her mouth and sucks, touches her tongue with his, alternates between tiny kisses and deep kisses until Siw feels dizzy.

They sit there for some minutes, exploring each other's lips and tongues. Max places his hands on Siw's temples, caresses the back of her head; she strokes his cheeks, grips the back of his neck. It's impossible to know how long this will last or what it might come to mean, but oh, that *first kiss*! It definitely hit the spot!

In the end it's all too wet and sweaty and a bit sore and, well, long-winded. They pull back and look each other in the eye.

'Yay,' says Siw.

Max nods. 'Yay.'

Before the inevitable embarrassment and inability to work out what to say kicks in – what is there to say after a kiss like that? – Max gets to his feet and holds out his hand.

Siw takes it, and because she thought he was just helping her up she lets go when she is standing, but he tightens his grip. They walk. They are holding hands. Siw feels a lump forming in her throat, and gives a little cough.

If you start crying now, I'll kill you!

She doesn't know who or what she is going to kill. She imagines a little machine operator, like the one in that Pixar movie, who always makes a point of starting up the crying machine at the wrong moment. This time, however, she manages to stop him before he – or she, it must be a she – has got going. Siw's eyes remain dry.

They go up Galles gränd and past the cultural centre and art gallery, blasted into the rock. At Stockholmsvägen they turn left and stroll past the Kinnarps premises, which now stand empty, the Montessori school, and the Chinese restaurant. Siw has never eaten there, because there is something vaguely grubby about the place.

They have been holding hands for five minutes without uttering a word since that mutual 'Yay'. Maybe it's time to say something? Siw points to the hangar-like building across the road. 'That's where I work.'

Max nods and looks at the Flygfyren retail park, where only the sign displaying its generous opening hours is lit up. 'What's it like?'

'Fine.'

They've talked so much during the evening, gone into some really deep stuff – how come they've been struck dumb since the kiss? Siw has nothing against walking along in silence, or indeed holding hands, but she still thinks it's weird. Surely they ought to have *more* to discuss now?

They continue alongside the churchyard and pass the chapel where the software developer Niantic, perhaps somewhat insensitively, has located a *Pokémon Go* gym. Sometimes there can be around twenty people on a raid among the gravestones. The thought makes Siw take out her phone. She is greeted by an egg, and an 'Oh?'

Max does the same. Siw has two eggs to hatch, Max five. Only a couple of ten-kilometre eggs remain unhatched after their long walk. They stand by the churchyard gate for a little while sorting things out before they set off again. Siw makes an effort to get the conversation going. There is one matter she wants to clear up.

'Charlie,' she says.

'Mmm?'

'What he said, when he was sitting in the tree. Don't you feel as if people have become . . . something has changed. Within a very short time.'

427

'Yes, maybe. In the town centre.'

'Exactly. I haven't really thought about it until now, but it's as if everyone feels the same as Charlie, although not to the same extent. It's all a bit more . . . depressing.'

'Or unkind. People are less kind.'

'Yes, and maybe that's because of how they feel. There's that business at the riverside restaurant, and there have been more reports in the local paper of people who've been . . . unpleasant to one another in different ways. In the town centre.'

'Why do you think that is?'

'It's just an idea, but I thought it might have something to do with the container. Both you and I felt that there was something about it, something bad – beyond all the dead bodies inside it.'

'That's true. But what is it?'

'I haven't a clue. But it's definitely . . . something.'

They have passed the tyre workshop which Niantic insists on calling 'The car on the roof', even though the VW Beetle that used to be up there was taken down many years ago. The Thai kiosk is closed, and an unusually repulsive smell drifts over from the recycling containers, as if someone has decided to recycle a corpse.

They continue up the hill, following Siw's daily route from work, and she is beginning to feel nervous. She will be home soon, and what should she do then? The machine operator doesn't seem to know which buttons to press, but fortunately she avoids both the one for crying and the big red one with 'Panic!' written on it. However, she can't help pumping the anxiety pedal. Siw's hand slithers in Max's grip as her palm starts to sweat.

They stop in the street outside Siw's apartment, which gives her a reason to let go of Max's hand and discreetly wipe her own by nonchalantly slipping it into her back pocket.

'This is where I live,' she says, pointing. 'That's my balcony.'

'Okay. Shall we go and sit on it for a while?'

That's how easy it can be, sometimes.

4

Siw invites Max in and manages to refrain from apologising for the mess, because she knows it is only her exaggerated need for tidiness that would refer to one newspaper on the table and two unwashed wine glasses in the sink as 'a mess'.

Max looks around her living room. 'This is lovely,' he says. He nods in the direction of her knitting basket and adds: 'Suffering for your art.'

Siw is amazed that he remembers the comment from one of their very first . . . But then it's not that strange, she remembers it, why must she always . . .

Calm. Remain calm.

She tries to pull herself together and take charge; she is in her own apartment after all. 'Right, this is what we're going to do.' She points to the sofa. 'You sit down there, I'll pour us a glass of wine, then I'll play you a selection of Håkan tracks that will make you change your mind about him.'

'Oh no,' Max says. 'We are *not* going to do that.'

'No? So, what are we going to do then?'

'This is what we're going to do.' He gently takes her head between his hands and kisses her again. The thought that pops into her head is *Yes!*, and for a moment she sees the machine operator staring greedily at the panic button. Then she gives herself up to the moment.

This kiss is even better than the first, if that were possible, because their mouths are now familiar with each other. Plus, they're not in a public place, so their hands are allowed to join in the game. Siw caresses Max's back, hips and stomach, and discovers that his body is as taut and muscular as his arms.

How can I be with someone like this?

Max's hands are all over Siw, and at that point giving herself up to the moment becomes more difficult, because she has to use a huge amount of mental energy in order not to be embarrassed. Okay, so she's lost three kilos, okay, her tread on this earth is a little lighter, but beneath another person's hands she feels every single excess kilo, beneath Max's fingers every bulge, every spare tyre is an abomination and something inside her just wants to yell, *Don't touch me! Don't remind me of how ugly I am!*

But Max doesn't seem to think she is ugly. His caresses are gentle and skilled – he doesn't knead her flesh like Sören does – and he is making small sounds of pleasure, as if the impulses from his fingertips are giving him great enjoyment. Siw begins to relax, and when he takes her hand and leads her to the bedroom, she actually feels *lust* through the veils of self-reproach. She *wants* this.

They start to undress each other. When Siw is down to her bra and pants she switches off the bedside lamp so that the room is in darkness. Max switches it on again, and so it stays on. They continue to stroke newly discovered areas, and the veils fall as the lust grows stronger and Siw stops thinking. She is only her body, that body is hers regardless of what it looks like and it is here now and *Yes*.

'Yes,' she says.

'Absolutely,' Max replies, gently laying her down on the bed. 'Shall I . . . ?'

'I've got a coil.'

'And . . .'

'Exactly.'

It may be that generations of women in Siw's family have given birth to only one child, a daughter, but she doesn't take any risks, and she especially didn't want to take any risks with *Sören*. She is *not* going to think about Sören now, that would be the direct opposite of a compensation fantasy.

Siw gasps when Max enters her. His hands flutter over her skin, giving her such intense pleasure that she starts shaking. In order to stabilise herself she wraps her legs around his hips, throws back her head, closes her eyes and rocks. Stars burst into life behind her eyelids. Yes. *Yes!*

Afterwards they lie on their sides facing each other in the gentle glow of the bedside lamp, gratefully stroking the bodies that have allowed them to experience what they have just experienced. *That was so lovely*, Siw thinks over and over again, like a mantra. *That was so lovely, that was so lovely.*

'That was so lovely,' Max says.

'Mmm.'

'I'm ready for my lesson now. On Håkan.'

'I don't want him here now,' Siw replies. 'Not yet. Maybe later.'

She refuses to think about the fact that she has to work tomorrow. No chance. Only this night exists, and it is going to last forever. They lie with their faces close together, stroking each other's cheeks and searching for eternity in each other's eyes. Forever.

'Sibyl,' Max says, gently pushing a strand of hair out of Siw's eyes. 'You're the most beautiful person I've ever seen.'

Siw finally breaks down. The button is pressed, the tap is opened. The tears begin to flow, and there is nothing she can do about it. She hides her face against Max's chest and pulls him close.

'You must be blind,' she whispers. 'Blind, blind, blind.'

SUICUNE

ON ALL THE FRONT PAGES

A press conference had been announced for ten o'clock on Sunday morning. The Norrtälje police, together with colleagues from Stockholm and a couple of experts, were going to give the latest updates on the container found in Norrtälje harbour, with twenty-eight dead bodies inside.

Because of the interest in the case, the conference had to be moved from the police station to one of the meeting rooms in the council offices. All the national media were present, plus a relatively large number of international representatives. Swedish Television was broadcasting live. The news value had gone up another notch since Donald Trump had tweeted an image of a bleeding container two days earlier, with the words 'Sweden's open borders policy kills twenty-eight people. So tragic.'

First up was a forensic specialist from the National Forensics Centre in Linköping, who was able to confirm the preliminary analysis. A number of people had died due the lack of life's necessities – fluid, oxygen, food. A few had died of heart failure, presumably caused by extreme stress. Others had fallen victim to lethal force, mainly to the head.

A spokesperson from Immigration Services spoke about what was happening to the bodies. The service was doing its best to trace relatives, and the aim was to return the deceased to their respective homelands for burial. When asked whether the victims would have been permitted to remain in Sweden if they had been alive, the spokesperson said it wasn't possible to make a collective judgement.

The local police didn't have much to add. They were essentially hosting the press conference, as the investigation had been taken over by the relevant national department. All they could do was appeal for a calm and sensible approach, because the last few days had seen an increase in both violent assaults and suicide. On two occasions firebombs had been thrown at the refugee facility on Albert Engströms gata.

And so to the most important point: the investigation itself. The press officer from the National Operations Department gazed out authoritatively at the assembled company of a hundred or so journalists, and began by dropping a bombshell: they had found the ship that had transported the container. The vessel, along with its captain and crew, was currently being held in Ålborg, Denmark.

After gathering eye witness accounts from along the coast, the Swedish police had been able to home in on the vessel concerned: a smallish cargo ship by the name of *Ambrosia*, registered in the Netherlands. An international search had been launched, and five days after the container appeared in Norrtälje, the Danish maritime police had found the ship.

The Spanish captain and the eight Filipino crew members denied all knowledge of people smuggling and container dumping. Eventually, with the help of an interpreter fluent in Chavacano, the Creole dialect spoken by the crew, they were confronted with photographic evidence, witness statements and even a fragment of video footage taken on a mobile phone, showing the container being loaded in Algeciras in Spain. At that point the dam broke, and everyone blamed the captain, although their accounts were full of contradictions. This in turn loosened the captain's tongue, and his statement was judged to be more reliable.

The crew had begun to grow more anxious after the ship had passed through Öresund. The captain didn't know how the idea had taken root, but his men had become increasingly convinced that *Multo* was inside the container. When asked what this meant, the captain answered in Chavacano. The interpreter explained that Multo, like many figures from folklore, could be seen in many different ways. The name came from the Spanish word for death, *muerto*, so Multo could be a dead person, a ghost, or Death itself in the form of the ultimate horror.

When the ship reached the south coast of Sweden, the crew refused to have anything more to do with the container, even though its intended destination was much further north, in Sundsvall. Nor was the captain allowed to open the doors to provide food and drink to the unfortunate individuals locked inside, who could be heard banging on the walls. If Multo got out, they were all doomed to die – the crew and the passengers. Better if it was just the passengers, in that case.

The paranoia grew as they sailed north. When they reached the shipping lanes leading into Stockholm, the crew demanded that the captain dump the container in the sea and let Multo sink to the bottom along with it. When he refused, he was put in chains, and the first mate took command.

As they prepared to heave the container over the side with the help of a derrick, the nervous first mate caught sight of a maritime police surveillance launch in the distance, which made him veer into the Norrtälje inlet.

436

Once the worst of the panic had subsided, the captain managed to negotiate a compromise. Instead of dropping the container into the sea, they would dump it ashore as soon as they found a harbour deep enough to allow them to berth. The captain hoped someone would find the container and be able to help those locked inside. The crew were sceptical, because that would mean releasing The Horror onto those who opened it, but then that was *their* problem. The Swedes.

And so one night in early September the container was dumped on the quayside in Norrtälje harbour, to be discovered a few hours later by Harry Boström and his dog Tosse.

POST-FESTUM

I

'Grandma, where is Philippinia?'

'It's called the Philippines. It's . . . Why do you want to know, Alva?'

'Because the people who left that box came from there.'

'What box?'

'The con . . . contai . . .'

'Container?'

'Yes. They were from Philippinia.'

'I thought you were watching children's programmes.'

'This is more interesting.'

Anita gets up from the kitchen table, where she has been absorbed in *Dagens Nyheter*'s Sunday crossword, and goes into the living room. On the television a man with short, steel-grey hair is explaining that yes, a number of children died due to lethal force, and no, the police are not taking any supernatural factors into account. Anita finds the remote and switches it off.

'Grandma, lethal force to the head means hitting someone really hard over the head so they die, doesn't it?'

Anita ignores the question and carefully lifts down the globe from the windowsill. It's a bit loose on its stand, ever since Alva tried to get it to spin at seventeen hundred kilometres an hour after Anita told her that was the actual rotation speed of the earth.

'Here,' Anita says, pointing to a group of islands in the Pacific. 'That's the Philippines.'

Alva studies the area as if it is a code she must crack, then she gives the globe a half-turn and points. 'And this is Spain?'

'Mmm.'

'And where's Öre . . . Öresund?'

Anita shows her the sound in the Baltic Sea. Alva sits there for a moment, her eyes darting between Spain, the Philippines and Öresund, then she announces laconically: 'They were a long way from home.' She draws a line with her finger from Öresund to the Philippines and adds: 'Almost as far as they could possibly be. Maybe that's why they went crazy.'

Anita sighs. 'People don't have to be crazy to kill one another. They do it anyway.'

Alva wrinkles her nose and gives Anita a look that equates to a wagging finger. 'Mummy doesn't like it when you say those things.'

'It's the truth.'

'No, because they didn't kill anyone. They just believed there was a ghost in the box, so they didn't want to open it. The sailors from Philippinia, I mean.'

'It's the Philippines. So, what's all this about lethal force to the head?'

Alva sighs theatrically at her grandmother's failure to keep up to date. 'That was the people *inside* the box.'

439

'Container.'

'Whatever.' Alva holds up her hand and frowns as she concentrates hard, counting on her thumb and forefinger. 'So, *they* came from Syria and Afghania. They were refugees. We should feel sorry for them.'

'Afghanistan.'

'You know what I mean!' Alva spreads her hands wide. 'Stop correcting me all the time! Show me where Syria and Afghaniastan are.'

Anita shows her, and Alva has two more locations to add to the previous three. She spins the globe, her finger tracing the routes between the countries while her lips move. Finally she shakes her head and says gloomily: 'It's a strange world.'

Anita doesn't contradict her.

Half an hour later, Alva wants to go home. Anita looks at the clock. 'We said twelve o'clock. It's only eleven.'

'What does it matter?' Alva says. 'An hour here or there?'

Anita smiles at Alva's use of an expression that was originally hers. At the moment her granddaughter is in an experimental phase when it comes to language, picking up words and phrases, testing their usability and effect then either discarding them or keeping them for a shorter or longer time.

'True,' Anita says. 'What's an hour here or there?'

2

The blinds in Siw's bedroom allow the morning sun to draw a burning line diagonally across the room. Siw's bare left shoulder is in such a position that the line catches the curve, turning her skin a shimmering pink.

440

Max is lying on his side with his arm tucked underneath the pillow, contemplating this miniature sunrise as he tries to capture a feeling, any feeling at all. It's like fishing for cuddly toys in one of those grab machines at the fairground. Just when he thinks he's got hold of something and tries to lift it out of the tangled mass, it slips from his grasp and falls back.

Is he happy, sad, in love, regretful, satisfied or wanting more? He doesn't know. The only thing he can say for certain is that he's in a strange bed, and lying with her back to him is Siw, with whom he had sex the previous night. He feels no desire to leave, but no great desire to stay either.

How different the situation was during the night. Long periods passed, periods he found it difficult to remember because he had simply been *there*, without reflecting, weighing up, considering. He had been alive, without asking why. Things have changed in the morning light, as he waits for a feeling. He thinks of Conor Oberst, who said it was so simple in the moonlight, but it's so complicated now.

Siw lets out a little puff of air, and a subtle change in her posture, a hint of tension in the muscles at the back of her neck, tells Max she is awake. And yet she doesn't turn over. Maybe, like him, she is trying to gather up the fragments of the night in order to examine them by the light of the new day and assess their content.

Max lies still, gazing at the glowing curve of her shoulder which dwindles and disappears as she rolls onto her back. Siw pulls the sheet up to her chin and briefly meets Max's eyes. 'Hi.'

'Hi,' he says. 'Good morning. Did you sleep well?'

'Mmm. How about you?'

'Yes. Really well.'

Siw nods, and Max nods back. They have both slept well, a

441

small note of positivity. Neither of them has lain awake, sweating and asking themselves *what have I done?* Siw glances at the alarm clock; it is just after eleven. 'I have to say something.'

'Go on.'

'My daughter, Alva. She'll be home at twelve. And don't take this the wrong way, but . . . I don't want you to be here then. It would only confuse her.'

This wasn't what Max had been expecting. He hasn't made any attempt to link the current situation to life in general. He is in an emotion-free moment with no limits. Clearly things are different for Siw, and maybe this lack of limits is possible only for those without children.

'Okay,' he says, swinging his legs over the side of the bed. 'No problem.'

'You're not disappointed?'

'No, no. Of course not.'

He has put on his underpants and is searching for his socks when a key is inserted in the front door. He and Siw look at each other, eyes wide. Before Siw has time to speak, Max has gathered up his clothes and crawled under the bed. Alva's feet appear in the doorway, then she runs over and jumps up to join Siw. 'Mummy!'

Max curls up as close to the wall as possible. He bundles up his clothes and rests his head on them. He has never been sure whether his life is a tragedy or a comedy, but right now it's a bedroom farce.

3

Seen from behind, the figure sitting on one of the wooden benches by the river down below the Roslags Museum could easily be taken for an alcoholic. The hair is lank and messy, the posture slumped, and there are two beer cans on the bench beside her. Seen from the front, it is only Anna Olofsson. Hair of the dog and all that.

Enough now, for fuck's sake.

Anna takes a good swig from one of the Falcon Bayerskt she bought from ICA Kryddan. The lukewarm beer washes over her dry gullet and brings some relief to her stiff limbs.

After the satisfying performance on the jetty, when Marko threw the tosser into the sea with his phone and everything, Anna had remained sitting on the hard planks with Johan while Marko loudly ended his friendship with the three arseholes from Stockholm. Lukas had eventually been allowed to get out of the water; he had continued to moan about his phone until the three of them trailed off to their hotel and Marko went to take care of his sister. Anna and Johan fetched a box of wine and returned to the jetty.

What had they talked about? Anna takes another swig and peers at the sunlight, reflected in the slow-moving waters of the river. She can't really remember, but it must have been *something*, because they'd stayed there until the first dark pink clouds heralded the arrival of the dawn over the Kvisthamra inlet. Their limbs cracked and creaked in protest when they finally stood up and took the empty box back to the house, which lay in silence. They said *Bye* and *Be in touch* on Marko's terrace, and on the way home Anna had to resist the siren call of every bush she passed: *come to meee . . . sooo soft . . . reeest . . .* She crashed into bed at six, only to wake four hours later with a pounding head, an itchy feeling all over her body, and the word *beer* glued to her tongue.

They'd probably talked about life. Anna remembered Johan saying something about how the bowling hall was a like a cocoon, but he would never evolve from the pupa stage to become a butterfly.

443

Anna had repeated the words 'pupa stage' with great seriousness, and they had toasted the idea. They had toasted a lot of things. Talked crap. She had no problem with that part.

It was the other stuff that bothered her. Anna generally has no time for regrets, but the previous evening had been . . . a bit much. She had a vague memory of throwing herself at Marko, as if she were observing from the outside, but the person who did all that was definitely her.

Enough now, for fuck's sake.

Another swig of beer, another attempt to smooth all the sharp edges inside her body. How many times has she had that thought since she started drinking seriously when she was fourteen? The day after, that is. A hundred? Two hundred? Days wasted drinking weak beer, eating pizza and bingeing on some box set. It was okay when she was fifteen, eighteen, but now she was *twenty-nine*. Enough, for fuck's sake.

Anna studies the grim-faced falcon adorning the can as the traffic roars by along Stockholmsvägen and the birch trees rustle their leaves, dried out by the summer. 'Quaaack, quaaack!' say the ducks on the river. Will she be sitting on this bench in thirty years' time, thinking the same thing? A sour-faced old woman with a dodgy liver, possibly in the company of some toothless old man who will give her a cuddle in exchange for a swig of her booze.

She puts her head in her hands and groans. She has never been in a long-term relationship – or any relationship at all, to tell the truth. She has had men ever since she lost her virginity, when she started drinking. Often as many as three. Not *at the same time*, for God's sake, but men she has juggled, played off against one another.

She was the talk of the school from the age of about fourteen. Not when she was around – no one dared – but there were exaggerated

444

rumours about what she got up to, and her phone number was scrawled on the walls in the toilets, next to a list of the services she offered. Occasionally some idiot actually rang her.

On this Sunday morning, as Anna sits on the bench feeling as if she is wearing a concrete baseball cap and tries to look into her inarticulate heart, she acknowledges once again the simple yet paradoxical truth: the reason why she can't cope with relationships is her all-encompassing fear of being *lonely*. How about that? To be so afraid of not being with someone that you can't be with someone.

'Quaaack, quaaack!' say the ducks. They sound agitated. Even the birds are annoyed with her.

You feel lonely only when you've been dumped. Before that you are simply yourself, as in self-sufficient and self-assured, but if you enter into a long-term relationship with another person, then you always run the risk of one day being dumped, left, found wanting. Lonely.

There is an image that haunts Anna. At the care home where she works there is a woman who is ninety-one years old, Greta Gustafsson – known as Garbo, of course. When Garbo was coming up to her ninetieth birthday, the staff wondered if they should make some special arrangements, perhaps book the dining room for a little party? No, no, *don't go to any trouble for my sake.*

Nobody came to visit Garbo on her big day, and when she didn't appear at dinner Anna got worried and went to see what was going on. The door of the old woman's room was ajar. Anna peeked in and saw the image that will not leave her.

Garbo had set her little kitchen table beautifully, and had put on her best dress. Another member of staff must have helped her, because a ready meal for one was all laid out. Lit candles, a small bottle of wine. So far so good. What brought a lump to Anna's throat was what she saw on the opposite side of the table.

445

The framed photographs of Garbo's children, her sister and her late husband that normally hung on the wall were now lined up along the edge of the table, all facing the lonely woman who raised her glass in a toast, murmured something and took a sip of her wine.

Anna had never seen a more striking picture of loneliness, and she stood there for a moment, her forehead resting on the doorpost. *Everything shall be taken away from us.* Can we live on memories, can we really live on memories? Anna got her answer when she pulled herself together, knocked and entered the room.

'Excuse me, Greta . . .'

Garbo gave a start and turned towards her. For a second Anna saw straight into a grief and loneliness so deep and yet so paltry that her heart crumpled in her chest. Then Garbo regained her self-control, forced warmth into her eyes and plastered on her usual smile.

'Yes, Anna?'

'I . . . I just . . .'

Garbo was one of the easier residents, insofar as she was rarely ill, never complained and appreciated the help she received. A contented old woman, or so it seemed, but in that second Anna had glimpsed the black, faceless despair concealed behind the mask.

'I just wondered if you'd like some company?'

'No, no. You have your work to do.'

'But I could—'

'Absolutely not. I'm sitting here reminiscing, that's all. I'm fine.'

Anna had walked away, her hands feeling strangely empty. As far as she knew, Garbo had three children. As far as she knew, none of them were dead. And all three of them deserved to be publicly flogged.

'Quaaack, quaaack, QUAAAACK!'

The agitated racket makes Anna raise her head. On the other

side of the river stands a five-year-old girl, with a woman who is presumably her mother. The child is holding a chunk of bread, and she is tearing off small pieces and throwing them into the water.

A dozen or so ducks have joined the party a metre below the girl's feet, a party that resembles one of Stig's drinking binges in the early hours of the morning. The birds whirl around, quacking angrily and pecking at one another as much as the morsels of bread. Feathers are ripped out, wings flap and the water foams, while the girl laughs and scatters another shower of crumbs over their heads, like a capricious goddess bestowing her gifts on her ecstatic worshippers.

Then things change. Simultaneously, as if on a given signal, the ducks spread their wings. They clatter over the water, flapping furiously, then take off. In seconds the quacking mass of feathers is up on the path, surrounding the child. *Nearer my God to thee.* They peck at the bread in her hands. She drops it, screams and moves closer to her mother.

The ducks are not satisfied. Like an oppressed mob who have suddenly realised their own strength and got a taste for blood, they waddle rapidly after the girl and peck at her white fingers.

'Shoo, shoo!' the woman shouts, hitting out at the bobbing heads as the girl sobs and hides her face in her mother's coat. The birds are still after her, but one of them grabs hold of the mother's index finger. The woman screams and jerks her hand away from the sharp beak. Her finger is sticky with blood, and her expression changes.

She takes a deep breath, draws back her foot and launches a vicious kick. There is the sound of a soft crunch, and the duck flies through the air with limp wings before landing in the river, its head lolling helplessly as it is carried downstream.

Hatred and triumph burn in the woman's eyes as she stares at the

447

hissing birds. She seems to be considering another attack, then she comes to her senses, seizes her daughter's hand and flees towards Tullgränd with the ducks waddling after her. A gull swoops down and steals the piece of bread.

Anna hears the sound of laughter beside her. She has been so caught up in Roslagen's version of *The Birds* that she has failed to notice someone joining her on the bench, in spite of the fact that the man in question is so huge that one of his legs is inevitably touching hers.

'Ducks with attitude, eh?' says Ewert Djup, digging out a plug of snuff from beneath his top lip, examining it carefully then flicking it into the river. 'Fucking birds.'

Even though Ewert made it possible for Anna to get through primary school thanks to his very existence, she is not comfortable in his presence. He radiates a latent air of violence; it's like standing in front of a tiger's cage when you're not sure if it's locked. Sixty years in the service of criminality has made his features harden and his eyes grow cold. His nose is crooked, thanks to an incident in the distant past when someone was still brave enough to take him on. He smiles at Anna, revealing an unnaturally white set of false teeth that makes her shudder inside.

'Birds,' he says pensively, before launching into one of his many stories. In the eighties he and his brother had a little place down by Spillersboda, did Anna know that? Anyway, everything was fine and dandy except for one thing: the fucking gulls. As soon as the sun rose the fuckers started screaming, and they didn't stop until darkness fell, sometimes not even then. They crapped all over the jetty, the boat, everywhere. What to do? They tried plastic snakes, stuffed owls, they threw stones, shot at them with air rifles.

In spite of herself, Anna is interested. The thought of the two hefty brothers setting out a variety of creatures to try to scare the

448

birds away and firing air rifles while grinding their teeth at the gulls is so far from the image she has of them that she wants to hear the rest of the tale. Ewert seems to notice, because he leans back, his belly sticking out from under his brown leather 1970s jacket. 'Bastard birds,' he says, and falls silent.

Anna obligingly gives him the response he is fishing for. 'So, what did you do?'

What the brothers did was to acquire several tons of gravel and a few kilos of herring. Two dynamite cartridges on the rocks beneath a pile of gravel, the herring strewn on top. They ran the detonator cable round the back of the cabin and waited. When forty or so gulls had gathered to fight over the fish, Ewert pressed the plunger all the way down.

'Bastard birds,' Ewert says again, and sniggers. 'We lost a couple of windows, but it was worth it. Scraps of gull hanging from every bush – my theory is that *that's* what frightened off the rest of them. If we saw a place festooned with bits of guts, fingers, brains and so on, we wouldn't be too keen on hanging around, would we? Anyway, it was quiet after that.'

'Have you still got it? The cabin?'

'What? No. Some fucker came and burned it down a year or two later. We got him, though.'

Ewert nods to himself as he watches the dead duck slowly drifting towards Kvarnholmen. *We got him, though.* Maybe it was a matter of guts and fingers there too. Or 'a little trip'. The conversation has taken a turn that reminds Anna of who she's talking to, and she wishes Ewert would get to the point.

'So,' he says, clasping his hands behind his head and spreading his trunk-like thighs, encased in a pair of stonewashed jeans. 'How come you're sitting here boozing at this time of day?'

'It's only low-alcohol beer,' Anna replies, as if she's worried that Ewert might *tell Daddy*.

'Mmm. And Acke gets out on Wednesday.'

'He does.'

'How much do you know about the . . . circumstances?'

'What circumstances?'

Ewert runs a sausage-shaped finger over his spider-veined nose, on which odd hairs are sprouting like thistledown on a block of granite. 'Well, you know he was caught. By customs. With three kilos. Of hay. From Hamburg.'

'Yes.'

'He hasn't said anything else? To you?'

'No – like what?'

Anna isn't keen on the way Ewert is looking at her. It makes her feel . . . exposed. Nothing to do with taking off her clothes, this is something different, something deeper, and she can't help averting her eyes.

'Mmm-hmm, mmm-hmm.' Hard to believe, but Ewert manages to make this sound menacing. 'The thing is, over in Hamburg, he'd been given the money to buy five, and I've had confirmation that he did buy five. But when he got to customs . . . suddenly he only has three. How would you explain that?'

'I've no idea,' Anna almost whispers, without looking at Ewert.

'One might suspect that two kilos have been . . . spirited away, so to speak. And that your brother intended to sell those two kilos himself. Take a higher price for the three kilos, maybe fiddle around to make a bit more. I don't know. You're his sister. What do you think?'

Ewert's reference to Anna's relationship with Acke doesn't bode well; it's as if this automatically means she's involved in Acke's

450

lunatic attempt to con the Djup brothers – something that just isn't done.

'Honestly, Ewert, I haven't a clue. Not a clue.'

'Hmm. Maybe, maybe not. But the street value of two kilos is around two hundred thousand. The three kilos confiscated by customs – well, sometimes you just have to roll with the punches. But going behind our back, trying to cheat us – well, that's something else. Two hundred thousand. And with the normal interest, that makes three hundred. Thousand.'

Anna doesn't quite know what Ewert means by *the normal interest*, which sounds anything but normal to her, but she knows that the brothers have been involved in moneylending, among other things, and to paraphrase the Lannister family motto, a Djup always calls in his debts.

'Why . . . why are you telling me this?' she asks in a small voice.

'I just wanted to let you know that your brother owes us three hundred thousand kronor. That's his situation. At the moment.'

4

Where the hell am I?

When Marko opens his eyes he is disorientated for a few seconds, as if he's been kidnapped, and when the black hood of the night is pulled off his head, he is in an unfamiliar place. He feels as if he is falling through space. Then he recognises the Kvisthamra inlet, and the terrace strewn with the detritus from last night's party.

He had felt obliged to offer Maria his camp bed, and had made do with a sun lounger with mouldy cushions that he'd found in the cellar. He is in the middle of the area where the pool might one day be, and rusty springs creak as he sits up and massages his stiff neck, his mouth contorted in a lion-yawn. His palate feels sticky and his tongue is swollen.

La dolce vita.

He drags himself off the chair, with its metallic death rattle, and goes into the kitchen where he drinks a litre of water straight from the tap, then stands there leaning on the draining board, head down.

After the incident with Lukas, the Stockholm gang had fled. Marko had remained sitting on the terrace, drinking glass after glass of wine while attempting to examine his life, with an uncharacteristic lack of focus. After an hour or so he gave up peering at his metaphorical navel and drank more wine, idly swiping through Tinder and getting seriously pissed off with all the duck-faced girls who looked exactly the same.

He considered joining Johan and Anna, who were still sitting at the end of the jetty, but the effort involved in conducting a normal conversation was definitely beyond him. Instead, he went and fetched Maria, who had collapsed under the apple tree, and put her to bed. He drank more wine and then he found the chair and that was the end of the story.

He pushes away from the draining board and wonders whether to do a few press-ups to get going, but his brain has been replaced by a bowling ball which is rolling around in his head, banging into the inside of his skull with a shuddering clang. This is a day worth remembering. Marko never, ever gets a hangover, because he is never drunk. When it comes to partying around Stureplan in Stockholm he keeps his consumption down to a level that would allow him to drive a car next morning, if he so wished. Right now it's doubtful whether he could even ride a bike. He sluices his face in cold water. *Backfired last night. What the fuck does that mean?*

Maria is curled up on the camp bed, wrapped in Marko's sleeping bag. He is still angry with her, but in her sleeping, defenceless face he sees the little girl she once was, and his anger begins to abate. Lukas is the one who ought to . . . ought to what? A number of violent scenarios involving blood, shit and vomit flicker through Marko's mind, and he feels a little better.

He goes back outside and starts to clear up the mess, dropping cardboard, plastic and fag ends into a rubbish bag. Here and there people have spilled wine, staining the pale wood. He's just finishing off when he hears shuffling footsteps behind him.

'Marko?' Maria is standing in the doorway, still wrapped in the sleeping bag. Her hair is like a bird's nest, her make-up has run and her eyes are swollen – heroin chic. When she yawns, thick strands of saliva stretch between her lips. 'What time is it?'

'About ten.'

Maria pulls a face, as if this confirms her worst fears. She staggers over to the sun lounger and flops down on it, the springs screaming in pain. 'Where did you sleep?'

'There.'

'*Here?*'

Maria examines the chair as if searching for some indication that Marko is telling the truth, then she frowns and looks around. 'Where are the city boys?'

'They left.'

'After . . . ?' Maria waggles her index finger in the general direction of the jetty and whinnies like a foal.

'It's not cool.'

'It really is.'

Marko is about to make some acidic remark about Maria's culpability in the situation, but decides he can't cope with an argument.

453

Plus, there's no denying it: it felt so good, throwing Lukas in the sea. Maria leans back and shades her eyes with her hand against the sun sparkling on the water. Marko digs out a cigarette stub from between two planks and drops it in the bag. When he looks up, he sees that Maria is staring at him. He spreads his arms wide. 'What?'

'Marko,' Maria says in an uncharacteristically serious tone. 'What do you really want?'

'What do you mean?'

'Well, those three . . . Lukas and thingy and whatshername. They all want one thing. Do you want the same?'

'I don't understand.'

Maria takes a deep breath, then exhales. Her eyes narrow in concentration. 'Okay, so if we say that a person is defined by their dreams, what they want . . . I'm guessing those dickheads want a loft apartment in Vasastan, a Jag in the garage, a share portfolio and some peach-arsed Botoxed trophy girlfriend that they can cheat on. What do you want?'

'Not that, anyway.'

'No. But that's kind of what you've got. That life. That dream.'

Marko snorts. 'You mean, my life is superficial, because I go after status and money? That's a very superficial analysis in itself.'

'Is it?'

'Yes. And what do you suggest I should do instead?'

Maria makes a sticky, smacking sound with her tongue and shrugs. 'No idea. Get a job with the bank here in Norrtälje or something. Move back home.'

'Firstly this isn't my home, and secondly . . . How much do you think I'd earn? A quarter of what I do now? A fifth?'

'And? Don't you remember what Dad used to say when we'd done something kind of immoral?' Maria lowers her voice, imitating

Goran's trembling, admonitory tone. '*Your soul is in danger, my child.* That's the way it is, Marko. Your soul is in danger.'

5

Johan is sitting on the hill. On the bench where he and Max, then he and Marko used to sit. It's really only a plank of wood with no backrest. He has a sheaf of papers on his knee. He turns to the last page and reads.

'He stood by the window staring at the tall, nondescript trunks of the pine trees with their pale green crowns. Then he glimpsed a movement among the branches. An angel or a devil poked its nose out and beckoned him. *Come.*'

Johan looks up and gazes at the aforementioned pine trees. No movement, nothing beckoning him. Just pine trees. The clock on the church tower is showing eleven thirty. On the top of the water tower something is growing – possibly more pine trees. He once wrote a Lovecraft-inspired story about a slimy deity that made the water tower its home.

The biggest problem with reality is its lack of imagination. Human beings have to supply it themselves. Johan sometimes envies Max or even his mother their capacity for delusions. Admittedly these are and were mainly a torment to them, but still: the ability to genuinely see something *beyond* . . .

Johan can read Lovecraft and Kafka, he can make things up, but deep down he knows that only paltry reality exists, with its pine trees and more pine trees. He weighs the well-thumbed pile of paper in his hands and feels a sudden urge to stand up, take a few steps forward and hurl the whole lot over the edge of the hill and down onto Tillfällegatan, to watch the pages flutter over the town like injured doves of peace.

And then! Someone catches sight of a sheet of paper, picks it up and begins to read. *Oh my God!* The person in question is desperate to read more, runs around and finds another page. On the way he or she bumps into others who also have one page or two, and are hunting for more. The whole of Norrtälje is in uproar! People rush around searching for pages, swap with one another, stand in groups reading aloud. It's fantastic, unbelievable, where has this gift come from? The residents of Norrtälje raise their eyes and up on the hill stands Johan, silhouetted against the sky . . .

Yeah. Right.

He sighs and gets to his feet. It's a good job daydreams are free, otherwise he'd be flat broke by now. With the bundle of pages clasped to his chest, he negotiates his way across the overgrown hill, which no one seems to take care of anymore. The stone steps leading down to his apartment block have kind of sunk, and snow-berry bushes are encroaching over the sides.

One of the questions Anna asked him during the night on the jetty was *What are you going to be when you grow up?* He had been danger-ously close to confiding in her about his dreams of being a writer. It was her directness, the way she simply takes things as they are that finally made him tell her about Marko. The fact that he and Anna were fellow sufferers in their hopeless love for Marko also played its part.

But the subject of being a writer was a step too far. From the odd comment he had learned that Anna had barely read a book in her whole life, unless she was forced to do so. He assumed that Anna, like many people who don't read, regarded writing as something magical, or possibly suspicious and pretentious. So he had kept quiet about his dream, because that was all it was: a dream.

456

He takes out his phone, which now contains Anna's number plus a horrible profile picture taken with a flash out on the jetty. Her skin deathly white in the harsh light, drunken red eyes edged with tear-smudged eyeliner and mascara, her mouth a smeared blotch. He feels a sense of relief. Anna looks like everything he has always despised. During the night he crossed a line and became friends with a monster.

Friends?

Yes, and that's okay. The wine and the heightened atmosphere had helped, but their long, meandering conversation had felt weirdly *pure*, without barriers or reservations. He had talked about his mother's mental illness, Anna had talked about her criminal family as if these were perfectly normal topics for discussion between two strangers. When it was time to say goodbye, they had swapped numbers. Johan wasn't a fan of unnecessary physical contact, but they had even hugged. For several seconds, and it had seemed natural, just one of those things. So yes: friends.

He sits down at the bottom of the hill, still clutching the bundle of pages to his chest. This is what he has, this is his consolation and his dog and maybe that was why he decided to take it out. Let it have a bit of fresh air in the great outdoors, which it had never seen before. A first step out into the world, which will never be followed by a second step.

Totally bonkers.

He has to be at the bowling hall in an hour, to prepare for the afternoon's league games. That's the reality. He stands up and heads for the door of his apartment block. Before he goes in he shows the world the bundle of pages for one last time. There isn't a soul in sight, and only the pine trees whisper their approval.

457

6

With exaggerated enthusiasm at the prospect of buying ice cream from the Flygfyren shopping mall, Siw has managed to persuade a reluctant Alva to go with her, and Max is able to wriggle out from under the bed. He quickly gets dressed and is about to leave when he stops. Siw and Alva should be away for at least twenty minutes, giving him time for a little snoop around.

He doesn't know what he's looking for as he slowly wanders from room to room in Siw's clean and tidy apartment. Perhaps an impression, a sense of who she is as manifested in the home she has chosen.

Only forty or so books in the bookcase, mainly Swedish crime novels by female authors. A large number of films – fantasy, thrillers, romantic comedies and a Chaplin box set that takes up a third of one shelf.

One problem with the breakthrough of Spotify is that you can no longer check out someone's record collection in order to find clues about their character, and soon books and films will no doubt go the same way, thanks to their respective streaming services. Eventually only the classic bathroom cabinet will remain.

Max wanders into the kitchen and finds the box of Itrim powder. Otherwise, everything is in its place in drawers and cupboards, glasses and plates neatly stacked, knives hanging in a row from a magnetic strip. Max scratches his unshaven chin as a vague feeling of unease makes its presence known in his stomach, and he tries to remember a line of poetry.

He pushes open the door of Alva's room, but doesn't go in. By leaving him alone in the apartment – even though it wasn't really her choice – Siw has kind of given him permission to look around. Alva has not. Max merely notes that Alva's sense of tidiness isn't quite as well developed as her mother's, then he closes the door and moves on to the living room.

The rocking chair, the knitting basket, the two-seater sofa, the small TV, the Röllakan rug. There is absolutely nothing striking, nothing to catch the attention, except possibly for a certain excess of candles, and he is no wiser than when he began his tour. The line of poetry suddenly appears.

The mysticism of suburbia is the lack of mystery.

That's exactly how it feels – hence the unease. Siw's apartment is so completely normal and transparent that . . . no, that's not it. Max rubs his eyes. Okay, so what would he have *wanted* to find? Something that . . . wasn't perfect. A tangle of cables, a drawer full of random bits and pieces, a bunch of mouldy beetroot. Something that . . .

Yes!

Something that resembles Max himself.

There is quite simply no room for him here. That's what it is. He feels less like a spy and more like an intruder, someone whose footsteps are tainting the ground on which he walks. The suggestion is so strong that Max suddenly thinks he might be wearing his outdoor shoes, and has to look down at his feet to check.

The thought of outdoor shoes gives him the push to leave. Just one last thing. He rummages in the knitting basket and picks up a half-finished jumper in a child's size, which he holds up to the light from the window. He stands there for a long time, examining every stitch, until he becomes aware of a salty taste in his mouth, and realises he's crying.

He lets go of the jumper with his left hand, places his hand on his heart and tries to *feel*. But there is nothing there – no sorrow, no joy, no longing. He is simply crying, without knowing why. A couple of tears land on the jumper as he replaces it in the basket. 'Stop it,' he whispers to himself. 'Why are you crying?'

It's a long time since he last cried, and now it's happening, it's pretty irritating not to know why. Max wipes the tears from his cheeks and goes into the hallway, where it takes him a while to find his shoes, which have been pushed underneath the shoe rack. He opens the front door, then turns back. This time he is aware of the tears before they reach his mouth.

7

Siw is so unused to getting what she wants that she doesn't know what to think. As she heads for the shopping centre with Alva, her brain has got stuck on a scene from last summer, and it keeps playing over and over again.

Håkan's last encore at Ullevi. Siw had thought it was over when fireworks lit up the night sky over Gothenburg to the sounds of 'You'll Soon Be There'. Her sheer joy jumped up another impossible notch when the closing scene from *Modern Times* began to play on the big screen behind Håkan. Chaplin's tramp and the girl, walking hand in hand along the road. It was *perfect*.

And then another encore. It had just gone on and on. The audience of thousands had kept repeating the same line: 'If you want me, you can have me so easily', and Siw had swayed with the crowd, singing at the top of her voice and feeling all her carefully guarded barriers coming down, until the only thing to be said about her and her life was contained in that one simple line.

If you want me, you can have me so easily.

She can hear the voices in her head right now, feel the pleasant numbness in her body. *If you want me . . .* It's not about the meaning of the line; she doesn't even know if it's true. It's the sense of being part of a moment that lasts forever.

'Don't they?'

Alva's voice cuts through, and the irritable tone makes it clear to Siw that she has missed something.

'Sorry, darling – what did you say?'

Alva rolls her eyes and shakes her head, and Siw knows what that means: *why don't you concentrate, Mummy*, but for once she reiterates her comment without issuing further reprimands.

'I said that when people are scared, they do stupid things. Don't they?'

'I suppose so – why?'

'Because as I said *before*, the people in the box tried to get away because they were scared of misery and war and those who drove the boat were scared of ghosts and that's why it all turned out the way it did.'

Siw is struggling to understand what Alva is talking about. The box? The boat? Ghosts? Then the pieces fall into place, although the mention of ghosts is new to her. She sighs. 'Has this come from Grandma?'

Alva shakes her head. 'I was watching *Piggley Winks* but it wasn't very good so I changed channels and there was this man talking about the box.'

'The container?'

'Oh, for heaven's sake, you're both as bad as each other! Why was Grandma so weird before?'

'When?'

461

'In the hallway. Just before we came out.'

A faint blush, which fortunately slips beneath Alva's radar, colours Siw's cheeks. When Siw managed to steer Alva away from the bed, she had come out into the hallway just in time to see her mother pushing Max's shoes under the rack. Anita had given Siw a look; Siw had shaken her head, which made Anita raise her eyebrows and snort, which in turn made Siw let out a groan. A virtually silent exchange, which, of course, had attracted Alva's attention. She had looked from one to the other and said: 'What? What?'

However, Siw is grateful for Anita's uncharacteristic sensitivity. If Alva had spotted the shoes, she wouldn't have given up until Max had been forced to crawl out from under the bed, and then things would have got *really* tricky. Now it's just the usual: Alva suspects something is being hidden beneath the surface, and is diving like a tern attracted by a flash of silver.

'I noticed,' she says. 'Grandma was weird. And you were weird. Why?'

Siw attempts to think of an explanation, but it collapses before it even reaches the drawing board. She is used to getting her eight hours, but last night she slept for maybe three, and her brain feels woolly. After they'd made love, Siw had played Håkan to Max, and then they'd sat on the balcony talking, wrapped in blankets. Drunk more wine.

It was a course of events unlike anything Siw had encountered before. In her previous relationships, or whatever the correct term was, Siw had acted as something for her sexual partners to rub themselves against, empty themselves into. And knead, in Sören's case. Lovemaking had never led to a softer, gentler mood where there was a different kind of intimacy, as it had done with Max. During those early hours of the morning Siw had experienced sex as something greater than an itch that needed to be scratched – for the very first time. It was overwhelming and a little bit frightening.

She can't explain any of this to Alva, so she plays the card she very rarely uses: 'Grown-up stuff.'

As expected, Alva is furious. She clenches her fists and grinds them against her temples as she spits out her words: 'Aargghh! That's *cheating*! It's not *fair*!'

She stomps off ahead of Siw in high dudgeon, but Siw doesn't have the energy to defuse the situation. Hopefully the ice cream will cool down Alva's rage.

If you want me . . .

The evening at Ullevi had been wonderful, and the time she had spent with Max on the balcony had had something of the same character. Leaning against him, wrapped in a fluffy blanket in the candlelight, with the wine slipping through her veins all the way down to her pleasantly tingling sex, she had felt her own boundaries and those of the moment begin to dissolve, as if she were inside eternity, as if she were part of it.

So, what was frightening about that?

The fact that she wanted more, and didn't know if she could have it? No – just like with Ullevi, she had accepted while it was going on that *this is now and it will never happen again*, and presumably she and Max were not the type who would end up together, as it says in the same song.

It was more the sense of dislocation that this completely new experience brought with it, the fact that life and its possibilities looked different from what she had imagined until now. She felt a real loss of control, and if there was one thing she didn't like, it was losing control, being pushed off balance.

Yes, she thought. *I've lost my balance. Totally lost my balance.*

Alva stops a few metres away from the revolving doors at the shopping centre, and as usual she is studying the big staff photograph framed in a heart. Siw is included in the photo, which once made Alva insist that Siw was a *celebrity*.

When Siw joins her Alva points to the picture. 'There are more boys than girls.'

'Maybe. What kind of ice cream would you like?'

However, Alva has no intention of allowing herself to be diverted. Her first comment was only meant to prepare the ground, and perhaps in revenge for Siw's unfair answer earlier, she asks tearfully: 'Is one of *them* my daddy?'

'Alva, I've told you—'

'I think you're *lying*.'

'Well, it's not one of them, I swear on my honour.'

'Hmm. I want a Ben and Jerry's.'

'Do you know how much one of those *costs*?'

'You've only yourself to blame. Cheat.'

Alva stomps off towards the entrance, and Siw follows her after a last glance at the photograph. They may not be the most stylish guys in Roslagen, posing in their checked shirts, but she would have preferred several of them to be Alva's father instead of the real one. Anyone at all, in fact.

LITTLE BASTARD

I

Siw and Anna didn't know it at the time, but 2011 would turn out to be the year when they did certain things and made certain decisions that would affect their lives for many years in the future.

During the spring Siw had managed to buy the apartment on Flygaregatan, with her mother's help, while one of Stig's 'business associates' had transferred his lease on the scruffy two-room apartment on Stockholmsvägen to Anna. She had thought it was temporary, like the job she applied for at the care home after a few years stumbling along as a personal care assistant. Seven years later she is still in the same apartment, still doing the same job.

Siw had studied sociology at school, with the intention of training to be a social worker. That still hadn't happened, but when she started work at the shopping centre in the autumn of 2011, she was planning to stay for six months before going to college the following spring. That didn't happen, partly because she fell pregnant. It was all Johnny Depp's fault.

Both Siw and Anna were big fans of *Pirates of the Caribbean*, ever since as fourteen-year-olds at the Royal cinema in Norrtälje they had held their breath and laughed themselves silly at Jack Sparrow's antics. They were also in agreement that the films had got steadily worse, and hadn't even bothered to go to see the fourth in the series when it was shown in the spring.

However, during the autumn the release of the film on DVD and Blu-ray coincided with Stig acquiring a top-of-the-range home movie system. This was a few years before fifty-five-inch became standard, but according to Stig's motto 'If we're going to do it, we're going to do it properly', he staggered home with a Samsung sixty-five-inch, plus a surround system with a subwoofer that brought the worms to the surface in the garden, if he was to be believed.

Sylvia had calmed down slightly over the years, and she contented herself with muttering something about 'penis extension' before happily – well, not quite – flopping down on the enormous sofa and working her way through the huge collection of war movies that Stig had swapped for an unused black bathtub.

One Friday evening when Anna knew that the house was empty, she and Siw went round there with a copy of *On Stranger Tides* to check out both Stig's impressive installation and Johnny Depp's imitation of Johnny Depp. Anna had bought two bottles of rum in honour of the occasion. The brand? *Captain Morgan*, of course. According to Anna, the big advantage of a home cinema was that you could smoke and drink all the way through the film. At the age of fifteen she had been banned for life from the National Cinema in Rimbo after doing exactly that. The fact that the building was owned by the Swedish temperance movement didn't help.

The vast black TV screen dominated the living room, and Anna and Siw gazed at it with sceptical reverence. Anna fetched two glasses and a bottle of cola. Siw used her index finger to show how little rum she wanted, and Anna poured twice as much. When it came to her own drink, she merely added a dash of cola to her almost-full glass before tackling the remote controls lined up on the coffee table. After ten minutes of fruitless navigation between menus and channels, Siw picked up the instruction booklet. After another fifteen minutes, they managed to bring up the start screen. By this time Anna had finished her drink and poured herself another.

When Penélope Cruz first appeared on the screen, Anna raised her glass, spilling a small amount of rum on the leather sofa, and said: 'Not my thing, but if it was I wouldn't mind scissoring *her*.'

The film really wasn't very good. The story about the search for the fountain of youth felt contrived, and Jack Sparrow's manipulative behaviour, which had been so funny the first time, just felt . . . affected. The only good thing was Penélope.

'Shit,' Anna said after less than an hour, emptying her third glass before throwing her head back. 'Johnny Depressing, I'd say. He's sending me to sleep.' Five minutes later, she was indeed asleep. Siw dutifully stayed where she was and watched the rest of the film, even though the two considerably weaker rum and Cokes she had drunk made it difficult for her to follow the unnecessarily complex plot.

Just as Anna started to snore, the front door opened and Siw stiffened. Among the many words that could be used to describe Anna's family, *unpredictable* was high on the list. When a member of the family entered a room, you never knew what to expect: sunshine and smiles, or thunderclouds and curses. Plus, the situation could change in seconds.

Someone grunted in the hallway, and heavy footsteps approached.

Siw held her breath as if that would allow her to remain undiscovered when Acke lumbered through the door. He peered at the screen from under his fringe.

He shook his head at Johnny Depp, who was chattering like a chimpanzee. 'This is crap.' He plonked himself down on the arm of the sofa next to Siw and exhaled a blast of what she thought was whisky.

'Have you seen it?' she asked him.

'Ages ago. Pirate Bay. Crap.' He looked at Anna, who was sleeping with her mouth wide open, a string of saliva trickling from the corner of her mouth. He grinned. 'Pissed, is she?'

'Something like that.'

Siw glanced at Acke, whose black hair hung down over his eyes. His face was angular and pitted with pock marks after a severe bout of acne when he was fifteen. Now, two years later, he was almost clear. He gave Siw a crooked smile in a way that her mother would have called *sneaky*. Just for the sake of something to say, she asked: 'How are things?'

'Crap,' he replied, scratching a bulging crotch that was only inches from Siw's face. 'Beata dumped me. I was looking forward to a real fuckfest this weekend, and now . . . pff.'

Acke rubbed his nose; maybe he'd taken something to enhance the effect of the whisky. His eyes, peering vaguely at Siw from behind the curtain of hair, suggested that this might be the case. Siw turned her attention back to the screen, but she could feel his gaze burning into her cheek, which, of course, flushed red.

'Shall we fuck?' Acke suggested.

'Absolutely not.'

Acke had made the same suggestion when he was fifteen and his face looked a lot like a pizza, but Siw's rejection back then had been less about his appearance and more about the fact that he was Anna's little brother, and technically a child.

Now his complexion had improved and the lines of his face had hardened, and if it hadn't been for something sharp and ferrety about his features, he could have been described as handsome. His question evoked a cloud of distaste in Siw's belly, but also a tingle in the place her mother referred to as *where your thighs meet*.

'You're blushing,' Acke informed her. 'You want to.'

'I'm blushing because you're stupid.'

'Come on, Siw – why not?'

'You know why not.'

'My sister's asleep.'

'It's not *that*.'

'Then what? Nobody needs to know.'

Acke leaned over and licked the back of her neck. The cloud grew. The tingle became more intense. Acke took her hand and placed it on his crotch. There was something pretty big inside his jeans, sending heat throbbing through her palm. He nuzzled her earlobe and she gasped.

It was three years since she had been with Niklas from the motor vehicle programme. Three years without the warmth of someone else's flesh inside her. When Acke stroked her inner thigh a fire started in her chest. The smoke rose upwards, obscuring her ability to think clearly. 'Not here,' she whispered.

Acke blew in her ear, took the hand that was resting on his crotch, and pulled her to her feet.

Siw glanced at Anna, who was still sleeping loudly, and went with Acke to his room. Her brain was suspended over the fire, helplessly rotating on a spit as it whimpered: *No, no, no, not a good idea, not a good idea.*

469

The bedroom was illuminated only by a thin red rope light above the window. When he closed the door behind them, Siw could barely see her hand in front of her. Acke made short work of getting undressed, and in no time he was standing naked before her. Siw's eyes had quickly grown accustomed to the gloom, and she stared at Acke's large, erect cock, which looked somehow unreal on his skinny body. He clicked his fingers. 'Come on, your turn!'

Not a good idea, not a good idea, not a good idea.

Siw was grateful for the dim light, because she felt as if her entire body was blushing when she took off her clothes. She had to wiggle her broad arse to get her jeans down, and when she unfastened her bra, her breasts flopped out like water balloons. Acke didn't seem to care. He pushed her towards the bed, and when the backs of her knees touched the frame she fell backwards with a frightened squeak. Acke grabbed hold of her legs and parted them.

'I'm not on the pill,' Siw gasped. 'You need to . . .'

Stop. You need to stop.

Acke reached under the mattress and produced a condom. He tore at the packet with his teeth and managed to rip the rubber as well. When he started rummaging under the mattress again, Siw rubbed her eyes, came to her senses and clamped her thighs together.

'Acke, I don't want this.'

She placed her hands on either side of her hips and pushed herself up into a sitting position. Acke abandoned his search, grabbed her breasts and forced her down again.

'Acke, no! No!'

Acke spluttered and a few drops of saliva landed on Siw's cheek. With unexpected strength he pushed her legs apart, lurched forward and thrust into her. There was nothing pleasant about it, nothing at all, because the small part of Siw that had reluctantly felt warm and open was now cold and closed. There was only violence and a mechanical process as Acke thudded into her. Once, twice, three times.

Siw wanted to leave her body, she wanted to become an impenetrable lump of iron, and above all she wanted to scream, but she didn't do it, because the sight of Anna in the doorway would make her die of shame. She clamped her lips together to hold the scream in as her head banged rhythmically against the wall.

Four times, five. Then Acke's body arched and he groaned. Wet, sticky warmth poured into Siw, then Acke collapsed on top of her like a marionette whose strings have been cut. He stayed like that for five seconds, then said, 'Fucking hell,' and pulled out of her. There was a faint squelching sound, and another drop of liquid landed on Siw's cheek.

She had just been raped, but she wasn't thinking about that as she lay there with her hands clasped on her chest as if in prayer, staring up at the dark red ceiling with tears in her eyes. She was actually thinking: *Idiot, idiot, idiot*, referring to herself. When she stopped thinking *idiot*, she thought: *Please, God, don't let me get pregnant.*

When Acke's semen began to trickle down her leg, he said with disgust in his voice: 'You can go now'.

Without a word Siw gathered up her clothes and crept out through the door. She could hear the deafening cacophony of cannon salvos from the living room, so loud that the floor was vibrating as she scurried into the bathroom like a terrified animal. She locked herself in, avoided looking at herself in the mirror, and got in the shower.

She spent several minutes directing the flow of water at her vagina; there seemed to be no end to Acke's sperm. She rubbed with her fingers, she wept, she almost pushed the shower head

471

inside to sluice away the potentially lifegiving, lethal secretion as best she could. She wanted to delete, rewind the tape, undo what had been done.

When she returned to the sofa ten minutes later, Anna was still asleep. She woke up when Siw sat down, and looked around blearily. 'Have I missed anything?'

Yes. You could say that.

Siw clenched her fists over her belly, where the seed that would become Alva had begun to grow.

2

If Alva has Johnny Depp to thank for her conception, then her continued existence can be traced to a ship in a bottle. The ship is a miniature model of Silja Line's flagship *Galaxy*, and the bottle once contained Absolut vodka.

How the ten-centimetre-tall ship got in through the bottle neck that measures three centimetres in diameter unfortunately lies beyond the remit of this narrative. Feel free to choose your own method. The key point is that the ship formed part of a campaign in the spring of 2011, and was given to those who booked a group trip for twenty people or more.

The Human Resources department at Flygfyren had arranged just such a trip to perk up their employees. Two trips, in fact, because half the staff were needed to keep the store open on each occasion. The first voyage was on the Sunday, two days after Acke's attack on Siw.

She hadn't expressed an interest, partly because she didn't like being on a packed ship where glassy-eyed passengers were funnelled along the shopping mall like pigs to the slaughter, and partly because she had a tendency towards seasickness.

On the Saturday she changed her mind and emailed the contact person to say she'd like to come, if there was a place. The answer came quickly: 'There is a place! Let's go crazy!' Siw wasn't sure she wanted to go crazy, but she felt the need to get away, cut loose, do something outside the box. There was also an element of fantasy about sea breezes. She couldn't shake off Acke's assault. If she could just stand right at the front of the ship in the prow and give herself up to the chilly wind blowing off the Baltic Sea, she would feel better. Less dirty. Something like that.

There was no going crazy, no seasickness, no cleansing, just transportation to Finland and back, with an overnight stay in a tiny cabin that she shared with Kajsa-Stina from the fish counter. Siw tried to hang out with the others in the nightclub, but after the second beer her inner voice informed her that getting drunk would take her in the wrong direction, plunging her into darkness.

She went back to the cabin, where Kajsa-Stina had opted for an early night with a bottle of mint liqueur. The older woman expounded at length about her rheumatoid arthritis, drank glass after glass and exhaled in a series of belches until the inside of the cabin smelled like a box of After Eight. Then they went to bed. Siw lay awake for a long time, listening to the steady thrum of the engines, the vessel cutting through the waves. She saw herself as a lone ship passing over the black sea, all lights extinguished. Did she have a stowaway on board?

Her period failed to materialise three weeks later, but it was another two weeks before she bought a pregnancy test, because she didn't want to *know*, and be forced to make a decision. Eventually

473

she pulled herself together, and after peeing on the plastic stick, she could see the answer in the little window.

Now what?

She sat on the closed toilet lid with her head drooping. She'd already known, to be honest. A week or so earlier she had started to feel sick in the mornings, and her breasts were tender when she pulled on her tight overalls. The signs had been there, but they were only signs. Now the truth was in her hand, blue on white.

Now what?

Siw wasn't against abortion in principle, but at the same time she found it hard to see herself allowing someone to cut away the life that was fighting to grow inside her. Although they wouldn't be cutting at this stage, would they? Did that ever happen? It was probably more like some kind of . . . flushing out. She shuddered at the very thought.

On the other hand. Could she imagine being . . . *a mother*? She tasted the word, said it out loud: 'Mother'. The only association it triggered was with her own mother, and she had no intention of being like Anita. She changed tactics and said, as casually as possible: 'Have you heard? Siw's going to be a mother.' It sounded insane. She might as well have said: 'Have you heard? Siw's going to the moon.'

Admittedly she'd had vague hopes of one day having a family, a child of her own, but not *now*, and there could be no prospect of building a family with Acke. He would be as suitable a father as he would be for the role of astronaut on the aforementioned trip to the moon. In fact, he might be better as an astronaut. No, this was her decision and hers alone.

And so the weeks passed as she weighed up the arguments for and against. There was really only 'against'. Her accommodation would be terribly cramped, she would be short of money, she wouldn't be able to continue her education as planned. She would be exhausted from lack of sleep, she would hardly have any time to herself. On the 'for' side there was only a hypothetical baby that she didn't know, and she couldn't imagine how she would react to this child. She knew what she had to lose, and she had no idea of what she might gain.

Ten weeks had passed by the time Siw slammed her inner fist down on an imaginary table on her way to work. *Enough!* The only rational course of action was to . . . remove the human being-shaped clump of cells that was threatening to devastate her life. She would call during her lunch break, make the appointment.

Her shift on the checkout passed in a mixture of euphoria and nausea. It was going to happen! She would put this unpleasant episode behind her, tie it to a brick and drop it into the well of oblivion in her consciousness as if it had never happened. No harm done, life goes on, keep smiling.

Lunchtime came. Siw had decided to eat first, then make the call. Her usual seat was taken when she walked into the canteen with her microwaved meal, so she chose a table by the window. She had only just started to eat when she spotted it on the window ledge. The ship in a bottle. *Galaxy.* The ship she'd travelled on.

She sat there staring at the detailed model, resting on a choppy sea made of blue plastic, its beautifully painted hull, white clouds in a pale blue sky. It fascinated her. There was something there. Something she had failed to consider. Then she saw it.

Regardless of what she had thought at the time about the cleansing properties of the sea breezes, she hadn't had the slightest desire to go on that trip. The reason she went had been completely different: the possibility of an alternative version of her pregnancy that didn't

475

include Acke. A zipless fuck with a half-drunk Finn that she'd never intended to go through with, but it *could have happened*.

She had gone in order to acquire a made-up father for a child whose existence had yet to be confirmed at that stage. This father had been essential, because she had already known that *if* she was pregnant, then she would keep her baby.

She studied the model ship in the bottle. In her mind she went inside, recalled being in the cabin before Kajsa-Stina arrived with her mint liqueur, the Finn who groaned and thrust, made the bunk creak and squeak before leaving, never to return.

Apart from the bit about the groaning and thrusting, this was the story she would serve up to her child and anyone else who asked. *Have you heard? Siw's going to be a mother!* Yes. She certainly was.

THE WIND SPEAKS

Here I am again. You shouldn't be surprised, because I am eternal and omnipresent. Not even when the sea is as still and smooth as a mirror am I completely absent, just as the sun is still present when it is hidden by clouds. You might say there is no wind, yet somewhere a poplar leaf will tremble at the top of a tree.

The wind of change is blowing across Norrtälje, a metaphor that has little to do with me. I can bring down tall trees and make ships founder, but I am not capable of bringing about change of the kind we are talking about here. I am, however, the very best reporter, because I can poke my nose in wherever I like.

So. On my journeys I have noticed, among other things, that autumn has come early to the deciduous trees growing along the river. Limes and maples don't usually let go of their leaves until late October, allowing me to play with them for a while before I tire of the game and drop them in the river. This year the surface of the water was speckled with yellow in the middle of September, and by the end of the month the branches were bare. There were some days when I didn't even have time to touch each individual leaf as it drifted to its eternal rest.

And the brown trout, the pride and joy of Norrtälje as it passes up and down the river – where has it gone? All I have seen are upturned, white bellies floating along on the current, disappearing among the mass of leaves.

In Society Park the ground is unstable and some areas have been cordoned off for fear of sinkholes. Sinkholes! Hundreds of thousands of people have walked here for centuries, but now and only now does the ground threaten to open up beneath their feet.

At night someone is sneaking around on the periphery of the park and chopping down trees. Recently the perpetrator has started removing a ring of bark from the trunk so that the tree slowly starves to death. This is someone who hates both nature and people.

Some residents have noticed that the cobblestones on the walkways along the riverside have begun to move and poke up so that they become a trip hazard for the unwary, but so far I am the only one who can make out a faint tilt in the north wing of the hospital, which is slowly, slowly sinking down towards the riverbank.

There are many things wrong, and if I had hands with which to grip, I would happily offer my help, but as it is, I can only watch as cracks open up in one of the bridges, as the runestone known as Brodds sten begins to lean, and whole chunks of the riverbank come away and tumble into the water. We must speak frankly: Norrtälje is falling apart.

So far I have mentioned only the physical, practical irregularities. I am no connoisseur of the human psyche; I leave that kind of thing to psychologists and writers. I can only report on what I see on the outside, and what I see now is antipathy and irritation, a discontent with life that is evident in both facial expressions and body language when people are near the river.

In the same spirit of frankness, I must also tell you that what is in the river is *The Horror*. This horror was in the black sludge that oozed out of the container and down into the harbour inlet, and from there it found its way into the river, where it is now emitting the fumes that bring about its destructive effect.

You might point out that horror is a concept, and not something that can take on a physical form. Allow me to remind you that this is the wind talking. I too can be reduced to a concept in order to describe the movement of the air, but here I am anyway, as concrete as letters printed on paper. And I am telling you it was the horror that came out of that container.

To what extent this horror arose as a consequence of the terror the people inside the container felt, or if it was a stowaway that created this terror, is not for me to know. However, the little I have learned about the human mind tells me that cause and effect are often connected in a self-reinforcing hall of mirrors. You are complex, not to mention extremely troublesome creatures.

WHAT THE RIVER DOES TO US

I

'... and Bowser kidnaps Peach and then he takes all the lovely things in the world because he wants them for his wedding to Peach but she doesn't want to marry him because he's big and ugly and so Mario has to rescue her.'

Alva nods to herself and licks her Daim ice cream like a cat, allowing only the very tip of her tongue to capture the tiniest morsel. Ever since she went over to see a friend a few days ago and played what she refers to as *Mario Oddsy*, the word 'Switch' has passed her lips with increasing frequency. She talks about the device as if it were a minor deity, capable of creating miraculous revelations and eternal bliss.

Siw has checked it out and discovered that the deity costs about four thousand kronor, so unfortunately eternal bliss will have to wait until they can afford it. She also thinks that for one thing, Alva is too young for her own games console, and for another, she has a tendency towards monomania. When she was allowed to play *Angry*

Birds on Siw's phone for a while, she became so obsessed that she neither saw nor heard anything around her, and would sit there for hours unless Siw intervened.

They turn off Glasmästarbacken onto Tillfällegatan. Alva leads the way, and Siw knows exactly what she is up to. Alva's eyes are unseeing as she licks her ice cream and imagines herself in *Mushroom Kingdom*. Suddenly she regains her focus, looks sharply at Siw and asks: 'How do you know they're dead?'

'What . . . Who?'

'My grandfather and grandmother.'

'Your father told me.'

'When?'

'When we met.'

'When you *slept* together.'

A month earlier Alva had come home after spending the evening with Anita, and had explained in detail how babies are made – the vagina and the penis and the sperm, the whole lot. Siw didn't really have any objections, and the only amendment she made to Anita's information was that sex can be very nice when you're old enough, which Alva refused to believe. Sex was grown-up nastiness, and she had no intention of ever going there. Okay, maybe when she'd retired, but not before then.

Alva stops and gazes at a Lego Friends set displayed in Dubbelboa's window. She doesn't say anything, but gives her mother a dark look, no doubt preparing the ground for what is to come. It is no surprise when she turns into Lilla Brogatan.

As they approach the sculpture known as Folkflinet, Siw begins to feel uncomfortable, aware that something is going to happen. She stops and looks at the depiction in metal of a person thumbing their nose. Norrtälje's pillory used to be situated here, but fortunately

Siw's Hearings don't extend that far back in time. If they did, she wouldn't be able to go to work, because the town's place of execution was located where the Flygfyren shopping centre now stands. No, this is something else.

On Strömgatan, only about ten metres away, some kind of row is going on. Five young men are waving their arms at one another with jerky movements, their voices drowned out by the rushing of the river. Quite a lot of Afghan guys train at the gym, and as far as Siw can make out, two of the five belong to this group. The other three are presumably native Swedes.

She can't tell what the argument is about, but one of the Afghan guys is gesticulating with his phone and pointing at it as if to indicate that he has pictorial evidence of something, which seems to infuriate the Swedes. The heated exchange of words descends into pushing and shoving, faces are contorted in revulsion. The guy with the phone is kicked in the stomach. He doubles over and one of the Swedes grabs his phone, hurls it at the building behind them. Shards of glass and plastic rain down on the tarmac.

The other dark-haired guy aims a punch at the one who took the phone, but the biggest Swede gives him a hard shove, sending him flying backwards into the fence along the riverside; he almost tips over it. The Swedes exchange high fives, stamp on the phone for good measure, then continue on their way towards the harbour, leaving the two Afghans sitting slumped on the path.

Siw would like to do something, say something, be a better representative for Sweden, but she can't think of anything, plus her body is still preoccupied with the perception of the Hearing, which has nothing to do with the scene she has just witnessed. In spite of its unpleasantness, it wasn't bad enough to evoke a Hearing.

Alva hasn't noticed a thing. She is standing on the bridge with her back to Siw, looking down at the river as it races along, bubbling over the rocks. Her shoulders are slumped, her back bent. When she sets off towards the square with the same gloomy posture, Siw follows her, hoping to console her if possible. Instead, she stops dead halfway across the bridge.

Fucking world.

Alva continues along Lilla Brogatan, and Siw is overwhelmed by terror at the thought of the planet on which her daughter will grow up. It isn't just about the quarrel, it's much bigger than that. The increasing polarisation, the winds of the far right blowing through the world, the entire ecosystem which is going to hell, the extinction of whole species, the rising seas. A world and a human race that are busy eating themselves up, that is what Siw has to offer her daughter. Her lungs contract as if she is cowering in the expectation of a blow, and suddenly she can't breathe.

Out of the horror that has exploded in her chest, a picture emerges. All the leaders of the world, all the climate-blind industry magnates and all the rabid nationalists, lined up on the old airfield, which is now the football pitch. Siw is standing on her balcony, gazing down at the thousands below. Then she nods and presses the detonator in her hand.

The charge placed in the middle of the group explodes. A shower of red, shredded flesh spreads in all directions; scraps and larger pieces of suit fabric are caught by the wind and carried up into the sky. Siw leans on the balcony railing as a wonderful, lukewarm mist of blood moistens her face. The pitch is covered in a carpet of man-gled internal organs, gleaming in the sunshine. A few top politicians from the very edges of the group crawl out with mutilated bodies, but they soon stop moving. Peace and quiet settle over the field.

That showed you.

Siw blinks, struggling to understand what has come over her. Violent fantasies are not her thing, and she loathes horror films – all types of violence, in fact. Maybe it's to do with that sense of disconnection she felt before.

Alva has stopped halfway to the square, and is beckoning to Siw. She still looks pretty miserable. Siw pulls herself together and goes to join her daughter.

'What's wrong, sweetheart?'

'What if we get poor and have to move and can't afford to buy food?'

'There's no danger of that. I don't earn much, but it's enough.'

'But what if you die?'

'I'm not going to die, Alva.'

'What if my daddy comes and kidnaps me?'

'I would never let that happen.'

'No. Because then I'd kill him.'

Siw raises her eyebrows. This is a completely new variation in Alva's countless ways of tackling the problem of her father. She has never expressed any fear of the ghostly figure in the background.

'What made you think of that?' Siw asks.

Alva shrugs and straightens her shoulders. 'I just did.' Apparently forgetting what she has said, she carries on towards the square with lighter steps, and Siw follows on behind.

As Siw suspected, the draw is the gaming store. Alva presses her nose to the window, staring at a large cardboard figure of Mario and a somewhat wild-eyed rabbit.

'Oh, Mario,' Alva sighs, on the verge of tears. 'Oh, the rabbit.'

'Darling, you know we can't—'

'I know, Mum, I *know*.'

One positive aspect of Alva's dream of owning a Switch is that she has stopped going on about the rabbit in the pet shop, and instead shifted her attention to the fictional version, which according to the title of the game is *Raving Rabbid*. She lets out a sob and caresses the glass with her finger.

Siw knows her daughter. Apart from her stubbornness, Alva has patience. If Siw is not mistaken, this performance is merely one step in a longer campaign to break down Siw's defences, and it is not impossible that she will succeed. Eventually.

Alva seems to have retired from the fray on this occasion. She turns away from the store and skips away over the cobbles, humming a tune – presumably from *Oddsy*. Siw looks at her skinny body, bouncing along full of a child's energy; listens to her cries of 'Yoo-hoo!', and a little of the melancholy she felt on the bridge returns.

Skip along, my darling, until the real Bowsers come and take all the lovely things in the world.

2

Anna's balcony measures three square metres. It offers a view of a car park and the facade of a building stained by exhaust fumes over the years. Along the edge of the balcony there is a sheet of corrugated metal, its flaking paint an unidentifiable shade somewhere between beige and grey. It is topped by a railing so rusty that it turns your palms brown if you hold on to it. A thin crack runs diagonally across the concrete floor, and here and there the odd piece has broken away. A line of dirt in the corner by the wall, cobwebs everywhere. A rickety metal table with an ashtray, fag ends floating in the rainwater. A folding plastic chair that is never taken indoors, and which has acquired a pale brown film after years of exposure to the weather.

Why this detailed description of Anna's balcony? Well, because she is sitting there, and she feels exactly the way it looks. She leans back on the plastic chair which squeaks reproachfully, and sucks listlessly on her cigarette. A woman in her seventies is sitting on a balcony in the apartment block opposite. She too is smoking, while her gaze rests accusingly on a bicycle lying on its side.

You and me, hun.

As if the woman has heard her, she glances up and meets Anna's gaze. For a fraction of a second there is confusion, a short circuit in Anna's brain, and she is looking at herself through the woman's eyes. She is the woman, or she will be. A shudder passes through Anna's body as she returns to herself. There is a hiss as she drops the fag end in the ashtray.

One of her workmates at the care home has a favourite expression. When too many members of staff are at home with the kids because they're sick, or are signed off sick themselves, she likes to say: 'The situation is untenable.' It can't go on, everything is going to collapse. But it never does. It just gets a little worse.

However, Anna's situation at the moment is exactly that – untenable. She can't go on like this. Ewert Djup's implied threat was a black stone dropped into her already overflowing goblet of life's difficulties. It spills over the rim, and she feels as if she is about to dissolve.

She gets up and goes indoors. Her decor is provisional, a collection of temporary items that she had planned to leave behind when she moved. The worn, scruffy sofa, the stained coffee table, the moth-eaten rugs. She hates this apartment, which isn't even her own.

Dust bunnies swirl around her feet as she crosses the living room and goes into the bedroom. The bed is the one she had as a girl, and it doesn't have a sprung mattress. She feels it sag as she flops down and buries her head in her hands.

Outside the window, grubby from exhaust fumes and acid rain, the never-ending traffic on Stockholmsvägen rushes by. At night her bed often vibrates when the buses trundle past, and their headlights make patterns on the ceiling through the broken blind. Drunken men, shouting and singing, keeping her awake.

Men, Anna thinks. *Men.*

She is so tired of them. Bone-weary. It is their stupidity and lack of consideration that have sabotaged her life, from her father Stig's dabbling with criminal elements to her own pointless relationships with idiots driving EPA tractors, and Acke's crap with the Djup brothers which she has now been dragged into. She bangs her hand on the bed in frustration, and a cloud of dust particles whirl up into the air.

The panoply of men and boys who have messed up her life pass through her mind, ending with the image of miserable old Folke Gunnarsson in the care home, a concentrate of male repulsiveness distilled through a long life in the service of bitterness. *Foreigners go home, let's just get down and dirty . . .*

So. What is she going to do? She has no savings and nothing of value to sell, except possibly her body, and that isn't an option. At the age of sixteen she provided certain sexual services on a couple of occasions when she was drunk, in return for 'petrol money' for her moped; the revulsion that came over her when she sobered up is not something she intends to experience again.

So. Should she simply let things proceed, until her little brother Acke is chained to the towbar of the Djup brothers' Volvo, bellowing with fear? That isn't an option either.

The only possibility is to ask her family for help, which she really doesn't want to do. There is no rhyme or reason as to why Anna in particular should be responsible for Acke's wellbeing, but that's the way it's been ever since he was a little boy, and that's the way it has stayed. She is the one who must make his case. The idiot's case.

Anna would like to sink through the uncomfortable mattress. She feels very low, and decides to deal with it as she always does: by partying. Within five minutes she has called three girlfriends from Rimbo who live in Norrtälje, and arranged a night on the town starting in Little Dublin. The choice of companions has dwindled over the years as people settle down, and these three are neither her first nor second choice – it's more a matter of scraping the barrel. But at least they can drink.

She puts down the phone and drums her fingers on her knee. She has a long afternoon ahead of her. She ought to do the cleaning. She doesn't want to do the cleaning. The state of the apartment is a kind of protest, a way of kicking against the reality of living here. On the rare occasions when she does clean up, it feels like a defeat, an acceptance of the provisional as something permanent.

What can she do?

Anna thinks, then suddenly her face lights up and she slaps her thighs. She knows *exactly* what she is going to do.

3

For the first time, Anna is walking along the corridors of the care home when she isn't here to work. The paper bag containing two Danish pastries rustles in her hand, and she feels like an intruder. It doesn't help when Reza, who only works weekends, gives her an enquiring look. Anna shrugs – *that's just the way it goes*. She continues to Berit's room and knocks on the door.

'Yes, yes! Come in!' Berit calls out, her tone indicating as usual that she has been disturbed in the middle of important work.

Anna opens the door and finds Berit busy with her laptop. She looks irritably in Anna's direction, but her expression softens when she sees who it is.

'Oh, it's you! People are running around like lunatics!'

'They're only doing their job.' Anna waves the bag. 'I brought pastries!'

'Good. The cinnamon buns in this place are lethal for my false teeth. Come here.'

Berit pulls herself up into a half-standing position, and Anna gives her a quick hug. Siw's grandmother doesn't have the old-woman smell of nappies, bedsores and bad breath due to rotting teeth – more an old-lady combination of talcum powder, mothballs and cocoa.

Anna makes coffee and sets out the pastries on a plate. Berit smiles at her. 'Is this when I find out what it's like to be an Olofsson?'

'Maybe.'

Berit tilts her head to one side. 'Is something bothering you, sweetheart?'

Anna hesitates, then tells Berit all about the conversation she had with Ewert Djup, the dangerous position her little brother has got himself into thanks to his idiotic behaviour, and her own responsibility for sorting out the situation.

'You lost me there,' Berit says. 'Why is it your responsibility?'

'You asked me what it's like to be an Olofsson, and there you have a perfect example. That's just the way it is. He's my kid brother, and it's up to me to look after him.'

'You mean, there's a family loyalty you can't free yourself from by swearing a sacred oath, like they used to do in olden days?'

'Well, I wouldn't put it quite like that, but . . . yes.'

'Hmm.' Berit brushes a few flakes of pastry from her lips and points to a chest of drawers where a number of framed photographs are displayed. 'Look at those photos. Tell me what you see.'

Anna gets up and studies a dozen or so pictures in different sizes and from different periods of time. 'I recognise Siw,' she says. 'And Alva. And that must be Anita when she was young.'

'She was a miserable cow even then. Carry on.'

'And these women – I assume one of them is your mother?'

'Wrong.'

'Okay. So is one of the men your father?'

'No. The one on the far right was my husband – Anita's father.'

'You don't have a picture of your parents?'

'No. Guess why.'

'Maybe because . . . there wasn't one?'

'Oh, there were plenty. I threw the whole lot away. Because I didn't like my parents. They weren't nice people. As soon as I was old enough to take care of myself, I refused to have anything more to do with them. Stopped regarding them as my family. The other people in those photos are friends. Most of them are dead now, but I regarded *them* as my family.'

Anna returns to the table, where Berit is looking at her so sternly that Anna lowers her eyes and shrugs. 'So you think I ought to cut all ties with my family?'

'I'm not saying that, but I do believe you should think hard about where your loyalty lies. You didn't choose your family. During the course of our lives we bump into lots of people who just happen to be there. Nobody says you have to take them on.'

Anna sits in silence for a long time, considering what Berit has said. She understands and even agrees with her logic, but she can't summon up the feeling that would make it possible for her to act differently from the way she knows she must. She is stuck fast.

'So,' Berit says, brushing her palms together. 'What are you doing tonight?'

Anna outlines her plans, which makes Berit shake her head gloomily. 'I'd be very careful, if I were you.'

'What do you mean?'

'I don't know how much Siw has told you about this . . . gift we have in our family?'

'The Hearing?'

'Mmm. Yesterday I went into town with the mobility service minibus, thought I'd shuffle round with my wheeled walker and do a bit of shopping. I didn't stay long, because . . .' Berit runs her hand over her forehead in a graceful gesture to indicate her brain. 'Siw's Hearings are strong and direct, mine are more . . . comprehensive, and what I heard on Tillfällegatan . . .'

She shudders at the memory, and her false teeth make a faint clicking sound as she chews the air in an effort to find the right words. 'There is so much *anger*, both now and in the future. So much screaming, the thud of so many bodies hitting the ground. It's falling apart.'

'What's falling apart?'

'Norrtälje.'

4

It is eight thirty in the evening and Anna has already sunk a few beers with accompanying shots, and has about two beers to go before the oblivion and numbness kick in. The anger Berit talked about has not yet expressed itself in violence, but there is something in the air, in the tone of conversations and the movements of people all around. A tension.

She is sitting at a table for four with Johanna, Emma and Elin, who were part of her outer circle at primary school. When she contemplates them through alcohol's incipient tunnel vision, she sees three slightly worse versions of herself. Rimbo trash. They are all overweight to varying degrees, thanks to junk food and boozing at home. They are all wearing too much make-up, with backcombed bleach-blonde hair and brightly coloured blouses with or without ruffles, straining over their busts. Both Emma and Elin are personal carers visiting clients at home, while Johanna is signed off sick following a burn-out she suffered as a childminder.

At the moment she seems anything but burned out – more like on fire as she tells them about a recent Tinder date, nostrils flaring.

'. . . and after, like, ten minutes he's, like, "Are those your tits?" and I'm, like, "No, I borrowed them from my granny", and guess what he said? "Can I have a feel?" I mean, "Can I have a feel," like I'm an avocado or something he wants to check the quality of before he—'

'Hello, girls! Hello!'

The man has been trying to attract their attention for ten minutes, but they have studiously ignored him. He's in his forties, and his idea of getting dressed up for a night out is a plumbing company

T-shirt with the logo 'Pipes R Us'. He is having difficulty focusing, and saliva sprays from his lips as he turns to his two friends to complain.

Johanna's story ends in the usual way – she ends up in bed with the guy and it's a disaster. They move on to discussing the problem of men who use someone else's online profile picture, then claim that they used to look like that a few years ago.

'Hey, hey! What the . . .'

Using the table for support, the man gets to his feet. As he staggers past behind Anna's back, she hears the clink of a belt buckle. He positions himself with one hand on Anna's shoulder, while with the other he hauls out his penis and bangs it down on the table.

'There you go!' he says with an unpleasant grin. 'What do you think of that?'

The organ is only a couple of centimetres from Anna's right hand. She feels the urge to form a fist and flatten the limp piece of flesh even more, but decides it's not worth the trouble. Divorced from sexual activity, the male member is such a *ridiculous* object, but the man doesn't appear to realise this as he stands there dry-humping the edge of the table, looking very pleased with himself.

Men. Men. Men.

What does he expect? Does he think they're going to leap to their feet, hands on their cheeks, delightedly shrieking: 'Oh, wow! Look at that! Aren't you amazing?' Incel men must think that the simple fact of having a cock is like a free pass to the Gröna Lund amusement park, where all the attractions are open 24/7, *come and get it!*

A security guard grabs the guy by the shoulders and drags him towards the door. He struggles to shove his dangling organ back into his pants as he yells: 'Fucking bitches! Cold-hearted fucking . . .'

An icy shard of pain pierces Anna's right eye and continues into her brain, as her companions hurl abuse at the man. The headache settles inside her skull like a cold rag, and she rubs her eyes as three indignant voices blend together.

'What an idiot . . . Seriously, what was he thinking? . . . Does he expect us to . . . I mean . . . Has he never heard of #MeToo?'

The man's friends have become very interested in their drinks, and are staring into their beer glasses. One even has the grace to blush. Anna finds herself thinking he's actually quite sweet and maybe . . .

No. No.

Something falls through her, or perhaps she falls through something. In the harsh light of the headache she sees herself sitting where she is sitting, surrounded by friends who are not friends, on an evening like a thousand other evenings. She is going to drink too much, and tomorrow she will be hungover, and so it will all begin again.

During the course of our lives we bump into lots of people who just happen to be there.

That's exactly how it is with Emma, Elin and Johanna. They happened to be in Rimbo during a period when wasted evenings with cigarettes and low-alcohol beer by the old tennis courts were what counted. Sniggering, swearing, talking about boys. Twilight, the smell of wet leaves. Nothing wrong with that, but now? Now?

Anna stands up. 'Sorry. I just remembered there's something I have to . . .'

Emma opens her eyes wide. 'What? You're not *leaving*, are you?'

'We've hardly started!' Elin wiggles her half-full beer glass as if to show how much is left.

'I have to . . .'

Anna doesn't know what she has to do, apart from getting away from Little Dublin and everything it represents. She has to start

494

somewhere else, pick up a new thread, anything, but she has to get away. Now.

5

For as long as Johan can remember he has had a problem with being in the present. The first time he became aware of this was during registration after the summer holidays, when he started in Year Four. The teacher read out his name, and he raised his hand and said: 'Here'. When he lowered his hand, he felt a sense of regret, as if he'd lied.

While other names were called out and his classmates cheerfully answered 'here', Johan experienced strong doubts. Was he really *here*? He ran his fingers over a cross carved into his desk; he pinched his forearm. Yes. The indications were that he was here, but in that case why didn't it feel that way? And where else was he?

As time went by, Johan realised that the root of this feeling, or rather non-feeling, was his constantly whirling thoughts and fantasies. He found it difficult to keep his internal and external lives apart, a milder version of the syndrome that plagued his mother. It didn't matter whether the condition was genetic or learned behaviour, he was going to have to keep the phenomenon in check if he wanted to live a comparatively normal life.

That is why he loves to write. Or no, let's settle for the fact that writing *eases* his sense of disconnection. When he is sitting at his computer chiselling out a story, he no longer feels fractured. His internal world immediately finds its expression in the external form of words on the screen, and he is even able to achieve a state of harmony. Balance.

But now it is Saturday night in the bowling hall. Johan lifts the basket out of the deep fat fryer and tips the chips onto a plate. His movements are well-practised and mechanical, and his thoughts are free to wander. He thinks about swapping *hand* for *hound* in familiar expressions.

He's my right hound. Not bad. *Give me your hound.* Better. He flips the burger on the griddle one last time, then places it on a roll with a slice of cheese, adds gherkins and a squirt of dressing. Done. He picks up the plate and is on his way when he suddenly stops. *One hound doesn't know what the other is doing.*

Johan is still giggling when he puts the plate on the bar in front of Olof Carlgren, known as Bowling Ball Olle because of his hobby and his physical shape. Olle peers at him through tiny eyes embedded in rolls of fat and asks: 'Something funny?'

'One hound doesn't know what the other is doing.'

'Right. What are you talking about?'

'That expression . . . oh, never mind. Eighty-nine kronor.'

After taking Olle's payment, Johan walks around collecting plates and glasses. It is unusually quiet for a Saturday night, and only four lanes are occupied. *Take my hound and let us be friends.* Johan is heading for the kitchen with a loaded tray when he hears a voice close by. 'Hey.'

Anna is standing next to the boxing machine with her hands pushed deep in the pockets of a bomber jacket. There is something fragile about her face, as if the skin beneath her eyes is unusually thin.

'Hey,' Johan says, lifting the tray. 'I'll just . . .' He stops himself, then says: 'One hound doesn't know what the other is doing.' Anna snorts, and something of the fragility melts away. Johan continues into the kitchen, grateful for the tray, which neutralises the question of whether to hug or not. When he returns Anna is sitting at a table. 'Can I get you anything?' he says. 'A beer?'

'I'm fine, thanks. Now what's that song by Håkan Hellström, Siw's favourite . . . mmm-hmm-hmm-hmm, *put your hound in mine.*'

'Not bad.'

'Not bad. Yours was better.'

At the next table Olle is attacking his burger with enthusiastic grunts. Johan slides into a chair and lowers his voice. 'How are you?'

Anna rests her cheek on one hand. 'You know, my friends just asked me the same question and I said fine thanks, no problem.'

'But . . . ?'

'But actually, things are pretty bad.' Anna runs her hand over the table, brushing away invisible crumbs. 'I don't know why I decided to come here . . .'

'It's okay.'

'Yes. I guess it is.'

A group of boys who have finished playing are standing by the counter, and Johan goes over to sort them out. As he takes their money and prints off their scorecards he glances at Anna, who is now sitting with both hands cupping her cheeks, like a crying child in a mass-produced 'art' print. She doesn't know why she has come here, and he doesn't know why he's pleased that she has, but that's the way it is. He picks up a glass, gets a bottle of Coke out of the chill cabinet and joins her again.

'Coke?'

'Thanks.' Anna frowns as she concentrates on pouring the drink. She takes a sip, then says: 'It's just that life, everything, it all seems so, I don't know . . .'

'Hopeless?'

'Wow. Yes, hopeless. I've never used that word, but yes. No hope.

It's as if there's a thick fog and I can only see a metre in front of me. One day at a time, kind of.'

'Mightn't there be something good beyond that fog, though?'

'There might, but I can't see it. I've got nothing to hope for. Have you?'

Johan can't say that he has hopes for his novel, since he doesn't have the courage to do anything with it, yet it is still there like a distant, shimmering possibility. The faintest glow, a lighthouse in the fog. However, this isn't something he can consider putting into words while sober, so he replies: 'No. One step at a time. Until you reach your final goal – the crematorium.'

Anna lets out a bark of laughter. 'You're even more depressing than me!'

They sit in silence for a while. Pins are knocked down and Olle chomps on his chips. Eventually Johan says: 'Isn't it possible to find something? Something to give you hope?'

'Like what?'

'I don't know, but something that will provide . . . direction. Something to build up.'

'Like training? Education?'

'That's one example.'

Anna chews on a strand of her black hair, then says: 'Direction. Yes, maybe.'

'This is the way I think.' Johan is venturing into dangerous territory here. 'That my life is a story. Is it a sensible story? Believable? Are the main character's actions consistent? Do I care about him? It creates a kind of . . . order when I think like that. As if there is a line, a progression after all.'

'And do you like it? This story?'

Now it is Johan's turn to snort. 'I wouldn't exactly rush out to buy it, but it's what I've got.'

Anna nods, finishes off her Coke, then places her hands decisively on the table and gets to her feet. 'Time I went home.'

'What are you going to do?'

The skin beneath Anna's eyes no longer looks thin. 'Clean.' She raises her index finger as if to request silence. 'One more thing. How does it go now . . . *It trembles, your childish hound that I kissed . . .*'

Johan holds up his hand and Anna gives him a high five.

6

By quarter to ten the last players have departed, and Johan leaves it to Ove to close up. Walking home along Baldersgatan, he feels unusually contented. He doesn't even stop to spit on the Social Services' office sign, or to piss in their flowerbeds as he usually does. He just keeps going.

Johan's comfort zone is so strictly limited that it closely resembles a padded cell. He is very reluctant to change his familiar routines, which allow him to live in a parallel reality inside his head. Anything that comes from the outside and disturbs the balance is potentially destructive.

And yet: Anna. Ever since high school he has avoided the type of person she represents. Those who laugh too loudly, who take up too much space in a thoughtless, slobbering way, who always get too drunk. White trash, if you like. So how come he found her visit to the bowling hall so uplifting?

Maybe his unexpected closeness to her means he is taking a step away from that padded cell, venturing into the corridor or maybe

499

even the park, an opportunity to breathe a little fresh air. The fact that he originally despised her makes the step even greater, and creates a sense of freedom that Johan has not experienced for a long time.

The clusters of rowan berries glow red in the white light of the LED street lamps on the way down the hill leading to the bus station. He runs his fingers over them and thinks *autumn*, and the word doesn't mean dying and withering, but open skies, multi-coloured leaves and a nostalgia that doesn't hurt. He is in the bright part of his thoughts.

Your childish hound that I kissed.

He cuts through the bus depot and passes the library as expressions and song lyrics bounce around in his mind. *I wanna hold your hound.* He turns down into Hantverkargatan and continues towards the square. When he reaches the fountain he turns right for the bridge, texting Anna as he walks:

Five grubby little fingers on a grubby little hound.

The reply comes immediately in the form of a smiley and a thumbs up. Johan has never sent a smiley in his entire life. Imagine that.

'Hey! Hey!'

Johan has almost reached Harry's Restaurant when he hears a voice behind him. He stops and turns around. Two guys with what Johan thinks of as Afghan haircuts are jogging towards him from the direction of the square. One points to Johan's hand.

'Hey, can I check out your phone?'

There is nothing remarkable about Johan's iPhone 6s, except possibly that the screen isn't cracked, so he says: 'Why?'

The guy shrugs. 'I just want to look. Give it to me.'

As he holds out his hand, his companion takes a step closer to

Johan, and there is no doubt about what is going on here. The second guy places a hand on Johan's shoulder. 'Don't be stupid. Give him the phone.'

Johan's heart begins to pound, and he presses the phone to his chest as it buzzes with an incoming text. He automatically glances at the screen and sees **A bird in the hound is worth two in the bush**. He laughs nervously, and all he can think of is that if he loses the phone, he will also lose Anna's number. The hand on his shoulder tightens its grip and the outstretched hand makes a *give it here* gesture, at the same time as its owner says: 'Swede smashed mine. I want yours. Give.'

The hand moves from Johan's shoulder to the back of his neck and he feels invaded, as if someone has come stomping into his padded cell in muddy boots and he hates it, but he can't do anything to defend himself. He is about to give up the phone when a large man in a leather waistcoat, his arms covered in tattoos, emerges from the tapas bar next door.

'What's going on here?' he says, folding his meaty arms over his chest.

'Nothing,' says the first guy, lowering his hand as the grip on Johan's neck loosens. 'No problem here.'

'Looks like a bit of a problem to me,' the man says, turning back to the bar and shouting: 'Hey! We've got some apes out here nicking bananas!'

Two men of the same calibre get up from their table and head for the door. The Afghan guys exchange glances, then take to their heels. Before the bikers have reached the pavement, the Afghans are in the square, heading for the harbour.

The man waves his friends away and pats Johan on the back. 'Are you okay?'

'Yes,' Johan replies tonelessly. 'Thanks.'

'No problem. We have to stick together, fight the invasion of the apes. Look after yourself.'

The man goes back into the bar, says something that makes his friends guffaw. Only now does Johan realise his whole body is shaking. No one has ever tried to mug him before; he has never had his integrity *damaged* in the way that just happened.

The phone almost slips out of his sweaty grasp. He puts it in his pocket and continues on unsteady legs. On the bridge he is struck by the thought that the Afghans might simply have run around the block, and are waiting for him at the end of Tillfällegatan. His legs feel even weaker, and he leans on the railing.

The invasion of the apes.

Johan pictures an army of men with thick black hair, cropped at the sides and long on top, pouring in across the borders, breaking into houses, looting and raping as they laugh and jabber in Arabic. He sees them waving ISIS flags, forcing the residents of Norrtälje to their knees in the main square before going around and systematically cutting each person's throat with their long knives, while their ape-chatter rises to the clock tower, which has been transformed into a minaret.

Fear turns to rage, and Johan stares down into the coal-black waters of the river as he sees himself attacking the telephone thief with a hammer, smashing his crooked fucking teeth to bits, placing his balls in a vice and tightening it until he howls for mercy and then *squish* and blood spurting and spurting everywhere. The whole fucking lot of them. Bring out a hundred thousand vices, squish all the apes' balls. That will be a hymn of praise to Allah, thank you very much.

Strengthened by his burning anger, Johan lets go of the railing and crosses the bridge. He continues along the street, so preoccupied with increasingly bloodthirsty scenes of retribution that he forgets to be afraid. The worst of his fury cools as he makes his way up Glasmästarbacken, but he is still so cross that his neck feels constricted.

When he gets home he takes a beer out of the fridge and drinks it while pacing up and down. Then he has another, but the tension in his neck refuses to go away. There is only one thing he can do.

Johan opens his computer and logs into the Roslagen group under his alias, SvenneJanne. Then he writes a piece, a long piece about what has just happened to him and how he thinks certain problems should be solved. Slowly the constriction eases. By the time he copies and posts his contribution, he is completely relaxed.

7

If there's one song Anna loathes, it's the one about turning that frown upside down. The fantastic thing is that it's her mother who created this antipathy. Sometimes when Anna was particularly cross or disappointed, Sylvia would croak out those lines without for one second changing her own miserable expression.

The bit about how the mouth ought to laugh and be happy is especially unpleasant. Anna imagines a gaping mouth, laughing and singing *tra-la-la* while terrible deeds are being planned within the body it is attached to. Hence the reason for the fear of clowns.

So how come Anna is humming that ghastly tune as she polishes the bathroom mirror? Layer after layer of ground-in dirt is transferred to the cloth in her hand, until her reflection is of HD quality and indistinguishable from the reality. And that reflection shows an Anna who is contemplating her work with a smile of satisfaction.

She has shaken out the rugs and vacuumed. She has done all the washing up and scrubbed the draining board with Ajax. She has taken out the rubbish and wiped down all the cupboard doors. She has *not* tackled the oven, which is another matter entirely, but in time it too will find itself under attack. Anna has made up her mind.

It was what Johan said about direction. At the moment Anna can't see herself embarking on some kind of training course or making a radical change to her life that will enable her to progress. What she can do, however, is clean up the crap that is clouding her vision.

Maybe it all started with that thought about *men*. All those idiots with their stupid grins, a plug of snuff just visible beneath the top lip, who have stood in her way when she has wanted to move. Then there's the alcohol, the booze that has made her wobble when she could have gone in a straight line. She wants to clean up, let the fresh air in, and the apartment was the closest task to hand. She needs to accept that this is what she has, and it is as good a place as any to begin.

In a way, Anna is turning that frown upside down with every stroke of the cloth. Whether it becomes a *story* that anyone other than a patient in a coma would listen to is debatable, but you have to start somewhere, and even a thousand-mile journey begins with a kick up the arse.

The question of Acke and the Djup brothers will have to wait; each day has enough trouble of its own, as the Bible says. She smiles as she squirts Toilet Duck beneath the rim of the bowl. Maybe she'll become one of those wise old buggers who simply disgorge platitudes day after day? Unlikely but not impossible.

She gives a little snort of laughter as she thinks, *Five grubby little fingers on a grubby little hound.* For a play on words to be funny, it has to create a funny picture. Anna's phone rings. The grubby little dog with a gloomy expression and fingers instead of claws lingers in her mind as she goes into the living room and picks up her phone. The screen gives her two pieces of information that should be incompatible. 1: It is one o'clock in the morning. 2: The caller is Siw. She has never phoned later than eleven, so the first thing Anna says is: 'Hi, hun – how are you?'

A shuddering sigh, then Siw replies: 'Okay. I just can't sleep.'

'Is this to do with Max?'

'No. Yes. Maybe.'

Anna curls up and makes herself comfortable on the newly vac-uumed sofa. Regardless of what she has decided about her own life, she has no intention of giving up her interest in gossip and relationship problems, which ultimately are the only things that *are* interesting.

A few years ago she might have said: 'Spill the beans – give me all the juicy details,' but she made a decision when she left her friends from Rimbo. Plus, she knows it wouldn't work on Siw, with the coyness she regards as integrity. Instead, Anna simply says: 'Tell me. How did it go?'

'It went well.' A subtle change in Siw's voice lets Anna know that she is blushing. So it went *very* well. Then comes the inevitable: 'But . . .'

'But?'

'But I just feel . . . I mean, what function would I fulfil in his life?'

'Function?'

505

'Yes. Everything has a function, doesn't it? Last night when we . . . did what we did, and then when we sat and talked, I felt as if . . . I had the right to be there. I was fulfilling a function. But then this morning, I'm not sure . . .'

'So do you *want* to be a function? Think about Sören – you weren't much more than functional as far as he was concerned. A melon with a hole in it would have worked just as well.'

Siw lets out a little sob. 'Don't say that.'

Anna bites her lip and adds *cynical banter* to the list of things she is going to try to refrain from. 'Sorry – that wasn't fair. But you know what I mean. You've got it all wrong. Love isn't about functions, it's about . . .'

Anna pauses and Siw says: 'Go on, Anna. Tell me what love is about.'

'I don't fucking know, but it's definitely not functions.'

There is a silence as Anna tries to work out if she actually has a definition of love, but all that swirls to the surface are the platitudes she isn't yet ready to disgorge, plus the grubby little dog.

Eventually Siw says: 'I feel . . . unhinged. Displaced. I can't sleep. It's as if I'm a little bit outside myself. This is not good.'

'Do you like him?'

'Yes, I like him a lot. But it's as if I can't allow myself to feel that way.'

'Because you don't have a function?'

'Yes.'

'Even though your function is pretty clear.'

'Is it?'

'Yes – to be the one who likes him a lot. I reckon that's the best function you can have.'

'Although that kind of depends on him feeling the same way.'

'Yes, that's the tricky bit.'

'Goodnight. I'm going to sleep now. Or at least I'm going to try.'

'Goodnight. You're right about one thing, anyway.'

'Which is?'

'You are unhinged. Goodnight, sweetheart.'

THE MEMORY OF A MEMORY

I

It is Max who has sent out the question on Discord, and a dozen people have turned up for the raid at Brodds sten. Better than expected at seven o'clock on a Sunday evening, when the raid boss is no longer a novelty. Max himself already has four Entei, one with almost perfect stats, so the raid is mostly about collecting points and being part of a context.

Max has never understood why Brodds sten is there. The runestone, which stands on the slope leading down to the river near the bus station, is a replica of a stone that wasn't even there in the first place. One hundred per cent fake ancient monument, yet it is still one of the sights of Norrtälje. Maybe those responsible hope that people will forget over time, and begin to treat it as the real deal.

Twilight has fallen and the temperature has dropped. Damp veils of mist are creeping up the slope, and the mood of the group beneath the bare elm trees is not the best. The usual small talk and comparison of captures just isn't there. People are staring at their screens with grim concentration as the raid counts down to Start.

The countdown can be exciting, particularly when it involves a new raid boss, but for the first time Max thinks it seems ominous, as if it were counting down to some kind of catastrophe. He doesn't understand where the thought has come from, but the closer it gets to zero, the more anxious he feels.

Needless to say, nothing happens. Entei leaps out and the players' respective Pokémon stand in a circle and attack. Because Entei is fire, Max has mainly chosen water Pokémon, with a fully primed Vaporeon at the head. In less than a minute Entei has been defeated and the capture takes over.

Whether it's down to some rotten logarithm, Murphy's Law or plain bad luck, very few succeed in catching the fire dog. There is sighing, puffing and blowing, and lots of groans until a twelve-year-old boy raises his clenched fist and shouts: 'Yes, yes, yes!'

'Shut the fuck up,' growls a forty-year-old man in a tracksuit, who doesn't already have Entei and is about to throw the last of his balls.

A gasp passes through the group, and people glance at one another. It is perfectly acceptable to show one's excitement, but 'shut the fuck up' is not part of the everyday vernacular. The boy looks frightened. The man continues to throw balls, and in spite of *excellent* hits, does not succeed in his mission.

'There's no need for that,' a woman says to the man, who now appears to want to hurl his phone into the river.

'What the fuck's it got to do with you?' The man waves his phone around, revealing the sweat patches under his arms. 'It's so fucking unfair. That kid over there, what's he on? Twenty? He chucks a couple of balls that aren't even *nice*, and he gets it. I'm on forty, I fire off four *excellent* curveballs in a row, and . . . nothing. It's not surprising I'm annoyed.'

'Can you hear yourself? You're a grown man, for goodness' sake!' the woman replies.

The man is about to respond even more angrily when a neatly dressed woman in her thirties who works for the council suddenly yells: 'Fucking *hell*! Cock!'

Another collective gasp. As there are children in the group, this kind of language is tacitly forbidden. Just as it is acceptable to show excitement, members are also allowed to get annoyed. But there are limits.

The woman who reprimanded the man turns to the woman from the council. 'Maybe you should consider your use of language.'

'I'm considering where you can shove your phone, bitch.' The younger woman turns her back on the group and marches away. Everyone exchanges apologetic or embarrassed looks before dispersing, without even having checked who's managed to capture the boss.

Max has been so preoccupied with the behaviour of the group that he still has four balls left. He uses a Golden Razz Berry with each and manages to snare Entei with the very last one. When he looks up, everyone has gone.

What was that all about?

He has seen both the man in the tracksuit (PuttePelle3) and the woman from the council (MjauVoff) on earlier raids and they have never behaved like that. They have been quiet and pleasant, like most of the others. Max thinks about the deep unease he felt during the countdown, but it doesn't make him any the wiser.

'There's something,' he whispers to himself as he slips the phone into his pocket. 'There's definitely something.'

He wanders down the slope towards Elverks Bridge. When he reaches Kvarnholmen he stops and gazes out across the river. The café where Maria works is nearby. This is one of the river's fast-moving sections, and the water makes a rushing sound as it races over smooth stones which reflect the glow of the street lamps, making them resemble hundreds of predators' eyes, staring up at him from the riverbed.

The shark is coming for him. The muscle of death darts out of the depths, its black eyes contemplate him with indifferent hunger, he is nothing more than a piece of meat floating in the endless sea. The horror rises in Max's chest, his throat contracts . . . and then Micke Littletroll is there with his chainsaw, lopping the top off the problem. The soufflé of fear collapses and his breathing slows. Max continues across the bridge.

It is years since he thought about the shark in that way, as something present and threatening, an incarnation of his imminent death. It is a terrible and defining event from his past, but that's all it is. An abstraction. But here on Kvarnholmen something happened to make that forgotten fear flare up. Max presses his hand to his chest; his heart is still beating faster than it should.

There's definitely something.

When he reaches Tullportsgatan and stands beneath the elm tree where he last stood with Siw and Charlie, his heart rate is back to normal and he is struck by a realisation. His parents are away on a cruise for a month, and the house is empty. Instead of turning right for Stockholmsvägen, he turns left. There is something he wants to try.

2

When Max passes Marko's house, he sees that there are lights on. He is not in a hurry to carry out the test he has in mind, and there is something *luxurious* in having Marko around for the moment, so he takes the opportunity.

As he approaches the house, the front door opens and Goran and Laura emerge. Max hasn't seen them for several years, but recognises them immediately. Laura's hair has gone grey, but she still has that same aura of warmth and security. Goran's body is marked by a lifetime of hard work, but he moves with dignity. Max looks around, struck by the urge to flee. He has no idea why, but a bolt of embarrassment shoots through him.

Before he has time to do anything, Goran spots him and raises a hand in greeting. 'Max! Are you coming to visit our . . . what's the word? Ah, yes, *lunatic*. Our lunatic son?'

Goran shakes Max's hand and Laura gives him a brief hug as Marko watches from the doorway. They chat politely for a moment, and Max can't shake off the desire to run and hide. Marko's parents turn to leave, and on the way to the gate Laura raises a warning finger. 'Don't get carried away now, Marko!'

'Carried away with what?' Max asks as he joins Marko.

'Oh, we've been talking about furniture and so on. If it was up to them, it would be online auction sites all the way.'

'And if it was up to you? Bukowskis?'

Marko grins and jerks his head towards the house. 'Come in.'

Max takes off his shoes in the hallway, but still his footsteps echo softly off the bare walls as they walk through the empty rooms. Marko points to the kitchen, where the leftover booze from the party is lined up on the worktop. 'Do you want anything? There are three wine boxes and about twenty cans of beer.'

'No, I'm fine, thanks.'

They pass through the living room, where Marko's camp bed is made up, and continue out onto the terrace. Max stands there with his hands in his pockets gazing out over the garden, which is visible only as overgrown contours in the darkness. What he says next comes as a surprise to both of them.

'I've been wondering . . .' – although he hasn't been wondering at all – '. . . if you need any help with the garden. If so, I can take it on. Be your gardener.'

Marko looks at him searchingly. 'No, I don't think that will be necessary.'

Max grunts and spreads his hand, encompassing the chaotic mess in front of him. 'It is necessary, I can promise you that. It's not that I need the job, but . . . look at the state of the place.'

'I don't mean it like that.' Marko lowers his eyes and seems to be on the point of explaining further, but instead he shakes his head and changes the subject. 'So, how did it go with Siw yesterday?'

'That's a question with no simple answer.'

'Let's pretend we're teenagers. In which case there is *one* simple answer.'

'Okay, it went well.'

'Good. I think you needed that.'

Max makes a hacking sound that vaguely resembles a laugh. 'What a fucking cliché!'

Marko shrugs. 'Maybe. But I thought you seemed, I don't know, like, dried out or something.'

'Dried out?'

'Yes. Would you like to see the rest of the house?'

513

The words have struck home. While Max allows himself to be steered from room to room, the words *dried out* have been scrawled in luminous spray paint on the walls of his consciousness. During this entire unnaturally warm summer, when not nearly enough rain has fallen, Max has fought an unequal battle against drying out, and there are many plants he has failed to save. Flowers, shrivelled to a mere shell of themselves, shrubs with bare branches like fingers, desperately reaching up into the sky for help. Is this what his internal landscape looks like, and is it visible on the outside for others to see?

'I assume this will be Maria's,' Marko says as they enter a fifteen-square-metre room, containing nothing but a bare bulb hanging from the ceiling. He goes to the far corner and sinks down onto the floor, with his back resting against the wall. Max takes the opposite corner. They look at each other. The space is reminiscent of a cell or an interview room, a void where words carry more weight. If there is anything that needs to be said, then now is the time to say it.

'The thing is,' Marko begins, 'you might be the most important person in my life.'

'Me?'

'Mmm. You.'

The luminous spray paint fades, and Max fumbles in the darkness, trying to understand what Marko means. After what happened on the silo, Marko could be regarded as the most important person in Max's life, because otherwise Max wouldn't have a life, but how can the reverse be true?

'I don't understand. There must be loads of people, your mum and dad . . .'

Marko holds up a hand to silence him, then tucks his hands between his thighs. 'I mean, you're the one who's had the greatest

514

influence on my decisions. It started when your dad sorted out a job for mine, if you remember?'

Oh yes, Max remembers, and now he realises where that incomprehensible urge to run away came from. A penny that has been rattling in the slot for years finally drops as Marko goes on: 'Ever since then I've been competing with you. I was determined to do everything you did, but better.'

'Well, you've certainly done—'

'Wait. This house. Do you know what I actually wanted to do? I wanted to buy *your* house. That time on your terrace, when your dad and mine . . . I wanted to erase it, wipe it out by taking over the place where it happened.'

'Marko, I'm sorry . . .'

'Don't be. It's not your fault. But it is a fact. You've set the direction of my life. And enough is enough.'

They sit in silence in the bare room, looking at each other. The incident on the terrace plays on a loop in Max's mind, and he finds that he remembers it with astonishing clarity. It is seared onto his memory as something significant – he just didn't realise how significant.

'Marko,' he says eventually, 'I rake up leaves and deliver newspapers. You have nothing to worry about.'

Marko lets out a snort of laughter and shakes his head. 'Man, oh man, oh man. Idiot. Don't you get it? When you offer to be my gardener . . . in some weird way, you still win.'

'How?'

'I don't actually know, but that's the way it is. That I do know.'

When Max emerges onto Drottning Kristinas väg it is dark. A veil of dampness hangs in the air, creating haloes around the street lamps and making the tarmac shine. He pushes his hands deep in his pockets and heads towards the house where he grew up.

The conversation with Marko has shaken him. At junior school he thought it was cool to have someone to compete with, and he never suspected how Marko viewed their relationship. And Johan? How much did Max really care about his wretched circumstances? How often was he really there to offer support? Only when it suited him, to tell the truth.

I am an egoist. I have always been an egoist.

The street is deserted, and the only sound is Max's listless footsteps on the black tarmac. Thick cloud hides the light of the moon and stars. A chill creeps under his clothes, and Max feels so irredeemably lonely that he wraps his arms around his body.

The memory of the memory of the shark returns. The loneliness of that moment, spread across all the days of his life. A lump of meat in the great darkness, no human life anywhere in sight. The black waters of the Norrtälje river slipping over slimy stones, the loneliness in the eyes looking down at them.

Shit. Shit.

Max touches his eyes to check if he is crying. He feels as if he is crying, but there are no tears. He has a sudden urge to run to Siw's apartment, but the impulse collapses as quickly as it arrived. He has nothing to offer, he is a person who cannot even cry.

There are several lights on in his parents' house. There have been a number of break-ins in the area, so they have installed a timer that switches lamps on and off in different rooms to give an illusion of life. Max could do with a timer like that.

The gate squeaks as he pushes it open, and as soon as he takes two steps the motion-sensor outside lights come on. Max peers into the harsh brightness and feels as if he has been caught, an unauthorised person with no right to be here. Someone will come and remove him at any second. He pulls himself together, shades his eyes with one hand and unlocks the front door. Once inside, he quickly keys in the code to deactivate the alarm. The outsider has gained access. The house has been captured.

He goes through the rooms, switching on all the lights. The cleaner must have been in recently; the place smells of detergent and polish, and every surface is shining. It looks like a photograph in an estate agent's brochure. There is a ghostliness about the total lack of ghostliness, and Max himself is the ghost.

He stops and looks at the sofa, where he had his vision of the man putting the barrel of a shotgun in his mouth. He goes into the kitchen and runs a hand over the marble island where he used to drink juice and eat biscuits after school. Not a speck of dust on his fingers. He sits down on the step stool where he would some-times keep his mother company while she was preparing dinner. He glances at the cooker but he can't see her, nor can he see himself sitting on the stool; he just knows he did it, a theoretical knowledge.

He goes upstairs and stops outside his room. The sticker with the raised hand and the words 'No entry for unauthorised personnel' is still on the door, and makes him hesitate before he pushes down the handle.

The room hasn't really changed since he moved to Stockholm to begin his studies at the School of Economics. The film poster for *The Commitments*, which was his favourite for a long time. The computer is gone from the desk, but all the plastic figures from *The Lord of the Rings* are still on their shelf, and his student cap is hanging on its hook. The only big difference is that the room is now used for storage, and there are several cardboard boxes piled up in one corner.

Max sits down on the bed, which is covered with a patchwork quilt made by his grandmother. He looks around the space where he spent so much of his childhood; he hasn't been here for over five years. As he had suspected and feared, he feels absolutely *nothing*. It could just as easily be the empty room where he and Marko sat and talked a little while ago. The same applies to the rest of the house. Nothing to distinguish it from Marko's desolate surfaces.

In the same way as he was theoretically able to see himself perched on the step stool as a little boy, he knows in theory that this is his childhood home, but he doesn't feel it. It is just a place where he happens to be, and in every way that matters he has no childhood home.

He gets up and positions himself in front of the full-length mirror. From the age of twelve, when he lost his fear of the visions, he would stand here and interview himself, inspired by *The Commitments*, asking admiring questions about his own brilliant future.

Now the figure in the mirror is gazing at him with a certain amount of scepticism. It nods like someone who has finally had its suspicions confirmed, and says: 'So, you're back.'

'Yes,' Max replies. 'I guess I am.'

'You seem disappointed?'

'Yes. I suppose I'd hoped for some kind of . . . confirmation.'

'Of what?'

'Of the fact that I am capable of a pure emotion. And that's what nostalgia is, wouldn't you say?'

MirrorMax frowns. 'I'm the one who's asking the questions here.'

'Sorry.'

Silence. MirrorMax looks Max up and down, and doesn't appear to like what he sees. He sighs. 'Why are you bothered about emotions? You never used to be. It was the future that mattered. What's happened?'

'Siw. Has happened.'

'Siw? The fat girl?'

'Don't say that. She's . . . I think she's . . . my chance. If I can just cope with seeing her.'

MirrorMax shrugs. 'You know what you have to do.'

'Do I?'

'Yes. Otherwise you wouldn't be talking to me.'

'The medication. I have to stop taking my medication?'

MirrorMax is clearly annoyed, because Max has asked another question. Max sits down on the bed once more and stares at his hands, which have begun to shake.

Stop taking the Lamictal.

Max has been taking the anti-anxiety drug for so long that he has no idea what Pandora's box of suppressed shit might be hidden away in his consciousness; what slimy, crawling creatures might be released if he stops.

But is it really the all-encompassing braking mechanism it is supposed to be? It didn't protect him against the experience on Kvarnholmen, for example. The fear that seized his heart had been the old, unmedicated kind.

He can argue back and forth as much as he wants, but something must be done if his relationship with Siw is to have any chance of becoming something real. Right now it's as if he is wearing a hazmat suit, or making love with oven gloves on. He needs to set aside his protection and trust that the attacks won't be too severe. He gets up and returns to the mirror.

'Okay, you miserable sod,' he says. 'You're right. Thanks for the advice. You won't be seeing me again.'

LOYALTY

Anna has taken a day's leave, and on the Monday morning she goes out to her car, a bright red Golf 96 in the residents' car park behind the apartment block. She bought it from Stig at 'mates' rates' four years ago – eight thousand kronor. Which was fine, except that Stig had paid five thousand, so Anna clearly wasn't much of a mate.

The door rattles when Anna slams it shut. The car has that kind of old, musty smell that doesn't exist as an air freshener. A hint of oil and petrol, a whiff of upholstery that has been rubbed by many backsides, and is now in the process of eating itself.

And yet Anna likes her car, which she calls Satan because of its colour and general malevolence. With a little under four hundred thousand kilometres on the clock, it has developed many little quirks. The handbrake has to be jammed on with a stick, the windscreen wipers work only sporadically and definitely not when it's raining, the fan is always full on. Among other things.

But it almost always starts, and with a triumphant roar from the cracked exhaust pipe Anna pulls out onto Stockholmsvägen and turns left. The radio was already toast when Anna bought the car, so she has to rely on herself for entertainment. She plays Johan's game for a while, and laughs out loud when she comes up with *if you're happy and you know it, clap your hounds*. In fact, she is so pleased that she has to pull over and send him a text before driving on.

When she leaves the motorway at the Rösa interchange, her thoughts turn to Siw, who has become *unhinged*. Anna has never felt that way. She has certainly *fancied* or even been in love with some guy, but the truth is that she has never had a relationship with a boy or man who has been anything other than . . . yes, a function. If anyone has got to her, it has been Siw.

Anna doubts this is because she hasn't met 'the one', and in her darker moments she sometimes thinks she is incapable of love, something that doesn't sit well with her fear of being alone. However, she is repulsed by the idea of making herself vulnerable, allowing someone to poke their grubby little fingers *on a grubby little hound*.

Siw is different. Ever since they started hanging out in high school, Anna has known that Siw's defences are fragile, and has made a point of protecting her. She has also done her best to harden her friend, with only marginal success. And now this Max has got under her skin. One thing is certain: God help him if he hurts Siw, because then he will have Anna Olofsson to deal with, and he doesn't want to know what that would involve.

Anna drives into Finsta, where St Birgitta had her visions and stood up to the king a thousand years ago. Girl power with God on her side, yeah. This inspiring thought is followed by a depressing realisation about her own situation, or rather Acke's. No one has their back. What the hell is she going to do if Stig and Sylvia refuse to help? No idea. Not a clue.

She doesn't feel any better when she reaches Rimbo twenty minutes later. There is actually nothing wrong with the little town, where everything is centred on the main street like in cowboy films, but whenever she comes back she feels *trapped*, like an animal that has managed to escape from its cage, yet voluntarily returns.

She drives past the former swimming pool; she and her friends once got hold of the key and spent the night there, floating on lilos, smoking and drinking vodka straight from the bottle in a budget version of Beverly Hills.

The Chinese restaurant, which has never got around to fixing its misspelled sign, 'Chines Restaurant'. The toy shop where she used to pinch *Magic* cards and sell them to older boys in the schoolyard. Pizzeria Miami, whose depressing decor she has spent days staring at with hungover eyes.

This is your life.

Friends who stayed here have said that stories are still told about Anna Olofsson, and maybe she should be proud, but the main emotion she feels is anger. Her childhood was a fucking *war*, and if she felt like it, she could claim that she is suffering from PTSD, boo-hoo, and that's why she has trust issues.

She turns onto Närtunavägen and heads for the family small-holding, which is on the other side of the lake known as Långsjön. She slows down for the last part, because the forest is crawling with suicidal creatures of all sizes. No one even raised an eyebrow when Sylvia or Stig arrived home with broken headlights or a dented bumper after close contact with a deer. Stig even kept a bolt gun in the boot, because things got so messy with an axe.

Anna's heart sinks as she drives into the yard and sees Lotta's van with the bonnet open. The text on the side reads 'Pitstop Pennsylvania – American Stuff'. Lotta is the member of the family who is least well disposed towards Acke and his activities; everything will be more difficult if she's around.

Anna switches off the engine and the Golf dies with a shudder. When she opens the car door, she hears a metallic clang and sub-dued swearing from the front of Lotta's van. Stig is leaning over the engine and seems to be trying to remove something that doesn't want to be removed. 'Come here, you little bastard.' Either that or a mouse has found its way in.

'Hi, Dad.'

Without returning her greeting or raising his head, Stig says: 'Give me a hand with this.'

Anna joins her father and peers down at the engine, which reeks of 5-56. The smell is forever associated with her childhood, because Stig always had so much stuff that was covered in rust. The con-nection to one battery terminal is dark brown with corrosion, and shiny with 5-56. Because of the awkward angles it's hard to turn the nut. Anna grabs an equally rusty spanner and holds the bolt firm so that Stig can use both hands to loosen the nut. A minute or so later, he is able to lift out the battery. Anna's hands are brown and impregnated with 5-56. She wipes them on an old rag, while Stig carries the battery over to the garage, where he has a charger.

A very typical homecoming; nobody 'shows off' in the Olofsson family. It's a few months since Anna was here, but nobody makes a big thing of it. You just join in with whatever's going on, take life as it comes.

Stig emerges from the garage wiping his hands on his oil-stained overalls, and goes so far as to say: 'So. You're here.'

'Yes. It's been a while.'

'Has it? Maybe you're right. We don't exactly go around counting the days, you know.'

A word that often crops up with unhappy children who later become unhappy adults and need therapy is *unwanted*. Anna has never felt unwanted, because neither Stig nor Sylvia paid the children enough attention to sabotage their mental health. The five siblings grew up more or less feral and to a certain extent without parental input, but they were never subjected to obscure demands or expectations.

'Will you want dinner?' Stig asks.

'No, I probably won't stay that long.'

'Right. So, what are you doing here?'

'There's something we need to talk about. Something important.'

'Fine. Come inside then.'

Maybe not unwanted, but definitely unwelcome. However, Anna isn't offended, because she knows that Stig and Sylvia's basic attitude is that other people exist mainly to cause trouble.

Stig turns his back on her and heads for the house with long, supple strides. He is approaching retirement age, but there is no sign of that in the way he moves, which Anna resents slightly. She has been looking forward to the day when her parents start to become frail and in need of help so that she can tell them where to go, but it seems to be taking a while. Stig has a bit of a pot belly and a certain puffiness in his face, but that's all. Anna gives her hands one last rub and follows her father.

If the marzipan odour of 5-56 is one of her childhood triggers, the smell inside the house is another. For Anna, it means *home* in spite of everything, and is hard to dissect. There's coffee, earth and sweat, which taken together smell a bit like blood, but there is also smoke from the wood-burning stove, and something crispy, electrical from the radiators, which perhaps adds up to the smell of fire. Anna's childhood home smells of blood and fire.

Sylvia and Lotta are sitting at the kitchen table, each with a cup of coffee. An open bag of cinnamon buns lies between them; it seems to have been ripped apart by a lion. As soon as Lotta catches sight of Anna, she rolls her eyes. 'Oh look, little Miss Slimfit has come to visit!'

'What the fuck are you talking about?' Sylvia asks. If an excess of subcutaneous fat counts as a sign of age in Stig, then Sylvia has gone in the opposite direction. Her already angular face looks almost cadaverous. Her cheekbones are even more prominent, and her skull is visible beneath the thin skin, like a sneak peek of what she will look like when she comes back as a ghost.

As if she is revealing a shameful secret, Lotta says: 'Haven't you heard? Anna's started *working out*.' She spits out the final words, along with a shower of cinnamon crumbs.

The revelation does not achieve the desired effect. Sylvia looks from the crumbs to Lotta and says: 'Maybe you should consider doing the same, fat lump.'

Anna clamps her lips together to stop herself from smiling. This too is a typical situation. Because their parents' attention was such a rare gift, war broke out between the siblings whenever it did appear. Everyone wanted to be the person in the limelight, wanted that tiny fragment of affirmation and acknowledgement. The occasion when Sylvia took Anna with her to crush the headmaster was the stuff of legend, and however jealous Anna's siblings might have been, they never tired of hearing the story.

So even though Anna often thinks that she will let her parents rot alone in their beds in the autumn of their lives, she can't help feeling a childish satisfaction when her mother takes her side. Since the scales appear to have tipped in her favour at the moment, she takes the opportunity to sit down and say: 'We have a problem.'

She briefly explains what has happened to Acke, and what he has done. She goes into more detail about her conversation with Ewert

526

Djup, and the three hundred thousand he claims Acke owes him. When she has finished, Lotta crams another cinnamon bun into her mouth and says: 'You said *we* have a problem. In what way is this *our* problem?'

'Because we're a family.' Anna looks at Stig, who holds her gaze and even gives the smallest of nods as she goes on: 'And things are looking bad for Acke if we don't do anything.'

Stig opens his mouth to speak, but Lotta gets there first. 'Okay, in that case, I just want to make it clear that if you're going to chuck three hundred thousand at that idiot, then I want the same.'

'Shut your ugly gob,' Sylvia snaps. 'Nobody's chucking any money at anyone.'

'But Mum,' Anna says, regretting the word as soon as it crosses her lips. Sylvia's expression darkens and she holds up her index finger. 'I've said it before and I'll say it again: I am no one's fucking mum. If you've got yourself in the shit, then you can crawl out of it on your own.'

'It'll be the towbar for Acke,' Lotta says, wiping the corners of her mouth. 'A little trip.'

Anna is so angry that she falls into the family jargon when she turns to Lotta. 'If it were your fat arse they were going to drag behind the car, I wouldn't fucking care, you could grease the road all the way to Grisslehamn with your blubber, but—'

'That's not going to happen,' Stig says.

'No,' Anna says, ducking as Lotta throws a cinnamon bun at her head. 'So, what is going to happen then?'

'They'll give him a job. To pay off the debt.'

'What kind of job is worth three hundred thousand? Murdering someone?'

'Yes. Or a couple of people.'

527

Anna's jaw drops and she looks from one member of her family to the others. 'Are you serious? Are we going to let the Djup brothers turn Acke into a *murderer* just because you won't . . . So he'll end up spending the rest of his life in jail?'

'Doing a job like that doesn't necessarily mean spending time in jail,' Stig says calmly. 'It depends on how well you do it.'

'Right, and how *well* do you think Acke is going to do it? As you've frequently pointed out, he's an idiot. I love him, but he's as thick as pig shit, and we all know that. So what the fuck?'

'In that case, you'd better help him,' Sylvia suggests. 'Since you're so smart. And so keen.'

Anna presses her fingers to her temples. 'You want *me* to help Acke kill people – is that what you're saying?'

'I'm saying nothing, but hear this: we can't magically produce three hundred thousand, because we don't have it. End of.'

A lump forms in Anna's throat, making it impossible for the words to reach her mouth. When she stands up and leans on the table, her hands get covered in sticky crumbs, and all she can manage is a whisper: 'You talk about loyalty. So how the hell can you be such *traitors*?'

TAKE GOOD CARE OF HER

I

Siw's pockets are full of stones – that's how she feels as she walks to work on Monday morning. Her shoulders slump with the weight, her back is bowed. The stones are her dashed expectations, pulling her down to the ground. As soon as a person begins to hope, she also gets to know hope's shadow-sister, disappointment. For years Siw has marched along, hopeless and with empty pockets. Now she is out of kilter, barely able to keep her balance.

She hasn't contacted Max and Max hasn't contacted her. She thinks it is his responsibility to make the first move, because they were at her place. Thanks for your hospitality, kind of. Or she is just cowardly or old-fashioned or pathetic or soft in the head and #MeToo and incel and *surely he could at least send a text?*

She passes Clas Ohlson where they are promoting lamps, 'light up the autumn darkness'. Siw loves candles, rope lights, decorative lighting, and she tries to feel angry with Max because the campaign's image of a cosy living room with multiple light sources doesn't touch her at all. Angry is better than sad, but she can't do it.

Most of all she wishes she could accept the events of Saturday night and Sunday morning for what they were: a special time, something wonderful that came and went, a memory to cherish, but she can't manage that either. It meant far too much to be packaged up in that way. An emotion she had never before experienced was woken within her, and it refuses to go back to sleep. There's nothing she can do, except stagger on with the stones of disappointment in her pockets, and longing tearing at her chest.

Siw looks up at the poster of the staff enclosed in a heart, she unlocks the door and walks along the deep red corridor, the birth canal into work, she stops at the sign that proclaims 'We love good food', adorned with magnets in the shape of little hearts. It's as if there is a horrible pink filter in front of her eyes, and all she can see is love, love, love in all directions, but there is none for her.

In the changing room she puts on her uniform while gazing out of the window. That enormous, black surface, the ventilation drum and . . . the gull. Siw stands so close to the window that the tip of her nose is touching the glass as she tries to recall a thought. The idea that the gull was her soul. Oh well, in that case nothing has changed. The gull is sitting in the same place, and her soul is as desolate as always.

Maybe it's just there for decoration? Maybe it's stuffed? The gull, I mean.

Siw smiles to herself and straightens her back a little. She can do this, of course she can. The gull is sitting in the same place, and now Siw is going to do her job, as usual. Life goes on, whether she is out of kilter or not.

It is nice to blip herself into the checkout, nice to smile

professionally at the customers with their endless stream of goods to be scanned, nice to let her hands work and to be a fully functioning person in the world instead of a sack filled with stones.

After work she and Anna are going to the gym. The last time they worked out Siw was able to manage five kilos on several of the machines – progress that is not dependent on the whims of other people. She has lost four kilos and started to ease up on the powder diet. She is going to be strong, she is going to be the strongest, she is going to be a fucking Pippi Longstocking of self-sufficiency.

Siw has just scanned a chicken salad and an orange juice without raising her eyes when a voice says: 'Hi'. Max is standing on the other side of the conveyor belt wearing his overalls, and all Siw can come up with is: 'What are you doing here?'

Max points to the chicken salad. 'Buying lunch.' Siw looks at the plastic box as if it might give her a clue as to how she's supposed to behave. Neither the salad nor the juice offer answers to any questions, apart from what Max's lunch habits might be, so she opts for: 'Aha.'

After a quick glance at the customer behind him, Max leans closer to Siw and lowers his voice. 'Listen, I'm sorry if . . . Oh, never mind. Would you like to meet up? After work?'

'I can't, I'm going to . . . tomorrow?'

'Okay, fine. Tomorrow. That's good. Not the best. But good.'

'Why not the best?'

'Because that means it's another day before I can see you. Be in touch re time and place, all right?'

Max picks up his lunch and blows Siw a kiss. She can't reciprocate because her hands are tightly clasped beneath the belt. Her chest and the back of her neck feel hot and sweaty and her heart is tumbling over and over and the stones are falling out of her pockets and the idea of self-sufficiency is out of the window.

Another day before I can see you.

2

'He's pretty . . . ahhh . . . keen then?'

Anna is talking while using the pec deck machine. This is her last rep, and she uses the footrest to release the weights in a controlled manner before standing up. Siw takes her place and adjusts the lever, adding five kilos. Anna whistles and looks around. 'Who are you showing off to?'

'No one. And I don't think anyone here would be terribly impressed by someone taking fifteen.'

'*Someone taking fifteen*,' Anna imitates. 'You've started speaking the lingo and everything. But back to Max. Did he really say that?'

'Well, we both have names,' Siw says. 'And we're talking to each other. But then we're fucked.'

'What are you talking about?'

'We definitely wouldn't pass the Bechdel test.'

Siw does her ten reps slowly and confidently. Anna is better at stomach and thighs, but there is a frenzy in her movements that doesn't suit the pecs. Maybe it's because Siw is using a machine with something *male* about it that she suddenly sees, or rather hears, how very *girly* their conversation is.

'I couldn't give a fuck about Bechdel,' Anna replies. 'Or Schrödinger's cat. *And* his dog. Are you in love?'

'Yes. I think I am.'

Anna claps her hands in the coquettish way that doesn't match the rest of her personality; perhaps that's why she's so fond of the gesture that makes her into someone else.

'What about you?' Siw asks. 'How are things?'

Anna lowers her hands and her face falls. She shakes her head. 'Not great, actually. I hate my family and I never want to see them again. Do you know who the Djup brothers are?'

'I have an idea, yes.'

'Acke, you know Acke . . . He's done something which means he owes them three hundred thousand.'

'What kind of something?'

'Doesn't matter. But unless he can cough up the money, he's in deep trouble. I don't even want to tell you what they'll do to him.'

'And why is this your responsibility?'

Anna pulls a face and frowns at Siw. 'You too? He's my kid brother. You might not understand that because you haven't . . . but that's just the way it is.'

'So, what are you going to do?'

Anna looks defiant, just like she used to do in school when she was about to cause someone real problems.

'I've got an idea. A really good idea. Shall we finish with the rowing machine?'

Anna clearly has no intention of going into more detail about her really good idea, so they wipe down the pec deck and amble over to the rowing machine, which turns out to be occupied by a man who is sitting typing something on his phone. Anna recognises him; he often fishes in the river. They wait. A friend of the man passes by and they chat for a minute or so, then the man returns to his phone.

Anna goes up to him. 'Excuse me, can we use the machine while you're busy?'

The man slowly raises his head and looks Anna up and down.

'No.'

'But you're just sitting there. Maybe you could do that some-where else?'

The man thinks for a moment. 'No.'

Anna looks at Siw, eyes wide with disbelief, then turns back to the man. 'Are you serious? What's your problem? This isn't like fishing, you know. Other people are waiting.'

The man sighs and stands up. He is considerably taller and fifty kilos of muscle heavier than Anna. There is a vague, unfocused anger in his expression as he leans down to Anna, looks her in the eye and says: 'And?'

Siw tugs at Anna's arm. 'Come on – let's not bother.'

To Siw's relief, Anna seems to have picked up on the threat emanating from the man, and allows herself to be pulled away. The man makes a faint growling noise before sitting back down with his phone.

'What's the matter with people?' Anna says. 'It's as if . . . I don't know.'

'I'm changing the subject,' Siw says as they go down the stairs to the changing room. 'Mum's stepped up so often lately, I was wondering if . . . you might be able to look after Alva tomorrow evening?'

'Is it because of Max?'

'Yes.'

'No problem.'

FROM THE RUSHING OF THE RIVER

Marko has spent Monday shopping. When he discussed the furniture issue with Goran and Laura, at first they insisted they didn't want anything, then they started talking about online auction sites, and after a period of hard negotiation Marko finally managed to push through IKEA. An order with home delivery has been placed, but it will be a few days before the goods arrive.

Two things that weren't part of the order were a bed and a kitchen table, because his parents think the ones they have are perfectly fine. Marko doesn't agree. Their double bed wasn't new when they bought it sixteen years ago, and the same applies to their table, which is also too small for the kitchen in the new house.

Marko has realised that it is pointless to try to persuade his parents to let him upgrade their furniture, and therefore it is better to present them with a fait accompli. If they want to sell the stuff in their beloved online auction, then they can do so.

The 160cm bed with a double-sprung mattress was a bugger to haul up the stairs to what will be Goran and Laura's room. He also took the opportunity to buy pillows and a duvet, along with an extra set of bedding so that he can sleep there himself, then change the sheets when it's time for his mum and dad to move in.

When he'd bought the bed he drove his hired van to Mio, where he picked up a kitchen table and chairs, two standard lamps and a rug. And an armchair. The last item is the only one he's unsure about. Goran loves his flaking leather armchair, which over the years has moulded itself to his body as he sits there shaking his fist at Serie A on TV. Oh well, it's a big house, there will be room for the new chair somewhere, and at least Marko will have a comfortable seat for the time being.

It is seven o'clock and Marko has just got home after returning the van to Circle K. Everything is in place, and he sits down at the kitchen table with a cup of instant coffee. The table is about twice as big as the old one, and also has an extra pull-out leaf.

Goran and Laura have relatives scattered all over the world, and occasionally everyone gets together, but so far it has never happened in Norrtälje, because there wasn't enough room. That can change now. Marko smiles to himself as he pictures Goran showing siblings and cousins around the house, while complaining with ill-concealed pride about Marko's profligacy. Then a big party around the fully extended table.

Marko is sitting there gazing into space, hearing the hum of conversations in different languages filling the house when the doorbell rings. He opens the door to find Maria outside. She has dark circles beneath her eyes, and her normal elegant posture is gone. She almost looks like an ordinary person.

'Can I come in?'

Marko takes a step back into the still empty hallway and lets his sister in. She shuffles along and lets a bag slip off her shoulder and land on the floor with a thud, then she heads for the kitchen. Without commenting on the new acquisitions, she sits down. 'Is there anything to drink?'

'You mean . . . ?'

'Yes.'

'From the party, right. What would you like?'

'Anything.'

Something in Maria's tone suggests that she would prefer spirits, but Marko decides that isn't appropriate. Instead, he fetches a wine box from the pantry, and opens the pack of wine glasses he also happened to pick up in Mio. When he places the half-full glass in front of Maria, she says: 'Wow, you've got wine glasses now.'

'Very observant.'

Only now does Maria look around. She points to the table and chairs and nods before taking a big gulp of wine. She puts down the glass and slumps on her chair.

'So how are things?' Marko asks. 'It was your first day at work today, wasn't it? At the café?'

Maria nods, her expression suggesting that she is confirming a regrettable fact. She rubs her eyes and sighs. 'You can't imagine.'

'Stressful?'

'I have no problem with stress. Well, I guess I have these days, but . . . it's not that.'

'So, what is it?'

Maria takes another gulp of wine and rolls the glass between her palms. 'People are so. Fucking. Horrible. I thought . . . you know, in the world of modelling there's so much envy, rivalry, constant name calling. And little digs. I thought I'd be getting away from all that now I'm in the real world. But it's actually worse here.'

Marko pours himself a small glass of wine and sits down next to his sister. He doesn't know what she imagined the 'real world' would be like, but in his experience people's elbows are pretty sharp there too.

'Maybe your expectations were . . . misplaced.'

Maria empties her glass and shakes her head. 'You don't understand. When I say horrible, I don't mean impolite or miserable. I mean really . . . vile. I put a cup and saucer down on a table and it rattles. This guy says: 'Do you have to make so much fucking noise?' I weave my way between two tables, and a woman says can I stop pushing my fucking tits in her husband's face. I give a kid a glass of juice and he wants to know why I stink. And an old man called me . . . Can I have a drop more?'

Marko obliges, but pours her only a quarter of a glass. 'What did he call you?'

'A wog whore. I didn't think anyone actually said that kind of thing. And it's not just . . . Everyone is so unpleasant to everyone else. They won't step aside for anyone, won't let anyone use a spare chair at their table. And that's still not the worst of it.'

Maria finishes her wine and leans forward, her head in her hands. Her shoulders shake and she lets out a sob. Marko strokes her back. 'What is the worst of it?'

Maria takes a deep breath, pulls herself together. When she raises her head, her eyes are full of tears. 'I hardly ever think about my childhood, those years when we were refugees. But today . . .' She makes a circular movement with her hand in the air, as if she is turning an ancient film camera.

'The café is on an island out in the middle of the river. That rushing sound is there all the time, and I don't know, it was as if . . . everything came surging forward out of that rushing. All the shitty little rooms we lived in. Germany, Holland. How I was scared of the police the whole time, the fact that I never had anyone to play with, and I don't know if you remember Dolly . . .'

'Your doll.'

'Yes. Because I didn't have anyone else, I played with Dolly and she was my best friend and she *really* was and I consoled her when I was frightened and I slept with her and she was . . . she got left behind. At a bus station in Aachen or some other shithole.'

'I remember. You were upset for weeks.'

'Yes. And today . . . This is crazy, but through that rushing sound I could hear Dolly calling for help. I saw her being torn apart by two dogs on a cement floor and blood poured out of her when the dogs ripped off her arms and she kept screaming and screaming for me and asking me why I'd left her.'

The tears are pouring down Maria's cheeks now. Marko grabs the roll of kitchen towel and tears off a couple of sheets for her. She wipes her eyes, smearing the paper with kohl and mascara. She takes a deep, shuddering breath, then exhales as her expression hardens. She clenches one fist in front of her face.

'And at the same time it's just an image of all the crap we suffered, for years and years. My early childhood is nothing but shit. And I also heard in the rushing of the river all those indifferent voices of case workers, police officers yelling at us, people shouting abuse at us in the street. And I was filled with such . . . *hatred*. As the day went on and that rushing grew louder and louder inside my head and people carried on being horrible . . . I swear if I'd had a machine gun, there would have been a massacre.'

Maria's eyes are burning with such fury that her tears almost evaporate with the heat. Before she can launch into another tirade,

Marko places a hand on her arm. 'In that case, maybe you shouldn't be working there?'

Maria snatches her arm away. 'I won't let those bastards break me. Or my childhood. I'm going to . . . get harder, you understand? I'm going to become a fucking *weapon*. Cold steel. They'll see!'

THE MONKEY AND THE SPANNER

I

'Is Mummy meeting the guy?'

'What guy?'

'*You* know. The one who drives the thing that cuts the grass.'

'Oh. Yes, that's the guy she's meeting.'

'Good. Have you got any sixes?'

'Go Fish.'

Alva rummages around among the cards spread out on the kitchen table as if she really can feel a difference between them by stroking the backs of the 'fish'. She picks up one card, looks at it, then snorts and adds it to the bunch in her hand.

This is the third game they've played, and Anna is bored to death. Why are so many kids crazy about Go Fish? It ought to be against the law to teach the damned game.

'Have you got any queens?' Anna says. Alva rolls her eyes, groans something about cheating, and hands over three. To Anna's relief, Alva then throws down the rest of her cards and announces that she's done.

'Okay, so what shall we do? Watch a movie?'

'No. We're going to play.'

'Play what?'

'You know. *Play.*'

'Can't we just talk?'

'No. Play.'

What Anna enjoys most is sitting and chatting with Alva, because the child has such clear views on how the world functions, and she's very funny. Alva also likes Anna's tales of adult life and how dotty the old people in the care home can be. Playing and making up stuff isn't Anna's strong point, to put it mildly, and it is with the shambling gait of a prisoner that she trails after Alva into her room. She sits down on the floor opposite Alva and is presented with a Mutant Turtle figure.

'That's the Little Mermaid,' Alva informs her. 'You're her. I'm Elsa.' Alva picks up an impossibly slender doll representing Elsa from *Frozen*.

Anna looks at the masked turtle in her hand. 'Are you sure this is the Little Mermaid?'

Another eye roll. 'I don't have the real Ariel, so you have to *pretend.*'

'Right.'

'Go on then – say something.'

'Like what?'

'Oh, for goodness' sake! This is Elsa, so you might say: 'No, no, Elsa, you mustn't freeze the sea, because then all my fishy friends will turn into . . . fish fingers.'

Anna laughs and Alva glares at her. 'What?'

'Nothing, it's just . . . fish fingers, that's . . .'

'Play!'

They carry on for about ten minutes until Alva declares that Anna is *super bad* at playing, with the clear implication that she is a great disappointment as a childminder. Anna says: 'Everyone who knows the answer, put up your hound.'

'What?'

'Well, you take, like, a phrase, an expression, and you swap hound for hand and hounds for hands, like, "If you're happy and you know it, clap your hounds, clap clap."'

Alva giggles. 'Clap your hounds . . .'

'Try to come up with one yourself while I make a quick phone call.'

Anna goes into the living room, leaving Alva staring at the floor with deep concentration. She calls Johan, who answers almost right away. 'Hi.'

'Hi. Listen, you're good at making up stuff, aren't you?'

'I think so – why?'

'I'm looking after Alva, Siw's daughter, and she's into . . . well, fantasy games and that kind of thing, I just can't do it.'

'So you want me to—'

Alva hurtles out of her room, shouting: 'I've got one, I've got one! Are you awake, Lars, are you awake, Lars, have you washed your hounds, washed your hounds . . .'

Johan laughs. 'That was good. So you're playing that game?'

'I was desperate. Hang on a minute.' Anna lowers the phone and turns to Alva. 'Listen, I've got a friend who's brilliant at making stuff up. Would you like him to come over?'

Alva nods, and Anna sighs with relief. 'She says yes. Can you? Do you want to? Are you brave enough?'

'Mmm, as long as you don't build me up too much before I get

543

there. I'm not sure I'm *brilliant.*'

'Compared with me, you absolutely are. Come as soon as you can.'

Anna gives Johan the address, and he says he'll be there in fifteen minutes. When she ends the call she sees that Alva is staring searchingly at her. 'What?'

'Mr Brilliant,' Alva says. 'Is he your boyfriend?'

'No. Definitely not.'

'Do you *want* him to be your boyfriend?'

'No, I don't. And it can't happen.'

'Why can't it happen?'

Anna doesn't think Johan would appreciate her discussing his sexual orientation with a child, and desperately searches for a way out of her dilemma. Before she can stop herself, the words are out of her mouth: 'Shall we play Go Fish while we wait?'

2

Johan arrives exactly a quarter of an hour later. Alva is wary at first, standing very close to Anna while Johan takes off his shoes and jacket, following every movement as if to make a preliminary assessment of his character. When Johan has finished, he says: 'I've heard that there's someone here who's bad at fantasy games.' He looks at Alva. 'Is that you?'

Alva shakes her head ferociously, then points an accusing finger at Anna before focusing on Johan once more. 'Why have you got a plait?'

Johan turns his head so that his hair falls over his shoulder. 'It's actually called a ponytail, but that's kind of weird, isn't it? In that

544

case, my head must be a pony's bottom.'

Alva covers her mouth with her hands and giggles, glancing at Anna – *did you hear what he said?!* However intelligent and mature Alva might be, she still shares a great deal of humour with her contemporaries, and 'bottom' always hits the mark. The ice is broken. 'Would you like to see my room?'

Johan follows her and sits down on the floor. Possibly with the aim of making a direct comparison, Alva does exactly the same as she did with Anna. She presents Johan with the Mutant Turtle figure, informs him that it's the Little Mermaid, while she is Elsa.

'Okay,' Johan says. 'But you know what? The Little Mermaid is on a secret mission, and that's why she's disguised herself as a turtle. And you know what else? This mission is *so* super secret that she's disguised herself as a *masked* turtle!'

Alva nods eagerly and tells him that Elsa is also on a secret mission. She is going to freeze the whole of the Little Mermaid's sea, and turn her friends into fish fingers.

'But why, Elsa, why?' Johan asks in a high voice.

'My people are starving,' Elsa replies. 'They need fish fingers.'

'But can't we go hunting for food together?' the mermaid suggests. 'I know a place where enormous meatballs grow.'

'Meatballs don't grow,' Alva objects. 'They're made from animals that get whatdoyoucallit, *minced up*.'

'These meatballs grow on trees,' the mermaid insists. 'Because they're vegetarian. The only problem is that they're guarded by a *slime dragon*. What shall we do?'

Anna follows the conversation open-mouthed. Alva looks up at her and jerks her head, which means something along the lines of *watch and learn*. Then she raises an eyebrow, a gesture which indicates even more clearly that Anna's presence is no longer required – or desirable.

Anna settles down on the rocking chair in the living room and brings up Facebook on her phone. It's a long time since she posted anything, but she can see on Messenger that her friends from Rimbo have posted a couple of comments about Anna's behaviour when they last met. Inviting them and then walking out – what a thing to do!

Her thumb hovers over the screen for a few seconds, then she blocks all three of them. It feels so good that she also goes into her contacts list and deletes their numbers. She is about to delete several more people, but stops herself. One step at a time.

She puts down the phone and leans back, rocking gently as she listens to the murmur of Alva and Johan's voices in the next room. She can pick out the odd word about explosions, danger, and a sea of turds. She smiles to herself, closes her eyes and falls asleep. She doesn't know how much time has passed when she is woken by Alva, who is standing in front of her in pyjamas.

'I'm going to bed now.'

'Goodness, what time is it?'

'Half past eight,' says Johan, who is sitting on the sofa.

'What – so you've played for . . . an hour and a half?'

'I wanted to carry on, but Johan said it must be my bedtime, which it isn't actually, because I usually go to bed at eight o'clock.'

'Yes, Siw told me. How did it go with the . . . slime dragon?'

Alva looks apologetically at Johan, as if Anna is asking about old news.

'Fine,' Johan says. 'It turned into an ordinary dragon when we fed it some glue.'

'Good to know.'

Alva gets into bed and settles down with the covers pulled up to

546

her chin. Anna sits on the floor next to the bed, and Johan leans on the doorpost. Anna strokes Alva's hair. 'Would you like me to read something or sing or . . .'

'No. I want Johan to tell me a story.'

Anna looks enquiringly at Johan, who comes over and sits down beside her. 'Okay,' he says to Alva. 'What do you want the story to be about?'

'What do you mean?'

'You tell me two things that have to be in it – anything at all. For example, a hippo and a football, or an alien and a torn towel. You understand?'

Alva nods and she screws up her face in concentration, then says: 'I want a monkey and . . . and . . . a spanner!'

Johan laughs. 'Do you know what a spanner is?'

'Of course I do. A man came to our school to fix the radiator. He had a great big one.'

'Okay.' Johan thinks for a few seconds. 'Here comes the story of the monkey and the spanner.'

He embarks on a long, complicated tale about a monkey who finds a spanner in the jungle. The monkey doesn't have any friends, and it tries all kinds of things with the spanner. It doesn't seem to be edible, but it's quite useful for peeling bananas. The monkey tracks down the machines that are felling trees in the jungle, and uses the spanner to sabotage them. He gets better and better at wrecking the machines. One day he reaches the coast, where a ship lies stranded because its engines are broken. The monkey jumps on board and repairs the engines. The captain, a nice man with a great big beard, asks the monkey to come along as an engineer, and because the monkey is lonely, he accepts.

There are several adventures at sea in which the monkey and his

547

spanner save the day. Eventually the ship docks in Sweden. The monkey is tired of life at sea, so the captain suggests he should go and live with the captain's daughter.

'And that,' Johan concludes, 'is how Mr Nilsson came to live with Pippi Longstocking. I assume you know who Pippi Longstocking is?'

'Of course. Mummy's read it to me. But how did Pippi's horse, Little Old Man, come to live with her?'

'We'll save that for another time,' Johan says. 'Goodnight.'

'Goodnight,' Alva replies. 'And by the way . . .' She raises her index finger. 'That Håkan, the one Mummy likes, that song where he . . . wait . . . I've got it! Never take your hound from the one who loves you!'

Johan laughs. He holds up the palm of his hound and Alva slaps it with her little hound. Anna says goodnight too, and when they have left Alva's room with the door open just a little bit, she lowers her voice: 'I've never heard that story before.'

'It's . . . apocryphal,' Johan says.

'Sorry?'

'I made it up.'

'What, just now? While you were sitting there?'

'Yes.'

'So if I, like, asked you to tell me a story about . . . a punk and a hearing aid, you could do that?'

'I expect so.'

'Okay, go for it!'

Johan smiles wearily. 'I think we've had enough stories for tonight. It takes its toll on the brain.'

'Mine would explode. And the story still wouldn't be any good. Would you like a glass of wine?'

'That would be nice, but I have to be up early in the morning. The engineer who maintains the machinery is coming. Another time? Seriously, that's not just a throwaway remark – another time, okay?'

'Okay. And thanks for your help.'

'No problem.'

A brief hesitation, then Anna takes the initiative and gives him a farewell hug. As Johan's departing footsteps echo in the stairwell, Anna shakes her head and whispers: 'The Monkey and the Spanner. Wow.'

3

The aromas emanating from the pizzeria make Johan's stomach rumble, and he considers picking up a Quattro. However, it's almost nine o'clock, which is closing time, and he doesn't really want the pizza feeling in his body. It's delicious while you're eating, but afterwards you often feel heavy and slow, which is not desirable now that Johan is feeling clean and light in a way that he hasn't done for a long time.

There is something liberating about playing with a child when you really get into it. The game has no other purpose but itself, you just have to go with the flow, see where it leads, and somehow in the process you are washed clean. Johan genuinely enjoyed playing with Alva, because she came up with lots of her own ideas that sent the stories shooting off in an unexpected direction.

And *The Monkey and the Spanner*, that was a great success. Ever since Max and Johan used to play on the hill, Johan has known that he has a gift for spinning coherent tales about fantasy worlds. Maybe he ought to be writing something like that, rather than his gloomy, ponderous Norrtälje novel?

However, right now that isn't what's occupying his mind as he cuts across the football pitch towards Carl Bondes väg. Rattling around in constantly changing combinations is *The Punk and the Hearing Aid*. He can't help it. Set up a bar in front of a high jumper and say 'don't bother about that'; sooner or later he or she will jump, just to see if they can. The same applies to those few words that have dripped into his ear like poison, and refuse to leave him.

Has the punk developed tinnitus from attending too many deafening concerts, or does he just use the hearing aid as an accessory? Does he play himself? Is he a guitarist, for example, and can't hear what he's playing, so it becomes maximum punk? Then he gets himself a hearing aid and is horrified by the way it sounds . . . *No, wait!* Johan has just turned into Carl Bondes väg when he clicks his fingers.

The punk has a hearing aid because he is an *old* person with poor hearing. But punk was in the 1970s, so the punk can't be older than . . . hang on, imagine an eighty-year-old man in a care home who has just discovered punk! He's crazy about the Ramones, the Sex Pistols, Ebba Grön. But because of his poor hearing he has to play the music really loud, and the other residents complain . . . or maybe it gets them going too?

Johan laughs as he pictures a gang of old people with wheeled walkers, joining in with 'I Wanna Be Sedated'. Actually, that's not a bad title for the story. Old age is the period in life when you can ditch any consideration for others and embrace anarchy. Just imagine a group of people who actually do it!

He thinks about the lyrics of 'I Wanna Be Sedated', the references to not being able to control the fingers or brain. Perfect! He begins

550

to walk faster, and by the time he reaches Glasmästarbacken he is almost running. He has to get home and write this down while everything is so crystal clear in his mind.

In the hallway he simply drops his outdoor clothes on the floor and hurries to his desk, opens up his computer. His emails appear as the start page and he sees that lots of people have commented on his most recent post. He hesitates, but curiosity takes over and he logs in.

There are over seventy comments, and Johan reads them with a sinking feeling in his stomach. The hate pouring from the screen is like nothing he has ever seen before. Not directed at him, the writer of the post, but at immigrants in general and Afghans in particular.

Okay, so Johan's words were written in the heat of the moment, and maybe he used a few unnecessarily harsh phrases such as 'thieving Blackheads' and 'grinning Muslim bastards', but the comments are on a completely different level, suggesting that the doors of refugee centres should be nailed shut and firebombs thrown through the windows, and that Muslim women should have their vaginas stapled together to stop them having so many kids. Doesn't this page have a moderator?

Virtually everyone is praising SvenneJanne for telling the truth, being a brother in the struggle. He is given extra credit for coming up with the term 'Blackhead', which is a guaranteed classic.

Johan closes the page and sits quietly for a while, with his fists clamped to his chest. Yes, he thinks the number of refugees allowed into the country should be limited, but that's because of the difficulties with integration, not because Muslims, for example, are worse people. However, he has to admit that that's how it came across in his article.

He doesn't know what he can do. He giggles nervously, rubs his

551

eyes, undoes his ponytail and ruffles his hair. There is nothing he can do. He has let the monster out of the box, and now it is growing of its own accord. He can only hope that it will eventually die due to lack of nutrition. He has no intention of writing any more posts, despite the comments urging him to do so.

He goes into the bathroom, rinses his head in cold water under the shower and dries it with a bath towel, rubbing so hard that he can feel his hair thinning. Then he sits down at the computer again and begins to write.

After half an hour he has forgotten about having to get up early in the morning. After another hour he remembers, and decides he doesn't care. After four hours he has written an eight-page story about the pensioners in the Long Life and Happiness care home, who dig punk so much they're getting feedback in their hearing aids.

I Wanna Be Sedated is the perfect title, but for the moment he calls it *The Punk and the Hearing Aid*, and sends it to Anna as an attachment to an email. His message says: 'Challenge accepted'.

I KNOW A HILL
WHERE I USED TO GO

I

Max and Siw have arranged to meet by the open-air stage in Society Park. Siw is a few minutes late, because her hairdresser Lisa spent a ridiculous amount of time telling her off for not taking better care of her hair. Siw asked Lisa to take it easy with her treatments and sprays, but she is still surrounded by that smell you only get in the hair salon, and which proclaims *here I come – I've made an effort!*

As soon as she enters the park she sees the gangly figure sitting on one of the benches in front of the stage. Dusk is falling, so she can also see the glow of the phone in his hand. Suddenly she stumbles, and has to grab hold of a tree to stop herself from falling.

Something similar has happened many times over the past few days, and she thinks it's connected to the sense of being off-kilter. In a bewildering way it is as if she is walking two centimetres from her own body, which means that she sometimes misses precision

553

movements. Hits the wrong keys on the till, fails to spear a piece of macaroni with her fork.

Sometimes the phenomenon fades, but then Ghost-Siw re-appears, hovering alongside her but not fully integrated with her. Yes, that's exactly what it's like. She is going around with a ghostly sensation of being *possessed*, albeit by a different version of herself. She doesn't understand it.

Max turns his head when he hears Siw approaching, and she says: 'Sorry I'm late'.

'No problem.' Max points to the stage. 'I've taken the gym. Do you want to put anything in?'

Siw gets out her phone. Because both she and Max belong to Team Mystic, she can add a Pokémon to defend the gym. She sees that Max has chosen a hefty Gyarados, and as a joke she chucks in Plusle, who looks tiny next to the scaly sea serpent. Max checks his screen. 'Wow. Strong team.' He puts the phone away and stands up. 'Shall we go?'

'Where?'

'There's something I want to show you.'

When he comes over and gives her a quick hug, she hears the *Pokémon Go* music playing faintly from his pocket.

'Listen, why don't we switch off *Pokémon*?' she suggests.

'Good idea. It's just a habit.'

'I know.'

They both turn off *Pokémon* and exchange a fleeting smile. It feels a bit awkward, and Siw is finding it hard to grasp that the man in front of her has been inside her apartment, and inside her as well. That all feels very remote, standing here with their sharply delineated bodies.

'How are you?' Max asks as they set off.

'I don't know. Somehow it's as if I'm . . . not quite myself.'

'As if you're someone else?'

'It's hard to explain, it's as if I'm me, yet not really me.'

Max snorts. 'A while I ago when I was on Tinder, I met this girl. She flatly refused to believe that I was me. She sat there looking from my profile picture to me and back again, and just *refused*. Even though she didn't know me . . . Sorry, I'm gabbling. I'm a bit nervous.'

'So you were on Tinder?'

'To be honest, it was only that one time. It doesn't suit me at all, but I suppose I thought I ought to give it a go. How about you? Have you ever been on it?'

'God, no.'

Max's admission that he is nervous has enabled Siw to relax a little. They have emerged onto Bergsgatan, and Siw points to the stage, barely visible in the darkness beneath the trees. 'I was in a play there one summer.'

'Wow – you were an actress?'

'That's overstating it a bit. It was one of those old comedies – *Panic on Pythagoras*, it was called.' Max laughs and repeats the title of the play, which was just as bad as it sounds, and Siw goes on: 'I played the maid. I had loads of stuff to carry around, and exactly two lines: "No, the factory owner isn't home at the moment", and "Can I tempt you with a top-up?"'

They are on the way up Glasmästarbacken and Max's laughter echoes between the buildings. Siw thinks he is laughing too loudly and for too long – it wasn't *that* funny. She looks at him and he stops himself by putting his hand to his mouth. He takes a couple of deep breaths, then says: 'Sorry, I'm not quite . . . myself either. Your hair looks nice.'

Why is it that as soon as someone mentions your hair, you have to touch it? Siw quells the urge and draws her coat more tightly around herself instead, which makes Max ask if she's cold. Siw says yes, maybe a little.

Max puts his arm around her shoulder and gives a quick squeeze, then starts frenetically rubbing his hand up and down her back. Like the laughter, this is *too much*. Is he really that nervous? Siw moves to one side to get away from his almost aggressive touch.

'I've been listening to Håkan quite a lot over the past few days,' Max says, taking no notice of Siw's evasive action. 'Through my headphones at work and so on. I've completely changed my mind. I get why you like him so much. Fantastic. Really . . . really good. Especially the album with the title song "It will never be over for me"; there are so many tracks on there that . . . that . . .'

Max's voice fades away and he quickly glances around, as if to check if they're being followed.

'That?' Siw asks.

'What?'

'That what?'

'I don't know.'

Max crosses the road, and Siw has to break into a run to keep up. He continues up the hill with his hands in his pockets, head down, apparently unaware that he has company. He suddenly veers off into the car park in front of the three-storey apartment blocks, hurries between the buildings.

Siw's heart is pounding with the effort of following him. She stops and looks up at Jansson's newsagent's, considers giving up and going home. If she is possessed by a ghost, then Max seems to have been taken over by a demon; she hardly recognises him. While she is hesitating, Max turns around and comes back to her.

'Sorry, I was in a hurry,' he says. 'But I really want you to . . . I want . . . come here.'

He leans forward and plants a kiss on her lips with such fervour that their teeth collide. Siw rubs her mouth. 'What are you doing?'

'Sorry. Sorry. I will explain, but . . . please come with me.'

Siw shrugs and follows Max up some steps edged with snowberries, onto a pine-clad hill where simple benches are dotted among overgrown shrubs. Max walks about fifty metres in the direction of the centre, then stops.

Norrtälje is spread at their feet, sparkling in the September darkness, with the silhouette of the water tower rising majestically into the sky like a watching giant. They can see all the way to the square, with odd cars speeding along Lilla Brogatan. Yellow light pours from the windows of the old fire station, and is reflected in the waters of the river.

Max spreads his arms wide, encompassing the hill behind them. 'This is . . . the land of my childhood.'

'I thought you lived near Marko?'

'I did, but we hardly ever played there. We were always here, me and Johan. He lives over there, and we came here nearly every afternoon, as I remember it, and made up different stories. As soon as I think about my childhood, it's this place that comes into my mind.'

Siw looks around. The light from the town is enough for her to see that there's nothing remarkable about the hill, it's just a spot like any other, somewhere in Sweden. But it's not what things *are* that create our memories, but what we make of them.

'Why did you want to show me this?' she asks.

Max pulls off a big yellow maple leaf, one of the last still clinging to its branch. He pinches off tiny slivers. 'So you'll know. If I say,

"On the hill Johan and I once found . . .", then you'll know what kind of place it is, and I'll know that you know what I mean. Hang on, is that right? Yes. And . . . yes! Now! I have to . . .'

He stops picking at the leaf, comes and stands by Siw and points down towards the harbour, where the balconies of the brand-new homes are adorned with light ropes. 'You remember the silo?'

'Who doesn't? You told me you and Johan climbed up it and—'

'That's not it. Well, it is. But there's something else.' Max's hands are shaking. He tears the leaf into two halves, stares at them, then nods eagerly and goes on: 'Ever since that time, when I was twelve years old, I've felt like there's a . . . space. Something missing. A vacuum. As if I don't have a chance of being whole again until I find what's missing.'

'You told me,' Siw says. 'What I did outside the library, with the buggy – you saw the incident, but you didn't see me.'

'Yes, but I've been thinking about it, and I've realised that in a wider sense too . . .' – Max brings the two halves of the maple leaf together to form a whole – '. . . you're what's missing. For me. A vacancy arose, so to speak, and you're the only one who can fill it.'

Siw wants to say something, but her vocal cords have tied themselves in a knot. She clasps her fingers together and presses her hands against her stomach while she gazes down at the harbour and summons up the old silo in the darkness, sees the boys clambering up it, sees the buggy rolling down the library steps, a few seconds that were so critical. Eventually she manages to speak: 'Wow.'

'Yes. And when I was at your place the other morning, the only thing that made me feel real emotion was that sweater you're crocheting . . .'

'Knitting.'

'I can't tell the difference, but whatever. It was the only thing

558

that was . . . incomplete, the only thing that resembled me, and I got the idea that with you . . . this is difficult . . . but that over time, stitch by stitch, with you I might eventually be . . . complete, if I can, if I can do it . . .'

Max has dropped the torn leaf and is waving his hands around as if the words are attacking him from all directions and he has to defend himself, make choices in order to come out with coherent sentences. Siw grabs his wrists and pulls him close. 'It's okay, Max. I understand. Kind of. Come here.' She raises her face to kiss his lips.

'Wait.' He pulls back a fraction. 'Just one more thing. Then fuck it. On Saturday, when we were together. It was wonderful, but at the same time it was . . . theoretical knowledge. The fact that it was wonderful. And in the morning, I couldn't . . . anyway. I've stopped taking my medication. That's why I'm like this. It's really hard, but I want to be able to feel what I'm really feeling. For you.' He looks shyly at Siw, then adds: 'I want to be able to love you.'

Then fuck it. They kiss each other until their mouths taste of metal. Siw breathes in through her nose and September's melancholy sweetness spreads through her body, making her light and drunk on the future. She wants Max to show her more of his places, she wants to show him her places, and she wants them to find places that belong to both of them.

Their lips part and Siw presses her face to Max's chest in a firm embrace. At last she understands the experience of being two versions of herself. On the one hand, the person she *is*, on the other, the person she *is for Max*. Only now does she see them, as the two versions slide together with an almost audible click. She is herself again. She is where she is meant to be. For always.

2

They stand side by side looking down on Norrtälje. Siw switches between regarding her home town as the better part of Roslagen, which is how it likes to market itself, and a picturesque prison, a secret outpost of the local jail. Standing on the hill with Max, the town sparkling at their feet, it feels more like a promise than anything else, the arena for what will be her love story. She blushes at her own thoughts, and is grateful for the fact that even when her cheeks feel like burning hotplates, they don't actually *glow*.

'Shall we take a stroll?' Max asks.

'Mmm-hmm.'

The ground is covered in moss, slippery and treacherous in the darkness. They take each other's hand and find their way to the steps, which are far too narrow to allow them to walk side by side. Still they don't let go. Max rests their interwoven fingers on his shoulder and leads the way. Siw follows, and the difference in their height combined with the angle of the steps means she can keep her arm outstretched. This is a new experience. Everything is a new experience.

They wander down Glasmästarbacken hand in hand, then turn left before the river and pass Rurik's Ship, the Viking vessel on its stone plinth, sailing east towards the harbour inlet.

'Rurik,' Max says. 'What do you know about him?'

'Nothing. I only know one amusing fact about the Vikings: they ate toadstools.'

'Why?'

'No idea.'

They continue along the path by the river, speculating on possible reasons why the Vikings might have eaten death-cap mushrooms, if they did. It's not important. The important thing is that they are finding their way to a tone, an understanding of how to talk to each other, whether it's light-hearted or serious.

Siw is closest to the river, and its rushing is like a constant whisper in her right ear. When they are approaching Skvallertorget via Strömgatan, she remembers the fear she experienced at the state of the world, and tightens her grip on Max's hand.

'What's wrong?'

'I just . . . Do you think everything's going to go to hell?'

'Maybe,' Max says in a subdued voice. He lets go of Siw's hand so that he can thump his chest, then goes on: 'Sorry, I've got such a . . . it's some kind of . . . panic.' He leans against the nearest building, head down, taking short, shallow breaths.

He is very close to the spot where the Afghan guy's phone was hurled at the wall; there are shards of glass on the ground, shining in the glow of the street lamp. His back heaves as he tries to take in air, and Siw is overcome with fear.

She might think that Max is lovely and funny and wonderful to be with, but she doesn't know this other side of him, doesn't know how it might manifest itself now he's stopped taking his medication. The demon could have many different faces. Maybe Max can be nasty, contemptuous, violent, make her life hell.

A torrent of images pours into Siw's mind, images of Max in the grip of his illness, capable of hurting her more deeply than anyone else, simply because she has such high hopes for their relationship. Or has she? Maybe this is just a stupid crush, created by her lack of knowledge about love? She could be deceived, exploited. The sweet warmth in Siw's heart starts to be corroded by fear.

Max pushes himself away from the wall with a groan and looks at Siw. In his eyes she reads the same fear that she is feeling. Max presses his clenched fist to his chest and says in short bursts: 'You. Have to. Fight. Against it.'

He is right. The fear is always lurking, ready to dictate our thoughts and actions. Siw knows this better than most. So many times she hasn't dared to make the shortest leap, for fear of falling; she has always chosen the safe, familiar option. You have to fight against it. Dare to hope.

She goes over to Max, glass crunching beneath her feet as she presses herself against his back and gently places her hands on his chest, breathing in a steadier rhythm than him. They stand quietly like that, and each breath Max takes is deeper than the previous one, until he is once again breathing normally. He turns, caresses her cheek. 'Thank you. I don't know what . . . I just got so scared.'

'I understand. Me too.'

They take each other's hands and set off again. As they are passing Folkflinet, the site of the pillory in times gone by, Siw points to the metal sculpture and says: 'Everything is about fear.'

'What do you mean?'

'The pillory used to be here. People always try . . . anything that doesn't fit in, anyone who isn't like the rest of us, has to be excluded and shamed. Preferably eradicated.'

'That's how we validate ourselves. Who we are. By saying "that's not us".'

'Exactly, although really we're afraid, because that's exactly what we are. Something that doesn't fit in.'

Max looks at Siw with an expression she can't interpret. There is appreciation in it, but she's not sure if it's because of what she's said, or because a checkout assistant from Flygfyren is capable of

562

that level of analysis. 'What?' she says. 'Didn't you believe I could think thoughts like that?'

Max smiles. 'One of the things that interests me most right now, Siw Waern, is finding out what kind of thoughts you can think.'

Siw isn't sure if that's an answer, but it will do for the time being. They carry on past the shoemaker's and the tailor's, and the old wooden bridge that featured in *Kalle Blomkvist: Master Detective*. They are close to the river all the time, and there is something about that rushing sound in Siw's right ear that is bothering her. It penetrates her brain, settles like a cold fog over all the warm thoughts she wants to think.

When they are opposite the tourist office, something finds its way through the rushing, something that is connected to it. Siw stops and grips the railing, clenching her jaw as the Hearing drowns out every other noise. Agitated voices, the rustle of clothing, the thud of bodies, shouts, then a splash, the sound of bones shattering, a scream abruptly cut off.

'What is it?' Max asks.

'Here,' Siw says, making a sweeping gesture. 'Something is going to happen here. Or has already happened.'

'When?'

'I don't know. I told you – I don't know. But someone is going to end up in the river somewhere around here. And die. I think.'

'Do you want to wait?'

Siw shakes her head. 'It could be tomorrow. Or the day before yesterday. I've stopped trying to work it out. But I want to get away from here – now.'

'Espresso House?'

'Anywhere. As long as we get away from here.'

They turn into Öströms gränd and Siw is glad to leave the rushing

563

sound behind her. With every step they take she feels more in synch with the loveliness of this evening, and can't understand her baseless fear. The relief is so great that when they reach Posthusgatan, she presses her body closer to Max, and feels moved to flutter her eyelashes like Lady in the Disney cartoon on Christmas Eve.

Bella notte.

3

They each order a cappuccino, Max with an extra shot of espresso, and find a table where they can sit side by side on a sofa. Max takes a sip of his coffee, wipes the foam from his upper lip and says: 'I don't understand how you can be so cool about it.'

'About what?'

'Your . . . Hearings, wasn't that what you called them? When I have my visions, it's something else.'

'It's not so . . . it's kind of like wearing noise-cancelling headphones. You select that function, virtually every other sound disappears and I hear only . . . what I'm meant to hear.'

'I think you're cool anyway,' Max says, kissing her cheek.

Both cheeks begin to burn. Siw glances around and a little voice inside her shouts: *Look! I'm sitting in a café with a fit guy, and he just kissed me!* However, no one has taken any notice of this world-shattering event: the fact that Max has indulged in a PDA for the first time. Does this mean they're a couple now?

'I just don't know what it's for,' she says.

Max plays dumb. 'Kissing?'

'No, I know exactly what that's for.' She leans towards his lips, thinks: *Steady on, this could be ridiculous* and settles for a chaste kiss

564

before going on: 'This . . . gift. Okay, I once managed to prevent something. *Once.* No, twice if we count Charlie. But like just now, by the river – what's the point? What am I expected to do? All that happens is it creates an intense feeling of unease, precisely because there's nothing I can do. And besides . . .'

Siw wishes she could simply flutter her eyelashes, but among many other things Max is the only person she's met who not only believes what she is saying, but can also understand. Anna believes her, but she will never be able to understand. Not completely.

'Besides?' Max prompts her. He doesn't seem to mind talking about it.

'Alva.' Siw gets a lump in her throat. 'One day this will happen to her, and she will have to go around with all this terrible knowledge, all the things she can't do anything about. I just hope it takes a long time. She's so little.'

'Mmm. Although she seems tough. And funny. She might cope better than you think.'

Siw sips her coffee and sits back. 'You should hear her. "Are you meeting *the guy*, when do I get to meet *the guy*?" She liked you when we met on the football pitch, and now she thinks it's unfair that I'm keeping a secret from her.'

'I'd love to meet her. When you think the time is right.'

Siw feels dizzy. She was just chatting, pleased to be able to talk about something other than her troubles; this is a lot to take in all at once. 'I'm just going to . . . powder my nose.'

Max guffaws at the anachronism, worthy of *Panic on Pythagoras*. Siw gets to her feet and somehow manages to walk to the loo, where she sinks down on the seat without opening the lid.

I'd love to meet her.

But it wasn't that, it was what came next: *when you think the time is right.* That means Max sees a long-term future with her, which shouldn't come as a surprise after what he said on the hill, but it's still overwhelming when it's a throwaway comment rather than part of an emotional moment.

When you think the time is right. Max likes Alva and wants to meet her, but it's going to happen in the 'right' way, a way that will form the basis of a relationship between the three of them. Siw can't get her head around all the implications of that simple sentence, but one thing is very clear: Max is serious.

Siw whimpers and covers her face with her hands as a shudder runs through her body. Part of her wants to prise open the window above the toilet and flee, but for one thing, she would need another six months on the powder diet to get through the small space, and for another, it's a stupid idea. Why is it so scary to see her dreams come true?

The fear that comes over her now is completely different from the icy, scrabbling terror she felt down by the river; this is more like the trepidation you feel when a newborn baby is placed in your hands. You are afraid of dropping it, hurting it, doing the wrong thing and seeing that precious life slip through your fingers. A wet thud on the concrete floor, and it's all over.

Siw takes a couple of deep breaths, gets to her feet and splashes her face with cold water. She clings to the washbasin, looks in the mirror, then raises a stiff index finger. 'Pull yourself together, Siw Waern! If you fuck this up because you're such a coward, then . . . then you'll have me to deal with!'

'And who are you?'

'Trust me, you don't want to know. Now get out of here!'

Siw dries her face with a paper towel and tries to think Lady-thoughts. *Bella notte.*

566

When she emerges from the toilet, Max is sitting exactly as she left him, with his arms resting on the back of the sofa. Siw rejoins him and says: 'Unbelievable.'

Max looks around as if the 'unbelievable' applies to something Siw has just seen, which indeed it does. She points to him. 'You've been alone for a few minutes, and you *haven't* taken out your phone.'

Max shrugs. 'We said we weren't doing *Pokémon.*'

'You do know your phone can be used for other things?'

Max grins and is about to answer when his mouth stiffens in a terrible grimace. His eyes roll upwards and his hands clutch the back of the sofa. His body arches and he kicks the table over, sending cups and saucers crashing to the floor. The hum of conversation around them stops while Max emits deep groans, as if he is in the grip of a hungry incubus.

'Max, Max, what is it?'

His legs are still kicking out, and the heel of his boot smashes a coffee cup. Siw crawls onto the sofa so that she can place her hands on his chest, but at that moment the attack is over. Max collapses with one last groan, and lies there with his legs and arms spread. A drop of sweat trickles down from his hairline and reaches his eye just as his focus returns.

'What happened?' Siw asks. 'Did you see something?'

Max nods and holds out his hand to Siw, who helps him to his feet. He wobbles, clears his throat and says: 'I saw what you heard. It's happening now. Any minute.' Without letting go of Siw's hand, he runs towards the door. As he pushes it open someone shouts after them: 'Hey! You need to pay for the damage!'

They race along Posthusgatan, heading for the river.

567

4

It is not screaming they hear as they hurtle down Öströms gränd, but a cacophony of cackling and quacking, as if someone has tipped a sackful of ducks and fighting cocks into the river, and the battle is in full cry. Siw looks at Max, who spreads his hands wide as he continues to run. This noise wasn't part of Siw's Hearing or his vision.

They reach the river and lean over the rail to get a better view. The racket is coming from the water, which is boiling with movement. At first they can only make out silhouettes by the inadequate light of the street lamps, but as their eyes get used to the gloom they can distinguish flapping bodies and a shadow jerkily moving back and forth across a thick, fallen tree branch.

'A beaver,' Max says. 'It's a beaver.'

Siw has never heard of beavers in this river, but it can't be anything else with its flat tail, chunky body and hamster-like face, its teeth snapping at the ducks flying around it, pecking and screaming out their fury.

A couple of ducks are already dead. One is jammed between two branches, wings outstretched like a fallen cherub, while the other is drifting away on the current. Siw follows it with her gaze, and sees a dozen or so people gathered on the bridge twenty metres away, enjoying the spectacle.

This is not what I heard.

She turns to Max to ask him exactly what he saw, but events take a new turn. On the other side of the river, three boys aged about ten come running from Smala Gränd, arms pressed to their chests. When they come closer, Siw recognises one of them from

Pokémon Go Roslagen. They open their arms and piles of stones fall to the ground, ranging in size from a ping-pong ball to a fist. They pick up as many stones as they can hold in their hands and start bombarding the beaver.

'Mattias!' Max yells. 'Mattias, stop that!'

The boy takes no notice. He hurls a large, sharp stone that hits the beaver on its back. The animal is knocked sideways into the water, and the ducks take the opportunity to peck at its head. When the beaver manages to scramble back onto the branch, its flank is black with blood in the faint light. The birds know that it is weakened, and intensify their attacks.

Siw turns to Max. 'What . . .' but he is already running towards the bridge. Siw hesitates. She sees a man jogging down to the boys, who haven't noticed anything because they are fully occupied with aiming at the beaver. It has been hit by a couple more stones, and barely defends itself when the ducks go for its eyes.

'What the fuck are you doing, you little bastards!' the man roars, his face contorted in a mask epitomising the concept of *hatred*. In a single movement he picks up Mattias, lifts him to chest height and throws him into the river.

The boy's arms flail and the stones fall from his hands as he sails through the air. His screams blend with the frantic quacking of the ducks as he lands on his back with a loud splash, scattering the birds in all directions as if a grenade has exploded in their midst. Up on the bank Mattias's companions are fleeing from the man's furiously waving arms.

When Siw sees two more men approaching from Smala Gränd, she too begins to run, because the situation is now starting to merge with what she heard earlier. One final glance at the river: fortunately Mattias has landed so far out that the deeper water has received his body rather than the rocks. He is whimpering and swimming towards the spot Siw is now leaving, with the aim of intervening if she can. The agitated cries of adult voices that formed part of her Hearing are coming from behind her as she reaches the bridge.

More people have gathered, and are loudly discussing the unfolding events. Their voices vibrate with rage; at the moment the bridge is occupied by a lynch mob. From down below comes a scream that Siw recognises, and she knows it's too late. She pushes her way through to the railing just as the man who threw Mattias in is punched in the chest. He staggers backwards, scrabbling at thin air for something to hold on to, then tumbles over the edge.

Siw sees the sharp protruding rock just waiting for his head to strike it. She closes her eyes tightly as the man's scream is cut off by the splash, then the crunching sound she heard half an hour earlier. The crowd around her cheer loudly.

Siw opens her eyes just as Max appears up by Smala Gränd. He takes in the scene before him, then turns and walks away. The two men are standing open-mouthed as if they can't believe what they are seeing, staring at the man lying motionless in the shallow water, his lips frozen in one last scream. On the other side of the river Mattias is scrambling out across the rough edging stones, sobbing helplessly. Blood is seeping through the back of his T-shirt in a couple of places.

The crowd on the bridge disperses, apart from a few individuals who stay around to call the police and offer themselves as witnesses. The birds fly or paddle away. The performance is over. Siw leans over the railing and sees a shadow slowly gliding by. The dead beaver bumps helplessly into a couple of rocks before continuing on its way out to sea.

Ten minutes later Siw and Max are sitting on the bench next to the fountain in the square. 'It's as you said,' Max begins. 'What the fuck is the point of having this "gift" when there's nothing you can do? And that was actually the longest advanced . . . warning or whatever you want to call it that I've ever had.'

'If we'd stayed by the river, we'd have been in time,' Siw says.

Max tosses a pebble into the stone sculpture, which resembles a baptismal font. 'I sometimes wonder . . . Even when I was little I wondered why I never . . . tuned into people who *almost* died. Either who is going to live and who is going to die is preordained, or I tune in a little while later, when what's going to happen has already taken place.'

'But that wasn't the case tonight. You saw it, we ran, then it happened a minute or so later.'

'Yes – just enough so we didn't have time to do anything. As if we were *meant* to sit in that café precisely so far from the bridge, as if we were *meant* to stand there gawping like idiots before . . . If I'd run over the bridge straight away, I could have . . .'

Max is slumped forward, his hands waving pointlessly in the air, lips gabbling manically. Siw puts her arms around him and hugs him. 'Max. Hush, Max. It's okay.'

Max tries to twist himself free. 'It's *okay*? We've just watched a man die, and we were the only two people who could have done something about it, but instead . . .'

Siw tightens her grip. 'Seriously. We can't change the course of the world, it's insane to imagine that we can. People are responsible for their own actions. And remember Charlie – sometimes it is possible to do something.'

Max's stiff muscles relax a little. 'Yes, but would he have gone through with it if we hadn't come along? Would he really have killed himself?'

'You saw it happen.'

'Yes, but I saw the buggy too. I'm beginning to suspect that *you* can change things, but I can't.'

'Why would that be the case?'

'Because you're a sibyl. You have something that's . . . approved. Authorised by fate, or however you want to put it, while I'm just a poor bastard who has visions that achieve nothing apart from tormenting me.'

'Max . . .'

'Wait. I was inside the head of the guy who fell into the river. Do you know what his final thought was, before he cracked his skull on that stone?'

'No. That's not something I can access, as you know.'

'*Pity the fucking kid didn't die.* That's what he was thinking. Not in words, of course, but his head was full of images of Mattias's head sticking up from a filled-in hole in the ground, with sharp stones being thrown at it. His skin tore, his eyes fell out and blood gushed from his mouth as his teeth were knocked out. A ten-year-old boy, he was thinking that about a ten-year-old boy, and then he stopped thinking. Thank God.'

Max is on his feet now, pacing back and forth in front of the former City Hotel. He rubs his scalp ferociously, then slaps his head so hard that the sound echoes across the square. 'If only it would disappear, if only I could get rid of it!'

Siw sighs, stands up and grabs his hands, which are moving around as if they have a will of their own. 'Max. Look at me.'

His eyes fix on hers and stay there. She aims for a point beyond the veil of angst and says: 'You must have made a choice. At some stage you must have chosen to live with this instead of going crazy, yes?'

The veil is drawn aside and a distant look comes into his eyes. 'Yes. It was a cloud. That reminded me of an elephant. Rearing up on its hind legs.'

'Okay. Think about what you decided back then. How it felt. What you maybe promised yourself. Hold on to those things. They are what's important.'

Max nods slowly and his hands go limp in Siw's grip, before he gently withdraws them, then wraps her in his arms.

'Thank you,' he whispers into her hair. 'That was . . .' He breathes in through his nose. 'Have you been to the hairdresser?'

'Yes. And if you promise to try to stay calm, you're welcome to come to dinner the day after tomorrow, on Thursday. Dinner with me and Alva.'

Max releases her and steps back, his hands resting on her shoulders. 'Are you sure?'

'I'm sure. It feels . . . right.'

MAI PIÙ

I

In the autumn of 2016 Maria had a shoot in Ragusa on Sicily, as one of the faces of Dolce & Gabbana's spring collection. Her career had passed its peak and she was no longer *prima faccia*, just one of three supplementary models. But still: Dolce & Gabbana. By that point Dolce's name was sullied by accusations of exploitation, and the brand was seen as slightly lame, even passé in the fashion world. Not by the general public, though, and therein lay the problem. D & G had become a mass-market product.

The plan was to regain credibility by launching a more exclusive and daring collection with the working title *la ferocia*, ferocity, and it was Maria's dangerous, luminous green eyes that had got her the job.

She was flown from Milan to Catania with the remains of the previous night's cocaine rush swirling around in her body, and the dance floor's EDM beat still pounding in her ears after only a couple of hours' sleep. When she left the airport, she immediately turned around and headed for the baggage claims area to collect her suitcase. Then she remembered that she didn't have a suitcase. Probably not, anyway.

A driver was holding up a sign with her misspelled name on it, and Maria flopped down on the back seat of an Audi A4, which was pretty much standard within the industry, and immediately fell asleep. She was woken an hour and a half later when the driver took a hairpin bend at speed, causing her head to bang against the window.

She opened her eyes and looked out. Blinked. Thought she must be in the middle of a bad trip, coming down from last night. Rubbed her eyes, looked out again. The car was driving through a *perpendicular* town. Higgledy-piggledy stone houses appeared to be piled on top of one another to form a wall, reaching up to the sky. She cleared her throat and asked the driver, her voice hoarse from too many cigarettes: '*Cosa é questo?*'

'Ragusa!' the driver exclaimed, letting go of the wheel so that he could wave his hand at the wall made of houses. 'Ragusa Ibla!'

As they drew closer Maria could see that, in fact, narrow, winding roads led up between the buildings, roads so narrow that the driver had to fold in his wing mirrors in order to get through. After a meandering route that almost made Maria throw up, she was dropped off in a large, sloping square.

She had a vague memory of a message informing her that her destination was the Piazza del Duomo, Cathedral Square, and judging by the enormous church about fifty metres away on the western side, she had arrived. The driver pointed to the steps of the cathedral, where lights were already in place for the shoot.

Maria nodded and set off. She had been so out of it in the morning that she had put on stilettos. Under normal circumstances

575

she had no problem conducting herself with dignity however high her heels might be, but there was something about the angle of the square combined with the tilt inside her own head that nearly made her stagger; the cathedral seemed to be looming right over her.

She heard an angry tooting and jumped back, almost falling over as a little train filled with tourists snaked its way across the square. A middle-aged man at the back shouted, '*Ciao, bella ragazza italiana!*' after her. She gave him a Bosnian finger.

When she looked up she saw that the entire team was now gathered on the steps watching her antics, along with a hundred or so curious onlookers who had come to see what was going on. Maria straightened up and used her willpower and high-heel training to cover the last few metres without any further mishaps.

The team consisted of eleven people, only five of whom appeared to have a specific role. Make-up, hair, lighting, clothes, runner. The rest wandered around fiddling vaguely with this and that. Maria was shown into a tent where she was carefully made up, styled and dressed, without any input from her apart from raising her arms.

She asked who the photographer was, and the make-up artist answered with deep reverence in her voice: 'Sergio Al'Uovo'. Maria sighed. Despite his incomprehensible name – Sergio of the Egg – he was one of the most respected and highest paid in the industry. Tall, shaven-headed, muscular, hyperaesthetic and as camp as Christmas. She had worked with him on a couple of previous occasions, and it hadn't been a pleasant experience. To put it simply, Sergio had difficulty regarding people as anything other than usefully animated objects.

Maria emerged from the tent in a dress that Jane might have been wearing before she met Tarzan, after wandering around in the jungle for several days. A long slit that was more like a tear revealed Maria's legs, and the upper part of her left breast was also exposed as a shoulder strap was missing – presumably stolen by a monkey.

Sergio was waiting, and he was in a foul mood. As soon as he saw Maria he slapped his head and rattled out a stream of rapid Italian. She didn't understand a word, but was steered straight back into the tent to have her make-up redone.

When she came out again, Sergio scowled at her and spread his arms wide, as if to say: *see what I'm expected to work with!* The upper part of the square was now full of people, with almost everyone holding up their phones with or without selfie sticks.

Maria took her place on the steps and awaited The Egg's instructions. Sergio took a few sample shots to assess the light, barked at the guy who was in charge of the lamps, then took a few more shots until he decided he was satisfied. He turned his attention to Maria, who fired up her professional smile. She knew it looked virtually natural, and she also knew she could hold it until she fell asleep. Sergio shook his head and shouted: '*Anima, stronza! Vita, eh!*'

Soul, bitch. Life.

Maria tried to inject more soulfulness into her pose and her smile. She pictured Tarzan in the form of Alexander Skarsgård, swinging through the jungle in order to sweep her up in his muscular arms. Sergio covered his eyes as if she was causing him pain, and yelled: '*Che idiota!*'

The people in the square laughed. Maria was used to being shouted at and bullied, but not so publicly. Her smile was becoming something of a strain. She put her hands on her hips in a pose that was meant to be challenging. Sergio shook his head and came storming up the steps.

'*La ferocia, stronza! La ferocia,*' he hissed so close to her face

577

that drops of saliva landed on her lips. He grabbed her hips and twisted them into position as if he were a chiropractor. He placed one hand on her bottom and the other on her stomach to push her pelvis forward.

Maria had never experienced this kind of treatment, although she had heard of it happening to others. Because Sergio was gay, which meant there couldn't be a sexual motive, he thought he had the right to handle women's bodies however he wished.

'*Sei eccitata e feroce, capisci?*'

You're horny and ferocious, get it?

Maria nodded and was about to say that she understood perfectly when Sergio squeezed her pussy so hard that a fabric-covered finger actually penetrated a small distance inside her. The men down on the piazza cheered, and Sergio repeated: '*Eccitata!*'

Before Maria had recovered from the shock, Sergio slapped her twice across the face, bringing tears to her eyes. '*E feroce! Ya!*' he said, returning to his camera.

Maria wanted to run away, but mostly she wanted to fight. Was it for this that she had endured all the kicks and blows in the playground – to be publicly humiliated by a bald-headed sadist? She wanted to smash that half-a-million camera down onto his shiny head, watch the blood splatter the cathedral steps.

She didn't fight. She didn't run away. Instead, she channelled all her rage into her expression, sending laser beams from her eyes into the lens in the hope that they would burn away Sergio's corneas. The camera rattled like a machine gun, and when Sergio straightened up he was beaming. '*Facile, eh! Che belleza!*'

Afterwards, when Maria was sitting in the make-up chair with her face covered in cold cream while an assistant wiped the blusher from her cheeks, the tears began to flow. She had never been so humiliated, so deeply objectified. There and then she made a sacred vow to herself: it would never happen again.

2

Having a job and at the same time completely avoiding objectification is an impossibility. Working means fulfilling a function, hiring yourself out. In the past it had been Maria's face and body that were the goods in question; now it was her hands and feet. In and out with trays, cups, cutlery and plates. Laying everything out, clearing the tables, fetching and carrying. However, rather than a form of objectification, Maria thought of it as a mechanisation of herself, which made it easier to accept. She could be an efficient, impersonal machine, carrying out its pre-programmed movements.

Could be. But wasn't allowed to be, because of the way the machine in question looked. The eyes of many men lingered on her for far too long, and the nauseating sense of being objectified came creeping in. A few guys, both her own age and older, had glanced at her bare ring finger and asked what she was doing after work. Maria had replied that she would be taking care of her five kids. That bit she could cope with.

The nastiness she had described to Marko was much worse. The aggression in people's voices, the filthy looks they gave one another, and particularly the way the women treated Maria. Scowling faces when a sandwich didn't taste exactly as they'd expected, complaints about coffee that was too weak, too strong, not hot enough.

The customers in the café sat there with sour expressions, searching for the tiniest detail to complain about. If they couldn't find anything, they started on the other clients. Harsh words had been exchanged on more than one occasion, but so far altercations hadn't led to physical violence. Maria thought it was only a matter of time.

And the rushing sound. That alone was enough to drive a person crazy. The constant gushing and gurgling as the river made its way across the rocks, dividing around the island where the café was situated.

When Maria was fourteen she had seen the film *Poltergeist*, the white static on the TV where the ghosts appeared. This was the same, but with sound instead. Through that rushing Maria heard the voices from her past that had mocked and frightened her, and she moved among the outside tables with a little shiver of fear constantly trembling in her chest. If she hadn't had to go indoors at regular intervals to collect orders, she would have broken down.

The outdoor area was open for only one more week before it closed for the season, but Maria didn't think she could last that long, so she had started to do something she'd never expected to do again: she had started to pray.

Goran and Laura were no devout Christians, but they were religious enough to seek out a Catholic church wherever they found themselves. They would go to mass from time to time, and Maria would accompany them. During the early years in Norrtälje she had often attended the monthly mass held by the diocese of Our Lady in St Mark's church in Grind. This was partly because Marko had no interest in religion whatsoever, and partly because the mass, along with the journey to and from the church, was the only time that Maria had her parents to herself. She also discovered that she actually liked the ceremonial aspect, the magic of the ritual itself. And the prayers. She prayed at bedtime more or less every night until she was thirteen.

If the mass was a way of being with her parents, then the prayers provided an opportunity to be by herself, focus her diverse thoughts on something greater, and find peace. At some point after she turned thirteen worldly matters increasingly occupied her mind, and she forgot about praying.

But now it's back. It's the prayers versus the rushing sound. As Maria moves among the tables she gabbles the prayers she remembers from her childhood inside her head, in both Bosnian and Swedish. Verbal rosary beads as a defence against disintegration.

Ourfatherwhoartinheavenhallowedbethyname . . .

It works pretty well, partly because the prayer in her mind shuts out most of the rushing, and partly because the act of praying evokes that little girl on her knees by the bed, making Maria more amenable and indulgent when customers act up. The unpleasant remarks trickle away over the protective shell of the prayer.

It is the lunchtime rush, and even though the temperature is only twelve degrees, half of the outside tables are occupied. People are grunting and griping over the time it takes for their food to arrive, angrily stirring sugar into their cappuccinos. Maria is flitting from table to table with the prayer on repeat in her head, when a woman points to the river and calls out: 'Look! What's that?'

Many faces turn in the direction of the water, including Maria's. Something is floating along, something . . . hairy. A lot of objects drift by on a daily basis – leaves and branches, but also dead birds, both garden birds and ducks. Once there was a squirrel.

But this is bigger. People get to their feet and go up to the railing to see better. Disgusted cries of 'yuck!' and 'what the *fuck*' can be heard, because it is a dog. A medium-sized dog, maybe a cocker spaniel, bloated and with a yellow lead trailing behind it.

A man aged about fifty who had remained seated stands up to join the others. As he passes Maria his hand slides over her bottom and gives a little squeeze. A red mist descends over her eyes.

Never again.

There are many unpleasant aspects to working in the café, but so far sexual harassment has not featured. In Italy inappropriate comments and hands that just happened to land in the wrong place were the norm, but either the Swedes have a different character, or #MeToo has actually had an effect. But here it is: a man who thinks he has the right to treat her as an object for his own fantasies, squeezing her flesh as if he were assessing the ripeness of a mango.

Maria is empty-handed at the moment, so she spins around with the intention of slapping the man across the face and knocking him to the ground. She's perfectly capable – she's done it before. As she takes a deep breath, she spots something over the man's shoulder – a soft glow, completely different from the September greyness seeping down from the sky.

She lowers her hand. The pervert wheezes on his way. The tables are empty now, apart from the one furthest away by the bridge. Jesus is sitting at that table. The glow Maria can see is the halo emanating from his face, from his infinitely empathetic smile. He looks exactly like the picture Goran and Laura have in the living room. Jesus beckons her over.

Maria shakes her head and takes a step backwards, begins to gabble a prayer until she realises that this is absurd. He's sitting there, she can speak to him directly instead, but still she backs away. Because it's not him. Because she's going crazy.

A tinge of regret comes into Jesus's eyes, but his smile does not falter. He seems to be at least as capable as Maria of holding it – he could easily get a job as a model. He raises both hands as if to say *do not be afraid*, and when Maria continues to shake her head the gesture turns into *no matter, we have plenty of time.*

Over by the railing people have started to moan about the fact that the dog's lead has got caught up, and the dead animal is now bobbing up and down just below the café. A whiff of the gases produced by putrefaction reaches Maria's nostrils just before she backs around the corner and flees into the kitchen.

MY LIFE IN YOUR HANDS

Hi Johan,

I'm so impressed by your skills. How the hell did you manage to come up with a story like that from just a few words? The Punk and the Hearing Aid. *Brilliant. I laughed out loud several times when I was reading it, especially when the guy from the council comes to visit and they sing that song by Ebba Grön. Fucking amazing. I don't know how you do it. I don't read much, but if you come up with anything else, feel free to send it. I promise to read it. And I'm sure I'll love it.*

Hugs from your biggest fan,

Anna

Johan and Anna have arranged to meet at the pizzeria with the curious name 'The Pasta Expert' on Stora Brogatan. Okay, so they serve pasta too, but above all it's a pizzeria. The decor is ultra-spartan and the cosiness factor zero, but the prices are low, the pizzas are good, and after all, Johan and Anna don't have the kind of relationship that requires a cosy setting.

It is just before eight and Johan is a few minutes early. He takes out his phone and rereads Anna's email. It's not exactly literary criticism, but it's the first thing anyone has ever said about something he's written, and it gives him a warm feeling in his chest.

He has gone over the pros and cons umpteen times and even had difficulty sleeping before he made his decision: he is going to let Anna read his novel. The bundle of paper is stuffed into a nylon sports bag at his feet, and its presence is like an underlying anxiety, a caged animal. As he sits there in the pizzeria he goes over all the arguments for and against one more time, and realises that actually he hasn't made up his mind at all.

This is a worrying time for Johan. In today's local paper he read about an attack on the refugee centre on Albert Engströms väg. During the night someone had nailed the front door shut, then thrown a petrol bomb through a window. They had sprayed 'Blackheads go home' on the wall.

Fortunately the fire hadn't caught, and it ought to be possible to laugh at the idiot responsible. Why spray a message on a building you're attempting to burn down? And why tell the refugees to go home at the same time as trying to murder them? But Johan isn't laughing. He wishes he'd never written that post.

Anna arrives just after eight and manages to cheer him up a little by insisting he stands up, then giving him a bear hug and telling him he's 'an absolute genius' and repeating how impressed she is that he was able to make up such an amazing story from so little, like making soup out of a nail.

Johan orders a Quattro Stagioni, Anna a Capricciosa. As they wait for the food, Anna says: 'I shouldn't really be eating pizza. Don't tell Siw.' Johan pretends to zip his mouth shut.

'So,' Anna says. 'What are you up to?'

'Nothing special,' Johan replies, as his novel mewls like a new-born baby in his bag. 'The usual.'

'What's the usual? Tell me about a typical day at work.'

Johan talks about his job in the bowling hall, throws in a couple of anecdotes about the funny habits and superstitions some people have, and the constant complaints about the oil patterns. Anna laughs, and Johan begins to relax. The judgement he made about her intelligence the first time they met has turned out to be completely wrong. Okay, she's no intellectual, but she is whip-smart and she can make connections in a second. *If you're happy and you know it, clap your hounds* is one of Johan's favourites in their game, which is now a regular thing. As soon as either of them comes up with a new line, a message goes flying through the ether.

Their pizzas arrive, and they eat in silence for a while. Several times Johan checks with his foot to make sure the bag is still there, that it hasn't grown legs and wandered off. Whenever he hears the nylon fabric rustle, a stab of anxiety pierces his chest.

Am I going to do this? Have I got the nerve?

'How about you?' he asks. 'Anything going on with you?'

Anna takes a swig of her Coke Zero, which she acknowledges is a meaningless gesture in relation to the pizza, then nods. 'Yes, actually.'

'Tell me.'

Anna takes a deep breath and shakes her head, as if she can't believe what she's about to say.

'I'm going to get a qualification.'

'Wow – in what?'

'Physiotherapy. As you know, I work with the elderly. I enjoy it, but at the same time . . . it's a bit depressing, just keeping them going. I'd like to be able to *do* something to improve their lives. So

586

yes, physiotherapy. I already did a course in health and social care, and it seems my grades are good enough.'

'Wow again – does that mean you're going to university?'

'Yep. Uppsala in the spring, if everything works out. Three years.'

Johan raises his glass of regular Coke in a toast, and Anna clinks her glass against his.

'To being brave enough to put yourself out there,' he says.

'Cheers – but I'm scared, don't think I'm not!'

My turn! yells a voice from the bag. *This is the perfect moment! Do it!*

Johan is about to bend down and pick up the bag, but some kind of psychosomatic paralysis prevents him from doing so. He feels a sharp pain at the base of his spine, and he groans and straightens up.

'What's wrong?'

'Bowling. Industrial injury.'

'So you have time to play?'

'Yes. Sometimes.'

It is several months since Johan picked up a ball with the intention of knocking down pins. In spite of the pain in his back, he is fascinated by his body's ability to manifest his mental state.

'Talking about playing . . .' Anna gestures towards Johan's phone on the table. 'Could you teach me *Pokémon Go*?'

'*What?* I thought you hated *Pokémon Go.*'

'Well, it's . . .' Anna shuffles uncomfortably. 'It's this business about having friends and exchanging presents and so on. I'd like to be able to do that with Siw. And you, for that matter.'

'Is that all?'

Anna pushes aside the last third of her pizza. 'No. It's also because . . . I've sort of gone along in the same rut. Never really dared to try anything new, never . . . put myself out there, like you

587

said. So now I'm giving it a go, which means questioning things I previously took as read. Like *Pokémon Go*. Will you teach me?'

In a way that Johan doesn't understand, Anna's startling request to learn *Pokémon Go* is the straw that breaks the camel's already half-broken back. With a grunt of pain he lifts the sports bag onto the table, takes out the wad of paper and hands it to Anna, who reads from the first page: '*Roslagen Metamorphosis*.' She wipes her fingers on a serviette, then looks at Johan. 'What's this?'

'It's my life. Which you are holding in your hands.'

Now it is Anna's turn to say, 'Wow,' with a wry smile. 'That doesn't sound pretentious at all. And what does metamorphosis mean?'

'Transformation. Yes, it is a bit pretentious, but it's kind of true. It's partly a version of my own life, a heightened version, and partly . . . that's where my hope for the future lies.'

Anna flicks through the sheets of paper, reading a few words here and there. 'Is it a novel?'

'I find it so difficult to . . . It's a story. And you wanted more stories.'

Anna's lips move as she reads a couple of sentences. Something makes her smile. 'Okay. But don't you think you should . . . I mean, I don't read books. Has Max read it? And Siw is much more—'

'Nobody's read it. You're the first person I've shown it to.'

'I see. Why? Why me?'

'To be honest, I don't know. Maybe I was flattered by your email about the story I sent you, and maybe . . . I don't know. I just want you to read it. And tell me what you think. And talking of scared, I'm shit scared now. A part of me wants to snatch it back and tell you to forget the whole thing.'

Anna doesn't seem to have heard the last part of Johan's comment, because she is absorbed in a section of the story. Without addressing his fears, she says: 'But shouldn't you, like, send it somewhere so it can become a book?'

'A publisher. Yes. But I don't think I'll ever be brave enough to do that, because . . .'

'They might not like it. And you'd be completely devastated.'

'Something along those lines, yes. And please, try to read it as quickly as you can, because I'm going to be totally . . .'

Johan jerks his head around to illustrate extreme nervousness. Anna nods and runs her hand over the front page, which is creased and grubby after six months of messing around.

'I'll start tonight,' she promises. 'And you'll teach me *Pokémon Go*, okay?'

'It's a deal. Excuse me. I think I need to go to the toilet and throw up.'

THE KEY TO HOME

I

The house is finished now, or at least as finished as it can be without the things that Goran and Laura want to bring with them from the old apartment. Marko wanders from room to room, trying to imagine his parents' everyday life, see if there's anything missing in order for it to work properly. He has bought wardrobes and bed-side tables, several lamps, chests of drawers, rugs for every room. Side tables, storage solutions. Washing machine and tumble dryer. Among other things.

And yet he feels as if something is missing, something he can't identify, which is why he is walking around like a detective, eyes narrowed, attempting to suss out what has been removed from the crime scene or what ought to be there, but isn't. He is waiting for a revelation, a moment of inspiration – *aha, she had a dog! So where is the lead?*

After a good hour he has failed to solve the mystery, and finally resigns himself to the faint suspicion that what is missing is a *connection*. The house is nothing more than a space containing a number of objects that carry no memories, and therefore lacks life. Hopefully Goran and Laura will be able to change that.

The sad part is that Marko feels exactly the same about his apartment in the city, and he has no desire to return to its exclusive, sterile rooms. Before he came to Norrtälje he had planned to spend a week or two sorting out his parents, then he would pick up the threads of his Stockholm life from where he had left them. Now he isn't sure he wants to do that.

Several factors have led him to this point. The incident with Lukas and Markus and the realisation that he doesn't want to have the same crap ambitions as them, the knowledge that his almost lifelong rivalry with Max is over, but above all the sense of having simply raced ahead without even considering whether there is solid ground beneath his feet. He has no firm base, no roots – he is lost. He is like this house, an empty space waiting for its real contents. The feeling is not entirely unpleasant, because it also allows for a tremor of potential. Something new might happen.

What happens now is that his phone rings. The display shows 'Mum', and as soon as Marko answers Laura says: 'Marko, you need to come over. There's something strange about Maria.'

Marko sinks down on a kitchen chair. 'What do you mean, strange?'

'She's locked herself in her room and refuses to come out. I think she's drinking.'

'Okay – on my way.'

Marko has been worried ever since Maria told him she was working at the café. He doesn't think she is capable of holding down an ordinary job. She depends on the spotlights, the camera lens, the admiring looks. Simply plodding along quietly is not in her nature as Marko knows it, and now she has crashed after four days of what is reality for normal people. She can be very wearing.

2

'Maria? Maria?'

Marko can hear Maria moving around in her room, and when he presses his ear to the door he thinks he hears the sound of a glass being put down. Her voice is groggy when she answers: 'What do you want?'

'I want to talk to you. Can you open the door?'

'No chance.'

Goran and Laura are hovering behind Marko. He turns and spreads his hands wide, but Laura waves him on. Marko sighs. His parents ought to know as well as he does that Maria is as stubborn as they come. If she digs her heels in, they are buried deep in the ground. Purely to show that he's trying, he tweaks his approach.

'I *need* to talk to you.'

'Why?'

An opening – and one last chance. Putting his mouth to the tiny gap between the door and the frame, he says: 'Everyone knows why and everything will be perfect.'

He hears a sound between a snort and a sob, and a couple of seconds later the key is turned. Laura opens her eyes wide and mouths: 'What did you *say*?' Marko shrugs and says: 'The hat is yours,' which leaves his parents even more confused. They don't remember. He opens the door and immediately closes it behind him.

'That was cheating,' Maria says, flopping down in the little armchair in the corner. She picks up a glass containing a golden liquid and takes a large swig. Marko perches on the bed. 'What's happened?'

With the slack neck muscles of the drunk, Maria lets her head droop towards her shoulder as she wiggles the glass back and forth, peering at the reflections of the light in its golden contents. Her laptop is open on the bed next to Marko. On the screen he sees a person reaching out a helping hand to someone who is beneath the surface of the water. The hand is in sharp focus, its owner blurred yet familiar. When Marko checks the name of the website, he understands why. *Encounters with Jesus.* He points to the computer. 'I thought you'd given all this up.'

'So did I.'

'But?'

'But ... you know perfectly well. Jesus never gives up on a sinner.'

She raises her glass again and Marko says: 'Maria, stop drinking. What are you talking about?'

To his surprise, she decides to co-operate. She puts down the glass and looks up at him with her bloodshot eyes. She waves her hands around her ears and says: 'My job. Is sheer hell. People ... people are such ... fucking arseholes. All day, just , ... *che palle*. And that river, it's like ... Treo? Alka Seltzer?'

'You need a painkiller?'

Maria dismisses the suggestion with an exaggerated wave of her hand. 'No, no, *no*. I mean, it's like working inside a glass with a tablet dissolving.' She makes a rushing, bubbling sound, saliva spraying from her lips. 'All the time. All. The. Time.'

Marko glances at the screen again, at the long-haired, smiling figure reaching out, *come to me, I will raise you up*. 'But what does that have to do with Jesus?'

'I've no idea, but that's where he comes. To that fucking place.'

'Jesus comes . . . to the café?'

'Mmm-hmm. He's been three times so far. He wants to talk to me, but I don't want to talk to him.'

'Right . . . why not?'

'Because I don't think I'll like what he's got to say.'

Before Marko can say or do anything, Maria grabs her glass and empties it in one swig, but when she goes for the half-full whisky bottle he manages to swipe it before her hand gets there. She pouts and slumps back in her chair.

Marko weighs the bottle in his hand. What is it they say? *Swings and roundabouts.* If Maria has spent years developing a drug habit, she's unlikely to be able to get herself clean without some kind of transitional prop.

'I realise you don't believe me,' Maria says. 'Why would you? I don't believe I believe . . . no, hang on. I don't even believe I believe it myself.'

'But you are a believer, aren't you?'

Maria snorts. 'I haven't been to church or prayed in, like, fifteen years, so it's a bit like saying you're a dog owner even though you haven't had a dog for . . . fifteen years. Although . . .'

Marko puts the bottle on the floor, as far as possible from his sister. He leans forward. 'Yes?'

His tolerant attitude arouses Maria's suspicions, and she stares at him for a long time before she speaks. 'I started praying. To help me get through. But only like a mantra, like . . . what would you call it . . . gabbling. Gabbling in my head. And then he turned up. Just sat there looking at me, wanting me to come over to his table.'

'And what did you do?'

'I was shit scared, of course, because that kind of thing just doesn't happen. I ran into the kitchen and stood there shaking until they pushed me out with an order. By then he was gone, and everyone was completely . . . because there was a dead dog there.'

'Instead of Jesus?'

'No, for fuck's sake – that's irrelevant. But today he came back. Twice. And I . . .' Maria's whole body tenses and she clutches the arms of the chair, then whispers: 'Marko. What if he's the Devil?'

Marko almost laughs, but successfully reduces the impulse to a strained smile. 'Why is it more likely to be the Devil than Jesus? I mean, I'm not a believer, but I still think Jesus is a considerably more credible figure than the guy with horns and a tail.'

'That's what you think?'

'That's what I think.'

Maria gets up and comes over to the bed. Marko discreetly moves the bottle with his foot, but she takes no notice of his manoeuvre. She sits down beside him and brings up a series of testimonies, images of blurred or glowing figures.

'These people,' she says, waving her hand over the posts, 'are almost always in seriously stressful or hopeless situations when Jesus appears to them. When something terrible has happened, or is about to happen. When they feel like shit. There isn't one single person who was enjoying a cosy Friday evening in front of the TV with the family, and suddenly Jesus is sitting there wanting to know what they're watching. No, it's always . . . when he's really needed. And I don't know, me and my situation . . .'

'So believe,' Marko says.

Maria tears her attention away from the screen and looks Marko in the eye. '*What* did you say?'

'I said *believe*. You did it when you were little, and if it helps to ground you, to find your footing, then why not? Carry on praying and believe in what you see.'

'You don't think I'm crazy?'

'I do, but not because of this.'

Maria laughs and playfully punches his shoulder before turning back to the figure who is saving someone from drowning. Marko strokes her hair and quietly picks up the bottle, then gets to his feet and heads for the door. As he leaves the room he hears Maria whisper to herself: 'There you are . . .'

3

When Marko emerges from Maria's room with the half-full whisky bottle, his parents are in the living room. Laura nods at the bottle and brings her hands together in silent applause. Goran still looks worried. Marko briefly fills them in on Maria's situation, leaving out her visions and explaining that she is going through a minor religious crisis, which makes his parents' expressions lighten.

He puts the bottle on the kitchen worktop and tries to identify an unpleasant, tickling sensation in his stomach – it's as if a fly is buzzing around in there, its wings stroking his abdominal tissue.

Then he works it out. The feeling is hard to define because it is unusual for him, but what he is experiencing is *envy*. Even if there is an element of craziness in Maria's resurgence of belief, Marko envies her because it puts her in contact with her past and makes her more complete. While he is just . . . what is he? He doesn't know, and therein lies the problem.

When he returns to the living room, Goran and Laura are sitting on the sofa talking, their heads close together. Marko's gaze is inevitably drawn to the picture of Jesus on the wall above them. It is hard to imagine this smooth, glowing figure as a regular in Maria's café, but according to her that is what's happening. Marko shakes his head and is about to sit down in an armchair when he catches sight of the key hanging below Jesus. His jaw drops and he stands there staring for so long that Laura asks: 'Marko, what's wrong? Have you seen a ghost?'

No, Marko has seen chickens. Before the family fled from the farm when he was four years old, his favourite place was the little henhouse. Laura has often said that if Marko was nowhere to be found in the house or garden, you could be sure to find him there. There was just enough room for him to stand upright beneath the pitched roof, surrounded by warmth and the quiet clucking of about twenty chickens. He can still hear the sounds, the smells fill his nostrils, he recalls the total security he felt in that henhouse.

He sits down, points to the key. 'The farm. It's still ours, isn't it?'

Goran brings his hands up to his temples then spreads them as if to indicate an exploding head. 'It's nothing but ruins, my son. I've told you before. Blown to pieces, and the henhouse – you remember the henhouse?'

'That's what I was thinking about. I know it's gone – but the land must still be there?'

'Yes,' Laura says. 'If we wish to claim it. No one else is living there, but it's basically worthless. Why do you ask?'

Marko doesn't answer. The henhouse has acted as a catalyst for a chain reaction in the form of a picture reel spooling through his mind. The sun setting behind the hills of Mostar, the cows' moist muzzles, the scent of grass on their breath, the rabbit hutch and the lop rabbit called . . . *Rambo*, that was it. The squeal of the rusty pump in the yard, the flakes of metal that stuck to his palm, the way he could just about lift the bucket. The front door opening, the worn step with a deep gash in it, the smell in the hallway . . .

'Mum,' he says. 'Dad. The house is ready for you to move into at the weekend, if that suits you.'

'Oh dear,' Goran says, waving a hand in the air. 'Sixteen years we've lived here. Don't think we're ungrateful, but it's hard, my boy.'

'I was wondering about that. Have you ever really felt at home here? Is this your home?'

Goran and Laura exchange a look which suggests that at some point, possibly quite recently, they have discussed this.

'There's a good word in Swedish,' Laura says. '*Hemmastadda*. We've made ourselves *hemmastadda* – at home. But no – *home* is that ruin.'

Marko gets up and takes down the key, leaving a darker, key-shaped silhouette on the wallpaper. He holds up the key as if he is about to perform a magic trick. 'This was the front door key, wasn't it?'

'Yes,' Goran replies sadly. 'But there's no lock for it to fit, because there's no door anymore.'

'I'll get a door,' Marko assures him. 'And then I'll ask a locksmith to make a lock that this key will fit.'

'Sounds expensive,' Laura says. 'Don't go spending money on our account. That won't make the place any more like home. We'll hang it on the wall in the new house, just like here. It's better that way.'

Goran nods in agreement, but Marko says: 'You don't under-stand. I mean, a new door and a new lock at our old farm. When it's no longer a ruin.'

Laura realises what he means and looks shocked, while the penny has yet to drop for Goran. He is staring at Marko as if he is still expecting that magic trick. 'How is that possible?'

'Tata, I'm going to go down there. And renovate the place.'

A heated discussion ensues, followed by attempts to dissuade him by raising objections about the size of the project, the cost, the difficulty of finding tradesmen, the lingering ethnic tensions in the area.

Nothing has any effect. Marko has made a decision. As soon as he saw the key, which evoked the henhouse, which in turn triggered the picture reel, he knew that he had found his Jesus, the belief that will enable him to place his feet firmly on the ground and keep them there.

Now the rivalry with Max has come to an end and he has achieved more or less everything he set out to do, it is time to set new goals. In spite of its grand scale, the renovation of the old farm is only one step in a much bigger project. Maybe one day Marko will return to the life he is now living, but for the time being there is something else he has to do. He looks at his parents and summarises it with the simple words: 'I'm going to be a Yugo.'

LET GO

Anna is taking a walk outside the gates of the prison. It is Friday, just before one o'clock, the time of Acke's release. She wants to make sure that no one else is waiting, a person with less peaceful intentions than her. She can't see a soul, and returns to her Golf in the car park, as close to the exit as possible.

She winds down the window so that she will be able to hear if another vehicle arrives, then picks up Johan's novel. She's just over halfway through the three hundred pages, and of the few novels Anna has read in her life, she thinks this is the best.

The portrayal of the boy is heart-rending, and a scene in the council offices where he is met with coldness and a total lack of understanding actually made her cry. During that night on Marko's jetty Johan told her a bit about his mother, and Anna is impressed by the empathy with which he describes her. Insanity as a struggle to make sense of the world.

It isn't purely autobiographical, because there are sections where the boy's fantasies and the mother's delusions come together in a parallel reality called The Area. It is more real than this world, with the critical difference that everything that happens in The Area

600

happens for a reason and has a meaning, while this world comes across as random and empty.

Anna can understand that Johan doesn't want to expose himself to the risk of being – Google has taught her a new word in relation to publishing – *rejected*, but it's such a shame. In her opinion, publishers ought to be fighting over this book. Although what does she know, maybe the story goes off the rails at the end? Only one way to find out.

She reads a few pages. Ten past one; the gate hasn't opened, and no other car has arrived. She checks her phone to see if Acke has texted her, or if the dashboard clock is wrong. No text, and the clock is correct. She sighs. This is the same old crap, the crap she'd sworn to fight her way out of.

Since she decided to go to university in the spring, Anna has carried out an assessment of her life to discover which *team* she belongs to, in *Pokémon* terms. Without giving the matter any thought, she has been part of Team Olofsson until now. The disappointment over her parents' failure to step up and help has made her demand a transfer with immediate effect, even though she doesn't have anywhere to go at the moment.

However, she knows which team she is planning to join, and she calls it the Helping Team. She's going to be one of those people who helps others, thus making the world a slightly better place. It's not a matter of megalomania; she knows that her contribution will consist of making the lives of a few elderly residents a little more bearable in physical terms, but so what? She will do her bit for the team, and she will know why.

Anna puts Johan's novel back in its nylon bag and looks over at the gate. She has no idea what can be done about Acke and the Djup brothers. She was so angry at being let down by her parents that she formulated a crazy plan that involved stealing the gold Stig has hidden away; she knows exactly where it is. She has since dropped that plan – she has no intention of getting involved.

It is now twenty to two, and Anna's extended lunch break only lasts until two. She gets out of the car and goes over to the security post. A woman in the prison service's black uniform points to a microphone in the reinforced glass, and Anna says: 'Hi, I was supposed to be meeting my brother Acke . . . Anders Olofsson. He was due to be released at one o'clock.'

The woman asks to see Anna's ID, then turns to her computer. 'He checked out at eleven,' she says, as if she's talking about a stay in a hotel.

'Are you sure? Why?'

The woman shrugs. 'It says "special reasons" here. That's all I know.'

'Okay. Thanks.'

It's not hard to work out what those special reasons are – the same reasons that made Anna take a good look around when she arrived. But why hasn't Acke sent her a message?

Anna gets back in the car, but freezes before she turns the key in the ignition. The Djup brothers have eyes everywhere, and maybe those eyes were privy to the prison's routines. Maybe they were informed about the change of time, and were standing here waiting at eleven?

Anna sends Acke a text, then tries calling. The signal rings out, but no one answers. She shudders as she pictures Acke's phone ringing next to an injured body that has been taken for 'a little trip'; she hears her little brother's screams as the Djup brothers piss on a back that is a single open wound.

She is so upset that she drives a hundred metres with the handbrake on. Only when the smell of burning rubber penetrates her nostrils does she realise why the car sounds so weird. She releases the brake, takes a deep breath and tightens her grip on the wheel.

Please, God, don't let them have taken him.

The idea of stealing Stig's gold no longer seems quite so crazy.

SCREWED LIKE A PSYCHOPATH

I

It is surprisingly easy for Max to live without Micke Littletroll, at least as long as things are going well and he can follow a routine. Take the newspaper deliveries this morning. The first thing he saw when he picked up his bundle of the local paper was the news filling the entire front page: the man who'd been pushed into the river and died. It had been in the online edition the previous day, but hadn't made it into the print run until Friday.

Max had sat down on a step and read all four pages and looked at the pictures, while a wave of despair rose inside him, with no chainsaw on hand to lop off the top. Eventually he had screwed the paper into a ball and squeezed it, while his body shook uncontrollably in the throes of a panic attack.

If I hadn't gone to the café, if I'd run straight away, if I'd run a bit faster . . .

Incapable of moving, he had stared out into the morning darkness until it took on a physical dimension in the form of an inky liquid that threatened to seep into him. The dead man's final thoughts splashed around in the ink, the stoning of a ten-year-old boy down to the last detail, watched with repulsive enjoyment.

Then Max managed to do something he had never thought possible: he evoked the effect of Lamictal by the power of suggestion. It helped that he had created the image of Micke in the past, so now he visualised the little troll, the whine of the chainsaw, the lopping of his emotions. It made a difference. It wasn't as effective as the drug itself, but enough to get him on his feet and moving.

The paper round itself was fine, because it was the very epitome of the concept *routine*. Pull up on his bike at the door of an apartment block, count out the right number of papers, up the stairs, fold the papers, put them in mailboxes, down the stairs, onto the next. When he'd finished and dawn was beginning to nudge at the horizon, he felt more or less like a normal person.

Home for coffee and a sandwich before he set off for his second job in the park. At this time of year he was mainly occupied pruning trees and shrubs. The finishing touches to the more sensitive trees took place during July, August and September, while cutting back elms and maples that had grown too big was a job for late autumn. Normally there would have been quite a lot of leaf-blowing too, but because the summer had been unusually dry, the trees had begun to drop their leaves back in August. By September their branches were more or less bare.

The next incident happened at about eleven o'clock. After Max had had a go at the shrubs around the bus station with his hedge trimmer, he headed down to Society Park to check if the vandal had been out and about overnight. Some idiot had begun half-felling trees with a chainsaw, and on a number of occasions Max had had no choice but to complete what the idiot had started. Fell, chop, remove.

As he approached the sculpture known as *The Flight Across the Sea*, he could already see that something was wrong. It looked as if pale ribbons had been tied around some of the elms that flanked the memorial to the thousands of people from the Baltic countries who fled across the sea in the autumn of 1944. Max parked his buggy and went to take a closer look.

When he realised what had happened, a wave of anger surged through his body, much more powerful than the despair he'd experienced earlier that morning. The fucking vandal had ring-barked the trees. A paler band about ten centimetres wide encircled three of the trunks where the bark had been cut away. When the crown was prevented from supplying nutrition to the roots, the trees would wither and die of starvation. This would happen within a year or two, and there was absolutely nothing that could be done about it.

Max was so furious that he let out a huge bellow and stamped his feet up and down on the ground, as if he were sprinting in a race without actually moving forward. He boxed in thin air and bellowed again. Out of the corner of his eye he saw an elderly lady with a little dog turn and go back the way she had come.

'Someone's killing the trees!' Max yelled after her. 'What kind of fucking idiot would do that?'

The lady hunched her shoulders and hurried away, dragging the little dog behind her. Max kicked at the plinth on which the sculpture stood, and the pain in his foot cleared his head sufficiently for him to do exactly what he had done earlier: to *pretend* the medication was kicking in. He clenched his fists, lowered his head and focused all his energy on trying to summon up the troll he would prefer to do without.

After a couple of minutes his breathing and pulse had slowed. He unclenched his fists and examined the trees. There was nothing to be done. They would stand here dying for a couple of years until they became a danger to the public, because the root system was no longer capable of supporting them. Given that trees were sentient organisms, this was pure torture.

Max went back to the buggy and fetched his chainsaw. Might as well put them out of their misery now. The vandal had set Max's agenda for the afternoon. When the real saw roared into life it drowned out the remnants of his anger, leaving only sorrow. Max made the first cut.

2

The last tree has been chopped up, the saw sharpened and the buggy returned to the depot. It is five thirty and Max hurries home. He is due for dinner at Siw's at six, and he wants to shower first. As he is passing the florist's he nips in and buys a small bunch of tulips. Tulips might be uninspiring, but lilies are for funerals and roses are too much.

The nervousness comes creeping up on him in the shower, and grows while he is putting on his favourite shirt, pale blue with a floral pattern on the inside of the collar and cuffs. Jeans and a red woollen sweater. He hesitates between his best shoes and the more comfortable Ecco loafers he wears on a daily basis.

Comfortable. Secure. Calm. Cool.

He goes for the loafers. It is eight minutes to six when Max wraps the tulips in an old copy of the local paper, his hands leaving visible sweat marks. He has hardly eaten anything all day, because he wanted to get the trees finished; he's not sure whether the trembling sensation between his stomach and chest is down to hunger or fear.

If it's fear, then what am I afraid of? he asks himself as he hurries out of the door onto Kyrkogatan and jogs down towards the harbour with the tulips dangling at his side.

Because everything he said to Siw up on the hill was true. With her he has felt for the first time since Cuba that there is the possibility of a life with a meaningful forward movement, instead of a stagnant pile-up of the depressing patchwork quilt of almost identical days. He is afraid of messing it up. Of behaving like an idiot. He is afraid that Alva won't like him. He is afraid of everything that can go wrong.

It is five past six when Max reaches the tunnel leading to Siw's place. He has to fight a constant urge to turn around and run back home, and he goes for the same method that Ross used to get Chandler to his wedding to Monica.

Go up to that door there. No problem. Go up one flight of stairs. Cool. Ring the doorbell. You can do this. One step at a time.

The door opens. Siw is wearing tights, a knee-length checked skirt and a white blouse. Before they've even said hello, Max holds out the tulips and says: 'Tulips.'

That's when he understands. He and Siw have been on long walks, they have saved Charlie, they have made love, they have talked on the balcony. They have stood on the hill and looked down on Norrtälje, they have watched a man die in the river and they have hugged in the square. Special moments, some of them magical. And now the time has come for them to *play normal*. Do what people do. This is what Max is afraid he won't be able to achieve. I mean, surely you're not supposed to say 'tulips' as your first word? What are you supposed to say?

Siw smiles at his obvious nervousness, which seems to make her

608

relax. She asks him in, and while he is taking off his shoes, Alva appears in the hallway, points at him and says: 'Aha! So it was you!'

'What was me?'

'The guy – you were the guy!'

'Alva,' Siw says. 'You already knew that. You said Anna told you.'

'Mmm-hmm, but now I can see it with my own eyes!'

Alva is wearing joggers and a T-shirt with a picture of Shaun the Sheep, whose ears are angled downwards, almost exactly matching her own skinny plaits.

'Do you like Shaun?' Max asks.

'Mmm. He's funny. Do you know how to play?'

'Not now, Alva,' Siw says. 'Dinner is almost ready.'

Siw goes into the kitchen and Max hears running water and the rustle of paper as she unwraps the flowers and arranges them in a vase. Alva remains where she is, hands by her sides, preventing Max from passing her. He sits down on a stool and nods at her top. 'Have you seen the one with the Were-Rabbit?'

Alva shakes her head. 'No. But that's not Shaun the Sheep, it's Wallace and Gromit. Your friend is good at playing.'

'My . . . who's that?'

'Johan. He is your friend, isn't he?'

Max resists the urge to shake his head at Alva's strange assertion, and instead nods before asking: 'How do you know Johan is good at playing?'

'He was here. He played with me. He has a very good imagination. How about you?'

Max is rescued by Siw, who emerges from the kitchen wiping her hands on a towel. 'Anna looked after Alva when you and I met up. And she invited Johan over.'

609

'She did,' Alva confirms. 'He told me the story of the Monkey and the Spanner. Do you know it?'

Max hasn't spoken to Johan for a couple of days. Clearly a long race has been run since the raid by Wind Thingie, when Johan claimed that Anna hated and despised him, and insisted that he didn't care. A marathon at least. Alva manages to get through half the story about the monkey and the spanner before it is time to eat, and she quickly fast-forwards to the bit where you find out that the monkey was actually Mr Nilsson.

Siw has made fish stew with saffron. Alva eats the fish, but pushes aside the prawns, which judging by their size were bought individually. She states firmly that they are, in fact, the wrong size, and therefore not *real* prawns.

'So what size are real prawns?' Max asks tentatively.

Alva shows him using her index finger and thumb, then asks what Max's job is. He tells her about the newspaper deliveries and his work with the trees, hoping that Alva won't show an interest in the vandal who is going around ring-barking. She really wants to hear about his buggy, and there isn't much to say on that score. She gazes at him thoughtfully, and Max suspects that he is being compared with Johan and found wanting.

'You work a *lot*,' Alva informs him.

'I suppose I do.' Max feels that there's a *you're boring* in there somewhere. His shirt collar is starting to feel rather tight, and he can't help running his finger around it in a giveaway gesture.

Siw notices his discomfort. 'Okay, Alva, enough with the interrogation. You need to let me and Max have a chat too.'

'Just one more thing,' Alva says. 'What *else* do you do? When you're not working?'

Max searches through his meagre leisure pursuits, trying to

find something that will capture her interest. 'I play *Pokémon Go*, which—'

'I know,' Alva interrupts him. 'So does Mummy. *All the time.*'

'Right. Er . . . I've got a Switch that I—'

It's like pressing a button. Alva gives a start and leaps out of her chair, eyes wide. 'You've got a *Switch*?'

Max is confused; he glances at Siw who rolls her eyes, then nods encouragingly.

'What games have you got?' Alva asks after Siw has made her sit down again.

'At the moment I'm playing . . . I'm not sure if you know it, but it's called *Kingdom Battle* and—'

'The Rabbids!' Alva exclaims. 'Oh, the Rabbids! And Mario!'

'Exactly. You have to . . .'

Max outlines the background story, how the Mushroom Kingdom is invaded by the irreverent Rabbids, and how you have to combat them through a series of different worlds. Alva hangs on his every word as if he were a prophet speaking the One Truth. It feels a bit like cheating, but Max's shirt collar has stopped chafing, and he has been given a breathing space where he can hopefully prove that he *is* worth hanging on the Christmas tree, even if he doesn't have Johan's imagination.

He ends by saying: 'If it's okay with your mum, then maybe I could bring it with me sometime so you can try it out.'

A pang of guilt. If telling her about the Raving Rabbids felt like cheating, then this is more like buying Alva's affections through technology, since he doesn't have a personality to offer.

But I have. I just need a little time.

Alva is, of course, ecstatic at the suggestion, and Siw agrees as long as she doesn't start nagging about having a Switch of her own any more than she already does. Alva promises that this will definitely not be the case, and the atmosphere around the table has turned in Max's favour when the doorbell rings.

3

Christmas magazines, Siw thinks as she excuses herself from the table, where Alva is continuing her cross-examination on the subject of Nintendo. She wishes that Max and her daughter could have bonded over something other than video games, but it's good that they've found common ground, and that there may be more to come in the future. Because there is a future, Siw is increasingly convinced of that. The very fact that Max found the courage to come here in spite of his unmistakable anxiety shows that he is willing to make the effort.

In the hallway she begins to wonder whether sex might be on the cards once Alva has fallen asleep. It feels a bit embarrassing, or even dirty, but she has to try to get used to such considerations if she and Max are going to be a proper couple. Alva's presence is a fact, and she and Max can't limit their sexual activity to the times when they are alone. They are going to have to deal with the situation.

Siw unlocks the door. She usually buys something from the first child who comes calling, and this year she is thinking of a calendar for herself and a Bamse the Bear annual for Alva. She smiles warmly and opens the door.

The smile freezes. Acke is standing there. If Max was anxious, then Anna's kid brother is on another planet. The hood of his black top is pulled right up, and his dilated pupils are darting jerkily from side to side while his fingers twist and turn around one another as if he were rolling snot balls with both hands.

'Hi,' he says, pushing his way in without waiting for an invitation.

'What are you doing?' Siw hisses. 'You can't just—'

'Shut the fuck up. Close the door. Lock it.'

'No. You need to leave.'

'Not happening.' Acke continues into the apartment without taking off his shoes. 'Seriously. Lock the door. There are people who . . .' His voice softens a fraction. 'I mean it. Lock the door.'

Siw listens, but she can't hear anyone in the stairwell. She doesn't know what to do. Should she run out into the street, call the police, shout for help? She had forgotten that Acke was due to be released today, but she could never have imagined that . . .

Call Anna.

That's the only possible solution. Anna will have to come and take care of her kid brother, who is clearly under the influence. Dilated pupils – does that mean heroin or amphetamines? Siw can't remember, and does it really matter? A drug addict is in the same apartment as her daughter. Before she has time to do anything, she hears Acke's voice from the kitchen: 'Well, isn't this a cosy little family gathering.'

Siw walks into the room just as Alva asks: 'Who are you?' Acke gives Siw a cunning look. 'Hasn't your mum told you?'

'Alva, go to your room.' When her daughter doesn't react immediately, Siw grabs her arm, which makes Alva whimper. Siw gives her a push. 'Alva, go to your room now. And lock the door.'

Maybe it's the last sentence that finds its mark and makes Alva realise that this is serious. Looking frightened, she runs to her room and Siw hears the key turn. Acke grins. 'What's wrong, did you think I was going to—'

'I didn't think anything. You need to leave.'

Acke sinks down on the chair that Alva has vacated. His fingers are still twisting, and now his feet are drumming on the floor.

Max stands up and leans across the table. 'Didn't you hear what she said? She wants you to leave.'

Acke jerks a shaking thumb at Max. 'Listen to him! Is this the man of the house, or what? Do you know who I am?'

'I don't give a fuck who you are. Siw doesn't want you here, and that's enough for me.'

Acke points towards Alva's room, where Siw assumes Alva has her ear pressed to the keyhole. She just manages to close the kitchen door before Acke says: 'I'm the kid's father, so I don't need your permission to be here, you fucking wimp.' Max looks enquiringly at Siw. She lowers her eyes, and Acke lets out a croak of laughter. He smacks his lips and says: 'Give me some water. Mouth's as dry as a badger's arse.'

Max moves around the table. Acke pushes one hand into the pocket of his hoodie just as Siw gets a Hearing. The sound of something that must be a knife being driven into flesh, Max screaming in pain. Clearly Max's visions don't extend to himself, because he stands in front of Acke, arms folded across his chest. His voice is far from steady as he says: 'Get out of here now.'

'And if I don't? Who's going to make me? You?'

Rigid with fear, Siw stares at Acke's pocket. It could happen in two seconds or a minute or an hour. An hour seems unlikely. What was it Max said?

You can change things, but I can't.

'Max,' she says firmly. 'Acke is right – I need to talk to him. I'd like you to leave.'

Max's lips twitch. '*Me?* But you said—'

614

'Forget what I said. Go. I don't want you here.'

The hurt look in Max's eyes is a blade that cuts Siw's heart to pieces. Acke's foot-drumming intensifies and his hand remains in his pocket. His expression is repulsively triumphant. 'You heard what she said. Off you pop and let the grown-ups have a little chat.'

Max clamps his trembling lips together and spreads his hands. He is about to speak, but simply turns his back on Acke and heads for the hallway. Acke manages to deliver a kick to Max's backside that makes him wobble. Siw grabs his shoulder and says quietly: 'Max, it's—'

Max shakes off her hand and picks up his shoes. When Siw follows him, Acke snaps: 'You stay right where you are. No whispering and conspiring out there. Or shall I go and have a word with my little girl in the meantime?'

Siw's shoulders slump and she returns to the kitchen with her bleeding heart pounding and squelching in her chest. Acke points to the tap. 'What happened to the water? I'm dying of thirst here.'

While Siw is filling a glass she hears the front door open and close. Slam. Acke knocks back the water in one, wipes his mouth with the back of his hand then says: 'Lock. The front door.'

Within minutes Siw has become a slave in her own home. She does exactly as she's been told. She looks at the spot where Max's shoes were, hears him say 'tulips' as he clumsily slipped into her life. She lets out a sob. She must be able to sort this out, once she has the chance to explain.

Call Anna.

Yes, but her phone is on the kitchen worktop, and Acke is hardly likely to let her call anyone. When she returns to the kitchen, for the first time she fears for her own safety and that of her daughter. Even without whatever is currently stimulating his central nervous

615

system Acke is volatile, and at the moment he should probably be regarded as a wild animal whose next move is totally unpredictable.

Therefore, in spite of everything, it comes as a relief when he points to the chair next to him. 'Sit down. Sorry if I was a bit harsh back there, but I'm in a real mess.' He takes his hand out of his pocket and pours himself a glass of wine, which disappears as quickly as the water.

Siw perches on the edge of the chair and waits. Acke frantically rubs his eyes, scratches his head. He's put on several kilos of muscle since Siw last saw him, but still looks terrible with his sunken cheeks and dark circles under his eyes.

'I'm in deep shit,' he goes on. 'The short version is that if I can't come up with three hundred thousand, I'm fucked.'

'Right.'

'*Right*, you say. You don't get it. This is serious – deep, deep shit, and totally fucked. Do you know the Djup brothers?'

'Anna's mentioned them.'

'Has she now? Did she tell you what they do to people who can't pay their debts?'

'I don't think so.'

'No, because if she had, you'd remember, believe me. I need three hundred thousand and I need it now.'

'Acke, I don't have that kind of money.'

Acke makes a circular movement above his head with his index finger. 'This apartment – what's it worth? One and a half million? Two? You must be able to take out a loan against it.'

For the first time since Acke arrived, Siw's fear and despair gives way to a healthy dose of outrage. 'You come marching in here, kick out my friend, frighten my daughter, and now you want me to borrow three hundred thousand kronor to—'

616

Acke holds up his hand to stop her. '*Our* daughter, let me remind you.'

Siw is so taken aback that she finds it difficult to formulate a sentence. 'You have never, not for one second have you ever . . . you've never given her a thought, have you?'

'Well, no,' Acke admits. 'But maybe I should start? Engage with her. What is it they say? Be present in her life.'

'Is that a threat?'

'Take it however you want, but I need that money.'

Siw gets up, goes over to the worktop and picks up her phone. 'I'm calling Anna. Or maybe I should call the police?'

Acke runs a hand over his face; he suddenly looks exhausted. He slowly stands up. 'Call whoever the fuck you like. But think it over, Siw. I need that money, and . . .' Acke sighs, shuffles uncomfortably. 'Okay, let's try it this way: Please? I'm begging you.'

Siw selects Anna's name from her contacts list. As the signal rings out, Acke adds: 'I'm going now. But I'll be back. If you want to take that as a threat, then be my guest.'

Siw follows him into the hallway and cancels the unanswered call. Acke unlocks the door and steps out into the stairwell. Before closing the door behind him, he says: 'Nice kid, by the way.'

4

'Mummy, who *was* that? He was horrible.'

Siw is on her knees outside Alva's room with her daughter in her arms. Alva is hugging Siw with one arm and Poffe with the other. If Siw had ever considered telling Alva the truth, any such thoughts have just gone out of the window. Better a daddy in heaven who

617

throws down a cuddly fox toy than the 'horrible' figure who has just been sitting in her kitchen.

'Acke. He's Anna's little brother.'

'*Our* Anna?'

'Yes. Our Anna.'

'He can't be her little brother – he was big and horrible.'

'Well, he is.'

'But why was he here?'

'Because . . . he wanted to borrow some money.'

'Did you let him?'

'No.'

'No, because we haven't got any money. Not much, anyway. Not enough to afford . . .' Alva clamps her lips shut to prevent the word she is thinking of from escaping, then glances towards the kitchen. 'Where's Max?'

'He left.'

'Is he coming back? With . . . the Switch?'

'I hope so. I just need to . . .'

Alva's body has stiffened now that her immediate need for solace has been met. Siw lets her go, takes out her phone and clicks on 'Max'. She writes:

Sorry about what happened. I had a Hearing. Something terrible would have happened to you if I hadn't made you leave. I had no choice. Call me.

A few seconds later her phone rings. Siw's heart leaps, but the display shows 'Anna'.

When Siw answers, Anna says: 'Hi, I was in the shower. I thought you were spending the evening with Max.'

'I was, but . . . Acke showed up.'

'Acke? At your place? Why?'

618

'He wanted money. Three hundred thousand.'

Alva opens her eyes wide and mouths: WHAT? THREE. HUN-DRED. THOUSAND?

'From *you*?'

'Yes.'

'But . . . but . . .'

Siw feels as if she's trapped in a corner, and wishes she'd told the truth long ago. However, this is not the time, with Alva right beside her and her heart in bits. She feels a physical pain in her chest, and she is finding it hard to breathe. *Is there something wrong with me? For real?*

'I just thought I'd let you know.'

'Fuck. I'm so sorry, Siw.'

'It's not your fault.'

'I've been looking for him, he's . . . it's not good if he's out and about, I think they're watching him.'

'The Djup brothers?'

'Yes.'

Siw shakes her head. 'But didn't they . . . that song, "We Live in the Country", some farmers who . . . weren't they the Djup Brothers? It sounds a bit ridiculous.'

'Trust me, Siw – these guys are anything but ridiculous. Did Acke say where he was going?'

'No.'

'Fuck. Oh well, at least it's not your problem. I'd better . . . Speak soon, hun.'

Siw ends the call and listens to Alva's outraged exclamations on the astronomical sum. She can see something of Acke's pointed features in her face, the shape of her eyes when she narrows them. A part of him is an ineradicable part of her.

Not my problem? If only that were true.

619

5

When Acke gets to the bottom of the stairs, he peers out through the glass in the main door. It is hard to see anything with the stairwell light on, and he sinks down with his back to the wall and his head in his hands.

Going to see Siw had been an impulsive act born out of desperation, after he'd tried everything else. He has spent the day hiding in Anna's storage facility in the basement; he has keys, because she has allowed him to stash a few bits and pieces there. He's called everyone who might be able to help him, and been given the cold shoulder. They all know his situation.

Acke lowers his head, the ligaments at the back of his neck crunching. The speed he took to help him pluck up courage is still swirling around in his body, turning his bloodstream into ant runs where thousands of eager little feet are scampering up and down, preventing him from collapsing in a state of apathetic terror. He will need more very soon, somehow. Preferably enough so that he can overdose and escape the whole shitty mess, but he's never heard of anyone snorting themselves to death on speed, which means he'd need to inject and that's a line he hasn't crossed yet, but if he got hold of some heroin . . .

His thoughts are spinning, keeping pace with his fizzing blood, and his fingers are drumming on his knees. He isn't proud of what he did to Siw, or the fact that he frightened the kid, but neither is he ashamed of himself. There's no room for shame in his current predicament; it's simply a matter of survival.

He had found out what was expected of him on release while he was still behind bars, and had been given a foretaste to make things clear. He still has bruises on his back following an attack in the shower, when he was beaten with bars of soap wrapped in a towel, and his left thumb is just about usable after being trapped in a vice in the workshop.

Acke has said it hundreds of times by now: he has no idea what happened to those two kilos. They disappeared somewhere between the purchase in Hamburg and customs in Trelleborg, and the most likely scenario is that the seller conned him. Once the deal was done he offered Acke a really good spliff, and somewhere in the fog that followed he must have taken back two packets, and by the time Acke left he was too out of it to notice.

He grinds his teeth and indulges in one of his many fantasies detailing what he would do if he got hold of that German arsehole who called himself Klaus. When Klaus is hanging upside down from a metal swing frame, having been whipped into submission, the stairwell light goes out. Any sudden change makes Acke jerk into life. He is on his feet in a second, peering out into the darkness. Nothing.

The plan right now is to go back to Anna's. He would never take the risk if the basement didn't have a separate entrance at the back of the building. He can spend the night there and hope that tomorrow brings a better idea, or a softening on Siw's part. He doesn't have much faith in either option, but what else can he do?

Pointlessly hunching over, Acke slips out of the door and tries to stay in the shadows as he turns left and enters the tunnel leading out of the courtyard. He is halfway along when a tall, bulky figure steps out, silhouetted against the lights of Flygaregatan. Acke's lungs contract and the air is pushed out of him in a squeak. He can't tell if it's Ewert or Albert, but it's definitely one of them. The brothers rarely do their own dirty work, so they must regard Acke as a particularly sore point.

Acke doesn't think any of these things. He doesn't think anything. As soon as that familiar shape appears, there is only blackness inside his head. Acke squeaks, turns and runs. After three steps he cannons into an equally tall, bulky figure, barely visible in the gloom.

'Dearie me,' says Albert Djup, slapping Acke across the ear with his enormous palm. A shrill ringing noise fills Acke's head and he staggers sideways and leans on the wall to stop himself from falling. He gropes for the knife in his pocket, but maybe the blow has upset the nerves in his ear that control balance, because he is suddenly overcome by a feeling like seasickness, and throws up over his trainers.

Albert lets him finish before he grabs Acke's hood, yanks his head back and delivers another blow that numbs half of Acke's head.

'Fear not, for the Lord is at hand,' Ewert intones. A handkerchief wipes the vomit from Acke's lips before being pushed into his mouth. There is a ripping sound and a length of duct tape is wound twice around his head. Acke is dizzy, barely aware of what is happening. He gulps, swallows and tries not to throw up into the handkerchief and possibly choke.

Albert holds on to him, removes the knife from Acke's pocket and slips it into his own. Another ripping sound, and Acke's feet are bound together as if he were standing to attention. Next, his hands are secured with cable ties. Ewert looks him up and down and nods.

'Ready to go,' he says before setting off, leaving Acke alone with Albert, who distractedly picks his nose while humming a tune that Acke vaguely recognises. His heart is pounding so hard it must surely be visible, like a clenched fist punching from the inside of his chest. His legs have turned to jelly, and he is only standing up because Albert is holding him under one arm.

Acke says: 'Mmmfff,' and Albert replies: 'Shut the fuck up.'

The sound of an engine, a car reversing up to the tunnel's entrance. A Volvo 740. The jelly turns to liquid and Acke almost manages to collapse, but Albert tightens his grip and says: 'Time for a little trip.' He picks Acke up in his arms as if he were a small child, carries him to the car and drops him in the boot.

'Nightie night,' Albert says, slamming the lid. Everything goes black.

6

Acke lies there in the darkness. He can hear the clink of metal objects around him; he can smell oil and 5-56. His attitude to throwing up has changed. He tells himself to do it, in the hope that he will choke and avoid what is to come. He achieves nothing more than a spurt of sour bile that shoots down his nose.

He cries. He shits himself. He bangs his head against the metal floor of the boot in the hope of knocking himself out. He howls in despair and shits himself again.

He doesn't know how long the drive lasts, he is in that timeless space where pure fear lives, but at some point the sound of the engine changes and the car slows down. The tyres crunch over gravel. The engine is switched off with a final shudder. Heavy footsteps, the boot is opened.

Ewert Djup is standing there. He bends down towards Acke, but stops dead and waves his hand in front of his nose. 'Jesus Christ, what a stench!'

'Don't you remember?' Albert says. 'Used to be pretty standard.'

'Now you come to mention it . . .' Ewert clicks his fingers. 'Of course! We always put down newspapers!'

Albert tuts sympathetically. 'The trouble is, we've got rusty.'

'Yes, but then it's a while since someone tried to put one over on us.'

'True. Very true.'

Acke shakes his head, tries to protest, *I didn't, I'd never dream of, I can explain*, but all that can be heard are muffled grunts, and his inability to communicate makes fresh tears flow. The brothers heave him out of the boot and chain his bound hands to the towbar, his face looking up at the starless night sky.

Please God, just let me die.

'Okay,' Ewert says, studying Acke. 'Time to go. Coming along for the ride?' He grins at his own joke, and is on his way to the driver's seat when Albert says: 'Aren't you forgetting something?'

Ewert clicks his fingers again. A button is pressed, there is a hissing sound, then a lively melody played on the accordion before a group of men start singing about living in the country and buying a horse.

The car starts, the engine roars. The exhaust pipe blows out smoke right next to Acke's head, but he can't smell any fumes thanks to the stench of vomit that still fills his nostrils. He stares up at the sky, tries to make his consciousness become one with the darkness. Detach. Disappear. He doesn't succeed. And so they are off, while the namesakes of the brothers Djup continue to sing about their rural concerns; now they are buying a cow.

Acke groans as sharp gravel tears his skin. He pushes his feet down hard and arches his back. The car accelerates. The soles of his shoes bounce over the uneven surface and gravel chips hit the back of his neck as he tenses his stomach muscles to the utmost in an effort to keep his bottom and back off the ground.

The car veers to the right and Acke's legs jerk sideways. The ties securing his wrists pinch as he is thrown off balance, and he whimpers in pain as his right hip is dragged across the sharp gravel for a few seconds before he manages to lift himself again. A veer to the left, and the other hip gets the same treatment. He feels warm blood trickling across his stomach.

How long? How long can I hold out?

If Acke was in any way capable of reflecting on his situation, he might feel a paradoxical relief that the fear is gone for the moment, replaced by sheer survival instinct. The only thing that matters is to retain control of his feet, to keep his stomach muscles sufficiently tensed. The tens of thousands of sit-ups he has done in the gym and in his cell will help, thank you very much, but before long those muscles feel like a single taut string that is bound to break.

The Djup Brothers have moved on to the purchase of a pig.

Sweat is pouring over Acke's body, and his backside is slowly, relentlessly dropping towards the unforgiving gravel. He can also feel it on his feet. His shoes have been worn down, and soon his bare soles will be exposed to the stones.

Snot flies out of his nose and he grunts and pushes himself upwards for one last time, his muscles screaming with pain. He manages a few centimetres, but can't hold his position. He can hear the fabric of his jeans scraping across the ground. He is just about to give up and let himself be shredded when the car slows and stops.

The singing farmers have now moved on to imitating all the animals they have acquired. Then the song comes to an end, the engine is switched off, and the car door opens. Acke hangs helplessly from the towbar, with sweat pouring into his eyes. Ewert appears, puts his hands on his hips and nods.

'You did well there,' he says, unhooking Acke's hands. 'Although I think you might need some new shoes.'

Is it over? Have I survived?

Ewert grabs hold of Acke's legs, swings him around and attaches his feet to the towbar. He nods pensively. 'Although the second round is worse, of course.'

Acke screams beneath the tape as he pictures the *second round*. No possibility of escaping the gravel, just the inevitable progression to a torn, bloody mess. He screams and screams. Ewert puts one hand behind his ear, frowns and calls out to Albert: 'Can you make out what he's saying?'

'Same old, same old, I imagine.'

'I expect you're right. But let's check.'

Ewert inserts his fingers under the duct tape and his long nails scratch Acke's lips as the strip of tape is pulled down. Acke gasps for breath, and can't form a single word.

'Did you want to say something?' Ewert asks. 'Or shall we get going?'

'No, no, no,' Acke pants. 'It wasn't me, you have to believe me, I was conned, I . . .'

Ewert sighs. 'We've heard it all before. If there's nothing else, then—'

'I'll do anything,' Acke says. 'Anything. Anything you want, as long as you let me go.'

Ewert looks at Albert, then at Acke. He crouches down so that his knees are level with Acke's head, and leans forward. 'Anything?'

'Yes, yes, yes. Anything.'

There is a click as Albert opens Acke's flick knife and slices through the tape securing his feet, which drop to the ground with a dull thud. 'Well then,' Ewert says. 'We'd better see what we can come up with.'

Siw stares at the beautifully laid table, the half-eaten dinner. There is something deeply depressing about the sight, because it is her hopes and dreams that lie there, exposed and abandoned in the glow of the candlelight. She can't bring herself to clear away and wash up, because she is still clinging to the tiniest spark of hope that Max will come back, so dinner can sit there going cold, a monument to failure.

Acke. Fucking Acke.

Why did he have to choose tonight to show up and ruin everything? Siw would have been happy to see him behind bars for life. She has never told him that Alva is his daughter, but no doubt he has done his sums, and there are certain likenesses. If nothing else, then Siw's behaviour this evening must have confirmed his suspicions.

Fucking Acke.

Is she going to have to deal with him from now on? Since he attacked her, she has done her best to exclude him from her thoughts. If it weren't for Alva's constant questions, Siw might be able to regard her daughter as the result of a virgin birth. Now that has become even more impossible. The bastard is out and about.

Hot tears prick Siw's eyes as she impotently shakes her fists at the table. She wishes Acke would disappear from the surface of the earth, and indulges in a fantasy where she lures him to Society Park and watches him vanish into a sinkhole. Slurp, slurp, problem solved. As she is visualising Acke's fingers scrabbling for purchase, her phone rings. The display shows 'Max'. She swallows her tears, clears her throat and answers.

'Hi,' Max says in a neutral tone. 'I got your text.'

'I just wanted to . . . I'm so sorry about how things turned out, but I heard . . . You would have been stabbed.'

'I get it, of course I do. Was it true, what he said about Alva?'

Siw takes a deep breath. She has never actually told anyone what happened. It requires a considerable effort on her part to grab those scrabbling fingers and drag Acke up out of the sinkhole so that everyone can see him. She lowers her voice to a whisper. 'Yes. He raped me.'

Max inhales sharply. 'I'm so sorry, Siw.'

'Don't be. I got Alva. The problem is that I got him too. Can't you come over?'

There is a silence on the other end of the line, and Siw holds her breath. If only she could *cut* Acke's appearance. Regard it as an unnecessary and barely credible scene that doesn't even belong in the 'extras' section. Pick up the threads where they left off.

'To be honest . . .' Max says, and Siw squeezes her eyes tight shut. Nothing good can come of a sentence that begins with *To be honest*, and her fears are confirmed when Max goes on: '. . . I don't think I can. You know how I feel about you and everything that entails, but the way things are now I've stopped taking my medication . . .' Max's voice breaks as he concludes: '. . . I just can't do it.'

'Please? Can't you try?'

Siw can hear the suppressed tears when Max replies. 'I daren't. It's too messy. I'm afraid I'll say or do something that . . . I don't trust myself. Too chaotic. I'm really sorry, Siw. About everything. We'll sort this out, but . . . not now. Goodnight. Bye.'

Max ends the call. Siw stares at the display; his name flashes and is gone. A blank, black screen that reflects only her own face, terrifyingly lit from below by the candles. Feeling numb, she puts down the phone and begins to clear the table. A sinkhole opens up in her chest, and her longing screams as it is dragged down into the depths.

She scrapes fish stew into the compost bag. She rinses the plates and stacks them in the dishwasher. She is busy transferring the remainder of the stew into a plastic box when Alva comes into the kitchen.

'Why are you crying, Mummy?'

'I'm a bit upset.'

'Because Max left?'

'Yes. Among other things.'

Alva goes up to Siw and rests her head against her mother's waist. Siw puts down the spoon and strokes her hair. Alva places her hand on Siw's and says: 'He'll be back.'

'Do you think so?'

'Mmm. Have you kissed?'

'Yes.'

'Then he'll definitely be back. With the Switch.'

THE SOUND OF A CAR CRASH

|

'Boomshakalaka!'

Marko makes a 'clean sweep' gesture with his right arm while the screen above his head shows an animation of pirates firing a cannon ball and clearing a deck of pins, as the word 'Strike!' appears. This is his first strike on his ninth throw. Three of his balls went straight into the gutter, and he is hopelessly behind. But a strike is still a strike.

Max picks up his ball. Marko goes over to Johan, who gives him a high five and says: 'Nice. You're on the way. How did the move go?'

'Lots of carrying and even more sighing, but at least they're in now, and so is Maria. Not that she helped much; she spent most of her time complaining. I don't know what's wrong with her.'

'So, are you going back to Stockholm now?'

Marko scratches the back of his neck and glances at Max, who raises the ball to his chin. 'I'll tell you later.'

Max takes two fluid steps forward, swinging the ball backwards at his side before sending it away with a slight screw. It looks as if it's going to be perfect, but it leaves two wobbling pins standing.

'Rubbish!' Marko yells. 'That's not how to do it!'

It is Sunday and Marko has finally been persuaded to play. In spite of his rude comments, he is seventy-five points behind Max and one hundred and thirty behind Johan, who has missed a strike only twice. Johan offered to play with his left hand, but Marko turned him down on the basis that then it would be even more galling to lose.

After Max has knocked down the remaining pins for a spare, Johan bowls his ball, which appears to meet no resistance whatsoever, giving him his seventh strike. Marko doesn't look happy, but can't help smiling when Johan points to the animation and says: '*Hörövarhepp.* The pirate ship.'

Marko picks up his ball. 'You remember.'

'Of course. It's probably the funniest thing you've ever said.'

'Okay. Watch this – time for the killer blow.'

Marko's 'killer blow' consists of hurling the ball in a straight line with all his strength. If the pins had been the old type with a wooden core, they might have been damaged by the projectile, but the new ones are solid plastic and can stand the pressure. Unless they're pulverised.

Johan pulls a face as Marko's ball hurtles through the air two metres above the lane, landing with a crash that shakes the floor before continuing its journey towards the pins. It veers sideways, touches the outermost pin without knocking it down, and finally lands in the pit with a thud.

'Cock,' Marko says, causing a flutter in Johan's chest. The expression makes him think of Anna, who hasn't yet said anything about his novel. This means he is living in a constant state of mild panic.

They end the game and Johan fetches three beers from the fridge. They sit down at a table and clink bottles. 'Crap game,' Marko says, not unexpectedly. He takes a swig then turns to Max. 'So, how did it go with Siw on Friday?'

It is surprising that Marko agreed to play, and even more surprising that he is taking his comprehensive loss so equably. Something has happened to him since the round of minigolf. Max sighs and runs his finger around the top of the bottle. 'You could say it went . . . a bit wrong.'

'In what way?'

'I can't talk about it – it's to do with Siw's background, so it's up to her to . . . But it's a bit . . . diff . . . ah!'

Max's face crumples and he puts his right hand on his heart, squeezes hard. His legs stiffen and his head is thrown back as he makes a terrible groaning noise.

'Shit,' Marko says. 'Is it that bad?'

Johan leaps to his feet and grabs hold of Max's shoulders to prevent him from sliding to the floor. The attack is short-lived, and after only a few seconds Johan feels Max's muscles soften. His eyes begin to focus once more.

'Did you see something?' Johan asks.

'Yes.' Max coughs. 'I got shot. Well, someone got shot.'

'Where?'

'Here. In the heart.'

'No, I mean where – in town?'

'Down near Broddsten, what's it called – Zettersten Park. The path by the river.'

Marko takes out his phone. 'Shall I call the police?'

'No. I'm pretty sure there were people nearby.'

'So, who fired the shot?'

632

'I've no idea. It's quite a long way from here, so it's . . . unclear. The whole thing. But someone got shot. With a pistol.' Max waves a hand wearily in front of his face. 'Forget it. I can't deal with it right now.' He takes a swig of his beer, and Johan and Marko do the same.

They sit in silence for a while, then Marko says: 'Shit, have people starting shooting one another now? What's happening to this town?'

'Seriously, Marko,' Max says. 'Not now. There's so much crap going on and I . . . I just can't deal with it. Not now.'

'Okay. In that case, I've got something to tell you. Johan asked if I was going back to Stockholm, and I'm not. I've booked a flight to Sarajevo on Wednesday.'

'Sarajevo?' Johan repeats. 'In Bosnia?'

'I hope so, otherwise I've made a big mistake.'

'What are you going to do there?'

Marko interlaces his fingers, stiff from bowling, then straightens them out with an audible crack that makes Max wince. 'The thing is, I'm fed up of trying to be a Swede. I'm so well integrated that it makes me want to throw up.'

'I'd say you *are* a Swede by this stage,' Johan says.

'Not entirely. There's something that . . . anyway, I've decided to try to become a little . . . unintegrated, if such a word exists. Go back to my roots, all that stuff. I'm going to see what's become of our farm, find out if there's anything I can do.'

'Wow,' Johan says. 'But can you still speak . . . what is it? Serbo Croat? Bosnian?'

'*Naravno.* Of course. A couple of weeks down there and I'll be a full-on Yugo.'

'Cheers to that,' Max says, clinking his bottle against Marko's.

'*Živjeli. Živjeli*, brother.'

2

An angel or a devil poked its nose out and beckoned *him. 'Come.'*

Anna puts down the last page of Johan's novel and remains sitting on the sofa for a long time. She once saw a novel described as 'affecting' and didn't really get what that meant – after all, it's just a story, letters on paper. Now she understands, because that is exactly what Johan's narrative has done: it has affected her, just as one is affected by illness or misfortune, which is exactly what the novel is about.

The amazing aspect, which has sometimes made Anna put down the text and simply breathe, is how these everyday or exceptional torments are elevated to something magnificent or especially meaningful when they are seen in the light of The Area. A psychotic episode with a fire extinguisher becomes a heroic battle against the shadow creatures known as Krav, which threaten to swallow up both the boy and his mother.

The New Testament.

Yes, there are similarities. The elevation of a revolutionary's painful death on the cross to a greater narrative about humanity's struggle to raise itself above its earthly restrictions and find salvation.

Anna doesn't quite express herself that way, because she isn't exactly steeped in the Bible, but she feels that reading the story has given her something more than just following an exciting tale. It's as if she has had a spiritual experience, as if she has been immersed in something much greater than letters on paper. Maybe it helps that the action takes place in Norrtälje, so she is able to follow the boy every step of the way.

Her blood is fizzing, she can't settle. She picks up her cigarettes and lighter and goes out onto the balcony to calm her euphoric restlessness with nicotine. She has just lit up when she sees a familiar figure striding towards the apartment block.

'Acke! What the fuck!'

The sound of her voice makes Acke jump as if he has been caught out doing something really bad. He looks up and raises his hand. 'Hi, sis.'

'What are you doing here?'

'Coming to see you, of course.'

'Why are you coming from the back of the building?'

Acke shrugs. 'I just am.'

'You'd better come up. Idiot.'

Anna takes a long drag of her cigarette, then stubs it out. The reason for Acke's unusual approach is presumably because he's afraid the main entrance is being watched. *Let's hope it isn't*, she thinks. *Otherwise that might be the last I see of him.*

She pushes Johan's novel under the sofa cushions before opening the door. She hears footsteps on the stairs, so clearly Acke hasn't been kidnapped en route. *And relax.*

If she hadn't visited Acke so often in jail, she would hardly have recognised him. The figure that comes plodding up the stairs is many kilos of muscle heavier than the normal guy who went in, and is even harder to link to the overenergetic, skinny kid who ran round and round a pole pretending to be a planet.

Anna waits on the landing with her arms folded. Acke gives her a crooked smile and opens his embrace. 'Do I get a hug?'

Anna shakes her head and goes back into her apartment with Acke trailing behind.

'Are you mad at me?' he asks as he kicks off his shoes.

635

'What the fuck was all that business with Siw? Why did you go to see her?'

'Oh, that. I was a bit stressed.' Acke goes into the kitchen and sits down. 'Have you got a beer or something?'

Anna opens the fridge and gets out a can of Falcon Bayerskt, which she slams onto the table in front of her brother before taking the chair opposite him and nailing him with her gaze. Acke opens the can with exaggerated slowness, has a gulp or two, grunts with satisfaction and wipes his mouth with the back of his hand.

Anna doesn't understand. Acke is sitting here as cool as a cucumber; he didn't even lock the front door behind him. None of this makes sense.

'You were *a bit stressed*?'

'Mmm.'

'But you're not stressed anymore?'

'No. I'm not stressed anymore.'

'Why not?'

'Things have sorted themselves out.'

'What things?'

'Just things.'

Acke nods as if to underline the veracity of his statement and takes another swig. Anna is far from satisfied. 'So Ewert Djup showed up and threatened me . . .'

'Oh – sorry about that.'

'. . . and as far as I could make out, you were going to be in a hell of a lot of trouble if you couldn't come up with the money he thinks you owe him.'

'True.'

'So? Have you done it?'

'Done what?'

'For fuck's sake, Acke! Have you paid him the three hundred thousand?'

'Kind of.'

'What do you mean, kind of?'

'We've . . . worked out a payment plan.'

'A . . . I've never heard of the Djup brothers accepting a—'

'No, well, that's the way it is.'

Acke nods again and empties the can. He crumples it and tosses it into the sink with a clatter. Anna frowns and jerks her head in the direction of the draining board. 'Who the fuck does that nowadays?'

Acke shrugs and gets to his feet, says he has stuff to do, just wanted to show his pretty face to his big sister, they'll talk later. Anna follows him into the hallway. As he puts on his shoes she asks: 'But why Siw? Why didn't you come to me?'

Acke straightens up and when he reaches out to stroke her cheeks, she doesn't pull away. 'You haven't got any money,' he says, running his finger from her ear to her chin. 'And you ask too many fucking questions.'

He turns away. He is about to open the door when Anna says: 'Are you going to murder people?'

'What?'

'That's what Dad thought. That you'd have to murder people to pay off your debt.'

Acke stands with his back to her, and she can't read his reaction. After a few seconds he says: 'Dad's an idiot,' and walks out. Anna listens to his footsteps echoing in the stairwell. The spiritual unease she felt after reading Johan's novel has now given way to an extremely concrete variant. It is Acke's calmness that is making her feel anything but calm. Something is seriously wrong.

637

3

Typical. #MeToo can sweep across the country and every politician can claim to be a feminist, but if the football pitch is overbooked, which teams have to move to the ordinary patch of grass outside the fence? The girls, of course.

Not that Alva and her teammates seem to mind. They are dribbling happily between the cones that have been set out, passing clumsily to one another. Siw is watching from the bench next to the rampart, the bench where she and Anna usually meet. Alva is clearly one of the weaker players, but she isn't the weakest. That position is occupied by a plump little girl who tends to trip over her own feet whenever the ball comes anywhere near her.

Siw is slightly embarrassed by her thoughts, which aren't too far from Schadenfreude. She looks down at her phone and presses the message icon. She knows it's pointless. If Max had texted or called, there would be a little red '1' above the icon, and yet she can't help herself. The system might have gone wrong. But there is nothing.

It is Sunday, just under forty hours since Acke's ill-timed appearance. Max should have had the chance to sort himself out by now, and Siw is slightly annoyed with him. She probably prevented him from being stabbed, possibly killed, and what thanks does she get? Silence. She has no intention of making the first move.

She shivers. She can sit here in the biting wind nursing her pride, but it still hurts. Max might be a nervous wreck, but she wants him to be *her* nervous wreck. The silence is taking its toll on her mental health, because it means she has to use her imagination. Her brain is constantly buzzing.

'Messi!' shrieks one of the girls, and receives the response:

'Asllani!' Siw rubs her hands together and opens *Pokémon Go*. The gym behind her is Team Instinct, and she spends a while conquering it for Team Mystic. She fights off all the Pokémon and is about to install Vigoroth as defender when something makes her look up.

The other girls in Alva's team are still running around in their hi-vis vests, but Alva is standing stock still. Her arms hang loosely by her sides, her mouth is open and she is staring wide-eyed at a point diagonally behind her mother.

Siw looks over her shoulder, but the only thing in that direction is the roundabout at the junction between Drottning Kristinas väg and Carl Bondes väg. A van is just coming off the roundabout, heading towards the Flygfyren shopping centre.

The van? Is that why Alva. . .

Her chain of thought is interrupted when Alva claps both hands over her ears and screams. The girls stop chasing balls, and Siw runs to her daughter.

'What is it, sweetheart? What happened?'

At first Alva refuses to take her hands from her ears or open her eyes, which are shut tight. Siw assures the trainer that everything is fine, then speaks softly and gently to Alva. Eventually Alva removes her hands, opens her eyes and says: 'It's the truck.'

'What truck? The van?'

'No, bigger.'

'A lorry?'

Alva nods, then frowns. 'One of those that carries petrol, stuff like that.'

'A tanker? I haven't seen a tanker.'

'Me neither. But I *heard* it.'

A shard of ice pierces Siw's heart. It has happened. Alva has experienced her first Hearing. But why didn't Siw hear anything?

Keeping her voice as calm as possible, she asks: 'Why did you scream, sweetheart?'

'Because it was so loud. It really hurt my ears.'

'What was so loud?'

'The . . . tanker. When it whatdoyoucallit . . . exploded. It really hurt.'

A tear trickles down Alva's cheek. Siw hugs her daughter and rubs her back until Alva relaxes. Siw loosens her grip and takes Alva's hand. 'Let's go and sit on the bench for a little while.'

'But I've got training . . .'

'Just for a minute or two.'

Alva resists, but eventually allows Siw to lead her to the bench. Siw drapes Alva's jacket around her shoulders. 'Tell me exactly what you heard.'

'So, this truck came along, one of those . . .'

'Tankers.'

'Yes. It came from that direction.' Alva points towards the gym. 'Then it came along here.' Alva's finger follows Carl Bondes väg. 'And then it braked, and then someone screamed, or maybe someone screamed and then it braked and then it whatdoyoucallit *skidded* and then there was a huge bang when it . . .' Alva turns her head and looks at the rampart. 'I think it hit that . . . lump there. What is it?'

'A rampart.'

'What's it for?'

'I'll tell you later. What happened next?'

'Then there was lots of noise and splashing and liquid pouring out and then . . . then there was a huge bang. Like a thunderstorm, but louder.'

'The tanker exploded.'

640

'Yes.'

Siw takes a deep breath and glances towards the spot where Alva said the tanker would be. She can't understand why she didn't hear anything herself. She takes Alva's hands, which are cold from sitting still, and rubs them with her thumbs. 'Okay, sweetheart, let me explain. What you heard . . . is something that's going to happen in the future. It could also be something that's already happened, but not in this case; we would have known about it. That means it hasn't happened yet, but it's *going* to happen.'

'I know.'

Siw is so taken aback that she lets go of Alva's hands. 'You know?'

'Yes. I knew when I heard it.'

Siw runs a hand over her chin. Alva's relationship to her gift is clearly going to develop in a completely different way from Siw's. She takes her daughter's hands again. 'Okay, that was unexpected. But the problem is that you never know *when* it's going to happen. It could be in a few minutes . . .' – Siw's eyes flick towards the gym – '. . . in a few hours, or tomorrow, or the day after tomorrow. Do you understand?'

'No.'

'What do you mean, no?'

'It's not like that. This is going to happen in a week. Seven days. That's a week, isn't it?'

'Well, yes, but . . . how can you know it'll be in seven days?'

Alva shrugs. 'I just do.'

'Are you certain?'

'Absolutely certain.'

'And do you know what time?'

'No. But definitely seven days. I want to go back to training now.'

Siw is about to protest, but she is so taken aback that before she can work out what to say, Alva has shot off to rejoin her teammates. Perhaps it's just as well. Siw needs to think.

If it's as Alva says, then that explains why Siw hasn't had a Hearing. She has never been able to hear more than three days into the future. Possibly four, once. On top of that, Alva is fully aware of the implications of her special talent, and is able to predict a fairly exact point in time. If all of this is true, then her gift must be considerably stronger than Siw's.

The force is strong with this one.

Siw is struck by a childish impulse to do what she has always done when a Hearing is involved: to run to Grandma and tell her all about it. She will go to see Berit, explain what's happened and that all four of them are now sibyls, but for the moment Siw is the adult who must deal with the situation.

Apart from anything else, she must take into account that a tanker is going to explode here in a week, with significant danger to human life. In spite of her promise to herself, one thing is clear: she has to contact Max.

ESCALATION

I

It is Monday morning and Maria is dreading going to work. In recent days she has been frightened by people's extreme unpleasantness, but now she is mostly afraid of herself. She has started to have such horrible fantasies about the café's customers. When she puts down a meatball sandwich in front of a sour-faced man, she sees herself smashing the plate and slicing off his downturned lips with a shard of porcelain. And so on, and so on. Her days pass in a cloud of violent fantasies; maybe that's what enables her to function, in spite of everything.

And then there's Jesus. Five times he's shown himself. Since the outdoor dining area closed he has chosen a new regular table, right at the back of the room. No one except Maria takes any notice of him, and when a couple sat down at the same table as the Saviour on one occasion, he simply disappeared into thin air. Maria is the only one who can see him, but that doesn't make him any less real.

She hasn't spoken to him, because she is afraid of what he might say. Presumably he can see inside her head, and knows that she is a bad person with bad thoughts. He is there to bring Maria back to the straight and narrow, and at the moment she can't cope with walking that particular path.

Moving house at the weekend was sheer torture. Theoretically, Maria knows that Marko has done something amazing by buying and kitting out the new house, but from a practical point of view it's a fucking nightmare. The acquisition of such an ostentatious place has more to do with Marko himself than his parents. Or his sister.

In spite of the fact that Goran and Laura have expressed their sincere gratitude, Maria can see that they are lost in their over-the-top residence. They wander aimlessly through the sparsely furnished rooms; all that is missing is the sound of clanking chains to make them the very epitome of restless souls. Maybe things will improve over time, but right now their luxury home is making them homeless. Again.

The move hadn't even got underway when Marko announced his next lunatic project – travelling down to Bosnia to restore the family farm. Maria restricted herself to sighing when he revealed his big plans and waved the key to their old front door, but secretly she has two thoughts regarding the project.

Thought number one: it is a much better idea than the purchase of the show-off house. Goran and Laura never complain unnecessarily, but there is a special tone in their voices when they talk about the old farm, a nostalgic melody with its rhythm made up of tears shed in the past. To be able to return there, if only for a holiday, would heal something within them.

Thought number two: although she would never admit it to Marko, she really appreciates having him around. However much she moans about his big-brother-act, it's nice to know that he's *there*. That she has someone to turn to if the floor gives way and the whole thing collapses, and recently she has felt it beginning to crack beneath her feet. This is not the right time for Marko to leave her, but she would never say that to him.

Maria picks up her wallet, phone, and the keys to the café. She says goodbye to Goran and Laura, who are sitting at the enormous kitchen island with a cup of coffee. They seem to be enjoying themselves just as much as if they were in the waiting area at A & E.

Fucking Marko, Maria thinks. *You crush people with your goodwill.*

She is in a bad mood all the way to the café, and it doesn't improve when she reaches Tillfällegatan and hears the rushing of the river. Yet another day inside that infuriating noise. Can't someone come and dry it up? Many times a day she is seized by the urge to run outside, grab hold of the railing and scream at the river: 'Can't you shut the *fuck* up for once?'

Before she goes into the café she stops and looks over at the far side of the river, the place where someone was shot the previous day. The blue and white police tape is still there, cordoning off an area of about thirty square metres, and the path is discoloured with a dark fluid. Maybe someone turned their fantasies into reality? Maria shakes her head and unlocks the front door.

She is the first to arrive. The place is empty, apart from the table in the far corner where Jesus is sitting. He is wearing a white linen tunic and an equally white robe. When he smiles at her, his teeth are very white. Maria runs a hand over her eyes. Jesus is still there. She rubs her eyes. Jesus tilts his head on one side. She considers hitting herself on the head. Instead, she goes over and sits down opposite him.

'Okay,' she says. 'What do you want?'

'I am here for you,' Jesus replies in a voice so gentle it seems to

645

have been filtered through honey. He speaks Swedish, of course; what else would you expect?

'And why me?'

Jesus shrugs, sending a billowing wave through the fabric of his robe. 'My mother was also called Maria.'

'That's not a reason. There are lots of people called Maria. What is it you want with me?'

'To help you.'

'I don't need any help.'

'Yes, you do.'

Okay, so Jesus is up to speed with the situation, as he should be. Any ordinary person can see that Maria is having a hard time, so it would be a blow if the Son of God couldn't. Maria puts her reservations to one side for a moment. 'How can you help me?'

'You are tormented by your thoughts.'

'Yes. And?'

'Don't do it.'

Maria raises her eyebrows. This at least is unexpected. But does Jesus really know what she is thinking, does he know about the horrible images that fill her mind every day? She soon has her answer. Jesus says: 'I had similar thoughts. When they tortured *me*.'

Maria's eyebrows go up a little further. 'Do you mean on the cross?'

'Mmm.'

'That's not what it says in the Bible.'

For the first time since he appeared to her, Jesus's lips curl into a contemptuous sneer instead of a smile.

'*The Bible.* How would the idiots who wrote that know what I was *thinking*? They got most things wrong, and they made up a load of stuff. Okay, the bit about driving the moneylenders out of

646

the temple was more or less correct, I really did lose it that day, but otherwise . . . pff.'

Jesus flaps his hand as if he were waving away a particularly irritating bluebottle. Maria can't help being fascinated. *Lose it*. She is more surprised at his choice of words than his knowledge of Swedish. Then again, something happened to the disciples that made them able to speak different languages, so Jesus must have been able to as well.

'So . . . you also had this kind of fantasy?' she asks.

'All the time. I mean, the Romans were one thing; in a way they were just doing their job, albeit a little overenthusiastically, but do you know who I'd *really* have loved to fry slowly?'

'No.'

'Those idiots who were allowed to choose who should be released, me or Barabbas. Even Pontius Pilate wanted to let me go, but oh no, free Barabbas and up on the cross with Jesus, they shouted. Doesn't make sense. What fu . . . what absolute idiots. If I had them here . . .'

Jesus clenches his right fist and shakes it as if he were crushing something hateful. This is not at all what Maria had expected; this version of Jesus is much more to her taste than the one that emerges in the Bible. She is about to delve deeper into how he can help her when the door opens. Maria turns her head and sees Kitchen-Birgitta come in. When she turns back, Jesus has vanished.

Oh well. No doubt there will be more opportunities.

'Have you seen this filth?'

Berit gesticulates towards her computer screen, where she has the Roslagen portal open. Anna leans over and glances through the article. 'An ordinary evening in Norrtälje' is about someone, presumably a guy, who has been the victim of an attempted mugging by two Blackheads, as he calls them, but was saved by the timely intervention of a Swede.

The text is dripping with contempt for people who live on the goodwill of Swedish institutions, yet at the same time conduct a low-intensity war against Sweden and the Swedes. Zero tolerance is proposed. The smallest offence, for example shoplifting, and the individual is sent back where they came from. Steps must be taken before it is too late, otherwise Norrtälje will soon go the same way as Malmö. Tolerance is all very well, but zero tolerance is better. Signed SvenneJanne.

'That's . . . horrible,' Anna says.

'Mmm, and do you know what's even more horrible? The number of people who agree with him! Hundreds of them in the comments box. One of them even hints that he was the one who started the fire at the refugee centre as a tribute to this SvenneJanne.'

Anna clears away Berit's lunch dishes; she decided to eat in her room today, because she couldn't cope with, quote: 'sitting there with all the dribbling old fogeys'. Anna stacks the plate, glass and cutlery in the dishwasher, then returns with a cup of coffee – one lump of sugar and a dash of milk, just the way Berit likes it.

'There's a very unpleasant atmosphere,' Anna says. 'It's as if attitudes are . . . hardening.'

'Exactly.' Berit points to Monday's paper, which is on her bedside table. 'And now people have started shooting one another.'

Anna has already read the article with growing unease. The shooting down by Broddsten took place about half an hour before Acke showed up at her apartment. The perpetrator was wearing a hoodie, and has not yet been found. It's a common item of clothing and proves nothing, but Acke was wearing a hoodie when she saw him from the balcony, coming from the wrong direction. According to the article, the murdered man had no known links with the criminal fraternity, but Anna suspects that if the police dig a little deeper, then Ewert and Albert's faces will emerge. They will, of course, have a rock-solid alibi for the time of the shooting.

'What is it?' Berit asks. 'You look worried.'

'No, it's just . . . there's a lot going on.'

'Indeed there is.' Berit blows on her coffee before taking a sip. She smacks her lips contentedly. 'By the way, Siw and Alva are coming to see me the day after tomorrow.'

'Cool. Any particular reason?'

Berit frowns. 'You think they need a *reason* to visit this old bag?'

'Yes. I presume you pay them to turn up.'

Berit bursts out laughing and puts down her coffee to avoid spilling it. 'Joking aside, I got the feeling there was something – possibly to do with Alva. I have my suspicions, but we'll see. And yes, I do slip Alva the odd note now and again. I don't think that's why she comes, but better safe than sorry, eh?'

'You've got nothing to worry about. She thinks the world of you.'

'It's okay, I'm not fishing for compliments. Anyway, how are you? What are you up to?'

Anna doesn't even consider sharing her fears about her little brother, partly because she doesn't want to spread groundless suspicions, and partly because it's too big a subject, and she has other residents to take care of. Instead, she mentions the other thing that has been occupying her recently.

'I read a novel,' she says. 'An absolutely fantastic novel.'

'Author?'

'It was actually written by a friend, so it's just a pile of loose sheets of paper. But it's the best thing I've ever read.'

'Hmm. I didn't know you had friends like that.'

'You mean, because I'm thick?'

'More of an imbecile,' Berit says with a warm smile. 'What fun! Is she – your friend – going to get it published?'

'It's a he. And he's afraid to try.'

'Then you'll have to persuade him. Do I detect . . . ?'

'No, you don't. Time I got back to work.'

Anna stands up and strokes Berit's hand. Berit nods towards the computer. 'If that SvenneJanne has to write, then he'd be better working on a novel instead.'

3

Max and Siw meet at the Espresso House after work on Tuesday. They avoid the sofa where they sat last time, even though it's free. The situation is different now, and they sit down opposite each other at an ordinary table with a cappuccino each. Siw clears her throat and says in an almost formal tone: 'First of all I have to say that this isn't about us.'

Max looks amused. 'No?'

'I mean it. On Sunday, at football training . . .'

Siw explains what happened when Alva's gift came to life, and how it differs from her own. She has spoken to her daughter, and Alva has told her that her Hearing was so detailed that it also evoked images, and that was why she knew the vehicle was a tanker. Plus, she knows which day it's going to be.

'Unbelievable. The force is strong in this one.'

'*With* this one,' Siw corrects him. 'Very funny, but that's exactly what I thought at the time. Anyway . . . I went past that exact spot today and I'm still not hearing anything, but Alva insists she's absolutely certain.'

'Okay. And . . . ?'

'I think you know.'

'You want me to be there on Sunday to warn you before it happens.'

'Or to prevent it from happening, if possible. There are so many kids on the football pitches on Sundays, and this is going to be very close by.'

'Good point, but preventing things doesn't seem to be my strong point. Remember when we were last here and the guy in the river . . .'

'Yes, but that was before Alva.'

Max looks searchingly at Siw. 'You really believe this.'

'Yes. Or I believe that Alva believes it. If it turns out to be wrong, then so much the better, but it's impossible to do nothing when she's so convinced.'

Max nods. 'I agree. And it would be wonderful if we could put this gift to a positive use for once. So yes, I'll be there.' He runs a hand over his forehead, as if he is wiping away imaginary beads of sweat. 'Shit. We're sitting here chatting about this as if it's just a matter of stepping in as a football coach.'

'How else would we talk about it?'

651

'I don't know, but it's like there should be some kind of *Avengers* language to discuss this sort of thing.'

'Although actually it's just a matter of stopping that tanker before it happens. Remember Charlie. We can do it.'

Max clicks his fingers. 'Speaking of Charlie, he called me. He's going out in the boat for the last time this season on Saturday, and wondered if we'd like to come along.'

'Do you want to?'

'I think so. You?'

'Yes.'

A certain shyness comes over them, and they both fall silent. In spite of Siw's introductory assertion that this conversation wasn't going to be about their relationship, it has drifted in that direction. There is an elephant in the room and an angel is walking over their graves. Siw takes a sip of coffee and keeps the cup in front of her face in a childish attempt to hide.

It is Max who eventually acknowledges the elephant's presence. 'That . . . person who showed up at your place. Is he really Alva's father?'

'Yes. Like I said.'

'And he would have stabbed me?'

'That's what I heard.'

'Not exactly Father of the Year.'

'He hasn't had anything to do with Alva. Not a thing.'

'So, what did he want?'

Siw tells Max about Acke's threat and his ridiculous demand for money, and that there has been no sign of him since. As far as Siw is concerned, he might as well be dead. The very idea of Acke poking around in her life and having any contact with Alva brings tears to her eyes. Max covers her hand with his on the table.

'Thank you, Siw. I'm sorry I overreacted. It struck a raw nerve. It's because of my medication, the fact that I'm not . . . But I'm getting better and better at dealing with it, learning to differentiate between reasonable and unreasonable feelings.'

Siw nods. 'Why do we have to suffer so much . . . I can't help wishing I could protect Alva from all this. Lock her away in a room so she doesn't have to deal with it.'

'That's exactly what they used to do with people who have special gifts,' Max says. 'Lock them up and throw away the key. Or burn them at the stake. The world doesn't want to know about people like us.'

People like us. Hounds like us.

Siw strokes Max's fingers with her free hand. 'Shall we carry on?'

'Of course. What is it your friend Håkan says? What else would we do? We'll take it slowly.'

Max leans across the table and Siw meets his lips with hers. It is not a passionate kiss, just a gentle contact to seal an agreement. They are going to carry on. Slowly.

'Okay,' Max says when their lips have parted. 'So, how do we stop a tanker?'

4

A couple of hours later Anna and Johan meet at The Pasta Expert, which is becoming their regular haunt. The lighting is clinical, the tables reminiscent of a school canteen, but the atmosphere is enlivened by a colourful mural which is meant to represent Italy, but looks more like Germany, with a log cabin and a waterfall. They have each ordered a simple pasta dish, and Johan is finding it difficult to eat because the space where the food is supposed to go is full of fluttering butterflies.

They have chatted for a while about this and that, particularly about what is happening to Norrtälje. It's not just that people are behaving badly; the town itself seems to be in decline. Cracks have appeared on one of the bridges – Faktoribron – and it might have to be closed for repairs. Cobblestones on Stora Brogatan have become uneven and are a real trip hazard. The plinth beneath the statue of Nils Ferlin has sunk, and the entire sculpture is in danger of collapse. It is as if Norrtälje's foundations are disintegrating.

But the butterflies in Johan's stomach are nothing to do with any of this; as far as he is concerned, Norrtälje can implode. His novel, on the other hand . . . It is fifteen minutes since they met and Anna still hasn't mentioned it. In the end Johan can't help himself. He tries to adopt a casual tone and fails completely. His voice cracks when he asks: 'So, how about the novel? What did you think?'

Anna puts down her fork and wipes her mouth with a paper napkin. She must be deliberately doing everything so slowly, keeping him on tenterhooks. A flash of the old repulsion he felt towards her flares up in his chest, making the butterflies flap their wings in a mad panic.

'Well,' Anna begins, nodding *slowly*. 'I don't know how to put this . . .' *If you say it was 'interesting', I'll throw up*, Johan thinks before Anna continues: 'I don't really have the words for this kind of thing, but okay . . .' She holds up her right hand and starts to count off the points on her fingers.

'It's the best book I've ever read. I thought it was absolutely fantastic. I loved the language. I didn't want it to end.' That's four points. She hesitates, the index finger of her left hand hovering over the little finger of her right. 'And . . . oh yes! You're super talented. So thank you for letting me read it.'

Johan is floored, just as he would have been if Anna had said the direct opposite. He can't take it in. He's sitting here with someone who has read his – reality-based, but even so – creation and thinks that . . . no, it's too much.

'So you . . . you liked it?' he says feebly.

Anna crumples up her napkin and throws it at him. 'Which bit didn't you understand? I loved it. The title sucks, but everything else is perfect.'

Perfect.

Johan stares at his spaghetti carbonara. It is impossible to eat. The butterflies have gone, replaced by a chaos that reaches all the way to his fingertips. It is as if he has spent his entire life in the shadows and now, just now, someone has caught sight of him for the first time. It is overwhelming.

'Okay,' Anna says. 'So, what happens next?'

'I . . . I don't know. I have to digest this. There's still a lot to do. With the book, I mean.'

'No, there isn't.'

'No?'

'No. I mean, I'm no expert, or what's it called, critic, just an ordinary reader, but surely that's what counts? It needs to be something that ordinary people want to read?'

'Well, yes, but there are parts, certain places where—'

Anna sighs, shakes her head. 'I knew you'd be like this. I knew you'd start picking away at something that's already brilliant, and possibly ruin it in the process. It won't do, Johan. So I've sent it off.'

Johan's heart skips a beat, and once again he is finding it hard to take in what Anna is saying. 'You've . . . the manuscript? Where?'

Anna shakes her head. 'No, it looked pretty battered, so I made two copies at work. Sent it to Bonnier and Norstedts. I checked online, and they seem to be the biggest. Is that right?'

Johan grabs his head to stop it from falling off. Everything he has longed for and everything he has feared has been compressed into a time frame of a couple of minutes through Anna's words and actions. He whispers: 'You're joking. Tell me you're joking.'

'Nope. You would never have got your arse in gear, so I took it into my own hands.' Anna laughs. 'Not your arse, I wouldn't . . . but the book. I enclosed your address and phone number. Oh, and I suggested changing the title to *The Boy Who Hated the Council*. Good, eh?'

'*The Boy Who* . . .'

'Yes, because that's what it's about. Among other things. And it's a cool title. I'd certainly be interested in a book with that title, whereas *Roslagen Metamorphosis* – no thanks.'

Johan is having difficulty breathing. He pushes away his plate, folds his arms on the table and rests his head on them. Out of everything Anna has said, two words stand out. *Bonnier. Norstedts*. He pictures someone, maybe at this very moment, placing Johan's novel on a desk and starting to read. What does he or she think? What does the desk look like? Where is the light coming from?

Johan concentrates on taking in air. His windpipe is constricted and he is wheezing like an habitual smoker. He tries to think, but the only thing that comes into his mind is the image of that person looking over the text that forms his novel. It is impossible to tell what the person's opinion is.

Johan manages a deep breath, giving his brain a little oxygen to work with. When did Anna send the manuscript? How long will it be before someone reads it? How long before he hears something? If

656

the time since he gave Anna the novel until now has been a period of anxious waiting, what will it be like now that he's anticipating a verdict from a *publisher*?

Anna scratches the back of his neck with her fingers. 'Seriously, Johan – what's the worst that can happen?'

Johan raises his head, runs his hand over his face. 'That they don't want it.'

'Okay, and? Then you'll know.'

'What will I know?'

'That they're soft in the head, because it's an amazing book. But there are more publishers – loads of them. I checked. And I'll tell you another thing: there's a whole load of authors who've done really well even though they were – I learned a new word – *rejected* lots of times. Like the guy who wrote the vampire book.'

'*Let The Right One In.*'

'Him, yes. All the publishers went, like, "yuck, we don't want this", and the very last one he sent it to . . .'

'I know, but—'

'There is no but. You didn't dare, and I get that, so I did it for you.'

Johan groans. He sits for a long time slowly shaking his head, as if the movement might erase what he has just heard. A crumpled serviette hits his ear and he looks up.

'And let me tell you something else,' Anna says, licking tomato sauce from the corner of her mouth. 'You're going to thank me one day.'

The air is chilly when they emerge onto the street, and Anna zips up the thick cardigan she is wearing under her coat. Johan doesn't seem to be bothered by the cold, or anything else. He staggers along Stora Brogatan in the direction of the square with a distant look in his eyes. The nylon bag containing the original manuscript dangles from one hand.

'Listen,' Anna says, nudging his shoulder with hers. 'A little perspective, okay? I've sent your story to a publisher. The sky hasn't fallen in.'

She had foreseen Johan's reaction, but not the intensity of it. There is something deeply egocentric about his exaggerated reaction to the posting of a bundle of paper, as if the world has stopped and is holding its breath before the apocalypse, which Anna finds slightly irritating. She realises there are things she just doesn't get, but for fuck's sake . . .

Johan comes out of his trance. 'No, I know. I do know really, but . . . it feels as if I've been dumped stark naked in the town square.'

'So, is it better to cower in a corner fully dressed?'

Johan stops outside the window of the På G restaurant, where a number of people are sitting alone at tables sipping a beer. He wraps his arms around his body as if he has only just become aware of the cold, and shivers. 'So. I think what you did was good, even if it was very . . . self-indulgent.'

'I don't know what you mean.'

'Ruthless, then. But even if I can't quite bring myself to believe it, maybe you're right. Maybe I will thank you one day. Right now, though . . . you have to understand. It's as if someone has suddenly told you you're going to be compelled to appear in the next series of *Paradise Hotel* or something.'

'You *watch* that?'

'No, but I know what it's about. I think. Kind of . . . making yourself vulnerable.'

Anna puts on an indeterminate accent and says: 'Just say no, man.'

'What? Why . . . ?'

She waves away his question. '*Ex on the Beach*. I'll show you on YouTube sometime. But I do get it. Kind of. Although in your case, it's more like you've longed to be on *Paradise Hotel*, but never had the nerve to send in an application.'

Johan sighs. 'I guess you're right.'

They carry on walking. When they reach the sculpture with running water outside the bank, Anna says: 'And there's another difference. I'd have a one in a million chance of being picked to splash around in some pool like a walrus, but you . . . your chances are significantly higher.'

Johan is about to respond, but is interrupted by loud voices further down the street. Over Anna's shoulder he sees a small crowd outside the cinema. Anna also turns to look.

Eight or ten people are involved in a noisy altercation. The group splinters into jerky movements and flailing arms as the confrontation becomes physical. It's difficult to hear what they're saying over the sound of running water, but they're definitely not having an intellectual discussion about the film they've just seen.

Anna and Johan continue along Stora Brogatan until they are level with the Nordea bank. The intensity of the disagreement has increased, and the two of them stop in order to avoid being dragged into whatever is going on. It seems as if a group of immigrants and a group of Swedes have clashed, and insults such as 'monkey boys' and 'fascist fuckers' bounce off the walls of the surrounding buildings. Johan grimaces when he thinks he hears the word 'Blackheads'.

He gestures towards Lilla Torget. 'Shall we go . . .'

He doesn't get any further. Both he and Anna give a start as a shot is fired. One of the guys with black hair staggers backwards, falls and bangs his head on the display case showing the film posters. The glass shatters and shards rain down on him, and he collapses on the cobblestones.

Johan hears yelling in a language he doesn't understand, followed by the deafening report of another shot. One of the Swedish guys clutches his stomach and sinks to the ground in front of the Vita M clothes shop. The tone of the loud voices changes from anger to panic. And pain. The young man who has been shot in the stomach is kicking out with his legs, roaring as blood seeps out between his fingers. The black-haired guy lies motionless, his friends leaning over him.

Johan grabs his phone and calls the emergency services. A woman answers immediately. 'Emergency, how can I help?'

'Norrtälje. Outside the cinema. Shooting. Two people . . . have been shot.'

He hears the clatter of a keyboard as the woman asks: 'Is this happening now?'

'Yes. Two men are lying on the street. Outside the cinema.'

'So this is the Royal on Stora Brogatan?'

'Yes. Is there another?'

'Another what?'

'Cinema. In Norrtälje.'

The woman ignores his pointless question. 'Help is on the way. Can you give me your name?'

Johan hesitates, realising that he is going to get dragged into all this whether he wants to or not. He will probably be required to give a witness statement. However, it probably doesn't matter whether he reveals his name or not; the police wouldn't be up to much if they couldn't see what number he was calling from. 'Johan. Johan Andersson.'

'Okay, Johan. Please stay on the line until the police arrive and you can tell them what you saw.'

'I didn't see much, I just—'

'Are there any other witnesses?'

Johan looks at Anna, who is watching the unfolding horror with her mouth hanging open. He thinks for a couple of seconds, then says: 'No. Not as far as I can see.'

'Thank you, Johan. In that case, you must understand that your observations are extremely important.'

'Er, yes, I . . .'

He lowers his phone and whispers to Anna. 'Get out of here, otherwise you'll be dragged into this shit. I'll stay.'

Anna hears Johan's words, but doesn't understand them. Her gaze is fixed on the gang of young men, whose hostility seems to have dissolved after finding its outlet in violence. She takes a few steps, stumbles over a cobblestone, but manages to keep her balance as she moves towards the combatants, with Johan hissing: 'No, nooo!' behind her.

Norrtälje police station isn't far away, and flashing blue lights can already be seen coming from the direction of Hantverkaregatan. The members of both gangs exchange agitated remarks before three from one group and two from the other flee towards the main square on either side of the street, as if they have temporarily agreed a truce in the face of an external threat. Only the two victims remain, each

661

with a friend. The yelling and jeering have been replaced by groans of pain and helpless sobs.

The black-haired guy isn't moving at all. His face is turned to the side, and a shard of glass is embedded in the back of his head. Blood is pouring out into the gaps between the cobbles. Anna looks up and sees that he is lying below the poster for *The Nun*. A demonic female face with burning eyes gazes with satisfaction at the tragedy before her.

Anna shifts her attention to the guy on the other side of the street. He is curled up in the foetal position, still clutching his stomach. He too is bleeding profusely, and his blood is also finding its way into the gaps between the cobbles. Soon the two streams will meet in the middle in an involuntary fraternisation of pain.

Sobs and groans mingle with the rushing of the river, which just keeps on moving, paying no heed to the actions and sounds of humanity. Fear fills Anna's chest as she bends down to see the fallen Swede's face, which is contorted in mortal fear and harshly illuminated by flashing blue lights as the police and ambulance arrive.

She can't help it. In spite of what she has just witnessed, Anna feels a surge of relief. The man lying on the ground is not Acke. None of the men who are still here are Acke. None of those who fled were Acke.

A shooting has just taken place, and Acke had nothing to do with it. Therefore, he didn't necessarily have anything to do with the previous shooting either. For some unknown reason, people have started shooting one another in Norrtälje, but there is no longer anything to suggest that Acke is a perpetrator.

Car doors open and close. Anna straightens up and gets ready to make her statement.

AS WE PASS THROUGH TIME

I

THE BEST GRANDMA IN THE WORLD it says on the coffee mug Berit is raising to her lips. She received it from ten-year-old Siw on her sixty-second birthday, and it makes Siw happy to know that it was one of the items Berit insisted on taking with her when she moved into the care home. It marks the strength and longevity of the connection between them.

Alva sips her juice and contemplates the mug. 'Hmm.'

'What, sweetheart?' Berit asks, putting down her coffee.

Alva, who has an unusually clear grasp of relationships, points to the mug. 'That. You got it from Mummy, didn't you? Because you're my mummy's grandma just like Grandma is my grandma.'

'That's right.'

Alva turns to Siw. 'How can you know that Great-Grandma is the best grandma in the world? I mean, she's the only one you've got. There might be others who are better.'

Berit bursts out laughing and picks up the mug. 'You're absolutely right.'

'I am. Because to be honest . . .' – Alva lowers her voice a fraction – '. . . I'm not *completely* certain that my grandma is the best in the world.'

Berit covers her mouth with her hand to prevent herself from spraying her great-granddaughter with coffee. She swallows with some difficulty, coughs, and has tears in her eyes as she says: 'It sounds as if Anita won't be getting a mug.'

Alva shrugs. 'You never know.'

'Maybe you could find one that says *Possibly the best grandma in the world*?' Berit suggests.

'Sounds like a good idea. Do they exist?'

Siw raps on the table. 'Excuse me, can we talk about what we're supposed to be talking about?'

Siw had phoned Berit that morning and explained briefly what had happened to Alva on Sunday. It was easier that way; if she'd done it while Alva was around, Alva would have insisted on supplying endless details and clarifications that had no relevance to the key issue, which was the unexpected extent of her gift.

Berit gently runs her index finger over the words on the mug and says to Alva: 'I believe your mummy has told you what you are?'

'Yes. A sibyl.'

'And you understand what that means?'

'Yes. I can hear into the future. But I already knew that.'

'She understood as soon as it happened,' Siw chips in.

'Can you try to explain *how* you knew?' Berit asks.

Alva purses her lips and wrinkles her nose. 'No. I just knew. I heard that . . . tanker and the explosion and I knew it wasn't real because it hadn't happened yet. Although it really hurt my ears!'

664

'And you know it's going to happen on Sunday?'

'In four days. Is that Sunday?'

'Yes.'

'Then it's on Sunday.'

Berit clasps her hands together, puts her elbows on the table and rests her chin on her knuckles as she gazes at Alva, who becomes uncomfortable under her scrutiny, and pulls a silly face. Berit pulls the same face. 'Last Sunday you knew this incident was seven days away. How did you get the number seven? How did it show itself?'

Alva folds her arms, frowns and lowers her head, which is what she does when she's thinking as hard as she can. Siw and Berit exchange a glance: *our little girl*. There is tenderness but also unease in that glance, because neither of them can be sure of what Alva's version of Hearing involves, or how they can help her to deal with it.

Alva raises her head and draws on the tablecloth with her index finger. 'What's the name of this instrument? It has lots of wires and you pick at them with your fingers and it goes plinkety-plonk and makes music?'

'You mean, strings?' Siw says. 'Like on a guitar?'

'Mmm. But more, lots more.'

'A harp?'

'Don't know. Can I see a picture?'

Siw googles 'harp', clicks on 'images' and selects one. Alva nods. 'Yes. That's it. A harp.'

'Okay.' Siw puts down her phone, leaving the image of the harp on the screen. 'And why is it important?'

'Because . . . because . . .' Alva wiggles her fingers in the air as if she is plucking an invisible harp. 'Because of the way it sounds. It's like loads of different plinkety-plonks, and when they come together it sounds like music. Although it's only plinkety-plonks.'

'And you can hear each . . . plink and plonk?' Berit says.

'Yes. Although it's super hard to explain, because there are a lot more strings than on that one there.' Alva points to Siw's phone. 'Several thousand super fine strings, and they all have to plink and plonk in exactly the right way to play a melody.' Alva scratches at her temples. 'Oh, it's so *difficult*!'

'I think I understand,' Berit reassures her. 'For something to happen, many small factors have to work together, and eventually that leads to something much bigger than the sum of all those factors.'

Alva frowns. 'What did you say?'

'I think I said roughly the same as you, but in a slightly more complicated way. And the fact that you know it's seven days – is it because you can hear exactly how many strings have to plink and plonk, and how long it will take before it becomes a melody?'

'Yes. Although that's not the weirdest part.'

'It isn't?'

Alva glances guiltily at Siw. 'I haven't said anything to Mummy, but I can *do* something as well. Something very strange.'

Berit also looks at Siw, who raises her eyebrows and turns her palms upwards. *Haven't a clue.* Since Sunday she and Alva have talked a great deal about what happened, and Siw has told her daughter everything she knows, and shared several incidents from her own past. The story of how she climbed up on the roof to talk to the men who were clearing the snow made Alva squeak with fear, but the child hasn't said a single word about being able to *do* something special.

'What is it you can do, sweetheart?' Siw asks gently.

Alva frowns at her mother and grandmother, then extends both her hands. 'I just know, okay?'

666

'What is it you know?'

'That things will work better if you hold my hands.'

2

Siw has never regarded her gift as anything other than an alternative way of perceiving reality, a sixth sense if you like. Just like the other senses, it is something that simply exists, like the air she breathes and the sky above her head. When she and Berit each take one of Alva's hands, she feels something she has never experienced before. The gift becomes a physical presence inside Siw's body, and she can feel it coursing through her like a parallel bloodstream.

She gasps in amazement, and she can see in her grandmother's eyes that she too is feeling something completely new. It is like suddenly catching sight of her own gift, an object with a physical presence in the room. No, that's wrong. Siw's special gift has no substance that can be touched, but she is experiencing it as clearly as if it had, and what makes that gift perceptible is the fact that Siw can feel it pouring out of her and into Alva.

She looks at her daughter, but Alva is completely focused on the coffee mug bearing the words *THE BEST GRANDMA IN THE WORLD*. Daughter, mother and great-grandmother sit holding hands and something indefinable and primal is flowing between them, three ancient trees with interwoven roots, using one another's power and making it stronger. The flood grows in its intensity. A trickle becomes a stream, becomes a river, becomes a torrent merging with the sea and a shudder passes through the room, a microscopic tremor that makes reality quiver. Alva lets go of their hands and Siw and Berit let out a long breath.

'There you go,' Alva says. 'I knew it would be better if we did it together.'

'What . . . what did we do?' Siw asks, turning to Berit who is staring at the middle of the table. The coffee mug is gone. Stupidly, Siw reaches out and touches the spot where it was, but her fingers pass through thin air. 'Where's . . . the mug?'

Alva points. The mug is upside down on the draining board. Siw is at a loss. Does Alva have some kind of power like *Carrie*, can she transport things with the power of her mind? If so, why didn't Siw see the mug moving?

'What did you do?' she asks.

Alva pinches her nose. 'It's hard to explain.'

'I think I understand,' Berit says. 'In about fifteen minutes a member of staff would have come in and washed up the mug. I'm guessing Ifan, because he always puts it there to dry. So what you did . . . you moved the mug into the future.'

'Mmm. Does Ifan have a bracelet that jingles?'

'Now you come to mention it, yes, he does.'

'Then it was him.' Alva frowns. 'I mean, no . . .'

'It's going to be him,' Berit helps her out. 'Or it was going to be him. Now it's already happened.'

Alva sticks the end of one plait in her mouth and has a little chew, then says: 'It's crazy.'

'It is,' Berit agrees.

Siw hasn't said a word, because she is dumbstruck. How can her daughter and her grandmother sit here chatting about what has just taken place as if Alva had scored from the penalty spot or done something else unlikely and *crazy*? What she has just witnessed is a miracle. With the power of thought, Alva has forced open a gap in time and space, then pushed an object through it. This is more than a special gift, this is . . .

'Magic,' Siw says. 'It's magic.'

'Yeah,' Alva says, tossing back an imaginary mane of hair. 'And I'm Hermione.'

Siw has read the first two Harry Potter books aloud to Alva, but paused when it came to *The Prisoner of Azkaban*, in spite of her daughter's protests, because she thought it was horrible. Siw realises that as far as Alva is concerned, what she has just done is merely a pale imitation of the everyday magic that is carried out with a shrug in the books, which Alva regards as documented truth.

Siw doesn't know where to start; it seems unlikely that Alva, or she herself, has the right language to deal with this issue. Instead, it is Berit who takes the practical approach.

'Why did you want to hold our hands?'

'You know.'

'I think I do, but how would you describe it?'

'Because . . . when I've done it myself, it only works on little things. I can do it with a piece of Lego, but not Duplo. An ordinary pen, but not a thick pen – what's it called, a marker pen. A troll that you stick on the end of a pencil, but not Poffe. And when we were talking about the mug, I thought: *I'll move that*, but then I knew I wouldn't be able to do it by myself, like Hermione can.'

The corners of Alva's mouth turn down as she considers the feebleness of her gift compared with that of her idols. Siw's head is spinning, but she pulls herself together and manages to ask: 'But how do you do it? If you move a piece of Lego in this way, then you haven't moved it with your hand.'

Much to Siw's surprise, Alva understands the problem and must have thought about it, because she replies: 'Mmm, I know. It's

669

tricky. I have to think really, really hard, like this: *In a minute I'm going to pick up that piece of Lego and put it over there.* I think about it so hard that the other way of moving it kind of disappears. I have to kind of . . . fool myself. Then it works.'

Berit stabs at Siw's phone, bringing the screen to life, then gazes at it for a few seconds. 'Can you explain how this is connected to the harp?'

Alva sticks the ends of both plaits in her mouth and adopts a grim expression, not unlike the girl who has recently started school strikes for the environment beyond Sweden's borders. She waggles her head from side to side, as if she is regretting the demonstration which has led to so many difficult questions. Eventually she removes the plaits from her mouth. 'No more questions, okay? But the mug . . . to move it from the table to the draining board takes a few plinkety-plonks, a few . . . *notes*. Notes, that's what I mean – isn't it? And I can kind of *play* that harp and change things. It's as if I miss out a load of notes, and yet the melody is the same. Or, no, I pretend to play so that bracelet jingles . . . no . . .'

Siw places her hand on Alva's before she grabs hold of a plait yet again. Alva looks at her in surprise. 'I've got it! What's it called when you press a button on the remote and everything speeds up?'

'Fast-forward?' Siw suggests.

'That's it! I fast-forward – but super fast, as if I'm playing the melody so fast that you only hear one note. And then it happens. Boom.'

'But how can you—' Siw begins. Alva holds up her hand, and Siw responds by raising her own to show that she is giving in.

Berit reaches for her coffee, remembers it isn't there, shakes her head and asks Alva: 'Did you do anything nice in school today?'

They chat about everyday things until the door opens and a

670

barely audible jingle indicates that Ifan has arrived. He greets the little group around the table with a nod, then spots the mug on the draining board.

'Oh, you've already washed up,' he says. 'Thanks for that.'

'You're welcome,' Alva replies.

THE ROOT OF EVIL

I

Anna isn't well on Thursday morning, and calls in sick, which is
a rare occurrence. She feels exhausted and weak; she can barely
summon up the energy to make a cup of coffee. Maybe it has something to do with what she witnessed outside the cinema the previous
evening, or maybe she is actually coming down with something. It
doesn't matter, the symptoms are real enough.

When the coffee is ready she sits at the kitchen table, shoulders
slumped, and drinks it while she reads the online edition of the
local paper, *Norrtelje Tidning*. The foreign guy, who was an Afghan
refugee with a temporary residence permit, was already dead when
the ambulance arrived. The Swedish guy is in a critical condition.
The police have been unable to establish the cause of the shooting.

The incident isn't the only one that happened on the same evening.
A woman was raped down by the Roslagen Museum, not far from
the spot where Anna had her conversation with Ewert Djup. The
perpetrator left the victim shocked and bleeding in some bushes,

then fled on his bicycle. The police would appreciate any relevant information. Outside the theatre a man was beaten up by two other men, apparently as a result of a dispute about a tin of snuff.

In his editorial Reidar Carlsson raises the issue of the senseless and escalating violence that is now prevalent in Norrtälje. He demands that the police are given greater resources and increased powers in relation to paragraph nineteen of the Police Act. Stop and search should be allowed without a specific reason, because a large number of guns seem to be in circulation. He also brings up the broken window theory, which states that the visible decline of an area creates an environment that encourages further crime and disorder. This is rapidly becoming the case with Norrtälje, where parts of the town centre are falling apart and . . .

Anna closes her laptop. She doesn't need to read any more to grasp what she already knows: *everything is going to hell*. The knowledge has been embedded in her body since last night and is on a constant loop in her mind: the shard of glass protruding from the young man's head, the nun's burning eyes, the two bloodstreams mingling together. She doesn't think it will ever go away.

Without thinking, she takes a big gulp of the freshly brewed coffee and scalds herself. The pain livens her up a little. She cools her mouth with cold water from the tap, and also dabs her eyes. Better. Maybe the violence she saw at close quarters has entered her like a psychosomatic virus. She rubs her eyelids with her wrists, then goes over to the balcony window and looks out. She remembers Acke coming from the wrong direction, and is struck by a thought.

The keys.

There is an entrance to the cellar on that side, and Acke has keys to both the front door and the cellar, because Anna has allowed him to store a few bits and pieces. She goes into the kitchen and

rummages in the glass bowl where she keeps all kinds of stuff –
batteries, paper clips, keys to a bike that got stolen, a hairband, and
right at the bottom the keys to the cellar. She hasn't been down
there for years.

She becomes increasingly nervous as she goes down the stairs,
and she can't understand why. Even if it turns out that Acke is living
in the cellar, and is sleeping in there right now, it's not as if her kid
brother is a danger to her. No, but there's something about going
down into a cellar to search . . . She's probably seen too many films.

It's a relief when she sees that the padlock to her storage area is
in place. She tugs at it and establishes that it has been clicked shut,
which means that Acke can't be in there.

Unless . . .

Unless the Djup brothers went after Acke, in spite of his assur-
ances, found him, killed him and locked his body in . . . Anna
gives herself a little shake. Because of what happened yesterday,
she is seeing possible violence in everything. After she'd given her
statement to the police, every single person she met seemed to carry
the threat of imminent assault or worse, and she had hurried home
with her head down.

Pull yourself together.

Anna unlocks the padlock and leaves it hanging there as she
switches on the light. There isn't much in the storage facility: Acke's
two boxes, a box containing Anna's winter clothes, plus a barbecue
she bought for the balcony. She used it once before the neighbours
complained and pointed out that it wasn't allowed under the ten-
ancy agreement.

However, two things have changed since she was last here. Two
jackets are lying on the floor with a depression in the middle suggesting that someone has sat there, and a sports bag with the Swoosh

logo is next to Acke's boxes. Anna nods to herself. At some point Acke has hidden here, and left a couple of items behind. Hardly surprising.

She picks up the bag; it is unexpectedly heavy. She opens the zip. At first, she can't understand what she is seeing – a cluster of black metal. Spare parts? Tools? She reaches in and gasps when she realises what she is holding. A pistol. The bag is full of guns.

There are grooves in the barrel of the weapon in her hand, and it is marked with a star. Several numbers are etched into the side, along with the words 'Zastava Yugoslavia'. Anna feels around inside the bag; there are at least another twenty guns, plus several boxes of ammunition.

She closes her eyes, recalls the scene outside the cinema. She can't be sure, but one of the men who ran away pushed a gun into the waistband of his jeans, and she thinks it at least resembled the gun she is holding now. She flops down on the jackets and stares at the nondescript bag with the innocently smiling Swoosh logo.

We've worked out a payment plan.

Anna doesn't know how much a pistol is worth, but presumably selling them forms part of the payment plan. Acke is the arms supplier to Norrtälje's ongoing civil war. Anna groans and drops her head into her hands, forgetting that she is still holding the gun. Pain stabs through her head as her eyebrow meets cold metal.

'Fucking Acke! Fucking idiot!'

She throws the gun at the bag, and under different circumstances it would amuse her that her aim is true, and with a rattle the pistol rejoins its brothers in arms.

What the fuck am I going to do?

Isn't there an amnesty if you hand in guns to the police? Can't you do it anonymously? But how anonymous is anyone in Norrtälje?

675

And if she did that, presumably Acke would be in deep shit. But so what? Is Anna simply supposed to accept that her kid brother is going around handing over guns to people who feel like shooting someone?

Guns don't kill people. People do.

Right. And a hammer doesn't knock in a nail, but it's bloody impossible to do it with your bare hand. Then again, it isn't impossible to kill someone with your bare hands, although it's a lot harder. Guns kill, full stop.

So? Anna stays where she is for a long time, her eyes fixed on the bag. It's only about twenty chunks of metal, but she feels as if she's staring at a collection of poisonous snakes. Right now it is her responsibility to make sure they don't escape and cause more devastation and death. And yet still she sits there, dragged into the Olofsson family's shit once again, in spite of her determination that it wouldn't happen.

Her head spins when she finally gets to her feet, and she hauls the bag up to her apartment with sweat pouring down her face.

2

After half an hour of googling, Anna more or less knows what she is dealing with. The guns in the bag are Zastava M57s, calibre 7.62 x 25, which tells her nothing except that they're pretty powerful. The Zastava is a copy of the Soviet Tokarev semi-automatic pistol and was produced under a licensing agreement for the Yugoslav army, in vast quantities.

After the civil war, tens of thousands of pistols were in circulation with no form of control whatsoever. Criminals and 'entrepreneurs',

676

both from the former Yugoslavia and from the west, travelled around the rural areas of the divided, poor country and bought pistols for two to three thousand kronor apiece. On the black market in the west a single gun could bring in as much as thirty thousand, particularly in areas where the supply was limited.

Like Norrtälje, for example.

The situation was pretty much perfect. Anna had once heard Stig say that Norrtälje and Rimbo were crap markets for guns. Plenty of people went hunting, and if you really wanted to shoot someone, there was always a rifle around.

In the town of Norrtälje, an incomprehensible conflict situation had flared up in a short time. Many of the residents wanted to arm themselves, the supply of guns was almost non-existent, and *ta-da*, there stood Acke with a bag full of goodies. Party time, Anna assumes. How many guns had the bag contained to begin with? She also learns that the amnesty only applied during a short period in the spring, for some reason.

She has shut down the computer and spent some time pacing up and down when the doorbell rings. Before she can get there, it rings again. And again. Outside the door stands Acke, dripping with sweat, his eyes wild and staring. 'Have you got them, have you got them?'

'What?' Anna says icily, even though there can be no doubt what Acke is referring to.

'Don't.' Acke manically scratches his cheeks and tries to push past, but Anna stands firm. 'Please, for fuck's sake, please say you've got them!' When Anna neither answers nor moves, Acke shoves her hard and rushes into the apartment.

Anna closes the front door. The bag is in the living room, and she finds Acke sitting on the floor, breathing hard and rooting around among the guns – a pathetic sight. Anna sits down on the sofa. 'What the fuck are you doing?'

Acke continues to rummage. 'Told you. Payment plan.'

'They're all there, Acke. Don't you realise what you've done? People have started shooting one another in Norrtälje, and it's your fault.'

'I can't help it if they want to shoot one another.'

'Seriously? Have you turned into some kind of American right-wing extremist? You don't believe what you just said.'

Acke seems reassured by what he has found in the bag. He takes off his jacket, wipes his face with his shirt, then perches on the edge of the armchair, one foot jiggling up and down. He shrugs. 'So? Everyone is responsible for their own actions. If someone wants to buy a piece of hardware to defend themselves, or even kill someone else, then that's on them – it's nothing to do with me.'

Anna flops back against the cushions. This debate is meaningless, and is dragged up every time some teenager goes into their school with a semi-automatic weapon. And? Should we ban knives as well? And hammers? They can also be used to kill. No, it's people's *attitude* that needs to be changed. Not that the NRA or any other gun lobby makes the slightest effort to change attitudes, but the argument and the respective positions are locked in. However, Anna can't help trying again: 'I saw two guys get shot last night, presumably with that shit you're selling. Are you telling me they'd have been shot anyway?'

'Stabbed maybe, how the fuck should I know. Shit – you were *there*?'

'Yes, and it was awful. People have gone crazy and you're supplying them with guns – how can you defend that?'

Acke's foot stops moving and he leans towards Anna, his elbows resting on his thighs. 'Okay, so maybe you can tell me what I'm supposed to do instead?'

'Well . . .'

'The Djup brothers, they . . . never mind, but it was either this or a little trip. Do you understand what that means?'

'Well, I know . . .'

'No, you don't. You know nothing. I'm not too keen on this either, but I have no choice. If I don't do it, I'll be found torn to shreds under some fucking bush.'

Anna doesn't know if it's whatever she might be coming down with, but she suddenly feels sick. She knows exactly what *a little trip* involves, she understands Acke's dilemma, and the inevitability of the situation is making her nauseous. Wearily she asks Acke how he ended up here, and now that everything is out in the open, he is happy to tell her.

In the late 1990s the Djup brothers sent a Serbo-Croat speaking courier to Serbia, where he bought about fifty guns for next to nothing. However, this turned out to be something of a miscalculation, because the pistols were hard to sell for exactly the reason Stig had given – there were plenty of other guns around.

After selling enough to cover the costs, with a certain amount of difficulty, and after a deal with a bikers' club had gone belly-up, the pistols ended up in the attic of one of the brothers' 'business associates' to wait for better times.

And there you go – as if by magic, those better times came along! The atmosphere in Norrtälje deteriorated to breaking point, and suddenly owning a gun was an attractive prospect. A visit was made to the attic, and it fell to Acke to take care of distribution. The brothers wanted fifteen thousand per gun, and whatever Acke managed to get on top of that would be used to pay off his debt.

Acke had thought the whole enterprise was hopeless, but he had to give it a go. Via old friends he spread the word that there were pistols for sale. These friends chatted to friends who chatted to friends. People began to get in touch, and to Acke's surprise some were willing to pay as much as thirty thousand. He'd even made one sale for thirty-five.

'So, this is where we are,' Acke concludes his story. 'I've already paid them one hundred and eighty. When I get to three hundred I'll stop and return the guns that are left. Goodwill, kind of. Well, I might sell one to give myself a head start, but then that's it.'

Goodwill, Anna thinks. *He's talking about goodwill.*

'How . . .' she begins, but is hampered by a surge of bile filling her mouth. She swallows hard. 'How many have you sold?'

Acke peers into the bag and counts on his fingers. 'Eighteen. No. Seventeen.'

'*Seventeen?*'

'Yes.'

Seventeen black pistols slithering around among the violent residents of Norrtälje, seventeen black barrels, snake eyes that can stare at anyone until that person falls down dead. Anna presses a hand to her mouth, leaps up and runs to the bathroom.

She just manages to drop to her knees and open the lid before the vomit comes pouring out of her. The retching continues until nothing but bile is left. She rests her forehead on the cool porcelain and takes deep breaths. She thinks about the boxes of ammunition in the bag, every cartridge with the potential to penetrate someone's body, tear that person's internal organs to pieces. Hundreds.

A massacre. He's facilitating a fucking massacre.

Until now the shootings have involved one person at a time, but what if someone goes crazy and decides to empty the whole magazine into a crowd? Anna should have acted differently. Dumped the bag outside the police station and run away, anything.

She hauls herself to her feet, rinses her mouth in the basin, drinks straight from the tap. When she returns to the living room, Acke has gone, taking the bag with him.

3

Maria's life has been a little easier since she accepted Jesus, if not in the conventional way. It's not about an open hand leading her towards the light, more like a clenched fist that acknowledges her darkness.

When she unlocks the door of the café on Friday morning, Jesus is in his normal place in the corner, but he looks anything but normal. His clothes are in tatters, he has scratches and grazes on his face and arms, and he is wearing a crown of thorns, its sharp spikes causing blood to trickle down his forehead. Maria takes a seat opposite him and asks: 'What happened?'

Jesus gives her a grim smile. 'I thought you'd read the Bible.'

'Yes, but . . . that was a long time ago.'

'Time has no meaning. It never stops happening. Have you read *The Divine Comedy*?'

'No.'

'You should. It's much better than the Bible. The sinners in hell constantly relive their torment; it's like a circle, over and over again.'

Maria frowns. If she has understood correctly, Jesus of all people is sitting here *blaspheming*. 'Are you trying to tell me you're in *hell*? That's kind of hard to believe, if you'll forgive me.'

Jesus wipes away a drop of blood that has reached his eye. 'You can believe what you want – I'm just telling it like it is. Absolutely, I'm in paradise and all that jazz, but on another level I'm in hell.' Jesus gestures towards himself and his condition to underline the truth of his words, then adds: 'It will never end.'

Jesus has had a good two thousand years to think about this and has presumably considered the same question, but Maria can't help asking: 'Is there no way out?'

'Yes, if only I was allowed to defend myself. A cudgel, a knife, anything. You can imagine how I've dreamed of kicking the Romans' arses.' Maria giggles, which encourages Jesus to continue. 'I'm supposed to be the sacrificial lamb, enduring his agony without complaint, but I dream of once, just once, wiping those sadistic grins from the faces of my torturers. But I'm not allowed.'

Jesus lowers his martyred head and shakes it dolefully. Maria doesn't know if she's overstepping the mark, but she reaches across the table and places her hand on Jesus's. 'I'm so sorry.'

'Don't be. This is my role and I guess it has some kind of purpose, if I've understood correctly. But never let it happen to you.'

'How could it happen to me? I'm not the Son of God.'

'I don't mean specifically *that*, but similar things happen to ordinary people too, every day. Don't let it happen to you. Be ready. Don't let them oppress you. Fight.'

The last word lingers in the air as Kitchen-Birgitta opens the door, nods to Maria without the hint of a smile, and disappears into the kitchen to make a start on lunch.

Fight.

During the day the staff do their best to avoid one another as usual, and Maria suspects that they have all come up with their own internal strategies in order to cope with the situation. Maria now has Jesus at her back, and that feels good. Her violent fantasies become less acute and more like the morbid tales that she and Johan used to make up back in the day.

During the lunchtime rush she actually revives one of their old favourites, the Cannibal Princess, and lets her feast on a couple of particularly annoying small children. Slurp, slurp as she sucks up their intestines; crunch, crunch as she munches on their little fingers as snacks.

When the lunch battle is over and the café is more or less empty, Maria gives herself a break and sits down at a table with the local paper. She reads about the shooting, the rape and the assault the previous evening with a sinking feeling. Norrtälje is turning into a dangerous place to live in.

'Hi.'

Maria has been so absorbed in the article that she hadn't noticed the door open and close. Anna is standing in front of her. She looks like shit. Maria stands up, gives her a hug and asks her to sit down.

'How are you? You don't look too good.'

'No,' Anna says. 'I think I might be ill, or . . . I don't know what to do.'

'Tell me.'

Anna puts her phone down on the table and points to the newspaper, where the shooting is the lead story. Because it happened so late, there is only a picture of the blood outside the cinema and a brief report. Anna tells Maria what she witnessed, then she sighs. She goes on: 'And the worst thing is . . . I have to tell someone. Siw's at work, and . . . promise you'll keep this to yourself?'

'I promise.'

'My brother is behind the whole thing.'

Maria's eyes grow wider and wider as Anna tells her about the stash of guns, Acke's activities, and her fears that someone will lose it completely in a crowd and cause a massacre. What should she do?

'I don't know,' Maria says, leafing through the newspaper. 'But under the circumstances this doesn't seem like a very good idea.'

She shows Anna a full-page advert for a hastily arranged event. There is talk of 'Dark Times' and 'Norrtälje's Soul', and without coming right out and saying so, this is clearly intended as a response to the apparently unstoppable decline that has affected the town recently.

So: a Festival of Light! For the coming Wednesday everyone is encouraged to use their imagination and skills to construct a vessel that can carry candles. Rafts, boats, anything at all that will float, adorned with candles. The vessels will be launched by the bridge, Faktoribron; they will then drift down the river, spreading their warm glow over the residents of Norrtälje who will gather along the banks of the river.

'There's your crowd,' Maria says.

Anna rubs her forehead. 'Yes. Although who's to say . . . it's only me who . . . fuck, what am I going to do? I can't . . . he's my kid brother.'

'Mmm. Speaking of which – if you're feeling better this evening, Marko is flying to Sarajevo and we're having a little gathering to say goodbye and so on. Six thirty at our place. If you feel up to it.'

'Yes. Thanks. But what shall I do?'

'It doesn't sound as if your brother is open to reasoning, so . . . If you can't somehow get hold of that bag, I don't think there's much you can do.'

Maria rummages in her handbag, digs out a pack of painkillers and gives two to Anna. 'Right now I think you ought to take these, go home and go to bed. There's drinking water in the toilets.'

Anna nods wearily, gets up and shambles off to the toilets. As soon as she is out of sight Maria picks up Anna's phone. It is locked with a simple pattern that Maria happened to notice during Marko's party. She unlocks it and brings up the contacts list. 'Acke' is at the top. Maria scribbles down the number on a napkin, which she tucks in her chest pocket.

When she told Marko she was broke, that wasn't quite true. She has put a little money aside for an emergency. This is an emergency. She is sure that Jesus would agree.

DIVORCES

I

During the past few days Marko has made an unexpected discovery: to resist is a greater adventure than to possess. He has spent years dedicating himself to an entirely predictable quest for status; he now owns a wardrobe full of designer labels in a luxury apartment on Stureplan, with a top-of-the-range car in the garage. The acquisition of these items hasn't given him a fraction of the excitement and sense of adventure he is experiencing now, as he is about to leave them behind.

He has paid a quick visit to Stockholm to collect his passport and a few things that might be useful on his trip. The aforementioned wardrobe doesn't contain a single item of clothing that is fit for purpose, apart from underwear, so he assumes that he will have to shop in Sarajevo and dress down when he arrives. He can hardly wander around in a bespoke Caruso suit clearing rubbish.

He has contacted an aunt who still lives in Mostar and has a room to rent, but he is planning to spend the first few nights in a hotel while he works out the lie of the land. He stumbled to begin with during the conversation with his aunt, but after a few minutes his Bosnian came back to him. It will be fine.

His last evening in Sweden. At Laura's suggestion he has invited Max and Johan over to say goodbye. Anna and Siw turn up too, along with Siw's daughter Alva, much to Goran's delight. He immediately hurries down to the cellar to fetch a box of Maria's old toys.

Laura has brought canapés and sparkling wine, which feels exactly right to Marko. This is something to *celebrate*. With true Bosnian generosity she has made at least twice as much food as they can possibly eat, so there is plenty for the unexpected guests too.

Marko contemplates the assembled company, munching on *sucuk* sausage and sipping bubbly. Max and Siw are chatting with their heads close together, so presumably there is something going on between them. Anna looks tired, but Johan makes her laugh; the hostility between them seems to have disappeared completely. Only Maria is standing alone, eyes narrowed, chewing her lips.

It's strange. Marko has only been in Norrtälje for a few weeks, but already the years in Stockholm feel like a distant dream. During the party he had a premonition, but now it is perfectly clear: these are the people with whom he belongs, not the financial whizz-kids in Stockholm. And now he is going to take a huge step away from them, possibly towards yet another new identity. It is an adventure and his chest is fizzing with more than sparkling wine as he goes over to join his sister.

'Are you okay?' he says. 'You seem a bit . . . distant.'

'I'm good. Everything's good.'

'Will you be able to manage without me?'

Maria smiles mysteriously. 'I will now.'

'What do you mean, now?'

687

'Just – now. Don't worry. I'll be fine.' She looks away, and her gaze falls on Goran. This time her smile is more open. 'Check out Dad.'

It is not without a pang of nostalgia that Goran digs out Maria's dolls and princess dresses. His son is about to leave them once again, and Maria's childhood is in the distant past. Everything is vanishing or changing. It is some small consolation to have Alva here, giving the dolls new life.

He picks out a ghost-like doll that Maria liked to use to scare other children at Halloween, but Alva recoils and says: 'That's horrible! It's like death!'

'Don't be afraid,' Goran reassures her. 'There's no need to be afraid. Do you know why?'

Alva pricks up her ears. 'No. Why?'

'Because fear . . . is about things that are going to happen in the future. Do you understand? We are afraid of what *might* happen. This doll can't do anything. And we can't influence the future.'

'Yes, we can.'

'What do you mean?'

Alva makes eye contact with her mother, who for some inexplicable reason gives her a warning look, and Alva says: 'It doesn't matter.' She takes the ghost-doll and examines it from different angles. 'Actually, it's not that horrible.'

'No,' Goran agrees. 'And do you know what I've learned? Do you know what people are most afraid of?'

'Monsters.'

'No, what people are most afraid of is fear itself. They are afraid of being afraid. Isn't that strange?'

Alva tilts her head on one side and contemplates Goran, then announces: 'You're a funny old man.'

688

Siw steps in immediately. 'Alva! You can't say that!'

'But he *is*!'

'It's fine.' Goran picks up a Barbie doll. 'Do you know who this is? This is the princess – Princess Moonlight, who only goes out at night and is friends with all the animals in the forest.'

'Mmm,' Alva says. 'Although you do realise it's actually Barbie, don't you?'

Max sits down on the sofa next to Siw. He tucks a strand of her hair behind her ear, and together they watch and listen as Goran and Alva make up a story with the dolls. It is wonderful to see a man who is normally weighed down lighten up and relax; even his back, hunched from years of hard work, seems to straighten a little as he walks Barbie across the cushions searching for her magic wand. Max feels unusually . . . what? Uncomplicated. As if things are simple at the moment, even though they are certainly not.

'We're coming along tomorrow,' Siw says.

Max has been so caught up in the story of Princess Moonlight that he doesn't understand what she's talking about, then he remembers. Charlie. The boat trip. 'Great. He suggested eleven o'clock.'

'That works. Do you think he'll have a lifejacket for Alva?'

'I'll ask him.'

'Good. Have you thought any more about . . . Sunday?'

'Mmm. I've borrowed a "Road Closed" sign from work. The plan is to put it out as soon as I know the tanker is coming, and then I'll run.'

'And I'll speak to the trainers,' Siw says. 'Although I have no idea how I'm going to convince them.'

'I think they might be easier to persuade when you tell them the children might be in danger.'

'Which children are in danger?' Alva asks, gesturing to Goran to indicate that the game is temporarily paused.

'We don't know,' Siw says. 'But *if* the tanker comes along when you've got training . . .'

Alva nods, and Goran looks confused. 'What tanker?'

'It's a long story,' Alva informs him. 'Let's play.'

Anna's laugh is a little too shrill, and Johan can see tiny beads of sweat along her hairline. 'How are you really?'

'I don't think I'm very well,' Anna says, placing a hand on her forehead. 'But there's something else. I'll tell you later.'

'Does it have anything to do with what happened outside the cinema?'

'You could say that – but it's not what you think. Have you had any . . . after effects?'

Johan takes a gulp of sparkling wine, which goes up his nose and makes him sneeze, giving him a welcome respite. The truth is that he has suffered significant after effects, feeling guilty and finding it difficult to sleep.

It is, of course, impossible to work out the causes and effects that eventually led to two people lying shot on the pavement, but somewhere along the line there is Johan's post 'An ordinary evening in Norrtälje,' and the cursed reference to 'Blackheads'.

Just before he came to Marko's he logged onto the Roslagen portal and tried yet again to find a way of deleting the post. He even sent a message to the administrator and asked them to do it. So far his efforts have been in vain, and the post continues to generate enthusiastic acclaim.

He rubs his nose. 'No. Not really.'

'Congratulations,' Anna says. 'I can't get rid of the image of those

690

two bloodstreams flowing together. The way that something kind of beautiful is actually just ugly.'

His flight leaves at nine thirty, so at seven fifteen Marko picks up his suitcase and says his goodbyes. Goran hasn't had a drink so that he can drive Marko to the airport and bring the car back.

Before getting into the passenger seat, Marko stands for a moment looking at the people gathered on the steps. He remembers driving into town less than three weeks ago in the hope of *returning like a winner* like the victor in *Mario Kart*; instead, he was struck down by an attack of diarrhoea.

This is a lot more stylish. His family and friends are waving and beaming at him as he gets ready to break free, with The Adventure shimmering in his chest. Marko flashes one last Zlatan-smile, raises his clenched fist above his head and shouts: 'Yeah! Wario wins!' Then he gets in the car.

2

Anna and Johan leave Marko's house together. When they reach the crossroads of Bergsgatan and Gustaf Adolfs väg Anna suddenly feels weak and has to lean on an electricity box. She doesn't have a very high temperature, but she has hardly eaten anything today, and she has just poured a couple of glasses of bubbly into her empty stomach.

'Shit,' Johan says. 'You look rough.' He waves in the direction of the white buildings on the hill leading down to the harbour. 'Do you want to come home with me? I've got Ibuprofen.'

'It's usually tea.'

'I've got tea as well. I think.'

'No, I mean . . . Oh, forget it. Yes please.'

Johan puts his arm around her for support as they set off. Anna rests her head on his shoulder. She is perfectly capable of walking on her own, but it's a long time since she did this with anyone other than Siw, and when consideration is offered it's stupid to refuse it.

Johan's grip on her is surprisingly firm, and his fingers are strong. Maybe it's the bowling that has made his right arm a more impressive part of his body. Anna closes her eyes, revels in the moment and asks: 'Are you, like, totally gay?'

Johan snorts at the expression. 'Totally.'

'That's a shame.'

He gives her a hug as if to confirm that he feels the same. As they draw closer to the houses he asks: 'What was it you were going to tell me?'

'Ibuprofen first. And tea. Then I'll tell you.'

Johan's apartment is like Anna's in that it contains nothing more than what is absolutely necessary – barely even that. At least Anna has a few rugs. When they have taken off their outdoor clothes, Johan says: 'Go and sit down while I make the tea.'

Anna shuffles into the living room, where there is a sofa but no coffee table, and a desk and chair, plus a decent-sized TV to which a Playstation 3 is connected. There are several games on the floor, the covers showing men with big guns. Anna sniffs. Acke used to like Playstation 2, and she remembers the covers of the games showed men with big guns. Some things never change.

She is on her way to the sofa to collapse, but diverts to the desk and Johan's computer. Thinking about Acke has led her to think about the guns, and she wants to check the local paper's homepage to see if there have been any further events similar to what happened outside the cinema.

She sits down with a grunt and opens up the laptop. The Roslagen portal is open on the screen, the homepage Berit often refers to. Anna types *norrteljetidning* in the search box and is about to press Return when she sees something in the top right-hand corner that stops her in her tracks. 'Logged in as: SvenneJanne.'

What the . . .

'Do you want honey?' Johan calls out from the kitchen.

Anna doesn't answer. She moves the cursor to 'My posts' and clicks. Twenty or so posts are listed on the screen, with titles like 'Eurabia is coming closer' and 'Beggars do not enrich our culture'. Up at the top she finds 'An ordinary evening in Norrtälje'.

Johan comes into the living room. 'Do you want to—'

Anna spins the chair around and points at the screen. 'Are *you* the one who's been writing this shit?'

Johan frowns. 'Do you usually poke around in people's computers?'

And there's the answer. Anna is lost for words. She slowly shakes her head and looks back at the screen, where 'Radicalised Beardy Boys' jumps out at her. Johan steps forward, slams the laptop shut and tucks it under his arm. The only thing Anna can think of to say is: 'Who *are* you?'

'What do you mean, who am I?'

'You're . . . you're one of those who . . .'

'One of those who what?'

'Who . . . who . . . *hate*.'

Johan flops down on the sofa clutching the laptop; it's not clear whether he is trying to hide or protect its contents. He purses his lips. 'Just think about that attempted mugging – it was actually something that happened and it really upset me, it was all a bit too much. So I've tried to . . . get rid of it.'

Anna's chest aches as something special that had been building suddenly collapses with a deafening crash. She presses her fist into her ribs and says: 'But . . . Eurabia, beardy boys, enriching our culture, it's . . . it's *that*. All that crap.'

'And it's that attitude that is so unfortunate. It means no one can discuss certain matters. Signal words. And suddenly you can't even chat anymore.'

'No,' Anna says, using the desk for support as she gets to her feet. 'No, that's not true.'

As she slowly heads for the hallway, Johan puts down the laptop, gets up and places a hand on her arm. 'Anna? Surely we can at least talk.'

She shakes off his hand, looks him in the eye. 'Don't touch me.'

While she is putting on her coat and shoes, Johan stands in the living room doorway becoming increasingly agitated.

'It's exactly this kind of reaction that makes everything so polarised. Someone sees a trigger word and the warning lights immediately start flashing: 'Racist, racist!' But I'm not . . . If you actually *read* what I've written . . . Okay, so there's a certain amount of clickbait in the titles, but I do try to be nuanced and . . . Don't you realise that your reaction is incredibly intolerant?'

Anna opens the front door. 'I have read what you've written. Intolerant, Johan? Seriously? Goodbye.' She slams the door behind her and walks down the stairs. When she emerges into the yard, she is overcome by exhaustion. She sinks down onto a stone step and hides her burning face in her hands. Tears seep between her fingers.

Fucking hell.

On one side there is Johan, whose posts have definitely contributed to the current atmosphere in Norrtälje, and on the other there is Acke, supplying guns and making that atmosphere literally lethal. It is a shit storm, and Anna is sitting in the middle watching it happen. To hell with the whole lot.

She grabs the railing and pulls herself up. She glances up at the apartment block and sees Johan standing at a window. She gives him the finger and staggers onto the street.

HOW THE SEA BREEZES BLOW

Charlie's boat is in Gräddö, just over twenty kilometres outside Norrtälje, so they have arranged that he will pick up his passengers by car outside Siw's apartment at eleven. The weather is a bit miserable and the temperature ten degrees, so Siw makes sure that she and Alva are wrapped up warmly.

'*No*,' Alva says when Siw tries to cram a hat with ear flaps onto her head. 'That's a baby's hat.' She tosses the offending item up onto the shelf and digs out her favourite, the one with the Jansson Metals logo: *We bow to you.*

Shortly before eleven the doorbell rings. Max is standing there with a carrier bag. He and Siw hug briefly before Alva appears, focusing on the bag. 'What's in there?'

'The Switch.'

Alva's eyes widen and she says: 'In a *carrier bag*?' as if Max is guilty of heresy by transporting the precious relic in anything other than the ark of the covenant which is its carboard box. She peers into the bag and discovers that Max has also brought a game. She clutches her head and shouts: 'OMG! Mario! The Rabbids! Can we play now?'

'We're going on a boat trip,' Siw reminds her, glaring at Max when Alva replies: 'I don't want to go on a boat trip, I want to play Rabbids!'

'When we get back,' Max assures her. 'It has to be connected up to the TV and so on. It takes a while.'

'Promise?' Alva holds up her index finger. 'You're not going to sneak off again, are you?'

'No.' Max laughs as he puts down the bag on the hall table. 'Promise.'

Siw fetches the picnic basket she has prepared. Alva doesn't take her eyes off the Switch until Siw closes the door and takes her hand. As they walk down the stairs Siw makes a conscious effort to think: *this is going to be a nice day*, instead of thinking about the tanker, an ever-present threat that is getting closer.

It didn't help when she had her own Hearing near the rampart yesterday evening on the way home from Marko's. Tyres and metal screeching over tarmac, a reverberating crash, gushing liquid, and then the deafening explosion. Alva had looked at her mother as she stood there, fingers outstretched. 'You heard it, didn't you?'

'Yes. And I understand why you screamed.'

A nice day. Each day has enough trouble of its own. A nice day.

When they emerge onto the street, Alva tucks her free hand into Max's. He glances at Siw with something approaching terror, but Siw simply smiles and raises an eyebrow. *There you go.*

'Swish me,' Alva demands.

'Sorry?' Max says.

'Swish!' Alva's legs give way so that she is dangling from Max and Siw's hands. Siw has no idea where she learned this trick, because she has never, ever walked between two adults holding their hands, but she is clearly determined to make the most of the opportunity.

Max understands what is required of him. He looks at Siw. 'One, two and . . . threeee!', at which point they swish Alva up in the air. She waves her legs and screams with delight before she lands. 'Again!'

They manage four more swishes before they reach Drottning Kristinas väg, where Charlie is waiting for them beside a dark blue Volvo 240. His face lights up as soon as he sees them and he spreads his arms wide. 'My saviours in my hour of need! My angels!'

'Who's the weird guy?' Alva whispers.

'That's Charlie,' Siw informs her. 'He's the one who's taking us out on his boat.'

'Is he drunk?'

'No, he's just happy.'

Charlie gives Max and Siw a bear hug each before crouching down in front of Alva. 'And what might this little lady be called?'

Siw sees Alva's nostrils twitch as she sniffs Charlie's breath to make sure he really is sober. 'My name is Alva. Do you always talk like this?'

Charlie roars with laughter. 'No, only when I'm in such esteemed company. In you get.'

Max sits in the front, Siw and Alva in the back. When Siw is helping Alva with her seat belt she sees her nostrils twitching again as she takes in the unfamiliar smells of oil, years of cigarette smoke, and something that is probably fish. As the car begins to move, Alva leans closer to her mother and whispers: 'This car smells of old men'.

They turn onto Kapellskärsvägen. Max and Charlie are discussing possible routes for the day's outing. Siw looks out of the window and tries to relax. A crash barrier has appeared along the middle of the road since she was last here; that must have been . . .

almost eight years ago. On the way to the Finland ferry and Alva's imaginary conception.

In Södersvik Charlie takes the old Kapellskär road to Gräddö. The trees on the island of Rådmansö have coped with the dry summer rather better than those in Norrtälje; some even have a few greenish-yellow leaves still hanging on. As they are driving through Södersvik Alva spots a sign and yells: 'Bakery! Cakes! Can we buy some cakes?'

Charlie stops and they go into the combined bakery and café, housed in the former village store. Handwritten labels list the ingredients in the eye-wateringly expensive eco-friendly sourdough bread, and the whole place is more Södermalm than Roslagen. Alva makes her choice. The amount Charlie pays for four cinnamon buns would easily have covered four meals in McDonald's, but he doesn't complain. They get back in the car and continue their journey.

They pass Rådmansö church and the village of Rådmanby, where they see a somewhat cryptic sign in front of a huge pile of gravel: 'Private gravel! I can see you, you thief!' Five minutes later they turn into the car park at Gräddö marina. They put on their lifejackets and head towards the sea.

This late in September the harbour is only half full of boats, because many have already been taken out of the water for the season. Charlie sets off along a jetty and gestures proudly towards a large wooden gig with seats along the gunwale. 'There she is – the apple of my eye!'

'He really likes her,' Siw explains before Alva can ask.

Alva looks sceptically at the gig. She has never been out to sea before, and Siw isn't sure what she'd expected Charlie's boat to look like. Alva tugs at Siw's hand. 'Mummy, I think that's really dangerous.'

Charlie laughs and holds his belly like a policeman in an old comedy film. Then he grows serious. 'Young lady. I would never put you in danger. You do know that your mummy and daddy saved my life?'

'Max isn't . . .' Alva begins, then clamps her lips shut, trapping the words inside. She gives Max a funny look, and Siw guesses that she is considering the possibility that Max actually *is* her father. Or at least might be, one day. Max doesn't say anything either.

After a certain amount of persuasion, everyone is seated, including Alva. She starts to ask: 'How did they save . . .' but her voice is drowned out by the throb of the engine. Siw hasn't told her about Charlie's suicide attempt, and she would prefer not to. Since the Hearing Alva has become preoccupied with death.

With one hand on the rudder, Charlie manoeuvres out of the marina and on towards the inlet. The noise of the engine makes normal conversation impossible, and Charlie puts his mouth close to Max's ear as he tells him about the islands they pass. Alva sits with her hands in her lap, staring grimly ahead as if it is only her willpower that is keeping them afloat.

After ten minutes Siw feels completely relaxed, and even Alva's posture is starting to soften. It is very pleasant, chugging along slowly, and the sound of the engine is slightly soporific. Siw allows her thoughts to drift, and the boat enters the inlet, passes through the harbour where the container stood, and continues to the river.

The river.

It has occurred to her before; at first it seemed that all the violence had occurred in the town centre, but on closer consideration it appears to be concentrated on the area close to the river. The attack on the Afghan boys that she herself witnessed took place right by the river, and when she was crossing the bridge . . . She remembers the fear she felt that metamorphosed into murderous fantasies.

The boat has reached a stretch of open water and the north-easterly wind has freshened. Siw notices that Alva is shivering. 'Are you cold?'

'Mmm.'

Siw goes over to Charlie and shouts in his ear: 'It's a bit cold – Alva is shivering!'

Charlie immediately kills the engine. 'We can't have that! This is far enough, and if the young lady will allow me to . . .'

Charlie flips up his seat and pulls out an old padded jacket, which he hands to Alva. She stares at it, nostrils twitching again. Even from a distance Siw can tell that the jacket *smells of old men*, but Alva clamps her lips shut and puts it on. It is so big that it envelops her entire body when she draws up her legs.

They drift along with the engine switched off. Charlie points towards the harbour where a lifeboat is moored. 'Räfsnäs,' he says, before moving his finger to indicate a lighthouse several hundred metres out. 'Tjockö. How about some coffee?'

Siw pours coffee into the cups she has brought with her, and gives Alva a glass of juice which disappears into the jacket-tent. The bag of cinnamon buns is passed around, and the buns turn out to be almost worth the exorbitant price.

'I've been thinking,' Siw says, relishing the taste of cardamom. 'All this stuff that's going on in Norrtälje – everything seems to happen near the river.'

'The same thing occurred to me,' Max says. 'But—'

Charlie interrupts him. 'Er . . . I don't know if I told you, but I used to work at the River Hotel, and that was where I started to get dark thoughts that led to . . .' Siw clears her throat and glances meaningfully at Alva. Charlie nods. 'Anyway. I've left now, and life is good. But my colleagues . . . I met a few of them the other day, and they said that as soon as they get to work it's as if a darkness comes over them, and it was at its worst when the outdoor dining area was open. Nobody wanted to be there, because the customers were even more miserable and aggressive. And it's right by the river.'

'But what's the reason?' Max wonders. 'Is it poisoned or something?'

Alva pokes her head out of the jacket's opening. 'What are you talking about?'

'The river,' Siw says. 'We think maybe there's something in the river, but we don't know what it is.'

Alva's little hand emerges, clutching her cinnamon bun. She takes a bite and gazes thoughtfully at the lighthouse, then says: 'It's probably a monster.'

'Nobody's seen a monster in the river.'

'Of course not, because it's an *invisible* monster. Can we go home to the Switch now?'

They finish their coffee and buns, Charlie starts the engine and turns the boat around, and they chug back towards Norrtälje, which might have a poisoned river at its heart.

Or an invisible monster.

The voyage home passes without incident, and Charlie drives them back to Norrtälje. Alva gives an unexpectedly fine performance when she shakes Charlie by the hand and thanks him for the trip. Then she races indoors to the much longed-for Switch.

I SPIT ON YOUR GRAVE

I

When Maria locks the café door it is already pitch dark outside. She glances in through the window and sees Jesus sitting at his table, illuminated only by an LED light rope on the ceiling. He raises his hand, waves goodbye. Maria waves back.

She can't understand why it took so long before she started talking to him; the conversations with the Saviour are the only thing keeping her on the right side of insanity. He understands her rage, because he shares it. She has learned that Jesus is not only disappointed in those he refers to as 'my people', but in *all* mankind for whom he is forced to sacrifice himself. During the conversation before Maria closed up, Jesus said that man is merely an advanced form of vermin, incapable of anything but destruction. Perhaps Maria wouldn't go quite that far. *Perhaps.*

The river rushes by with its bubbling madness behind Maria as she turns and sets off along Kvarngränd. She doesn't think she can carry on working at the café for much longer, not even with Jesus's help. She has just started to consider possible alternatives when she hears rapid, shuffling footsteps and sees two shadows peel away from the darkness by the liquor store's loading bay. Men, but . . .

They have no faces.

Maria takes a deep breath so that she can scream, but a gloved hand covers her mouth as she is dragged towards the loading bay. One of the faceless figures holds up a kitchen knife in front of Maria's face and says with a Russian accent: 'You keep quiet, bitch, or I cut your throat.'

During her years as a model Maria has had quite a lot to do with Russians, and in spite of the desperate situation, she can tell that the accent sounds fake. Two pretend-Russians are forcing her face down onto the platform, her cheek is scraping against the concrete.

The guy with the knife jumps up onto the loading bay and puts one hand on her head, while the other pulls down her jeans and knickers. She hears the clink of his belt buckle, then he says: 'You little cunt, I'm gonna fuck you so hard and make you suck my dick.' He actually says 'fook' and 'sook'. The guy holding Maria's head pipes up: 'And then it's my turn.'

The wind blows across Maria's naked backside. Her body is in uproar, a torrent of stinking lava flows through her stomach and makes her shake, but in the middle of that torrent there is an ice-cold chord, vibrating with the sound of Jesus's voice.

Don't let it happen to you. Fight.

When a hot penis begins to poke at Maria's chilly vagina, she reaches into her bra with her right hand. Her fingers grip the Zastava. She got it from Anna's brother – 'mates' rates', twenty-five thousand wisely invested kronor.

The guy in front of her is panting with arousal, and when he straightens up to get a better view of the rape, the pressure on

704

Maria's head eases a fraction. She jerks free and spins around just as the guy behind has begun to thrust into her. There is a faint popping sound and he staggers backwards, his erect cock swinging from side to side. Maria aims the gun at the guy with the knife. 'Drop it. Now!'

'No understand,' comes from the featureless face. Maria considers shooting him in the leg, but that would attract unwanted attention. She's not done yet. Instead, she hits his knee with the gun, as hard as she can. He cries out in pain and drops the knife.

'Get out of here,' Maria says. 'Run. Or I'll kill you.'

The nylon stocking over the guy's face crumples as he grimaces before hobbling away as fast as he can. Maria turns to the would-be rapist and finds herself looking into the barrel of a pistol identical to hers. He has managed to pull up his underpants over his bulging cock, but his jeans are still round his ankles, like Maria's. He edges closer with little pixie steps until the barrel is no more than half a metre from Maria's face. Her gun is in her hand, down by her side.

'Put the pistol down,' he says in Swedish. 'Drop it, you fucking whore.'

'Oh, so we're speaking Swedish now, are we?' Maria nods at his Zastava. 'And you've got one of those too?'

'Drop it. Now.'

Maria shakes her head and raises the gun so that it is pointing straight at his face. 'Identical pistols, yes. But there is a difference. The little catch on yours is down, while mine is up. If your thumb moves a single millimetre to release that safety catch, I will shoot you. Give it to me.'

The gun in the guy's hand begins to shake as Maria's fingers close around the barrel. She takes it off him and throws it under the loading bay platform.

'What are you going to do?' he asks.

'It's more a question of what *you're* going to do. You can start by removing that stupid stocking.'

The guy looks around as if he is searching for a way out, or is afraid there might be a witness, then he pulls off the nylon stocking. His hair is standing on end and his face is shiny with sweat, but Maria recognises him as one of the café's most unpleasant customers. He has often leered at her.

'Been planning this for long?' she asks, and as he opens his mouth to answer, she goes on: 'Forget it. Pull up my jeans.'

'What about mine?'

'They're fine as they are. Get a move on. Down on your knees.'

She waves the Zastava and the guy drops to his knees. He shuffles forward, his jeans dragging over his ankles. When his nose is inches from Maria's pubic hair, she presses the barrel of the gun to his temple. 'See anything you like? If you touch me, I'll blow your head off.'

Using his index fingers and thumbs like pincers to make sure he doesn't accidentally brush against her skin, he manages to pull up her knickers and jeans. When he makes a move to stand, Maria cracks him across the head with the gun. 'Stay right there!'

His voice breaks and tears spring to his eyes as he looks up at Maria. 'What . . . what are you going to do?'

'I already told you – this is about what *you're* going to do.' Maria grips the gun with both hands and holds it in front of her crotch. 'You're going to suck my cock.'

'No chance.'

'Okay. In that case you can bend over the loading bay, and I'll pull down your pants and fuck you in the arse with it. *Then* you can suck it. Does that sound better?'

The guy lowers his head as if he is praying. His shoulders shake and he sobs: 'Please . . . please . . .'

'I'm being kind to you. I should have shot you ages ago, you fucking waste of space. And I *will* shoot you if you don't do as I say.'

He looks up at Maria, and something in her green eyes seems to convince him that she is serious. He places his lips around the barrel of the Zastava.

'Work it,' Maria says, and he moves his head back and forth so that the barrel glides in and out of his mouth. Maria groans with not entirely simulated pleasure. The butt of the gun is bumping against her crotch, and the sensation is not unpleasant. She likes this. God, she likes this! The lava that was flowing through her body now surges into her brain, mingling with the rushing of the river until her head is red hot with intoxication. The guy continues to whimper and sob.

Maria lets go of the gun with one hand, grabs his hair and pulls him towards her while she thrusts forward with her hips. There is a crunching sound as the pistol smashes a couple of his front teeth before shredding his palate. He makes retching noises and tries to pull away. Maria yanks his hair. 'Don't even think about it. And if you throw up on me, I'll shoot.'

With blood pouring from the corner of his mouth, he carries on sucking, slurping and slobbering as his saliva wets the black metal. Maria throws back her head and looks up at the stars. *What a wonderful evening.* This is how it should be. At last she has worked out how it should be and what she is going to do.

As if blood, tears and saliva weren't enough, thick strings of snot are now finding their way along the sides of the gun and onto Maria's hand. *Time to put a stop to this.*

707

'Oh,' she moans. 'Ooooh.' She ramps up her faked pleasure a little more before whimpering: 'Oh baby, I'm coming . . .'

He spits out the barrel and lurches backwards, holding his hands pathetically in front of his face. 'No, no, don't do it . . .'

Maria raises her eyebrows and adopts a surprised tone of voice. 'Really? But I thought *all* girls liked giving blow jobs?' She takes out her phone. 'Look at me.'

He daren't do anything but obey, and Maria takes a photograph of him before kicking his arse as hard as she can. She spits on him and says: 'Get out of here, you bastard.'

He scrambles to his feet and pulls up his jeans. He opens his mouth, and Maria can see the jagged edge where his teeth have been broken. He staggers off in the direction of Gröna Gränd and disappears into the darkness. Maria watches him go. *Vermin. Nothing but vermin. I'm going to exterminate the lot of them.*

She retrieves the other gun from beneath the loading bay platform and tucks it into the waistband of her jeans. Before she walks away she glances towards the café. Jesus is sitting at his usual table. He smiles at her, gives her the thumbs up.

2

Maria spends a couple of hours wandering back and forth along the paths by the river, listening to the rushing water and allowing increasingly revolting images to fly around inside her mind. After only fifteen minutes she begins to regret not shooting her attacker. A gun barrel up against each eye, then fire. In the best-case scenario the head would explode and Maria's face would be showered in blood and brains.

708

Maybe that's why she is walking by the river? Waiting for the two guys to return and make a fresh attempt on someone else? If that happens, she will shoot them in the crotch first, *then* in the head. Let some time pass between the shots to make sure they suffer. But they're unlikely to come back; presumably they've had enough for tonight.

She hasn't decided whether to report the incident and show the photograph to the police; she's not sure she has the strength to get onto that particular merry-go-round. The question of her gun would inevitably come up, and that's not a good idea. The perfect solution would be for the guys to reappear so that she can shoot them, eliminate the risk for other women in the future.

She keeps walking, thinks about how vile people are. The first person who comes to mind is the actor Hans Roos, and she is struck by the urge to get on the bus to Stockholm and execute the fucker. However, the remains of his career, with his damaged face, were sunk by #MeToo, when several women spoke up about the assaults they had suffered at his hands, so he's well and truly fucked anyway. That doesn't preclude the possibility of a warm bullet in the cock at some point in the future, but not tonight.

The river rushes and sings about men and women who have abused their power during Maria's modelling career, disgusting film producers and rich men's sons with wandering hands, dead smiles and ice-cold eyes. And now there are all the customers who come to the café, with their nasty comments and condescending attitude. Fucking bastards, every last one of them.

A middle-aged man is coming towards her, the corners of his mouth turned down, hands in his coat pockets. He definitely looks like a rapist. Maria stares at him, grabs hold of the gun in her waistband and hopes he will try something. However, he simply passes by and says: 'What the fuck are you looking at?'

When he has gone a few steps, Maria turns around, draws the gun and aims at the back of his head. Rage against the whole world and all the people in it bubbles and boils in her chest, and she is on the point of firing, but comes to her senses. That isn't how it's going to happen. So how is it going to happen?

At about ten o'clock she texts Laura to say that she is staying over with a friend, then she goes back to the café and unlocks the door. There is a two-seater sofa near the table where Jesus usually sits. Maria fetches a blanket and a cushion and curls up with her knees drawn up to her chest, after sliding the guns under the sofa.

To hell with the whole fucking lot of it.

Marko had once talked about 'the thorn of command'. Maria doesn't remember exactly what he said, but when someone with power forces another person to obey an order by dint of their authority, then a thorn is created, and you can only get rid of it by passing it on to someone else.

Throughout her career people have pointed and yelled at Maria, telling her how to walk, how to stand, how to be. The days in the café mean non-stop acquiescence to the commands of others. Inside she is a pincushion, studded with deeply embedded thorns, and it is going to take radical action for her to free herself.

The river flows through Maria's head as she considers possible scenarios. After a while she hears the rustle of fabric and realises that Jesus has arrived. He speaks to her of the apocalypse and the destruction that will justifiably come upon mankind.

Jesus's voice and the rushing of the river combine to form a pleasant hum that accompanies Maria into sleep, where she dreams of blood, fire and annihilation.

CAUSE AND EFFECT

I

The first football training sessions begin at eight o'clock on Sunday morning. At a quarter to eight Max takes up his post on the bench by the rampart. He is wearing long johns under his jeans, a thick padded jacket, a woolly hat and gloves. This could be a long day.

He has spent the night with Siw. After a few hours of *Kingdom Battle*, where Alva grasped the principles of the strategic game astonishingly quickly, they had a simple dinner of spaghetti with cheese sauce. Low-fat cheese, please note. Siw has cut down on the powder, but is still calorie-conscious. At bedtime Alva asked Max to tell her the story of the Monkey and the Spanner. When he said he didn't know it she requested a story about a polar bear and a balloon instead.

Sitting next to Alva's bed, Max tried with increasing desperation to come up with a tale involving the required elements. He couldn't think of anything except a polar bear sitting on a melting ice floe with a balloon in its paws, which wasn't much of a story. How did Johan do it?

On top of all that he suffered an attack of dizziness, something that had happened from time to time since he came off his medication, and had to lean on the side of Alva's bed for support and sit with his head down for quite some time. Alva had sighed and said: 'I think we'd better call Johan'.

With a huge effort Max had straightened up and asked if she'd like to hear the story of the Leopard Who Lost a Spot. The book already existed, but Alva hadn't read it, and she accepted his offer. It worked, and she laughed out loud when he got to the part about the monkey falling into the pot of paint he'd used to cover one of the leopard's spots. Max breathed a sigh of relief and said goodnight.

Then things became a little awkward until Siw went for the default option and asked if he would like a glass of wine. Max said yes, and then everything was much easier. They talked about what might possibly be in the river, and about Max's conviction that something *metaphysical* had oozed out of the container.

'What do you mean by metaphysical?' Siw had asked. 'Do you mean something . . . philosophical?'

'More like a . . . how shall I put it . . . a condensed feeling. A feeling so strong that it becomes something else.'

'Like if you love someone – you love them so much that it becomes the *idea* of love?'

'Kind of, but absolutely not love. The opposite, in fact.'

'Hate?'

'Yes. Or fear. Or both. I don't know.'

Gradually the conversation moved on to less serious matters. When Max got up to leave, Siw said he could stay over if he wanted to – which he did. They had carried on talking in bed, then made love quietly so as not to disturb Alva. Nothing earth-shattering, but it had been a pleasant evening and night in a relationship that was gradually beginning to mature.

Max was used to waking early, and didn't even need to set his alarm. He got up at five thirty, went home and got ready for a day on watch. He made sandwiches and a flask of coffee, put on warm clothes. All perfectly normal. It wasn't until he picked up the 'Road Closed' sign that his preparations diverged from an ordinary outing to the forest.

And now here he is, on duty. The first children wearing long-sleeved tops and with tights under their shorts have started kicking a ball around on one of the pitches. There is no frost on the grass, but Max can see his breath when he exhales through his mouth, and plenty of steam coming from the coffee he pours with hands that are only shaking a little bit.

He is nervous. Apart from in Charlie's case, Max has never managed to stop a predetermined course of events, and he has no idea what is going to happen. He feels a constant quivering in his chest, as if a tanker is rumbling through his internal tunnels on a permanent loop.

The previous evening he and Siw had discussed whether it might be better to stop the football training instead – but how? If they said there was going to be an accident or a terror attack, would anyone believe them? Could they pour some noxious liquid over the pitch? Like what? And how would they get hold of it? They might manage to stop Alva's team from training, but what about all the others?

No, the best option is to avert the incident, which is why Max is sitting here now, warming his hands on his coffee cup as the minutes tick by. Plus, this is the first time he's known in advance that he is going to have a vision, which also makes him uneasy. He doesn't like the visions, not one bit.

The minutes turn into hours. The temperature climbs by a few degrees, and Max is able to take off his hat and gloves. Teams follow one another onto the football pitches, and shortly before eleven Alva's teammates begin to gather. Just like the previous Sunday there is no room for them on the fenced-in pitches, so they are forced to play on the grass down below, closer to the rampart and the roundabout. *Shit*. At ten to eleven Siw and Alva arrive and sit down beside him.

'How's it going?' Siw asks, stroking his thigh as if to say *thanks for last night*.

'Fine.' Max leans forward so that he can look at Alva. 'You can't hear anything else? Anything about the time, for example?'

Alva shakes her head, scowls at Siw and says: 'I wanted to play Rabbids this morning, but Mummy wouldn't let me. Would you let me?'

Max glances at Siw. 'I think that's up to your mum.'

'It's *your* Switch!'

The argument continues, until Alva has no choice but to accept that as long as the Switch is in their apartment, it is Siw who decides when she can play. At that moment they realise that Alva's teammates are getting ready to play, and Max turns to Siw. 'Time for your speech.'

Siw sighs and nods, her lips clamped together. Then she and Alva get up and set off across the grass.

2

Siw has spent all morning racking her brains, trying out variations of what she ought to say in order to achieve the maximum effect.

714

She doesn't like speaking in front of people, and she is even less keen to reveal her special gift. However, they have to believe her – at least enough to take action.

The six- and seven-year-old girls in Alva's team have already started warming up by passing to one another under the supervision of the two trainers, Kristoffer and Lotta. Kristoffer is the brother of one of the players, and Lotta is his girlfriend. They are both twenty. Siw goes up to them, wishing she could stick her fingers in her mouth and whistle. Instead, she says to Lotta: 'Excuse me, but there's something I need to say. To the whole team. And you.'

Lotta raises her well-plucked eyebrows, and Alva adds: 'It's *important*.'

'Okay.' Lotta blows her whistle twice, then points to Siw. 'Alva's mum wants to say something.'

Fourteen pairs of eyes swivel in Siw's direction. She takes a deep breath and begins. 'The thing is, something *might* happen. Something dangerous. An explosion.' She nods towards the roundabout. 'Over there.'

Everyone looks at the roundabout, and Kristoffer asks: 'What do you mean?'

'I know this sounds weird, and don't ask me how I know . . .'

'I know too,' Alva pipes up.

'Yes, well, anyway. The important thing is that you run. A tanker is going to come along that road, and as soon as we know it's coming, *if* it comes, then you have to run. Siw points away from the roundabout. 'Over there, towards the rugby pitches.'

'Aussie rules,' Kristoffer informs her. 'This is crazy – why are you doing this? You're scaring them.'

The girls don't look particularly scared, so maybe this is about Kristoffer's fear of crazy women. Siw expected this reaction, and

715

was able to come up with only one response: 'All I'm saying is that there's a *risk*, okay? There's a risk of an explosion, and if the tanker comes along, you have to run.'

The odd giggle is heard. Alva fixes her gaze on her teammates. 'Everything my mummy just said is true. If that tanker comes, we have to run, because otherwise we'll *die*.'

That hits home. The giggling stops, and several of the children glance uneasily at the road. Kristoffer raises a couple more objections, and intimates to the team that Alva's mum is perhaps not all there, then Lotta steps in. 'Surely we can do what she says? I don't expect anything will happen, but if it does . . .'

Siw gives Lotta a grateful look as she gives her boyfriend a gentle nudge. Kristoffer shrugs and keeps his eyes fixed on the ground, muttering something about utter madness. Lotta turns to Siw. 'We'll do it. If and when.'

'Thank you.'

Siw glances at the main pitches where the older children are playing. Should she warn them too? Without any personal connection to either the trainers or the kids, she is unlikely to convince them, plus they are further away from the explosion. Which isn't going to happen, is it?

Is it?

3

Roger Folkesson, who lives in Björnö, is on his way to Arlanda with a load of aviation kerosene, thirty-five cubic litres splashing around in the aluminium tank of his four-axle truck. He is in a bad mood. His wife Carina was unusually distant when he called her this morning before leaving the depot in Östhammar. She has been oddly unresponsive over the last few weeks, come to think of it, ignoring his caresses and loving words.

He has just taken the wrong exit off the roundabout from Vätövägen and is now heading for the centre of Norrtälje with his hazardous load. Not that he's worried about an accident, he's never even come close, but it's against the law. All it takes is for some super-keen cop to glance out of the police station window, and he'll be hit with a hefty fine.

Roger continues towards Kapellet. When he reaches the bridge over the river, all his dark thoughts are focused on one clear image: Carina in the arms of Svante Berggren, their next-door neighbour. The bastard has called round far too often lately; Roger once found him sitting in the kitchen drinking coffee with Carina when he got home from a long shift.

Of course.

A few ducks rise into the air from the river on Roger's left-hand side, and he smiles bitterly as he sees Svante and Carina enjoying themselves in bed, while he is out earning money to support the family by the sweat of his brow. Fuck it!

Roger slams his hands on the wheel as he passes the police station; he no longer cares whether anyone might see him. He carries on up Stockholmsvägen as he takes out his phone and calls Carina. She doesn't answer. No surprise there – she's too busy being mounted by that fucker Svante with his fucking Mercedes.

Roger stops for a red light at the junction between Stockholmsvägen and Gustav Adolfs väg. By the time it turns green, he has made his decision. Instead of going straight on, he turns left. He got away early this morning, and he has time to nip home to Björnö and catch the two of them red-handed.

The image of Svante's fat arse bobbing up and down between Carina's generous thighs makes Roger see red. A crafty grin spreads across his lips as he passes the Contiga Hall. He indicates right, then checks his phone: twenty past eleven.

He turns onto Carl Bondes väg, keeping half an eye on the road as he begins to formulate a message to Carina. He is going to tell her that he will be a few hours late, lull the fuckers into a false sense of security, make them think they can lie there relaxing for as long as they want, maybe have another go.

He will pick up the axe from the woodpile on the way in; no, wait – the chainsaw! Brilliant. He will charge into the bedroom where they are indulging themselves in the pleasures of the flesh, revving the chainsaw – Svante will shit himself on the spot! Perfect.

Roger has clumsy fingers, and it is with some difficulty that he writes: **wll be a bit late tday not hme til . . .** Suddenly he becomes aware of a movement in his peripheral vision. He looks up. Ten metres in front of him some lunatic is standing in front of a road sign, waving his arms. Roger drops the phone and yanks the wheel to the left.

4

It is nineteen minutes past eleven when the expected vision hits Max. He sees himself falling sideways in the cab of a truck, sees his hands clutching the wheel with white knuckles, feels the pressure on his chest and throat as he hangs from the seat belt while the truck slides across the carriageway, the screech of metal on asphalt slicing into his ears. The image of a chainsaw chopping off another man's penis is wiped from his mind, giving way to the chalk-white expanse of ice-cold fear. The last thing he sees is an elderly lady with a wheeled walker; she has stopped at the crossing by the roundabout and is staring at him with her mouth wide open. Then an explosion shatters his eardrums before he disappears in a sea of red.

When Max comes to his senses he finds himself lying flat out on the ground underneath the bench. Over by the football pitches Siw is standing staring at him, hands clasped to her chest. Max gets to his knees and looks over towards Gustav Adolfs väg. A tanker indicating right appears just beyond the hangar-like structure of the gym.

Max waves his arms at Siw, *go, go!* before standing up and grabbing the road sign. The tanker turns into Carl Bondes väg. It is forty metres away. Max can hear Siw shouting behind him: 'run, run!' He places the sign in the middle of the road, confident that the driver has plenty of time to brake. But something is wrong. The driver's attention is elsewhere, and he doesn't even appear to have seen the sign that is now only twenty metres in front of him. Max hesitates, then positions himself in front of the sign and waves his arms frantically.

Only when there are about ten metres between them does the driver finally notice Max. He brakes, lurches to the left, and the tyres skid across the carriageway. Max covers his mouth with his hands as the huge, shiny silver tanker begins to tip over, coming straight for him. He hurls himself to one side and feels the draught on the nape of his neck as the back end of the tanker passes just behind him with a metallic screech. Max lands on his stomach on the grass just as the tanker cannons into the rampart with a deafening clang, not unlike a cathedral bell.

He drags himself to his feet and runs. Fifty, sixty metres away he can see the backs of Alva's teammates, arms flailing as they run towards the rugby pitch, or . . .

Aussie rules, he thinks as he runs. *They'll be fine, they . . .*

Then comes the explosion. The cool September day is lit up by a phosphorescent flash, the thunderclap hits Max's ears, leaving behind a high-frequency whistling at the same time as a red-hot wave breaks over his back, hurling him forwards. His feet leave the ground and he flies several metres through the air. When he lands face down with a crash that knocks the breath from his body, he sees the trainers, Siw and the entire football team go down like skittles ahead of him.

He can't hear anything through the whistling, but he can smell singed hair and feathers. The back of his body feels as if it has been dipped in boiling oil, and when he manages to turn his head he sees that his padded jacket is on fire. He throws himself onto his back and rolls from side to side in order to put it out.

Everything around him is fire. Heat sears his face when he looks towards the roundabout, which is an inferno, with a twenty-metre-high flame roaring up into the sky. A shard of metal buries itself in the grass next to Max's head with a burning hiss, followed by a loud thud as a bigger chunk lands a couple of metres away.

Max crawls away on all fours. He doesn't get far before his limbs buckle and he collapses.

5

The blast wave makes Siw totter forwards a few steps before she goes down head first, along with the trainers and all the girls. She hears little squeaks of terror, but no cries of pain. She raises her head and sees Alva looking at her, wide-eyed. She asks: 'Are you okay?' and her daughter nods. Presumably everyone is okay.

But Max . . .

Siw turns and sees Max rolling around on the grass as if he is in agony, and her heart contracts. He is no more than thirty or forty metres from the inferno; Siw can feel its heat on her skin even though she is so far away. She pulls off her jacket and holds it in front of her face as she runs towards him. She sees him get up onto all fours.

He's alive. He's going to make it.

It is as bright as a perfect summer's afternoon. Brighter. Several of the trees closest to the roundabout are burning like torches, illuminating the yellowed grass. The bench next to the rampart is on fire. The heart of the blaze itself is a wall of yellow-white light, like a sun that has fallen to earth, but a sun that is spewing out black smoke, which is rising into the sky and obscuring the real sun.

Siw's forehead hurts and her tears turn to steam before they can fall when she sees Max collapse. She holds one hand above her eyes for protection and narrows them as much as she can; she can barely see as she makes her way towards him. When she is a couple of metres from him, she can't help looking.

Oh my God.

The back of Max's padded jacket is a smoking crater of melted nylon and blackened feathers, and beyond the top layer she can just see the charred fabric of his shirt, and red, shiny skin. Only odd dark clumps of frazzled hair cling to the back of his scalp. The nape of his neck is bright red.

'Max? Max?'

He responds with a groan. Siw grabs hold of his hands and drags him away from the fire. Every panting breath is agony, and her throat dries out. Max's jacket slides easily across the grass, but after thirty metres the shock catches up with Siw, and she falls over.

She hears shouts and screams behind her, running footsteps approaching. She crawls close to Max and puts her face right next to his.

'Max? Max? Are you okay?'

Max lets out a sob. A tear appears in the corner of one eye and trickles down his cheek. He curls up and weeps. Siw wipes away the tears. 'Ssh, ssh. You did what you could. You tried to prevent it.'

'No,' Max whispers. He opens his eyes, which express irreparable sorrow. He shakes his head feebly. 'No, I *caused* it.'

A FIRE HAS BEEN LIT
FROM MY RAGE

It is quarter past eleven, and at the café the lunchtime rush has just begun. Customers are sitting at tables looking miserable, making snide remarks and throwing barbs when something isn't to their liking, sighing and groaning. In other words, everything is just the same as always, but today Maria can face it with equanimity. She has a plan, formulated in the early hours of the morning together with Jesus, a plan which will set her free.

Okay, so she's probably going to end up in jail, but she will be free in a different, more essential way. She would rather sit in a cell with the pincushion inside her emptied than rush around in her everyday life, suffering a constant barrage of sharp pricks. Today is the day. She serves up sandwiches and salads with a nasty little smile on her lips.

Just you wait.

At twenty past eleven, something unexpected occurs. A deafening bang like a thunderclap is heard from the south, and the floor vibrates. Maria has no idea what it might be, but she takes it as a sign. For once the café's clientele look at each other briefly, before giving up on a possible sense of community engendered by the incomprehensible and dive back into their screens to search for facts. Kitchen-Birgitta emerges from her domain.

'What was that?' she asks, looking around as if the source of the noise is to be found in the café. She is sixty years old, and not conditioned to turn to a screen as soon as something happens.

'Go and have a look,' Maria suggests. Birgitta wipes her hands on her apron and heads outside. One might almost think that Jesus has a finger in this particular pie, because the bang – whatever it was – came with such perfect timing.

Maria slips into the kitchen and closes the door behind her. Birgitta's territory is neat and tidy; every surface not currently in use is spotlessly clean. The key elements for Maria's purposes are a toaster and a microwave, plus a gas hob that runs on a cylinder.

During the morning Maria has thought through the course of events, and she doesn't waste time hesitating. She unscrews the hose from the liquefied petroleum gas cylinder, which responds with a loud hiss. She also opens the tap on the reserve tank; her nostrils are soon filled with the cloying smell.

Because she isn't sure about the line between fact and fiction, she takes the precaution of delaying the explosion with ruses from two different films. She pushes a newspaper into the toaster and switches it on, à la Jason Bourne. The microwave is at head height above the toaster; Maria tosses in Birgitta's deodorant spray and presses 'Start' à la Catwoman in *Batman*, when she stands in front of the sea of fire and says 'Miaow'. Maria looks around as if she is searching for a third option.

Get out now, before it's too late.

Just as she turns to leave, or rather run, the newspaper catches fire in the toaster, but nothing else happens. She lets her arms drop

724

to her sides. She has pictured herself running away from the café, hopefully reaching a safe distance before all hell breaks loose and every single bastard customer is consumed by the fire. *Miaow.* Then the police can come if they want to.

Presumably the amount of gas has to reach a critical mass before it explodes. How do you know when that is? In films they always seem to know. Okay, what if she barricades the outside door and lets everyone in the café be gassed to death? Hardly – they could just open a window and climb out. She could stand guard and shoot those who try to escape. It's a possibility, but it's less satisfying. Less spectacular.

She decides to make one more attempt. She digs out another copy of the local paper and folds it tightly. The smell of gas is getting stronger, and she feels a little dizzy as she walks towards the toaster. As she reaches the worktop she hears a loud metallic click, whereupon the microwave explodes.

The door shatters and a shower of broken glass flies into the right-hand side of Maria's face like a swarm of angry wasps. There is a loud whistling in her right ear, and the pain in her head is indescribable. She staggers backwards, falls and hits her head on the draining board. A curtain of red comes down over her eyes, and at first she thinks the gas has caught fire, but then she realises she can still hear the hissing with her left ear.

Turn it off, turn it off.

She tries to get to her feet, but her legs refuse to obey. She fumbles around at the cupboards above her, but can't find anything to hold on to. Warm blood is running down her neck from her face, tickling her collarbone. When she manages to open her left eye, the kitchen is swaying back and forth like the characters in *The Hat is Yours.*

Maria topples sideways onto the floor. The red curtain is now pulsating, as if she is inside a living heart. That's a nice thought. A warm, pleasant thought. She can rest inside that thought, even sleep. Wake up with Jesus. Mmm.

Someone is shouting and screaming, an older woman by the name of . . . what was her name? Kitchen-Birgitta, that's it. Now she is in the kitchen, as she should be. Mmm-hmm. The sounds change. The hissing stops, a window is thrown open. Someone is touching Maria.

'What are you doing, what have you done?' the person shouts in her ear. Before Maria loses consciousness, she manages to part her lips and whisper: 'Miaow.'

DEVASTATION ENDANGERING
THE GENERAL PUBLIC

I

Gunvor Abrahamsson is due to be transformed from the Solgläntan care home to a nursing home; her needs have become so complex that the staff have neither the time nor the training to meet them. Because Gunvor absolutely did not want to move, they have bent the rules – but now the first bedsores have flared up, and there is no longer a choice.

'Nooo, nooo!' Gunvor screams when the paramedics arrive to transfer her to a stretcher. 'Help me, God! Don't let them put me away!'

Anna tries to console the old lady by stroking her hand, but Gunvor's arms are flailing and Anna can't get to her. A lump of sorrow in Anna's throat makes it hard to swallow. In most cases when a resident has to be moved to a different kind of care facility it is because of worsening dementia, and the person in question is barely aware of what is happening. In other cases the patient is so

727

frail that it no longer matters to him or her where their final days will be spent, and some residents simply don't care.

But then there are exceptions, like Gunvor. Those whose minds are clear, but whose needs make their current situation untenable. In a way they feel like refugees, who after living in a country for several years are suddenly informed that they are to be deported. It is an assault.

'Anna!' Gunvor yells as the paramedics lift the stretcher. 'Please, Anna – don't let them take me!'

The lump in Anna's throat grows bigger, and she has tears in her eyes when she finally manages to grab hold of Gunvor's hand. Gunvor has lived here for eight years, and is one of the few residents that Anna regards as a friend. This friend is now being taken away from her, sent to death's waiting room.

Anna whispers the only words she can say: 'I'll come and visit you.'

Gunvor's eyes are wild and pleading as she shakes her head. That doesn't mean that she is rejecting the idea of visits, but that *it won't be the same*, and, of course, she is right. Something special is ending right here, right now. Anna wipes her eyes, kisses Gunvor's fingers then lets go of her hand. The old lady is carried away. *This life*, Anna thinks. *This fucking awful life.*

She doesn't know if it's a good thing or a bad thing that she took on an extra shift this Sunday to replace a colleague who is caring for a sick child. Probably good, in spite of everything. Even if it hurts, it would have been worse to be parted from Gunvor without a word of goodbye. *This life. A series of separations.*

The last few days have been shit. Ever since Anna left Johan with her middle finger sticking up in the air, she has been really low. There was something about him, something she really liked;

he made the future seem a little brighter. But she cannot, *cannot* hang out with someone who has those views, because that would be the same as endorsing them.

Anna has never been involved in anti-racist protests – or anything else, come to that – but she has the simple view that people should try to be nice to one another as far as possible. That kind of White Power talk is the direct opposite of nice, so it doesn't matter how much she likes certain parts of Johan when other parts are shit, because shit gets everywhere.

The ambulance doors have just closed when there is a noise that sounds like thunder. A vibration passes up through Anna's body from her feet, and the windows around her rattle. Her immediate thought is: *This is the Lord showing his anger at the way Gunvor has been treated.* Then a number of car alarms start going off, which doesn't seem to fit with the emotional outpourings of a God Anna doesn't even believe in.

So, what was it?

The lights above the doors of several rooms begin to flash, and the more able residents emerge into the corridor and look around, seeking an answer to the question Anna has just asked herself. Petrus Pettersson, Solgläntan's eighty-five-year-old prankster, rubs his hands together and exclaims: 'What a bang!'

Anna knows that Petrus spent his working life on construction sites, so she asks: 'Are they blasting somewhere?'

Petrus shakes his head. 'If they are, it's without any kind of insulation. Completely unprotected. No chance.'

Eira Johansson, who has sat in the corridor doing nothing all morning, suddenly comes to life: 'Terrorists! It's terrorists!'

Anna leaves them to their speculations and heads for Berit's room; the light above the door is flashing. Under normal circumstances

729

Berit would have come out under her own steam to see what was going on, but a cold has kept her in bed for the past few days. When Anna walks into her room, Berit lowers her phone and says: 'Can you call Siw?'

'Why?'

'That explosion, it came from over by . . .' Berit waves in the direction of Siw's apartment, 'and now she's not answering her phone. Maybe she'll pick up if it's you.'

Anna hadn't realised where the blast had come from, so she hadn't been worried about Siw, but now . . . *Doesn't Alva have football training on Sunday mornings?* She fishes out her phone and makes the call, but with the same result as Berit. She sends a quick text:

The explosion? Let me know you're okay.

Berit's eyes are fixed on the window. 'Oh my God – look at that.'

A thick black column of smoke is rising into the sky. It's hard to be sure, but its source seems to be somewhere near the old airfield.

'I'll go and check,' Anna says.

Berit is wringing her hands. 'Call me as soon as you know.'

It is almost eleven thirty and Anna is due to take her lunch break anyway, so she pulls on her jacket and runs down the stairs. As she passes the Roslagen Hotel she hears the sound of sirens from over by the airfield, and fear clutches at her chest. She can't imagine what has gone on, but the idea that her best friend might be dead . . . Might have been blown up . . .

That's the kind of thing that happens to other people. In countries far away from here.

A choking, chemical burning smell hits her nostrils, and as she turns into Drottning Kristinas väg she hears shouts and screams along with the howl of the sirens. She clenches her fists and lengthens her stride.

Gunvor. Johan. Not Siw too. Please, not Siw.

2

'. . . and I'm not saying that immigrants are worse than us in any way; have I ever said that? As far as I'm concerned, we could take in any number of immigrants if there was a simple route to integration, and if everyone who came here was willing to go along with it. No problem. All Swedes might be chocolate brown in a hundred years – so what? No problem. I don't believe in any of that genetic crap. But it's partly the economy we're talking about here, and then there's the culture – people with no intention of embracing Swedish values are coming over here . . .'

Ove gazes at one of the little red cottages inside the bowling hall and lets his thoughts drift away. Over the past few days Johan has been on a constant verbal crusade against all the *fucking idiots* who don't share his views. It's as if he is trying to justify himself to someone, and that someone is not Ove, who rarely responds. It's easier that way.

Johan, however, is only just getting going. His argument is clearly laid out before him like a chain of coloured lights, which he switches on one at a time. After the unwillingness to embrace Swedish values come the refusal to shake hands, honour killings and the oppression of women, with a quick detour into sexual assaults at music festivals, teenage gangs, a word about the general *coarsening* of society and . . . Ove raises his head and looks around, frowning.

'. . . a simple thing like shaking hands. If we as Swedes . . . what's wrong?'

'Didn't you hear?' Ove says. 'It sounded like an explosion.'

'An explosion?'

'I think so.'

Johan shakes his head and is about to continue his lecture, but Ove gets up and walks over to the main door. The bowling hall has been open for half an hour and so far no one has come in, which is normal for a Sunday. Johan wraps his hands around his coffee cup.

Ever since Anna gave him the finger, anger has been bubbling inside him. He should have followed his original instincts as far she was concerned. She's nothing more than a stuck-up judgemental bitch who can't even listen to reason. Like so many others. Mention the word 'Muslim' and they cover their ears and run away. Is that what you'd call a democratic conversation? *Those* are the kind of people who create polarisation and hatred.

It's as if something is sitting inside his chest, whimpering. He bangs his clenched fist hard in the general area of his heart; he feels like crying. This makes him so angry that he almost hurls his coffee cup at the wall.

'Look at this!' Ove shouts from the open door. 'Jesus, just look at it!'

Johan stands up and rubs his arms. It's not only the whimpering, there is an itch too. Something is scratching him from the inside, making him scratch back. He would never admit it to anyone, but he has started to feel a bit . . . sick in the head. Something is wrong.

'Look!' Ove says again as Johan joins him. An apocalyptic column of black smoke is rising from central Norrtälje, darkening the sky.

'What the fuck is that?' Johan says.

732

'I told you – there was an explosion. Do you think it's one of those terrorist attacks?'

Even if Johan would happily speculate along those lines, there is usually something more likely. He takes out his phone. 'The council's probably cut through a gas main.'

He brings up the online edition of the local paper and scrolls down. He can't find anything, but when he refreshes the page after a minute a brief note has been added – 'explosion in central Norrtälje' – but no details.

Ten minutes later a reporter at the scene reveals that a tanker has exploded, and that the police have taken away a person 'suspected of causing devastation endangering the general public'.

'What does that mean?' Ove wants to know.

'Presumably you were right. It's something to do with terrorism. Someone has deliberately caused this.'

'In *Norrtälje*?'

'Welcome to reality.'

3

My face. My face. My face.

Ten minutes have elapsed since Maria's failed attempt to blow up the café, and all she can think about is the part of her body that has earned her a living for the whole of her adult existence: her face. Is it ruined?

The right side of her head is a single burning pain, and her T-shirt is covered in blood. There is a buzzing noise inside her skull, and the pressure is unbearable. She is still sitting on the kitchen floor. Birgitta has called an ambulance and been told that there may be a delay, due to another incident. Something big. Slowly, slowly Maria raises her right hand from the floor and cautiously touches her face.

Her cheek is swollen and prickly from the myriad tiny shards of glass embedded in the flesh. It hurts when she winces in disgust and lowers her hand. It's impossible to tell how bad it is, but her modelling days are definitely over. She might be considered for a campaign aimed at raising money for victims of torture, but that's probably it.

Birgitta has spent the last five minutes getting rid of customers and closing the café. She comes back into the kitchen, folds her arms and looks at Maria. 'What were you trying to do, you crazy woman?'

The right side of Maria's mouth is paralysed and her voice is thick when she answers: 'Blow up the whole fucking place.'

'Including me? Were you going to blow me up too?'

'Didn't think about that. Not really.'

'You didn't think about that. I see. It doesn't seem as if the ambulance is coming, so I'll drive you to the hospital. And then I'll go to the police station and report you.'

'Fine. What do I look like?'

'What do you look like?'

'Yes.'

'You look terrible – what do you expect?'

Birgitta helps Maria to her feet and drapes Maria's arm over her shoulders, because she is having problems with her balance. Maybe she has damaged part of her inner ear. Birgitta leads Maria through the café, still ranting. The words come pouring out of her, accompanied by the rushing of the river.

'I'm not saying that I knew something like this was going to happen, but I sensed you were going to be trouble, my girl. I know who you are, and I imagine that's why you think you're too good for this place, and for us ordinary people. I've seen how you go around despising everyone and everything, so I assume it doesn't matter who dies, because we're all nothing but shit on the bottom of your shoe.'

They emerge from the café and the daylight stabs Maria's eyes as she looks over at the liquor store's loading bay. She considers telling Birgitta what happened the previous evening, but decides it isn't worth the bother. Without uttering a word in her defence, she tumbles into the passenger seat of Birgitta's old Volvo. Birgitta gets in and glares at her before starting the engine. Maria closes her eyes against the agonising brightness of the sky.

When she opens her eyes again they are on Lasarettsgatan, but she has no idea how they got there. Perhaps she fainted. The buzzing and the pressure inside her head have abated slightly, and she is thinking more clearly. Birgitta glances at her, and asks in a pleasanter tone of voice: 'How are you feeling?'

'Not so good.'

'*Why* did you want to blow up the café?'

'Because . . . people are so horrible. I just . . . everything was kind of black and I just felt . . . hatred. I felt only hatred.'

'But that doesn't mean you can—'

'No. I know that. I know that now. But not then.'

There is no warning, it is like pressing a button and a dam bursts. Tears begin to pour down Maria's cheeks, everything that has been building up for such a long time comes flooding out of her in the form of unstoppable sobs. What will Goran and Laura say when they find out that their daughter attempted mass murder? What will happen to her?

'And you decided this morning?' Birgitta asks as she turns into the emergency department car park.

'No,' Maria snivels. 'Last night. Two guys tried to rape me . . . they were wearing masks and they—'

'Oh my God! Have you reported this?'

Maria shakes her head. 'Something inside me broke, that's the only way I can explain. And then I wanted to . . . smash everything else.'

Birgitta parks and helps Maria out of the car. The reception area is empty, but as soon as they walk in a nurse appears, glances at Maria and asks: 'Was it the tanker?'

'What tanker?' Birgitta says.

'Come with me and we'll . . . So, what's happened to you?'

Maria takes a deep breath, but Birgitta gets there before she can answer. 'A microwave oven exploded. I've no idea why.'

The nurse nods and helps Maria into a cubicle. Maria pauses and turns to Birgitta. 'Where . . . where are you going now?'

'Home,' Birgitta says with a sad little smile. 'Where else would I be going, under the circumstances?'

4

When Anna rounds the bend on Drottning Kristinas väg, she begins to sense the extent of the devastation. By the roundabout a hundred metres away lies a huge, distorted metal skeleton surrounded by enormous flames, and Anna's jaw drops when she realises that the burning torches only fifty metres from her are actually trees.

Her chest begins to hurt as she jogs closer, and she pulls the neckline of her top up over her mouth to protect her from the toxic smoke. The flickering glow of the fire mingles with the flashing blue lights of the emergency vehicles; more sirens are approaching. When she is level with Siw's apartment she sees that the pizzeria sign has been torn off, and that one of the restaurant's windows facing the roundabout is shattered.

Siw's block is the last one with its windows intact; every window in every building closer to the devastation is broken. Anna leaves the road and runs over to the football pitches, where a crowd has gathered. In the background the firefighters are working to extinguish burning properties on Carl Bondes väg. Everything within a fifty-metre radius of the roundabout has been crushed, burned, or is ablaze. The only exception is the rampart, which, of course, was constructed for exactly this kind of situation. The bench, *their bench*, is a charred remnant. Police cars and ambulances are parked further up the road.

Anna pushes her way among the people, her eyes darting everywhere as she searches for Siw's dark mop of hair. A weight is lifted from her shoulders when she spots Siw, one hand on Alva's shoulder. Max is there too, and the atmosphere is anything but calm. People are pointing and yelling, and most of the anger seems to be directed at Max. Anna jogs over, arriving at the same time as two police officers, striding along authoritatively.

One of the officers points to Max. 'Several witnesses have stated that you were responsible for this.'

Max turns, and Anna inhales sharply when she sees that his shirt is burned and in tatters, the skin beneath it dark red. Max rubs his face with his hands. 'I was actually trying to . . .' His shoulders slump and he shakes his head. 'It doesn't matter. Just do what you have to do.'

'Nice of you to give us your permission,' the officer says, grabbing hold of Max's arm. 'You need to accompany us to the station.'

'I think,' Max says, showing them his back, 'I need to go somewhere else. First.'

The officers exchange a few remarks, then beckon over a paramedic. While Max is standing with his back to the police, he gives Siw an intense look and draws a finger across his lips like a zip. Siw looks as if she is about to protest, but then she nods. Alva is staring at the ground with an expression of total concentration.

Anna asks: 'What happened?' Siw waves her away as if she were an irritating insect. Anna forgives her. The situation seems particularly difficult. She takes out her phone, writes **Siw & Alva OK**, and sends the message to Berit. When she looks up, the police officers and the paramedic are leading Max over to an ambulance.

A young man of about twenty is about to go after them, but is held back by a girl the same age. He shakes her off and points to Siw. 'She knew about it too! She was in on it! She told us – you heard her! She told us exactly what was going to happen!'

'Yes,' the girl agrees, 'but then why would she—'

Alva raises her head and takes a step towards them. 'It was me who said it in the first place,' she says, placing her hands on her hips. 'I told Mummy it was going to happen, and that was why she told you. Because I said it.'

The young man angrily shakes his head and wags his finger at Siw. 'It happened because *he* did what he did. Your friend, or whoever he is.'

'Mmm,' Alva says. 'That was a mistake.'

The young man waves his hand in the direction of the twisted metal on the roundabout, the burning buildings and trees. 'A mistake? Is that what you call this? A *mistake*?'

'Mmm. It's hard to explain. I'm very sorry.'

Alva raises her arms and Siw picks her up, lets her daughter rest

738

on her hip. Alva clings to Siw's shoulder and tucks her head into the hollow beneath her collarbone.

'I know it sounds crazy,' Siw says. 'But we knew this was going to happen. We've known for a week, and we were trying to prevent it, but . . . it went wrong.'

Anna can't keep quiet any longer. 'It's true. Ever since Siw was little she's been able to . . . see things that are going to happen. And Alva can do it too.'

'And who are you?' the young man asks. 'Are you also . . . oh, fuck it. Okay, so you can see into the future. Okay. So tell me what I'm going to do next.'

'It doesn't work that way,' Siw begins. Alva raises her head, stares blankly into space for a few seconds, then says: 'You're going to take out your phone and call your mum and tell her everything's all right and in the picture on your screen she's wearing a white uniform so maybe she's a nurse, yes, she must be, because you ask her if any of the people injured in the accident have been brought in. That's what you're going to do, although maybe you won't do it now, because I've said it. That's what's so difficult.'

The young man had been about to interrupt Alva, but now he closes his mouth with an audible click and simply stares at the little girl, who once again hides her face.

His companion asks him: 'Was that what you were going to do? Call Gunilla?'

He nods and makes a few lame gestures in the air in front of Alva, as if he is freeing her from invisible cobwebs. Then he spreads his arms wide and gives up. His companion looks at him with triumph in her eyes, as if she has known this all along.

739

The explosion on the roundabout, which would be a topic of conversation in Norrtälje for many years to come, claimed only two victims, which is incredible. One was the driver of the tanker, Roger Folkesson, and the other was Lisa Lundberg, aged eighty-five, who had been standing no more than twenty metres from the detonation. The twisted remains of her wheeled walker were found on the blackened site of what used to be J R Finance Ltd; Lisa's charred body was thirty metres further away near Kvisthamrabacken. A hundred or so residents would attend her funeral, which without the explosion would have been a solitary affair, since she had no living relatives.

A number of people in nearby properties suffered minor burns or were injured by flying glass, and one person driving along the road was badly bruised when his car was tipped over by the blast wave. His Labrador, who was travelling in the boot, broke a paw.

Apart from the fatalities, the most severe damage caused was of a secondary nature. A man living on the third floor of Drottning Kristinas väg 23 was on his balcony at the time; he saw, heard and felt the explosion, which almost knocked him off his feet. This particular individual had a sick fascination with fire, and the incident sent him into a frenzy of wild excitement, which made him race down the stairs in order to see this miracle at close quarters. In his agitated state he didn't look where he was going. He slipped and almost fractured his skull on the concrete steps. He was found half an hour later by a neighbour, but his injuries were not life-threatening. His main complaint was that he hadn't got a good view of the fire.

There had been plenty of people on the football pitches, and even though the police didn't issue any information, Max's name began to spread via gossip and social media as early as Sunday afternoon. He was the *perpetrator*. The killer. The destroyer. The forum on the Roslagen portal went crazy with hate-filled tirades and speculation on the perpetrator's motive.

The predictable Islamophobes tried to whip up a discussion about the Caliphate's most heinous act on Swedish soil, but it quickly died out when it became clear that the person in question was a son of Norrtälje with no links to radical Islam. The Islamophobes weren't convinced, but became a marginalised group.

A more popular theory was the suggestion that this was an environmental protest directed at the use of fossil fuels, but it was hard to explain why the perp would want to cause the uncontrolled burning of several thousand litres of aviation fuel. Everyone had seen and felt the effects of the toxic cloud above the town – no environmental benefits there.

The simplest and most favoured suggestion was that this had been 'an act of insanity'. The fact that the perpetrator had had a 'Road Closed' sign with him was a problem, however – it couldn't have been done on the spur of the moment. No, but surely even insanity can involve planning? A little bit, at least?

It was a couple of days before a truck driver joined in the discussion and added fuel to the fire, if you will pardon the expression. He'd read about the tanker travelling through the centre of Norrtälje, and pointed out that this was against the law. Plus, if the tanker was supposed to be delivering to Arlanda, then why did it turn onto Carl Bondes väg? There was no rhyme or reason to it. And another thing: if the tanker took an apparently random route, then how could this Max guy know about it in advance? None of it made sense.

Soon the conversation took another turn. Someone on the football pitch had heard talk about seeing into the future – that Max had seen what was going to happen and had actually been trying to prevent the accident, but had failed.

Needless to say, many dismissed this as nonsense, but according to the principle of Occam's razor, the theory had one clear advantage: it was simple and it explained everything. You just had to ignore any reservations regarding supernatural abilities. Some people were able to do so, and even put forward the possibility that Max was a tragic hero.

Max knew nothing about any of this. After his injuries had been cleaned and dressed, he was remanded in custody on Sunday evening prior to a preliminary investigation getting underway, on the basis that there were reasonable grounds to suspect him of causing devastation endangering the general public, with a possible sentence of six to eighteen years in prison if it was judged to be a serious crime, otherwise three years.

6

'Six to eighteen years? Fucking hell!' Anna shakes her head and puts down her wine glass so that she can stroke Siw's back. 'That's crazy!'

'It's the same as for an act of terrorism,' Siw says, waving in the direction of the roundabout, which is still cordoned off with blue and white police tape. 'Like when that guy drove his truck into the crowds on Drottninggatan.'

'But that's completely different!'

'Not according to the law. And I know you mean well, but please don't stroke my back. I feel . . . crap. I was the one who started all this, and Max is the one who's paying for it.'

A few people are moving around inside the cordon, and several have gathered outside. Their faces are illuminated from below by burning torches which have been lit to commemorate the tragedy, which took place eight hours earlier. Siw feels completely detached from herself.

As far as she is concerned, the practical consequence of the explosion is that two plant pots were blown over on her balcony. The plants weren't even damaged, and now she's sitting here sipping wine with her best friend, while Max is in a cell.

Anna keeps on stroking Siw's back. The gesture bothers Siw because it is so misplaced. She ought to be flogged, made to run the gauntlet or at least be interrogated and asked to explain herself. But there is nothing. She has *got away with it*, and she feels ashamed. She can understand the concept of criminals who long to be caught and punished.

'Okay, how about this,' Anna says. 'What if Max had been there by pure chance? If he'd seen what he saw, that the driver was going to crash – don't you think he would have tried to stop it?'

'But *he* was the one who—'

'Yes, well, forget that for the moment. So, he's by the rampart. The tanker is coming. The football pitches are full of kids. Of course he tries to stop it.' Anna taps her index finger on the table to underline her point. 'The *difference* is that the kids wouldn't have had any warning, so they wouldn't have had time to get away.'

'Anna, that doesn't work.'

'Yes, it does, and you know why? Because you've no idea whether the tanker would have crashed anyway.'

'That's true, but—'

'No. No buts. Tell me the two of you wouldn't have done any-thing, as you seem to think you should have done. Just said, *oh no, we mustn't mess with the future, and anyway, I'm sure it's not going to happen.* What if the tanker had come along and crashed and exploded and Alva and all her teammates had been burned to death? How do you think you would have felt then? A bit upset, possibly? A bit worse than now, perhaps? Fucking awful, maybe?'

'You shouldn't swear.' Alva has got out of bed and is standing in the balcony doorway wrapped in her duvet, clutching Poffe.

'Can't you sleep?' Siw asks her.

'No. And I think Anna's right.'

'Have you been listening?'

'Yes, because I've been thinking about all this too. And what I've thought is that when I heard . . . before, I mean – I didn't hear . . . Max shouted, "Stop, stop!" at the driver. This morning, I mean. I didn't hear that a week ago.'

Anna spreads her hands in a *there you go* gesture, then gives Alva the thumbs up. Alva would normally do the same, but not this time.

'Or maybe it's like you said, Mummy – what was it you said?'

'That we can't hear or see each other. Or ourselves.'

'Mmm. That *could* be true.' Alva frowns, a deep furrow appearing on her forehead. 'Although that's just weird and it makes me feel dizzy thinking about it. Is Max in prison?'

'He's going to be questioned, and he might have to stay in custody if they decide not to let him go.'

'Right. Can I play on the Switch?'

'Not now.'

'No, but tomorrow. If Max is in prison.'

Even though the events of today have clearly had an impact on

744

Alva, she has an enviable ability to move on. Siw says: 'I'll ask him, if I'm allowed to go and see him tomorrow.'

'Say hello from me. Tell him I think he's nice, and I hope he won't end up in prison. Tell him that.'

'I will. Goodnight, sweetheart.'

'What a kid,' Anna says when Alva has returned to her room. 'She's the best thing you've ever done.'

'She is.'

The question about the Switch could be seen as insensitive, but it came as a relief to Siw, because Alva has been closed-off and deep in thought all day, and has only wanted to talk during brief periods. Siw is worried about how this might affect her daughter in the long term.

'Acke . . .' Anna begins, and Siw almost jumps because the name has been uttered so close to *the best thing you've ever done*, as if there is an association. Is there? Does Anna know? Is she about to bring it up? No, Anna is off on a different tack. 'You know all those guns that are around in Norrtälje at the moment? He's the one who sold them, to pay off his debt to the Djup brothers. The fucker had hidden an entire arsenal in my storage unit in the cellar. He's moved them now, of course.'

'Wow.'

'Yes, wow. And that's why . . .' – Anna taps the screen of her phone and brings up a page from the local paper, which she obviously had ready – '. . . this worries me.'

Siw takes the phone and reads about the Festival of Light on the river, the launch of assorted vessels carrying candles which is to take place on Wednesday, in three days' time. She looks up at Anna. 'It seems to me . . . me and Max . . . that all this aggression is to do with the river, in some way.'

'What do you mean?'

'All the bad stuff happens near the river. Alva says there's an invisible monster in the water, and while I don't believe that . . . something is going on.'

Anna clicks her fingers. 'Shit, I'd forgotten about the ducks!'

'What ducks?'

'It was the morning after Marko's party. I saw a flock of ducks on the river, and they were behaving completely . . . they attacked a mother and her little girl who were feeding them. And then there were those guys who got shot outside the cinema, and . . . Jesus, you're right!'

'I think I am.'

Anna points to her phone, where the article is still on the screen. 'In which case, I'd say that this festival is a bad idea. A really bad idea.'

CONSEQUENCES

I

After thirty-seven large and small shards of glass have been removed from the right-hand side of Maria's face and the doctor has talked about her guardian angel, because her eye is undamaged, she is admitted for observation in case of concussion. Ten of the wounds in her cheek needed two or more stitches, and the doctor was honest with her: yes, it would have a negative effect on her appearance, but it probably won't be as bad as she feared. And regenerative treatment is available.

'What kind of treatment?'

'Plastic surgery, in layman's terms.'

As soon as Maria enters her room, she knows she can't stay there. The pressure inside her skull increases, and when she thinks about the doctor who seemed so good and honest, she now realises that he is an insensitive pig, and that the nurse pushing her wheelchair is so ugly she's barely good enough to use as manure. Then she hears the rushing through the window, which is ajar. The room is right next to the riverbank.

'I don't want to be here.'

The nurse sighs, rolls her eyes and purses her lips. 'Is the room not up to madam's standards?'

'No, it isn't. I want to be as far away from the river as possible. If you put me in here, I'll jump out of the window.'

'This is the only department for—'

'I'll jump out of the window. I mean it. I might not even open it first.'

The nurse mutters something disparaging about spoiled patients, but goes off to make a call. Maria wheels herself backwards into the corridor, so that she at least has five metres between herself and that bloody river.

She hasn't the slightest idea *why* this is the case, but she has become more and more convinced that the river and its rushing are at the root of her problems – maybe even *all* the bad things that are happening. Birgitta's behaviour was the definitive proof; her attitude changed completely during the short drive to the hospital.

Unlikely and inexplicable, but Maria intends to act accordingly. If you've heard that a river is heaving with crocodiles, you don't ask how big they are, what colour they are, if they're hungry, or if they even exist, because you can't see them. You just don't go swimming in that river.

The nurse returns and sourly informs Maria that there is room on the oncology ward at the opposite end of the hospital, 'unless of course madam has a problem with cancer patients too.'

'I love cancer patients. And I can get there under my own steam.'

'That's not how we do things here.'

In line with Maria's newly acquired insight, the nurse softens the further they get from the river. By the time they reach oncology, she is almost pleasant. After sorting out Maria's bed, she leans closer and whispers: 'There's something about the north wing, by the river. We generally have a good atmosphere in the hospital, but over there . . .' She shakes her head. 'How can it have anything to do with the river?'

'I've no idea,' Maria replies. 'But that's the way it is.'

When the nurse has gone, Maria sits quietly for a long time, gathering her strength before calling Laura. Half an hour later her parents arrive, and as soon as Goran walks in and sees her, he bursts into tears. He squeezes her hand and kisses it. 'My girl, my little girl – why didn't you say anything?'

'About . . . about what?'

'The cancer. Why did you . . . all alone . . . you look . . . what have they done to you . . .'

'Dad, I haven't got cancer.'

'But you're on a cancer ward . . . oh my goodness.'

For simplicity's sake, Maria says: 'There was no room anywhere else. It was an accident at work, that's all.'

It takes a while before Goran accepts that cancer is not eating away at his daughter. Laura pulls up a chair and looks searchingly at Maria's face, which is still swollen and covered in a dressing.

'Your appearance,' Laura says, pointing to her own cheek. 'Is it going to change?'

'Yes. For the worse.'

'And how do you feel about that?'

'It's okay, Mum. Honestly – it's absolutely fine.'

2

'How are you?'

'I thought it would be worse.'

'What do you mean?'

'I once had . . . an experience. In a confined space. I thought this would be . . . but it's okay. It's okay.'

Siw takes Max's hand, which is lying limply on the table between them. 'Max, I'm so sorry.'

'It's not your fault.'

'In many ways, it is.'

'No. When there's no alternative course of action, it can't be anyone's fault. It just can't. How's Alva?'

'Pretty good, but she spends a lot of time brooding. She says hi. And . . .'

Siw looks at the floor, and pink roses bloom in her cheeks.

'And?'

'She asked if she can use the Switch.'

For the first time since Siw arrived, a fleeting smile crosses Max's lips. He nods. 'She can use it as much as she wants, as long as all this wasn't an incredibly elaborate plan to get hold of a Switch.' He raises his free hand, gives a joyless smile. 'I'm joking, of course.'

'How did it end up like this?'

'I've thought about that, of course. I think the problem lies in the fact that we can't see ourselves. Or each other.'

'Like that time when I . . . the buggy. By the library. You couldn't see me then.'

'No. And during those seconds when I was inside the driver's head, I didn't see myself step out into the road, I just . . . or rather he just . . . swerved.'

Siw squeezes Max's hand more tightly. 'Maybe it would have happened anyway?'

'Yes. He was angry because he thought his wife was having an affair with the neighbour. He was texting, and his mind wasn't on the road. That's the possibility I'm clinging to, but then I keep coming back to the same conclusion: I was the one who made it happen.'

'I just don't get it,' Siw says. 'I've never . . . The only time I managed to intervene was with the buggy. And Charlie, of course. And on both occasions it worked.'

'So maybe I'm the problem. Or the combination of the two of us.'

'Don't say that.'

'I don't mean it that way.'

Silence falls between them. Siw gazes at the porridge-coloured walls, the wooden table into which someone has carved *FUCK*, and Max's custody suite clothing – tracksuit bottoms and a white T-shirt. 'So, what are you going to do?'

'I'm going to tell the truth, but leave out you and Alva.'

'You're going to tell them you can see into the future?'

'Yes, I'll just exaggerate the length of time.'

'It won't work.'

'No, I know. I already said all that in the first interview, and now I'm booked in for a full mental health assessment.'

Siw chews at a cuticle. She doubts whether a claim of paranormal abilities will be enough to get Max's sentence commuted to psychiatric care rather than prison, and would that really be better? As far as Siw is aware, there is no time limit on compulsory care.

'Maybe I can do something,' she says.

751

'Like what?'

'I'm not telling you, because you'd try to stop me. But I might be able to do something.'

'Siw, I don't want you to—'

'I know, I know. Listen, Max, it's a bit weird to bring this up now, but I'm going to say it anyway. Whatever happens . . . do you want me to wait for you?'

Max snorts and shakes his head, not as an answer to her question, but as a reaction to the melodramatic or filmic aspects of the situation in which they find themselves. It's barely even realistic. He looks at Siw for a long time, then he says: 'Yes. I want you to wait for me.'

'Then I will.'

DEGREES OF BROKENNESS

I

It is six o'clock on Monday evening when a disability transport service taxi stops in the square known as Lilla Torget. The driver lifts a wheeled walker out of the boot. Alva slides out of the passenger seat and races around the fountain while Siw helps Berit out of the back seat. The driver brings the walker over and asks if they can manage now.

'We can manage,' Berit says, gripping the handles. 'Pick us up here in an hour.'

Berit has recovered from her cold, but Siw can see her legs shaking as she slowly moves towards the Little Bridge.

'Are you sure you can do this?' Siw asks.

'Stop nagging. If I was about to drop dead, you'd hear it in advance, wouldn't you? Crash, bang, one old lady down – have you heard anything like that? No, you haven't. Where shall we start?'

This is about the Festival of Light. Berit hadn't followed the news while she was in bed with her cold, but as soon as she read about the event she called Siw, who, of course, already knew and had lain awake half the night trying to come up with a plan.

On the one hand, Siw is extremely hesitant about any attempt to prevent a preordained course of events, making herself into a catalyst rather than a saviour. On the other hand, it would be wonderful to atone for what happened with the tanker, now that public flogging is no longer allowed.

But if something does happen, what can they do? When Siw told Berit about her suspicions regarding the river, Berit said she'd been thinking the same thing. They can't be the only ones. There must be plenty of people in Norrtälje who have joined up the lines between the hot spots of violence and seen the river snaking through the pattern, but being aware of the problem is not the same as being capable of dealing with it.

As they slowly make their way towards Skvallertorget, Siw realises how bone-weary she is. It's not just the lack of sleep. The shock of Sunday's incident is screwing itself into her, bit by bit, and she is beginning to feel unreal, dissociated, affected by PTSD. Her body is moving, but her mind is trailing behind like a tired old dog. This morning she considered calling in sick, but sensed that she would feel worse if she sat around at home all day, so she went to work and carried out a zombiefied pantomime of her duties. Then she visited Max. And now she is here.

When they reach the bridge and stare down into the rushing water, a spiteful little thought pops into Siw's head: she envies Max. Imagine just sitting in a cell, not having to worry about anything except existing.

And brooding. Brooding, brooding.

All the horrible images that have plagued her during the night come hurtling back with full force. The column of fire, Max's red-raw back, the children falling like skittles, and the old lady . . . the little old lady she glimpsed by the crossing, the burning trees, the inferno she had helped to create, the hell she had brought to this earth like a malicious demon, the fear . . . Siw opens and closes her hands, and for a moment she finds a perverse pleasure in having been a part of causing such chaos . . .

The river.

Alva and Berit have also narrowed their eyes as if they too have been struck by terrible thoughts, and Siw says: 'Whatever you're thinking about, try to stop. It's the river that's making you do it.'

Through sheer mental force Siw pushes away the images of herself as a demon grinning with satisfaction, and replaces them with the first thing that occurs to her as a counter-balance: her favourite scenes from *Friends* on a loop. Ross puts his fingers to his temple and says, 'Unagi', Phoebe sings about Smelly Cat, and Joey makes an entrance wearing all of Chandler's clothes.

She doesn't know what strategy Berit and Alva are using, but she can see from their more relaxed expressions that they are succeeding. Alva points to the skewed statue of Nils Ferlin a hundred metres away. 'Let's go over there.'

Siw helps Berit with the walker over kerbs and muddy patches of grass, while Rachel teaches Ben practical jokes and Chandler plays 'Cups' with Joey and Monica exclaims 'I *know*!' for the umpteenth time. As they approach the statue the internal sounds of so many people's pretend-friends disappear, to be replaced by screams, screams. Swearing, shouting, bodies pushing and being pushed, falling.

Siw jumps as the first shot is fired. Someone cries out in pain. Two more shots are heard, clearly separated, before war breaks out in earnest. It is impossible to tell how many shots are fired, if they are close by or far away; everything is simply a sound-porridge of loud bangs, screams, shouts, running feet, bones breaking as people are trampled in the rush, the splash of blood, dying gasps.

Both Berit and Alva have stopped dead, wide-eyed, listening to exactly the same thing. The sounds die away, the footsteps fade into the distance and all that remains is the rushing of the river and the groans of the injured. Then the Hearing is over, and Siw reminds herself that they now have access to an additional piece of information.

'Alva – is this going to happen on Wednesday?'

'In two days. Is that Wednesday?'

'Yes.'

Berit looks as if her legs are about to buckle. Siw supports her, helps her to sit on the walker's seat. The older woman is pale, and beads of sweat have broken out along her hairline. 'Oh my God,' she says. 'That's the worst thing I've ever heard. A massacre. In Norrtälje.'

Alva is chewing on her lips, terror in her eyes. Siw hadn't wanted to bring Alva, but her daughter had insisted. Siw crouches down in front of her.

'Now do you understand why I thought you should stay at home?'

'Mmm.'

'Was it horrible, all those people who—'

'Yes, but that's not it.'

'So, what is it then?'

'The thing in the river. I *heard* it.'

'What . . . what did it sound like?'

'It's hard to say.' Alva stuffs the end of one plait in her mouth and chews on it, then says: 'Imagine you're eating a really juicy, sticky orange. And giggling at the same time. Like that.'

Maria is discharged from the hospital on Monday afternoon, and Anna picks her up in her Golf. The first thing Anna says when she opens the passenger door and sees Maria's face, which covers the colour spectrum from yellow to blue, is: 'Jesus – will they be able to fix you?'

Maria gets in and closes the door behind her. 'The doctor says I'll never be a ten again. But probably a seven, possibly an eight.'

Anna contemplates Maria's undamaged left profile before starting the car. 'From this angle you're still a ten.'

As they drive out of the car park, Maria says: 'You know, in a way it's almost nice. I know that I am, or was, beautiful, and I know how that sounds, but in fact, it's like having a frog on your forehead. Whatever you say or do, all anyone can think about is that fucking frog. I'm not complaining, the frog has provided me with a good living, but I'm really, really tired of it. It will be cool to see what people actually think of me.'

'They might think you're an arsehole.'

'They might. But then I'll know, and I can try to change.'

'People don't usually say that kind of thing.'

'Listen, can you just let me look on the bright side here?'

'Absolutely.'

In order to avoid the river, Anna turns into Götgatan instead of Lasarettsgatan. 'Is it true what you said on the phone? That you were trying to blow up the café?'

'Yes.'

'I didn't ask the natural follow-up question at the time, so I'm asking it now.'

'Why? I could say that Jesus told me to do it, but basically it was just hatred. Blind, bottomless hatred of everything and everyone.'

Anna shakes her head. 'Why does everyone have to hate so much?'

'It's the last line of defence,' Maria says. 'When you've used up all your other options. When you're nothing anymore, when you have nothing. At least you still have your hatred.'

'Shit, that was deep.'

'You see – not just a pretty face. Have you heard from Johan?'

'Speaking of hatred . . .'

Maria turns towards Anna, and out of the corner of her eye Anna sees the glow of the street lamps casting shadows over the scabs and stitches. Maria's lips are swollen too. She asks: 'What do you mean?'

'I don't want to go into detail, but Johan has a lot of hatred within him, and I don't think it's his last line of defence. It's just the way he is, and I can't cope with it.'

Maria sits in silence for a while; she doesn't speak until they turn into Gustaf Adolfs väg. 'Hatred isn't the essence of Johan, deep down. It's more of a carapace. A shell of hatred that he wears. I don't know why, but . . . You have to understand that he's my brother. He's like a brother to me. I'm on his side.'

'I'm not sure you should be. You've gone soft since you had your face remodelled. Tell me about Jesus instead.'

3

'. . . and three hundred,' Ewert Djup says, placing the last bundle of notes in the carrier bag. He nods pensively and turns to Acke, who is standing with his hands clasped together over his crotch. Ewert grins. 'Getting ready for a free kick?'

758

'We're okay now, aren't we?' Acke says. 'The debt has been repaid, so we're good, right?'

Ewert ignores the question and asks one of his own. 'How many did you sell?'

'All of them. Except that last one in the bag.'

Ewert lets out a low whistle. 'How many were there? Forty? So you must have been able to put a fair amount aside for yourself as well.'

'Yes, but you said that was okay, right?'

Ewert takes the Zastava out of the sports bag, inserts a bullet and points the gun at Acke. 'If you say "right" once more, I'm going to have to shoot you.'

Acke hears Albert snort behind him. They are in a disused factory outside Rimbo, and somehow the proximity of so much rusty metal is contributing to Acke's nervousness. The whole place exudes *threat*, and he just wants to get away. However, the brothers are enjoying their game with the helpless mouse, and don't seem inclined to stop.

'So you've armed Norrtälje,' Ewert goes on. 'I read the papers, and I get the impression that you've been . . . less than careful in your choice of customer.'

'There were never any . . . You never said anything about . . .'

'No, we didn't. But you have to be able to think for yourself.'

'You told me to sell the guns and give you the money and I've done that so now we're good, right?'

'Oops.' Ewert raises the gun and squeezes the trigger. Fortunately the safety catch is on, and no bullet penetrates Acke's skull between his tightly closed eyes.

'The calm amidst the storm,' Ewert says, putting down the gun and folding his hands over his stomach. 'Let me explain. You've paid your debt, that's correct. But one fact remains. Do you know what that is?'

'No . . . no?'

'You tried to put one over on us. Owing someone money is one thing. You pay it back, and everyone is happy. But trying to swindle someone in . . . and I say this with all modesty . . . in *our position*. Dearie, dearie me. That's not good. Not good at all.'

'But I've explained—' Acke begins. He doesn't get any further before the back of his head receives a hard blow from something that is probably rusty and almost certainly made of iron. He is hurled forward and the floor rushes up to meet him, bathed in dazzling white light before everything goes black.

When the world starts to reappear on the edges of Acke's consciousness, its character has changed. Judging by the air entering his nostrils and the sounds caressing his eardrums, he concludes that he is outdoors. His hands and feet are bound, he is lying on his stomach, and he hears the rattle of little stones that move when he tries to turn onto his back. Acke doesn't want to open his eyes in order to participate in what is going to happen. He knows that he will have to open his eyes at some point. He opens his eyes.

The moon and stars cast their pale light over what Acke at first thinks is a perpendicular rock face. Then he sees the strips of earth and stones, the wide grooves made by diggers. He's in a gravel pit, which explains a lot. He is lying on a pile of gravel. Ewert and Albert are standing at the edge of the forest fiddling with something by their car, chatting happily.

It's all so bloody unfair. He's done what was asked of him, fulfilled his side of the bargain. Because written agreements are impossible, mutual trust is essential for criminal activity, and what the brothers are doing now is a violation of . . . whatever codex there might be. Honour among thieves, perhaps.

Ewert's heavy boots crunch across the gravel as he strides over and contemplates Acke, hands in his pockets. Acke wishes he could twist over onto his back, he feels even more exposed and undignified to be lying on his stomach with his arse in the air, as if he is offering himself up to be whipped or raped.

Fortunately Ewert doesn't appear to have any such intentions. With a groan he crouches down and rests his elbows on his knees. 'You don't get it, do you? You don't realise what's going on.'

'What I realise is that no fucker . . . I mean, people *know* I've sold those guns for you. If anything happens to me, then no fucker is ever going to want to work for you again.'

Ewert sounds genuinely upset when he replies: 'Oh, Acke. Did you actually *tell* people? Do you really think that was appropriate?'

'Well, I might not have mentioned your names, but . . . people know.'

'In my experience, people know exactly as much as it is healthy for them to know. You'd be surprised at how confused people can get when they find themselves looking down the barrel of a gun, for example. Suddenly they know nothing.'

'Nobody's going to—'

'Shut up. Call me old-fashioned, but I think you have the right to understand why what is going to happen to you is going to happen.'

'What's going—'

Ignoring Acke's unfinished question, Ewert continues: 'We've spoken to our contact in Hamburg, and he says that you definitely intended to keep those two kilos for yourself, that you boasted about—'

'That's a lie!' Acke yells. 'He's a liar!'

761

'That's possible. Entirely possible. But he's a significantly more important business associate than you are. *Significantly*. So at the end of the day . . . I suppose you'll just have to blame capitalism, that's all there is to it.'

Acke is no longer listening. One single phrase has taken over his brain. *What is going to happen to you.* It doesn't bode well, and Acke throws himself fruitlessly from side to side while Ewert finishes what he has to say. 'And with regard to people's unwillingness to work for us, you could well be right. But giving them the impression that it's okay to fleece us is worse. Much worse. So . . .'

Ewert spreads his hands to indicate that the explanation is over and brooks no contradiction. He groans again as he straightens up, then he looks at Acke and rubs his palms together.

'What are you going to do?'

'Actually, it's quite amusing,' Ewert says with a laugh. 'In a way, you could say I took inspiration from your sister.'

'What, who? Anna?'

'Mmm. I bumped into her down by the river and there were some ducks there that . . . anyway. I told her what Albert and I once did when we had a problem with some gulls. And then it struck me: maybe we could do the same if we have a problem with a person? So here we are.'

Ewert points to a thin line on the ground that Acke had thought was a shadow, but now he sees that it is a cable running from the pile of gravel on which he is lying to a block of stone twenty metres away.

'There are four dynamite cartridges under this pile of gravel, and the detonator is behind that stone over there, and . . . well, you get the idea. It's all perfectly straightforward.'

If looking down the barrel of a gun can make a person confused, then the prospect of being blown apart makes all rational thought disappear. There are no longer any words to utter or think and Acke simply roars, swallowed up by the fear of *destruction*. Ewert signals to Albert, and they both lumber towards the block of stone.

Once they are out of sight, Acke falls silent. He has perhaps a few seconds left of his life. He raises his head and looks at the crescent moon up above the treetops. He takes a deep breath, inhaling the nocturnal smells of vegetation, pine needles and moss. He is totally present in the moment.

Then a shock passes through his entire body, a blow to the stomach that forces the air out of him before he becomes a part of the air. The explosion shatters his eardrums a fraction of a second before it tears the rest of him apart. Then there is nothing but an echo in the forest, followed by a great silence.

4

'*If* my daddy is in heaven,' Alva says, contemplating Poffe's beady glass eyes, 'I don't actually think you can throw things down from there. But I believe it *anyway*, even though I don't really believe it. It's weird.'

'That's just the way things are sometimes,' Siw says, pulling the duvet up to her daughter's chin. 'For example, we do things even though we don't expect them to lead anywhere. Because we somehow still believe.'

'Are the police going to believe Max?'

'No, because nobody believes it's possible to hear or see into the future.'

'Although it is.'

'Yes. We know that, but not many other people do.'

The characteristic furrow appears in Alva's brow. 'But what if the police could believe in that other way? Believing even though you don't really believe?'

Siw smiles and strokes Alva's forehead. 'You're amazing. That's an excellent description of exactly what I've been thinking. That's why we might go to the police station tomorrow. If that's the right place to go.'

'I've never been to the police station. Mummy? What are we going to do about all those people? The ones who are going to shoot each other?'

'I have no idea. Maybe we shouldn't go there at all. I'm not sure it's up to us to do something.'

'We can tell the police.'

'We can,' Siw says with a weary sigh. 'But will they believe us?'

'Are you tired, Mummy?'

'Yes, sweetheart. I'm very tired. It's all been a bit much over the last few days, hasn't it?'

'I'm tired too, but not sleepy. You don't need to tell me a story, though. Oh!' Alva sits up in bed. 'I know what you can do! Call Johan so he can come and tell me a story!'

'We don't know each other in that way.'

'So, in what way do you know each other?'

'Not well enough to ring and ask him over.'

'That's a shame. He was fun. I like Max more, but Johan is more fun. Actually, I like them both just as much, but Johan is more fun.'

5

Johan is sitting in front of the television with the GameCube control in his hands and a half-full bottle of whisky beside him, feeling anything but fun. In spite of the fact that he is pretty drunk, he easily wins the cups in *Mario Kart* against the computer-generated players. It's no challenge. He considers moving to Time Trials instead, but shuts down the game and removes the disc before taking another slug of whisky.

Everything is shit. Marko has gone to Bosnia, Max is in custody and Anna wants nothing to do with him. He lost contact with his other childhood friends a long time ago. He has no one.

Fucking idiots, he thinks, without knowing who he is referring to. Possibly every single person who exists on the planet, all those who have unconsciously conspired to make sure that he has absolutely no one to turn to in his misery. He tries to cry, but without success.

He looks up at the ceiling. He has never had a main light, so the hook sits there like a naked, upside-down question mark. *Do you want to do it?* It is astonishing that the idiots who build houses still fit strong hooks on ceilings when they *know*. The constant temptation, the nagging question.

Not only is his chest aching with misery, his flesh is crawling with a directionless unease that cannot find an outlet, an extended panic attack that makes the night ahead of him seem endless, impossible to endure. Once again his eyes are drawn to the hook. He has a nylon rope. The thought of putting an end to this shit once and for all, achieving peace . . . But who will then experience this peace?

Semantics. He has another drink. *Splitting hairs. This isn't about peace. It's about the absence of shit.*

765

He inserts *The Wind Waker* disc in the console. He has already gone through it from start to finish, collected all the available heart pieces, so now it's just a matter of spending a little time in that world, sailing for pleasure, so to speak.

He places Link in the boat and adjusts the direction of the wind so that it is blowing away from the land. He sets sail and races away. He can see a few pirate ships on the horizon, and heads towards them. When he is within range he brings out the cannon and fires off a salvo that makes the skull and crossbones flags shudder.

The Sea Scouts are attacking.

He manages a smile that is more like a wound in his face, slicing all the way down into his heart. There was a time when he and Marko sat here side by side, there was a time when a future existed. Sixteen years later he is living in that future, sitting drunk and unhappy in front of the TV on a Monday evening, sailing on the same sea as back then.

The pirate ships have been sunk and the sea is empty. The sky darkens and a strong wind blows up; the rain begins to hammer down on Link, sailing along in his fragile craft. For the first time Johan is struck by how *alone* the figure in green is. The little boat, the dark sea, the menacing sky, the empty horizon, not an island in sight. There is nowhere to go. *The Wind Waker* is a tragedy.

Johan takes in the sail and puts down the control. Link bobs up and down on the waves, not moving in any direction. Johan goes into the kitchen and finds the blue nylon rope in the bottom drawer. He carries a wooden chair into the living room and ties one end of the rope to the hook with a granny knot. He has no idea how to tie one of those knots they use when they're going to hang cattle rustlers in cowboy movies, but surely an ordinary running knot will be good enough to get the job done?

Pathetic.

He has another swig of whisky and contemplates his work. It's totally irrelevant, of course, but the simple running knot looks pathetic. He could easily check online, find out how to make a proper noose, but that would merely be postponing the longed-for moment. He glances at Link, who is still bobbing up and down on the black water.

Goodbye, my friend. You will never make it home now. Thanks for all the enjoyable hours we've spent together.

Johan clambers onto the chair and puts the loop around his neck. Should he leave a note? The usual stuff is something along the lines of *this is my own choice and it's nobody's fault and blah blah blah.* That's not the way he feels. Quite the reverse – it's *everybody's* fault that he is standing here in his own dark sea, and the only direction he can take is downwards. He closes his eyes, lifts his heels.

He is about to step out into emptiness when the sound in the room changes. The pleasant and somehow salty melody indicating that it is now morning is coming from the game. Johan opens his eyes. The storm has abated, the sea is calm and bright. Link is holding on to his oar, waiting to be guided, waiting to set his course. Johan tilts his head on one side and stares at him.

Yes, Link is alone and all directions are equally valid. But you might just as well say that he is *free.* It's a question of how you choose to look at it. If one direction doesn't work, then you try another.

The chair wobbles and an icy bolt of fear shoots through Johan's chest before he manages to stabilise himself. He now has no interest whatsoever in dying. He removes the noose, climbs down from the chair and settles in front of the game. He sets sail once more. The sun rises in the sky, the music plays and the boat glides through the

767

blue water. Soon an island appears in the distance. Silent tears pour down Johan's cheeks. As long as you continue to live and sail on, it is possible to make fresh choices. That is what it means to be free.

Thank you, Link. Let's go home.

768

BETTING IT ALL ON A MIRACLE

I

It has taken Siw an hour of calling, waiting in queues and patiently telling various people that she has vital information concerning the tanker explosion, and no, it's not something she can explain over the phone. Eventually she manages to arrange a meeting with the two investigating officers, a man and a woman.

'And that's everyone who's . . . I don't know the right term . . . working on the case?'

'Yes. We also have a prosecutor who's in charge of the preliminary investigation – the person who gives us the job, so to speak.'

'Can he be there too?'

'She. I don't think she'll have time – it's my colleague and I who are actually conducting inquiries.'

Siw had to content herself with this, and at ten o'clock she is at the police station with Alva. Eva Meyer looks sceptically at Alva's *Jansson Metals* bobble hat, then says, 'You didn't mention bringing a child.'

'It's essential,' Siw says.

'My name is Alva,' Alva states.

After a brief hesitation the inspector shows Siw and Alva into a small, windowless room with an oval table and six chairs. She invites them to sit down and asks if they'd like a drink.

'Have you got juice?' Alva wants to know.

'I think so.'

'What flavour?'

'Orange, if I'm not—'

'I don't like orange. Is there any strawberry?'

'Alva,' Siw says. 'This isn't a café.'

Alva looks sternly at Siw. 'I *know* that, Mummy. But she *asked* me.'

Eva Meyer laughs and says that she's going to fetch her colleague. Within a minute she is back with a rotund man aged about sixty, with the biggest sideburns anyone has seen this side of the 1970s. He has kind, twinkling eyes and looks more like a wily farmer than a detective. His name is Henrik Bang. Eva Meyer, on the other hand, has the physique of a marathon rummer. She looks *sharp* in a way that is not unlike Alva's appearance. She places a small tape recorder on the table and asks if they have any objection to the conversation being recorded. They do not.

'Could we start with your full name and ID number,' she says.

'Erm . . . Siw Märta Elisabeth Waern. Eighty-nine, zero four, fourteen, twenty-four, eighty-five.'

'Alva Berit Waern—' Alva begins, but is interrupted by Meyer.

'Your mother's details will do, thank you.'

'But I know mine.'

'Okay – go on then.'

'Alva Berit Waern, eleven, ten, nine. They're good numbers, aren't they? Although the last ones—'

'That's fine,' Eva says, turning back to Siw. 'So, you have information about the tanker that exploded?'

'Yes. The person you've arrested, Max Bergwall – he claims he can see into the future, right? And that's why he did what he did, to prevent the tanker from exploding?'

'I can't go into the details of the investigation.'

'No, but I was there when it happened . . .'

'So was I,' Alva pipes up. 'I got blown over.'

'And I *know*,' Siw goes on, 'that he's telling the truth. He saw in advance that it was going to happen, and he tried to prevent it.'

'If you were there,' Henrik Bang says, 'you should have a pretty good picture of the course of events, which hopefully will match the accounts of other witnesses.'

'Okay,' Siw replies. 'We can go into all that . . . it's difficult. But I came here with my daughter because I want to demonstrate to you that what Max says is true.'

'That he was trying to stop the tanker?'

'No, that it's possible to see into the future. That's the main reason we're here.'

Eva and Henrik exchange a glance. Does Siw sense *social services* and *child protection issue* in that look?

Henrik scratches his nose. 'So, you're claiming that you can see into the future?'

'Yes, I can . . . or rather . . . oh, it doesn't matter, but my daughter is much better at it than me.'

'Yep,' Alva confirms.

That might well have been the end of the conversation if it weren't for the fact that Eva has taken a liking to Alva, who perhaps reminds her of herself when she was little. She decides to play along for a while. 'And how is this . . . demonstration going to work?'

'It would be best if the two of you came up with something yourselves,' Siw says. 'But otherwise . . . You could go into another room, for example, and write something on a piece of paper, then Alva will tell you what it says.' She turns to Alva. 'You can do that, can't you?'

'I think so. If it's not too complicated.'

Henrik is confused. 'I don't understand – are you planning to show us some kind of magic trick?'

'You're welcome to suggest something completely different – anything that will convince you that the only possible explanation is that Alva can tell what is going to happen in the future.'

Henrik and Eva look at each other, and once again the situation is on a knife edge. Henrik straightens his shoulders and Siw can see that he is about to say, *We don't have time for circus tricks*, or something similar, but Eva gets in first. 'Okay.' She gives Alva a cryptic smile and takes out a notebook. 'I'm going to go out into the corridor and write something, then I'll come back in. Yes?'

Alva looks at the notebook and for a couple of seconds it's as if her eyes have become transparent. 'I know what you're going to write.'

'I haven't decided yet.'

'It doesn't work that way.'

'How . . . never mind.'

Eva leaves the room. Henrik is sitting with his arms folded, his eyes rather less kind and twinkly now. He shakes his head slowly.

'Is it fun being a policeman?' Alva asks him.

'Some days more than others.'

Eva comes back into the room, with the closed notebook in her hand. Before she has time to sit down, Alva says: 'I don't know that word. *Chortling*. It sounds funny.'

Eva stands perfectly still for a couple of seconds before flopping down on her chair and opening the notebook so that her colleague can read what she has written. He frowns with his bushy eyebrows and looks from Siw to Alva to Eva. 'I don't understand. Is this some kind of practical joke the three of you have cooked up?'

'I've never met these two before today,' Eva says. 'Alva, how did you do that?'

'It's hard to explain. Because in one way I just hear the pen moving across the paper, scratch scratch, but in another I can kind of see what it's writing.'

'Even though it hasn't happened yet?'

'Yes. And I knew as soon as we met you that you would believe us, at least a little bit, but that he . . .' – she points to Henrik – 'wouldn't. Not yet, anyway.'

'I think we'd better call Helena in,' Eva says.

'Who's Helena?' Siw asks.

'Helena Forsberg. She's the prosecutor who's in charge of the investigation.'

2

Eva goes to fetch the prosecutor and Alva continues to toy with an unimpressed Henrik. Among other things she confides in him that she is thinking of becoming a police officer when she grows up, which is news to Siw.

'That's an excellent idea,' Henrik says. 'You'll be able to lock people up *before* they've had the chance to commit a crime.'

'Can you do that?' Alva asks in amazement.

'No, of course you can't.'

'So why did you say it, then?'

The woman who arrives ten minutes later with a folder under her arm is about forty, and looks as if she has come straight from the hairdresser's. Her hair is perfectly styled, her make-up is faultless, and she is wearing a pencil skirt suit. Siw guesses that the prosecutor's office in Norrtälje is not her end goal in life.

'So,' Helena Forsberg says, sitting down at the table, but before she can continue Siw remembers an important point that she has to make. She raises her hand, requesting permission to speak, and Helena gives her a brief nod. It is clear that she is in charge now.

'There's something important I forgot to mention,' Siw begins. 'I don't know if Alva will manage to convince you or not, but everything that happens stays in this room. I do *not* want Alva analysed by some psychologist, I don't want any investigation into her gift, I don't want this to become some Stephen King story, to put it simply. Can you promise me that? We're here to prove that Max is telling the truth, nothing else. Okay?'

'I don't think that will be an issue,' Helena says, crossing her legs and resting her hands on her thighs in a movement that looks well practised.

'Because you don't believe us,' Siw replies. 'But if you do start to believe, can you promise me there will be no follow-up?'

'I can guarantee that I have no interest whatsoever in promoting children with paranormal abilities. Your daughter will not become an *Eleven*.'

Siw's jaw almost drops. Not only did the woman in front of her understand her reference to Stephen King, but she has clearly seen *Stranger Things* too. Does it bode well or ill that she is familiar with the supernatural as fiction?

'As I said to the detectives earlier, it's best if you come up with something yourselves – anything at all that will make you believe us.'

'Eva told me, and it sounds like a reasonable way to demonstrate,' Helena replies, picking up the notebook. Alva's eyes change for a couple of seconds, then she says to Henrik: 'I know what you're going to write.'

Helena frowns. 'How did you know I was intending to give the notebook to Henrik?'

'Because I can see into the future,' Alva explains in a tone that suggests she would have liked to add *stupid*.

Helena hands the notebook to Henrik, who sighs gustily but takes it. Siw says: 'Before we start, is there anything we can do to increase the chances of you believing us? If you want Alva to wear a blindfold, or earplugs – or both – that would be—'

'Maybe you could go and sit in the corner over there,' Helena says to her. 'And leave your phone on the table.'

Siw can't see what difference that will make. Do they think she's hacked into the security camera in the corridor, streamed it to her phone, and is then able to pass on information to Alva through inaudible whispers? Whatever – Siw does as she is told, after checking with Alva that it's okay.

Henrik leaves the room. Alva sits straight-backed in the middle of the long side of the table, with Eva and Helena on the opposite side, gazing at her as if she were a rare animal or an authority on some obscure topic.

Alva looks at Helena. 'Do *you* know if there's any strawberry juice?'

'There might be raspberry.'

'Raspberry would be fine too.'

Henrik returns, clutching the notebook to his chest as if he is afraid that Alva might be able to see through the cover with her X-ray vision.

'Okay, let's hear it.'

'You're a bit of a cheat,' Alva informs him. 'Because you haven't written a word. You've written Y, Z, T, V, A, and you've drawn a terrible picture of a dog. I'm not even sure it is a dog – it might be a cat.'

Henrik's lower jaw quivers, then it seems to lock. His lips move, and at first no words come out. Eventually he manages to stammer, 'Y . . . you sh . . . should know.'

Alva looks at Siw – *would you listen to this* – then explains with exaggerated clarity: 'I am not a mind-reader'.

Helena has taken the notebook from Henrik and opened it. One hand flies up to her mouth and stays there for some time before she lowers it. 'I think it's meant to be a dog.'

Alva shrugs. 'If you say so. Can I have some juice now?'

3

Before she can have her juice, Alva has to do another demonstration. This time Helena writes 'Alva' and does a surprisingly good sketch of Alva, possibly to prove that not everyone in the police service has zero artistic talent. Alva correctly predicts what the picture shows, and asks if she can take it home with her. She can.

She gets her raspberry juice, and drinks half the glass straight away. Siw returns to the table, and Helena moves to the short end, as if she is now presiding over the meeting. She clasps her hands together and begins: 'Okay. So, if we accept for argument's sake that such a gift exists, and that Max Bergwall possesses it too – he claims he saw the tanker explode *a week* in advance.'

This is a critical moment. Siw has made it clear to Alva that she

776

mustn't say she was the one who had the Hearing, thus involving Siw. The problem is that Alva finds it difficult to hide her light under a bushel; if she's done something amazing, she wants to tell everyone.

To Siw's relief Alva gives a huge sigh and says admiringly: 'Yes. He's fantastic.'

'Mmm-hmm.' Helena opens her folder and picks out a sheet of paper. 'Siw Waern. We were actually intending to call you in anyway.'

'W . . . why?'

'We have a couple of statements from parents of children in the football team. Apparently the children said you told them in advance what was going to happen, and that you shouted at them to run just before the accident took place.'

Alva glances at Siw. This is exactly the situation they were trying to avoid by persuading the trainers to keep quiet, and exaggerating Max's gift. Siw's cheeks flush red. 'I trust Max.' Hoping to divert any suspicion that she might be lying, she adds: 'I . . . We're a couple.'

'He's the guy,' Alva clarifies.

Siw decides it's better to tell the truth after all – or something close to it. 'And a few days earlier, I also heard that it was going to happen.'

It's too much for Alva. 'Me too! A whole week beforehand!'

'So the three of you were involved,' Henrik says, leaning across the table.

Siw isn't sure how to interpret *involved*, but feels she has no choice but to nod. 'The three of us knew it was going to happen, yes. And that was why I told the children to be ready to run.'

'I told them too,' Alva chips in, adding: 'I told them they'd *die* if they didn't run!' This may have been a tactical error.

Henrik looks triumphantly at Eva and Helena, who seem less inclined to accuse Siw. Helena spreads her hands wide. 'What you did is hardly a crime, and what your daughter has shown us today – well, it puts things in a different light, at least as far as I'm concerned. Possibly.'

'It was still Max Bergwall who caused the tanker to crash,' Henrik insists.

'But if we say . . .' Eva begins. 'If we say it's . . .'

'Not you as well!' Henrik snaps.

Eva ignores his contribution. 'If Max could see into a future where he caused a tanker to crash, then why didn't he just stay away?'

'That's the tricky part,' Siw replies. 'You can't see or hear yourself in these . . . visions.'

'So if I've understood correctly, Max doesn't actually know whether he was responsible for the crash, or whether it would have happened anyway?'

'That's right,' Siw has to admit. 'But he knew it was going to happen somehow, and he was keeping watch so that he'd be able to warn the girls in Alva's football team when it was getting close.'

The room falls silent, apart from a scraping sound as Henrik scratches his sideburns while staring at his unsatisfactory drawing of a dog. Eventually Helena says: 'There are no precedents.'

'What are pressidens?' Alva wants to know.

'Similar cases in the past, that can provide guidance. I've never heard of anything like this.'

'Not surprisingly,' Henrik says sourly.

Helena stands up and holds her hand out to Siw. 'Thank you for coming in. We'll probably contact you again, but in the meantime we have plenty to think about.'

778

When Siw stands up and shakes Helena's hand, Alva tugs at her sweater. 'The guns, Mummy. Tell them about the guns.'

'Oh God, yes, how could I forget? This might help you to . . . accept what we've said. On Wednesday, almost certainly during the Festival of Light, near the statue of Nils Ferlin – there's going to be a mass shooting, and several people will die. All of these guns that are in circulation will be used. I don't know if you can search people, or cordon off the area, or . . . The best thing would be to postpone the whole event, but I presume you won't do that. For God's sake don't assume that *I* have arranged all this for some bizarre reason, because if that were the case, then why would I tell you so that you can stop it?'

'So around Gustaf II Adolf's Park?' Eva asks.

'Yes. Are you planning to act on this?'

'I think so.'

'Good. That's a relief.' Siw takes Alva's hand, ready to leave.

'One last thing,' says Helena, who has been doodling absent-mindedly in her notebook while Siw was talking. 'I've read the books, seen the films, and we have the usual paradox. So, you tell us about this, let's call it hypothetical, shooting on Wednesday so that the police can prevent it. And if they do prevent it, stop it from happening, then you haven't actually seen into the future.'

'Please,' Siw says. 'Don't start.'

4

Interview with Max Bergwall, suspected of causing devastation endangering the general public. The interview is conducted by DSI Eva Meyer and DI Henrik Bang. Also present: Prosecutor Helena Forsberg, leader of the preliminary investigation.

EVA MEYER

Max. On the twenty-seventh of this month you placed a 'Road Closed' sign in the middle of Carl Bondes väg, then positioned yourself in the path of a tanker approaching from Gustaf Adolfs väg. This led to the vehicle in question leaving the carriageway and subsequently exploding. Is that correct?

MAX BERGWALL

Except for the implied causality, yes.

EVA MEYER

By causality, you mean you are opposed to the description of your own role in the course of events?

MAX BERGWALL

If we stick to official legal language, we can say that I am opposed to the *confirmation* of my role in the course of events.

HENRIK BANG

I don't think we need to get into legalese. To put it simply, you don't admit that it was you who made the vehicle crash?

MAX BERGWALL

As I said before, I believe it would have crashed anyway.

EVA MEYER

On what are you basing this assumption?

MAX BERGWALL

As I said before ... okay, fine. The driver suspected that his wife was being unfaithful, and just before the crash he was texting her, saying that he'd be home late, even though he was actually on his way home hoping to catch her red-handed. His attention wasn't on the road, and he was upset.

HENRIK BANG

How can you possibly know this?

MAX BERGWALL

Because I was inside his head before the crash.

EVA MEYER

You were 'inside his head'? You told us that you have the ability to see into the future, but—

MAX BERGWALL

Can I borrow your notepad and a pen?

HENRIK BANG

Time for another magic show . . .

　　[Pause. The sound of a pen moving across paper.]

MAX BERGWALL

There you go – that's the message he wrote. If I remember correctly, 'wll', 'tday' and 'hme' were misspelt exactly as I've written them. You can check with his wife. And what do you mean, *another* magic show?

HENRIK BANG

How could you know that the tanker was going to take that particular route?

MAX BERGWALL

Because . . . I've already told you this. Because I saw it in advance.
But I wasn't inside his head until immediately before the crash. He
was on that road because he was heading home to Björnö to try to
catch his wife out.

HENRIK BANG

How do you know he lived in Björnö? Were you friends?

MAX BERGWALL

Oh, for God's sake . . . Yes, we were best friends and we'd planned
all this together, right down to the details of the message he was
going to send. Can't you hear what I'm saying? I was inside his
head. I know the name of the neighbour his wife might have been
cheating with – Svante something. Berggren! Svante Berggren. He's
got a big fat arse, if you want to check on that too.

EVA MEYER

You have to understand that this business of being able to see into
the future and finding yourself inside someone's head is a little
hard to swallow.

MAX BERGWALL (sighs)

Yes, I know. Sorry if I . . . but that's just the way it is. I can't do
anything about it.

HENRIK BANG

There is absolutely no scientific documentation to prove that the
ability you describe exists in reality. Nothing. Nowhere.

MAX BERGWALL

What do you expect me to do about that? And wasn't there something in the Soviet Union in the 1970s?

HENRIK BANG

Possibly not the most reliable source.

MAX BERGWALL

I'm afraid if you're looking for the reason, that's all I can say. I saw the crash in advance and I tried to prevent it.

HELENA FORSBERG

If I could just intervene. If we accept that you have this ability: could it be that you saw the crash and the explosion in advance, but not your own role in the incident?

MAX BERGWALL

That's . . . possible. But I don't think so. As I said, the driver was upset and distracted. I've gone through the memory as carefully as I can, and I'm almost certain that he would have come off the road a few seconds later in any case. What made you think of asking me that question? Does it mean you believe me?

HELENA FORSBERG

It means I'm trying to keep an open mind.

MAX BERGWALL

Okay, thank you for that. Could you please check the message that the driver sent? I've gone over the whole thing again and again, and I've come to the conclusion that out of everything I saw and

experienced, that's the only thing that can be proved. If we discount
Svante Berggren's big fat arse, of course.

HENRIK BANG

Do you think this is funny?

MAX BERGWALL

No. I'd like to ask you a question. Can you think of a single reason
why I would deliberately try to cause an oil tanker to come off the
road and explode? And if so, why would I take a 'Road Closed'
sign with me? And why would I . . .

EVA MEYER

Yes?

MAX BERGWALL

Nothing.

EVA MEYER

Why would you make sure that the children on the football pitches
were warned in advance?

MAX BERGWALL

Oh, so you know about that.

EVA MEYER

Yes. Which means you are not suspected of having deliberately
caused the explosion, but of having caused it through negligence.
It's still a serious crime, but considerably less so than if you did it
with intent.

MAX BERGWALL

Thank you for that, but I did not make it happen. It would have happened anyway. Almost certainly.

EVA MEYER

However you look at it, and whatever we can make ourselves believe, that 'almost' is a problem.

MAX BERGWALL

I'm not denying that, but nor can you deny – and believe me, I've tried to come up with alternative scenarios, but without success – you can't deny that what I'm saying has the advantage of explaining everything.

HENRIK BANG

Apart from the fact that it's completely ridiculous, of course.

MAX BERGWALL

Yes, but there's a line of poetry: 'In the absence of natural meeting places, we gathered in unnatural places.'

HENRIK BANG

And what's that supposed to mean?

MAX BERGWALL

That if there's no reasonable explanation, then you should at least consider an unreasonable one.

PREPARATIONS

I

It is not possible to say that Siw sleeps well on Tuesday night. After she and Alva have talked for a long time about what they are going to do on Wednesday and Siw has said goodnight, she collapses into bed and falls into a kind of stupor. It can hardly be called sleep; it is more a trance born of exhaustion that holds her motionless in its grip until she wakes ten hours later, feeling anything but rested.

Over breakfast she and Alva continue to discuss the plan that will be put into practice that evening; it seems very risky to Siw. The fact that it involves Anita doesn't help; Siw is going to call on her before work.

'Tell her I said she has to come,' Alva says, slurping her cereal and milk. 'Then she'll do it.'

'You think?'

'As sure as night follows day.'

Alva's faith in both herself and the plan, which is mostly her own work, seems boundless. In Siw's opinion, there are far too many unpredictable elements, plus it is undeniably dangerous. She still hasn't given her daughter her final approval.

They say goodbye outside the door of the apartment block after Alva has assured her mother that she is perfectly capable of walking to school on her own – 'I have been ever since I started.'

'I know, but I like coming with you.'

'Fine. Don't forget to tell Grandma that I . . .' – Alva adopts a stern expression and puts her hands on her hips – '. . . I *order* her to come.'

'That might be counterproductive.'

'I don't want to learn any more new words. I know pressidens now. That's a bit like an example.' Alva's face lights up. 'Maybe you could tell Grandma that she has to come because of the pressidens?'

2

On Wednesday morning Max is questioned yet again. His information about Roger Folkesson's final text message has been checked; it turned out to be correct, down to the misspelled words. A photograph of Max was shown to Roger's devastated wife, and she confirmed that she had never seen this person.

It seems to Max that Helena Forsberg is increasingly open to the possibility that he is telling the truth, and to a certain extent the same applies to Eva Meyer. Only Henrik Bang continues to stubbornly embrace a conspiracy theory that is equally complicated and meaningless, simply because he refuses to accept *the other*.

'But in that case, how do I know all this stuff about Roger?' Max asks. 'Okay, let's assume that against all the odds we were friends without his wife's knowledge, and we cooked this up together. If so, why? If he wanted to drive off the road and blow up his vehicle and himself, he didn't need my help to do it. And as I've now discovered, it's not even legal for a tanker to take that route, so how the hell could I know that it would come along, and with such certainty that I took a "Road Closed" sign with me?'

'You just said it yourself,' Henrik says. 'If the two of you had cooked it up in advance.'

'But *why*?' Max spreads his hands in despair. 'That is one hundred per cent unreasonable.'

'It's precisely that *why* we're investigating here. And what was it you said yesterday? If there's no reasonable explanation, then you should at least consider an unreasonable one.'

'I didn't mean it like that.'

'I know you didn't mean it like that, but I just can't buy the unreasonable explanation you're trying to sell. Therefore . . .'

This goes on for another thirty minutes, with most of the impetus coming from Henrik. Both Eva and Helena are reluctant to join in the dance around the unacceptable object in the middle of the circle, namely Max's ability to see into the future.

Henrik makes a couple of references to magic and circus tricks, and Max realises that Siw and Alva have been in touch with the police to demonstrate that the impossible can be possible. He is both touched and anxious, but is assured that Siw is not suspected of anything.

Towards the end of the interview, Helena takes over. 'One thing I don't understand: once again, if we accept that such abilities exist, then there are at least three people here in Norrtälje who possess them. So from a purely statistical point of view, there must be quite a lot of people with such . . . qualities throughout the country. Why do we never hear about them? Why don't they make use of their special gifts?'

'Maybe the answer is sitting right here,' Max says, pointing to himself.

3

While Anna is changing Berit's bed, she hears the old lady speaking on the phone.

'Yes, hello, hello. My name is Berit Waern and I'd like to order a disability transport service taxi for six o'clock this evening. The Solgläntan care home. To the main square. In Norrtälje, yes. Thank you, thank you.'

Anna tucks in the last corner. 'Going out on the town?'

'Not really. It's this Festival of Light.'

Anna straightens up, looking horrified. 'You're not going to that, are you? There'll be crowds of people and . . . I think . . .'

Berit raises a hand to silence her. 'I know, I know. And that's exactly why I'm going.'

'What do you know?'

'That there's going to be violence.'

'And you're planning on joining in? With your wheeled walker?'

'No, I think I'll have to manage without my walker. Can you look in the wardrobe, please, see if you can find my Wellingtons?'

4

Johan has a late lunch at the bowling hall. He is heartily sick of the greasy diner food they serve here – burgers, chips, hash. The fatty croque monsieur into which he is now sinking his teeth is no exception, but today it tastes pretty good.

He hasn't yet emerged from the revelatory sensation of *being alive*. The idea that anything is possible as long as you continue to live; any decision can be reconsidered. Ever since his experience with Link on the black sea, it is as if fresh clarity has seeped into his brain, and he has spent a great deal of time considering himself and his life choices. He has concluded that a great deal of his dissatisfaction with his existence stems from the fact that he has simply *reacted*. Things have happened to him and he has reacted and thought as a consequence of whatever it might be.

To continue the comparison with Link, it's as if he has sat in the boat kind of fending off the waves, rather than grabbing the oar and setting his own course. He is going to try to change this. Exactly how this will work in practice he doesn't know, but he intends to try.

He has just finished his sandwich when his phone rings. It's an unknown number and he is about to reject the call, but in line with his new way of thinking, he wipes his messy fingers on his jeans and answers.

'Hello?'

'Good afternoon. Am I speaking to Johan Andersson?'

'Yes.'

'Excellent. My name is Sissela Rhenberg and I'm a commissioning editor with Bonnier . . .'

THE FESTIVAL OF LIGHT

I

The vessels carrying candles are due to be launched at seven o'clock, and people begin to assemble by the river a good half hour in advance. However, the positivity and sense of community that the organisers had been hoping for are notable by their absence. There is a lot of pushing and grumbling, particularly in the vicinity of the bridges, as people try to squeeze through to the best spots.

There is a particularly bad atmosphere in the square that bears Nils Ferlin's name. The police have blocked off the area with crush barriers, which enables them to search members of the public before letting them in. Four people have already been taken to the station because they were carrying guns for which they didn't have a licence. No doubt there are more guns out there; several individuals slipped away when they realised they were going to be searched.

Two factions have formed: those who think the police's actions are justified, and those who think this is a disgusting infringement of civil liberties by the fucking pigs. The tension between the two groups is becoming more heated, which once again shows how complicated it is to tamper with the future. By seeking to avoid a problem you can accidentally create it, as if there were a higher power deciding our fate.

Those who have vessels to launch have been asked to meet at Faktoribron. The aim is to work together to produce a collective celebration of light – well, that's the idea, but there isn't much evidence of mutual co-operation so far. People are making disparaging remarks about one another's vessels and trying to sabotage them. A rubber craft is punctured, a mast is snapped, a rope light is chopped in half. Here too the mood is approaching something dangerous, and the only collective feeling that is growing is anger.

By some tacit alcoholic communication, those with booze have gathered on the seats and benches by the river opposite the cinema. The irritability and mulishness that often comes with drinking is heightened, and some people are staggering around with the sole purpose of bumping into others in order to start a quarrel.

It is ten to seven, and the banks of the river are *boiling*. Thousands of onlookers are twisting and turning, shoving others to get some space, shaking their heads at how fucking awful it all is. One little increase in the temperature and the whole thing will erupt, explode. The launch of the vessels could well achieve the exact opposite of its stated purpose, triggering chaos instead of a sense of wellbeing and togetherness.

It is at this point that a strange quartet can be seen approaching from the main square. Four females of different ages, from a little girl with tight plaits to an elderly woman using a wheeled walker. Side by side they turn into Nils Ferlins gränd and continue towards the river. They are all wearing Wellington boots.

They are an impressive sight, and in spite of the general agitation the crowd parts to let them through. Slowly they make their way to the spot where a flight of stone steps leads down to the water. The elderly woman leaves her wheeled walker there.

2

'This is madness,' Anita says. 'What if you fall in the river, Mum?'

'Then you'll just have to fish me out,' Berit replies, placing her right arm around Siw's neck and her left around Anita's. She summons all her strength and pushes her human crutches towards the steps.

'I don't understand why we have to do this *now*.' Anita is clearly embarrassed as she looks at all the people who are staring at the little group. 'Surely any other day or time would have been better?'

'I told you,' Alva says. 'This is when it can be heard. When it *eats*. And the more people—'

'I thought you meant—'

Siw places her foot on the first step, and gently brings Berit down with her. 'Mum. We've already explained. It lives on fear. You said you'd help.'

'Yes, because Alva was so . . . But I didn't understand . . .'

'For God's sake, Anita!' Berit tentatively moves her foot, seeking the next step. 'Pull yourself together!'

Alva is right behind her. 'Yes, Grandma – for God's sake!'

'Madness,' Anita repeats, keeping a firm hold of her mother. 'A monster in the river that lives on fear. Madness.'

Nothing more is said until all four have made their way down the steps and are standing with the water swirling around their ankles. People on the opposite side around the statue of Nils Ferlin

793

have begun to take an interest in the performance. They shout and whistle, and Siw sees a police officer step forward and yell something.

She has seen the crush barriers and the increased police presence in the area, so Eva Meyer has obviously kept her word. As far as Siw is aware, it is not illegal to wade in the river, so she ignores the police officer's order, which is drowned out by the rushing of the water anyway. Alva looks around, narrowing her eyes.

Siw has to raise her voice to make herself heard. 'How do you know what to do?'

'It was that old man who told me.'

'What old man?'

'The one who played with Barbie.'

'Goran? Marko's father?'

'Mmm. He said that what people are most afraid of is fear itself.'

'Okay, but—'

'Quiet, Mummy. I'm concentrating.'

Siw looks at all the people along the riverbank. They had seemed amused to begin with, but now the attitude has reverted to the usual hostility. Some are gesturing to them, telling them to get out of the river, not to spoil the occasion, calling them a fucking pain in the arse, just like everyone else. One man is removing his shoes and socks, presumably with the intention of putting a stop to their nonsense. Alva squeezes Siw's hand and points.

'There.'

Siw can neither hear nor see anything, but the spot in the middle of the river four metres away is the perfect intersection between all the people jostling on its banks and bridges. The epicentre, the eye of the storm.

Anita and Siw are more or less carrying Berit now, and Anita continues to mutter about madness as the water gets deeper, pouring in over the tops of their Wellingtons and chilling their feet. Alva is leading the way now, the water up to her knees. She stops and points again, then signals to the others to gather around her.

Siw looks down. She's not sure if it's her imagination, but she thinks she can distinguish a sort of *thickening* of the water just in front of Alva's feet, something jellyfish-like, no bigger than a clenched fist, and her throat constricts with horror as her greatest fear takes over her mind.

Being burned on a bonfire. Tied to a ladder that is slowly lowered towards the licking yellow tongues. Her clothes burning away. Her hair catching fire. Her eyeballs drying out, exploding. Her skin beginning to blister and boil. Her lungs, seared with every breath. Life leaving her body. Fear of the image against which she has no defence.

'Help me, help me,' Anita whimpers, almost letting go of Berit, who slips sideways towards the surface of the water before Siw tightens her grip on her grandmother and is brought back to reality.

'It's only fear,' Siw says to Anita. 'It's not real. Don't think about it.'

'Come on!' Alva shouts. 'All of you – come on!'

They stand in a tight circle, arms around one another's shoulders, heads almost touching. They stare down into the gushing water. Siw can feel her mother shaking with cold, or fear – but she stands firm. Alva's hand clamps Siw's shoulder until it hurts, and Siw feels *it* begin to flow. It comes from Berit and Anita, it pours into Siw and on into Alva, whose grip tightens even more. They are like one single organism, a shared bloodstream, and Alva is its heart.

An invisible battle is taking place. An ancient strength from the four women directed down into the dark water, and an equally ancient resistance coming up from below. Siw feels an unbearable pressure on her eardrums, and the air around her seems to vibrate with the heat.

The bonfire is back. Siw is yet another sibyl who is to be burned to death to atone for her association with dark forces. The crowd that has gathered to watch her execution cheers when she screams out in pain. The blisters covering her skin begin to burst, her tongue shrivels in her mouth. One of the ropes binding her arms to the ladder burns through, and she plummets towards the fire. In a few seconds she will be dead.

Then she hears Alva's voice inside her head. *What people are most afraid of is fear itself, what people are most afraid of . . .*

The bonfire fades away. The heat consuming Siw's body is replaced by cooling water, eddying around her legs. The ropes around her arms become Alva's hand, squeezing her shoulder harder and harder. The pressure increases as whatever is in the river shrinks, turns into a single dot.

One last pinch from Alva that makes Siw gasp, and then it has happened. The presence in the river has disappeared. Alva wobbles and Siw pulls her close, presses her to her hip.

The man who has taken off his shoes and socks, jumped in and waded out is standing still, looking around in confusion as if he can't work out how he's ended up here. He looks at the four of them and asks: 'Are you staying there?'

'Not for much longer,' Berit replies.

'Okay. Can I . . . Do you need any help?'

'We're fine, thanks.'

Alva is clinging to Siw, who strokes her daughter's hair, then bends down. 'What did you do?'

'The same as with Grandma's mug,' Alva says wearily. 'I moved it. Into the future.'

'What . . . what future?'

'About a week. Almost two.'

'So . . . It will be back in two weeks?'

'No. It can't live for that long without food. If people aren't afraid. Of fear.'

'So . . . you moved it to a future where it doesn't exist?'

'In a way, yes. In another way, no. But I'm too tired to explain.'

Siw looks down into the clear, flowing water of the river. 'I thought it would be . . . big.'

Alva shakes her head. 'No. It's almost nothing.'

A cheer goes up and Siw raises her head. The vessels with their cargo of different-sized candles and lights have been launched, and their glow shines on the contented faces of the spectators. For a while Berit, Anita, Siw and Alva stay where they are, illuminated by hundreds of floating candles that are reflected in their eyes as they nod to one another.

We did it. We defeated The Horror.

Surrounded by bobbing, sparkling lights, they make their way back to dry land.

3

Johan arrives at Society Bridge a few minutes before seven. He stands for a while clutching the railing, gazing towards the newly constructed houses in the harbour. He remembers standing in this exact spot a while ago and being suffused with mindless hatred towards the people who had moved in there, and nothing has changed.

Fucking idiots, he thinks. *Coming here with their Stockholm money, thinking they can . . .*

Then it is as if a switch is flicked inside his brain. He blinks, tilts his head on one side. Something that has never occurred to him before: the houses are actually really nice. Modern, of course, but in a retro style that suits the harbour perfectly. On some of the balconies light ropes have been wound around the railings, which contributes to the warm, homely impression. Why should there be anything wrong with the people who live there?

He steps back, intending to cross to the other side so that he can watch the light vessels as they arrive. Then he sees a familiar figure leaning on the railing.

'Anna? Hi.'

Anna turns her head, looks him up and down. She doesn't say anything, but at least she hasn't walked away.

'Guess what? My book is going to be published. By Bonnier. You're the first person I've told.'

Some of the dismissive stiffness in Anna's shoulder eases. 'Congratulations. Cool.'

'And it's all down to you.'

'Not at all. You were the one who wrote it.'

Johan's heart is breaking. There is no one he would rather celebrate this with than Anna. Whatever she says, this is the best thing that has ever happened to him, and it wouldn't have been possible without her. The fact that they can't share the moment physically painful.

'And they also thought that *The Boy Who Hated the Council* was a much better title.'

'Great.'

He can't take any more. Johan drops to his knees on the asphalt in front of Anna, and grabs her hand.

'Forgive me. I've been an idiot. I'll . . . I'll change.'

Anna doesn't pull her hand away, but she says: 'People can't change just like that. You think the way you think.'

'I'll try and think differently. I mean it. I . . . stuff has happened. I've been stuck, and I'm starting to free myself. You're . . . I don't understand it myself, but I really want to be with you.'

A smile plays over Anna's lips as she looks down at Johan. 'Are you proposing?'

Johan's eyes dart from side to side, then he raises his eyebrows as if he has been struck by a very surprising idea. 'And . . . if I am?'

'Then you're crazy. Get up.'

With Anna's help he scrambles to his feet. He looks her in the eye and says: 'But seriously – why not?'

'There's one pretty obvious reason.'

'Yes, but you say you've had enough of men. So have I. Not that I want to be with girls, but I'm kind of . . . done. I just want to . . .'

'Come here.'

Anna opens her arms and they embrace each other. For the first time in goodness knows how long Johan feels such a sense of relief in his chest that it can only be happiness. He hugs Anna, holds her close. Across the river the light comes drifting towards them.

4

When all the vessels have passed by, many people linger by the river, chatting about what they have just seen. Everyone agrees that it was a wonderful experience that should become a tradition.

On the main bridge a woman has just bought a hot dog from a trader who has taken the opportunity to sell his wares. Her wallet is old and worn, and she doesn't notice that her credit card falls out as she tucks the wallet into her bag.

She has gone only a couple of steps in the direction of the main square when a man catches up with her and holds out the card. 'Excuse me – you dropped this.'

'Oh – thank you so much!'

'You're welcome.'

EPILOGUE

On Saturday, three days after the Festival of Light, Johan, Anna and Maria are heading towards Society Park. Suicune has just been released as raid boss, and several members of the Pokémon Go Roslagen group have arranged to meet at Wind Thingie.

Johan feels more light-hearted than he has done for years – or ever, in fact. On the way to the park he posted the signed contract to Bonnier, and as he walks along between Anna and Maria picking up random Pokémon, he is unusually present in the moment, which is almost painful. He is aware of every breath, the unevenness of the gravel beneath his feet, the scent of Maria's no doubt exclusive perfume.

Anna sighs, and Maria asks her what's wrong.

'Acke. I haven't heard from the bastard for days.'

'I thought you were going to let go of all that.'

'I want to. And I have, kind of. The problem is that it won't let go of me. How are you getting on with Jesus?'

'He's gone. I think it was just . . . something the river created inside my head.'

Johan looks up from his screen. 'Jesus? What are you talking about?'

801

Maria manages a strained smile. Only a small number of the injuries to her face needed stitching, but if she tries to move her face too much, she risks opening up the smaller wounds which are still healing. She still looks as if she is suffering an acne attack from hell.

'The Saviour punished me for my vanity,' she says, turning to Johan. 'Or I just went crazy. I don't know.'

She slowly shakes her head, and the effect is surreal. She goes from photo model to the bride of Frankenstein and back again in seconds. The doctors have said that it will improve significantly, but for the moment Maria is happy with her duality. She looks the way she feels.

As they cut across the grass they see that a large group has assembled around Wind Thingie. The irritation and hostility that had recently become the norm are gone, blown away by the wind coming off the inlet, and the pleasant small talk has returned. Johan scans the gathering and his jaw drops.

'Max!' he shouts. 'What the hell!'

Max and Siw are indeed standing close together by the edge of the quay, absorbed in their screens. Max looks up; he has dark circles beneath tired eyes, but he is *out*. Johan strides over and gives him a big hug. After a brief hesitation he also gives Siw a quick hug, which she awkwardly returns.

'What the hell!' Johan repeats. 'I thought you were on your way to the gallows? Why haven't you been in touch?'

'I got out an hour ago,' Max says with an apologetic gesture. 'Siw came to meet me and then . . . I was intending to call you when we're done here.'

'But . . . *how*?'

'I'm not completely certain.' Max gives Siw a warm glance before he goes on: 'But I think Siw managed to convince the police that certain . . . gifts do exist. They say I'll have to spend a month or so in an open prison for negligence relating to traffic or something, but that's all.'

Behind him Johan hears someone say 'negligence relating to traffic' in an ironic tone of voice. Two people from the *Pokémon* group are staring aggressively at Max. His role in the incident with the tanker is common knowledge, and it is doubtful whether he will be able to carry on living in Norrtälje. However, anything is better than *six to eighteen years*.

'How about you?' Anna asks Max. 'How are you coping with what happened?'

Max gently rubs his eyelids. 'It haunts me. And I guess it will continue to haunt me. There's nothing I can do; I'll just have to learn to live with it.'

Siw strokes Max's arm, a gesture that makes it clear she intends to help him with this. Anna looks around. 'Where's Alva?'

'Where do you think?' Siw puts on a childish voice. 'The Rabbids! Mario!'

Someone calls out, 'We're going in!' and Siw's eyes open wide as Anna whips out her phone.

'Are you *playing*?'

'Yes. Johan taught me.' Anna holds out her phone to Johan. 'What do I do now?'

'That's a raid pass. You use it to pay so that you can join in the raid. And we're a private group, so . . .'

When Johan has finished instructing Anna in the secrets of raiding, it strikes him that it was on a raid right here, exactly a month ago, that he met her for the first time and immediately disliked – not to mention loathed – her. Now he has more or less proposed to her.

'What are you smiling at?' Anna asks as bright blue Suicune hops across her screen.

'Nothing. How little we know. You have to attack now.'

'How?'

'Use your finger – like this.'

Anna stares grimly at her phone, tapping away with her index finger as if it were a matter of life and death. *More or less?* Johan thinks. He doesn't really understand how it has happened, but Anna is now one of the few people he genuinely likes. Sex has never been particularly important to him, so why be alone if you don't have to be?

Max and Siw are even closer now. Siw rests her head on his shoulder as she dabs idly with her thumb, bombarding the boss. Being alone doesn't seem to be an option there either. Only Maria remains a short distance away, watching the battling group with the crooked half-smile the undamaged side of her face can manage.

The raid is over, and everyone is focused on capturing Suicune. When Anna has thrown her last ball, she says: 'What? What just happened?'

Johan, who has thrown all his balls without capturing the legendary beast, glances at her screen and snorts. 'You got him. Congratulations. Beginner's luck.'

People start to drift away, chatting quietly and promising to meet up again on future raids. Johan looks around at his friends, takes a deep breath of the fresh autumn air and says: 'It's only Marko who's missing.'

'Speak of the devil . . .' Maria takes out her phone. 'This came through this morning.' She holds up the screen so that everyone can see. Marko is standing bare-chested in front of a house where renovations are in full swing; two men are busy fixing new tiles on the roof. The image is captioned: 'The Yugo is working hard!'

Anna uses her thumb and forefinger to enlarge the picture so that Marko fills the screen. She sighs longingly, which makes Johan laugh. 'I thought you said you'd had enough of men?'

'I'm prepared to make certain exceptions, plus I'm still thinking about that question you asked.'

'And?'

'And . . .' Anna points to her own screen, where Suicune is shining. 'So I've captured him – what happens next?'

'Nothing. We wait a month, then Raikou comes along.'

'Is that all?'

'That's life.' Johan takes Anna's hand and brushes her knuckles with his lips. 'I kiss your hound, Madame.'

THANK YOU!

The Kindness is a story about our reliance on one another. I want to take this opportunity to thank some of the people on whom this novel has in its turn been reliant.

My childhood friend Peter Wihlborg gave me a thorough guided tour of the bowling hall in Norrtälje and initiated me into the mysteries of oil profiles.

At the Flygfyren shopping centre it was Sandra Arfman who showed me around behind the scenes and made it possible for me to write about Siw's everyday life.

The wonderful years we spent living with the Adasevic family provided the inspiration for the Kovac family, although the Kovacs are not in any way modelled on the Adasevics.

My former publisher Jan-Erik Pettersson acts as the perfect, tactful editor, as long as I am careful not to mention anything about football.

My current publisher Pelle Andersson is the epitome of The Kindness, always a source of warmth and wisdom.

Jenny Bjarnar and Love Antell . . . Oh, for goodness' sake, the book is dedicated to you. There are limits.

807

Håkan Hellström sent encouragement and happily allowed me to use a number of lines from his songs as chapter headings.

Fritiof Ajvide and Emma Broberg read the manuscript at an early stage and offered valuable observations that made the book several pages longer.

Anna-Karin Andermo also read the text closely and found some inconsistencies and careless errors. The sharpest eyes in town.

Over half the book was written in Mario and Hortensia's kitchen in Cuba's finest *casa particular*, to which we constantly return. In memory of Zuqui.

And, as always, Mia, who listens to me reading aloud in the evenings while I am writing, and gives her thoughts when everything is finished. Without you there is nothing.

Thanks to everyone for kindness, friendship and love.